Doompoint

Sam Bates

Doompoint
© 2021 Sam Bates

Paperback ISBN: 978-1-7376929-0-4

Library of Congress Control Number: 2021915590

This is a work of fiction. Any resemblance to actual events or persons, living or dead, is entirely coincidental.

First Edition

Cover: © 2021 Ivan Zanchetta & Bookcoverart.com

Printed in the United States of America

https://sambateswriter.medium.com/
https://www.facebook.com/sambateswriter/

Pelias relaxed a little more and finally took note of the cold. It enveloped him and weighed heavy on his shoulders. Pelias noticed the king's long, unwashed, stringy hair.

"What are you thinking, boy?" King Endrew said, still stuck in place.

The young man shook his head in a solemn way. "It's a lot to comprehend, My Lord."

"Uragon was your friend. Tell me what you are thinking."

Pelias stumbled through the explanation: "The prince... he made a mistake – he erred and his mistake had a consequence to pay. I just... I only wish his consequence wasn't so... final."

"Did I do the right thing?"

"It's not my place to question you, King."

King Endrew finally turned, scowling. His robes swayed as he walked to his bed. "Damn it all, boy! Speak your peace. Your words cannot wound me... no more than I already am."

Pelias considered for a moment, squinting hard at his thoughts. "I don't know, My Lord. I honestly don't."

King Endrew waved away the knight's answer. "Leave me be for the night. Summon my steward. I need a fire." Pelias bowed and turned. He grabbed the knob of the door when King Endrew said to him, "Pelias, make sure you discard of all of my son's... *projects* properly."

"My Lord," Pelias responded. He left and began descending the stairs of the tower, his armor clinking with each step. He had lied to his king. Not wholly, but he had lied. King Endrew had *not* made the right choice. He was looking for faults where there were none. To Pelias, it was clear who was to blame. The truth behind the answer did not soften the blow.

He reached the bottom to see Wyll, King Endrew's steward – a young man of about fifteen with curly blonde locks - walking away. "Wyll," the Chief Commander called. The young boy turned and approached him quickly. "Bring logs for a fire. The King has grown cold..."

Chapter 1

"Do you ever miss the days where all we had to worry about was who to kill?"

Dane flicked his eyes at Amir. His friend's auburn hair and beard shimmered in the dim sunlight that streamed through a nearby window. Somehow, the man always managed to have a twinkle in his eye.

Dane grabbed a goblet of wine and took a long drink. "Sometimes," he replied. "Though, I preferred my life in-between The Legion and The New Dawn."

"The New Dawn's not too bad, but hopefully someone will assassinate Endrew soon, so we can be done with it."

"Don't say things like that." Dane's voice was sharp but calm. "Evie just made it out of the city. I don't need you getting me locked up before I can follow her."

Amir raised his hands in defense. "You're right. Sorry…" The two sat in silence and enjoyed their drinks for a moment, until Amir said, "When do you think you'll leave?"

Dane shrugged. He would have left with his daughter if it had not been so risky to do so. Amir's ties to The New Dawn were stronger than his own, and he was not as eager to abandon the city as Dane was. The two men had been inseparable for over twenty years, and Dane's gut tightened at the thought of leaving him behind.

Dane took another sip of his wine. "Next week, at the latest. You'll join me, won't you?"

Amir shook his head. "If I leave now, how many more magi will be massacred in the streets?"

Dane thumbed the old scar on his chin. "I can't stay, Amir."

"I'm not asking you to. You need to be with your daughter before she raises too much hell. I don't have any family, but I've got a lot of people counting on me."

"What if something happens?"

"To me?" Amir waved away the suggestion. "I'll be fine. I'm a lot tougher than you." Both men laughed.

A bell tolled in the distance, and their revelry was cut short. "We'd better go or we'll be late," Dane said.

The two men left Dane's house and proceeded down the hill toward the city square. Eden was a city of stone and wooden houses. Some of the buildings were built so tall that they rivaled some of the castle towers. The market was huge, boasting stalls with wares to meet people's everyday needs, but also had a strong selection of items the people of Akreya could not get anywhere else.

The market was situated in the center of the city, and so could be approached from any direction. Next to it was a new fighting arena where the citizens could bet on deathmatches that were held daily. An old arena had been converted into dungeons near the castle.

To the north was the wealthy district, filled with manors that dwarfed the modest homes of the commoners to the west. Also in the commoner's district were the tradesmen, such as blacksmiths, cobblers, and tanners. The biggest stables were in the commoner's district, though each entrance had stables near their gates.

In the southern quarter of Eden were the soldier's barracks, along with the banks, art houses, armorers and many other businesses considered too rich for the commoners. To the east, separated from the rest of the city by high stone walls, was Castle Eden. Housing not only the king, but the visiting lords and ladies as well, its towers touched the sky. Once a symbol of strength, hope, and security, the castle now loomed behind them, offering the perfect place for the king to spy on his subjects.

The streets were busy today, full from side-to-side, most going the same direction as them. The faces were grim – one or two were even in tears.

"The infection is spreading quicker. More and more people dying. More and more people losing loved ones," Amir commented.

Yet another reason Dane was relieved that Evie had gotten out of the city. "How many are to be executed today?" he asked.

Amir shrugged.

The crowd fanned out as they entered a square. Usually, this area was used by performers during festivals, and other times it was used as a meeting place between people. For several months there had been no festivals, and no one wanted to meet by the execution platform that had been erected there.

All around, people stood shoulder-to-shoulder, surrounding the elevated wooden platform in the center of the square. As the two pushed forward, they saw a group of about twenty standing single-file at the stairs leading up to the chopping block. The victims ranged from young to elderly, poor to rich. Most were scared, but a few were stone-faced – looking straight ahead or wide-eyed at the giant crowd.

"Do you see anyone we know?" Amir asked Dane, who was a bit taller than him.

"A couple." Dane furrowed his brow. "Jake – Statham's farm hand. What is he...seventeen?"

"I think so. Anyone else?"

"Yeah, shit...Marita – the baker's daughter."

"That's not good. Do you think they...?"

"I don't know."

"Looks like Bren's missing again," Amir glanced around for the executioner.

Dane nodded. "Think he got sick? Being around it, maybe he caught it."

"We should check on him later."

A man dressed in a plain green surcoat thundered up the stairs to the platform. He was a muscular man with short grey hair and a grey goatee. His leather boots were scuffed and withered. At his side was a sword with a plain hilt.

"Ladies and gentlemen," he shouted, "we bring before you a group of people deemed dangerous, unfit, or deserving of execution by the city of Eden and its King — Endrew the Giant-scalper. He has given me full authority to put that into action. Let us begin."

Amir looked at Dane and scowled, leaning in close to whisper, "If I haven't said it before, Braxon scares me."

Dane grunted his agreement. Braxon was a retired general who had been appointed by King Endrew to head a campaign several months ago — to hunt and kill any persons with the ability to wield magic in any way, called magi. Over three-hundred people had been executed under his orders.

Braxon continued, pointing at the first prisoner: "This girl — Marita Dammen — has been exposed as a magi. She is deemed too dangerous to be among the common people. She will die."

Marita burst into tears as a city guard grabbed her arm and led her to the center of the platform. Her wrists were bound in front of her and her brown hair was disheveled. At the front of the crowd stood her parents, holding each other and crying, the mother too grief-stricken to look.

"Kneel," Braxon said as he drew his sword. Marita obeyed. Previously numb to the situation, a look of defeat was now present on the young girl's face. Jake, the next prisoner to be executed, watched with stern eyes as Braxon raised his sword. The boy was lean and strong, and the way his eyes locked on Braxon reminded Dane of a wildcat.

Jake's gaze fell to his bindings and in a matter of seconds they mysteriously dissolved. He rushed forward, fist drawn back. When he attacked the guard closest to him, his fist seemed to flash through his skull. One second the guard was standing there and in another his face was hidden by an explosion of blood, brains, and bone. A rippling shockwave knocked the other soldiers and nearby prisoners down, some tumbling down the steps of the platform.

Quick to react, Braxon blocked Jake's next blow, which was aimed at him. Jake's blows flashed quickly, but Braxon dodged them with ease. Braxon grabbed his rag shirt and pulled him towards the edge of the platform. The young man fell over the banister and landed hard on the cobblestone ground. Braxon vaulted over the railing and landed near him. Jake's breath hitched as he gasped for air.

Braxon immediately lunged, sword raised. The blade plunged into Jake's chest. The boy spit blood and clutched the blade, causing his fingers to drip crimson. Jake stared defiantly at Braxon and gritted his teeth before shouting, "For King Ularon!"

Jake's grip tightened on Braxon's sword and the blade shattered. Braxon stumbled back and looked at the hilt of his broken weapon, a scowl on his face. Jake chuckled and more blood bubbled between his grin. Braxon growled and threw the hilt aside. He dropped down and began punching the boy in the face over and over.

Once he was mangled beyond recognition, Braxon stormed to the top of the platform, snatching the sword from the body of the dead guard. "If anyone here was feeling remorse for the magi we are executing, look to that boy as an example!"

The crowd was silent, the wind heard easily by the uneasy bystanders. Even Dane and Amir stared wide-eyed at the body of the young man. They glanced at each other silently.

Braxon continued: "That...filth was a traitor. You all heard him proclaim the name of Ularon the Profane, King Endrew's sworn rival to the west. The boy was a magi and a turncoat, and he deserved to die. Now, back to it." Without warning Braxon turned and used the sword to part Marita's head from her shoulders. Blood sprayed Braxon and stained his surcoat. Screams rang through the crowd.

"Monster!" Someone shouted. A few others imitated the cry. Dane and Amir looked at the crowd and saw some were crying, but everyone was flabbergasted. They all stared, either at the severed head of the baker's daughter, the mashed face of Jake, or at Braxon, who was already beckoning his next victim forward without pause.

A guard approached Braxon and whispered into his ear. The general's lip curled in disgust and he drove the blade into the wooden platform. He shouted, "Everyone! There have been reports of dangerous prisoners spotted in the markets. You need to proceed to your homes and lock yourselves indoors. The executions will continue once the situation has been handled. Go, now!"

People started shuffling through the square, slowly at first, but as realization of danger dawned on them, they became frightened. They bumped into Dane and Amir, who stood silent, looking around at the crowd. "We'd better leave, too," Amir suggested, turning and leading the way. "My home's closer. We can stay there until this is sorted out."

The two men walked more calmly than the rest of the crowd. Some people were even running and pushing others to the ground. As Amir knelt down to assist a man who had fallen, Dane heard the clopping of horse hooves. Braxon approached rapidly on horseback, aimed directly at Amir. Amir pulled the man to his feet just as Dane pushed him out of the way. The general thundered past without even a glance over his shoulder, leaving them to watch him ride away.

The two men soon arrived at Amir's house. Amir slammed the door shut and locked it as Dane closed the shutters on all the windows. Dane ran his fingers through his black hair as Amir poured two cups of wine. "Well, this is all...terrible," he said, holding out one of the cups.

Dane snatched it and downed the drink. "This is insane. Braxon has always been a fanatic, but he's getting out of hand." He poured himself a fresh cup and took a short sip. "We should set out tonight. Eden is no longer safe for us."

Amir shook his head. "I already told you I can't. There are still so many magi in the city. If I leave, they may never get out."

"You can't help anyone if Braxon takes your head off." Dane set his cup down on the table.

"I'll just lay low for a while. Stay quiet."

"I don't like it. If you were smart, you'd leave with me tonight."

Amir chuckled. "I've never claimed to be smart, Dane." He took a sip as he grinned.

"Well, well...my hunch was right." Dane and Amir both spun around to face Braxon, arms crossed, visor raised on his helm.

"How'd you get in here?" Amir asked, taking a ready position by instinct.

"You're under arrest for being a magi sympathizer," the general said, ignoring the question.

"You've made a mistake coming here alone," Dane said. "You're a little outnumbered."

"Threatening me and obstructing my work... You're accumulating offenses quickly. Time you were brought in." He whistled, and both the front and the back door were kicked in. City guards poured in, swords and maces drawn.

Dane picked up a chair and threw it at the nearest guard. Amir grabbed the wine bottle off the table and smashed it over another's head. Amir dodged the blade of the next man and pushed him aside. Dane wrenched a mace away from a guard and smashed it into the man's face. He slid backwards to avoid a jab from another and redirected his attack. He planted his hand behind the guard's head and slammed his face into a wooden support beam in the middle of the room.

"Dane!"

Dane turned to find Braxon standing over Amir, blood trickling from his head. The old soldier wasted no time. He rushed forward and intercepted Dane's mace swing, disarming him and tossing the weapon across the room. Braxon's studded gauntlet smashed into Dane's face several times before he was hurled over the table and pinned to the ground by two other guards.

Braxon sauntered into Dane's view, hands resting on his belt. "You're under arrest. I look forward to this interrogation." A grin spread across his face.

* * *

After the fight, the guards bound Dane's hands and put a sack over his head. He could not see as he was escorted to a wagon and transported around town, but there was no doubt in his mind where he was being taken — the old arena turned dungeon. All the cells previously housed the gladiators who fought in the spectacle, most of them underground. Occasionally, the executions of prisoners too dangerous to transport were held above ground where people could observe them from the stands.

Dane heard Amir across from him say, "Are the blindfolds so the people don't see you're arresting two innocent men?"

"Shut up!" One guard responded. The rest of the ride was in silence. It was a quick ride with no stops. Braxon's warning about the loose prisoners in the city must have been heeded. Had it all been a distraction?

Dane and Amir's heads remained covered as they were brought from the wagon into the prison. They were placed in separate rooms and left alone for a while. Dane tried to listen for anything but concluded that he must have been taken into one of the underground cells. He guessed it was about an hour later when he heard the metal door screech open and boots shuffle in. The sack was ripped off his head, along with a few of his black hairs. He grimaced and blinked

15

heavily at the armored man standing over him. "Where's my friend?"

The guard dropped a plate of slop in front of him. "Eat. Or don't. I don't care." He turned and walked away. Later, a different guard brought him a half-full bucket to defecate in.

With one of Dane's arms chained to the stone wall behind him, it made it difficult for him to get comfortable. At best he got a half-hour of sleep at a time, making for fitful rest. It was the next day when he was visited by Braxon. The grizzled general studied his prisoner with a smug grin. One hand rested on the hilt of his sword as he paced back and forth, his surcoat waving gently with his movements, still stained with the blood of the baker's daughter.

"That look in your eye..." Braxon chuckled dryly. "You think yourself a fighter. You want to fight me right now." Dane did not break eye contact, but he said nothing. Braxon squatted down in front of him. He tapped his breastplate. "Look at my armor... Go on, look at it."

Dane let his eyes fall reluctantly to the armor. Perhaps at one time it was shiny and brand new. Now, it was dull and littered with scratches, cuts, and dents. "Lot of wear, huh?" Braxon asked. "I earned every one of these. I've been thrown in the dirt, wallowed in muck, shit, and piss. I've been drenched in blood – my own *and* my enemies. I'm still trudging through the filth and I'm still showering in the blood of those who oppose me. I'm still here to brag about it. What do you think you could do to me, boat-mender? I would cut you down in seconds. So I suggest ridding your stare of that contempt."

Again, Dane said nothing and made no effort to change the way he looked at the older man. How had he known he was a boat-mender? There was another guard standing by the door who shifted under the weight of the awkwardness pervading the room. His eyes flicked nervously between Braxon and Dane.

Braxon leaned in even closer. "I've been watching you for quite some time. Your behavior made us single you out. We have scholars studying the common people constantly, searching for the characteristics that make someone a sympathizer of the magic-users. The scholars are the smartest beings in all of Akreya, and they singled you out… Tell me about your daughter."

"I won't waste my breath, since you know all about me," Dane said.

Braxon stood and crossed his arms, giving a short sigh. "Name: Evie. Age: fourteen. Hair: black. Eyes: black. Suspected magi capable of telekinesis, telepathy, and mind control. She spends her days working at Dammen's bakery. We know from the display a few hours ago that the Dammen family had a magi present in their family. It is plausible they knew your daughter to be a magi and employed her."

Braxon cracked his neck. "What we don't know is where or how your little Evie disappeared. Want to fill in the blanks?"

Dane shook his head. "I don't know anything about those things."

"Well, you don't seem very distraught that your daughter's missing."

"I trust her."

"Her, maybe, but the Dammen family has put a very sour taste in my mouth. When I'm done here, I'll go ask them about Evie. As a favor to you. I bet they know something."

"You don't have to do that, General. I'll look into it myself once you release me." Dane's stern gaze matched his interrogator.

Braxon grimaced. "I'll let you go, if you tell me about The New Dawn."

Dane shook his head again. "I don't know what that is."

"Don't play stupid." Braxon crouched down again. "I know that's what you sympathizers call yourselves. Tell me who else is a part of The New Dawn and tell me how you smuggle magi out of Eden! Tell me where they go and I will free you."

"I can't help you." Dane's vision flashed black as Braxon struck him. The man grabbed Dane by the chin and looked into his eyes.

"What did I say about playing stupid, Dane?" He punched him again. "If you don't want to help, that's fine." One more blow before he stood and walked to the door. "I will track down your daughter without your assistance, but know this: When I find her I will part her head from her shoulders. That's a promise. You can stay here and rot."

* * *

Dane was taken to the next floor of the prison. He was still underground, but this room was bigger. He could hear voices, but he did not know if they belonged to guards or other inmates. The guards escorting him dropped him on the ground.

Dane lay there for a few moments, listening to his own breathing and feeling the ache persisting in his face, until he heard someone sniff. He opened his eyes and turned his head to see Amir sitting against the wall, watching him. Dane forced himself to his feet and stumbled towards his friend.

"I see you had play time with Braxon as well," Amir chuckled.

Dane saw that dried blood crusted Amir's auburn beard. He slid down the wall next to him. "Did he give you the speech about his armor, too?"

"He did. What a prick." Amir chuckled again. Dane rubbed his wrist where the shackles had irritated it. "He obviously doesn't remember either of us."

"Why would he? We were just mercenary scum to him."

Amir nodded.

* * *

Someone near Dane let loose a shrill cry as their life was taken from them. Dane swiped a mace aside with his sword before using it to decapitate a dwarf in one swing. The battle lulled around him. He panted and looked at the looming castle, high towers appearing as fangs ready to end him.

Small black specks formed in the sky and it took him a moment to realize the danger. Dane fell to the snow, curling up and pulling the body of the dwarf he had just killed on top of him. He heard the arrows thud into the ground around him. The body he shielded himself with jerked and spasmed as it was pierced by the projectiles.

Dane threw the body aside once the volley ended. There were several more dead around him. He made his way up the hill toward the castle as fast as he could. All around him, his fellow Iron Fox Legion mercenaries fought it out with the opposing forces.

Any dwarf brave enough to confront Dane was promptly cut down as he continued pushing uphill. The mercenary found himself approached by another barrage of arrows, but this time he was able to dive behind one of the many boulders that dotted the area. As the arrows rained down around him, he was startled when someone dropped to the ground beside him, coming from over the boulder. He brought his sword up instinctively, but saw it was Amir.

Amir grinned and said, "These dwarves sure love their arrows, don't they? They tried to give me an ear piercing." He showed Dane his ear lobe, which was bloody and torn.

"Looks good," Dane quipped. "We're almost there."

"There?"

"The wall."

"Too bad it doesn't stop there."

"We'll have them where we want them."

Amir flicked the point of his sword with his finger. "This is where *I* want them." Dane moved to Amir's other side and peeked around the boulder. Another volley began, so Dane propped his back against his cover.

Amir punched him in the shoulder. "I know you want to get home to see your daughter, but don't let your guard down."

"I haven't even met her, yet."

"Which is a good reason to remain headstrong. You don't want *me* raising little Evie, do you?"

"Hell no!" Dane smiled. "Let's go. Don't get lazy on me!"

The two men charged forward, dodging spears, swords, axes, and other weaponry. They both cut down anyone in their way, watching each other's backs. They moved smoothly, like water or a choreographed dance, weaving through the enemy ranks and eventually arriving at the walls.

"Now what?" Amir asked as they watched the remaining enemy forces attempt a retreat into their castle.

"We wait for orders, I suppose," Dane replied, scanning the area to see that he and Amir were the only two of their forces that had made it that far.

"I'll take a rest, then. Have you seen my pillow?"

"No, but I see Zuko." Dane pointed with his sword. They watched as the captain of Endrew Giant-scalper's men cut a swath through the enemies too unfortunate to have made it safely inside the walls of Winter's Edge.

"I don't know why Endrew hired our merry little band if he's got men like Zuko," Amir said.

"Because he doesn't have enough of them," Dane replied. "He's at least thirty yards ahead of his men."

"Where are the rest of *our* men?"

"I saw Tocca and Laine before the first arrow volley. I haven't seen anyone else since then."

"We need them up here."

"We just need *more* men up here," Dane said.

"*Ours*," Amir insisted. "Endrew doesn't hardly trust us, but he needs us. I doubt his men like us stealing their glory."

Dane gave his friend a sideways glance. "Don't worry, I'll protect you from the Edenians."

"I'm glad you find the risk amusing. Remember what I said about letting your guard down."

Just then Dane pushed Amir to the ground as a battle-axe clanged against the stone wall where Amir's head had been. Dane stabbed the attacking dwarf in the gut with his longsword. He looked at Amir. "You were saying?"

"Ass," Amir muttered as he stood, brushing snow and mud off his trousers.

Zuko slammed into the wall beside them, panting and looking around franticly. "You Iron Fox guys are as good as they claim." He took off his helm and set it on the ground.

"Hello, Captain," Dane said, holding out his water skin to him.

Zuko took a quick sip. "I wish my company shaped up like yours." He handed the skin back and shouted at his men: "C'mon! *Do not* let the Iron Foxes beat you! You are King Endrew's men. Act like it!"

A scattered group of men trudged up to the wall – around half of them were Iron Foxes. Dane looked at the crowd. Covered in dirt, blood, and tattered clothes, some of them managed to smile. Some of these men could not be happier in the muck and gore. Dane was going to miss them.

"We've gotta get inside those walls. It's gonna be a long wait for the battering ram. The snow and arrow volleys won't do us any favors, either." Zuko frowned.

One of the Edenians said, "I say we wait. We can get some ladders up here and scale the wall."

"I don't like waiting. It gives the dwarves time to plan and regroup."

Amir sarcastically raised his hand. "I have a suggestion, but it's messy."

"Speak," Zuko said.

"Sewers."

Dane nodded. "Castle on a steep hill. Feces has to go somewhere."

"I'm going to guess the dwarves have tried to hide the grate. We just have to find it."

"Let's do it. I'll go with you. Alton, Maggard, with us." Zuko led the way.

Dane pointed. "Rendan, Perro." The seven men began walking the length of the wall, looking for anything out of place. They moved at a slow pace so as not to suddenly run up on a group of dwarves.

Zuko pointed ahead. "That cluster of foliage up ahead looks unnatural. I bet that's what we're looking for." They approached cautiously, weapons gripped tightly. "Alton, fire through the bushes."

A soldier with short brown hair and an athletic build stalked forward slowly, like an animal on the prowl, his boots crunching in snow. He drew the string back and let the arrow soar. They waited several seconds.

Zuko said, "Did anyone hear anything? I didn't."

"It certainly didn't hit the wall," Dane said. He moved past Zuko and began finding his way through the shrubbery. The others joined them and found a large iron gate in front of them.

"Smells terrible," Amir said, looking down at the dirty water flowing over his boots.

"Gate's locked," Zuko said, after grabbing and shaking it.

Perro — a broad-shouldered man with arms of solid muscle and a top-knot - shuffled past him and lifted his warhammer off his shoulder. "Pardon me, Captain. You might wanna cover your ears," he said before beating the metal lock with the hammer. It took several swings, but the gate obeyed the commands of the weapon and swung open with a loud snap. Perro waved the others along as he stepped inside.

"I've got a clean torch," Maggard — a small Edenian man - said, bringing it out from under his cloak. "I was able to keep it dry." He lit it and led the way down the tunnel. Everyone tried to move as quietly as possible, but every step resulted in a loud sloshing sound. They walked for several minutes and never found any enemies or traps. The sewer twisted and turned occasionally but did not present any challenges in navigating it, other than a foul stench.

"The dwarves seem like they forgot the sewer after they camouflaged it," Rendan said. "I thought dwarves were supposed to be clever?" The man had a look on his face like he was perpetually confused, but indifferent at the same time.

"That's halflings, you dunce," Perro replied. "Dwarves're fonder of the 'brute force' approach."

"So they're a smaller version of you?" Rendan chuckled.

"Shh," Dane told them. Straight ahead, everyone saw a glow cracking through the darkness ahead. When they got a bit closer, they could make out the shape of a ladder in the darkness. Maggard dipped his torch into the water and the flame went out with a hiss.

"This ladder has to lead into one of their public outhouses," Amir mused.

"When we get in there the first thing to do is move to the gate and raise it," Zuko said. "If we don't get reinforcements in here, we won't last long. I'll go up first. Weapons at the ready." The captain took off up the ladder and Dane followed next. As his head came up he heard a muffled thump. Zuko held out his hand and pulled Dane up, who had to step over the body of a dwarf. "He picked an unfortunate time to shit," Zuko said.

The others joined them not long after. Zuko left the door out of which he had been surveying and whispered, "The lever for the gate is on top of the wall. Dane, Amir, and I will sweep through as many dwarves as we can on the ground while Alton uses his bow to pick off any on the wall. Maggard, Rendan, and Perro need to fight their way to the lever. As soon as they are on top of the wall, Alton, I want you to join them. You'll have a good line of sight from up there. Once the gate is raised, we will retreat back for a well-earned rest while everyone else swoops in for our scraps."

"I like the way you think, Captain," Amir said.

"Let's get to it, then." Zuko stood and led the way to the door, throwing it open and immediately bringing his blade down into the neck of a dwarf, who fell to his knees. Zuko planted his boot into the enemy's surprised face.

The rest of the men filtered out of the outhouse and played their part. Alton loosed arrow after arrow, never having to use more than one on an enemy, while Maggard, Rendan, and Perro sprinted for the nearest set of stairs that led to the top of the wall. Perro made it first, rolling through a couple of dwarves, throwing them off the stairs. Rendan and Maggard covered his advance as the mercenary made it to the top of the stairs. A dwarf took a battle stance, attempting to block Perro's way. He swung his warhammer, sending the short man flying backwards and over the wall, his scream muffled by the crash and clang of the battle.

Dane, Amir, and Zuko fluidly cut through their enemies, parrying every attack and returning the blows every time. They watched each other's backs and before long they were far apart from the others. The dwarves failed to slow them as they pushed deeper into the castle grounds.

Alton fired an arrow into a dwarf that had raised his mace at Perro's back. The dwarf fell over dead as Perro reached the lever. He threw it and ran to the edge of the wall. He waved down at the soldier's below, calling them on as the iron gate began to slowly rise.

A crossbow bolt whistled through the air and tore into Perro's back. He looked down at his chest and saw the metal tip peeking through his leather armor. Perro reached up and fumbled weakly with the bolt before falling backwards into the lever, shoving it the opposite way and halting the rise of the gate before the opening was even three feet wide.

Alton spotted the dwarf with the crossbow and loosed his arrow before sprinting to join the other men as they held their positions. Both Rendan and Maggard were beginning to wear out as they held the high ground. "The lever!" Alton screamed. "Flip the lever!"

"Go!" Rendan said to Maggard as he drove his sword through a dwarf's heart. Maggard shoved one of the dwarves down, sending him tumbling down the stairs and colliding with other dwarves before turning and running towards the lever.

Rendan held the enemy at bay for a few moments until he felt something bite into his thigh. He parried an oncoming sword and threw the dwarf over the edge of the stairs. He looked down and saw a throwing-axe in his leg. He went to pull it out, but two more dwarves jumped him and stabbed at him with daggers. Rendan attempted to shove them away, but one of them laid a kick into the axe stuck in his leg. He growled and tried to resist, but both daggers struck home and he was stabbed multiple times.

Maggard stopped and rolled Perro's body off the lever before jamming it all the way in the other direction. Once again the iron gate started rising. Maggard turned to see multiple dwarves sprinting towards him, shouting and holding their weapons high. Maggard grabbed Perro's warhammer and flung it at them, knocking one of them flat on his back and making another dive for cover.

Two more dwarves fell to the ground as Alton's arrows buried into them. Maggard dodged under the swing of an axe and cut down the closest enemy. Another one fell as his blade bit clean through his leg, removing it and splattering blood on Maggard's boots.

Alton ran past Rendan's body, an arrow already notched and ready to draw. He crested the top of the wall in time to see Maggard get split in two by a greatsword. A shot to the neck from Alton's bow ended the attacker's life. Seeing no more threats, Alton looked over to see soldiers rushing to aid Dane, Amir, and Zuko, who were executing the few dwarves who remained in the open.

"Get the doors to the keep open!" Zuko ordered. "Winter's Edge is practically ours already." Zuko sheathed his sword and walked away.

"Well fought, Captain," Dane said, walking with him.

"I should be saying that to you," Zuko smiled. "You may only be a bunch of sellswords, but you are some of the best warriors I've ever fought beside. You have my respect."

"We'd rather have your gold," Amir said, joining the two of them. "Not yours, personally. But we do need someone's gold."

"King Endrew is an honorable man. He will deliver on his promise." The three of them stopped by the gate and leaned against the wall. "Truly...thank you. I've been away from home for too long. This war is much closer to being over now that Winter's Edge is ours."

"I understand what you mean. I'm done. This was my last battle," Dane confessed.

"Oh?"

"Dane here is a father now," Amir smiled. "Figures sellsword work isn't the healthiest thing he could be doing."

Dane nodded. "I'll be returning to Eden with my wife and my daughter, Evie."

"Congratulations," Zuko said. He held out his hand and Dane shook it. "Not only for being a father, but for going home. Hopefully I'll join you in Eden soon."

"I'll be repairing boats in Clifftown for work. Let me know if you need a job," Dane grinned.

"Kingsguard for me, hopefully."

"Captain Zuko!" A voice boomed.

Zuko pushed off the wall and saluted a man who came riding by on a horse. "General Braxon. Winter's Edge will soon be ours."

Braxon ignored him for several moments. He looked around at the soldiers and mercenaries scrambling around the castle grounds. His face was twisted in permanent disgust. Finally, he said, "Well done. The men say you took a small team and breached through the sewer."

"Yes, sir. Myself, Alton, and Maggard. Along with the Iron Foxes Dane, Amir, Rendan, and Perro."

"Put your men in for promotions, Captain."

"Alton's the only one of ours left alive."

"Then put him in for a promotion, as I said." Braxon looked away at the doors where the soldiers were trying to bust into the keep with hammers and axes.

"Sir, I would also like to request a bonus reward for Dane and Amir."

Braxon's head snapped back to Zuko. "Absolutely not. Why should they get extra money for doing the job we're already paying them to do? You'll be taking the credit on this one, Captain. I'll die before we shower these sellswords with more praise than they deserve."

"Sir?" Dane asked incredulously, his eyebrows raised. Amir observed quietly from behind Dane.

Braxon measured Dane with a look. "Fitting you 'Iron Rats' crawled through the sewer. I look at you sellswords and all I see is shit."

Chapter 2

The bolt on the door thudded and it swung open to have Braxon swagger in. "Thought you two would like some company."

Two more men were shuffled inside. One of them was taller than everyone else by at least half a foot, muscular, and broad-shouldered. His black hair was cut short and he had a goatee to match. He was around the same age as Dane and Amir. They recognized him as Bren – Eden's Sword of Justice.

The other prisoner was shorter than Amir and much younger than any of them, appearing to be in his early twenties. He was lean, clean-shaven, and his blonde hair was neat and even. He did not appear to have been in custody very long, unlike Bren, who was streaked with dirt.

"I hope you all don't mind sharing a cell. We've had to make more room. The campaign against the magi is continuing to be a success. Just an hour ago I arrested a family of bakers." Braxon looked at Dane. "I'll execute them alongside you." The general turned and left, and the other guards slammed and locked the door.

"I didn't expect to see you two here," Bren said, looking at Dane and Amir.

"I was thinking the same thing," Amir said. "We were wondering why we hadn't seen you for a while."

"What are you doing in here, Bren?" Dane asked.

The tall man sighed and leaned against the wall. "I refused to execute the sick." The younger prisoner sat down on the floor and closed his eyes, taking deep, relaxing breaths. Bren continued: "My job is to execute *criminals*, not the sick. Just because we don't know of a cure doesn't mean we should just take off their heads. I said so to the king. He didn't agree. Said we had to keep the disease from spreading. I told him to find someone else to take my place."

"He didn't like that?" Amir asked.

Bren raised his arms, displaying his shackles that dangled gently back and forth. "I don't think so."

"Endrew's crazy. Kind of makes me regret helping him win the throne."

"*King* Endrew," the young man said. "He is king. Respect that."

Amir looked at Bren and Dane. "I don't think that a man insane enough to start imprisoning magi and executing the ill deserves my respect."

"It's not his fault," the young man replied calmly. "He wasn't like this until...his son was killed. He was not a bad man until the prince was gone."

"Maybe not, but as for here and now he's daft," Amir said.

"I must ask you not to speak of your king that way."

"Or you might report me for slander and get me thrown in prison?" Amir laughed. "Sorry, kid, Braxon beat you to it." The young man closed his eyes and began meditating again. Amir looked at Dane who shrugged, and Bren, who wore a small grin on his face. Amir softened his look and said, "What's your name, kid?"

The young man took a few more breaths before opening his eyes and responding, "My name is Pelias."

Dane looked at his friend, whose eyebrows were now raised. Bren laughed. "You might know him better as Chief Commander of the Kingsguard."

Amir held out his hands in apology and chuckled. "I've never seen you without your armor, Chief Commander."

The boy waved his apology away. "Call me Pelias. I was relieved of my title as of last night."

"You're lucky our young friend is so forgiving," Bren chuckled, eyes gleaming at Dane and Amir. "Tell them what happened, Pelias."

"I suppose you two haven't heard. King Endrew placed Eden under martial law. No one is allowed in or out. Ten guards are posted at every gate leading out of the city. He claims this will help the spread of the infection and make it easier to round up any magic-users left inside the walls."

"So it's gotten worse, huh?" Amir asked.

"Yes."

"That doesn't explain why *you're* here," Dane said.

"The king's mental health was declining. It was hard to watch. Prince Uragon was my closest friend ever since I was a boy... When he was murdered, the King grew cold. I understood, though, because I felt the same way. I eventually came to grips with it, but King Endrew kept spiraling downward. I hated seeing it.

"He kept getting worse, and he outlawed magic use. Rounding magi up for execution was just the start of it. I drew the line when he enacted martial law. I was afraid the people would snap, that there would be more unnecessary death... Last night, while he was sleeping, I planned to assassinate the King. More to put him out of his own misery than for any other reason."

"King Endrew is dead?" Amir and Dane looked at each other incredulously.

"No, he is still alive."

"So you got caught? I'm surprised they didn't execute you on the spot," Amir said.

"I wasn't caught. As I stood by King Endrew's bed, holding my dagger in my hand, I remembered the oath I swore when I was appointed Chief Commander of the Kingsguard. I sheathed my dagger and reported my treason to the guard outside King Endrew's bedroom door. I handed over my weapons and was placed under arrest."

"You came here willingly? I wish we had gotten that choice." Amir crossed his arms.

"No doubt I will be executed within a few days." Pelias once again closed his eyes and began breathing rhythmically.

"King Endrew sure went off the deep end, didn't he?" Dane asked Pelias.

The Chief Commander nodded. "Losing a child will do that, I suppose."

"It still doesn't fit," Bren said. "King Endrew was always level-headed and focused. Sure, his son's death was tragic, but his reaction just seems so abrupt."

Bren, Dane, and Amir all looked at Pelias. The young man's eyes dropped to the ground as he said, "I don't think I could ever come close to comprehending what all he went through."

"Endrew took me in, at great risk to his reputation," Bren said. "I was exiled from my Tribe after most of them were slaughtered... Most kings wouldn't have even helped my people, let alone taken one as a ward. I was a scared but stubborn boy, raised in the wild and abandoned by the only people I knew. He gave me a life I never dreamed of having. To see him like he is now..."

"Is Braxon influencing him?" Amir asked Pelias.

Pelias furrowed his brow. "No, I don't think he is."

"I wouldn't be surprised if it was all that bastard's doing. How else would you explain Endrew's behavior? It matches the extremes of the general, that's all I'm saying." Amir eyed Pelias suspiciously as the boy averted his gaze, but he did not press any further.

No one spoke for a while. They wrestled with their own thoughts, realizing now that they too were blanketed in the shadow of their looming deaths. Dane thought about his daughter. What troubled him most was the fact that Evie may never know what happened to her father.

Amir sat next to Dane, but he kept to himself. Bren retreated to a corner of the cell and contemplated silently.

A few hours later, Amir whispered, "Dane." Dane looked up from his shackles. "You can say I was right."

"What?" Dane furrowed his brow.

"It's fine. You can say it. No hard feelings."

"What are you talking about?"

"I tried to tell you we needed to leave Eden. You didn't want to listen."

Dane chuckled. "*I'm* the one that said we should leave!"

"All right. If you refuse to apologize, I'll just haunt you after they cut off my head." Amir grinned.

"Good luck haunting another ghost."

Bren asked, "What's with the whispering? Secrets?"

"No. Just talking about how we're going to die. Would you like to join us?" Amir said.

"Is this really something to joke about?" Pelias asked.

"Why not?"

Dane said, "No doubt Amir will go down with a grin on his face."

"I have to come up with a really good last joke to tell."

"I don't think we have to die," Bren said, flicking his eyes to each of the others. "I've been in here a few weeks and I've noticed that whenever someone comes to deliver food or clean the buckets, one man stays at the door while the other comes inside. Two guards – that's it. Usually only a sword or club on both of them. Pretty easy to overpower, especially if there's four of us."

"They won't come here with only two men – that's stupid," Amir said. "If there's one thing Braxon doesn't allow, it's stupid people in his ranks."

"King Endrew's forces are declining," Pelias chimed in quietly. Everyone looked at him. "The sickness...it's floating through our army. More prisoners are brought in by the day and more soldiers are dying."

"If we *could* escape, would you come with us?" Dane asked.

Pelias took a moment to think before saying, "I took an oath. I already came dangerously close to breaking my vow. This is what my king commanded."

"King Endrew is frail-minded and he has abandoned you," Bren said. "Leave the city with us. We may need each other."

Pelias shook his head. "I don't know if I can..."

"Well I sure can," Amir said. "I helped Endrew win the throne he sits on. He owes me one."

"He's King. He doesn't owe anyone anything."

They debated what their plan of escape would be. They had barely settled on how they would go about it when they heard the jingling of the keys behind the door. They nodded to each other and spread around the room. The bolt was pulled back and the door ripped open. Braxon came thundering in with five other men.

Two of them rushed Bren and pinned him to the wall. Pelias, who was seated cross-legged on the ground, was kicked in the face by another guard, held down under his boot. One guard grabbed Dane and the other grabbed Amir.

Braxon stood in the center of the cell, smirking at Dane and Amir. "My day just got a whole lot better. Ask me why." Amir looked at Dane, but neither of them spoke. "Go on. Ask me why I'm happy."

Amir said, "Not that I actually care, but why- "

Braxon held up his hand and laughed. "I'm sorry. I forgot – dead men can't talk." He pointed at Bren and Pelias. "Your days are numbered, but you can have one more night. After that I can make you no promises."

* * *

Dane and Amir were bound and taken above ground, out into the open arena, where the dusty smell of tightly packed dirt and stale blood swirled around them. There were no citizens in the stands to witness their end. There were guards bustling about, preoccupied with other business. The Dammen family – a husband, wife, and daughter – were already standing there with a couple of other guards around a wooden pedestal. The wife and daughter were crying, and the husband stared at Dane with a pleading look on his face.

"Line them up over there," Braxon said, drawing his longsword. "Put the girl down on the chopping block." One of the guards forced the Dammen girl to kneel. Braxon pointed at her with his sword. "I will spare her life if someone tells me something I don't know about The New Dawn. This is the last chance you all have!"

"No, please!" Missus Dammen said, falling to her knees, hands clasped together. "I beg of you, spare her! Spare her! You've already taken one of our children from us!"

"Tell me what I want to know!"

Mister Dammen said, "Please, sir, I don't know anything! We don't know anything!"

Braxon pointed at Dane and Amir. "They do."

Mister Dammen looked at Dane. "Please! Tell him what he wants to know!"

"Tell me where you smuggled those people!" Braxon shouted.

Dane looked from Braxon to Mister Dammen. The baker's voice squeaked out a plea: "Please...we helped you. We hired your daughter. We let those people stay in our house – the ones that took your daughter away. Please, Dane...If you don't tell him, I will lose both my children! I helped your little girl. Now help mine. Dane!"

Dane studied the tears that dribbled down the man's face, rolling past his quivering lip. He sniffed and stumbled towards him. The baker dropped to his knees and planted his forehead in the ground at Dane's feet. He kept muttering in the dirt over and over.

Dane's brow was furrowed as he stood over the man. He clenched his jaw to prevent himself from spilling all his secrets. He let a small groan bubble up in his throat but shook his head. "I'm sorry. So sorry, Peter. I can't."

Mister Dammen looked up at him, cheeks and eyes bright red. "Go to hell."

Dane nodded.

"Dane-" said Amir from behind him.

"Enough!" Braxon interjected. "You had your chance." He raised his sword high.

"No, wait!" Dane shouted.

"Dane!" Amir shouted at the same time.

The sword fell and the Dammen girl's head rolled. Missus Dammen shrieked and dropped to the ground. Peter Dammen's eyes were glued to his daughter's body, which Braxon kicked aside. "The wife now." The guard tried to coax the woman to her feet to no avail. Braxon stamped forward and pushed the guard aside. He grabbed the woman by her hair and dragged her through the dirt to the block.

Missus Dammen asked. "Can I say something before you...?"

"No." In one fluid motion, Braxon brought his sword up and slashed through her neck.

"No!" Peter screamed.

"Him now."

This time the guard was more forceful. He kicked Peter in the rump towards the chopping block. He knelt voluntarily and looked up at Braxon. "You are a son of a bitch. I hope you burn for all eternity in-"

Braxon beheaded him in the blink of an eye, and did not think twice after it was done. He moved the body and pointed at Amir. "You."

Dane's eyes widened and stepped forward. "No, not him. Kill me, not him."

"Him," Braxon replied.

"No, no...I'll tell you. I'll tell you what you want to know."

Braxon grinned evilly. "Now we're getting somewhere. Only took three beheadings to get you to cave. Now – where do the magi go?"

"Okay, okay. They go-"

"Dane!" Amir interjected. Dane turned to have his friend head-butt him in the face, knocking him to the ground. "Shut up, old friend. I'll handle this."

Dane watched, horror in his eyes, as Amir strutted forward and knelt over the pedestal. He gave Dane a wink before looking up at Braxon and grinning. "You know, General, I look at you and all I see is shit."

One of the guards pulled Dane to his feet just in time to see Braxon swipe cleanly through his best friend's neck. Time stopped for Dane. His vision became unfocused, but he did not notice. Nor did he notice that his wrists began to bleed as he struggled against his bindings. He walked toward Braxon, his lip curled into a snarl.

A guard behind him kicked him in the back of the leg, knocking him to his knees at the pedestal. "Last chance, Dane. Your *very* last chance."

Dane looked at Amir's head, which was giving him a glossy stare. "I will see you in hell, Braxon."

"You'll be waiting a long time." Braxon lifted his sword before he was approached by another guard that sprinted up to him.

The guard was panting and his sword was drawn and stained with blood. "General – the magi have broken out of cell block F and are fighting their way up from underground."

"This won't take but a moment."

"Sir, that's not all. The infection – it's gotten worse. The dead are... They're coming back to life! They're overrunning the prison!"

"What have you been drinking, Corporal?" Braxon looked at him as if he were stupid.

"Sir...I know how it sounds. I don't know what else to say..."

"You'd better not be wasting my time. You, with me." Braxon motioned one of the other guards forward and looked down at Dane. "Sit tight. I won't be long."

Dane spent his next moments staring into Amir's dead eyes. His stomach was weak. He could vomit at any time. He could not stop his body from shaking. Tears welled in his eyes, and he fought them back.

He could feel the other soldier hovering around him. He was nervous, shuffling back and forth, occasionally glancing at the gate that Braxon and the corporal had disappeared through. The guard was startled, his hand dropping to the hilt of his blade, when the gate swung open. "Private! Private! Get the hell over here!" He rushed forward, leaving Dane alone.

Dane looked over at the gate. All he could see were soldiers hacking and cutting at something hidden in the shadows of the doorway. He looked back at the face of his dead friend. After checking for any guards watching him, he leaned back onto his knees. He struggled against his bonds but could not get free.

Dane got on his feet and started walking in the opposite direction from where the guard had gone. There was small door through which he had been escorted into the arena that he could go back through. He kept glancing over his shoulder but did not stop walking until he heard a dozen different men screaming behind him.

Dane turned and was shocked to see an enormous group of ragged-looking ghouls flooding into the arena. Their skin was grey and splotchy, and their eyes were solid white. They were groaning and growling, but worst of all was that most of them had dropped to the ground and were feasting on the dead soldiers who were fending them off mere moments ago, tearing flesh with teeth and ripping limbs apart.

Three of the monsters spotted Dane and began sprinting towards him. He tried to run but he could not take his eyes off them. He tried to back away, but his legs gave out underneath him. He could not bring himself to scurry away.

The three demons shrieked loudly, and Dane saw their blood-soaked hands and faces. Dane screamed defiantly back at them before Bren stepped in front of him. In his hands was a bardiche - a pole weapon with a giant curved blade on the end. He swiped one of the monsters aside and kicked another. He cut the third in half while Pelias helped Dane to his feet. Bren grabbed the one he had kicked away by the throat and studied it for a moment as its fists tried to swat at him.

Bren shuddered. "Disgusting." He drove the point of his bardiche into the demon's skull. He turned. "Are you all right, Dane?"

"I...I'm not sure, yet," he replied.

"Look," Pelias said, pointing. The one that Bren cut in half was wriggling in the dirt, reaching out for them, hissing and growling, all the while its guts stringing behind it.

"What in the hell...?" The three of them watched for a moment, but the scene only presented them with more questions and no answers.

"Let's get out of here," said Pelias, who was now in the glossy black armor of the kingsguard. A plain red cloak draped from his shoulder, a black-hilted sword hung from his belt, and a shield was cinched to his arm.

"Did you decide to leave with us?" Dane asked.

"There's still some good I can accomplish for the living." Pelias unlocked Dane's shackles and picked up a black shield from the ground.

Dane said nothing, rubbing the soreness from his wrists, casting sad eyes on Amir's remains...

* * *

The three of them made it out of the prison without any further incident. All the fighting had concentrated in the south side of the prison and they had avoided it by using one of the arena spectator exits in the north side. All the prisoners had escaped, and the soldiers had abandoned it – the ones that were smart enough to get out. The guards that did not make it were caught up in a vicious battle royale between the undead, magi, and other prisoners.

The three men stopped in an alley a few blocks away from the prison. "We need to get out of the city," Bren said.

"Eden is on lockdown, remember?" Pelias said.

"One step at a time," Dane said. "I need your help getting to my home to retrieve a few things."

The other two nodded and Dane led the way. Eden was completely different from what it was just a few short days ago. Some residents were fighting in the streets and those who were not watched the fighting from inside their locked houses. Small fires dotted the city, while some giant blazes engulfed abandoned houses and turned them into ash and rubble.

They stepped over dead bodies and around broken carriages as they got closer to Dane's home. They ducked into an empty house when they heard a dozen trudging footsteps approaching. Glancing out, the three men saw a group of soldiers led by General Braxon.

"Bastard's still alive," Dane muttered.

"I figured he died fighting in the prison," Bren said.

They heard Braxon shout a command: "Keep your eyes open for any ghouls running about.

Remember to strike them in the head. And show no mercy to any magi you encounter."

"We need to keep moving," Pelias said.

"I want to kill him," Dane said through gritted teeth.

"I don't think that would be smart."

"Pelias is right. Our chances of getting out of the city get slimmer the longer we hang around," Bren said.

They waited for Braxon and the soldiers to get down the road and Dane continued to lead the way. Before long, and without any other disturbances, they arrived outside his house. Dane held up his hand to stop them. "The door's already open."

"Someone's inside?" Bren asked, trying to listen.

"Yes. I don't have a weapon. I need you two to lead the way."

Pelias stepped forward, drawing his sword and pushing toward the doorway with his shield raised. After he disappeared inside, Bren followed. Dane walked in to find two men dressed in black with their backs turned to them. They were rifling through his drawers and cabinets.

The first man was a giant – even compared to Bren, whom he was at least a foot taller than. His head was shaved, and the straps of a leather mask wrapped around it. A battle-axe was slung over his muscular shoulders.

The second man had bronze skin and meticulously trimmed black hair. He was a dwarf compared to his companion, but a human by everyone else. A spear was propped against the wall next to him and a long black cloak around his neck.

The second man said, "This bum doesn't own a single thing worth looting." The giant grunted his agreement as the second man tossed a plate over his shoulder.

"Excuse me," Dane said. The smaller man grabbed his spear and spun around. The big man looked over his shoulder to reveal that the mask covered his nose and mouth, and had a design stitched into it that resembled mandibles on an insect. He turned the rest of the way and slowly put down the loaf of bread he had in his hand.

"Can we help you?" The spearman asked, holding his weapon in a relaxed grip as his eyes scanned them all from top to bottom.

Dane chuckled. "I would hope so. This is my house..."

"Gotta tell you, I've broken into better."

"Sorry to disappoint you. I haven't had guests in a while. Would you like me to show you to the door?"

The smaller man shrugged. "I'm okay here. Aren't you, Grunt?" The bigger man did not respond. "Forgive my friend. He's a bit antisocial."

"I don't know who you two are, but we *will* kill you," Dane took a step forward.

"What a terrible thing. With the shape the realm is in now, you're gonna go on a killing spree and we haven't even attempted to hurt you." The second man casually leaned on his spear. "Are you going to give us a reason to hurt you?"

Dane sighed, shook his head, and signaled for his friends to stay their weapons. "I don't have time for this. You're welcome to anything here, except for what I came here to get."

The second man screwed up his face and looked at Grunt. "I wasn't expecting that... I must look really tough."

The imposing giant narrowed his eyes at his companion.

"Do what you will with my home. I don't plan on ever returning." Dane walked past the two intruders and went into his bedroom. Bren and Pelias followed him, keeping their eyes on the pair of thieves.

Dane lifted the lid to a trunk that rested at the foot of his bed and lifted the bottom tray out to reveal a secret compartment underneath. The first thing his eyes drifted to was a leatherbound book of poetry that had been his wife's most cherished possession. He inhaled deeply and prayed for her memory to give him strength.

He lifted it and flipped through the worn and yellowed pages. Halfway through, his thumb caught and he pulled it open. Between the two pages was a withered buttercup that had been flattened for years. He picked the flower up carefully in both hands.

The flower had been a gift to Amir from an orphan girl the two had rescued during a vicious battle many years ago. She had followed the two of them around for days after that, particularly fond of Amir. One day, the girl was trampled by a horse, and Amir dropped the flower to the ground, unable to carry it and think of the girl.

Dane frowned. Amir had not even known that he had picked up the buttercup and kept it this entire time. Why he had done it? Had he planned on giving it back to Amir some day? The answer did not matter now. Both the girl and Amir were gone, along with his wife.

Dane put the flower back into the book and closed it gently. He sniffed and lowered the book back into the trunk, fighting off the forming tears that stung his eyes. He forced the memories out of his mind, refusing to let them cloud his thoughts.

Instead, he retrieved a longsword with a pointed pommel that was painted white, and orange to resemble a fox's tail. He placed it on the bed and then removed a hauberk — chainmail shirt — and grey armor of boiled leather. Even though the color had dulled, the sigil of the orange fox silhouette painted on the front of the leather contrasted the grey beautifully.

The smaller man stepped through the doorway to be met by Pelias with his shield raised. He ignored the Chief Commander and looked at Dane as he held his armor. "You're part of the Iron Fox Legion."

"I was," Dane said, tossing the article onto the bed.

"Now you're going back out there to find your brothers-in-arms."

"No." Dane found some of his other clothes and began changing behind a curtain.

"You're not much of a talker, are you?"

"You're too much of a talker," Bren said, gripping his bardiche tightly.

"Don't blame me. I spend all my time with him," he jabbed his thumb over his shoulder to indicate his associate. "If I don't talk, I go crazy. I call him Grunt, and my name's Koda. So... where are we going?"

"We?" Bren chuckled.

"If you are evacuating the city, we want in."

"Get lost."

Dane stepped out from behind the curtain adorned in his Iron Fox Legion armor. He picked up the longsword from the bed and began to wrap the belt around his waist.

Koda ignored Bren and addressed Dane: "You owe us one." Dane arched an eyebrow at him and waited for him to continue. "I didn't wanna tell you this for fear of appearing arrogant, but... Grunt and I ran off some rogues that we found here in your house. I think they were trying to steal from you." Grunt furrowed his brow at his companion and Koda shrugged at him.

"Thank you," Dane said, grinning slightly, cinching his belt tight, "but as I said, I don't plan on returning. I don't care about this place anymore." The sellsword strolled past the two strangers, tightening silver gauntlets over his fingerless gloves. "Bren, Pelias, let's leave." He walked out of his home, his two friends following him, Bren keeping his eyes on them.

"Can we come with you?" Koda asked.

Bren shook his head. "I don't trust you." He slammed the door after making his exit.

Koda looked at the giant and shrugged. "Right friendly folk. I think we're trustworthy." Grunt grunted.

* * *

"You two aren't obligated to come with me," Dane said as they slinked through the streets.

"The only other option is to stay here and die," Bren said. "I'm not ready for that."

"As I said, I can still do some good. I will help you and Bren get to your destination," Pelias said, striding faster to match their pace. "What exactly is your plan?"

Dane looked around for anyone nearby and stood straight. He sighed and placed his hands on his hips. "Over the last few months, I have been a part of The New Dawn. The group formed just after King Endrew outlawed magic and began imprisoning and executing anyone with any affinity to it. My daughter, Evie, is a magi and I joined The New Dawn so I could get her out of the city.

"We began smuggling magi out of Eden and escorting them to Etzekel – a sanctuary city in the northwest. It's a hidden city that most don't believe exists."

"Great," Bren said, hoisting his bardiche onto his shoulder. "You're part of this New Dawn, so let's go to Etzekel."

"It's not that simple. The magi leaders that rule it won't let us in unless we arrive at their gates with a magi in our presence."

"But your daughter is there."

"It doesn't matter to them. We have to present them with another magi to be allowed access to the city. They're very strict about their security. Paranoid, really, but can you blame them?"

Bren did not look pleased while Pelias scanned for danger.

"I do have a plan, though, if you both are still interested in joining me."

"How many times are you gonna ask us that?" Bren asked.

"You do realize that you will be assisting The New Dawn to some extent? That will put a target on your backs."

"Like we don't already. We've already fallen out of the king's good graces."

The two men looked at the Chief Commander, who shrugged his answer without giving it a second thought.

"Follow me, then."

Chapter 3

Ruddell's carriage began to rock back and forth and he was flung from his seat. He tumbled around in a fit of curses and flailing limbs, his golden necklaces rattling. He stood on shaky legs and pushed open the door, only to be grabbed by a walking corpse and pulled out onto the stone street.

The dwarf wrestled with the zombie and shouted for help as the monster attempted to sink its teeth into any part of his flesh. The creature's face ruptured as an arrow pierced the back of its head. The dwarf threw the corpse aside and struggled to stand under the weight of his own girth. He dusted off his long, red robe and spit, glaring at the elf standing near him.

Her hair was a dark red – perhaps unnaturally so. Her body was lithe, though the muscles underneath were hard and tested. She wore plain tan breeches and a green shirt, with a leather breastplate over her chest. A green headband hugged her forehead and she had an unamused look on her face.

Ruddell pointed at the bow in her hand and said, "You could have done that sooner! I'm paying you more than enough."

The elf squinted down at him. "I don't remember telling you to get out of the carriage, little man." She jabbed him in the gut with the end of her bow. "Get back in there and do everything as I say."

Without any argument, the dwarf climbed into the vehicle and locked the door from the inside. The elf climbed into the driver's seat, pushing the mangled body of the previous driver off and onto the ground. She collected the reins and urged the horses on.

Llanowar's wavy hair fluttered in the wind as she steered the horses through the city at a gallop. A city guard was grappling with one of the dead as they stormed past. The guard called out to them for help, but Llanowar ignored him. Though they had to dodge debris and people in the streets, they arrived at their destination in just a few minutes.

Ruddell's home sat back from the street. A patch of green grass was split down the middle by a walking path in front of the building. It was painted a dull russet and had two stories. Llanowar had spotted a hatch leading underground as they pulled up, and visions of the dwarf's possible wealth nudged at her brain.

Llanowar let go of the reins and dropped to the ground, bow slung across her back. She pounded on the door. Ruddell hesitated, but finally pulled the bolt and pushed the door open. He poked his bald head out of the carriage and took a few seconds to look to the left and right, up and down. Llanowar rolled her eyes and sighed before grabbing him by the collar of his robe and yanking him outside.

The dwarf glared up at her for a second as she said, "Welcome home, M'Lord."

"Well, what are you waiting for?" Ruddell waved his arms. "After you."

Llanowar looked at the three-story home looming over them. "You asked me to get you safely to your home. I did that." She crossed her arms and gave him a sideways glance.

"Oh, stop it. I know how you people are. I've got another pouch of gold with your name on it if you get me inside the house and then out of the city." Ruddell inspected her with an expectant gaze.

"Make it a bag and you have a deal." Ruddell nodded and Llanowar drew the small sickle that was sheathed on her hip. The elf immediately kicked the front door open and went inside. No one appeared, and the house was quiet. "What are we here for?" she asked when the dwarf joined her. She relaxed more when no intruders appeared.

"In the basement. I'll show you." Ruddell scurried past her and led the way through the house. He pulled a large ring of keys out from one of the folds in his robe and flicked through them, stopping in front of a solid metal door.

"You must keep a lot of treasure down there," Llanowar said, looking down at the dwarf.

"The most precious treasures I have," Ruddell replied. He found the key he needed and unlocked the door. He pulled the door open and skipped down the stairs. "Lilta! Cassandra!" The dwarf's slippers rustled on the stone steps as he and Llanowar descended into the basement.

Before they got to the bottom of the stairs, a black-haired human girl appeared. "Papa!"

Llanowar's eyes narrowed at the dwarf, flicking between him and the girl. She gripped the sickle a little tighter.

Ruddell quickly descended the rest of the way and embraced the girl. He only came up to her shoulders. "Sweet one!" Ruddell smiled and reached up, taking her face in both of his hands and pulling her down to plant a kiss on her forehead.

"What's going on outside, Papa?"

"Don't worry about that. We're leaving. My friend here is going to help us get out of Eden." Ruddell turned to the elf. "Llanowar, this is my daughter Lilta."

Llanowar squinted at the girl and then at Ruddell. "Daughter?"

51

Ruddell sighed and gave the elf a disappointed look. "Lilta, where is your sister?"

"Come see," Lilta pulled her father into the darkness. Llanowar followed and saw a ring of light shining from above. Ruddell and Lilta stood in it, looking up. "I told her she shouldn't use her powers, but she said she wanted to go look for you. I tried to stop her."

"Oh, no..." Ruddell stared dumbfounded up at the hole in the ceiling that led to his bedroom.

Llanowar saw the wooden ring above them was charred and scorched, with ember flecks still dotting the wood. "What happened?" she asked.

"Ruddell!" The dwarf flinched as Dane's head appeared in the hole, looking down at him.

"Dane! By the gods, you scared me half to death!" the dwarf said.

"Come upstairs. We have to talk."

Ruddell grabbed Lilta by the hand and led her upstairs, Llanowar close behind, with one last glance at the ring of cinders. Ruddell found Dane with Bren and Pelias, who were looking at the hole in the floor. Ruddell enclosed Dane's hand in both of his and shook it vigorously. "Good to see you, boy," Ruddell said.

"Hello, Sir Dane," Lilta said.

Dane smiled down at the eleven-year-old and said, "Now, you know I'm no knight."

"You have a sword and armor," the little girl replied, pointing at the fox on his chest.

He knelt to eye level with Lilta. "My friend there," Dane jammed his thumb at a doorway where Pelias had just entered, "he really *is* a knight." The girl noticed Pelias' shiny royal armor. She walked over to him as if caught in a trance and tugged at his red cloak. The young man turned and smiled down at the girl. Dane chuckled and looked back at Ruddell. "Your other daughter cut and run?"

Ruddell gave Dane a look that told him to be quiet and then glanced at Bren, Pelias, and Llanowar. "Can we talk about this with our present company?"

Dane shrugged. "I trust *my* guys – they already know about me. You?" He looked at the elven woman. The redhead met his gaze, an unimpressed look on her face.

Ruddell turned to Llanowar. "Two bags of gold if you never repeat what my friend and I are going to say." Llanowar nodded. "That's settled," said Ruddell as he turned back to Dane.

"I came to ask a favor. My companions and I were planning on leaving Eden and going to Etzekel. I thought we could both benefit if you and your daughters came with us."

"Because you need someone to get you into Etzekel."

"I do," Dane nodded. "My friends and I will protect you and your girls if you agree to come to Etzekel with us."

"Yes! I accept!" Ruddell looked at the hole in the floor. "There's a problem..."

"Cassandra is missing."

Ruddell nodded.

"Do you know where she went?"

"I just got here, myself," the dwarf said.

"Great," Dane muttered, scratching at the stubble on his face.

"I know where she is," Lilta said, walking back over to Dane and her father, leaving Pelias and Bren spectating from the corner.

"Where, child?" Ruddell asked.

"She said she was going to look for you at the bank."

Ruddell looked up wide-eyed at Dane. "Dane, I just came from there. It was crawling with those monsters, and a group of soldiers arrived as I ran away. Cassandra could be in real danger!"

"Let's go!" Bren and Pelias joined them as Dane gave the command.

"Llanowar, stay here and protect my daughter. We'll come back for you both."

"No," Dane said. "They come with us. After we get Cassandra, we leave immediately."

"Oh my..." Ruddell took a deep breath.

Llanowar climbed into the driver's seat of the carriage, forcing Pelias to slide down the bench from where he had been seated. The elf took the reins from Pelias' hands and looked at him. "I drive." Pelias looked down at Bren, who shrugged before handing his friend his bardiche – which would not fit inside the carriage - and climbing inside to join Dane, Ruddell, and Lilta.

"Do you know where to go?" Pelias asked Llanowar.

"I do," she replied.

Pelias awaited more information, but the elf did not offer it. He furrowed his brow at her but shook his head in silent resignation.

"Now, Lilta, when we get to the bank, you must stay here in the carriage where it's safe," Ruddell patted the girl's hand, which he grasped tightly.

"So do you," Bren said casually, looking out the window.

"Excuse me, Sir?"

"I'm no knight; don't call me sir. I said you must stay inside the carriage as well. We're going to be looking for a little girl. I don't want to have to look after you as well, Master Dwarf."

"That little girl is my daughter. I won't get in the way. I can defend myself." Ruddell huffed.

"Your powdered hands and silk slippers tell a different story." Bren finally looked at him. "I don't mean to be impolite, but if you want your daughter returned to you safely, you need to stay out of the way."

Ruddell looked incredulously at Dane. "Where did you find this ruffian?"

"While I was in prison," Dane replied. Ruddell blinked at him. "Bren was the Sword of Justice. He's very good at severing heads." The dwarf slowly looked back at Bren, wide-eyed. The big man bowed his head.

"Well, I suppose I should look after the carriage. You lot should be able to handle whatever is happening at the bank." Ruddell smiled nervously.

The rest of the ride was in silence. Lilta observed the now hectic nature of Eden with wide, innocent eyes. The city was less occupied every time they ventured out of doors. It appeared that most citizens had finally learned that staying in their homes was the safest place to be.

Occasionally they would pass a group of two or three of the undead, but they were preoccupied with the meals they had already obtained. Soldiers and knights were also very prevalent in the streets, but they did not bother to try and stop the carriage, as they were busy dispatching the ghouls or wrestling with rioters and looters.

They arrived at the Bank of Eden – a large stone building with thick iron doors that stood wide open. Llanowar and Pelias jumped down from the carriage. Bren took his bardiche from the young knight and scanned the area. As Dane exited the carriage, Ruddell shouted from the window, "Cassandra!"

"Quiet!" Dane growled. "We'll find her. Just stay put."

"I'll stay with them," Llanowar said.

Dane, Bren, and Pelias walked cautiously inside the bank. The marble floor was littered with scorched papers and droplets of blood. Dane looked around but saw no one – only the counter where the bank clerks would sit behind iron bars to handle the thousands of transactions that were processed every day. There were beautiful marble pillars and a stone staircase leading upstairs.

"That dwarf ran this bank?" Bren asked.

"He owns it," Dane replied, picking up one of the burnt pages of paper off the floor. "She was definitely here." He climbed a few of the steps and stopped on the landing. "Cassandra!" He began to climb the rest of the way when three city guards stepped out from a doorway underneath the stairs, one of them holding a brown sack that jingled with every move.

"Who are you two?" One of them asked, holding a one-handed axe by his side. One of the others leveled a crossbow at Bren's chest.

"We're looking for a little girl. My daughter," Bren lied. "She came here thinking she would find me. I work here, but I had already left."

The guards squinted. "Really? Why is there a kingsguard with you?"

"This gentleman offered to help me when I explained my dilemma to him."

"That so? What did this girl look like?"

Bren glanced at Dane, who was crouched on the stairs above the city watchmen. Dane pointed at Pelias and then tugged on a piece of his own hair. "Blonde hair," Bren said. Dane held up ten fingers, removed them, and then held up one more. "Eleven years old."

"We found a girl fitting that description, but..." the guard raised his axe and pointed it at Bren. "You're both under arrest. You, big man, for harboring a magi. And you, 'kingsguard,' for murder and theft of royal property. That armor's not yours! Come quietly and we'll escort you to your daughter."

Dane vaulted over the railing and crashed into the guard holding the crossbow, the weapon sliding across the floor. The other two guards were slow to react, and Bren and Pelias collided with them, knocking them to the ground and snatching their weapons away from them. "Brigands!" one of the guards shouted as he was pinned to the ground.

Pelias snatched the sack from the ground and untied the string. "And you call me a thief." Pelias turned the sack upside down and gold coins started spilling onto the ground with a loud, clattering echo.

"Where's the girl?" Dane asked.

"What do you want with a magi?" The guard looked at Dane. "Wait! I know you! I was in your house when the general arrested you! Yeah, you and that other fellow."

"In that case-" Dane punched the man in the forehead, knocking him unconscious. He looked at the second guard. "Where is the magi?"

The guard said, "We locked her in the vault downstairs."

"In a vault?" Dane raised his fist.

"We were gonna come back for her, I swear!"

Another punch and the guard was also unconscious. Dane looked at the third guard. "Any excuses?"

"No," the man replied, holding up his hands.

"Good." Dane pulled him to his feet and pushed him toward the door underneath the stairs. "Bren, grab the other two."

Bren slung one of them over his shoulder and dragged the other by the ankle. The four of them walked down a hallway that led to a flight of stairs leading downwards. They came into a room that housed thirteen vaults – six on each side and one at the very end.

"Which vault?" Dane asked.

"The one at the very end. Just spin the wheel and it'll open."

Dane walked forward, leaving the others behind. He spun the wheel and pulled the giant door open. As soon as there was enough room to squeeze through, a gnarled hand was clawing its way out. The zombie shrieked and tackled Dane to the ground. The creature flailed its arms, struggling to get a grasp on its meal.

The guard pulled a knife from his sleeve and slashed at Bren, still holding the bodies, but Pelias brought his shield crashing down onto the man's wrist, causing him to drop the knife. Pelias bashed him in the face with his shield, rushed forward, and severed the zombie's head with his sword.

Pelias sheathed his sword and offered his hand to Dane. "Is it dead?" He asked as he tapped the severed head with his boot. No reaction.

"The neck or above seems to work," Pelias responded.

Dane looked at the guard, who sat on the ground, wiping blood from his face. He stormed up to him and punched him. "Where is the little girl?"

"Fine, fine... She's in vault number seven." He coughed blood. "No more, please..."

Dane jerked him to his feet and shoved him forward. "You open it." The guard walked forward, reached out, and turned the handle to the vault. He gave it a tug and in the corner stood a blonde girl, scowling. Her hands were engulfed in flames, glowing orange in the shadow of the vault. In the depths of her eyes, a faint orange glow resonated.

The flames flickered more intensely as she glared at the guard and took a step toward him. He raised his hands in surrender and began backing away. Dane stepped forward, holding out a peaceful hand to her. He ushered the guard aside and knelt to eye level with her. Her eyes widened and the flames instantly extinguished. She jumped into Dane's arms and giggled.

"Sir Dane, you came to rescue me!" The girl's eyes shone with excitement. The circumstances that had caused her to end up inside the bank vault no longer concerned her.

Dane laughed. "Your father and sister are waiting for you outside. Let's go." He took her hand – cold to the touch – and started leading her. He paused and whispered to Bren and Pelias: "Handle them." He craned his neck at the guards.

Bren dropped the two bodies into one of the open vaults as Dane led Cassandra upstairs. Pelias grabbed the last guard by the arm and forced him into the vault. "Wait! We'll die in here!" the guard shouted, looking at both of them.

"We'll come back for you," Bren said, pulling the vault door.

Pelias – grinning – waved and said, "We swear." The guard screamed as the vault door shut and Bren spun the wheel.

As the two of them walked to the stairs, Bren looked down at the kingsguard, smirking. "You're not going to arrest me for that, are you?"

Pelias looked up at his friend. "They locked a little girl in a bank vault. Justice was done here." Bren chuckled and began up the stairs. Pelias stopped and looked back at the vault door. He thought about what he had just said and could not help but replay the events of the night before in his mind. Should he have killed his king, or did he do the right thing by sparing him?

Pelias was exhausted of thinking about it.

Coming out the door, Dane looked up from Cassandra and saw the two looters from earlier standing by the carriage. He pulled the little girl behind him and drew his sword. The giant man – Grunt – and the bronze-skinned one – Koda – both turned at the same time. Koda chuckled, leaning on his spear and pointing.

Ruddell poked his head out of the carriage and shouted at Dane, "Put your weapon away, boy! Bring me my daughter"

Dane gave the dwarf a sideways glance.

"Notice anything?" Koda asked, holding his arms out wide.

Dane's eyes danced around and he saw that there were more bodies on the ground than were there when they arrived. All the bodies were the grey color of the sick. Llanowar stepped out from behind the carriage. "We got surrounded," she said. "They helped." She pointed at the two thieves before climbing into the driver's seat of the carriage.

Dane scowled at Koda and Grunt as he sheathed his longsword. He took Cassandra by the hand and led her around them and into the carriage. He closed the door behind her and turned to the two men. "Did you take what you wanted from my home?"

Koda grinned and held open his cloak, where Dane's spoons, forks, and knives were strung along the inside. Dane raised an eyebrow at him. "Silverware is a sign of wealth where I'm from," Koda explained.

"Then don't expect any other rewards." Dane gestured at the passenger's seat. "Llanowar will babysit you."

Koda climbed up next to her and looked her over. "I don't think I mind at all." He winked at her and the elf rolled her eyes. Bren and Pelias caught the attention of Koda as they appeared. He waved and smirked at Bren. The big man sighed and shook his head. Pelias chuckled at his friend.

"Are we going to let everyone tag along?" Bren asked Dane.

Dane ignored him, motioned for Pelias to sit inside the carriage with Ruddell and the two girls. "I'll walk behind. Bren, you take the left side. Grunt, take the right." The masked man nodded and moved into position.

"Where are we going?" Llanowar called over her shoulder.

"Go to the western gate. It's time we left the city."

* * *

"Are you sure it has to be the western gate?" Ruddell whispered, his face right next to Dane's.

Dane nudged the dwarf away from him and resumed studying the gate. A small crowd of citizens were gathered around, shouting at the city guards that formed a palisade in front of the giant wooden drawbridge. Twenty guards were on the ground, their hands on the hilts of their blades. Three more were on top of the wall, protecting the drawbridge's lever.

"All of the gates are going to be under the same kind of protection," Dane said. "This one will get us headed in Etzekel's direction."

"Do you know where Etzekel actually is, Dane?"

Dane turned his head slowly to the dwarf. "Do you?"

"By the gods, you have no idea!"

"Keep your voice down," Dane hissed, looking over his shoulder at the carriage where his companions waited, observing the gate. "I know it's north-west."

"The New Dawn never told you or... or gave you a map?"

"You know I wasn't that deep into the operation. Why would they trust me with that sort of information?"

Ruddell grunted, remembering how the hierarchy of the organization had operated. "I suppose we can't blame them. It is a sensitive situation." The dwarf frowned. "Still... it would have been a big help."

Dane gave him a pat on the shoulder, pushed off from where he had been hiding behind a pile of stones at the corner of a blown-out building. Everyone turned to face the two of them. The girls were wide-eyed as they sat inside the carriage. Koda lounged up top in the driver's seat and Grunt stood under him. Llanowar was petting the horses and Bren and Pelias had been discussing strategies as they observed the bridge.

"The only thing I know to do is fight our way to the lever," Dane said. "We lower the bridge and get out. If we stick together, we should be able to move through quickly."

"What about the other people? What if they get in the way?" Bren asked.

"They'll be a distraction more than likely."

"Sounds good to us," Koda said. He grabbed his spear and jumped off the carriage, landing next to Grunt. "Just tell us who to gut."

"I don't think we have to murder the guards," Pelias said. "I could convince them that King Endrew ordered all of the gates be opened."

"You're supposed to be in prison." Dane gave him a sideways glance.

"Those men are foot soldiers. They may not know."

Dane looked at Bren, who shrugged. "Worth a shot," he said.

"I don't want to have to kill anyone," Pelias said, looking at the others. Koda rolled his eyes.

Dane said, "We'll try it your way, Pelias, but we need to be ready to fight." Ruddell climbed into the carriage with his daughters. Everyone dispersed – Llanowar climbed back into the driver's seat while the others moved out of the alley where they were parked and fanned out in the street.

Pelias moved alone through the crowd of citizens and approached the stone staircase that led to the top of the wall. None of the guards on the ground questioned him, though they did glance at him curiously. One of the soldiers got pushed by a citizen and the others jumped forward and began beating them back with their gauntleted fists. The crowd backed off and the violence did not escalate any higher.

Dane watched intensely from the edge of the street, leaning on the back of a bench. He glanced from the crowd to each of his companions. Koda and Grunt had melded into the crowd, trying to blend in – even though Grunt towered over everyone in the vicinity. Dane looked over his shoulder at the alleyway where Llanowar waited atop the carriage, reins in hand, while

Ruddell did his best to occupy his daughters' attention. Bren had found his way as close as safely possible to the staircase Pelias had climbed, staring after his friend, awaiting any sign of the situation going bad. Dane realized how much he would appreciate a joke from Amir.

One of the guards atop the wall hit his friend in the shoulder to get his attention and all three of them brought their right fist up and placed them over their hearts, followed by small bows. "Chief Commander," one of them acknowledged. "What can we do for you, Sir?"

Pelias returned the bow. "King Endrew has sent down word – the lockdown is over. He's lifted martial law."

The men looked at one another, surprise evident on their faces. "S-sir?"

"Lower the drawbridge." Pelias took a step forward. One of the men instinctively placed his hand on the hilt of his sword. Pelias stopped in his tracks and gave the man a wary look.

A different guard looked down at the man holding his sword and smacked his hand aside. "What the hell is wrong with you?"

Pelias raised his hand. "It's fine. No harm done. I appreciate a cautious sentinel." He smiled at them. He indicated the crowd below. "We need to lower the drawbridge and allow these people to leave before they do something foolish. I'll turn the lever myself, if you prefer."

"Not necessary, Sir," the man in the middle said. "I'll lower it immediately." The guards fanned out and the one grabbed the crank and began to turn it. The crowd began to shout and pump their fists in the air once they noticed the bridge beginning to lower. The guards on the street turned and stared as if they had never seen such a thing before.

Pelias sighed with relief and flexed his fingers. He peered over the wall and saw the bridge was about a quarter of the way down. He smiled and nodded at the guards. "Well done, men."

"What do you think you're doing?" someone boomed from behind Pelias. He looked over his shoulder at two men who donned the kingsguard armor. Pelias brought his fist to his chest and inclined his head. "Chief Commander, you're out of your cell," the same man said.

"Cell?" One of the guards asked.

Pelias turned to face the kingsguard. "Sir Donnar, Sir Mikel."

Donnar's head was shaved, but his black beard – flecked with grey - fell to the middle of his chest. He was a little taller than Pelias, but had far broader shoulders. Mikel was just a little older than Pelias. His hair was the color of wheat and trimmed short, like Pelias'. He looked at the Chief Commander with sad eyes. "Chief Commander," Mikel nodded at him.

"Raise the gate, you damn fool!" Donnar shouted.

"The Chief Commander said-"

"Raise it!" he shouted.

"Chief Commander?" the guard looked at Pelias.

Pelias sighed and closed his eyes, curling and uncurling his fingers around the strap of his shield several times. Donnar spoke again: "The Chief Commander was placed under arrest for treason. He conspired to kill our king, escaped, and is now trying to get out of the city. Now raise the damn bridge!"

The city guards looked to each other for answers, but they all shrugged or shook their heads.

Finally, the guard began cranking the lever in the opposite direction. The crowd began shouting louder in protest. Pelias took a deep breath and in one fluid motion spun and drew his sword, pointing it at the city guards. He heard the kingsguard draw their swords as well.

"Step back," Pelias ordered.

"Don't listen to him," Donnar barked.

The guards debated amongst themselves: "Do what he says."

"Who?"

"The Chief Commander of course!"

"But he tried to kill King Endrew!"

"Do you really believe that?"

"Sir Donnar says it's true."

"Sir Donnar is not the Chief Commander of the Kingsguard!"

Donnar finally boomed: "Enough! I will have all three of you whipped and beheaded right next to your Chief Commander!" The burly man lunged forward. Pelias blocked the man's blade with his shield and threw him aside. Mikel stood behind Donnar – his sword in his hand, but unmoving.

Bren, who had been distracted by the crowd, looked up to Pelias fighting Donnar. He stormed toward the stairs, but almost instantly the crowd dispersed and a riot ensued. Rocks and shoes were being thrown at the city guards, who in turn began beating people back with their fists. Bren tried to muscle his way through the crowd, when he saw Koda get swallowed up by it. Grunt lifted a man up by the collar of his shirt and threw him over everyone's heads. The mob had backed away from the giant man and were allowing the city guards to attempt to detain him. They surrounded the man with drawn weapons.

Bren looked up at Pelias, and then back at Grunt. He gritted his teeth and shifted the bardiche in his hands. He cursed and ran toward the city guards, ramming one in the back with his shoulder. He took a defensive stance next to Grunt, who snorted like a bull. In his eyes burned a fire, though he had not yet drawn his battle-axe. He looked over his shoulder for any sign of Koda but saw none.

Dane had drawn his sword and was moments away from joining Bren and Grunt in the fray when he heard one of the girls shout behind him. He saw Llanowar jump out of the driver's seat and approach a group of city guards who were attempting to tear Ruddell and his daughters out of the carriage. The elf had already drawn her sickle and she used it to slash one of the guards in the neck. The others spread out - one of them dropping Lilta on the ground – and drew their weapons.

"Now hold on, lass," one of the guards said. "There's eight of us and one of you. I don't think you wanna do this."

Llanowar pointed at the guard on the ground, who clutched at his throat as blood dribbled out. "Seven," she replied. She leaped forward, her sickle swiping in a wide arc, catching one of them across the face and causing him to stumble backwards.

A fist caught Llanowar in the cheek and she collided with the carriage. She scrambled onto the roof of the vehicle before a blade lodged itself into the wood right where she had just been. The elf rolled off the opposite side of the carriage. The city guards chased after her, only to find she had disappeared.

The door to the carriage crashed open and slammed into another one of the guards. Llanowar dove out of the carriage, slicing yet another man in the neck.

Again, Llanowar was sent soaring – this time by being bashed with a shield. She fell to the ground and was swarmed by the guards, who began to kick her with their armored boots.

Dane appeared and stabbed one of them through the chest. He was able to cut down one more before the other guards were alerted to his presence. They beat him back and away from Llanowar. Dane continued to shift backwards, drawing his opponents away from the elf.

The door to the carriage creaked open and Cassandra stepped out. She glared at the guards and in the blink of an eye her hands were engulfed in flickering flames. "Cassandra! Get back in the carriage, now!" Dane shouted.

"Magi!" one of the three remaining guards said. One of them took a step toward her. "You two get him. I'll get the little firefly."

Dane urged: "Cassandra-"

The little girl threw her hands forward and the fire erupted in streams, dousing the guard. He screamed and flailed wildly, cooking in his own armor. Ruddell and Lilta watched with wide eyes from inside the carriage. The other two guards turned and ran. Cassandra took several steps after them, but Dane wrapped an arm around her waist and hoisted her over his shoulder.

He put her back in the carriage and pointed a finger at her. "Don't do that again!" He shut the door and looked at Ruddell. *Watch her.* Dane sheathed his longsword and approached Llanowar, offering her a hand. She took it and spit blood. "Bring the carriage out of the alley but stay away from the drawbridge." She nodded and climbed into the driver's seat.

Dane turned to see that more guards had joined in defending the drawbridge from the mob. The citizens had finally joined Bren and Grunt and were fighting beside them. It was impossible to find Koda in the riot. Dane joined them, running in swinging.

A soldier grabbed Bren by the arm. He shook him off and Grunt picked the guard up and threw him into another enemy. Bren stepped around Grunt and stopped him from being hit with a mace, decapitating the attacker with his bardiche. Dane joined his two companions as their enemies received another batch of reinforcements.

Up top, Pelias pressed his shield into Donnar's stomach and shoved. Pelias ordered the three guards, who were still enthralled with the two knights in gridlock: "Get out of here!" They followed his instruction.

Donnar looked over his shoulder. "Mikel! Get up here and help me!"

Mikel stood still, watching the two men clash. His fingers flexed and unflexed again and again around the hilt of his sword. He did not fully believe that Pelias was a traitor, but it was not his place to say. He would do his duty.

Mikel stepped forward and erupted in a fury of a flashing blade and sparks that jumped when Pelias parried and blocked. Their blades locked, and Pelias saw sadness in Mikel's eyes. "Surrender," he pleaded.

Pelias did not respond but pushed him back as Donnar danced around him and brought his blade down. Pelias smacked his weapon aside with his shield and pressed his blade to his neck. The blood flowed over his blade when he slid it along the kingsguard's neck. Donnar cursed him with his last breath.

Pelias lowered his body gently to the ground. He looked up at Mikel, who took a deep breath. He sheathed his sword and, without a word, turned away.

Pelias' jaw dropped when a spear busted through Sir Mikel's skull. Koda grunted as he pulled his weapon from the knight's face.

"What are you stalling for? Let the bridge down," Koda said.

"He wasn't fighting back! You killed him!" Pelias shouted, rising to his feet.

"We don't have time for this!" Koda replied. "I really want to get out of this damn city."

Pelias scowled, walked to the lever, and began cranking. The fighting below continued as the drawbridge clicked and clanked as the chains holding it unraveled and let it rest securely over the moat surrounding the city. Pelias and Koda ran from the lever and quickly joined Dane, Bren, and Grunt in the middle of the riot.

With the bridge down, the mob had been rejuvenated and they pushed harder against the guards, overtaking them and storming out of the city. Llanowar brought the carriage up to her companions and everyone piled into and onto the vehicle. In a matter of seconds they were off at a gallop, rolling across the drawbridge and forcing the crowd to part for them. Some tried to join them on the carriage, but fell to the ground or were dragged for a few yards.

The companions looked around, trying to take everything in at once – the trees and their leaves, the dirt road beneath them, the running crowd, and each other. Eden had been on lock-down for only a couple of days, but it had been at least a month since Dane had seen the outside of the walls, now great columns of smoke rose out of the city behind them.

Koda grinned, having somehow managed to be the one to slide next to Llanowar on the bench. Grunt held out his hand to Bren in thanks as they both sat on the roof of the carriage. The Sword of Justice clasped the giant man's forearm and shook. The masked man nodded his head.

Ruddell held his girls tightly as he whispered calming words. The girls – ever curious – watched the scenery through the windows. Dane offered Pelias a drink from his water skin, but Pelias refused. Dane took a deep drink as Pelias leaned against the window.

Peering out, someone caught the young knight's eye. From the forest, a man in the armor of a kingsguard walked in the direction of Eden. The man locked onto Pelias' gaze. He had short black hair and a scar over one of his eyebrows. He had two war-axes hanging on his hips.

The most surprising thing was the man's face. The scar was normal – Pelias had been a witness when the man had received it. What made the Chief Commander take a sharp breath was the knight's grey, splotchy skin and his solid white eyes. There was a stain of blood around the knight's mouth.

Pelias murmured: "Sir Eins…"

Chapter 4

"He's waiting for you, sir," Wyll said, motioning at the door.

Braxon grunted. "How long has it been since he left his chambers?"

"Days, sir."

"Does he have wine in there?"

"Yes, sir."

"Good. I'll need it." Braxon walked to the door and stopped. "No interruptions, boy."

Wyll nodded and bounded down the stairs as Braxon pushed open the wooden door. He closed it behind him and walked purposely to the center of the room. He found his king on the balcony. His head moved slowly, intensely – to the point where Braxon was sure he could hear the grinding of the bones in Endrew's neck.

"There are a lot of fires down there," King Endrew said.

"The city guard has organized multiple fire-fighting squads. They'll be out soon."

"What does it matter? Let the city burn."

"I would advise against that, My Lord." Braxon stood tall, his hands clasped behind him.

"What have you come here for? What do you have to tell me?" King Endrew turned and walked into the chamber. He slammed the doors behind him, his long, stringy hair kicking up with the gust of air. He poured himself and Braxon each a cup of wine.

Braxon sighed. "It pains me, Lord, to report that Pelias has escaped the city."

King Endrew glared at the general and the wine flowed over the brim of the cup he held. He slammed the pitcher onto the table and spiraled the cup across the room. "You failed!"

"He had help," Braxon said, unfazed.

"Who?"

"We don't know the identities of all of them, but all the reports I heard said he was with a group of seven to ten. They overpowered the city guards and lowered the western drawbridge."

"And where were you?"

"The undead congregated around the Great Temple of Errit. A large group of people had gathered in prayer and became trapped inside. We rescued them with minimal casualties."

"I don't care about the temple *or* the undead! You let him escape!"

"I have no excuses, Lord. What would you have me do?"

King Endrew began muttering to himself. He turned his back to Braxon and started twiddling his thumbs quickly, his eyes darting around the room. Braxon could not discern what he was saying. He finally turned back to the general. "Pelias knows... He knows the truth, and he *cannot* be allowed to expose us."

"I will hunt him down for you, My Lord."

"Choose whatever men you want from the ranks."

Braxon smirked. "If you would allow, My Lord, I know just the ones suitable for this task..."

"Speak your wish and I will grant it."

"Give me The Ravagers, and then I will hunt down Pelias and all of his companions. I will wipe them out and defend your honor!"

King Endrew flipped through a pile of papers on his nightstand and grabbed his quill. He quickly scribbled his name in a flourish of his wrist and handed the paper out to Braxon. "Take this pardon down to the dungeons. Give The Ravagers whatever they require and go!"

Braxon took the pardon, bowed, and turned. He chuckled quietly to himself as he exited the room.

* * *

"By the gods, we have been blessed today, boys!" Rorn laughed loudly and slapped one of his cellmates in the arm. Through his smile, Braxon could see gaps where a few of his teeth were missing, and glints of gold where others had been replaced. His oily russet hair hung to his shoulders in knots, and his beard was stained yellow around the mouth from years of tobacco usage.

Braxon stopped and looked at each one of the prisoners. Dirty, hair unkempt, they smiled at him through chipped, cracked, and broken teeth. They all had scars — some were missing eyes, noses, or even entire appendages. Braxon sniffed and curled his lip at the barrage of foul stenches that erupted.

"If you don't like the smell, Sir Braxon, you're more than welcome to bathe us," Rorn said, laughing again.

"Perhaps this was a mistake," Braxon said, waving the pardon nonchalantly in the air before turning and walking away.

"'Ey! Whatchu got there?" One of the other prisoners barked.

Braxon stopped and turned. "It *was* a pardon. But I don't think you all deserve it."

"Sod off!"

"Why would His Majesty want to pardon us?" asked Rorn.

"Because I suggested it."

"Why would you do that?"

Braxon coughed – choked by the stench of the dungeon – and stepped forward. "I have a proposition – a deal which would be good for both of us." He turned and waved the guards off.

Rorn's eyes followed the guards out of the room and then he responded: "We ain't got nothin' to bargain with, Sir Knight. Nothin' the likes o' you would want."

"You are wrong."

"Let's hear this deal, then," A skinny man in the corner said.

"I can grant all of you this pardon. You will have full immunity to do as you please and you can never get in trouble with the law again."

A different man scoffed loudly. "Bugger off! We don't have time to listen to your hogwash!"

"This paper doesn't lie," Braxon said through gritted teeth, holding onto his patience. "Do any of you know how to read?"

The Ravagers all looked at one another but no one said a word. Off to the side – in a separate cage – a woman said, "Bring it here."

Braxon looked in the direction of the cage, which was blanketed in shadow, and approached. He had not even known she was there. He knelt to eye level with the woman. He could just barely make out her figure – skinny but muscular. Braxon raised the paper to the bars of her cell.

"Take it back into the torchlight," the woman said. Braxon did so. She took her time studying it. He heard her mouthing the words, occasionally craning her neck and squinting at a difficult word. When she did,

Braxon caught glimpses of long black hair that draped all the way to the floor, pooling by her hands. Finally, she consented, "It's legitimate."

Braxon rolled it up and walked back to Rorn and the others. "Would you care to hear the rest of what I have to say?"

"I'd be lyin' if I said you didn't 'ave my interest piqued, Braxon," Rorn said, now more docile.

"As I was saying: Immunity from the law. The only thing I require is that you fall under my command. You do as I order and you do it when I order it."

"Sounds too simple to me," the skinny man said.

"I'm not a complicated man. It does not interest me to scheme and plot. I present to you the terms I require. Accept them and I will free you."

"You haven't really told us why," Rorn said. "Why us? You have thousands of fighters like us under your command already."

"That's not true. I have *no one* quite like The Ravagers. For what I'm about to do, I don't need fighters - I need hunters."

"I think I get it now," Rorn said. "We're free to do as we please?"

"So long as you follow my orders."

Rorn nodded and looked at his boys. "Aye, we could do with stretchin' our legs."

* * *

There had been little conversation between the strangers since their escape from Eden. Dane had attempted to keep Cassandra and Lilta's spirits up with a little help from Ruddell. Bren and Pelias had whispered amongst themselves occasionally, while Koda chatted casually with his unresponsive companion. Llanowar had ignored all of them to the best of her ability, content to steer the carriage.

The seating arrangements of the vehicle had changed several times. Grunt and Bren now walked beside it on opposite sides. Koda had left his seat next to Llanowar after many failed attempts at conversation, and Pelias had taken his spot, the young knight equally quiet and unbothersome to the elf.

Dane stayed at the rear of the wagon, keeping an eye for any pursuers, though that seemed more unlikely as time passed. They had travelled at a steady pace for several hours, and this was the first time they had stopped to rest, pulling the carriage off the road.

Ruddell was sitting on the ground with his daughters. Grunt and Koda were out gathering firewood. Llanowar was hunting alone, and Bren and Pelias were tending to the horses. Dane knelt by the small creek to refill his water skin. He closed his eyes and focused on the cold water running over his fingers.

Dane said a quick prayer for Amir's soul. He did not know if it would do any good. He had never been a very religious man, but he had memorized the rites. As a mercenary, he had seen travelling priests say them over his fallen comrades. Dane took it upon himself to learn them. This was the first opportunity he had found to say the words for Amir, the first time to catch his breath.

Dane forced the thoughts of his friend from his mind and corked the water skin. He stood and walked back to the middle of camp at the same time Koda and Grunt returned with the firewood. Dane offered the skin to them. Koda set his bundle down and took it.

"Any trouble out there?"

Koda took a swig and offered it to Grunt, who grunted his refusal. Instead, he walked to the creek – his back turned to everyone – and removed the leather mask from his head. He cupped his hands and drank deeply. Dane and Koda both watched him for a moment before Koda handed the skin back.

"Couple of undead," Koda said. "We took 'em out."

"Just be careful – always," Dane said.

"I appreciate the concern, but Grunt and I can handle ourselves."

"You're not wrong there," Ruddell chuckled. "I've been trying to place where I've seen you two, but it's been so hectic I couldn't figure it out." Ruddell got to his feet and, grinning, wagged a finger at the both of them. "You two have made me a lot of money."

Dane gave the dwarf a questioning look.

"The arena," Ruddell explained. "I *never* bet against the two of you."

Koda bowed low, making a sweeping gesture with his arm. "We're honored, Master Dwarf." Grunt grunted with agreement.

Pelias said, "Then I suppose I can't fault you for your display on the castle walls. They don't teach you to practice honor and mercy in the fighting pits."

Koda turned and gave the young man a taunting grin. "More often than not, honor and mercy will come around to bite you in the ass."

"I'd rather die with my honor intact."

"Go right ahead."

"Enough!" Dane hissed. "Things are bad enough, don't make it worse."

Koda jabbed a thumb at Pelias and said in a mocking tone, "I don't think this one likes me."

"I don't." Pelias said, crossing his arms.

"We don't know each other," Dane said, "but for some reason all of our paths have crossed. For the time being, let's try and get along." No one offered a rebuttal, so everyone spread out around the camp they had made and kept to themselves.

Nightfall was fast approaching when Llanowar returned with her kills – six squirrels and two rabbits – which she dropped near Pelias, who was on the ground, building a fire. Koda came up beside her and said, "They say the way to a man's heart is through his stomach. You're going above and beyond."

She ignored him, walked over to the horses, and began inspecting them to make sure they had been properly taken care of in her absence. It was quite some time before anyone attempted to make conversation. Everyone ate their food quietly and stared into the fire or into the dark, watching for any danger.

Dane noticed the girls were starting to nod off, so he stood up and cleared his throat. He did not really know what to say to begin the conversation, so he said, "Thank you, everyone, for helping me out of the city. I don't think we could have done it without one another."

"You don't mean that." Koda grinned and waved Dane's words away. Koda was starting to get used to being ignored, but a silent look from Grunt made him avert his eyes and rid his face of the grin.

"I think," Dane continued, "that before we all travel any further, we need to discuss what our next move is, and we need to decide if we will stay together or not."

"Do we have to discuss this now?" Ruddell asked.

"It would be wise."

"Dane's right," Llanowar said. "It would be foolish to be unprepared. A plan is what we need."

Grunt grunted his agreement.

"We should go to Jalfothrin," Koda suggested. "The elves there will be better equipped to handle this."

"Wrong," Llanowar countered. "Jalfothrin's gates are sealed. They locked themselves away when news reached them of the sickness."

Koda sighed and looked into the fire. "Where would be the next best place to go?"

"The coast. We should acquire a ship and set sail."

"Leave Akreya?" Ruddell asked, as if he had never heard the concept before.

"Plenty of other continents out there. I say we go there before all the ships set sail – or they're stolen." Llanowar bit into a squirrel with fervor.

"It's not a terrible idea," Koda said, both he and Grunt nodding.

"Actually," Dane said, clearing his throat a second time, "Bren, Pelias, and I already had a plan in mind before we got out of the city."

Cassandra and Lilta were fighting sleep, taking in everything the adults were saying.

"Why didn't you start with that?" Koda asked.

"You'll understand in a moment why we couldn't trust you and Grunt at first. You, either, Llanowar. I apologize to all three of you."

"Are you sure we should bring them in on this, Dane?" Ruddell asked.

"Go bugger yourself!" Koda glared at him, no longer in a playful mood. "Grunt and I saved your life and your daughter's life back at the bank while you hid in your carriage, dwarf! Don't forget it!"

"Are you trying to start a fight with everyone?" Bren asked.

"I don't remember talking to you."

"Enough!" Dane said. "Koda – give me a moment to explain. Ruddell – I'm certain we should tell them. They've been nothing but helpful." Dane held his hand out to Cassandra. "Would you come here for a moment, dear?"

She was unsure. She looked at her father, who gave her a half-hearted smile, and then at Dane, who was also smiling down at her. She took his hand and climbed to her feet.

"Show everyone what you can do, Cassandra," Dane coaxed.

"I'm not supposed to unless it's an emergency," she replied, looking up at the sellsword.

"It's safe here, I promise."

Cassandra looked around at everyone, as if seeing them all for the first time. Dane patted her on the shoulder. The girl looked down at her hands and they flashed as they became encased in fire.

Llanowar merely blinked at the girl, having seen her powers firsthand. Koda and Grunt flicked their eyes at one another. Cassandra began playing with the fire, controlling it and twisting it into all sorts of shapes and patterns, her eyes a cloudy orange.

"Why did we make Pelias start the fire if she can do that?" joked Koda.

"Because of King Endrew's ban on magic, we had to protect Cassandra," Dane explained. "Ruddell and I are members of The New Dawn. We protect magi and arrange for them to get to safety."

"And that's why you couldn't trust us?" Llanowar asked. "You thought we would turn you in to the king?"

"We had to be careful."

"You were okay with that?" Llanowar measured Pelias, who was leaning against a tree at the edge of camp.

The Chief Commander of the Kingsguard was staring at the ground. He snapped his head up when he was addressed. "I... what?"

"Do you no longer care about your king?"

Pelias furrowed his brow. "I did dishonor myself by breaking my oath. But King Endrew also dishonored *himself* with the choices he's made. He should not have asked what he did of his subjects."

"I've said it before – honor's overrated," Koda said. "You think Grunt and I survived in the arena for eight years by fighting honorably all the time?"

"We're getting off-topic," Dane said. "Let me explain: The New Dawn escorts people to a magic-safe city named Etzekel. It's run by magi, but they won't let anyone in unless they arrive at the gates with a magi. If we get to Etzekel with Cassandra, we'll be safe."

"Why is that better than going to the coast? We'd just be locking ourselves inside another city wall."

"I *have* to get to Etzekel. My daughter is there." Dane patted Cassandra, who was still playing with the fire. The little girl looked up at him and the flames dissipated. She grabbed his hand and squeezed. Dane smiled at her sadly and ushered her back to where her sister had already fallen asleep.

"Pelias and I have already agreed to accompany him," Bren said.

"As have I," Ruddell chimed in. "Obviously, we'll need Cassandra to get inside."

"I think it would be smart if we all stayed together," Dane said. "We learned at the bridge that we're all skilled. We can survive together. But I understand if any of you want to leave. I don't have that option. I'm getting to Etzekel no matter what."

Grunt made a low growling sound to get everybody's attention, and then pointed at Dane and nodded. "If he's hanging around, I am too," Koda said. He stood and swept his arms wide open. "I find each and every one of you to be charming in your own way!" He looked at Llanowar and winked. She rolled her eyes and looked away.

"What about you, Llanowar?" Dane asked.

"I'll have a whole chest of gold arranged for you," Ruddell interrupted. Llanowar shrugged and Ruddell nodded, a wide grin on his face. "It's settled!"

Later in the night, Llanowar, Ruddell, and Koda relaxed around the fire while the others slept. Koda had tried to make conversation with the woman, but he had never met a more stubborn person in his life, even for an elf. The gladiator was surprised when Ruddell of all people was able to get her talking.

"Why do you sit like that?" the dwarf asked. "With your back to the fire, I mean."

The elven woman picked under her fingernail for a moment longer before responding, "Flames ruin your night vision. If a predator comes to attack us in the middle of the night, I'll be able to see it better."

The flames crackled and a cool midnight breeze shook the leaves over their heads. "You're worried about predators?" Koda asked. "Not soldiers coming after us?"

"You think they'll bother with us when they have so many other problems?" Llanowar scoffed.

"You don't know Braxon," Ruddell replied.

"He's crazy," Koda agreed. "Killing magi is his only mission." He looked at Ruddell, whose eyes held an anger he had not yet seen. Koda held his hands up. "I'm sorry, dwarf."

Ruddell looked at his daughters, two bundles snoring softly in the grass next to him. He sighed. "You're not wrong. I've been on edge for the last few months. I'm relieved to be out of Eden."

"Do they know?" Llanowar asked, sparing a look at the girls before bringing her eyes back to the darkness.

"What?" Ruddell asked.

"That they're not yours."

"Oh... Yes, they know. They're not stupid."

"I'm just trying to be considerate."

"I have a feeling that doesn't happen often," Koda said to Ruddell, "don't ruin it." He looked at Llanowar, but his teasing had no effect. He sighed and tossed a twig into the fire.

"They've been mine for a couple of years. I remember the day I adopted them. Happiest day of my life." The dwarf smiled at Cassandra and Lilta as they slept.

"What made you decide to do it?" Llanowar asked.

"I had never married, and I wanted a family. My money bought me a comfy house, but it was empty by myself."

"I'm surprised you adopted two girls. Most consider girls too much work."

Ruddell chuckled. "I came from a home of fourteen kids. I was the only boy. I'm used to dealing with girls."

Koda thought he saw a smile tug at the corner of the elf's lips, but she turned her head away before he could know for certain.

* * *

"Why does *he* get to stay cozy in the carriage?" Koda asked, raising his voice over the howling wind and beating rain.

"It would be ridiculous to have a carriage and not use it," Ruddell said.

Koda shot him a glare and pulled the hood of his cloak down even tighter. "You walk, and I'll ride, little man."

"No! You're already soaking wet. You'll ruin the seat!"

"You'd be better off staying silent, Ruddell," Bren said from the other side of the vehicle, frowning. He had no cloak to shield his body from the elements, and the droplets raced down his face. The retort on Ruddell's lips disappeared and his mouth closed. He put his arms around his daughters to garner a defense in being thrown out into the open.

Llanowar wiped the rain from her eyes and tugged her own hood down, groaning every time the wind would lift it off her head. Pelias, sitting next to her, had offered to take the reins, but the elf was reluctant to hand them over, mumbling something inaudible through the torrent.

Grunt, like Bren, had no cloak, but he paid no attention to the weather. The rain streamed off his mask in a funny way, dropping onto his strong chest and soaking his shirt. He trudged along beside Koda without complaint.

"We should have pulled off the road and packed ourselves in that wagon as soon as the rain started," Koda continued.

Dane called from the back, "We don't have time to waste on unnecessary stops. Braxon could be hunting us, you know that."

"Well, you could have mentioned last night that none of you had any idea where Etzekel is," Koda said, strolling along beside the carriage, sighing and accepting his fate in the rain.

"The New Dawn was pretty tight-lipped," Ruddell said. "It was only the highest members that were allowed to know the exact location of the city."

"What exactly did you do for the group?" Koda asked.

The dwarf draped out the window, smiling at the bronze-skinned man. "Most importantly, I provided The New Dawn with excessive funds. I also sheltered magi from time to time."

"A saint among men..."

"We're gonna have to get rid of the wagon," Dane said. "There's a village a few miles up the road. We can sell it and maybe buy a couple more horses with the gold."

"No carriage?" Ruddell whimpered.

"Etzekel is somewhere deep in the forest. No roads, so no carriage."

"But the girls will get tired easier."

"No, we won't!" Cassandra said, swinging her feet as she sat across from her father."

"Yeah! We're bored of riding in here!" Lilta chimed in. "Can we go out in the rain?"

Dane chuckled at the girls and the bewildered look on Ruddell's face. He did not notice Bren sidling up next to him. His bardiche was propped on his shoulder and rain droplets congregated around the hairs of his goatee. There was a serious look on his face that spread to Dane.

"Did you say a prayer for him?" Bren asked suddenly.

Dane's eyes fell to the dirt road turning to mud underneath his feet. "I did," was his reply. The two of them slowed their pace until they were out of earshot from the rest of the group. "He died for me. And Evie. And everyone in The New Dawn... I was ready to give up all my information, but he stopped me."

"Don't feel guilty, Dane."

Dane shrugged. "Amir was always stronger than me. Wasn't the first time he saved my ass." He took a swig from his water skin. "You were a friend to him, as well, Bren."

A smile flashed on Bren's face and then disappeared just as quickly. "He had a lot of friends."

Dane nodded. They left it alone after that, gradually joining up with the others as they crested the top of a hill that looked down on the small village called White Willow.

Thatch-roofed houses dotted the area, with a stable and a building that could either be a meeting hall or a temple being the largest structure. The village was lazy, with only a few people seen scurrying around tending to their labors. The whole area was quiet – no voices, no animals, no loud noises that could be associated with work of any kind.

"Not a village of early risers, huh?" Koda said.

Dane pushed to the front of the group. "It's midday. It shouldn't be like this. Everyone stay on alert." They proceeded down the hill as their eyes scanned their surroundings. Dane motioned for Llanowar to stop the carriage at the edge of the village.

Four people approached them from downhill, gesturing with friendly waves, ignoring the rain. "Greetings," a man in a wide-brimmed hat said, smiling.

"Hello," Dane replied. "We were looking to sell our carriage and purchase some horses."

"Is it stolen?" A woman asked, eyeing it suspiciously.

"No, Miss, it's mine," Ruddell said.

"Is there anyone who can accommodate us?" Dane asked.

"Well," the man in the hat said, "our stable master recently came down with illness, but he may be able to help you."

Dane looked at his companions, who returned the skeptical look. "Illness?"

"Nothing serious, just a fever and cough. I don't think it's contagious."

"If he's willing to help us, we would appreciate it."

The greeting party walked away, leaving the companions waiting at the perimeter of the village. "Something's not right with these people," Pelias said. Grunt grunted his agreement. "Most folk would offer strangers a place to get dry…"

"Let's just wait and see what happens. We can leave after we get the horses."

"Sickness, did you hear him?" Ruddell asked.

"I heard. Stay calm."

It was not long before the man in the hat returned to them. "Fernie wants to ask you a few questions about the carriage. If you'll follow me…"

Dane, Ruddell, and Bren followed the man while the rest remained with the carriage. The rain gradually lightened before ceasing as they were led downhill to the large temple building. A group of children sat on the stone steps, heads in their hands, looking dejected and bored. It was obvious from their plastered legs that they had been enjoying the mud. The man shooed them off the steps and kept walking.

Inside, the temple was dark, with only a couple candles in the corner. Dane, Bren, and Ruddell looked at one another when they realized that there were a dozen people scattered across the floor, bundled up in blankets, coughing into rags, and spitting into buckets strewn around them. Somewhere, someone was moaning as if on the peak of death. There was burning incense placed all around the room to try and hide the smell of vomit and other excretions.

Dane put his hand on Ruddell's shoulder. He could tell that the dwarf was about to object to being in the building, and Dane did not want to ruin their chances of selling the carriage here. They followed the man to the back of the temple, stepping over the people on the floor and offering quiet apologies.

The man they came to talk to looked like he had more than a fever. His skin was vividly pale, his eyes watery, and he was drenched in sweat. There were droplets of blood on the ground next to his face and he had a firm grip on the wooden bucket next to him.

"Fernie, these are the folks looking to sell the carriage."

Fernie coughed and spit blood into the bucket. "I… I've got Marleyn taking down a description of the carriage, she'll be back with the specifications of your vehicle… Until then, I have some…" He spit in the bucket again. "Q-questions about it." Fernie took a soaked rag and wiped his forehead, laying still for so long that Bren and Ruddell glanced at one another. Bren shrugged. Fernie snatched the rag off his head and said, "How long have you owned the vehicle?"

"About two years, I think," Ruddell replied.

"How often do you drive it in a week?"

"I never drive it."

Fernie clutched his head and grimaced. "You dunce... how often is it used?"

"Oh! Every day."

"Has it ever made any journeys of significant distance, or has it stayed in one city?"

"It was used only in Eden, until we came here."

A thin, young girl with thick, wavy blonde hair brushed past Bren. He caught her eye and offered a friendly smile, to which she blushed and let her eyes drop to the ground as she knelt next to Fernie, a piece of paper in her hand. She held it out to him, who smacked her hand away. "You think I wanna read in my condition?"

Marleyn dropped her head and stared at her scribbles. When she spoke, her voice was mousey. "The... the body of the vehicle is black lacquered wood with golden olive branch trim. Wheels and axles are in good condition, except the right rear wheel has a crack that runs the circumference of it. Reins and yoke also in good condition. Padded cloth bench seats on the inside, sewing starting to unravel on one side. Minor tears in the other. The doors on both sides creak when opened."

Fernie lay motionless for a while longer. Marleyn looked around nervously before poking him in the ribs. Fernie smacked her hand again. "Hands off me, woman. I'm thinking." He spit more blood into the bucket and then put his hand on her shoulder, pulling her down until she was almost lying beside him. He whispered in her ear and then draped the wet rag over his face.

Marleyn stood and straightened her dress. "If you'll come with me, I will pay you for your carriage." She averted her eyes and walked away.

The three men followed her out of the temple, casting last glances at the ill. "I'm glad to be out of there," Ruddell muttered. Marleyn led them towards the stables - which had a conjoined house - where Llanowar had parked the vehicle. "Llanowar, my dear, begin unyoking the horses."

"Hold on," Dane said. "Marleyn, how much is Fernie giving us for the vehicle?"

"If… if you'll just come inside we will discuss it." She looked at him and then immediately dropped her gaze again. Her blue eyes flickered with fear as she met his eyes and dropped them again. Dane held his hand at his side, his fingers spread out, shaking it slightly to get her attention. She gave him a pleading look, and Dane followed her sight as she dropped her eyes to his longsword. Dane gripped the hilt and swallowed.

Bren caught the gesture as well and slowly turned, taking in the village. There were no other villagers in sight. Pelias perked up and took a step toward them, hand on his sword. Dane shook his head at him. Ruddell looked up at all of them. "Perhaps I should stay with the carriage?"

Marleyn shook her head, looking more scared than before. She pushed the door of the house open and waved them inside. "Come inside and I will get your compensation."

Dane walked in first, looking at the doorways leading off on both sides, hand still on his sword. Bren ushered Ruddell in next and then followed behind, keeping an eye over his shoulder and on Marleyn. Dane noticed a bloodstain on the wooden floor under his feet.

Marleyn stepped in and shut the door, locking it behind them. She slid into one of the corners, pressing herself into it as tightly as she could, and hit the wall three times with her fist. Eight armed men stepped out of the rooms around them. Dane recognized a few of them - such as the man with the wide-brimmed hat, who held a pitchfork.

"What the hell is this?" Bren asked, glaring at them.

"Give us your weapons and you can leave alive," a bearded man said.

"Oh my!" Ruddell said, clinging to Bren's tabbard. "Take whatever you want!"

"If you follow through with this, you will die," Dane said.

Bren brushed Ruddell away and gripped his bardiche in both hands. "Don't discourage them, Dane. They deserve a beating."

"We don't wanna hurt you folks, we just need weapons," one of the bandits said.

"You're going about it the wrong way."

"Enough talk!" Another man shouted, pointing a knife at them. "We got sick people here and we got monsters roaming around these woods. Give us your weapons and get out of here!"

Dane was about to retort when a sharp scream pierced their ears. Everyone froze for a moment. "That sounded like Milly!" the man in the hat shouted. "Unlock the door, Marleyn." The girl did as she was told, throwing the door and retreating to her corner. The man walked out and looked around. "Hey, get out here, now!"

The other bandits left Dane and the others in the house, running out as if nothing out of the ordinary had just taken place. More screams followed, drawing Dane and Bren out of the building. All the people that had held them up were sprinting toward the temple where they had spoken with Fernie minutes before.

"What's happening?" Dane asked.

"We don't know. There was a scream that came from the temple and all of them started running over there," Pelias said.

"Good riddance," Bren said. "They tried to hold us up."

Ruddell ran out of the house, holding a box. "I got their gold!" he laughed. "That will show these brigands!" He ran and threw it into the carriage. "Let's go!"

"What about the horses?" Koda asked.

"Take them!"

"Wait!" Pelias said. "We're stealing from them?"

"Here we go again." Koda rolled his eyes.

"They tried to steal from *us*," Dane said.

Another scream led the others to see the bandits shoving each other out of the way to try and escape the temple. A couple of them fell down the steps, others leapt through the air, waving their arms and screaming. Out of the darkness of the doorway, a grey hand stretched out and clutched the doorframe.

Into the sunlight shuffled an undead, with grey skin and solid white eyes. The zombie stumbled down the stairs and latched onto one of the bandits who had fallen. It took a giant bite out of the man's leg. He screamed and attempted to beat it back with the mallet he was holding.

It was as if a dam had broken – undead after undead erupted out of the temple, spreading out through the village and searching for a meal. Marleyn stepped out of the building and gasped when she saw the threat.

"Don't look," Bren said, grabbing her hand and ushering her toward the carriage.

"Dane, we should help them!" Pelias shouted.

"We should get the hell outta here!" Koda interjected.

Dane looked at the villagers, who were struggling to fend off the monsters. He debated abandoning them until he saw a woman trip and fall to the ground. With an undead approaching her, Dane drew his longsword and ran forward.

"Let's go!" Pelias shouted, running forward and drawing his sword. Bren followed, leaving Marleyn next to the carriage. Grunt hit Koda in the arm and ran toward the fighting. Koda rolled his eyes and grabbed his spear and leapt off the top of the wagon, his black cloak flapping behind him.

Dane kicked the zombie to the ground and helped the woman to her feet. She ran off and Dane turned to see a man get grabbed and a chunk of his flesh pulled from his forearm. The mercenary decapitated the monster, but the victim fell to the ground, wailing and bleeding in the grass. The other companions joined Dane, ferociously fending off the undead.

Behind them, Llanowar pulled out her sickle and began cutting the straps that tied the horses to the carriage. "Lilta! Cassandra!" The girls ran over to the elf. "Hold these reins. Don't let the horses run! I'm going to get the others from the stable." The horses whinnied and danced around, tugging at the reins.

She raided the stables for some rope to bind the other horses. The animals stomped in their stables, panicked by the noise and sensing the fear in the people nearby. "Ruddell! Get over here and help me find something to tie these horses!"

The dwarf came crashing into her after rummaging through a chest. "I don't see anything!" he cried.

"I've already looked in there! I saw a shed behind the stables. I'll go check there; you check the house." The two of them split off from one another.

Ruddell wrung his hands nervously, creeping into the house at a snail's pace. "Anybody still in here?" he shouted. "I'll hurt you if you try to attack me!" He raised his fists to protect himself. Marleyn shot through the door behind him, causing him to jump forward and cling to the wall in terror. "Child! I think you gave me a heart attack!"

The human girl ignored him and shoved him toward one of the rooms. "There's rope and tack in there," she said. As the two of them were grabbing the supplies, they heard one of the girls scream.

They ran back outside, arms weighed down with bridles, reins, and rope. Ruddell gasped when he saw Lilta holding her shoulder while an undead scrambled to cling to her. Before they could react, Cassandra let go of her horse's reins and grabbed Lilta, pulling her sister away from the monster. The horses galloped away.

Lilta fell to the ground, blood bubbling up from under her hand. Cassandra stepped between her and the zombie. As her hands hung at her side, they erupted in flame. She glared at the approaching monster and raised her hands. The flame that engulfed her hands pulsed and flickered before leaping forward and encasing the undead.

Dane and the other companions approached, staring on in shock. Their weapons were soaked in blood and the bodies of the fallen were strewn behind them.

The flaming zombie stumbled backwards into the carriage, setting it aflame. Marleyn and Ruddell ushered the two girls away and watched with wide eyes as it shuffled forward, slowing down to a halt. The undead dropped like a sack of flour, headfirst into a pile of hay, letting out a loud shriek as it stopped moving. The hay flared and the fire licked its way toward a wooden beam that supported the stable.

The horses whinnied and neighed as the building slowly became a pyre. Llanowar ran up next to them, looking at the flames. She rushed forward and unlatched as many of the stable gates as possible, throwing them open as hard as she could. The horses galloped into the woods, thundering past everyone before they could attempt to gather them.

"Get away from the carriage!" Dane said.

They all gathered around Lilta, who lay on the ground as she held her wound. The little girl winced through tears and panted heavily.

Dane said, "We need to get her somewhere safe. Who knows if there's more undead in the area?"

Marleyn looked around. "No one is alive?"

"Just us," Bren said, shouldering his bardiche, panting and looking back at the bodies. "Sorry."

"Good." She crossed her arms and looked away from the dead. Bren furrowed his brow but said nothing.

"We need to go," Dane said, wiping the blood off his sword with a tuft of grass and sheathing it. "Grunt, will you..." he pointed at Lilta sprawled on the ground.

Grunt nodded and gently lifted her off the ground. Ruddell watched the giant walk away with his daughter, but the dwarf was hard-pressed to stand on his own. Cassandra grabbed his hand and tugged. He struggled to his feet, wiping tears from his face and following Grunt.

"We need horses," Ruddell stated, absent-mindedly.

"We're walking for now, my friend," Dane said, leading his companions into the woods where there were no roads.

Chapter 5

Braxon spread the ashes around. He flicked the residue off his fingertips and stood up. "This fire is fresh. They left sometime early this morning."

Aiya - the Ravager who had read the pardon in the dungeons - pointed at a pile of bones on the ground. "They have a hunter with them. A decent one, at that." She looked from the bones to Braxon, her thigh-length black braid swinging with the motion.

"So they won't be starving anytime soon," Rorn said. The stocky man spit, with some of it catching in his beard, and planted his hatchet in a nearby tree.

"Where's your tracker?" Braxon asked.

"Leyon!"

A skinny man pushed through the group of Ravagers. In his mouth was a piece of straw and on his shoulder was a wooden club with a black stone — obsidian — imbedded deep in the wood. He held the weapon out to Rorn, who took it. Leyon dropped to his hands and knees, studying the ground and brushing leaves aside.

"Did they get back on the main road?" Braxon asked.

"They had a wagon. Considering we haven't found it abandoned in the forest or on the side of the road, they would have no choice." Leyon took his club back from Rorn. "With a wagon, there's only two destinations they could get to. Bandimere or White Willow."

"It has to be Bandimere," Braxon said. "There's nothing in White Willow. It's a dead end."

"Unless they were going to ditch the wagon there and continue into the forest or the Platinum Plains."

"Will you be able to tell?"

Leyon sighed in a bored manner. "The right rear wheel on this wagon has a crack in it. I'll be able to tell which way they went."

Braxon waved his hand in a circle. "Let's move out!"

* * *

Dane put the rag against his water skin and turned it upside down for a moment. He wrung it out and handed it back to Cassandra. The little girl dabbed it gently against her sister's forehead. Ruddell sat on the ground, using his leg as a pillow for Lilta, and stroked her hair continually.

Dane left them alone and joined the others, who were gathered at the edge of the camp, where the light of the fire began to fade away. Koda leaned on his spear near Llanowar, who was sharpening her sickle. Grunt watched the forest for any disturbance while Bren and Pelias leaned against a couple of trees. Marleyn was hard-pressed to find herself away from Bren's presence.

Dane looked at each of them and sighed, scratching at the stubble on his jaw, stopping to feel at the scar on his chin. "I..." The words escaped him.

Koda swallowed and stared at the ground. "What... What do we do about her?" he asked.

Pelias answered: "We should just give it some time. Give everyone a moment to breathe."

"It only took a day for her to become...nothing."

"She's not dead, yet." Llanowar said, her eyes still on her blade.

"That's not what I meant," Koda said, exasperated. "But... she might as well be. We have no medicine. Soon, she'll be one of those things..."

"You shouldn't give up on her so soon," Pelias said.

"I don't want to, but I see where this is going. She has an incredible fever. Her skin is severely pale. Hitched breathing. Body aches. I've seen plenty of people die in the fighting pits and let me tell you that it's not always from a stab wound or getting your skull caved in." Koda stamped his spear into the ground to draw everyone's gaze as he pointed to where Lilta lay on the ground. "That's what a killing disease looks like."

It was silent for a few moments, save for the bugs, Cassandra's sniffles, and Llanowar's sharpening stone. Finally, Bren said, "Dane, she looks exactly like those people in White Willow did."

Dane nodded and looked at Marleyn. "How did all of your friends get sick?"

Marleyn brushed her thick hair out of her eyes and spoke quietly, "I don't want to think of them as friends anymore..." She held one of her arms, rubbing her hand up and down as she thought. "It started small – a couple of them had gotten attacked by monsters. Monsters that they described as people with pale skin and blind eyes, just like what they themselves turned into."

"So it's a fact... The sickness and the undead are correlated," Dane said.

"Has to be," Pelias interjected. "Think about the sick people in Eden."

"The sickness was in Eden for weeks. Why is Lilta turning so fast?"

99

"Younger, smaller... weaker," Llanowar offered.

"So she's gonna be one of those things, soon," Koda said. "Do we... you know?"

"Kill her?" Pelias said. "She's a little girl. She's innocent."

"Tell that to the zombie that made lunch out of her shoulder."

"Easy, easy," Bren said, putting a hand on Pelias' shoulder. "This is an unpleasant conversation for all of us."

Llanowar sheathed her sickle and stood from the stump she sat upon. "It would be merciful to put her out of her misery. When you are hunting and you bring an animal down, you immediately kill it. Anything else is disrespectful."

"But we didn't do this to her. It's not up to us," Pelias said. "That's murder."

"What would it matter if we waited for her to turn into one of those monsters?" Koda said. "That's just delaying the inevitable."

"We're not the only people here," Marleyn interjected. Everyone looked at her and she dropped her eyes. "Sorry."

"What makes you think you can speak as one of us?" Koda asked.

"Easy, Koda," Bren said, staring him down.

"If she wasn't such a coward, maybe Lilta wouldn't have been bitten. She's so damn mousy... If she had just spoken up, maybe..." He gestured toward the girl lying on the ground.

"Quiet," Pelias said, taking a step forward, putting a hand on the hilt of his sword.

"Now you're okay with violence, eh?" Koda said, grinning at the young man. "You wouldn't have lasted five minutes in the arena."

"This isn't the arena, and I don't need any dirty tricks to gut you, Koda."

"Enough!" Dane hissed through gritted teeth. Koda and Pelias said nothing but continued glaring at each other. "You can speak," Dane said to Marleyn.

She pointed at Ruddell and Cassandra. "That's her sister and her father. They should decide."

"Marleyn's right," Bren said. "None of us have any say about this."

Dane sighed again and nodded. "Ruddell," he called, "will you come over here for a moment?"

The dwarf made no move or made any sound. Dane looked at the others, who shrugged. He walked over to where the man and his daughters were gathered. Dane put his hand on his shoulder and shook it gently.

"Leave me be," Ruddell said.

"I know this is hard, but we have to talk."

"Leave me be."

"I'm sorry. I can't do that."

"Go with him, daddy," Cassandra said, looking into her father's eyes and giving him a small smile. She squeezed his hand. "I'll take care of Lilta."

Ruddell smiled back at her and stood, letting Lilta's head down gently to the ground. He walked behind Dane, his head down and hands folded inside the sleeves of his robes. "Hello, everyone."

"You doing all right?" Pelias asked.

"Not really." He lowered his voice and said, "I know what it is you lot want to talk about. You're not killing my daughter."

"Take it easy," Dane said. "We don't want that either. We want to discuss all our options."

"The options don't matter. None of you are touching my daughter." He glared up at all of them.

"There's no need to get hostile," Bren said. "We're all very sad about what happened to Lilta. We just wanted to know what you thought about the situation. Now we know."

"Now you know," Ruddell said, looking at each of them. "Mind your own business." Ruddell turned and fell to his knees, gasping for air. They all looked to see what had startled him and the breath in their lungs left them.

Cassandra stood over her sister, fire arcing out of her hands and coursing over Lilta's body. Ruddell screamed, ran toward her, and tackled her. They tumbled to the ground and Cassandra screamed.

Dane ran over and tried to wrestle the angry dwarf off the girl, but it took Grunt's strength to do so. The giant ushered Dane aside, lifted the dwarf by his belt, and walked away with Ruddell dangling in the air like a piece of luggage. Dane escorted Cassandra away from her sister and cradled her close to him.

"Do... do we put her out?" Koda asked. He, Llanowar, Pelias, and Bren stood around Lilta's burning body, their eyes wide. No one answered.

Grunt pressed the dwarf against a tree. The giant human dropped to one knee and looked Ruddell in the eye. He patted him on the shoulder, but Ruddell paid him no mind, unable to see through the curtain of tears that blocked his sight. He tried to brush Grunt's arm away unsuccessfully.

"We should put her out," Koda said with less doubt.

"We don't have time to dig a grave. There is nothing dishonorable about burning her." Llanowar said, blinking several times.

"But... she wasn't dead," Pelias responded, the fire flickering in his wide eyes.

Cassandra shouted, "Yes she was!" Dane held her back, but the girl tried to shove around him. "She wasn't breathing – she wasn't! I didn't kill my sister!"

"It's all right, Cassandra," Dane said, holding her tighter. Her body was shaking, but he did not know if it was because she was overwhelmed or angry.

She huffed and looked up at him, wiping a tear from her eye. "She asked me to do it, Sir Dane."

"What?"

"She asked me to put her to sleep. She said she hurt. She asked me to stop it. I did it. I loved her."

Dane felt the tears forming in his eyes, but he fought them off. He embraced her again and stroked her blonde hair. He looked over his shoulder. Bren and Llanowar gave him sympathetic gazes. Koda avoided his eyes, and Pelias could not tear his attention away from the burning corpse.

Dane felt Cassandra tug on his clothing. He looked at the sweet girl's face, the tears crafting trails on her dirty cheeks. "Is my daddy mad at me?"

Dane racked his brain for the proper answer, but the longer he waited to respond, the sadder Cassandra got. "He's just sad. It'll be okay, Cassandra." He looked over at Ruddell, whose dead eyes stared unwaveringly at the ground.

Koda scooped water out of the creek and splashed it on his face. There was an empty feeling in his stomach, and the cool water felt good. He stared at his glistening hands. They were shaking ever so slightly.

He knelt over the water and submerged his entire head. He felt it swirling around him, tugging at his black hair, bubbles popping up as he slowly exhaled through his nose. He heard something swish by his face, and the deafening rumble of someone approaching.

Koda flung his head out of the creek, water trickling down his face and onto his chest. He blinked droplets out of his eyes and reached for his spear. A large hand grabbed him by the shoulder.

Grunt was staring down at him, eyes as silent as the man himself. Koda retracted his hand, leaving his weapon in the grass. Grunt crossed his arms and took a step away. Koda wiped his face with the edge of his cloak.

"Crazy night, huh?" Koda asked.

Grunt grunted.

"I mean, no crazier than any other night here recently..."

The giant man blinked slowly, standing still as a statue.

"That girl..." Koda sighed. "... Should I have...?"

Grunt shrugged.

"You're no help..." Koda grabbed his spear and stood, leaning on the weapon. "I've been going through the whole thing in my head over and over. I'm not even sure if there's anything I could have done... probably, but... I don't know."

Koda remembered drying his face, but somehow there was still water stinging his eyes as he looked up at his friend. To most people, the giant's stare would have been unreadable and possibly even unnerving, but Koda could read him like a book and knew that the man empathized with him. After a moment of silent gazing, Grunt punched him lightly in the shoulder and walked away. Koda followed.

Later – well into the night – Dane lay awake. He rubbed his eyes and sat up, sighing. He propped himself against a log. He looked over at Pelias, who was keeping watch. The young knight was leaning against a tree with his arms crossed. His eyes surveying the darkness surrounding their camp.

"Anything?" Dane asked softly.

"Nothing," Pelias responded. He shoved off from the tree and approached the fire. "I don't like this."

"You'll have to be more specific."

"Wandering lost in the forest, hoping we end up where we intend to. It doesn't sit well with me."

"I understand," Dane said. "It sounds ridiculous to me – to search for a secret city that doesn't exist on a map. I have no choice. I don't know if I want to leave Akreya... but I know I can't do it without Evie."

"I'm following your lead." Pelias gave him a quick smile.

Koda said, "I can't sleep a wink with you two chattering on."

"Sorry," Pelias said.

Koda sat up, groaning. "I'm joking. Can't sleep anyway." He stood and stretched, looking around. Ruddell and Cassandra were both asleep – although at opposite sides of the camp. Koda thought about how the girl had cried herself to sleep only a few hours ago and grimaced.

Looking over, he saw Marleyn sleeping next to Bren. He grinned and jammed a thumb in their direction. "What's that about? Seems she's joined to his hip."

"Jealous of him?" Pelias teased. "Too bad you made yourself look like a fool earlier."

"She's gotta be almost half his age. But I'm much better looking, if you ask me." Koda chuckled and stumbled lazily to the edge of the camp to urinate. "I suppose I should apologize for what I said to her..."

There was silence for a while except for the chittering of nocturnal insects. A slight breeze picked up, causing the flames of the campfire to pulse in response. Koda returned to the warmth, placing a blanket over his shoulders.

"I have seen a lot of wicked things in the arena – I've *done* a lot of wicked things," Koda said, "But I think seeing Lilta burned by her own sister was the most horrendous thing I've ever witnessed."

"Keep your voice down," Pelias whispered. "You don't want Cassandra to hear." Pelias paused and closed his eyes. "I agree with you, though. Poor girl."

Dane said, "We need to be more careful tomorrow."

"What do you mean?"

"In White Willow – we left the girls alone. Lilta got bit, and Cassandra could have died too. It was tragic, and it can't happen again. Especially not to Cassandra. We need her to get into Etzekel. She's the only magi we have."

Koda looked away, picking up a rock and running his thumbs over it. Pelias said, "We'll all be more careful from now on. We can keep someone with her at all times."

"We all need to stay in teams. No one goes anywhere without someone to watch their backs. I don't want to lose anyone else." The three of them nodded in agreement.

"You two get some sleep," Koda said. "I've slept as much as I'm going to this night."

* * *

The next day was spent walking in silence. Ruddell had become a shell of a man. He trudged along with his eyes on the ground before him. He did not acknowledge anyone, just silently obeyed when instructions were given to him.

Cassandra tried her hardest to get him to talk, but he ignored the words she spoke. It was not long before the little girl's face dropped. Her bottom lip constantly quivered in an effort to fight off tears. Dane ushered her near the front of the group to walk with Marleyn, while Bren and Llanowar stayed in the back with the dwarf.

The weight of yesterday's events bared down on all of them. The only times they found solace were when they came upon the dead. After they were cut down, the silence resumed. No one could forget the burning body of the girl.

Close to dark, they found a cottage in the woods. One corner of the building had fallen, and the roof was on the verge of collapsing, but it would still provide more cover from the elements than they had gotten so far during their travels.

Approaching cautiously, Dane opened the door while Koda slipped in through the gap in the corner. Llanowar and Grunt circled around, but there was no one around – living or dead – inside or out. The companions piled inside away from the open corner.

Marleyn brushed the leaves and dust off the table while the others set the other furniture upright. The furnishings, though dirty, were still comfortable and a welcome change. There were even a few blankets that Llanowar waved the dust out of. The place smelled musty and damp, but that was no matter to them.

When the sun set, they lit a fire and huddled around the stone fireplace. Pelias kept his back to it, keeping watch while the others relaxed. Dane could tell that everyone was pleased to be under a roof, no matter how dilapidated it was, but they were still bothered by Lilta's sudden death.

Ruddell was still unresponsive. His face still drooped, his eyes empty as he stared at a bloodstain in front of his feet. The others ignored the red, but it was the only thing holding the dwarf's attention.

Marleyn sniffed and glanced up at Bren. He offered a small smile, but nothing else. She looked at everyone's faces, twisted in thought and reflection. She saw Dane thumbing the scar on his chin slowly, and it gave her an idea.

Marleyn cleared her throat to try and get everyone's attention and said, "Did you get that while you...?" She nodded her head at the sigil on Dane's chest.

He nodded and rubbed the armor with his fingertips. "Yeah. A guy with a hatchet tried to hit me in the skull. I was lucky to walk away with just this."

"Wow!" Marleyn said, smiling. "Do you miss it? Mercenary work, I mean."

Dane shrugged. "Not really. It was my only choice when I was a kid. Same goes for a lot of guys, but some of them just love to fight. That's not me. I grew out of it a long time ago."

"And yet here we are," Koda said. "Fighting's in our blood. Yours, mine, and Grunt's. We won't ever escape it."

"I'd like to believe I can," Dane said.

"You can do anything!" Cassandra said.

Koda said, "There was a time I wanted to believe that too. Growing up in the desert isn't pleasant. As a kid

I dreamed of getting away from it and finding a peaceful life, but that didn't happen."

"There's still a chance it could happen," Marleyn said.

"No, there's not. I accepted that a long time ago. Just like Dane here, kids in the desert don't have much choice to improve their station. I did some mercenary work myself to try and earn my way out, but all it earned me were some shackles.

"I fought hard and killed who I needed and got out of one arena. I finally got out of the desert, made my way to Eden where I was sure I'd live a life free of fighting. I was unable to find work, and I got tired of living on the streets, in the gutters, under bridges.

"The Edenian arena paid good. All I had to do was fight and kill again. Grunt and I were royalty to the fans. I ate well and had my pick of women, so I became a little more comfortable with the idea of fighting. It was certainly fancier fighting there than in the desert.

"Then all this shit happens and I find myself without work again. I tried to look on the bright side; maybe it was finally my time for a peaceful life. Ha! Look at the world now. I'll never do anything but fight. I've accepted that." Koda looked at Dane. "You should too."

Dane said nothing. He knew it would do no good. Koda could not be persuaded otherwise, his mind made up. Marleyn chewed her lip, and dropped her eyes to the ground.

"You're a real killjoy, you know that?" Pelias asked. "What if your life of fighting is meant to be spent fighting with hope of something better? Marleyn's right – you've still got time."

"I don't need a lecture from a spoiled kid who's spent his entire life in a castle with the other rich folks," Koda said, glaring at him.

Pelias scoffed and smiled sadly. "I'm not rich. Never was. Just lucky."

"Oh, I can't wait to hear this one."

"I lived on the streets just like you," Pelias said, looking him in the eye. "My parents died when I was barely old enough to take care of myself. I learned fast how to live on the streets, but those lessons were harsh, and I saw firsthand what happened to others who didn't learn."

Koda huffed. Marleyn asked, "So you were an orphan? How did you become Chief Commander?"

Pelias looked away, his eyes searching the darkness away from the fire. "Like I said, I got lucky... Right place at the right time... Prince Uragon snuck out of the castle one night. He got attacked by some dogs. I jumped in to help him, but I had no idea he was the prince.

"He took me back to the castle and told his father the story. King Endrew was so grateful that he took me on as a ward of sorts." Pelias snapped his fingers. "Just like that, my world was turned over. I didn't adjust very well at first, but I kept trying, even when people laughed and sniggered at me. I didn't give up."

"Oh, you poor thing," Koda said, rolling his eyes. "Lucky, indeed..."

Pelias' nostrils flared, but he said nothing.

Bren interjected, "It sounds like a blessing, Koda, but trust me, it's not easy learning an entirely new way of life while everyone does their best to keep you out of it, all because you weren't born to the right family."

"Hmm... Maybe not," Koda said, "but I'd like to try. That's all I'm saying."

"You had your own taste of royalty – said so yourself. Becoming a champion fighter in the arena is probably better than being plucked from your life and being dropped into something completely foreign."

"That happened to you?" Marleyn asked.

"Yes."

"And?"

"It was hard." Bren closed his eyes in thought, and the girl knew he would not speak any more about it.

She frowned. This had not gone the way she had envisioned. Instead of getting anyone to smile, they all sulked alone. Ruddell still stared at the bloodstain and Cassandra did nothing but glance at her father periodically with sorrowful eyes.

"Ruddell, are you okay?" Marleyn asked.

The dwarf mumbled something unintelligible, his head twitching rapidly. Marleyn patted him gently on the back, but he did not acknowledge the gesture. Cassandra sniffled and tried to quietly shuffle into a dark corner of the cottage unsuccessfully. Everyone knew she was retreating to cry in the dark, but no one said anything to her.

Llanowar stood up. "It's been a long day. I'll take next watch, but I'm not taking first."

"Get your beauty sleep," Koda said. "It won't take much."

As usual, the elf ignored him, stretching her arms over her head. As she did so, her shirt rode up slightly. In the firelight, Koda spotted strange markings on her side.

"What're those?" he asked, pointing at her skin.

"Tattoos," she said, dropping her arms to her side and glaring at him. "Never seen any?"

"Well, I've got a few myself... Kinda like that."

"They're elvish runes." She stepped away from her spot by the fire and grabbed a blanket.

"What do they mean?" he asked.

"Doesn't matter." She draped the blanket over her shoulders and dropped to the ground.

It was not long before everyone else had gone to sleep, spreading out on the cottage floor. Dane took first watch, but Marleyn could not sleep. With one arm draped over her forehead, she stared at the ceiling.

"Thank you for what you tried to do," Dane said, his voice soft.

Marleyn turned her head. His back was turned to the fire and he was looking towards the gap in the wall. "Are you talking to me?" she whispered.

He nodded. "You tried to cheer everyone up."

"It didn't work."

"Sometimes it doesn't. Doesn't mean it wasn't appreciated. They know what you tried to do."

Marleyn said nothing more. She looked back up at the darkness in the rafters.

* * *

"Dane! Wake up!" The voice stirred Dane from his stagnant position. He was on his feet in seconds, sword already in hand, head whipping side-to-side in confusion. He found himself alone in the cottage, and when he squeezed through the collapsed corner, he became aware of what had happened. The undead had come in a swarm — a larger group than they had encountered at White Willow.

Pelias jumped between him and another zombie, shoving it away with his shield and stabbing it through the face. He and Dane moved in sync, covering each other's openings. Dane noticed only he and Pelias were in the camp.

Worry and fear began to spread in Dane and it fueled his aggression. He shouldered into one of the zombies, knocking it to the ground before using his sword to split the skull of another. He stomped the face of the one on the ground, crushing it. "Where's Cassandra?" he shouted.

"I saw her with Grunt and Koda off that way-" Pelias pointed with his sword. "She ran off when the first undead broke into the camp. Ruddell bolted, as well. Bren and Llanowar went after him. Marleyn is with them."

"I'm going to make sure Cassandra is safe. She comes first!"

"I'll round everyone else up. We'll regroup with you all." The two men ran in separate directions, cutting down undead as they did so.

Dane weaved among the trees, decapitating and dismembering zombies as he danced. He was afraid. Not of the dead, but for how he might find Cassandra.

Rounding a tree, Dane ran into the arms of a zombie and they both toppled to the ground. The undead gripped his shoulders with amazing strength and leaned in for the kill. It got close enough for Dane to see flesh stuck in its teeth and smell its rancid breath. Dane grabbed it by the throat and held it at bay. His hand fumbled in the grass and dirt for his sword, but to no avail.

Dane gritted his teeth and brought the zombie's head down. Their skulls smashed together. Again and again, Dane head-butted the dead demon until it's blood and brains covered his face and it had stopped struggling.

Dane left his sword in the leaves and continued through the brush. He grew more exhausted as he sprinted, dodging low branches and the extended arms of the undead. Where was Cassandra? Dane struck out with his fist, caving in the face of a zombie, never slowing down.

Finally, he pushed through the bushes and emerged into a clearing. Grunt held three undead at bay while Koda thrust a spear through the skull of another. Cassandra stood between them, fear awash on her face. Dane sprinted as fast as he could and snatched Cassandra away from the monsters.

Koda turned and drove the blunt end of his spear into the head of a nearby zombie and then stabbed the point into one of the three that was assaulting Grunt. The giant man took the two remaining zombies and jammed his thumbs into their eye sockets. With his giant hands he dug his fingers into their skulls. He clenched his fists and their heads exploded, covering his hands in a sloppy, bloody mess.

Koda looked at Grunt. "You okay?"

Grunt simply grunted and pointed behind him. Koda turned to see Dane looking up at the three of them. He was holding Cassandra's arm out for them to see small scratch marks just above her wrist.

Dane, on his knees, let go of her arm, his own dropping to his sides. "I'm sorry," Cassandra sniffled. The girl held Dane's face in her hands. "I'm sorry," she said again.

There was a rustling noise from the bushes where Dane had come from. Bren, Pelias, Llanowar, and Marleyn emerged and walked over to them. Marleyn knelt next to Dane and presented him with his sword. "I found this."

Dane took it, stood, and sheathed it. "Thank you." He ran his fingers through his black hair and let out a long sigh. He thumbed the scar on his chin and noticed for the first time that the sun had crested the horizon. "Marleyn, can you bandage Cassandra's hand?"

The young woman nodded and took the gauze that was held out to her by Llanowar. Cassandra looked up at Dane. "Are you mad at me?"

"No…" It was not a lie, but he did not have the energy or focus to present his answer in a convincing manner. He motioned for everyone except Marleyn and Cassandra to step away out of earshot.

"Ruddell's gone," Bren offered.

"Dead?"

"Without a doubt," Llanowar said. She crossed her arms and pursed her lips. "Little bastard ran straight into a horde of zombies."

"Be respectful of the dead," Pelias said.

"Why? He was foolish. This isn't easy for anyone."

"He lost one of his daughter's last night."

"And he's going to lose another, but he chose to leave her alone. I'll not make excuses for a coward."

Pelias bit his tongue.

"What do we do now?" Bren asked. "We won't be able to get into the city."

Koda said, "Maybe we can find it before… y'know…"

"That's quite a maybe," Pelias said.

"Then perhaps this is where we part ways," Llanowar said, taking a step away.

"We've come this far together," Koda said hurriedly. Grunt gave him a sideways glance, before looking up to avoid meeting anyone else's gaze.

Dane said, "Koda's right. We escaped from Eden because of each other. I don't think we should be so quick to throw that to the wind."

"We don't have a magi… or, we soon won't." Bren said.

"We can figure something out."

"We have to try," Koda said.

"I *have* to succeed," Dane said. "I *will* see my daughter again." He looked at Llanowar. "I would like everyone's help. Please."

The red-haired elf scanned the faces of everyone as they awaited her answer. "Fine. I will stay with you for a little while longer."

A small smile appeared on Dane's face. He looked at everyone and nodded his thanks. They all turned to find Cassandra and Marleyn embracing. A wave of calm came over everyone, and for a moment they were able to ignore the groans of the dead off in the distance…

Dane pushed aside a net of thorns using his gauntlet. He allowed the others to proceed as he held the prickles at bay. The farther they travelled into the forest, the denser it became. The trees squeezed closer together, the branches hung lower, and the thorns and bushes drew in closer every mile.

Cassandra shuffled by on shaky legs. Her breaths had become raspy and she had no interest in her surroundings. Her eyes never strayed from what was directly ahead of her. Her skin was beginning to turn pale at only mid-afternoon.

Grunt walked behind to catch her if she happened to fall. Marleyn and Koda walked on either side of her. Marleyn had her arm draped over the young girl's shoulder. Koda cracked jokes when he thought the timing was right, but as her health declined, he slacked off – content to keep smiling for her sake.

"Marleyn," Koda said.

The young girl looked at him, and the smile she had donned for Cassandra slowly faded. She continued to glance at him, but never held eye contact.

Koda chuckled and shook his head. "You don't have to be afraid of me. I just wanted to apologize for what I said the other day."

"Oh... Well... Thank you, Koda." She smiled a little.

"You're still mousy, but I'm far from it, so I guess we complement one another. Besides, I'm used to talking my ear off at Grunt, so it's not much different with you."

Marleyn chuckled and looked at Grunt, who shrugged.

"Oh, and as a token of my apology..." Koda lifted one side of his cloak and reached inside. He pulled out a shiny silver spoon. "Take this." He pushed it into her hands, and she laughed nervously.

"Thank you, I suppose." She looked at it, attempting to be grateful.

"Silverware is a sign of wealth where I come from," he explained, "and with the world going to shit, that may be a treasure to you later. Who knows?" He laughed and looked down at Cassandra. A small smile was on her face, but her color was gone, and she could barely keep her eyes open. He sighed quietly to himself and patted her on the shoulder.

In the blink of an eye, Llanowar took an arrow from the quiver on her back, nocked it to the bowstring, drew, and fired, whizzing right past Koda's ear. Everyone stood at the ready, unsure of what she was shooting at. Through the foliage, a zombie pushed through. It stumbled and fell to the ground. Llanowar ran forward and retrieved her arrow from its skull. The others followed, leaving Marleyn and Cassandra slightly behind.

"Impressive," Koda said, grinning. "She's better than Yura, eh, Grunt?" Grunt nodded in agreement. "Did you kill her, or did I?" Grunt tapped his own chest. "You're sure?" Grunt nodded again. "Hmm..."

"What are you going on about?" Pelias asked.

"Yura was a pit fighter in Eden. She was pretty skilled with a bow." Koda winked at Llanowar. "Nothing like you, though."

"Just keep in mind how good I really am," Llanowar said, walking away.

Koda hit Pelias in the shoulder and held his thumb and index finger out with a small gap in-between. "Getting closer," he smirked. Pelias shook his head and continued walking.

"Help!" Marleyn shouted. She held Cassandra in her arms as the girl coughed up blood on the front of her dress.

Tears streamed down Cassandra's face. "It hurts," she said.

"Can we do something?" Marleyn asked, looking up at everyone.

"Turn her face down," Dane said, kneeling beside them. "She'll choke on her own blood." He helped Marleyn suspend Cassandra in the air as she hacked more blood on the ground.

Pelias grabbed a handful of his red cloak and tore a sizable strip off the corner. He held it out and Dane took it from him. He and Marleyn turned the girl back over after her coughing fit ceased and he used the piece of the cloak to wipe the blood from her lips.

Cassandra took long, shallow breaths and tried to swallow a couple of times before she succeeded. She said, "It's hot...so hot..." A tear fell from Marleyn's face and landed on Cassandra's cheek. "Let me go... Put me down..."

Dane and Marleyn laid her flat on the ground. She looked around at the dirt she rested in and smiled. "This is a good spot," she said. She closed her eyes and flexed her fingers. Fire materialized out of thin air and clutched at her body, scrambling around and consuming her corpse.

Dane rubbed his forehead and took a few steps back, his eyes locked on the fire, bumping gently into Pelias and Llanowar. The young knight patted him on the shoulder as Llanowar walked away and propped herself against a tree away from the group. Grunt looked at Koda out of the corner of his eye and Koda glanced at him before averting his eyes to his feet, wringing his hands at the same time. The fire reflected in his watery eyes.

Marleyn folded her arms close to her body as if she were cold. She stood as close to Bren as she could get. The big man made no move to turn her away. She looked up at him, dug into a pocket on her dress, and withdrew a small silver locket.

Bren took it from her when she held it out to him. His rough fingers skated across the trinket's smooth surface. He pressed the button on the side and it flicked open. Inside was a small portrait of Cassandra, Lilta, and Ruddell – all of them with wide smiles.

Marleyn said, "Cassandra gave me that when I treated her bite-wound. She told me that she knew she was going to die, but that she wanted us to remember her family. She told me to show everyone when she died so that we wouldn't be sad."

Bren passed it to Koda, who glanced at it and sighed before passing it to Grunt. Grunt studied it for a moment before handing it to Pelias and closing his eyes.

Pelias and Dane looked at it together, Dane moving his hand as if to take it from the young knight before letting it fall back to his side. Pelias turned and called, "Llanowar." The elf looked over her shoulder. Pelias walked to her and handed her the locket.

Llanowar rejoined the others, giving the trinket back to Marleyn. Marleyn looked at the portrait one more time before closing it and placing it back in her pocket. "Cassandra had faith in all of you, and she wanted you to know that you shouldn't lose hope. Keep going." Now that she had delivered her message, Marleyn reverted to her timid, quiet self, folding her arms close to her body again.

Koda said, "I know that we've already talked about this, but...since we left Eden, it only took two and a half days for a whole family to die."

"You're right. We *have* already talked about it," Pelias said. "Let's not back-track."

Dane held up his hand to stop Pelias. "I would like everyone to stick together as we had planned, but if anyone is having serious doubts, then by all means leave." He pointed at Marleyn's pocket where the locket was kept. "But Cassandra knew that her family could be remembered through us. I'll honor her and her family by finding mine."

Dane began walking away from Cassandra's smoldering body. Pelias, Bren, and Marleyn followed immediately. Llanowar hesitated - allowing some distance between her and the others - before proceeding. Grunt stepped in front of Koda and looked down at him.

"It happened again." Koda said, looking up at his friend. "*I* let it happen again. Why is this happening?"

The giant's eyebrows were raised. He took a deep breath before shaking his head and shrugging. He pointed at the others as they were walking away and made a short growling noise.

Koda nodded. "You're right, Grunt. I'm not letting anyone die again. Next time, I'm using my powers."

* * *

Fires dotted the landscape. Some were just embers while others roared and licked at the night sky. The air was cool, and an army of stars were visible. The screaming had finally stopped. Eden had fallen in a matter of days.

King Endrew buried his knuckles into the stone railing of his balcony. The army's fire-fighting corps had never come to fruition. The fire had consumed anything it could, leaving piles of rubble all around. What the flames had not been able to destroy, it had left its mark of black soot, staining the stone around it.

Where the fires burned brightest, Endrew could make out bodies draped across the crumbled remains of buildings and sprawled throughout the streets where upturned carts and broken-down wagons stood. The bodies were not just human. Horses, chickens, pigs, dogs, and cats had all succumbed to either the flames or the hunger of the dead.

After the city had been ransacked and all its inhabitants slaughtered, the undead had marched out of the gates, leaving the chaos behind. No one had come to check on the king for several hours.

Perhaps now that the screaming had stopped, he could finally sleep. It had been nearly a week since he had slept, and even longer that he awoke feeling rested.

King Endrew turned, his robes swishing at his feet. He rubbed his eyes as he approached his bed, throwing the covers aside and kicking off his slippers. He poured himself a goblet of wine and downed it entirely.

There was a pounding on the door. The king froze, holding his empty cup. The pounding persisted after a short pause. Endrew set the cup down on the table and waited. The pounding came again.

Who could it be? He had thought for sure that he was alone, the only living thing left in Eden. He looked around for a weapon but found none. Did he need one? His son and his capital were both gone, so what was here to live for?

At the insisting of another round of beatings, King Endrew walked to the door and ripped it open, ready to meet his fate. Before him stood his steward – Wyll. The boy was red-faced and his curly, blonde hair was matted with sweat.

Wyll rushed into the king's chamber, ignoring all formalities, and slammed the door shut behind him. His chest heaved as he leaned his back against the wood.

King Endrew turned and strode toward the wine again. He poured a cup and sipped. "You've disappointed me, boy," he said.

The steward took a few steps forward and bowed, his breathing nearly under control. "I'm sorry, My Lord, but I could not get to you. The dead were in the stairwell and I had to hide until they departed."

"I don't care about that. I was hoping that you'd come to kill me."

"My Lord?"

"What am I lord of anymore, boy?" Endrew asked, downing the rest of his drink. "The capital of my kingdom is utterly demolished, and no doubt the rest of the realm will be too. But that's okay, because I no longer have an heir to inherit any of this rubbish. So what am I a lord of?"

"I am bound to serve, My Lord. You still hold the title of King."

"Oh, begone with you, boy. I don't want to be king anymore, and I don't want to see your face again." Endrew poured another cup.

"You're releasing me from your service, Lord?" Wyll asked.

The king slammed the wine jug down on the table. "Take a hint, boy! Yes, yes, leave me! I don't want you around anymore!" He pointed out the door to the balcony. "Go perish somewhere out there! Just leave!"

Wyll bowed one last time. "As you wish." He opened the door and screamed, ducking under the swing of a war-axe.

Wyll rolled to the side and scrambled to the wall as Sir Eins stalked inside, the black metal of his Kingsguard armor clanking as he went. He ignored Wyll, who stared wide-eyed at the grey, decaying skin of the dead knight.

King Endrew moved around to the opposite side of the table, clutching his cup to his chest. The kingsguard locked onto him with his white eyes and trudged forward, holding a war-axe in each hand. The king realized now that he did not want to die.

Wyll stood up slowly, hugging the wall, and made his way towards the door. Endrew pointed at him and called, "Help me, boy!"

Wyll watched as the undead knight raised the axes and made his last few steps around the table. King Endrew screamed as the kingsguard began hacking away at him, the screams soon turning to gurgles of blood. Wyll ran out the door as fast as he could.

Chapter 6

"Who the hell are we huntin', General?" Rorn asked through a curled lip.

Braxon and the Ravagers stared at the remnants of White Willow. "Traitors to the king," Braxon snarled. He sifted through a pile of wood and ash that he suspected was the carriage they had been following.

Aiya, Leyon, and the other Ravagers inspected the bodies that lay before them. "I'm starting to think we should have stayed in prison," a concerned-looking elf said to another of his kind.

The other one replied, "Yeah. What in *vrodam* happened while we were locked up?" He looked at Braxon. "Where did all of the undead come from? Are they all from the plague?"

"That doesn't matter now," Braxon replied.

"I think it does."

"I don't give a shit about what you think." Braxon glared at him.

"If you won't tell me, I refuse to go any further under your command."

Braxon leaned in close to Rorn and whispered. "I don't like this one. Will you keep him under control, or shall I?"

Rorn looked at the elf. "I never liked him. He was always a whiner."

Braxon looked him in the eye. "You, or me?"

Rorn cleared his throat and approached the elf. He drew one of his axes and slashed open the man's throat. The only person to flinch was the other elf that had been talking to him. The others watched silently as the elf clasped at his throat as the blood bubbled from it.

Rorn wiped his axe on the executed elf's jacket before he slumped on the ground. He forced his weapon back in the loop on his belt and looked at all the Ravagers. "Listen up, you bastards: We were locked in a dungeon together for three years. Before that, we pillaged, plundered, and killed together for two. But that time together doesn't mean shit to me now. We all do what Braxon says. If someone wants to act contrary to that, you will be removed. Understood? Good."

Braxon added, "Don't ask any questions and do what I say when I say it."

Leyon called for everyone's attention and pointed toward the stables where a herd of zombies emerged from the forest. "Their armor is all pieced together. Their weapons, too," the tracker added. "They're bandits like us, General."

"They're infected. Take them out." Braxon muscled past everyone, drawing his longsword. "Don't forget to aim for the head!" Braxon and The Ravagers sprinted forward, letting out war cries.

Braxon pushed the first few undead aside so he could get to the center of the horde. His sword flashed quickly and precisely, decapitating and brutally cleaving the skulls of the monsters. Rorn, Leyon, and Aiya were the first to join him, but none of the Ravagers shied from the conflict.

Swords, clubs, and axes rose and fell with such ferocity that the enemies were dispatched in less than a minute. Rorn dropped his one-handed axes into the loops on his belt and dusted his hands off. Braxon pointed at some rubble and said to Leyon, "See what you can make of that. I think that's the carriage our targets were using."

Leyon propped his club on his shoulder and nodded as he strolled casually over to the rubble. Aiya planted her two-handed axe into the ground and looked at Braxon. She made a gesture as if she were stroking facial hair on her own face. "You have blood in your goatee."

Braxon took his time to respond. He cleaned the blood off his sword and sheathed it. "Not the first time. Not the last time." He turned and started walking away. "I want every single body in this village inspected." Aiya started immediately as Braxon walked up to Rorn. "Have some men look around for any supplies we can use. The people of White Willow won't need them."

"You got it," Rorn said, chewing on a piece of grass.

"Make sure you finish off that elf. We don't need another one coming back to life."

"Yes, Your Majesty," Rorn chuckled as Braxon walked away.

"Before you ask," Leyon said as Braxon approached, "yes – this *is* the wagon you're looking for."

"So, they left the carriage and continued on horseback..."

"Possibly, but I don't think so."

"Why?"

"There were five horses, but you said there were nine people in the group we're tracking."

"Then a few of them doubled up, so what?"

Leyon pointed at the hoof prints, following them for a few steps before he swept his arm in a wide arc. "Were you expecting the group to split up? Because every one of the horses went a different direction."

Braxon sighed and stroked his goatee. "It's gonna be a son of a bitch to follow each of those trails."

"You don't have to." Leyon swapped his club to his other shoulder. He led Braxon from where the horses had run away. "Look here. Going into the forest here:

126

nine sets of footprints. They belong to your prey. At least that's my guess."

Braxon studied for a moment, contemplated silently. "That would be the smart play on their part. They're doing what they can to lose us."

"They'll have to try harder."

"Well done, Leyon. Go help Rorn collect supplies. We'll leave immediately. We can't let them get too far away."

*   *   *

"...So there I was, alone and transporting a crate of gold bars through the desert when I was surrounded and held at sword-point by a gang of halflings, dwarves, and elves."

"So you lost the gold?" Llanowar asked as she and Koda trudged along at a steady pace. The forest remained thick and unaccommodating. It was still preserved in its natural way, with no man-made paths to guide them.

Koda chuckled. "Indeed. They sold me to some merchant who promptly resold me to the Pit Master to fight as a gladiator in the arena in Red Dune."

"It must have been horrible..."

"Wasn't all bad. I won my freedom, met Grunt, and we both ended up fighting in the arena at Eden. I never would've met him otherwise, I don't think. He's been a good friend. Saved my hide many times."

"Have you ever heard him speak?"

"Not a word. I've always been a talker, so it balances out." Koda laughed and Llanowar spared a small smile.

"I've lost gold too, you know?" The elf said, forcing herself to frown.

"What?" Koda asked, his smile twisting in confusion.

"Ruddell," she grunted. "He owed me coin."

Koda scoffed and shook his head, though his smile remained. "You don't have to convince me you're a hard-ass, you know? You don't care about that gold, and I know it. If it makes you feel better to pretend you're all fight and no heart, fine, but I'm not fooled by the act."

Llanowar sighed and flicked dagger-eyes at him, but kept her mouth shut.

Pelias matched his stride with the two of them. "Koda, can I speak with you for a moment?"

Koda gave him a suspicious look and slowed down. He stepped aside to let Bren and Marleyn pass by. After everyone was out of ear shot, he said, "I have finally gotten Llanowar to hold a real conversation with me. This better be important."

"I've been doing some thinking, and I wanted to thank you for what you did back at Eden. You saved my life on that wall. You can say otherwise, but I know you have your own code of honor. Thank you."

Koda took a moment to process. "You didn't have to thank me. Just...don't go around telling people I'm as soft-hearted as I am. You'll ruin my reputation." He grinned. "But I guess I should apologize for what I said the other night. I just thought you were another spoiled kid with a cushy life. I was wrong."

Pelias nodded. "So, are we on peaceful terms now?" he asked as he offered his hand.

Koda clasped it with his own and they shook. "Just to clarify, I was always on peaceful terms. It was you who got his breeches in a knot." Koda hit him on the shoulder and grinned again, walking away. Pelias could not help but smile as well.

Koda and Pelias joined the others. They rounded a tree and were flabbergasted by the sight before their eyes. The companions had broken through into a clearing. The sunshine seemed to be confined to this area alone, for when they were amid the trees, only a few rays could penetrate the foliage.

Scattered around the clearing were the grey corpses of the undead. The green grass was defaced with splatters and pools of blood, and the sun reflected brightly off the red. Quite a few of the bodies were smashed in a similar fashion to a squashed spider. On the other side of the bodies and straight ahead of the company, some entire trees were uprooted, others broken and leaving splintered stumps protruding out of the dirt.

Everyone maneuvered around the bodies and approached the trees. Dane reached out and brushed his fingers over some of the wooden spikes. Grunt knelt and inspected a log. The path of downed trees continued for a distance before stopping at the large, wide entrance to a cave.

"What could have happened here?" Bren asked.

"Something big, whatever it is," Koda said.

"A giant?" Marleyn suggested, her voice quivering.

Dane replied, "It's too far south to be a giant, but anything's possible."

"Such as dead people roaming around," Koda quipped.

"If we're still going to take this direction, I say we move quickly and take a wide birth around that cave," offered Pelias.

Llanowar called for everyone's attention. When they turned, they found some of the bodies that were uncrushed had reanimated and were attempting to stand. They got to their feet slowly, lazily, as their bodies readjusted to the actions again. Over a dozen zombies turned their heads and craned their necks at all the companions. There was a moment of hesitation before all the undead staggered toward them.

An arrow was lodged in the skull of the nearest zombie in the blink of an eye. Everyone rushed past Llanowar as she notched her next arrow. Pelias toppled an undead before moving on and allowing Grunt to move forward and stomp on its head.

Dane cleaved through a zombie's skull before dodging away from another that attempted to grab him. Llanowar took it down with another arrow. Bren decapitated two with one swing of his bardiche. Koda sidestepped him and skewered one undead with his spear. He forced it backwards and into another zombie.

With both of them pinned by the spear, he trapped them against a tree. Koda stepped aside as Grunt approached. The giant man reared his fist back and crushed the skulls of both zombies with one strike. Grunt removed the spear and tossed it back to Koda as the bodies slumped to the ground.

Behind them came a loud thump, a pause, and then another thump. With each pounding, the ground shook. As the others grappled with the remaining undead, Llanowar turned around. Her eyes got wide.

"Cyclops!" she shouted.

Everyone glanced over their shoulders, keeping the undead at bay. The cyclops was as tall as the trees, bare-chested and bald. Its single eye was solid white and its skin was grey. Its ankles were torn and bleeding with flaps of skin swirling around its legs with each step.

Blood stained its lips, dripping from its chin all the way down its neck.

The cyclops' flabby stomach bounced wildly with each step. It pushed the unfallen trees on the path aside as it moved; some of them sprung back into place, while others cracked like thunder and fell to the ground. It moved faster as it stomped closer.

Koda shouted, "Llanowar, move!"

The elf nocked an arrow and drew. She raised her bow to aim for the cyclops' eye and fired. At the same time, the undead cyclops stumbled and caught the arrow in its ear. It let out a mighty scream, spittle erupting from its mouth. It drew its hand back and let it go in a wide arc.

Llanowar was sent flying as the cyclops' hand caught her in its path. She spun in the air and disappeared into the forest with a shout. The monster raised its hand over its head and drove it down, ready to take out the entire group.

Dane's breath hitched and he shut his eyes tightly as he waited to be crushed by the palm of the cyclops. His death did not come. He was jolted out of his paralyzed state by the sound of Bren and Grunt both letting out war cries. Dane opened his eyes and panted heavily. His heart thumped wildly in his chest when he saw Grunt and Bren holding the monster's hand at bay over their heads.

Koda charged forward and imbedded his spear deep into the cyclops' calf. Dane grasped his sword tighter and leapt in the air, slicing the leviathan's wrist and making it draw back its hand. Blood fell from the sky and plastered them all. Grunt drew the battle-axe from behind his back and screamed, his eyes coursing with anger, veins pulsing on his bare head.

Bren picked Marleyn up from where she cowered on the ground. She clung to him tightly as he carried her to the edge of the clearing. He set her down and said, "Go find Llanowar! Make sure she's okay and stay away from any undead!"

"Go with her," Pelias shouted, picking his shield up from where he had dropped it. "We'll handle this!"

Marleyn and Bren ran off into the woods.

The cyclops uprooted a tree and tossed it with ease at the other four. Koda flipped over it while Grunt, Dane, and Pelias dove to the side or ducked under it. Dane and Grunt were the first to return to their feet. They each set their sights on one of its legs.

Grunt's monstrous battle-axe cleaved a deep bite into the knee of the cyclops and it dropped down. Dane buried his sword into its foot and jumped back to try and avoid a swiping hand. He was too slow, and Dane twisted in the air before colliding with the ground and throwing grass and dirt in the air as he slid into the base of a tree.

A monstrous hand opened wide and extended towards Koda. The gladiator threw his spear, and the weapon lodged itself into the meat of the cyclops' palm. Its fingers landed in the dirt around Koda, acting like a fleshy prison, but the butt of his spear buried itself in the dirt and gave him enough time to slip out of harm's way.

As the monster raised its hand again, Koda leaped in the air. "I'll take that!" he shouted, grabbing and ripping his spear out before landing and performing a series of rolls and flips to get out of range of the beast.

The cyclops brushed Grunt away as he reached out with the other hand to clutch at Dane. Pelias stepped in front of him, his feet spread in a solid stance, his eyes as unwavering as a stone rampart as they peered over the crest of his shield. Pelias' sword dug a path through the leviathan's palm, but it ignored the pain and snatched Pelias up.

Pelias' arms were pinned to his side as the cyclops squeezed and lifted him into the air, his legs kicking. His sword fell to the ground and he could feel his armor trembling as it fought against the weight of the monster's grasp. He struggled and tried to wriggle free, but he could not move a muscle. His breathing became more labored as he glanced around for any way to escape.

Koda looked up at Pelias and cursed. He saw Dane, staggering to his feet and picking up his fox-tail sword where it lay among the bodies. Grunt was not easily dissuaded, and he was back at the cyclops' feet, hacking away with his axe. The monster raised his other hand above Grunt and let out a shout.

With all his companions scattered, Pelias being crushed, and Grunt on the edge of getting flattened, Koda knew that he had no other choice. He took a moment and a deep breath. He squeezed the shaft of his spear as tightly as he could and then in a puff of black smoke, he disappeared.

Another cloud of smoke formed in front of the cyclops' face as Koda reappeared in mid-air. He thrust the point of his spear through the lone eye of the monster and into its brain. Koda dangled as he held onto the spear, a wave of the monster's breath caused him to sway.

Grunt removed his axe from its leg and ran away as the beast began to fall. He ushered Dane out of the way as the cyclops tumbled the rest of the way to the ground. Koda was separated from his spear as he was thrown when the head of the beast smacked a large rock.

Pelias ceased to be crushed, but he was still trapped under the hand of the creature. He stared up at the sky, allowing himself to feel amazed at the fact he was still alive. Grunt and Dane approached and, together, managed to lift the hand high enough to allow Pelias to squirm out from under it. The Chief Commander began the search for his weapon.

Dane dislodged the spear from the cyclops' head and tossed it to Koda, who had made his way back to them. "You're a magi?" Dane expected a quip in response, but Koda simply nodded. He dusted his hands off and looked to Grunt, who stood with his arms crossed. "You knew?"

Grunt nodded, and Koda confirmed, "He knew. He's the only one."

Dane sheathed his sword and glared at him. "Why didn't you tell the rest of us?"

"None of you trusted me. And I didn't truly trust any of you lot, either."

"What changed?"

Koda put his hands on his hips. "You're good people. And I...have enjoyed your company. Ruddell, Lilta, and Cassandra were good company as well, and they're gone. I didn't want anyone else to die."

Dane studied him for a moment. Pelias cut in, "We should go find the others. Llanowar could be hurt."

"We'll discuss this more later," Dane said to Koda. He nodded and gave his spear a quick twirl. Grunt gave him a light punch in the shoulder and made his friend smile again.

At about that time, Bren, Llanowar, and Marleyn broke through the tree line. "Is everyone all right?" Bren asked, dropping to one knee to take a rest.

"We're alive," Dane replied. He cast a glance at Koda but chose not to elaborate. "Llanowar, are you well?"

Llanowar gave a stone a light kick. "I'm pissed off." Everyone gave her a questioning look. "I missed my shot."

"We should keep going," Marleyn suggested, glancing around like a startled doe, "there's no telling what else could be out here."

The companions marched on at a steady pace, eager to distance themselves from the corpse of the cyclops, sure that the noise of the battle would draw more attention. They kept to themselves as they moved, but once they felt they were in the clear, they stopped and regrouped.

"Why did you keep it a secret?" Dane asked Koda.

"I'm sorry," Koda said. "When we escaped from Eden, we were strangers. Grunt and I didn't even know if we were going to hang around, so why would I tell you? But time went on, and I wanted to."

"Maybe Ruddell and the girls wouldn't be dead if you had just said something."

"What's going on?" Marleyn asked.

"What are we even talking about?" Bren echoed.

"Koda's a magi," Pelias said.

"You are?" Llanowar's jaw dropped.

Koda nodded.

"Why didn't you say something?"

"It was clear from the beginning that there wasn't a lot of trust among us. Why would I reveal my whole hand to players I didn't trust?"

"Because it could have saved lives!" Dane said.

"Calm down," Pelias said, holding a peaceful hand out to the others, taking up next to Koda. "You're all just angry. You need to look at it from his point of view. Which of us don't have secrets?" He cleared his throat. "And who's to say that if one of *us* hadn't made different choices that we could've saved lives?"

Koda blinked at the knight. "Thank you, Pelias." He looked back at the others. "Trust me, if I could go back and do things differently, I would. You have to believe me."

"Pelias is right," Marleyn said. "If I could go back, I would've told you guys about the ambush in White Willow sooner. Maybe then Lilta wouldn't have gotten bit. There's any number of things that any one of us could've done and changed the outcome. Let's not fight here."

Dane sighed. "You're right. Let's move on from it. At least we know all hope isn't lost for getting into Etzekel."

"Etzekel, you say," a suspicious voice interrupted.

Everyone raised their weapons and instinctively chose a different direction to defend. Their eyes darted around, but no one saw who the voice belonged to. Dane gritted his teeth and said, "Show yourself!"

"I'm not done studying you…" Llanowar spun and fired her bow up into the trees when she located the sound. Everyone paused, rigid, their ears pricked. "… Good shot. Wrong direction, but good form on your draw and release."

The voice now resonated from the opposite direction that Llanowar had loosed the arrow. Llanowar growled and fired another. The voice said again, "I'll reveal myself if you promise not to shoot me."

Everyone in the company glanced at one another for an answer, but they all remained as tense as ever. Dane called, "You have my word."

"I'm not sure how much that's worth...Dane."

Dane blinked and he felt as if he had been knocked in the head. He tried to recall the mysterious voice but no memories came to mind. His body somehow became tenser than it already was. Why could he not place the voice?

Out of the trees sauntered a muscular man with thick, messy brown hair and an unkempt brown beard. He wore simple brown rags with his arms exposed and his feet were protected with animal skin boots. A plain satchel was slung diagonally across his torso. As he walked, he tapped the ground with the blunt end of a silver trident.

"Marek!" Dane exclaimed. "You're alive after all these years?"

"It does look like it, doesn't it?"

Everyone else looked from Dane to Marek and back again, confusion on their face. Grunt was the only one that was not confused. Instead, his eyes were narrowed, glaring at the new arrival.

"How?" Dane asked.

"I guess your eyes were playing tricks on you." Marek walked forward and measured Grunt with a look. "I never thought I would see you again, Valyn."

"Valyn?" Koda said as Grunt crossed his arms, still glaring. "You must be mistaken."

"You think someone could mistake that beast of a man for another person? I doubt it."

Koda looked at Grunt. "Your name is Valyn?" His friend nodded, but refused to take his eyes away from the stranger.

"Dane, who is this?" Bren asked.

"He was a member of the Iron Fox Legion along with myself and Amir. We were on an expedition in the

Red Crescent Desert and got ambushed. He and a few others got left behind."

"I'm the only one that lived," Marek said. "I ended up getting sold into slavery and being sent to the arena in Camel Row. That's where I met him." Marek pointed at Grunt.

"Hm," Koda said, frowning. "Slavery, pit-fighting, Grunt - we have a lot in common. I don't buy it."

"Buy it, or don't. It happened."

In a motion quicker than the giant man should have been able to make, he shoved through everyone and swung at Marek, hitting him in the face. The blow sent him spinning and dropping to the dirt. Grunt cracked his knuckles and leered down at him.

Koda stepped next to his friend. "I'm guessing you weren't *great* friends..."

Marek wiped blood from the corner of his mouth as he used his trident as a prop to push himself to his feet. "I assumed we were. We fought together, killed together...and I won him his freedom."

Grunt reached behind his head and unbuckled the strap on his leather mask. The mask dangled in his hand as he dropped his arms to his side. He straightened and continued to glare at Marek.

The rest of Grunt's companions moved around slowly to try and catch a glimpse of his face, and they were left speechless.

Grunt's lips were gone, removed in a rough fashion that left jagged pieces of skin hanging over his exposed teeth and gums. Part of his cheeks were also removed to reveal that his tongue had been cut out. His nostrils had been slit and left to scar.

Marek studied his face and then looked at the mask. "I didn't know they would do that to you. I thought they would honor the deal." Grunt huffed and put his mask back on. He walked away from the group. Marek looked at Dane. "Looks like we've both made mistakes, old friend."

"So it would seem." Dane sheathed his sword.

"What's this 'deal' you're talking about?" Koda asked.

"I made a deal with the local magistrate that I could put together a team of fighters to rival his winning team. Valyn was on that team. If we won, we were supposed to gain our freedom, but the magistrate was a snake.

"He tried to go back on his word. Several of the people on our team were killed, and not just in the arena. Finally, I told the magistrate that if he would let Valyn go, he could keep me there. He agreed, and I stayed for another year before I broke out during a slave revolt."

Koda said, "But he didn't just let Grunt go without paying a price..." He looked up at his friend, who had lowered his eyes, no longer glaring daggers at Marek.

Marek stood. "I had no way of knowing, though I should have expected it."

As Marek picked up his trident, Dane asked, "Do you know where Etzekel is?"

"You're trying to get into the magic city?"

"We are."

"I know where it is. I stay there most of the time."

"How far away is it?" Llanowar asked.

"Not far. About half a day. Would you like me to take you there?"

"Would you?" Dane asked.

"I suppose." He began walking away. "Follow me."

139

Koda joined Grunt, who was fiddling with his mask, jerking viciously on one of the straps. "Are you gonna be okay, big guy?"

Grunt snorted like a bull.

"I don't know what this guy did to piss you off, but if you want I'll help you skin him. I just ask that you wait until we get inside Etzekel. I miss hot baths."

Grunt shook his head and began following the others.

Dane and Marek trudged on beside one another. Dane was silently appreciative to have found a familiar face while on this trek, though he was unsure of where he and Marek stood with one another. He had been under Dane's command when he was taken prisoner by a band of southern raiders. He did not know if Marek resented him for that, but he had agreed to show them to Etzekel, and that was enough for now.

It brought him a small amount of comfort that Marek knew the location of the magic city. Dane allowed Marek to lead him and his companions, content to follow someone else for once.

"Where's Amir?" Marek asked.

The question instantly brought Dane back down from where he was. *It was nice while it lasted*, he thought. "He's dead."

"I'm sorry to hear that. I liked Amir."

"He was executed right before my eyes."

"Executed?"

"Maybe we can talk about it later."

Marek nodded. "Suit yourself, old friend. Tell me later, or don't." He followed it up with a shrug.

Somehow, Marek's indifference was a comfort to Dane.

* * *

"This is home," Marek said.

Dane and his companions could not help but smile as they looked at the grey stone wall ahead of them. A wide moat ran the entire length of the wall, with a wooden bridge leading up to a plain iron gate. Atop the wall, a few guards had gathered to leer down at them, making no effort to allow them to pass.

Dane swallowed hard as he studied the place. He wanted to be inside now. Evie was there, and he needed to hug her and kiss her forehead and see that she was safe.

Marek leaned on his trident as he waited for the others to finish their gawking. "The trees are tall in this region, so the magi could build the walls high, but keep them low enough where they couldn't be spotted from the crest of a hilltop. The moat keeps animals and other undesirables away, and the strict laws regarding entry and exit of the city do the rest. It's much bigger on the inside, I promise."

"What are we waiting for?" Llanowar asked, her eyes flicking suspiciously among the men on top of the wall.

"I believe they're waiting for a magi to present himself." Koda stepped forward and extended his arms out to the side, clearing his throat.

"You're a magi?" Marek raised an eyebrow at him.

Koda glared over his shoulder at the interruption. "I am."

"Good for you." Marek tossed his trident to his other hand and waved his arm. "Let's see what neat trick you can do."

141

Koda cleared his throat and vanished in a puff of smoke. He reappeared in a tree above them, the black tendrils of smoke wafting through the greenery. "Eh? What do you think of that?" he asked, grinning.

Marek's eyebrows were raised, and he nodded his head, impressed.

"Can you vouch for your acquaintances?" A gruff man shouted from atop the wall, tipping his helm back and squinting his eyes for a better view.

"Of course," Koda replied. "I wouldn't be trying to get them inside this secret city if I didn't think they were secret worthy." He flashed invisible, and then he was standing amongst his companions again.

"Marek? That you?" the old man said, squinting harder.

"It's me," Marek replied.

"Why didn't you say so? What're we doin' wastin' time watchin' that lad's fancy tricks? You vouch for these folks?"

Marek looked at Dane for a moment before nodding. "I can, and I do. Now let me in, it's been days since I've slept in a bed."

"Did you bring anything good back with you?"

"Open the damn gate and find out, Herrold!"

"All right, but you better hurry. Been a lot of them dead folk around while you been gone. We ain't keepin' the gate open for long."

"Fancy tricks?" Koda muttered, frowning. "Besides, I thought you needed a magi to get inside?"

"That's what I was told," Dane replied. Before he could ask Marek about it, the man was already ten paces ahead.

To Dane, it felt like it took hours for the gate to climb up. His heart was pounding faster than it had since he had been imprisoned in Eden. He had been so consumed with protecting his friends and surviving to see his daughter that it hit him like a sack of stones that that moment had finally arrived.

Without any conscious thought, his legs started moving, slowly at first, but he was soon setting a brisk pace. The others followed suit and they soon crossed the open ground and stood on the bridge as they waited for the gate to rise the last few feet. Dane trotted inside, his head snapping from side-to-side, meeting the gaze of several strange faces. There was only one face he cared to see at this moment.

"Dane, hold on." Marek unslung the satchel from over his shoulder and passed it to Herrold, who had come down from the wall to greet them. The older man raised his thick eyebrows at the bag. "There are wild strawberries, mushrooms, and nuts in there. We can plant them in the garden. Pass them along, would you?"

"Aye," Herrold responded, popping one of the tiny berries into his mouth.

"Don't eat them all," Marek warned. "Help these people get settled." He indicated the companions as he joined Dane, who had stopped in his tracks, but was still looking around wildly. "Allow me to show you to your daughter."

Dane's head snapped to him. "You know my Evie?"

"I do. I intercepted her and one of her escorts outside the wall when she first arrived. I helped her get settled here, and she told me who her father was, what he did, and what he used to do. I knew it was you. I wondered when you would come after her."

"Please, take me to her."

Marek led the way without delay. Dane was not sure what he had expected, but Etzekel was far more developed than he imagined it could be. The magi and

The New Dawn had gone to great lengths to make the city fully functioning without requiring anyone to go outside the city's walls.

Marek explained: "Everyone that comes here gets a place to stay. Some have to share, but most get their own homes. There is a temple for the devout and a pub whenever people want to drink. We have our own garden for fruits and vegetables, and we also raise hogs and cows for meat. Our stable is small, but most avoid going outside the wall anyway."

"Except you?"

"Well, they need someone to go out exploring and scavenging. Most of the magi are afraid to leave and meet King Endrew's men. The New Dawn members that are here are mostly made up of the elderly, so they can't."

"Do the people here know about the dead?"

"I've told them, but they're so disconnected from it that they don't know what to think. They ignore it for the most part."

"If they saw them in person, they wouldn't be able to ignore it," Dane said.

By this time, they had weaved in and out of streets and alleyways, passing many people moving about the city, tending to their daily business. There were children, adult and elderly men, women, humans, elves, dwarves, and halflings. Dane could not think of a city he had been to that had been this diverse.

Finally, Marek and Dane stopped in front of a small, two story home. Marek smiled and gestured towards the door. "Enjoy your time with your daughter."

As Marek walked away, Dane wasted no time marching up to the door and pounding on it with his fist. He waited a moment, but he had little patience and returned to hitting the door.

He heard a familiar voice shout from inside, "Is the sky falling? Hold on and try not to piss yourself!"

It was not a moment later that the door was flung open. "From whom did you learn to talk like that, young lady?" Dane grinned.

The young girl that stood before him screeched to a halt. Her jaw dropped, and she looked her father up and down several times. In the blink of an eye, Evie launched through the air and wrapped her arms around Dane's neck. She squeezed as hard as she could as tears rolled down her cheeks.

Dane hugged her waist and suspended her in the air. He forgot about all he had been through recently, and he laughed and smiled wider than he had in weeks. He shuffled awkwardly inside, still holding her.

"I missed you so much, Dad!" Evie said.

Dane set her back on the ground and took her head in his hands, looking her in the eyes. "I missed you, too, sweetheart." He pushed some of her black hair out of her eyes before kissing her on the forehead.

"I've been so worried. You never sent any messages even though you said you would." She put her hands on her hips and glared at him.

Dane chuckled. "Spare me that look, darling. Just wait until you hear what I've been through."

"It better be good," Evie said, smiling wide. "You owe it to me."

Chapter 7

Later that evening, Dane sat at the kitchen table with Evie, enjoying a warm bowl of stew and a loaf of bread that she had prepared. The entire moment was refreshing for him – having a warm meal and finally a bath and a fresh set of clothes. The armor he had worn since leaving Eden had become dirty and smelled foul. Evie claimed she would wash and mend the leather for him after dinner.

Dane found himself unable to quit smiling. His daughter was safe and healthy, and he was with her. He had managed to escape the clutches of a tyrant who sought to harm him and those who he cared for, all while dodging the dead come to life. But that was behind him. No one could touch him or Evie now.

Dane took another spoonful of stew and ripped a hunk of bread off the loaf before popping it inside his mouth. As he chewed, he noticed Evie was lost in thought, frowning. "It's a delicious meal, darling. I missed your cooking."

She smiled at him. "Thank you, Dad." The smile was gone as quick as it came and she went back to staring at the table, lost in the lines traced in the wood.

Dane pondered a moment, setting his spoon to rest against the lip of the bowl and straightening in his chair, a faint smile on his face. "If I'm an inconvenience here in your beautiful home, I can venture back out in the morning."

Evie did not appreciate the joke. "You most certainly won't." Not even a cracked smile.

"What's wrong?" Dane asked.

She was silent for a moment, stirring her nearly untouched stew with her spoon. "Something happened to Amir, didn't it?"

Dane propped his elbows on the table. "How did you know?" He took a sip of wine.

"He would have been here with you, no matter what. You wouldn't have left without him, nor him without you." She looked her father in the eye. "He's dead, isn't he?"

Dane explained to her all the events of the past week. He described being arrested along with Amir, Amir's death, escaping, and fighting his way out of Eden all the way to Etzekel. He left no room for questions, spouting off everything he could remember while Evie sat silently and absorbed the tale.

Finally, at the end of the account, Evie said, "So he died for you?"

"He did," Dane replied. "And you and the other magi. With Braxon killing the Dammen family, I was ready to cave. Amir stopped me."

"Father, whenever you would tell me stories about you and Amir and the Iron Fox Legion, there was always a point where you would either say one of you was strong while the other was weak." Evie reached out and squeezed Dane's hand. "He guarded you when you needed it. He wouldn't want you to waste it."

Dane inclined his head, smiling slightly. "I know, sweetheart. I won't." He popped another piece of bread into his mouth and leaned over his bowl. "Tell me about your time here."

"It's been great!" She smiled. "I've gotten to know several people really well. I'll introduce them to you soon. I know the city well, too, and I spend a lot of my time helping Madagrett tend the gardens. She's a magi, like most of the people here. Dad, no one here is scared to use their powers – it's wonderful!"

"Have you been using yours?" he asked, raising an eyebrow.

Evie tried to hide her smile. "Some, yes, but only to be helpful."

"How so? Do the magi have you spying for them?"

Evie chuckled. "No, Dad. They've had me use my powers to read the thoughts of anyone who got terribly sick and couldn't speak. There was even one mute man that I've assisted communicating with."

"Maybe you can give a voice to my friend Grunt, then. He's unable to speak."

"Grunt? What's he like? What are the others like that you travelled with?"

"We call him Grunt because he can't speak. He wears a mask over his mouth, and he's the biggest, strongest man I've ever seen. His friend Koda fought beside him in the arena in Eden. Koda jokes constantly, and he's rough around the edges, but I feel like he's got a good heart. He's a magi, too.

"Then there's Bren. He was King Endrew's Sword of Justice, imprisoned for refusing to execute the sick. He's very level-headed and calm. His friend Pelias was the Chief Commander of the Kingsguard. He's young, but he's one of the most skilled fighters I've ever seen. He has a noble heart, but he's very serious, very stoic."

"Sounds like you, Dad," Evie chuckled.

Dane smiled and continued, "There's Llanowar, who I think you'd like. She's a very tough elf, and she's not afraid to speak her mind or tell someone if she doesn't like them. She was very wary of all of us to begin with, but she's warmed up to us some – except Koda, who is infatuated with her and makes no move to hide it.

"Finally, there's Marleyn. Poor girl... we picked her up in White Willow. Her whole village turned, and we had to put them down. She's attached herself to Bren, and she hasn't let go. She's sweet, very tender-hearted. I don't believe she would have made it without us..."

"Wow..." Evie sighed in admiration, thinking of all these people her father had come to know. "You've met quite some interesting characters, huh?"

"I have." Dane rubbed his scar with his index finger. "I don't think I would have made it here without them."

"I just wish Ruddel could have made it here with the girls. Cassandra and Lilta were so sweet." She frowned and pushed around some chunks of potatoes in her bowl.

"I wish they were here, too." His finger still ran over the groove in his chin.

"I want to believe that our friends are done dying, but... I just don't know."

"We're safe here. I'll do whatever I can to prevent anymore death. I promise." He pushed his chair back from the table and stood. "I need some sleep."

Evie jumped up so quickly that her chair fell over. She leapt into Dane's arms. "I'm so happy you're here."

Dane wrapped her in his arms and relished the moment. They separated and he set her chair back upright. "I am too, sweetheart."

* * *

149

Koda passed the jug of wine to Grunt. Etzekel's pub had a familiar feel to it, despite being cut off from the rest of the realm. It had comfortable furnishing and was stocked with product that was better than some of the swill they had downed in the past. There were about a dozen other people enjoying the pub, but a couple of them were getting up to leave.

Koda and Grunt had chosen a table in the corner and put their backs to the wall. They had spent the last few hours passing the wine back and forth and studying the different patrons that had come and gone. Their time in the fighting pits had made them less than trusting of strange places. A lay of the local land and its people was always their first objective when entering a new city.

After the time and one entire jug of wine had passed Koda came to his conclusion: "I've never seen a people *less* threatening than these."

Grunt nodded. Every person that entered the pub waved at the others and smiled as they ordered their food and drink. Some of them glanced at the corner where the newcomers sat, some still giving them a friendly wave or tip of the hat. Grunt gave a few short, sharp grunts before lifting his mask as little as necessary, hiding his scars with his hand, and downing what wine remained in his cup.

Koda poured more for him from their second jug. "I suppose you're right. They've earned the peace." Koda shook the jug before setting it down with satisfaction that they had enough to last a while. "Speaking of which, what's the story with this Marek fellow?"

Grunt cut his eyes at his friend and shook his head.

"Suit yourself. I just hope he's trustworthy. Dane seems to think so. But if you're still gonna try and kill him later remember to let me watch."

Grunt huffed a sharp breath through his nose, muffled by his mask.

"Dane hasn't let us down so far." Koda took another drink and watched the elven woman serving the customers. She smiled and chatted with a table while holding a serving tray in one hand. "I could see myself staying here for a bit. The people seem friendly enough."

Grunt raised his eyebrows.

"Not forever, no. I come from nomads. I've never stayed anywhere long. Not even when I was a slave."

Grunt shrugged and took another cautious sip.

"You've gotta tell me the story behind your scars someday."

Grunt cut his eyes at him.

"C'mon, we've been friends for years. I deserve to know."

The giant man stared into his cup.

Koda studied him for a moment, squinting. He could tell Grunt was reliving the memories as he stared into his drink. "You don't hate Marek because of the mutilation... do you?"

Grunt shook his head.

"Did he steal a woman from you?"

Again, he shook his head.

"He shaved your head and it never grew back, huh?"

Grunt glared at him and rolled his eyes.

Koda chuckled. "You're an interesting fellow, my friend. Maybe here we'll find a magi to restore your voice to you. Then you can be Valyn once again."

Grunt shook his head once more before tossing back the rest of his drink.

Koda tipped his cup back as well, stood, and pulled his cloak tightly around his body. He picked up the wine jug. "Mind if I take this?"

Grunt waved it away.

"I'll see you back at the house."

* * *

Llanowar studied the fletching on one of her arrows before cramming it back into the quiver with all the others she had already inspected. Her bow, recently polished, lay unstrung on the table next to the quiver. She picked up her sickle and began cleaning it.

The elf's eyes took note (for about the twentieth time) of the furnishings inside the tiny house that the magi had put her in. There were a couple works on the wall by Onthony Brey – a famous halfling painter with a penchant for illustrating lush forests and well-endowed women.

There were vases scattered about on nearly every table. If it was not flowers, it was scented candles. The entire place had a suffocating effect on Llanowar, but not because she was indoors. It was true that most of her kind were attuned to – and had a heightened compassion for – all things nature, but Llanowar herself had come to appreciate the changing of the times and the advancing of technology and civilization. Even still, the amenities were overbearing to her.

There was a knock at the door.

Llanowar carried her sickle with her as she approached the window that was next to the front door. When she peered out, she saw Koda was standing there with a jug of wine in his hands. Sighing, she pulled the door open.

Koda smiled at her and said, "You don't have to stab me – I brought the wine to share."

She rolled her eyes and walked back to the kitchen table. Koda followed and shut the door behind himself. "What do you want?" Llanowar asked.

"I brought you a house-warming gift." Koda reached into his cloak and grasped a wad of forks, knives, and spoons. They clattered as he set them on the table before her. "Did you know, that where I come from, silverware is-"

"Yes, I know." She held one hand up to silence him and rubbed her forehead with the other. Even still, she was unable to hide the tiny smile that formed on her lips.

"Will you share a drink with me?" She did not respond as she inspected all her weapons, shuffling the silverware out of her way. Koda continued: "Grunt and I spent three hours in the pub here. Everyone was very friendly. Wine's good." He slid the jug across the table toward her.

"If I drink will you stop talking?" Llanowar asked.

"Absolutely not," Koda smiled.

"Then I'm going to need this even more." She picked up the jug and took a long pull.

"You don't want a cup?"

Llanowar set the jug down and wiped her lips with the back of her hand. "Are you so proper that you need a cup to drink your wine?"

"Just after you," Koda teased.

"Then you'd better get your own wine." She took another drink.

Koda propped his elbows on the table and picked up one of the arrows. "So, do all elves learn how to shoot when they're children?"

"Not all of them devote their energy to shooting. I've seen some that were horrible at it."

Koda took the wine jug from her and sipped it. "All these years I thought all of you were born with the skill."

"Not in the least. There was one boy when I was growing up that was so scrawny he couldn't even draw the string. Another boy shot himself in the foot."

Koda laughed. "And you out-shot them all."

"No, not really. Most children that learn to shoot start when they are six. I didn't learn until I was eleven years old."

"How come?" He passed the jug back to her.

Llanowar took a long pull and paused for a moment. "I was born into a slave family. My tattoos you saw were markings."

"I guessed." Koda replied. "I didn't know elves allowed slavery in their culture, though."

"They don't anymore. My mother and I were some of the last slaves in Jalfothrin. We were owned by a vile man. He beat my mom – sometimes until she was unconscious – and if he felt she didn't learn the lesson he would keep the lecture going with me."

"That's awful," Koda said.

"He got his in the end," Llanowar shrugged.

"Did you...?"

She chuckled. "No, no. I didn't kill him. When Jalfothrin banned slavery, my master resisted the authorities. They threw him in prison where he ended up getting beaten to death by the other inmates."

"Wow. Nothing like sweet justice." Yet another sip for him. "So you were free and you learned how to shoot."

"I taught myself. My mother took me away from Jalfothrin since we were no longer slaves. I crafted my own bow, threaded my own string, and whittled my own arrows."

"I'm impressed."

"Your opinion means a lot to me," Llanowar teased.

"No, I meant that I'm impressed that you've actually held a conversation with me. Most the time, you ignore me." He smiled at her.

Llanowar shrugged. "Must be the wine."

"I'll start carrying it with me all the time."

They both laughed and took a few more sips, sitting and enjoying the company.

"I understand the life of a slave a bit myself," Koda said.

"I remember," she replied, nodding.

"Not as badly as you, don't get me wrong. I was free up until my early twenties, when I was captured and sold to that Pit Master I told you about. I wasn't a captive for long, and my chains actually led me to some good things, but I do understand the feeling of shackles."

Llanowar took a slow sip and eyed him curiously over the jug.

Koda stammered, "A-anyway, what I was saying earlier...about this place being safe... You should relax. I can tell you're uncomfortable in this place. Just...know that you have friends here. We didn't all spend weeks together in the wilderness for no reason I hope." Koda stood. "Enjoy the rest of that wine."

"Thank you." They smiled at each other as Koda shut the door behind him.

* * *

The cold water coursed over Bren's body. He let the wooden bucket fall from his grasp and make a loud bang. His breath hitched and he shivered as the chill wrapped his entire body. He ran his hand over the top of his freshly shaved head before reaching for a towel to dry himself with.

Bren put his breeches on and proceeded into the sitting room. Before his bath, he had already started a fire and now he seated himself on the couch to bask in its warmth. There was a soft rug under his bare feet, the couch was comfortable, and the fire was warm. Bren tilted his head back and closed his eyes. His smile was broken by a yawn.

There was a rap at the door and Bren sighed as he forced himself off the couch. He grabbed his shirt off the back of a nearby chair and slipped it over his head. "Pelias," he shouted, "you were starting to worry me, staying out that late." When he opened the door, it was Marleyn standing on the stoop instead of the Chief Commander. "Sorry, I thought you were Pelias."

Marleyn smiled shyly. "Just me," she said. She fidgeted with her dress and looked at the darkness all around.

"Would you like to come in?" Bren moved aside and held the door wide open. Marleyn shuffled inside and Bren closed the door behind her. "Come, sit and enjoy the fire." They sat together on the couch. "What brings you here tonight? Everything okay at your house?"

"Yes, everything is great. I just came over here because I wanted to thank you."

"Thank me? For what?" Bren cocked his head to the side.

"You saved me at White Willow. I don't think your friends would have brought me along if you hadn't already helped me. I was so frightened."

Bren walked into the kitchen and poured two mugs of ale. Marleyn studied his every movement. He came back with the drinks and handed her one. She took the mug and held it in her lap as Bren dropped back into his seat. "You haven't said much about White Willow."

"I don't even like thinking about it," she replied, dropping her eyes to the soft carpet underneath her feet. "The people there weren't always like that, you know?"

"Is that where you're from?"

"Yes and no." She turned the mug in her hand, running her fingertips over the surface. "I wasn't born there. I was born on the road." Bren raised an eyebrow and Marleyn blushed. "My parents were part of an acting troupe, I mean. They were nomads, travelling from place to place and putting on shows. They never charged a copper for any of their plays. They wanted to spread the joy of theater to everyone."

Bren smiled. "They sound like good people."

Marleyn nodded and looked away. She stared into the mug, a frown now on her face. "They were... We were on our way to put on a show at White Willow when I was ten years old when our troupe was attacked by a pack of wolves. There had to have been ten or twelve of them. They swarmed; everywhere you looked there were wolves."

157

"Wolves? They're not usually that aggressive if unprovoked."

"That's what everyone kept telling me afterwards... My father put me into our chest of props. The latch fell, and I was trapped in there for almost an entire day. The entire troupe was killed. Some hunters from White Willow found me later and took me with them."

"I'm sorry about your parents and your troupe," Bren said, taking a long drink.

"I called White Willow home after that. I loved the people there, called them family. Fernie was kind enough to let me stay with him. I worked for him in exchange. Years went by, but after the dead came through the first time, they started robbing people. It was like a heel-turn. No one seemed to question it... I guess you really can't know anyone fully, can you?" She looked at him.

Bren took a deep breath and shrugged. "Extreme circumstances make people do absurd things."

"Sometimes I wonder if my parents' spirits are watching me, disappointed that I helped them rob all those travelers."

"You did what you had to do to survive. That's what we're all doing. If you had set out on your own, it probably would have ended badly. I doubt your parents fault you for that."

Marleyn smiled and studied his eyes. "Thank you, Bren."

Bren nodded and the two of them sat in comfortable silence for a while. "You don't like ale, do you?" he finally asked, pointing at her mug. "You haven't drunk a single drop."

"I... I've never had it," she admitted.

"Now's your chance."

Marleyn smiled at him before eyeing the drink. She gripped the mug with both hands and raised it to her lips. At the same time, Pelias burst through the door. Bren jumped to his feet, tossing his mug aside and raising his clenched fists. Pelias was as startled by the two of them as they were of him. He was drenched in sweat and panted as he hunched over with his hands on his knees.

This was the first time in long while that Bren had seen Pelias out of his Royal armor. Now he wore plain breeches and a loose shirt that was patterned with sweat. Pelias raised a hand and huffed. "Sorry..." he stood straight and took a few quick breaths. "I didn't mean to interrupt." He looked at Marleyn. "I didn't know you were visiting."

Bren stepped toward him. "Pelias, is something wrong?"

Pelias furrowed his brow at him. "What? No, I was just out for a run."

Bren let his arms drop and he felt his muscles relax. He gave a half grin and a chuckle. "Don't come barging in here like that, then."

Pelias nodded but did not join in the jest. He looked around the room and scratched his head. He looked at Marleyn and pointed. "It seems you may have spilled something on your dress."

Marleyn looked at the front of her dress and said, "Oh no!" A wet blotch covered her chest. Bren took a towel from the kitchen and traded her for the mug of ale. Bren gave it to Pelias, who downed what remained of it.

Marleyn tried to sop up the spill to no avail. She sighed and clung to the towel. "I'd better go." She walked to the door and pulled it open. She turned around and smiled at Bren. "Goodnight." She nodded to Pelias and then closed the door as she left.

Pelias looked at Bren. "What the hell's going on?"

"What do you mean?" Bren took the mug from him and went to the kitchen to refill it and his own which he recovered from where he had thrown it on the couch.

Pelias followed him. "Between you and the White Willow girl."

"Her name is Marleyn."

"I know her name," Pelias said, pausing to wait for his mug to be refilled. "But why was she here?"

Bren handed him his mug and said, "Do you think that's any of your business?"

Pelias shrugged. "Perhaps not, but I think it's strange. You hardly know her. And she's half your age."

"You make it sound like we were... No, we were just relaxing and enjoying each other's company. As you should be." Bren took a drink. "What were you doing running at this time of night?"

"Just getting some exercise."

"We just spent weeks getting plenty of exercise in the wilderness. You should take a night to relax. Drink and sit by the fire."

Pelias raised his mug. "I'll say yes to the drink." He took a sip as he walked to the stairs that led to the next floor up. "I'm going to bathe." Bren took a sip and approached the couch, stopping when he heard Pelias call his name. When he turned, he saw Pelias crouched to look at him from the top of the stairs. "You do realize the poor girl's stricken with you?"

"You smell," Bren snarled at him. Pelias laughed and jumped to his feet.

The young knight was relieved to find a bath already drawn for him. Unfortunately, it had been prepared so long ago that the water was now cold. He drained his mug and looked around. *Wish I'd grabbed the whole jug*, he thought. He wasted no time stripping off his clothes and sinking into the bath. The chill of the water took his breath away, but he paid it no mind, letting the weight of breathlessness surround him.

As he settled in, propping his back against the tub, he closed his eyes and submerged his entire head. He focused on the water coursing through his short blonde hair and trickling off his scalp. He decided the water felt good and he found himself to be a new man with the sticky sweat washed from his body.

Pelias knew he needed to relax but it was not that simple. He had tried to relax, but that did not keep his mind from wandering. When his mind wandered, it always returned to thoughts of Eden and his life in the kingsguard. Was there something he could have done to help King Endrew and prevent the state that the realm was in now?

He could not find an answer that suited him or eased his anxious mind. He had tried running and doing push-ups. Neither of those worked, either. And so he returned to relaxing again. Hopefully the ale and a bath would work.

From what he could already tell, it would require either a warmer bath or much, much more ale...

Chapter 8

"Rise and shine. You don't want to waste the day away sleeping, do you?"

Pelias groaned and opened one eye to a squint. Marek and Bren stared down at him. Pelias sighed and rolled over, putting his back to them.

"Come now, don't be rude," Bren joked.

Pelias mumbled, "God forbid I get a proper day's rest."

"I think someone's feeling the effects of that ale last night."

Marek looked around the room to find multiple empty bottles scattered about. "And that ale. Oh, and that one, too." He chuckled to himself.

"Some of these were already here, I swear." Pelias' voice was muffled as he spoke with his face buried in his pillow.

"Ah, to be young again."

Pelias threw his legs over the edge of the bed and rubbed his face. A drum pounded inside his skull and his stomach churned. Bren gave him a cup. "Water. Drink." The young man downed it.

"I have news for you." Marek said.

"News?" At this point and time Pelias wished for no news of any kind. He just wanted a day with no goings on or trouble to hear about.

Marek nodded and grimaced. "Your king is dead. Murdered late last night." Pelias looked at the two of them. He tried to feign disbelief, but he had known it was coming. It had only been a matter of time.

"I... I..."

"Sorry," Marek said. "I just figured you would want to know. You are kingsguard, right? I recognized your armor."

"Yes. I was." Pelias smoothed his short blonde hair and forced himself to stand up from the bed.

"That's all I needed. If you'll excuse me, I need to go see Dane."

Pelias shook his hand. "Thanks for telling me." Marek nodded, turned, and left.

"Are you going to be all right?" Bren asked.

"I accepted a long time ago that my King was dead. I don't think I could have left Eden otherwise."

* * *

Dane sloshed the water resting in the basin in front of him. He dipped his fingers into the bowl of cream on the counter and began spreading it across his face. Just as he finished, there was a knock at the door. He rinsed his hands and opened it.

Evie giggled when she saw the great white beard her father had constructed. "I was going to see if you were hungry. Breakfast is ready."

Dane held up a razor. "I was just beginning to shave."

"All right, but hurry up. I want you to meet a friend of mine. I invited him to eat with us this morning."

"Who?"

"I'll introduce you to him when you come down for breakfast — so hurry up!"

Dane shut the door and — on his daughter's orders — proceeded to shave as quickly as safely possible. He studied himself in the mirror, running his

163

hand over his smooth cheeks. He had always appreciated the feeling of a fresh face.

When he came out, Evie was sitting on the edge of his bed, bouncing lightly up and down. "Who did you rob to be able to afford a mirror?" he asked.

Evie smiled. "Etzekel is wonderful, you'll learn. You don't have to be rich to have nice things here. There are skilled craftsmen of every trade here, and if they can't make it, it can be made by magic."

Dane ran a towel over his face one more time and put a shirt on. "I'm glad you've enjoyed being here. I've been worried about you ever since you left Eden."

Evie smiled at him. "Me, too, Dad. But I just reminded myself that you're strong and smart. I never thought anything bad had happened to you. I just thought you were slower than a turtle with only two legs!"

Dane chuckled and stretched as he soaked in the sunlight that streamed through the bedroom window. "It's going to be a beautiful day."

"Did you sleep well last night?"

"I did."

"Good. You can actually enjoy the day and explore the city."

"So, who's this friend you spoke of?"

"He's downstairs. Ready for me to introduce you?"

"Do I need my sword?"

"Dad, no! He's my friend. I don't want you to scare him."

Dane grinned. "Lead the way, M'lady."

Evie took the stairs in leaps and bounds, a wide grin on her face as she floated along. Dane was pleased by her jovial energy. Downstairs, he found a boy with a mop of red hair and freckles on his cheeks and arms seated at the table, smiling. He stood when Dane reached the table and stretched out his hand.

Dane shook it and smiled as Evie said, "Father, this is Caulen."

"Pleasure to meet you," Caulen said, bowing his head quickly.

"You as well," Dane replied. "You must be good friends with my daughter. She was in quite a hurry to introduce us."

"I am." Caulen and Dane sat down as Evie began placing the food on the table.

She said, "Caulen was one of the first people to talk to me when I arrived. He met me at the gate and he showed me around the city. Anything I needed he assisted me with. He was very helpful."

Dane nodded. "Then I'm grateful to you." He watched as Evie served Caulen. The two of them glanced at each other and smiled. Caulen blushed and looked away quickly – as if something had caught his eye. Evie pretended not to notice. Dane brought his wine cup to his lips to hide his own entertained smile.

To break the tension, Dane asked, "So, Caulen, are you a magi like my daughter?"

Caulen shook his head. "No. I have no gifts. Not that I'm aware of anyway."

"How did you come to be in Etzekel?"

"I was living with my aunt, uncle, and cousin. My cousin was a magi – she could turn liquid to solid in the blink of an eye if she touched it. She ended up killing a city guard in Jalfothrin who was..." He flicked his eyes at Evie, who looked up when he quit talking. "...trying to harm her and my aunt. My uncle and I were away working in a mine near the city so we didn't know anything about it.

"My aunt took my cousin and brought her to the mine. We took to the wilderness that moment. Came on this place completely by accident. Been here almost from the beginning. My aunt and uncle have passed, and my cousin disappeared into the forest a while back. I'm not truly alone, though. I know everyone, and I usually show the newcomers around."

"Sounds like a very important job," Dane said, taking a bite of his eggs.

"I'm the first person they meet, usually."

"How old are you?"

"Thirteen."

Dane nodded and took another bite.

"Evie told me you were a mercenary. I bet you've seen a lot of places." The boy's face lit up at the idea.

"In my time, I have seen a lot of things but I haven't been a sellsword in quite a while. I was a boat-mender in Clifftown, and I lived in Eden."

"Iron Fox Legion, correct?" Caulen asked.

Dane smiled. "Yes."

"They're the best as far as sellswords go."

"They were – until I left." They all laughed.

Caulen said, "Perhaps some time you could tell me about some of the battles you were in?"

"Sure. Some time."

Caulen nodded, grinning with excitement at the prospect.

"So what's the ruling council like here?" Dane asked. "I know The New Dawn is in charge, but *who* are the people actually running things?"

"It's supposedly a small group of magi elected by the higher-ranking members of The New Dawn."

"Supposedly?" Dane asked, raising an eyebrow as he chewed.

"I've only ever seen one — a halfling named Renwy. Rumor is that most of the council stay hidden because they're scared of Endrew's persecution."

"That's the whole reason the city was built — to be free of the persecution," Dane said.

Caulen shrugged. "That's just what they say. I don't know if it's true or not, but I know there are a lot of magi that keep to themselves in the tower."

"Hmm," Dane said.

"Things run pretty smooth here, so I don't care how they get it done," Evie said. "No undead, no death threats from zealots."

The reasoning was sound, but Dane could not shake the uneasy thoughts in his mind.

A knock came from the door. Evie left the two of them at the table to talk. "Oh, hello, Marek," Evie said when she opened the door.

"Good morning, Evie. Is your father available?"

"We're just eating breakfast. Come join us."

Marek nodded his thanks as he stepped inside. He greeted both Dane and Caulen and took a seat at the table. Evie prepared him a plate of food and placed it before him. "Thank you, dear."

"What can I do for you, Marek?" Dane asked.

Marek smiled at him. "I need to introduce you to a few people. Important people."

"Can't it wait a day? I was hoping to spend time with my daughter."

Marek chewed before replying: "Unfortunately, I don't make the rules. I'm just a messenger."

"At least let me finish my meal first."

"Of course," Marek said, smiling. "This is fantastic, Evie." She smiled.

"Oh!" Caulen exclaimed, startling everyone present. "Sorry," he said sheepishly. "I just realized that both of you were in the Iron Fox Legion."

Marek laughed. "We fought together through quite a few battles."

"Wow! Brothers in arms! Who's the better fighter?"

Marek and Dane glanced at each other, smirking. "That's a difficult question to answer," Dane said. "There are a lot of factors that go into a fight."

"Me," Marek interjected. Dane raised his eyebrows. "Dane put down his sword to start a family — and he has a charming young daughter to prove it." Marek indicated Evie. "I haven't stopped fighting."

Dane cleared his throat. "There was a reason I was your commander. I was more skilled back then than you will ever be." Dane teased.

"I suppose you're correct. Although… which one of us was it that took down that troll in Clifftown?"

"Even after all these years you're still hung up on that troll. You always fail to mention that it was a baby."

"Because a baby troll is still stronger than any man in the land. It's okay to admire me for my great feats, Dane."

The two of them laughed and Caulen was hanging on every bit of banter. "I want to hear this story."

"I'll gladly tell it," Marek said.

Dane pushed back from the table and stood. "Didn't you say I needed to meet some people?"

"Oh, I can make time for this," Marek laughed.

"I've heard you tell stories before. It will be well past dark before you have said 'the end.'"

Marek shrugged and stood. "Another time, Caulen."

Caulen sighed with disappointment. Evie began taking up the dishes. "Father, Caulen and I are going to go spend time in the gardens today."

"Be home before dark." Dane kissed her on the forehead. "Caulen." The boy nodded to him as he and Marek stepped outside.

"Nice day. I like it." Marek took a deep breath and stretched in the sunlight. The sky was a vibrant blue with only a smattering of clouds. Birds and insects were darting about.

"Who am I meeting?" Dane asked as he walked beside Marek. "It must be someone important. Back in the house you said that it wasn't up to you. You work for these people?"

"I work *with* them, for the most part, but they ultimately call the shots. One of them is the chief magi who oversaw Etzekel's construction. The other is a scholar who is gathering information on the undead. He's been performing studies on the infected and claims he has discovered some interesting things about them. Fair warning – he's kind of a strange fellow. An elf. I think he may be a bit touched in the head, if I'm honest."

Dane strolled alongside Marek as he led the way through the winding streets of Etzekel. "I didn't expect this place to be as expansive as it is," Dane remarked.

"It truly is something. I think magic has something to do with it."

"What do you mean?"

Marek grinned. "Think about it – Etzekel was erected less than a year ago. Caulen has been here almost the entire time and he says it was just as big when he arrived. It's impossible to build a city of this size in that amount of time. It has to be magical intervention.

I don't see why magic couldn't play a part on keeping the city safe under an illusion."

"Illusion?" Dane shrugged. "Maybe you're right. It makes no difference to me. I'm just glad to be with Evie again. Thank you."

"I didn't do anything. You practically found the place on your own."

"But you brought us to it, and you looked after her while I wasn't here."

Marek shrugged. "I didn't really do much, Dane. She's tough. She would've been just fine without me, and I daresay she'd make it without you if she had to."

Dane furrowed his brow.

Marek glanced at him over his shoulder and chuckled. "Now don't give me that look, Dane. It's something to be proud of. You raised a resourceful girl, a survivor."

"Hm," Dane said.

As the two of them rounded a corner, a scraggly man in rags threw his hands in their faces and let out a shrill scream. Dane jumped back, his hand instinctively dropping to his hip where his sword should have been. Marek pushed the man back against the nearest wall.

"The bell of the end-times tolls and beckons the dead from their graves! The bell of the end-times tolls and beckons the dead from their graves!"

Marek grabbed the man by his wispy beard and jerked his jaw around lightly. "Shut up, Nurey!"

"Soon you will be exclaiming that I was correct! It is written in The God Text that this day would come! Page one-thousand three-hundred and forty-seven! Verse eight! 'The bell of the end times tolls and beckons the dead from their graves! They shall urge forward and feast upon the unholy! Cover yourselves daily, brethren, for no living being can predict when the bell shall toll!'"

The man waved his hands around in a wild fashion as he shouted in Marek's face.

"I've heard it before, Nurey. Get the hell out of my face!" He gave his beard another tug and then pushed him harmlessly against the wall. "C'mon, Dane."

Dane walked after Marek, but eyed Nurey suspiciously as he passed. Nurey called after them, "Do not speak of Hell so freely, Marek! You may soon find yourself at its fiery gates!"

"Friend of yours?" Dane asked.

"That's Nurey. He's a priest of Haroun. You can find him preaching in the streets all day every day."

"The magi allow him to do so?"

"They made this city to be a haven. It's supposed to function as a normal city would. He's not breaking any laws. Why would they force him to stop?"

"I would think they wouldn't want him inciting fear in these people."

"Very few of these people ever leave Etzekel. They can't be allowed to forget what roams past these walls. The danger is ever-present." Dane shrugged. "If that answer doesn't please you, you may dispute with the magi themselves."

"I have been here less than a day. I have no business telling them how to operate their city." The two of them separated as a group of people walked down the middle of the street. When they came together again, Dane asked, "What's the deal between you and Grunt, if you don't mind my asking?"

"Grunt? Oh, you mean Valyn." Marek chuckled.

"I guess so," Dane replied.

"You remember how we parted?" Marek asked, his tone shifting.

Dane sighed and dropped his head. "Marek, I'm so sorry that happened. I thought I saw you die. I wanted to confirm it, but... I had too many men to command and... I couldn't risk all their lives. That whole place was a massacre."

"I didn't bring it up to make you feel bad, Dane. I forgave you long ago. Sometimes things happen that are out of our control. You did what a good leader does and saved as many as you could. Don't worry about it."

"Thank you. But still," Dane said, looking Marek in the eyes. "I'm sorry."

Marek nodded at him. "Anyway, you saw me get run through with a sword. After baking in the sun for a while, I was picked up by a caravan of merchants. They had no use for a broken mercenary, so they sold me to the magistrate of Camel Row, where I fought in the arena."

"That's where you met Grunt?"

"After a few years, yes. He was brought in as a recruit along with a few others. The magistrate orchestrated an event that was to be me, another gladiator named Vitora, and a team of recruits against a man named Hjolmar and his team of champions. The winners would gain their freedom.

"With this group of recruits, Vitora and I trained hard, and even though the odds were stacked against us – recruits versus champions – we still managed to come out on top. I lost several friends – even Vitora herself was killed. At the end of the last fight, there were only three of us left.

"Myself, Valyn, and Sir Ivan were supposed to be granted our freedom, but it had been a lie the whole time. The magistrate claimed he had never dared believe we would win, and he couldn't let all of us go after we had just massacred his best fighters, so I told him I would stay if he let Valyn and Ivan go. He agreed, and I thought that was the end of it. Apparently, they weren't so accommodating for Valyn, and I have no idea what happened to Sir Ivan."

"I can't speak for the knight, but Grunt should be thankful to you that he's alive," Dane said. "Do you want me to talk to him for you?"

"No," Marek said. "I don't blame him for being angry with me. If Ivan's fate was what I think it was, then that explains everything to me. He was Valyn's best friend and caretaker."

"Caretaker? What did he need a caretaker for?"

"He's had no violent outbursts?"

"What? No. Only when he's needed to." Dane furrowed his brow. "Marek, what did he need a caretaker for?"

Marek took a deep breath and looked at Dane. "I've probably said too much already. I'm just glad Valyn's alive, and that he's found such good friends." He smiled at Dane and said no more.

Was Grunt a cause for concern? Keeping a watchful eye on him might be wise. Marek had mentioned violent outbursts, but everyone had been prone to those recently, and they were quite necessary in these times. Dane shook his head. Marek claimed to trust him, and Grunt had been nothing but an asset to him since they had met, and he would not believe ill of him now.

After walking a while more, the two of them finally arrived at the base of a tall stone tower. A few balconies protruded along the outside of it. Dane pointed at the highest balcony and said, "From up there I'll be able to see the entire city."

"We're not going up. We're going down."

Marek pulled open a bare wooden door and led the way inside. The inside of the tower was devoid of any decoration. The walls were bare stone and to the left the carved steps led down; to the right – up. Mounted on the walls were torches at equal intervals. Occasionally a hooded figure would walk past them, paying the two warriors no mind.

"Who are these people, Marek?" Dane asked as he watched the fourth one go by. "They make me uneasy."

"Magi. Some of them are architects, healers, or sky-readers. Scholars – all of them."

"Are they dangerous?"

"Of course. They're magi. They can summon beasts from ethereal planes or control the elements of nature with the snap of a finger. But they've been hunted for long enough. They'll be the last people to try and attack you here."

Dane said, "Do they all hide their faces like that?"

Marek grinned at him over his shoulder and shook his head. "Not all of them."

After passing several side doors on their way down, they arrived at one at the very bottom of the stairwell. There were no markings to indicate what may lay beyond the threshold or to whom the room belonged. No noise could be heard coming from inside.

On the other side of the door, Dane found the room dimly-lit. Scattered about were tables with towering stacks of papers, scrolls, and books. There were vials and bottles of potions and poisons on shelves, vases and pots of foreign and rare plants all around. Two bodies – half-dissected – lay atop a couple of tables in one of the corners, whose stench mixed with the acrid, burning scent of the potions. Many tools and strange devices dangled from chains above their heads.

There were two people in the room: A halfling who could possibly have been very skinny but was

174

impossible to tell because of the layers upon layers of robes he wore. Dane suspected he was getting on in years, though he could not be sure because of halflings' quality of remaining youthful in appearance for all of their days. The other was a gangly elf who wore an off-set hat that flopped over the right side of his head. He looked rather focused as he mixed different ingredients in a jar with his back turned to everyone.

The halfling had been inspecting what the elf was doing, but when he heard Marek and Dane walk in, he turned and walked toward them with a smile and an outstretched hand. "This is the new arrival?" the halfling asked.

"It is," Marek replied, indicating Dane before moving on to spectate the elf.

The halfling took Dane's hand and shook. "Hello, my boy. My name is Renwy, and my friend lording over the concoction is Anandil."

"A pleasure. I'm Dane." Curious, Dane craned his neck to see what Anandil was mixing.

"Marek tells me you come from Eden?" Renwy inquired, still smiling.

"That's correct. It was a dangerous journey."

"Fear not, my boy. You are safe here – despite how the elf's laboratory may appear." He chuckled and sat down on a nearby stool.

Dane approached Marek and Anandil just as the elf sealed the jar and shook it vigorously. "Hello. My name is Dane."

"I heard," the elf said as he turned his back on him and walked over to a metal cage in the corner.

Dane furrowed his brow and looked at Marek, who shrugged. Dane followed the elf and saw a human man in the cage wearing only a pair of rough-spun sack cloth trousers. The man had long, shaggy hair and a rough blonde beard. He was skinny, but well-built and he was covered in hair on his arms, chest, and legs. His toenails and fingernails were jagged and uncut. He glanced again at the elf, who was stooped down and passing the jar through the bars. The man began to gulp the red liquid housed inside.

"You're wondering why I have a caged man in my laboratory," Anandil said matter-of-factly.

"As anyone would, I hope," Dane replied.

"I will explain it later, but first I must ask you some questions."

"Me?"

"Is it true you were a member of the Iron Fox Legion?"

"Years ago, yes."

Anandil took the now-empty jar from the scraggly man and walked back to the table. "Did you know the man named Brennon?"

"Of course. He was the founder of the Legion."

"Tell me about him."

Dane glanced at Marek, who was busy studying the different ingredients on the nearby table to notice. Dane said, "He was a good man. A good fighter and a good strategist, too."

"He sounds... 'good,'" Anandil mocked. "What else?"

Dane shrugged. "He always took care of his men."

"What else?"

"He was a good cook. Also, a good herbalist."

"What else?"

"What do you mean? The man's been dead for a long time. What does it matter?"

"Would you also describe him as crazy?"

"What? I prefer not to speak ill of a dead man."

"Was he crazy? Insane? Perhaps a bit 'touched in the head?'"

"I'm starting to think he wasn't the only one," Dane said, glaring at him.

Marek interjected. "Dane, just admit it. Brennon was a fine old man, but he was...off."

"So what? What does that matter now?"

Anandil reached for a book and dipped a quill in ink. He held the book in front of him, quill at the ready. "In what ways was he mental?"

"Dane, I promise you that all of this has a point," Renwy assured from his stool. "If you would be so kind as to answer my brazen friends' questions we will get there faster."

"Fine," Dane said. "Brennon always went on and on about how one day he was sailing and his ship crashed and washed onto the shore of some strange island. He would drone on and on about how the island was full of animals that could walk and talk and fight like people. He said he found their favor and they took him on as one of their own.

"They taught him different techniques for fighting. Sword techniques from the lions, spear techniques from the crocodiles... He claimed there were others, but we didn't believe any of it. No one did. We just humored him, is all.

"He returned to Akreya and formed the Iron Fox Legion. He was undoubtedly mental, but he was good at fighting so he trained others and eventually they came to be the best sellswords in the world."

"So, if he didn't find an island of talking animals, where did he go?" Anandil questioned.

"Who knows? Maybe nowhere. Hell, he could have simply dreamt the whole thing one night. I'm telling you, he wasn't right." Anandil, Renwy, and Marek all glanced at one another. "Don't tell me you think he was telling the truth," Dane said.

Anandil shrugged as he finished jotting notes in the book he held. "I don't know."

"What the hell is the point, then?" Dane asked. "I thought you all said I would understand?"

Anandil looked at Marek. "Has he always been like this?"

"What? Dry, snappy, intolerant of fun? Absolutely." Marek grinned.

Dane shot him a glare, but otherwise disregarded him.

Anandil walked between the two of them with his arm extended out in front of him. "This man – the one in the cage," Anandil indicated him. The man had yet to utter a word. "He has beast blood in him."

Dane looked at the prisoner, who looked him straight in the eye without shame. "What do you mean?"

"He's a werewolf," Marek said.

"A lycan," the man corrected him, his eyes flicking over to Marek.

"Same thing."

The man snarled at him.

"Uncultured beast. Perhaps you're ridden with fleas? In that case, I pity you." Marek chuckled and turned away.

Dane approached the cage. "I thought werewolves – lycans, I mean – had been eradicated for over two centuries?"

"We're still around. We've just gotten better at blending in..."

Dane felt a shiver creep down his spine at the words of this mysterious man.

Anandil said, "This is Harryck. One of the-" the elf glanced at the caged man, "- *supposedly* few remaining lycans in Akreya. We use him to test what effects the undead may have on his kind and in exchange we allowed him and his family to reside inside the city."

"Except you've kept me locked in this accursed dungeon since I arrived!"

"Harryck, we've been over this already. It's safer for your loved ones if you're not around until we are completely done testing on you."

Harryck jumped to his feet and grasped the bars of the cage in a white-knuckled grip. "I took the risk of letting you perform these experiments on me. I took the risk of never seeing my family again. How many times have you made me drink the blood? I haven't turned through any of it! Enough is enough, elf!"

Anandil jabbed his finger in Harryck's face. "I have but a handful of tests left to run. We can be done within the next couple of days, if that suits you."

Harryck let his arms drop and he crossed his legs and sat down again. "I suppose it's the best I'll get."

"That's the spirit!' Anandil walked away.

"I still don't understand what any of this has to do with Brennon," Dane said, following the elf.

"Beast blood," Anandil responded. "The same tests I'm doing on Harryck I have performed on a variety of wildlife. The results have always been the same. Animals — or those with beast blood — are immune to death's grasp. They can't be turned and won't be resurrected as a wight after death."

"All right? I still don't see the connection with Brennon."

Anandil let out an exasperated laugh and looked to Marek for help. "Dense! So dense!" He spun on his heel and got uncomfortably close to Dane. "Brennon found an island of anthropomorphic animals – beast blood! Dogs, rabbits, pigs, cattle – they've all been insusceptible to the undead – beast blood! Harryck is a lycan and unsusceptible to the undead – beast blood! It's all connected!"

"I told you – Brennon was a good man, but he was also unstable." Dane spoke slowly and deliberately. "Tell me right now what you are seeking from me. Out with it."

Anandil threw up his hands and turned to his alchemy table. Renwy took the opportunity to hop from the stool and approach Dane with his hands spread apart in a peaceful gesture. "What my long-winded friend is trying to get at, Dane, is that all of our research points to the fact that beast blood could be the key to fighting the infection plaguing the realm."

"I'm not hearing where I come into this," Dane glared down at the halfling.

Renwy kept his hands raised. "It's a long shot – I know – but Anandil, myself, and some of the other magi would like for you and Marek to form an expedition to try and find the island that Brennon claims he found. If we find the island and the animals, perhaps we'll find something else that can help."

"This is utter nonsense." Dane looked to Marek for confirmation, but he only shrugged.

"What else can we do?" Renwy pleaded. "We can't ask Harryck to infect everyone with the lycan curse. We've already asked so much of him. And how many people do you think would agree to those terms, anyway?"

Dane gritted his teeth. "This is utter horseshit. I have better things to do than chase the dreams of a dead madman with a halfling and an erratic elven scholar. Goodbye." Dane turned and slammed the door as he passed through.

Seconds later, Marek called, "Dane! Hold a moment." He caught up to him and matched his pace. "For what it's worth, I think it sounds crazy, too."

Dane turned on him. "Then what the hell did you bring me here for?"

"Just because something sounds crazy doesn't mean it isn't true. Surely you understand. Think of all the things we've witnessed across the realm. Goblins, giants, trolls..."

"You're just as insane as your friends back there."

"Before you go slinging more stones, just hear me out: I *do* think it sounds crazy, but stranger things have happened. Do you want to die behind these walls and never take a chance at reclaiming what the dead have consumed?"

"I'm here, my daughter is safe, and there are other people here that I care about. Dying here doesn't sound that bad."

"Evie, then. You could have a chance at opening this world up to her. She has a lot longer to live than you do, my friend. Don't you think it's kind of selfish to keep her locked behind these walls?"

"Selfish or not – I won't risk what little life I have left for this madman's quest when I can spend it with my daughter. I just got here!"

"I'm sorry to hear that," Marek said, and as he let Dane gain a significant lead on him, he added: "And Evie will be, as well..."

* * *

"This is amazing!" Caulen held the bow out in front of him and pretended to nock an arrow. Llanowar nodded, the smallest of smiles tugging at the corner of her lip. "Could you teach me how to shoot?"

"Perhaps. If your parents approve."

"My parents are long gone. All of my family is."

"Sorry to hear that," Llanowar replied, shifting uncomfortably.

Caulen shrugged. "Times are tough, and life doesn't get any easier. I want to be able to shoot so I can hunt."

"That's a good reason."

Koda chimed in: "She's the person to learn from, kid. I've seen 'er in action. Not a better shot in Akreya, I'll bet."

Caulen smiled more. "You *have* to teach me, then."

"We'll start tomorrow," Llanowar said.

Caulen handed her the bow back as Koda put his arm around him. "You know, I've fought with a spear ever since I was your age. If you want, I can teach you some techniques."

"No, thanks," Caulen said.

Koda removed his arm from the boy's shoulder. "Suit yourself. It was only a one-time offer. You blew it." Llanowar smiled and Caulen laughed at him as he walked away.

On the other side of the room, Koda found Bren chatting with Marleyn over some good ale, while Evie's eyes flicked between them both, all the while maintaining a grin. Pelias and Grunt were seated away from everyone else – keeping to themselves as if they were both mutes. Koda approached the two of them and offered a bottle of wine.

"Can I interest either of you in sharing a bottle with me?" Koda asked.

Grunt waved the offer away, and Pelias shook his head. "Please, no," the knight said. "I'm still getting over the drinking I did last night."

"Threw yourself a party, eh?" Koda chuckled. "I understand."

"Not exactly..."

Suddenly, Dane threw the door open and stopped short when he saw his home was full of people. "What is this?" he asked. Marek brushed past him as Evie approached.

"Did you hear what Anandil and Renwy had to say, father?" she asked.

"He did." Marek answered for him, casting a dissatisfied look at Dane.

"And?"

"I told you he wouldn't agree to it. Ale?" Evie sighed and pointed to a counter where there were still a few full bottles left. Marek made his way directly to the alcohol.

"You know the halfling and the elf?" Dane asked, glaring down at her. Everyone else had returned to their conversations without much thought as to why Dane was upset.

"I do. They run the city, more or less. You don't like them?"

"You read my mind." Dane picked up a bottle of wine off the table and looked around for a cup.

Evie handed him one. "I didn't have to. It's obvious."

"Don't use your power on me or anyone. And stay away from Anandil and Renwy. Those two aren't right in the head."

"So, you won't even talk about it?"

"I see no need."

"I think you should explain the situation to your friends and see what they think."

Dane took a sip of wine. "How did you even get them all here?"

"It wasn't difficult. Marek told me who you arrived with so Caulen and I went around the city while you were gone and told them that you had something to tell them."

Dane put his cup down on the table with unnecessary force and glared down at Evie. She grinned back at him. "I thought you were going to the gardens?"

"We did. Well, we went *through* the gardens while we were rounding everyone up."

"We're having a talk later."

"I figured as much." Her smile never faded.

Marek patted her on the head. "Sorry, kid."

"No problem." She shrugged while Dane poured himself another drink and downed it in one toss. "Father, it's rude to keep your friends waiting."

"Your daughter said you had something important to tell us," Bren said.

Dane noticed that everyone was looking at him. He sighed, set down his empty cup, and proceeded to tell everyone about the events of the morning. He told them about the laboratory underneath the tower, Renwy and Anandil, and the werewolf captive named Harryck. He relayed as much detail as he could remember – with Marek filling in a few grey areas – about the questions Anandil had asked about the Iron Fox Legion and Brennon. Finally, he came to the revelation of the beast blood, and how Renwy and Anandil wanted Dane to go in search of Brennon's legendary walking, talking animals.

Everyone was silent while Dane was speaking, not even bothering to take a sip of wine or ale. Finally, at the end of it all, Koda said: "Well, that's good, right?"

Dane looked at him with exasperation. "The elf is insane. Absolutely touched, Koda."

Marek cleared his throat. "I can confirm," he chimed in.

"But that doesn't mean that he's wrong," Evie interjected. "I have heard their proposal, and, while it may be far reaching, it doesn't mean that they're wrong. Stranger things have happened. Dragons used to reside in Akreya, yes?" She looked at everyone in the group.

Llanowar said, "Long ago, yes, but no one here has ever seen one."

"Exactly! No one here has seen a dragon, but everyone knows that they existed at some point in history. How can we be so easy to dismiss the beasts that Brennon claims to have witnessed?"

Koda chuckled and pointed at Evie. "I like you! But in all seriousness, I come from a family of magi. I've seen all manner of strange and twisted things. There is very little that would surprise me anymore. Not even talking animals."

Dane was about to speak, but Evie cut him off by saying: "So everyone understands what's being asked of them? Shall we take a vote to see what everyone thinks?" Dane glared at her, but she waved him off. "I know, I know. We're having a talk later."

She turned back to the others and said, "Renwy, Anandil, and the other founders of Etzekel have asked my father to form an expedition to find Brennon's beasts. Majority rules. Those in favor, raise your hands."

Caulen, Koda, Grunt, and Marek raised their hands along with Evie. That left Dane, Pelias, Bren, Marleyn, and Llanowar opposed. Five to five.

"Damn!" Evie exclaimed. "A lot of good *that* did." She jabbed her finger in Pelias' face, as he was the closest to her. "You! What's your objection?"

Pelias did not flinch at her accusations. He launched to his feet from where he was sitting. "Anyone who sets foot outside the city walls will die. There's no reason to leave. Don't even try." He walked to the door and opened it. "There's nothing but horror and devastation beyond the walls. Don't tempt it." He slammed the door behind him.

Everyone looked around at one another, unsure of that to do or say. Finally, Bren cleared his throat and put down his cup. "I'll go after him and see what's happened."

"I think everyone should leave," Dane said.

"This didn't go the way I planned," Evie offered.

Marek patted her on the head. "Sorry, kid."

It did not take long for everyone to clear out and leave Dane and Evie alone. "I know what you're going to say, Dad," Evie said as she closed the door behind Caulen.

"Nothing for tonight," Dane replied, pouring himself another cup of wine. "Go to bed."

Evie complied with no remark.

* * *

"Pelias!" Bren was following shortly behind him as the two of them walked back to their house. "Pelias, what was that? Why would you say those things?"

"They're true."

"What do you mean? You frightened everyone back there."

"Good. Maybe they'll heed my advice."

Bren grabbed him by the shoulder and stopped him. The younger man did not resist. Bren pulled him to the side of the street and they both leaned against a wall. "What's wrong with you? You've been acting strangely ever since we arrived here."

Pelias sighed and looked up at him. "If I tell you, you have to swear that you will *not* tell the others. Promise me."

Bren furrowed his brow at his young friend but nodded his agreement. "Fine. You have my word."

Pelias shuffled his feet and looked around. He held his tongue until a passer-by had made their way far down the road. "I know what the cause of the plague is."

Bren looked as if he had just been kicked by a mule. "Explain yourself."

"It is a long tale."

"We have nothing but time here. I need to know if you've gone daft on me, or if you are actually speaking truthfully."

"I'm not crazy," Pelias said, craning his neck around the big man to make sure no one was nearby. "I wasn't sure what I knew was true, but I know now."

"Out with it already!"

"Fine, fine.... King Endrew's son is not dead. Prince Uragon was banished – by his own father."

Wide-eyed, Bren asked, "Why would he do that to his own son?"

"Prince Uragon was performing dark magic. He was trying to raise legendary Akreyan warriors from the dead to strengthen his father's army to better fight Ularon and his rebels. He wanted to make an elite type of soldier that was tougher than the average man in every way.

"He had what he called 'projects' deep in the dungeons of the castle where he spent day and night practicing these rituals. I had no idea it was going on, and when I found out, I didn't think it would be possible. Uragon was no magi, so the dead would stay dead. Worst case scenario, the prince is utterly insane. But... somehow, he did it. I had to put his monstrosities down myself.

"King Endrew was disgusted by his son's practices and had to do something to stop him. He still loved him though, and so he banished him from the city and claimed that he had died. The action still weighed on him the same as if he had imprisoned or executed him. He had banished his own son to the ruin Doompoint in the Red Crescent Desert, and he mourned the decision every day.

"I was part of the squad that secretly escorted the prince from the city. It was a tough journey. We had to keep Uragon bound and gagged the entire way, but he did not resist, did not try to bargain with us. He sat as still and quiet as a monk with a vow of silence. It was chilling.

"At one point, we were attacked by bandits, and one of our own was slain – Sir Eins. When we arrived at Doompoint, we brought Uragon from the wagon, took the gag out of his mouth and cut the bindings around his wrists and ankles. I tried to speak to him, but he turned and trudged through the sand as the wind swirled around him. He disappeared into the darkness of the ruins without a word. Nothing has ever frightened me like that."

Bren felt the hairs on his arms bristle, and he swallowed hard. "You think he survived out in the ruins? I mean, Doompoint is deep into the Red Crescent. How could he have survived? His father practically *did* execute him."

"I thought the same thing, but as we were leaving Eden on that wagon, I saw the reanimated corpse of Sir Eins shambling towards the city. He looked directly into my eyes."

"I understand what you mean, but this infection could simply be a coincidence. Stranger things have happened in the realm's history," Bren said.

Pelias shook his head and slumped with his back against the wall. He sighed again and said, "No. I know in my heart that it's true. Before King Endrew had decided what to do with him, I went to visit Uragon in his dungeon. I tried talking to him as my friend, tried to persuade him to give up his dark magic. I tried to get him to confide in me. He did not speak until I was leaving.

"He said: 'My father is a weak man. Ularon will win because my father cannot do what must be done. *I* will do what is necessary for the realm and for my father, even if my father must be removed to do so.'"

"He meant to take his father's throne?" Bren stroked his goatee as he mulled over the realization.

"I don't believe he wanted it. In his own twisted way, I think he believed that if he killed his father before Ularon won his rebellion he could spare his father his honor." Pelias sighed. "I know in my heart that he resurrected Sir Eins to travel back to Eden and execute Endrew."

"None of this makes sense to me," Bren confessed.

"I don't think it ever could. The dark magic contorted Uragon's mind. It made him into something demented."

Bren gasped. "That's why the king grew to hate the magi so much! Magic corrupted his son."

189

"Yes."

"Pelias, we have to tell the others!"

Pelias pushed off the wall and jabbed his finger in Bren's face. "You promised to keep it a secret, as I've done. We need not concern the others with this news. There's nothing they can do. Everyone is happy here. We can't disrupt that happiness." Pelias turned and began to walk off.

"Pelias!" Bren called after him. "What do you intend to do?"

The young knight made no gesture or response. He walked away briskly with his head held high — his back and shoulders straight.

Bren squinted after his young friend, trying to ignore the pit that was forming deep in his stomach.

Chapter 9

"This wasn't here the last time I ventured this far." Rorn made a sweeping motion as he indicated the city they had found planted in the middle of the thick forest.

"Hm," Braxon mumbled, eyes squinted in study. He and the Ravagers crept along the tree line, inspecting the high walls as best they could to formulate a plan. "This has got to be Etzekel."

"How do you know the name?" Rorn asked, spitting.

"Magi have been fleeing to a hideaway for months. I didn't know where, but I've heard the name."

Leyon balanced on his heels underneath the shade of a tree with low-hanging branches. "Your six came here. No doubt about it," the lean man said. "The stranger they met after killing the cyclops must have led them here."

"I still wonder what happened to the other three," Rorn said.

"I can think of a few outcomes..."Braxon muttered.

Leyon and Rorn glanced at one another.

"What's the plan, General?" Rorn asked. "Are we stormin' the gates or scalin' the wall?"

"You'd have to be mad to try either one," Braxon said.

Rorn chuckled and nodded. "I've never claimed to be sane."

"This city is full of magi. Our group would get ripped apart if we tried anything direct. Give me time to study and weigh our options. Spread your Ravagers thinly around the perimeter of the entire city. No fires for anyone."

"Best think of something quick, General. The boys'll be gettin' antsy 'fore long."

Braxon snarled at Rorn. "Handle it."

* * *

Bren sipped his ale slowly as he enjoyed the morning breeze drifting in through the open window. "Where's your daughter this morning?" he asked.

Dane was stirred from his own thoughts, taking a deep breath to acclimate himself. "She's with Caulen - the boy who was here last night."

Bren nodded. "He was friendly. Is she fond of him?"

"I'm not sure. Romantic insights never came easily to me." Bren chuckled and took another sip. "Thinking back to all of the memories I had with Tabitha – Evie's mother – I can't remember a single time where I said anything romantic or would make a woman swoon. I honestly don't know why she ever loved me." He lifted his cup to his lips.

"I hope you aren't looking to me to explain how love works to you. Women rarely gave me a second thought once I told them I come from one of the northern tribes."

Dane chuckled. "They didn't appreciate the prospect of being in a harem?"

"Women in the midlands don't appreciate polygamy like their northern cousins do."

The two men shared a laugh and enjoyed their drinks. Everything was good and the morning was relaxed, but both of their minds were elsewhere.

Bren said, "Dane, I hate to break the mood, but about yesterday…"

"It's fine," Dane said. "We should probably discuss it."

"Do they really have a man chained down there?" Bren asked. "Underneath the tower?"

"In a cage, yes," nodded Dane. "It's appalling. There's no sunlight down there, though he seems to be fed well. It's terrible. They're holding him hostage over his family and forcing him to go along with their experiments."

"I'm beginning to think that this place is not what we thought it was at first."

"You may be right." Dane took another sip before refilling both of their cups.

"Have you thought about what other secrets Etzekel may hold?"

"I have. I wish I could ignore the thoughts and enjoy my time here."

"Perhaps we're in more danger here than outside."

Dane considered his words for a moment before remembering: "Did you ever talk to Pelias? What was wrong with him?"

Bren cleared his throat and peered into his cup. "I think he's just weary from the travel and… overwhelmed with this place and the information you gave us all yesterday. He also drank a good deal the night before, for what it's worth."

"I just hope his words didn't frighten anyone else. We don't need people on edge while confined to this place."

"I'm sure everyone understands."

There was a knock at the door. When Dane opened it, he found Renwy standing there smiling up at him. "Good morning, Master Dane. I've come to ask if you would like to join me on my morning walk of the city."

Dane looked at Bren, who shrugged. "Won't bother me. I suppose I should be going." He stood up from his chair and downed the rest of his cup. He walked past Dane and Renwy and stepped out into the street, saying his goodbyes.

Dane waved after him and shut the door. "Lead the way, Master Halfling."

They had not walked more than fifteen paces before Renwy said, "I want you to know that I understand why you feel the way you do about our request."

Dane adjusted his stride to match the struggling halfling but did not acknowledge what he had just said.

"You don't have to be so cautious around me, Dane. We're just talking. In confidence, I might add."

"I'm just eager to hear your explanation," Dane replied. A group of small children pushed roughly between the two of them, laughing and skipping along.

Renwy smiled after them. Dane – distracted by the children – felt a tug on his sleeve as the halfling reverted his course down a side street. "I thought that the two of us could discuss matters a little more casually if Anandil was not around. Not everyone gets along with him, I realize. And perhaps hosting our first meeting in his laboratory was not the proper thing to do."

"Some of my people are skeptical about the methods you employ in these experiments you've performed," Dane admitted.

"You mean Harryck. You say 'some of your people,' but what about you? How do you feel about it?"

Dane shrugged, refusing to divulge any more than that.

Renwy sighed. "Harryck knew what we required of him. We explained his obligations to him when we made the agreement to allow his family to reside here. I think his beast blood sometimes makes him...rash and abrasive. Read any old tomes or books and you'll see those characteristics certainly fit someone with his type of condition.

"I assure you that while he may regret his decision now, Harryck is being treated fairly and we are remaining within compliance with the agreement he made with us. Hopefully he will understand someday the part he played in ending this foul plague."

Dane and Renwy had made several turns during this short exchange and they now approached the gardens. At Dane's amazement, he found a wide variety of fruits and vegetables unlike anything that should have been possible. "How?" he asked. "Some of these plants don't even grow in the same season, yet here you have them all together."

Renwy indicated a chubby dwarven woman who was seated in the middle of the surrounding foliage. Her short legs were crossed as she rested on a blanket spread on the ground. She smiled and waved at Renwy as they approached. She stood to greet them.

"Dane, this is Madagrett. She oversees our gardens."

The dwarf curtsied for Dane and smiled. "Master Dane. Most people call me Maddie."

Dane, remembering Evie mention the dwarf previously, bowed his head in response. "Your garden is miraculous, Maddie. How do you do it?"

"Magic. I have always had a way with plant-life. I can communicate with it in a way. I just focus my energy and attention and it will grow. I really can't explain it past that." The dwarf shrugged. "Are you a magi?"

"No," Dane replied as he looked around in wonder at the different fruit trees surrounding them. "You know my daughter, though. She's a magi. Evelyn. Evie, I call her."

Madagrett beamed even more. "Evie is a joy to be around. Such a wonderful girl. She's very helpful to me. She should be around here somewhere with Caulen..." She pointed through the thicket of trees and Dane could see her and Caulen were planting seeds.

"Would you like to speak with her?" Renwy asked.

Dane shook his head. "I don't want to disturb them. Let's continue with our walk. Goodbye, Maddie."

Madagrett waved and said, "Best not stay out for long. Rain's coming soon."

After they walked well away from the gardens, Renwy asked, "Dane, what can I say to convince you to agree to the expedition?"

"Nothing. My daughter is safe and happy. I won't cause her any more grief by going on a wild goose chase."

"Is she truly happy, though? Trapped behind these walls? Knowing that the world could be changed, but her father is standing in the way of that?"

"Watch yourself." Dane glared down at him.

"I said we would have a discussion. I didn't say that I would refrain from speaking my mind. Follow me. We're almost to the gate." As soon as the words were out of his mouth, they heard a horn blow twice. The two of them rounded a corner to see several people dart about as the gate began to lift at the same time the wooden drawbridge was being lowered.

"What's going on?" Dane asked.

"The horn — if it blows once it means that a group of people are approaching the wall and need to be let in. Twice means the same, but that a horde of the undead are following closely behind. See how fast the bridge and gate are opened."

It was true. The bridge and gate were open and allowing passage in seconds, and as soon as the group was across, they were closed again.

Dane spotted Marek among the crowd. He approached Dane and Renwy and said, "Fifteen. It was a large party. They just happened into the area. They fled into the forest hoping the dead would be fewer. They had no magi, but a monstrous horde appeared while we were talking. I couldn't leave them out there."

"How many of the dead do you think are out there?" Renwy asked.

"I can't say for sure. Maybe a hundred.," Marek replied. "The sentinels are doing what they can, but it may take a while to thin them out."

"Very well," Renwy said.

Marek nodded to them and left to rejoin the group that had just arrived, hoisting his trident onto his shoulder. Rain began to fall lightly.

"Look at those poor people."

Dane studied the new group. They were all wrapped tightly in hooded cloaks and robes. Some of them sobbed and clung to passers-by. They were all disheveled, not unlike Dane and his friends when they had arrived.

Renwy said, "It sure seems like they're glad to have a safe place to come to." The rain suddenly shifted to bigger, heavier drops.

Renwy pulled a black hooded robe out from under his own and held it out to Dane. Dane took it and put it on, pulling the hood over his face. Renwy smiled. "It was my wife's. She was human like you." Dane raised his eyebrows. "I know – unusual for a human and a halfling to come together. Anyway, you can keep the robe. She's been dead for some time."

"Sorry to hear that," Dane replied, crossing his arms.

In a heartbeat, Renwy's demeanor changed. "Dane, I'll be upfront with you. The city is getting crowded. We soon won't have enough room for everyone who wants to be here. We'll have to start turning people away and getting rid of others unless we can extinguish the plague altogether. I hope you understand."

"I'm afraid I don't." Dane took a step away from the halfling and looked him up and down, his face fixed with irritation. He had an inkling of where this was going.

"We need you and your group to head the expedition. The magi here will never agree to go. They're scared. Scared of the undead that want to feast on them and scared of the living that want to hunt them. No one else but you and your friends can go."

"I've already made up my mind. The answer is no."

"Dane, I don't want to do this. Trust me. If you absolutely refuse to go on this expedition, I will be forced to remove you *and* your friends from the city."

"Either way, we have to leave Etzekel? If that's the case, we could leave and not do as you ask. I'm leaning towards that option, if you want to know the truth."

198

Lightning flashed over their heads as the rain continued to fall even heavier. Renwy glared up at him, the water droplets smattering his face as he had not raised the hood on his robe. "You misunderstand me, Dane. I will force you and your friends to leave. Your daughter I will keep here. You must agree to go and I will keep your daughter as collateral to ensure you do as we ask."

Dane straightened and uncrossed his arms. "You wouldn't dare. You couldn't."

"There are many powerful magi here in the city. Trust me – removing you would be no difficult task."

Dane's nostrils flared as he returned a burning stare at the halfling. "You son of a bitch."

"Call me whatever names you like, but you have a serious decision to make here. You have two days to discuss it with your associates. After that, we will begin the relocation process." Renwy turned and walked away. Without stopping, he added: "As I said, you can keep the robe. You may need it in your travels outside the wall."

* * *

Even after being in Etzekel for two days, Bren had spent most of his time cooped up in his home or with his friends, and so he decided to explore the city once he left Dane's house. The sun was shining, and the city was alive with many sounds, sights, and smells. Many people greeted him as he strolled through the streets.

Bren smiled and nodded at the passers-by. Occasionally he stopped and peered curiously at whatever goods a shop was dealing in. Even with persecution and plague threatening their lives, the people of the city operated as normal. Bakeries, smiths, jewelers, tailors, alchemists, and many others chatted with him when he stopped to look at their products.

He smiled when he found that Etzekel even had a library open to the public. It was a two-story stone building, and though large, it was not ornately carved or decorated like the library in Eden. It had a plain wooden sign advertising itself. It had been a while since he had been to a library, so he took to the steps.

At the top of the climb sat an elf with short blonde hair and an earring in each ear. He looked up from the book in his lap and smiled at Bren. "Hello, friend. Come to learn?"

Bren stopped and smiled. "I'm curious, is all. I didn't expect to find a library here."

"Wonderful, isn't it? Odd, though, how even when constructing the city, they thought to make a place for knowledge. Magic is good for what it does, but there is always something new one can learn." The elf closed his book and stood.

"Very interesting indeed. How did it come about?"

"The founders of the city brought the first selections with them. Since then, several of the newcomers have increased the catalogues with books and manuscripts from their own collections."

"I think I'll take a look." Bren nodded and continued the climb.

"Enjoy yourself, friend," the elf said, sitting down and reopening his book, only to be dismayed when a few light droplets of water splattered the page.

Bren opened the door and stepped inside of a well-lit room. The entire building was this single room, completely open and filled with several rows of bookshelves that were twice Bren's size.

Ladders could be found at the beginning of each row of shelves and could be moved from one end to another. Up above was a second-floor balcony that wrapped around the entire room. More shelves were filled there. He did not know what he had expected, but he could not guess how many books were inside the place. Very few of the shelves he saw were empty.

Bren was pleased at how many people were perusing the selections. Humans, elves, dwarves, halflings — all were engrossed in their hunt for knowledge and legends and stories. They were all about – the balcony, atop ladders, or seated on the floor as they searched. Some even sat atop the shelves themselves, cross-legged as they flipped through pages.

Bren ran his fingers along the spines of several books as he walked. The place was silent except for the occasional shuffling or someone replacing a book on a shelf or from someone clearing their throat or coughing. His footsteps sounded heavy in this place, but no one paid him any attention.

He walked among the aisles, taking in the smell of the parchment and paper, and the leather-bound volumes. He turned a corner and found a podium with the largest book he had ever seen. A lantern hung nearby to illuminate it. When he got closer, he found a placard that read, "Library Catalogue."

Bren's mouth dropped slightly as he flipped through a few of the pages. The entries were hand-written and listed in alphabetical order and gave specifics of where to find each book. Bren smiled in disbelief, thinking of the time and effort that had been put into this.

Suddenly, someone tapped him lightly on the shoulder. He turned and Marleyn gave a small wave, smiling up at him.

"Hey, Marleyn," Bren said, "Have you seen this?" He pointed at the catalogue.

Several people looked up from their reading and searched for whoever had spoken at full volume. Marleyn held a finger up to her lips, and Bren felt his cheeks get warmer. Her eyes shimmered at his embarrassment, and she beckoned him with the single finger at her lips.

He followed behind her, his eyes fixed on her thick hair and the way it bounced with each of her steps. Marleyn glanced over her shoulder at him and blushed. She led him out of the library and onto the steps.

The droplets that had begun when Bren entered the library had gotten bigger, splatting loudly against the street below the steps. The two of them huddled underneath the awning, watching the rain.

"That place amazes me," Bren said.

She giggled at him and said, "I found it just this morning. I didn't expect to find you in there."

"You don't think a Sword of Justice can read?" Bren teased.

Marleyn placed a hand on his chest. "No, it's not that. That's not what I meant."

Bren smirked at her. "I'm just too dumb, eh?"

She gave him a little shove. "Oh, stop that. I just didn't know you liked to read, is all."

"I was taken in by a king after being raised by the Bison Tribe. I had to learn to read, and then I read so I could understand the world better."

"That's fascinating, Bren." She looked into his eyes.

"The world of the Tribesmen is very small, very focused. They don't teach anything that doesn't pertain to the tribes. Only how to kill those not of the tribes."

"You haven't told me much about your life. Only that you were the king's Sword of Justice."

"It doesn't come up much."

Marleyn looked up at the sky, and seeing the rain was lessening, said, "I'd like to hear more. Will you tell me the story while we walk the city? I need to look for something."

"After you," Bren said, sweeping his arm down the stairs, "although, I think I'll save that story for another time."

"I wasn't intending to pry," she said as they began walking.

"I know. I'll tell you someday – maybe soon – but it's been a pleasant day so far, and those don't come around too often anymore."

"I know what you mean," she murmured. They reached the bottom of the steps and she looked up and down the street, thinking.

"What is it you're hunting for?"

"I'm looking for a chain."

"Chain?" Bren furrowed his brow.

"Just a small one."

"Like for a necklace?"

"Yes, one made of silver."

"I saw a jeweler on my walk a little bit ago. Follow me." He took her by the hand and led her back the way he had come.

Marleyn liked the feel of his hand enclosed around hers. She looked at his muscular arm and followed it up to his broad shoulders and then she studied his face, his sharp eyes, and shaped goatee as he walked intently. Her cheeks flushed and she looked down at the ground.

Before she knew it, they had stopped in front of a stall where an old dwarf was displaying all sorts of necklaces, bracelets, earrings, and anklets on a table. Marleyn knelt over the display, looking at each of them.

"They're all so beautiful," she said.

"Thank you," the dwarf said, smiling, his hands clasped behind his back.

"I would buy them all from you if I could, but this is what I need." She lifted a silver chain with no pendants or jewels attached. "How much?"

"Three silver pieces."

"I... I only have two." She said.

"I'm sorry, Miss," the dwarf said, holding out his hand to take the chain back.

Bren dropped a silver coin in its place. "There's the extra one," he said.

Marleyn gave up her two silver pieces and stepped away, smiling at the chain. "Thank you, Bren. This means so much."

"Most women would prefer the gold chains, or the jewels." The two of them strolled down the street at a leisurely pace.

"This is more important than any of that. It matches perfectly."

"Matches what?" he asked.

She stopped and dug into one of her pockets, and so he stopped and waited with her. She opened her hand and revealed the silver locket that Cassandra had given her in the forest. Marleyn attached the chain and held it out to Bren. "See?" she asked.

He took it and opened it to look once more at the portrait of Ruddell and his daughters. He smiled and closed it. Bren raised the chain over her head and slid it down around her neck, taking her hair in his hands and pulling it free of the necklace.

She smiled up at him, and he down at her. "Yes," he said. "It matches perfectly."

The two of them stepped closer to one another. Marleyn looked at his lips and then back up at him, her eyes wide. Bren put a hand on her arm and pulled her ever closer.

"Bren! Marleyn!"

The two of them snapped their heads down the street and stepped away from one another. Caulen marched towards them at a brisk pace. "Dane wants everyone to group up at Grunt and Koda's house. He didn't tell me what was going on, but he says it's important."

Caulen turned immediately and led the way. Bren and Marleyn looked at each other, worry on both their faces.

* * *

"Halfling dog! I'll put an arrow through his eye!"

Koda gave a sarcastic laugh. "Not before I put my spear through his belly."

Llanowar replied, "You chose in favor of the expedition yesterday."

"Yes. *Chose*. This halfling is taking that choice away from all of us."

Dane and his companions had gathered at Grunt and Koda's home to discuss what had transpired between he and Renwy. He had left Evie and Caulen behind. He did not want her to know anything until he was ready to tell her himself. At this point, he was not sure what to tell her at all.

"Is your friend Marek in on this scheme?" Bren asked.

Dane shrugged. "I don't know for sure, but I have to assume he is. He's involved with the workings of the city, though he claims not deeply. He brought a group of people inside the walls even though they had no magi."

"So maybe he's a good person?"

"He was a good person to have under my command, but that doesn't matter right now. I didn't trust him to be here with us. Not yet."

"Maybe we should just leave now," Koda said. "I don't want to go, but I won't do someone else's dirty work through bribery." He pointed at Dane. "We can take your daughter and get her out of here."

"I would rather still hurt the little man," Llanowar muttered. Grunt sounded his agreement with the elf.

"I doubt we can do either," said Bren. "Now that Renwy has revealed his hand he'll keep a close eye on all of us."

Marleyn spoke up: "I have a strange feeling that bad things will happen if we leave this city. No matter on whose terms. I don't want to leave… Bad things will happen."

Pelias cleared his throat. "If it's because of what I said the other night, I apologize. I wasn't thinking clearly. While I still think it's a bad idea to leave, I suppose we have no choice." The young man grimaced and dropped his eyes to his feet.

Everyone sat in silence, sipping wine or wringing their hands. They were all engulfed in their own minds.

Dane sighed. "We still have a little while before Renwy wants an answer. Let's all take our time and think on it. Perhaps an idea will spring to mind."

"Our options are limited," Koda said.

Dane nodded. "I know..."

Llanowar said, "I say we should still have a backup plan. Somewhere we can go no matter what happens."

"That's a good idea," Pelias agreed, "but where?"

"I don't think we should go back east," Bren said. "We know there's plenty of undead that way, and we may be unlucky enough to run into Braxon again."

"North?" Marleyn said.

Bren shook his head. "Nothing up that way besides the Tribes."

"Maybe that's not a bad thing," Pelias said. "We could build our own refuge in the mountains."

"Starting from scratch?" Koda said. "I don't like the sound of that. Why not south? There's not much in the desert, but I know it, and there's just enough life there that it won't seclude us from the rest of the realm."

"No," Pelias said, his back stiffening. "Not south."

"Why not?" Koda asked.

Bren looked at his friend. Pelias swallowed hard and cleared his throat. He opened his mouth to speak, but Bren answered first: "I don't think most of us could handle the heat." He smiled sheepishly. "I know I couldn't. I wasn't built for that." He chuckled.

Marleyn looked from Bren to Pelias, and then back to Bren. "Neither was I," she said.

Koda rolled his eyes. "Well this is great."

"Why don't we just continue going west, then?" Dane suggested. "Bandimere is the closest village from here. Let's just go there." He looked to the others, who nodded or shrugged. "All right, then. Everyone remember that. If we need to move on, we go to Bandimere."

* * *

Dane swung the door to his home open and stepped inside. He stopped short when he saw Marek sitting by the fireplace with Evie and Caulen. Marek stood up slowly and cleared his throat. He held out both of his hands to try and steady Dane, who was glaring at him as he shut the door.

"Dane… I didn't know. That wasn't part of the plan. Not *my* plan."

"What *was* your plan?" Dane asked. Evie and Caulen watched silently.

"I just wanted to try and convince you to go on the expedition. I truly believed it was the right thing to do, but I would *never* force you to go. Especially not by holding your daughter captive. Please believe me."

Dane threw off the robe that Renwy had given him earlier and took a step toward him. Marek shifted his weight to his back foot. He was unsure of whether Dane was going to attack or not. "Can you talk Renwy out of it?"

Marek shook his head. "No. I've been misled, as you have been. He claimed I was a close confidant of his, but I would have urged against this bribery if he had asked me. He knew I would have, and that's why he never said a word about it."

Evie said, "He's telling the truth, father."

Dane nodded and flicked his gaze at her. "I know." Looking back at Marek, he asked: "Do you have any idea how to get out of Renwy's deal?"

"No. He's serious. He came and told me about the talk the both of you had. I tried to protest and he had me removed from the tower."

Dane poured himself a cup of wine and dropped to the couch.

"Let's just agree to do it," Marek said. "That way we can smuggle Evie out of here somehow and then we can all decide what to do."

Caulen stood and said, "Dane, I will do what I can to help you get Evie out of here safely. I can watch over her while you go on the expedition, or I will help you get her out of the city, whichever you decide."

Dane nodded in acknowledgement and the boy seated himself again.

"Is anyone going to listen to what I have to say?" Evie asked. "Am I just a pawn in this game?"

"Of course we will listen," Dane said. "Just know that whatever opinion you have, the outcome affects everyone."

"I do understand that. That's why I think you should agree to the magi's offer."

"You still believe we should go on the expedition?"

"Do you remember what Amir said when he told you about the opportunity to assist The New Dawn? You told him that you didn't care about The New Dawn, you only cared about *my* safety. Amir said, 'We have a chance to help so many lives. You're focused on the one closest to your own heart, but what about the hearts of others?' Do you remember that?"

Dane nodded.

"This is the same thing. It's not ideal that we would be blackmailed by the magi into doing something for the greater good, but it's still the greater good. If you can forget about Renwy, Anandil, and the magi, you would be able to think about all the other people that this would help.

"If the magi are right and the beast blood can aid in ridding Akreya of this infection, then we have to put aside our bitterness and do it because it's the right thing to do. What's the point of living here in safety if so many others are going to suffer? We will have paid for our safety with their lives. There's a chance for all to know peace and we *have* to take it."

Dane could not help but think how much easier it would be to make this decision if Amir was still there, but he knew that Evie spoke in the same vein as his good friend. The man would quite possibly applaud the girl at her words. Even so, there was still much to think about.

"I understand what you mean and how you feel, Evie. I'll discuss it with the others and we'll all decide what course of action to take."

"Fine, but I want to be present. Caulen and Marek, as well."

Dane nodded. "Agreed. We'll decide together."

Chapter 10

It was early morning the next day and Koda was with Grunt enjoying the comfort of the pub. Koda, with his boots kicked up on the table, and Grunt with his head tipped back against the wall behind them, were approached by the elven girl who ran the place. She had been there every time that the two of them had visited and Koda began to wonder if she ever slept.

"Those folks over there tried to sit here this morning. I made them move." The girl smiled and brushed her black hair behind her long ear. Koda and Grunt saw some people wearing cloaks with their hoods up whispering amongst themselves. Koda saw them passing items around the table, but he could not see what they were. "I knew you two would be here before too long."

Koda smiled at the girl. "You know us so well for us being here such a short amount of time. Do you remember what we drink?" He held up his cup and shook it lightly.

"You spend more time here than you realize," she quipped, smirking at him. Koda grinned back at her, but out of the corner of his eye, he noticed one of the hooded people casting their gaze at him and Grunt.

Grunt tapped his cup twice on the table, his eyes looking lazily ahead. To anyone else it appeared that the giant man was lost in thought and mindlessly fidgeting, but Koda knew it was a signal. The two of them had been aware of the mysterious guests long before the barmaid had mentioned anything about them.

"Maybe they just like your mask," Koda said. He spoke quietly, but not so quiet that he appeared to be whispering sensitive information. "Maybe they're jealous and want to know where they can get one?"

Grunt glared at him and Koda raised his arms in surrender – a coy smile on his face. "So, you haven't really said a word about Marek…" Amused at his own joke, Koda chuckled.

Grunt sniffed and grunted.

"Well, he doesn't seem *that* bad. We'll see… Sometimes you just have to forgive people. Take me for instance-" Koda paused as the barmaid returned with a full jar of ale. He took it from her and poured himself a fresh cup. "-I forgave you for nearly getting me killed when we had that fight against the three lions. Remember? If you hadn't been able to grab that one by the tail when it jumped, I would have been kitty food. But you don't hear me going on about that anymore, do you?"

Grunt ignored him like so many times before.

"What time is it, love?" Koda called to the barmaid.

"Almost noon," she replied.

With that, both Koda and Grunt stood, dropped a few coins on the table and walked to the door – Koda offering a relaxed salute to the barmaid in passing. As they walked, they felt the eyes of all the hooded figures following them.

The pair strolled through the city at a brisk pace, purpose driving each of their steps. The streets were busy, but they maneuvered through the people with precision. Eventually they arrived outside a two-story home. Koda pounded on the door and was met by Pelias and Bren only moments later.

"Where's Marleyn?" Bren asked.

"She's with Llanowar. We're going to pick them up next," Koda replied.

And so, two became four and they proceeded to the next home a few streets over. Llanowar and Marleyn were already waiting for them by the front door. Marleyn waved at Bren, who returned the gesture with a light wave of his own.

"I understand why we're doing this," Llanowar said, "but won't it look more suspicious to the halfling if we travel the city in packs."

"We can't risk it," Pelias said. "Let the man think what he wants."

"Besides," Koda whispered casually, "I think Dane was right. Renwy *does* have people following us. Grunt and I were being watched at the pub, and they've followed us since then."

Marleyn looked over her shoulder to see who he was speaking of, but Bren stepped in her view. "Don't look. He's right – we're being followed. We don't want to spook them and make them more suspicious."

"Should we really be leading them along like this?" Marleyn asked. "What if they attack us at Dane's home?"

"That's already a possibility." Bren gave her a comforting smile as she looked up at him with frightened eyes.

When they arrived at Dane's home, Marek and Caulen were already there. Evie had prepared cups of wine for everyone along with slices of cheese and bread to snack on. Dane surveyed the room and felt relieved. He wished he could allow himself even a faint smile at his friends, but he could not.

"Thank you, everyone, for coming," Dane greeted them before taking a quick sip of his wine. "I suppose there's no reason to rehash the details of why we're here. I just have to ask what everyone thinks we should do."

Evie chimed in: "I've already told my father that I believe we should agree to Renwy's terms. I know it's not favorable, but we should just grit our teeth and do it. If the results of this expedition turn out how the magi expect, we could help a lot of people. That's more important than our pride."

"You know," Koda said, "I've lived most my life by the 'survival-of-the-fittest' rule and it hasn't let me down, yet... I don't like this."

"No one does, Koda," Dane said.

"We don't have a choice," Evie said. "If there's even a chance that we can save our home, then we have to take it."

Koda shrugged. "This may be the first noble thing I've done in my life. Let's hope it doesn't get me killed."

"Maybe you'll actually like it," Pelias said, grinning at him.

"We're all agreed, then? If anyone has any thoughts, now is the time." Dane asked.

Caulen and Evie glanced at one another and nodded. Pelias wrung his hands. Bren scratched at the stubble on top of his head while Marleyn bit her lip. Koda sniffed, staring at the ground, and next to him Grunt's arms were crossed, looking hard at Dane. Llanowar's chin rested in the palm of her hand while her index finger tapped at her cheek.

Marek cleared his throat and said, "I just want to say thank you for trusting me to be here."

Dane looked at him. "Evie trusts you. That's all I need to know."

"I won't let you down. Any of you." Marek glanced at Grunt before folding his hands in front of him and looking at the ground.

No one else spoke, though there were many hands wringing, and plenty of nervous fidgeting. The only replies were silent nods. "Very well." Dane took a long sip of his wine and handed his cup to Evie. "I'll go inform Renwy of our decision. You should all go home and pack what you need for travelling. He could commission us to leave immediately."

Pelias was already throwing the door open, walking with purpose, but he stopped and waited for the others. Everyone else was reluctant to leave.

Llanowar sighed and said, "Does anyone else feel like we're making a mistake?"

"Oh yes," Pelias replied, kicking the door gently shut and putting his back to it.

Marleyn looked at Bren and said, "I hope he doesn't send us away too soon. We only just got here."

Bren stood suddenly and cleared his throat. "Dane, I think we should talk about who's going to leave Etzekel."

"What do you mean?" Koda asked.

"Well, Evie can't go, correct? Renwy won't let her. She should have a couple of us stay here with her to watch her back."

Dane nodded as he pondered the statement, but Evie interjected: "I can watch my own back just fine. You all are the ones that will need the help! It's going to take all of you!"

"Bren's right," Dane told her, causing her to scowl. "But who should stay?"

They all looked at one another, though no one said a word.

"This is quite the predicament," Koda laughed. "None of us want to go, yet none of us want to stay."

Caulen stood. "I'll stay. Wherever Evie is, that's where I am." He stood next to her and crossed his arms. Koda laughed again, earning him a glare from the young boy.

Dane studied the two youths momentarily. Caulen's protection for his daughter brought him comfort. "Thank you, Caulen," Dane said, nodding at him.

Bren gave Marleyn a half-hearted smile. "You should stay..."

"What?" Marleyn furrowed her brow.

"You shouldn't put yourself in any more danger than you need to. You would be safer here than out there."

"What makes you so sure?"

"I don't want you to go outside these walls. I may not be able to protect you and stay focused."

"So you're going to leave me behind while you travel who knows how far and for how long?"

"I'll come back."

"You don't know that."

Bren sat down next to her again. "Marleyn, please... I'll come back." After a few moments of consideration, she nodded. Bren wrapped his arms around her and embraced her.

As everyone began filing out of Dane's house, Marek approached Grunt. "Well, Valyn, it appears we'll be fighting alongside one another again. I won't let you down this time." He held out his hand.

Grunt growled and ducked out of the door. Koda, following behind, looked at Marek with raised eyebrows. "I can't believe he said that to you! He's usually so polite."

*　*　*

Dane, donning his clean Iron Fox Legion armor, wrapped Evie in his arms and squeezed tightly. "I love you," he said.

"I love you, too, Dad." She smiled up at him. "Don't get too sentimental. You're acting like you won't see me again. You're just going to the tower."

"I take every chance I can to give you a hug," Dane smiled back at her. He let her go and placed a hand on the hilt of his fox-tail longsword, which hung loosely from his belt.

"Be careful."

Dane bowed and walked past her. He patted Caulen on the shoulder as he passed by and stopped by Marek so he could put his gloves on. "Any chance Renwy's thugs will jump me in a panic when they see me in this?"

"If they do, I'm sure you can handle it." Marek grinned.

"Thanks for watching the kids." Marek nodded and Dane opened the door. He was hoping for sunshine, but the sky was gloomy. He shut the door behind him and paused a moment until he heard Marek lock it.

With one hand resting on the pommel of his sword, Dane strolled at a brisk pace toward the magi tower. The thoughts racing through his mind put him on edge, and he eyed every passer-by on the street with suspicion. No one he passed gave off suspicious intentions, but he knew somewhere there was someone watching him very closely. He could feel their eyes tracking his path.

Dane glanced over his shoulder occasionally but made sure not to appear anxious. He reminded himself that he was simply going to talk to the halfling, because his demeanor was befitting someone who was on a mission to hurt someone. He reminded himself that this way, though undesirable, was the best way to keep everyone safe.

It was not long before he found himself at the entrance to the tower. He used his fist to give the door a couple poundings and stood back with his arms crossed. The door opened slowly and Dane prepared to explain his presence, but no one stood before him.

He gave one last longing look at the city street behind him before stepping into the dim staircase and making his descent...

*   *   *

Pelias took heavy, dragging steps down the stairs from the second floor. Bren glanced over his shoulder as he stuffed a blanket into his pack. "Back in the armor, eh?"

Pelias nodded, bundling his red cape underneath one arm. "Dane said to be ready. I like to be prepared."

"And yet, no pack..." Bren cinched his own closed.

Pelias pointed to the corner of the room, underneath an end-table, where a bag and his shield were resting. "I packed it the day after we got here."

"You really *are* prepared." Bren smiled.

Pelias did not respond as he trudged to the corner. He picked up his shield and slung the bag over his shoulder. He walked to the door and placed a hand on the knob. "Bren, I... I didn't know how to tell anyone, so I'm only telling you..."

Bren's heart immediately dropped into his stomach and he turned slowly to look at his younger friend. "You're leaving."

Pelias nodded. "I am."

"Why?"

"I believe if I can find Uragon and kill him, his dark magic will be extinguished."

"You can't leave now. We need you!"

"I'm hoping Renwy will give you all a few extra days to stay here in Etzekel. Maybe long enough for me to get to Doompoint and kill the prince."

"What if you don't get there before we set out? Someone could die!"

"I told everyone the other night that people are going to die if we set foot outside the walls. I believe that this is the way to minimize our losses."

Bren threw his pack to the ground and kicked it across the room. He pointed at Pelias. "Have you thought about anyone but yourself?"

"That's what I'm doing right now!"

"No!" Bren shouted. "These people — me and everyone that came here with us — we are all your *friends*. They wouldn't want you setting out alone. Let's at least discuss it with the others — cast a vote or something!"

"If there's a chance that I could have ended this sooner, or even prevented it in the first place, then I have to correct it. No one else needs to pay the consequences for my actions. You won't stop me. I'm going."

"Pelias, wait!" Bren lurched toward him as he opened the door. There was a large boom and the ground shook violently. The two friends looked at each other before running outside.

"Smoke — in the direction of the gate," Pelias pointed.

"I hear people screaming!"

As the two friends began running towards the danger, four hooded figures stepped in their way. From underneath their large robes, weapons appeared. Beneath their covers were an odd assortment of characters: an elf, a dwarf, and two humans. Their armor was mixed-and-matched – some heavy and some light. One of the humans did not wear any armor at all.

"Who are you?" Pelias asked.

"Ravagers!" the dwarf smirked.

"I thought you were all rotting in cells?" Bren asked.

"General Braxon needed us to hunt down some vermin. That'd be you," the elf said.

"Go back to your cells. I don't want to hurt you," Pelias warned.

The dwarf drew a pair of throwing axes from his belt and hurled both at the same time. Pelias jumped in front of Bren and deflected both axes with his shield. The first human rushed and Pelias parried his swing, redirecting him within Bren's range. Bren wrenched the dagger out of his opponent's hand and stabbed him in the neck with it.

Ahead of him, Pelias ducked low and swiped with his sword, cutting off the elf's leg and sending him tumbling to the ground. Bren finished him off with the dagger. The dwarf and the human rushed at the same time. Bren stood next to Pelias and threw his dagger at the dwarf, but he missed. Smirking, the dwarf ran faster, brandishing a hatchet.

"Bren!" Pelias tossed his shield to him before crossing swords with the human. Bren caught the shield and smashed it into the running dwarf's head, sending him sprawling to the ground. Pelias deflected a swing by the human before ducking and disemboweling him.

"Braxon pursued us this far? I thought for sure we'd lost him!" Bren exclaimed.

"And he's inside the city. We have to warn Dane." Pelias sheathed his sword and began jogging towards the tower.

Bren grabbed him by the shoulder. "Go get Marleyn and Llanowar and then meet with Koda and Grunt. I'll get Dane, Marek, and the kids. We'll all meet by the gate and fight our way out of the city together."

"I'll be faster. Why don't you get Marleyn?"

"You're a better fighter. She'll be safer with you! Go!"

Pelias nodded and the two separated, with Bren running to the house to retrieve his pack and bardiche.

* * *

The mysterious figures Dane passed as he descended the stone steps made him uneasy. None of them were bothered by him or curious of his presence and most did not react to him at all. Many of them carried armfuls of books or scrolls along with the occasional torch or lantern.

Dane kept a hand on the hilt of his sword but tried to appear comfortable. He could not shake the feeling that he was surrounded by enemies. He was placing a great deal of faith in a deceitful halfling.

Dane finally found himself at the bottom of the stairs. He pounded his fist on the wood before opening it slowly and continuing to knock. He found Anandil hovering over a vial of purple liquid that was emitting a faint colored smoke. He inhaled deeply.

Without turning, the elf said, "I don't remember inviting you here."

Dane ignored his tone and glanced around the room. Harryck watched him from his cage but remained silent. "You didn't. I was hoping to find Renwy here."

"What business do you have with him?"

"My *own*."

"Well, he's not here, so leave."

"Anandil, my friend, you have such a malicious tongue," Renwy chuckled as he stepped from behind a curtain. He held out his hand, but Dane ignored it. "To be fair, Dane, our business is also Anandil's."

"So, it's about the expedition?" Anandil turned and scowled. "You've decided to go?"

"My companions and I cast a vote. We *all* decided to go," Dane said, his hands curled into fists and rested on his hips.

"And all it took was a little blackmail," Anandil suddenly snatched the vial and downed the liquid.

"Now, now, Anandil. It's not necessary to antagonize our associate." Renwy patted Dane on the hand. "I hated having to do that to you, but we're desperate and I'll do anything to help my people. You understand?"

Dane glowered at the short man. "When would you like us to leave?" he asked through gritted teeth.

"Sooner, rather than later. Best to set off within the next couple of days."

From his cage, Harryck chuckled. "You need an extra pair of hands, Dane?"

"Silence!" Anandil threw the empty vial at the cage and it shattered, glass showering the human as he stumbled to the far side of his cage and knelt.

"Anandil!" Renwy scolded. He turned to Dane and smiled. "I apologize. The concoction he just drank is supposed to help ease the roaring flame that is his anger, but as you see it is slow to work."

"I'll go pack my things," Dane said, glaring at Anandil. "I'll let you know when we depart."

"Allow me to accompany you back to your home," Renwy said, shuffling to meet Dane at the door. He opened it for him and smiled, waving him through.

Once the door was closed, Harryck called, "Anandil... Something's happening outside. I can sense it..."

"Quiet, dog," Anandil replied as he returned to his vials and potions.

* * *

"I understand if you won't forgive me for what I'm doing to you," Renwy said. "I promise you no harm will come to Evie. She's been such a joy to have here."

"You're lucky she's a good person," Dane grumbled. "Better than you deserve."

"You don't even know me," the halfling said. "Perhaps one day."

"I hope not. Let's not speak of it anymore," Dane said. "And you can stop feigning politeness towards me. I know you're following me outside so you can call off the spies you have tailing me and my friends."

Renwy chuckled. "I didn't think they would pass unnoticed amongst you lot. Oh well, I was simply being careful."

"I don't trust you and you don't trust me. *That's* simple."

"After all this mess is behind us, though, I could see us being friends. Truly, I do."

Dane scoffed and kept trudging upwards. As soon as he opened the door, he found the dead bodies of the spies that had been following him. "Oh my!" Renwy said. Dane's sword was already drawn and he had stepped in front of the halfling.

Before them stood General Braxon - splotched with blood splatter - and a couple of vicious-looking thugs that were rummaging through the pockets of the dead bodies. Several plumes of smoke dotted the landscape behind them, and people were screaming and running for their lives around them.

"Braxon, you bastard!" Renwy shouted from behind Dane. "Why can't you just leave us all alone?"

"I have orders from my king. I *obey* orders." He pointed with his sword. "You're both criminals and I will bring you to justice."

"Renwy, get back inside," Dane said.

"No!" Renwy shoved past him and drew a knife. He shouted and charged at Braxon. Braxon stopped the slash of the knife by grabbing his wrist. He punched the halfling repeatedly in the face with his armored fist and then sent Renwy's knife stabbing underneath his own chin. Blood gurgled out of his mouth before he fell to the ground.

"Get him!" Braxon commanded. The looters took off towards Dane.

He ducked under the swing of a warhammer and stabbed the assailant in the thigh. He shoved him into one of the other attackers and deflected the sword stroke of the other. This left his opponent's back exposed and Dane's blade bit deep into him. The last attacker had recovered and was closing the distance between them. Dane dodged to the side and caught the man in the ribs with his sword.

Braxon came crashing towards him like a giant ocean wave and the two locked swords. "Tell me where Pelias is and I may take you in alive," Braxon said through gritted teeth.

Dane planted his foot into Braxon's stomach and shoved, throwing him backwards. Dane took several steps away. "Why do you want Pelias?"

"Orders," was all Braxon said.

"How did you get inside the city?"

"It was easy. We lured the dead outside the walls and waited for the right moment. Some of my Ravagers slipped in as innocents. The guards took no time to question them. They studied the place for a few days before bringing down the gate."

Dane's eyes widened. The band Marek had brought in!

Braxon laughed. "I've got more of my people leading another horde of undead here as we speak. They'll flood this city, and I will make sure *none* of you make it out alive!"

Great flashes of light interrupted Braxon's gloating as small shells of powder crashed at his feet, making loud popping noises and blinding him and Dane both. Dane felt a pair of hands grab his shoulders and lead him away, while a voice whispered, "Be calm. Run when your eyesight returns."

"Anandil..."

"I will distract him." The elf gave him a final push and Dane stumbled to the ground. He stood and rubbed his eyes until his vision began to clear. He had been moved to a nearby alley and he could see Anandil facing Braxon, brandishing a curved scimitar.

Dane took the opportunity and ran.

Evie glanced over her shoulder for what must have been the hundredth time since she had left the house with Caulen and Marek. Caulen ran behind her, his head swiveling back and forth on alert. Marek grabbed her hand and dragged her faster down the street. All the other civilians were running in the opposite direction.

"Evie, Caulen, step to it!" Marek barked, holding his trident in his other hand.

"I'm not leaving without Father!" Evie shouted.

"I'm not asking you to! I'm going back for him, but I need to get you two to safety first!"

"Isn't safety going to be the direction all of the other people are running?" Caulen asked.

"I want to find the others first. Get us all together," Marek replied. He reached out to several people that he recognized as they ran by, but no one stopped for him. "What's going on?" he shouted, but he was met with no replies. Finally, he saw Bren towering above everyone else on the street. Marek waved at him and they all stopped – huddling close but staying aware. "What's happening?" Marek asked.

"The gate's been destroyed," Bren began. "The undead are inside, along with General Braxon and The Ravagers."

"What?" Evie interjected. "That bastard! He won't stop hunting us!"

"No, he won't. He's in the city somewhere, but I haven't seen him."

"We need to leave, then," Marek said.

"Pelias is gathering the others and meeting at the gate. You should go there."

"What about you?"

"I'm going for Dane. Is he still at the tower?"

"That's my best guess."

Bren hoisted his bardiche onto his shoulder. "Protect the kids. I'll get Dane and meet the rest of you at the gate. Stay low until we're all together." Bren took off towards the tower before turning and shouting: "If I don't make it back, ask Pelias about Doompoint! Make him explain everything to you all! Promise me!"

Marek looked at him, perplexed, but gave an informal salute with two fingers. "Let's go, you two! Stay on my heels!"

* * *

Bren was alert as he approached the base of the magi tower. Several bodies littered the street around it. Bren stepped over the body of a dead elf whose hand clutched a scimitar and he shuffled around a halfling whose robes were stained with blood. The streets were quieter now since people had taken to hiding in their homes. He could still hear a good deal of ruckus coming from the direction of the gate, but where he stood it was less so.

Bren opened the tower door quickly, jumping back and bracing his bardiche in front of him. No movement or noise bellowed from inside and so he crept in, ready to counter any attack that was thrown at him. He looked up and down the spiral staircase. After recollecting a moment, he remembered Dane describing that he went down to reach the elf's laboratory. He took off downstairs at a brisk pace, taking one of the torches off the wall sconce and holding it before him.

Bren was astonished that he arrived at the final door without meeting any resistance. He shouldered into the lab, quickly scanning all the strange devices and plants scattered about. "Dane!" he called.

The voice that answered was an unfamiliar one: "Dane's gone."

Bren moved further into the room and found a cage that housed a hairy, beastly human. "You're the werewolf," Bren said.

"*Lycan*. Harryck is my name," the man grinned faintly.

"Dane mentioned you."

"You're one of his friends?"

"Yes." Bren stepped closer. "When did he leave this place?"

"Perhaps twenty minutes ago." Harryck let go of the cage bars he had been grasping. "It's difficult to keep track of time in this place..." The distant look in the man's eyes faded and he looked at Bren. "Something bad is happening outside, isn't it?"

"Yes. That's why I have to find Dane."

"Please, release me from my prison. I need to go check on my family. They're somewhere in the city." Bren gave him a sideways look, squinting suspiciously. "Please! What does it matter to you? We'll never see one another again after we get out of this tower. Please... my family..."

Bren contemplated a moment before nodding and breaking the lock with one swing from his weapon. He grabbed the gate and swung it open for Harryck, who walked out slowly, glancing around as if he had not seen his surroundings before.

"It's been a long time since I've been able to stretch my legs. Thank you..."

228

"Bren." The two men clasped forearms briefly before making their way towards the exit.

* * *

The trident soared through the air to spear a nearby undead and topple it. Marek jerked his weapon from where it was lodged and readjusted the pack on his shoulder. "Keep on me, kids!" He waved Evie and Caulen on as they dodged a stray zombie stumbling around the cobblestone.

"The gate should be right around the corner," Caulen said as he shuffled between Evie and the zombie to deliver a kick to the monster's chest.

A sharp whistle resonated from the rooftops above them. Marek spotted Pelias waving to get their attention. He pointed to an alley nearby and jabbed his thumb upwards. In the alley, Marek found a ladder that led up to the perch.

Once at the top, Grunt offered a hand to Marek, then Evie and Caulen after him. Koda, Llanowar, and Marleyn whispered amongst themselves nearby. Marek approached Pelias where he leaned against a chimney with his eyes affixed on the city gate down the street. A few people surrounded it, trying to contain the mess that had been made.

"Most of the undead have funneled deeper into the city," Pelias said. "General Braxon is here with The Ravagers."

"I met a couple of them on the way here," Marek said. "Braxon's still hunting, eh?"

Pelias nodded.

Marleyn tapped Evie on the shoulder. "Did you see Bren on the way here? Pelias said that he went to find your father..."

"We did. He was going to the tower." Evie smiled at her. "I'm sure he's going to be fine." The corners of Marleyn's mouth tugged in an effort to smile.

Koda, Grunt, and Llanowar moved closer. "What's our plan?" Koda asked.

No one answered. Pelias – his arms crossed – glanced at each of them and found their eyes all on him. He said nothing. He looked back to the gate and cleared his throat. "For now," he said, "we're not going to do anything. We have two people missing and we have to give them as much time as possible to get here."

"Pretty dangerous waiting with Braxon skulking around here," Koda said.

Pelias sighed. "...It's the right thing to do..."

From behind them, Dane shuffled onto the rooftop. Evie ran over and threw her arms around his neck. "We need to get out of here. Braxon is looking for us," he said.

"And he brought The Ravagers. Can you believe that?" Marek asked.

Marleyn stood up. "Wait, is Bren not with you?"

Perplexed, Dane scanned the roof. "No, I haven't seen him."

"He went to find you," she replied. She felt the tears welling in her eyes. "I hope he's safe..."

* * *

Bren and Harryck ran side-by-side up the stairs, taking them two steps at a time as fast as they could.

Bren had always warranted himself a fast runner on account of his long, powerful legs but Harryck was ahead of him by a couple of steps without difficulty.

"Here!" Bren said, stopping at the door. Harryck jogged back from where he had gone too far. Bren gripped his bardiche tightly. "I wish I had a weapon for you."

Harryck smirked. "I'll be fine. Trust me." He threw his leg in front of him, kicking the door open, and leapt out into the open. The elation he felt from being out in the open was short-lived. A wall of undead surrounded them. Soldiers, noblemen, hunters, and farmers all craned their necks to study the two living beings.

"We need to *move*!" Bren said as he led Harryck towards a nearby street. He shoved several zombies away with his bardiche, stepping over them as they stumbled to the ground. Harryck wasted no time following him.

Bren's bardiche cleaved clean through undead after undead as he pushed as fast and hard as possible. "This is the wrong way!" Harryck shouted. "My family lives *that* way!" He pointed as he ran.

"Let's focus on staying alive right now," Bren replied as he cut down another zombie.

"Shit, look out!" Harryck grabbed Bren by the shoulder.

Bren took a moment to analyze the view ahead. The path they were headed down was thick with undead – too many to fend off. Harryck pulled Bren down an alley beside them where there were no undead.

The two of them were putting a great distance between themselves and the zombies until they came to a dead halt. The walls of great brick buildings closed in around them as they scanned for any way out. No stairs, ladders, or even a low wall they could climb over.

"Go back, quickly!" Bren shouted, doubling back.

They did not get far. They turned one more corner and came face-to-face with a sea of undead all standing still and staring at them. As if rehearsed, they moved as one toward Bren and Harryck with slow, deliberate steps.

Both of them glanced at the other. "No choice but to fight," Harryck said.

"That's a losing battle," Bren said, flexing his fingers around his weapon. His eyes darted and he took rapid breaths. He was going to die, but he was going to die fighting.

"Maybe not… Forgive me later." Harryck grabbed Bren's arm and sunk his sharp teeth into his skin.

Bren jerked his arm away and gave Harryck an astonished look. "What the hell is wrong with you?"

"The transformation will happen fast. Just follow my lead." Harryck stepped in front of him and hunched over. Bren saw the hairs on his body begin to grow right before his eyes, turning into thick bristles. The man's arms and legs began to grow and distort in a grotesque way and he grew three times in size. His face pinched and expanded into a wolf's snout, his ears stretched and pointed upwards, and his teeth grew into mighty fangs.

Without hesitation, Harryck began to rip into the horde with his razor-sharp claws. Bren took one step forward before he felt a strange ripple that started in his stomach and flowed to the rest of his body. He dropped his bardiche and fell to his hands and knees.

Bren vomited and gasped for air. Peering down at his hands, his fingers grew longer, and the nails stretched into sharp claws…

232

Chapter 11

Bren's eyes shot open and he immediately turned his head to vomit on the ground next to him. He blinked slowly, paralyzed as he tried to remember what had happened. He stared at his hands and flexed his fingers before rubbing them deep into both his legs. It finally registered with Bren that he was back in the wilderness with no streets or buildings to be seen.

"How do you feel?"

Bren rolled over and saw Harryck leaning against a nearby tree. "What the hell happened to me?"

"Exactly what you think."

"You bit me... and now I'm..."

"I'm sorry, but I hope you realize I had no choice."

Bren sat up – too quickly. His head swam and so he clutched it in his hands. "My body... my skin feels like it's too big for my bones... like clothing that doesn't fit well. My skin is crawling all around and it won't stop."

Harryck knelt beside him and produced a skin of water. "Calm down. All those feelings are normal." Bren took the water and drank deeply.

"Will I get used to it?"

"Eventually. You won't black out after a while, either. The other good news is that you're now immune to the bite of the undead. Now, that doesn't mean they can't kill you. Let enough of them surround you and they'll rip you apart before you can do anything."

"Is this curse I now have more desirable than that one?"

"I get by all right," Harryck replied. "I understand this isn't desirable, but I had to make a choice. Kill me later if you want."

"I might just do that," Bren said through gritted teeth. He glared at the man from where he sat. "I can't believe this." He rubbed his head, feeling his calluses scrape against the stubble.

"I think you'll see that lycanism isn't so bad. I quite enjoy myself."

"Shut up!" Bren growled. "You had no right to do that!"

"How about a 'thank you' for saving your hide back there, eh? Because you weren't makin' it outta there in one piece otherwise, believe me. I'm not looking for a gift of appreciation or even your gratitude, but at least be realistic. You're alive because of what I did."

Bren sighed and sucked his teeth before his expression softened. He shrugged and then used Harryck as a prop as he climbed to his feet. "Where are we?"

"West of Etzekel, almost on the edge of the forest. Lake Wynt isn't much further." Harryck stood once Bren quit leaning on him. The big man stumbled a few more steps before holding his head again. "You'll feel better quicker than you think."

"Great," Bren muttered and spit on the ground.

Harryck took a sip from the water skin before corking it. "Bren, I didn't find my family in Etzekel."

"I'm sorry," Bren replied, glancing at him.

"I don't think they're dead."

"Maybe not."

"I know where my wife would take our son... The only place she would go is back to our village. There's a village of lycan's directly north of The Black Pillar where the Platinum Plains meets the Dragon Fang Mountains. Some of our people still reside there."

"An entire village? I was the Sword of Justice to King Endrew and I've never seen any village like you're talking about on any castle map."

"No shit, yeah? Why do you think lycan's are considered extinct nowadays? We don't like strangers and strangers don't like us… We got good at hiding."

"Then why did you leave?"

"Attacks by the wights were becoming more frequent. I thought I was doing the safe thing by moving my family to sanctuary. If she's not there, I don't know where she could be."

"Good luck to you." Bren held out his hand.

"You have to come with me, Bren," Harryck chuckled with disbelief.

"I guarantee that my friends won't be going to a secret lycan village that they know nothing about. It does me no good to follow you."

"You don't understand. You have to learn how to control your powers. You can learn to shift whenever you please, but if you don't it could happen at any time against your will. It's not like the myths. A full moon means nothing to our transformation. Do you want to wake up in a pool of blood with all your friends dead around you? Because that *will* happen."

"You're out of your mind!"

"I've seen it with my own eyes. I'm not fooling you — this is serious. I can teach you along the way, but we need to be in the safety of our own village. Think of your friends."

Bren sighed, feeling the cool breeze sweep around him. "How long will it take?"

"It depends on how strong your will is, but you can be back to your friends within two months."

"There's no other way?"

"Not if you want to live long or be around your loved ones."

Dane and his companions trudged along at a brisk pace. They had not stopped since slipping narrowly out of Etzekel, but he knew that they could not keep up this pace for much longer. Marek jogged at an even pace with him, his long hair jumping up and down with each step. Evie, Caulen, and Marleyn were behind them, with Koda and Pelias protecting either side. Grunt and Llanowar brought up the rear. Everyone had their weapons ready, having never put them away after battling through Etzekel's gates.

Occasionally they came upon a stray undead in their path but had met with little resistance. None of The Ravagers were to be found — presumably preoccupied with the sacking of the magi city. It had fallen fast in comparison to the time it had remained undiscovered.

They came upon a pond that rested in the middle of a ring of trees and Dane raised his hand to signal a rest. Caulen knelt by the pond and dipped his water skin into the cool water. Koda stood next to him, his arms crossed and a scowl on his face. "I already miss the pub back there..."

Caulen looked up at him. "It's not the best, but it's drinkable."

"Kid, I've had to drink camel piss to survive the desert. Didn't mean I had to like it."

Caulen left him to sulk by the pond and offered his water skin to Evie. She took a quick sip before handing it to Marleyn, who took a much longer drink. She handed it back and shook her head. "We should wait here for Bren."

"We're not far enough away from Etzekel, yet," Llanowar said, her bow in her hands with a nocked arrow at the ready. "Braxon could still catch us here."

"What if he's got Bren?"

"What could *we* do? The Ravagers are fifty strong. They're brutal warriors, and led by Braxon they have a strategic mind at their helm. Not to mention the undead we would have to repel."

"So we just leave him to die?"

Caulen put his hand on Marleyn's shoulder. "I'm sure he's okay. He's a warrior himself. He comes from the Platinum Plains, right? The Plains people are no one to fool with."

Marleyn sniffled and nodded her head. "Yes... Yes, you're right."

"We'll continue with our original plan to go to Bandimere," Dane offered. "He'll know we need supplies to sail. We'll wait there for him."

"Bren told me something interesting," Marek interjected, leaning on his trident. "Doompoint." He looked at Pelias, whose back was turned from everyone else as he surveyed their flank.

Every pair of eyes turned on him, following Marek's look, and he could feel the weight of their gaze. He dropped his head for a moment and turned towards them. "I was hoping to keep this a secret from you all."

"This sounds important. A secret kept from us by our own Sir Noble Knight?" Koda quipped.

"It was to protect you."

"Oh my, all the best secrets are hidden with that justification. Do tell." Koda crouched low, balancing on the balls of his feet.

Without interruption, Pelias retold his story to everyone. He left out no detail, explaining that Uragon was banished for practicing dark magic and made to look like he had died. He told of his journey to Doompoint, how Sir Eins had died, but reappeared to kill King Endrew in Eden.

"I know Uragon is behind this madness. I can feel it in my guts," Pelias concluded.

"Endrew banished his son for magic and that made him hate it," Marek mused. Pelias nodded.

"You knew this all along?" Llanowar asked.

"I knew Uragon was alive, but I didn't piece together everything that happened until we were in Etzekel. I was trying to maintain some level of loyalty to my king. I had planned to go to Doompoint alone and confront Uragon, but it appears Bren had a different idea."

"And it's a damn good thing he did!" Evie said. "You can't go alone! That's just dangerous and stupid!"

"She's right," Koda agreed. Grunt grunted as he nodded.

"Pelias, reconsider your plan," Dane urged. "We'll figure something out once we've had time to think and regroup with Bren. Don't do anything hasty until then, all right?"

Pelias nodded solemnly. "Fine, but I believe I can end this."

"You don't have to do it alone." Dane cleaned his sword and sheathed it.

"What if Bandimere is like White Willow?" Llanowar asked.

"I visited Bandimere a few times," Marek offered. "It's safe. They make do."

"Do they allow strangers?"

"I was a stranger, but they know me now. We'll be fine."

Everyone gave silent agreement before making their way around the pond and delving back into the forest.

* * *

Rorn laughed as he reveled in the carnage around him. The Ravagers were finishing mopping up the undead that roamed the streets of Etzekel, all the while searching their bodies for any treasure they could claim. They had herded so many zombies inside the city walls that the street was thick with their now motionless corpses. The cobblestone was slick with a heavy dose of spilled blood.

"What a damn day!" Rorn howled. "It's great to be splittin' skulls again! I wish there were more!"

Braxon looked around angrily. "None of these were the *right* skulls, Rorn. No sign of the Chief Commander or the mercenary. None of the ones King Endrew wants dead."

"We did what we were told. Not our fault your prey slipped away." Braxon glared at the man, causing him to raise his hands in defense. "They could still be holed up here...somewhere..."

Nearby, Leyon and Aiya shuffled out of a building with a dwarven woman bound between them – her head a disheveled tangle of brown hair. Fear permeated her face as she averted her eyes. Dried tears stained her face as she observed the dead surrounding them.

"We may have found another lead, Braxon," Aiya said, sidling up next to him. "Tell him, dwarf."

She glanced at each of the people surrounding her as she shuffled her feet and tried to think of what to say. Rorn eyed her as he wiped the fresh blood from his axes. Leyon dug around in his pack and tore a hunk of bread in half and started eating, disinterested in anything that was happening. Aiya and Braxon both stood with their arms crossed, leering down at her.

"Speak now, or I kill you," Aiya hissed.

The dwarf wrung her hands violently as she stammered: "M-my name is…is Madagrett. I tend the gardens here… Or rather, I did…"

"Magi?" Braxon interrupted.

"What?"

"You're a magi."

"How did you…?"

"Your hands," he pointed. "They're soft. Not gardener's hands at all."

"Yes, I am a magi."

He looked at Aiya. "What makes you think a gardener can help us?"

"Tell him what you told us," Aiya urged her.

"I heard some of your people talking about who you were looking for. The mercenary Dane, his daughter Evie, Chief Commander Pelias of the Kingsguard. I met a couple of them and heard about the others that they travelled with."

"I'm listening," Braxon muttered.

"They were commissioned by the head magi of the city to go on an expedition. I don't know what for, but I do know that they were to set sail from Port Trident on the western coast. They could be heading there. Or not. You've slaughtered everyone here. They have no reason to go there now."

"West, eh? Leyon."

Leyon nodded and tossed the bread over his shoulder. He picked up his club. "I'm already headed to check it out."

"I'll come with you."

"So, you'll spare me?" Madagrett called. "Since I've told you what I know?"

"No magi will be spared," Aiya replied, pushing her down to the ground.

Braxon trudged forward with a steely gaze as the dwarven woman cried out. As they walked, Leyon scooped up any jewelry or coin purses he found while never missing a single stride. "I like you. You know why?" Braxon asked.

The comment caught Leyon off guard. He raised an eyebrow and responded with a curious mumble.

"You don't talk much and you follow orders," Braxon said.

"I know who's in charge here," Leyon replied. "I appreciate your wickedness. No offense." In truth, Braxon did not take the words offensively at all. "Through wickedness you incite discipline. Rorn was a good leader, but only because he was the loudest and didn't shy away easily."

"*Was*?" It was Braxon's turn to eye his accomplice doubtfully.

"Rorn's time is nearing its end. He's much too foolhardy to realize the danger of our travels. He will be killed soon, and someone else will take his place."

"You want that job? You want The Ravagers?"

"I assumed you would take over full leadership of them."

"Perhaps while we search for Pelias and his cohorts. After that, I can't be seen mingling with degenerates such as yourselves. No offense."

Leyon scowled. "You don't care if you offend me. Luckily, neither do I. The opinions of others mean very little to me."

"Then you may just be the perfect man to lead The Ravagers..."

The conversation ended there as the two of them stepped through the city gate. Leyon inspected the ground for a few moments, weaving around the area by the bridge to get multiple angles. He knelt and ran his fingers through the grass on the other side of the bridge and then looked all about the surrounding forest.

"Interesting..." Leyon scratched his head again and stood, swinging his club a few times as he pondered.

"Interesting in a good way?" Braxon urged.

"It's amazing that so few managed to escape the city alive. It doesn't even look like very many tried."

"Foolish for them to build a city with only one gate."

"Fortunate for us. The giant man that was with Pelias escaped and he ran southwest. He was in a group, but I can't tell how many were with him. As cunning as our prey has been, however, I wouldn't say it's a long shot that Pelias and the mercenary are with him."

"But you're sure it's the giant?" Braxon hunched over to try and distinguish the footprints that Leyon was indicating.

"He's very hard to mistake. Very distinct stride. He's big."

"It sounds like we only have one option."

Leyon nodded.

"Fine, then we shouldn't waste time. Tell Rorn The Ravagers can rest for two hours. No longer."

* * *

The wind whipped the thick grass from side-to-side. The sun had just begun to stretch out from behind the storm clouds, and its light reflected off the grass like silvery-white waves swirling before Bren and Harryck. The latter stretched his neck and drew a deep breath in through his nose.

"I've missed the smell of the open fields," he said.

Bren replied, "It's been a very long time since I've been on the rolling plains."

"I'm surprised you've been at all. Most people avoid them because of The Tribes."

"I was born a member of the Bison Tribe."

"Then you're more dangerous than I thought you were."

"None of the three tribes are horrible people. Outsiders just don't know how to leave them alone."

Harryck stretched and yawned. "If you say so. I'd like to avoid them altogether, though, if you don't mind."

"I'm not gonna go looking for their attention. I'm more of an outsider than a Tribesman now, anyway." Bren grinned.

The two of them walked in relative silence for some time, making sure to stay alert for any sound of hooves that belonged to the beasts the Tribesmen rode. Aside from the occasional wild animal, their trek was undisrupted. After walking for about an hour, they came upon a solitary black stone pillar. It was scarred and weather-beaten from standing unattended for years.

"It's a shame that no one pays the pillars any attention anymore."

"Folk aren't as pious, I suppose," Bren replied.

"Someone is, though." Harryck stooped down and palmed a fresh apple that someone had left. "There's a whole basket of 'em. Lucky for us."

"Are you sure you want to take them? The Black Pillar represents the Arbiter of Mortals."

"Why should I care?" Harryck shrugged.

"He's in charge of every mortal beings' soul. They say when a person dies, the Shepherd of Souls has a duel with the Harvester of Souls, and whoever wins gets to claim that person. The Arbiter judges the duel. Do you really want to piss him off?"

Harryck scoffed. "Isn't he supposed to judge impartially? Surely he sees our need and won't hold it against us when our own duels of fate happen."

"Do as you wish. I won't have any part of it." Bren began to walk away.

"I didn't take you for a religious man." Harryck scooped up the basket and followed, crunching into one of the apples. "Juicy..."

Bren scowled at him. "I was the Sword of Justice for King Endrew in Eden. It was a duty I took very seriously. Before every execution I prayed to each of the Three Holy Ones. To the Shepherd I prayed that if the victim being executed was just, that he might swing his sword with all his might and take him under his care in Heaven. If the victim was cruel, I prayed that the Harvester might fight with the ferocity of a thousand wolves. And I asked the Arbiter to judge fairly so that whoever was correct would win."

"Most executioners just swing the axe," Harryck replied in-between bites.

"I didn't want the fate of their souls on my conscience."

Harryck shrugged and sunk his teeth deeper into the apple. Smacking his lips, he pointed. "We should swing out northwest now, or we'll be too close to The Elk Tribe."

"How long a journey is this?"

"At this pace, about two weeks."

"Can we move faster?"

Harryck chuckled and smirked at him.

* * *

"How far behind do you think Braxon is?" Koda asked as he knelt next to Dane in the grass as they paused in their journey later that afternoon.

"If we're lucky, it's going to take them at least an entire day to realize we're not hiding there. That's if they search nonstop. I think we're in the clear for now." He sniffed a wild mushroom that he plucked from the ground.

"Just how lucky would you say we've been so far, Dane?"

Dane looked him in the eye. "I'm not in the mood for your sarcasm right now."

"I'm being serious this time," Koda replied as Dane tossed the mushroom aside in disgust. "I don't think we're all on the same page here."

"What do you mean?"

"We should be heading straight west to the coast. Stopping in Bandimere is a waste of time."

"No one has made any plans, yet. Pelias isn't on board with the coast. Even if he does come around to the idea, we can't sail without provisions. Plus, we need to wait for Bren to catch up. All reasons to go to Bandimere. We need to catch our breath and collect our thoughts."

"I feel like Bandimere is going to be another White Willow or Etzekel. I would like to be able to stop running."

"And you think I don't?" Dane gritted his teeth as he leaned in closer to Koda. "I just want a place where I can think! We can rest and think and wait for Bren in Bandimere."

"You're not gonna like what I'm about to say, but we *cannot* wait for Bren." Dane glanced over his shoulder to see if Marleyn was out of earshot before glaring at Koda again. Koda nodded and stamped the butt of his spear in the ground a couple of times. "I understand how that sounds, but Dane, a lot of people have died already. You shouldn't expect Bren to be any different."

Dane's nostrils flared as he slowly stood. "We're moving out. Why don't you take the back of the line?" He walked off without waiting for a response.

Koda sighed and stood, hiking his spear onto his shoulder as Grunt walked up next to him. "Do *you* think Bren's alive?" Grunt shrugged as he watched Dane walk away.

"Me either, friend..."

Grunt jabbed a finger behind his back and Koda turned to see Llanowar teaching Caulen how to hold her bow.

"Like this?" the boy asked, a wide grin on his face.

"Pull more with your shoulders and back, not your arms." She straightened his back and kicked his feet apart. "Wider stance. You want to be as stable as possible."

"We're moving again, everyone," Koda said, trying to roust everyone into motion.

Caulen groaned, but Llanowar said, "You can practice drawing while moving. Perhaps you'll even find a squirrel to shoot."

"I'll get it on the first shot," Caulen smirked.

"I didn't even get my first kill on the first shot."

"Maybe I'll be better than you."

Llanowar laughed and shoved him ahead of her.

Koda fell into line behind Evie and Marleyn. Evie said to her, "Pelias looks completely lost in thought. He hasn't said a word since the pond."

"Maybe someone should try talking to him," Marleyn replied.

"Good idea. Go do that." She ushered her forward. When Marleyn was well enough ahead, Evie turned. "I read your mind, Koda."

"I feel violated, and not in the good way," Koda said with half the enthusiasm he usually displayed for his own jokes.

"I understand why you think Bren is dead, but I read everyone else's thoughts and they're all staying hopeful. You need to keep your thoughts to yourself."

"Hard to do when you read them like a book," Koda muttered.

"Shut it! Bren and Pelias saved my father's life back in Eden and he takes that very seriously. If Bren is dead, Dad will blame himself."

"That's crazy."

"That's just how my father is. Code of honor and what have you."

"If you ask me, I made the right call never having one of those."

"Pretend all you want that you don't, but you aren't fooling me. I can read you like a book, and not just because of my powers."

"Fine," Koda said. "I won't mention death to your father any more. But you better be careful - a few times he's come close to noticing the dead people walking around."

"He's thinking about the dead right now..." Evie stared sullenly at her father who walked ahead of her.

"You okay?" Marek asked as he walked beside Dane. He used his trident as a walking stick, pulling himself along at a healthy pace to keep up with Dane.

Dane replied, "I think I remember this spot from our days back in the Iron Fox Legion. Do you?"

The group was approaching a large, moss-ridden boulder that jutted into a high, sharp point above their heads. Marek pondered for a moment before a short laugh erupted from his gut. "I do, now that you mention it. Amir got drunk after that battle with the elven rogues we were chasing through the country. He stood up there, dropped his pants, and started pissing."

Dane smiled a small smile. "He said he was pretending to be a giant pissing down on us."

Marek was laughing heartily now. "O-only it had rained that morning, and he – he slipped on the wet moss up at the top there. Fell right into his own piss puddle." Dane nodded and the two shared in the laughs. "I *do* miss Amir. I wish I could have seen him once more."

Dane's laughter was short-lived.

"Did you... uh... did you say the words? For Amir?"

Dane snapped out of his thoughts. "What?"

"I remember you had me teach you the prayer. You wanted to start saying it on your friends' behalves. Did you say them for Amir?"

"I did."

Marek nodded. "I've forgotten them, myself."

"Hey, Dane! Marek!" Caulen came jogging up behind them, holding an arrow with a squirrel skewered on the end of it. "I got it on my first shot! Llanowar says I'm a natural!"

Marek grinned. "That's great. Let me know when you're strong enough to throw this." With blinding speed, he hurled his trident through the air and staked another squirrel to the trunk of a tree ahead of them. He laughed and patted Caulen on the arm before running ahead to retrieve his weapon. Caulen's shoulders slumped.

Marleyn had made no progress to console Pelias. As the two of them walked beside one another, she made small comments about the occasional irregularly shaped tree trunk, or an example of wildlife that skittered about. He responded with half-hearted agreements or disinterested grunts.

"You don't have to be ashamed of yourself, you know?"

Pelias gave Marleyn a skeptical look but did not reply.

She continued, picking her words carefully and deliberately: "You blame yourself for everything that's happened. That's a lot of weight to carry on your shoulders. I don't know everything, I'm sure, but I would bet that it's not your fault."

"Looking back, I had lots of chances to prevent things – or change them completely," said Pelias.

"Hindsight is always bothersome. It only allows us to reflect on our mistakes and missed opportunities." She wrung her hands as she spoke. "I wish I could have done something to keep the people at White Willow from robbing people."

"Not a lot you *could* do."

Marleyn nodded and bit her lip. "I still feel responsible, partly."

"You can't blame yourself for that. You had no choice."

"Exactly. So why can't you accept that for yourself?"

Pelias opened his mouth to speak, but no words formed.

"Like I said, I don't know everything, but I don't have to. If you could have done anything to prevent whatever deaths you feel responsible for, you would have done it – even if it cost you your own life. But what's in the past can't be changed. Only remembered and learned from."

"I didn't know you were such an inspiring speaker," Pelias produced a small smile.

Marleyn smiled back at him. "I didn't either." The two of them enjoyed the others company in silence for several minutes before Marleyn blurted out: "I'm worried about Bren…"

Pelias responded: "I am, as well, but I'm sure he'll be fine." She nodded silently, and Pelias continued: "I have to ask… why the fascination with him? I know he's a good guy, but I don't understand your infatuation."

Marleyn's cheeks flushed and she stammered as she attempted to reply.

Pelias chuckled. "It's all right. You don't have to be nervous. And you don't have to answer my question if you don't want to."

"N-no. I'll tell you. Back at White Willow, after the wights attacked and you all were leaving, Bren brought me along. He made sure I was safe – he didn't hesitate to drag me to my feet and take me away. I've gotten to know all of you now, and I like all of you, but in that moment, everyone's only concern was getting away. Everyone except Bren. He makes me feel safe."

Pelias nodded and smiled. "I get it. That's a good reason."

"What about you? Do you have a special lady? Or is Chief Commander of the Kingsguard not allowed to love? That's quite monkish, you know."

He shook his head. "No one prevented me from pursuing women except for myself. I took my job very seriously. My duties were my lovers."

"That's quite a bore," Marleyn jabbed.

"I was indebted to my king. I wanted to serve him perfectly and to be the most successful kingsguard in history... I am lost without my king and title..."

"I don't know what to tell you... To be Chief Commander at your age is an amazing accomplishment, and you'll be remembered for that. But I don't think that left you with any sense of reality. You need to find out what else is important to you besides the things you've lost. Find something that's still alive that's worth fighting for and protect it with all you have. One mistake, one loss, one defeat does not define you as a person."

Pelias looked at her but did not say anything. He kept trudging along, his kingsguard armor clanking with each step.

* * *

An entire day passed with little activity or abnormal sightings. Dane and his companions continued to move at a brisk pace, unsure of what followed. Braxon would not be able to find them this time unless he or his Ravagers had seen them slip out of Etzekel, and that was unlikely.

As they inched closer and closer to Bandimere, their surroundings transformed from dense forests to humid marshes. Their pace slowed as they now had to avoid the murky bogs that dotted the terrain. Evie had already stumbled and sunk knee-deep into the filth in the dim morning light and had been fuming ever since.

The thick fog that hung over them not only impaired their range of vision, but the humidity choked them and clung to their clothes, making them hang with extra weight. They were surrounded by all types of unknown creatures, evidenced by the strange noises that were emanating behind various trees and stones.

The trees in the swamps were bent and their branches drooped low as if trying to scoop up the company as they walked underneath them. Vines and moss clung to them, making them appear strangely threatening in the shadows. The sun could not penetrate the thick canopy above them.

"Marek," Dane said. He approached, tamping the butt of his trident into the ground in front of him before taking a step. "Fall back and make sure everyone is here. With the fog as thick as it is, we don't need to take any chances on losing someone."

"Stay put while I round them up," Marek replied before turning and walking away, jabbing the ground with his weapon.

Before Dane was a thin patch of land that cut down the middle of the marsh like a winding bridge. Being just wide enough for a person to walk on combined with the density of the fog made Dane wary, but he could not tell if there was a better way around. He decided to take the chance with the path before him.

The hairs on his arms and back of his neck suddenly bristled as a chill snaked down his spine. He instinctively reached for the hilt of his fox-tail longsword, but with deep breaths he surveyed as best he could through the fog. No imminent danger presented itself. He kept his hand on his sword, however; his gut had rarely done him wrong in the past. Dane wanted so vehemently to turn his head and check on the others, but something told him to avoid turning his back.

Finally, directly behind him, Marek said, "We're all here now."

Dane nodded. "We're going to take this path. Hopefully it leads us all the way across this marsh, but if it doesn't we'll turn around together."

"Why don't we just send a couple of us across to find out?"

"My gut says that's a mistake."

Marek shrugged as he leaned on his trident. "Makes no difference to me."

"I'll take the lead. You follow me, and the rest of us in this order: Koda, Evie, Caulen, Marleyn, Grunt, Llanowar, and Pelias. Weapons ready. Pass it along." Dane still did not look away as Marek explained the plan to the others. Dane drew his sword and flexed his fingers around the hilt several times.

"We're ready," Marek said finally. Dane heard Koda settle into place behind him.

"I don't believe this fog is natural," Koda said, lightly waving his spear through the air. "An illusion? Magic?"

"Let's just push through it," Dane replied. He stepped forward slowly, planting his foot firmly before moving the other. "Can you see everyone, Marek?"

Marek turned his head. "No. I can see Grunt, but Llanowar and Pelias are lost in the fog."

Dane groaned in antipathy. "I want a head count every so often. We're not going to lose anyone in this swamp."

The companions trudged along at a slow pace, but no one was lost in the clutches of the marsh or the grasp of the low-hanging vines and branches. Everyone was restless and the tension was heavy – due not only to the fact that the fog was so thick they could not all see one another, but also because they had not caught a glimpse of the sun in quite some time.

Time passed on, though no one could keep track of it.

"Does anyone else feel like we've been in this bog for days?" Koda asked.

"Perhaps we have. Who could tell otherwise?" Marek asked.

"It seems like the fog is lifting," Marleyn said.

"Everyone be quiet!" Evie snapped. "I can hear voices... A thousand thoughts racing around us all at the same time!"

"What's going on?" Dane asked.

"I don't know!" Evie clutched her head and dropped to her knees.

"We need to keep moving," Marleyn urged.

Dane halted the train. "Marek, swap with me. Keep your eyes forward." Marek jumped ahead, his trident in his hands and pointed forward. Dane skirted carefully by Koda and knelt in front of his daughter. "What's the matter?"

"Voices," Evie replied. "There are thousands of them in my head. I feel like my mind is going to rupture!"

"What are they saying?"

"All at once, I can't distinguish them from one another. They seem to be either frightened or angry."

"Either way, we need to get out of here. Grunt, can you carry her?"

Grunt nodded and took a step forward, but suddenly stopped as thousands of faint glowing lights rose slowly out of the water on either side of them. The lights were all different colors – blue, green, pink, red, purple, orange – every color imaginable. Soon everybody noticed the phenomena and their jaws dropped as the lights began circling them at blinding speeds and forming a beautiful tornado of color.

"I've never seen anything like this!" Caulen shouted over the rushing wind that encircled them.

"Fairies!" Llanowar shouted through the dissipating fog.

Evie stood up, and Dane grabbed her shoulders. "I'm fine now, the voices have dulled. They're inspecting us, trying to decide if we're good or evil."

"Can you tell them we're not here to hurt them?"

"I did. They said they must decide amongst themselves – humans, nor elves or even dwarves could be trusted by words alone. They are going to read all of our thoughts and judge each of us." She looked around incredulously.

"They can read our minds just like you can?" Caulen asked.

"Yes. They said they've never met a human that could communicate with them. They're pleased by it."

The fairies dispersed from the form of a tornado and swarmed in to inspect closer every one of the companions. Each person was surrounded by their own cloud of fairies until it appeared that they all had been adorned in a glowing suit of rainbow armor. Some of the company could not contain smiles or outbursts of joyous laughter at the magnificent beings.

They noticed that in the middle of each glowing ball of light was a small creature that resembled a shrunken elf – with tapered ears and bright, curious eyes. Though the creatures appeared elven, they had no discernable gender and wore no clothes to cover their bodies. Their bodies were supported by two sets of wings that resembled those of a dragonfly. They also observed that whatever color was emitted by the beings also matched their hair color, whether it was a deep purple or a bright red and everything in-between.

Grunt moved his arms slowly, but the fairies followed, drawn to him as if by an invisible magnet of energy. One of the fairies flew up to his face and inspected his mask. It reached out with a tiny hand and tapped the leather, confused by the fact that this human did not have a mouth or nose.

The fairies went about diligently inspecting each one of their visitors. A group of them gathered around Llanowar's ears and tugged on them, comparing her pointed ears to their own. A few of them ran their mouse-paw sized hands along Koda's bronze skin and stared bug-eyed at him before looking to their own ghostly pale skin. One of the fairies knocked on Pelias' armor while another dove inside his breastplate. He laughed as it scurried around, tickling his ribs.

"This is amazing!" Marleyn said as she reached out her hand to allow one to rest in her palm.

"Have you ever seen anything like this, Dad?" Evie asked.

Dane chuckled before responding: "I've never seen fairies with my own eyes. I'd heard the stories, but never..." He trailed off as he looked at the swirling colors.

"I would like to keep one, if I had a jar," Marek said. This earned him a slap on the nose, which was surely a mighty strike if only the attacker was a bit larger. He grinned and laughed. "I meant nothing by it."

"Well, what do they think of us?" Caulen asked.

"They approve of us all. They thank us for being such friendly visitors," Evie replied.

Suddenly, the demeanor of every fairy present changed. They all turned their heads simultaneously across the marsh to the south and stared at the encroaching fog. They bared their sharp little fangs and made low, rumbling growling noises.

"What the hell are they doing?" Koda asked, gripping his spear uneasily.

"They're saying that we should leave, that danger is approaching."

"What danger?" Dane asked.

Evie winced. "I don't know. I don't understand their name for it!" In the blink of an eye, all the fairies flew over their heads and away from the direction they had been looking. They all dove into the water in an arc of rainbow light, not leaving so much as a ripple to disturb the muddy waters. "They're...they're gone! I don't hear them anymore!"

"We should probably take their advice and leave!" Llanowar said.

"Leave? Should we follow them into the water?" Marleyn asked.

"No, let's keep pushing forward," Dane said. "Stick close to one another."

"Anyone else noticing that the fog is thick again?" Koda asked. He spoke the truth. With the fairies' disappearance, the fog had collapsed in around them. No one else acknowledged his comment, but everyone had noticed and they were all on edge once more.

Dane now led them at a pace quicker than before, placing his feet carefully but swiftly. "Everyone pay attention to your footing. The path is thinning!"

Through the fog, Llanowar shouted: "I hear movement in the bog! Whatever's in there is churning up a lot of water!"

"Stay alert, but don't stop!" Dane kept his eyes forward, pushing through the fog. Suddenly, he heard shouting behind him.

"Dad!" Evie yelled.

"What the hell is that?" Koda shouted.

"Grindylow!" Marek replied.

All the while, Dane heard grunting and the swinging of weapons. The strange, high-pitched chittering of a creature in pain followed shortly. Dane dug his heels into the soft ground underfoot and turned to run back to them.

When he cut through the fog, he found a monster with a bulbous head on top of a bundle of tentacles, with two long, spindly arms protruding out of either side of the bulb. Eight yellow eyes bugged out of its head and it had razor-sharp teeth in a wide mouth that stretched almost entirely around its head.

It had clutched each of Caulen's legs and was attempting to drag him underwater. Marleyn and Evie grasped his hands and were doing their best to fight the pull of the grindylow. Caulen gritted his teeth and was doing his best to keep his head above water. Both girls were slowly being dragged to the edge of the path.

Marek leaped into the slimy water and brought his trident down for the killing blow against the grindylow. Blood pooled around him in the marsh and he pulled Caulen to his feet, the water only coming up to their navels. Grunt pulled both girls away from the edge of the water by wrapping one arm around their waists.

Caulen came up coughing, wiping muddy water from his eyes and panting heavily. "I've never seen one of those things before!"

"A grindylow. They like to drown people – young people and children they'll target first, which explains you," Marek said as he patted him on the back.

"Someone should really-" Caulen's feet were ripped out from under him and he was dunked underwater.

"More grindylows!" Marek shouted as he sloshed through the water as fast as he could.

Dane and Grunt splashed into the water to aid them. "Llanowar, Pelias, stay with the girls!" Dane commanded.

In a puff of black smoke, Koda teleported into the water near Marek. He made ready to throw his spear but decided against it with the thickness of the fog. He growled through his clenched teeth and moved forward. His cloak tugged at his neck as it drifted behind him in the water.

As tall as Grunt was, he could move much faster through the water than the others. He soon caught up to Koda and Marek. As he ran past them, his arm shot into the water like a fisherman's spear and he caught Caulen by a trailing arm. He lifted him up out of the water and used him to tug the grindylow within his grasp. He grabbed a handful of tentacles and jerked the beast out of the water, spinning it above his head before cracking it back down onto the water like a whip. The grindylow ceased to move.

Though one threat was removed, three more grindylows darted through the water around them. All the monster's lurched toward Caulen. Koda was able to spear one before it could get a grip on the young boy, and Grunt grabbed another by the arm before pounding it in the eyeballs repeatedly with his bare fist.

Dane sliced the last one in half just as it reached for Caulen. Marek took the opportunity to unveil a secret he had been hiding. He held a hand out to his side and each of his fingertips glowed with a purple light. He flicked his wrist and streams of purple light flowed from his fingers before crossing over one another in mid-air to form a net. The net fell over Caulen, and when Marek clenched his fist, it enclosed around him. Marek kicked backwards through the marsh and pulled Caulen a safe distance away from the battle.

Marek flexed his fingers and the energy net disappeared in the blink of an eye. He draped one of Caulen's arms across his shoulders as the boy coughed up more water, groaning and holding his stomach. Pelias took Caulen's other arm and helped pull him back on land where he lay flat on his back. Evie and Marleyn gripped either of his hands and squeezed tightly as he was attacked by another fit of coughs.

A cloud of smoke formed next to Marek and Koda was there. He panted and wrung the water out of his cloak as he grinned at Marek. "You're a magi, too!" Marek nodded. "That was amazing!"

"That isn't all I can do. If I focus hard enough, I can make the energy beams sharper than any sword known to man – even sharper than the legendary Runadin. Dices my enemies like they were nothing."

Koda chuckled as Dane and Grunt climbed on land, dripping with water. Dane looked at Marek and said, "All that time in the Iron Fox Legion and I never knew you were a magi."

"Don't feel bad. No one did. It really helped me defeat that Clifftown troll." Marek grinned.

"*Baby* troll," Dane reminded him.

"Hey," Evie shouted. "Something's wrong with Caulen!" Everyone turned and saw that his skin was so white that everyone swore they could see through him. His breathing was labored and his eyes were fixed above. "He can't move!"

"It looks like he was bitten on the leg by that thing," Pelias said as he pointed.

Marek cursed as he leapt to his feet. "I've never seen this kind of effect from a grindylow bite. He's gone pale very fast. He may not have long."

Dane said: "Bandimere may be close enough, but we have to hurry! No time to waste!"

Grunt lifted Caulen gently in his arms and the company trudged onward with no rest.

Chapter 12

Everyone was on the brink of collapse. Their breathing was labored, and they were so exhausted that their limbs ached with every movement. They had not stopped moving since they discovered Caulen's wound – a wise choice, given that the boy had lost all color and was fading in and out of consciousness.

They had emerged from the marshes not long after that and had been running all through the night. Finally, they could make out faint torchlight mounted atop wooden walls as the sun just began to peek through the leaves of the trees.

"It's Bandimere!" Dane said. This bit of hope fueled them and they ran faster towards the gate.

A lookout on the wall shouted at them: "Halt where you are! What business do you have here?" The man squinted. "Marek, is that you?"

Marek did not respond, and they did not stop moving.

Koda disappeared in a puff of smoke and reappeared on the other side of the wall. "Please accept my apologies! We have a boy who needs medical attention. Do you have a healer in this village?" As he spoke, Koda was lifting the bar that locked the gates. He pulled the wooden barrier open himself.

Several people approached, startled by the abruptness of the situation, but also intrigued by it. Some drew their weapons and stood at the ready, but most sensed the urgency in Koda's voice and could feel that they meant no harm.

The rest of the company passed through the gate and looked around. The villagers looked at the frighteningly pale boy in the giant man's arms and glanced at one another. Finally, a woman said, "Follow me. I'll take you to Asira. She is our healer."

"Thank you!" Dane exclaimed.

They trailed after her as she led them through the dirt roads of their village. Small log houses with roofs of hay dotted the place in random fashion. The early morning was just beginning to roust people from their homes, and they gathered quite a following of stares. A few people rubbed their eyes – thinking the haze of the morning was playing tricks on them.

Finally, they arrived at a house that was nestled in a corner of the village by itself, away from any others. Smoke rose from the chimney and they could see light through the windows. "Good thing for you lot that Asira never sleeps," the woman said before pounding on the door.

It was not long before the door was pulled open by a slender woman with long, straight black hair, wearing a plain white dress. Several bracelets dangled on her wrists and on the backs of her hands were tattoos in swirling designs and symbols that also ran along her fingers. The tops of her bare feet were decorated in similar markings. Multiple necklaces etched with different, mysterious runes draped across the front of her dress. She appeared to be around Dane and Marek's age.

"Asira, these strangers need your help."

The woman took one look at Caulen and stepped aside, waving them inside. "Tell me what happened, quickly!" She spoke with a strange accent.

"We came through the marshes and the boy was attacked by grindylows," Dane said.

"He was bitten on the leg by one," Marek added, "but I've never heard of grindylow bites being poisonous."

"They are not," Asira said as she cleared a table for Grunt to lay Caulen on. She immediately began inspecting the boy, checking his pulse while feeling his forehead for a fever. "Show me the bite."

Marek rolled up the leg of Caulen's breeches. "What happened to him, then?" he asked.

"Was it the marshes to the east?"

"Yes."

"Those marshes are strange. The water itself poisoned the boy, more than likely. You don't ever want to get that water into an open wound." She placed her hand over the injury and held it there. A soft golden light broke through between her fingers.

"You're a magi," Dane said.

"Why haven't we met on any of my visits here?" Marek asked.

"Magi were hunted, until everyone forgot about us with the dead resurrecting. The villagers and I agreed not to advertise my presence."

"Can you save him?" Dane asked, indicating Caulen.

"Healing is my specialty, but sometimes it is not enough by itself to save someone. This boy is very far along. I can keep him alive, but if I leave him alone for too long, he will die."

"What can we do to help?" Evie asked.

"I need a special type of moss that grows on the trees around the village. I just used the last of my supply yesterday. If you will go fetch me some more, I can save him."

"How will we know if we have the right stuff?"

"It is a strange color. A dark red. Hard to see in the shadows. You had better take some lanterns, since the sun is still low." She pointed with her chin at a collection of lanterns hanging on hooks on the wall.

"Thank you! We'll hurry," Evie said.

After they gathered the lanterns, they walked outside. Dane said, "A few of us should stay behind and talk to whoever's in charge here so they know not to be wary of us. Marek, Pelias, come with me." The two of them nodded. "The rest of you stay in at least groups of two. Remember what dangers are out there and stay alert."

"I'm sorry to hear about your young friend." Tanken placed the knife he was holding on the table and reached for a rag to wipe the blood from his hands. A gutted deer carcass was sprawled in front of him. "But, if he has any chance to live, Asira can save him. I'm sure you have no reason to worry."

"I appreciate your words, Lord, but the world is nothing *but* worries these days," Dane replied.

Tanken's expression did not change. "You're right about that. Just call me Tanken. I'm no lord. I just do my best to guide the people here." Though Tanken was around Dane's age, deep lines ran across his face. His demeanor was serious, yet not unpleasant. Brown hair fell to his shoulders and he had a beard trimmed short.

"You seem to be doing well. From what little I've seen, the people here continue to live normal lives. Do the dead not walk here?"

"They do," Tanken responded, taking up the knife once again. "But not very frequently. Not as frequently as Marek says they do to the east."

"It's still true," Marek said.

"How do you do it?" Pelias asked. "Does some magic ward them away?"

"No, it's just luck, I suppose," Tanken said, shrugging. "I don't question it."

"This is the most peaceful place we've found yet. Even Etzekel was on edge compared to here. You can feel a difference."

"Etzekel?" Tanken's voice raised in curiosity, but he remained focused on the cuts he was making.

"The city we fled from," Marek responded. "It was attacked by bandits."

"I've never heard that name before."

"It was a secret city. Mostly magi resided there."

"I see..." Tanken pondered a moment. "It's sad when news of a secret society is not exciting enough to strike anymore questions. What with the dead roaming the land, all other accounts are mild in comparison."

"Sorry I couldn't mention it before," Marek said as he leaned forward on his trident. "But as I said — secret city."

"I understand." Tanken straightened again. "You and your friends are welcome to stay here. We could always do with a few more able bodies."

"Thank you," Dane said, bowing his head. "It will be good for us to rest for at least a few days."

"I thought moss only grew towards the north?" Koda groaned as he darted from tree to tree. His lantern swung rapidly in his hand.

"That's not actually true," Evie replied from nearby, kneeling at the base of a tree. Grunt was close to them, as well, keeping watch. He could not see where Llanowar and Marleyn had made off to. He made a short grunting noise to get the others' attention.

"What is it?" Koda asked.

Grunt swept his arm around and looked at the two of them.

"The girls? Well, when was the last time you saw them?" Koda asked.

Grunt shrugged.

"It's been a while," Evie said. "Should we shout for them?"

Grunt grunted and shook his head.

"He's right," Koda said. "We don't know what's out here..."

Llanowar and Marleyn had stuck together, their path leading them away from the others and behind a thick curtain of shrubbery. Neither of them thought to stay near their friends – both overtaken with the urgency to help Caulen.

They had begun to wonder if Asira was correct to say that the moss was close to Bandimere. They were not sure how far away they had travelled, but it was further than they hoped to wander. They pushed the thoughts from their minds and focused more on searching for the mysterious red moss.

"Llanowar, will you shine that lantern over here?" Marleyn was on her knees, shuffling through some tall grass that grew at the base of a nearby tree. Llanowar walked over and held it low for her. "Here it is! We've found it!"

Llanowar dropped to her knees beside Marleyn and the two girls began scrounging for every bit of moss they could. Having not been told how much Asira would need, they decided to take every bit that they saw. "That's all of it," Llanowar said.

"Should we head back or try and find more?"

"Let's head back with this. Perhaps it will be enough to get the healing process started. We can always come back."

Marleyn nodded and stood up. "Let's find the others."

The two of them began to walk back when Llanowar's arm shot out to stop Marleyn in her tracks. "Did you hear that?" she asked. Marleyn shook her head. "Take the lantern." As she passed the lantern off, the elf drew the sickle from her belt. She turned around, guarding Marleyn from whatever threat she believed stalked them in the waning darkness.

"Let's just keep going," Marleyn whispered.

As soon as Llanowar turned, she was smacked hard in the face with a club. She folded and fell to the ground. Before Marleyn could scream, someone dropped out of the tree above her and clapped a hand over her mouth.

"Don't scream and you may live, girl." The rancid breath of her captor accosted her with almost tangible force.

Marleyn's wide eyes scanned the trees as more people formed out of the shadows. All of them wore patched or mismatched armor with a wide variety of weapons. Finally, a man with grey hair and a grey goatee muscled through the brutes standing around. A longsword hung at his waist.

Marleyn knew who he was by listening to the conversations of her friends. This was the Braxon that she had heard so much about. His snarl and sour demeanor proved he was as menacing as she had imagined.

Braxon glanced at her but paid her very little attention. He pointed at Llanowar on the ground and gestured at a couple of the men around. "She had better not be dead, Leyon."

"I know better than that," a skinny man holding the club replied.

"Carry them both back to camp."

* * *

Dane, Marek, and Pelias returned to Asira's hut and were troubled to find that the others had yet to return. "You haven't seen any of them?" Dane asked.

"No," said Asira, not taking her eyes off Caulen. The boy was sweating profusely and was still deathly pale, but his condition had not deteriorated any further. "Go to that basin over there and bring me a ladle-full of water."

Dane turned and found the basin she spoke of. He dipped a nearby ladle into the clear, crisp water and brought it over to the table. "Do I use it to wash the sweat from his face?" he asked.

"It is for me to drink." Dane stood next to her and raised the ladle to her lips. She drank deeply and nodded her thanks to him. "You should probably get some for him, as well."

Dane did so, helping Caulen to drink. The boy was barely conscious, and Dane had to tell him to drink slowly. After he was done, he put the ladle back into the basin and walked to the door. He tightened his sword-belt and said to Marek and Pelias: "You two stay here and assist her with anything she needs. I'm going to look for the others."

He made his way through the village once more. The people there appeared to have grown accustomed to their new visitors rather quickly. Almost no one paid him any attention as he marched down the rut-filled dirt streets.

The man that stood guard at the gate stopped him. "You goin' out to look for your friends?"

"I am."

The man considered a moment, before groaning. "Well... all right, but you folks try not to make this a habit. We try not to open the gate too much unless it's an emergency."

Dane did not reply, and his silence made the guard uncomfortable. He quickly set to lifting the bar from the gate and swinging it open a little way for him. Once Dane's foot crossed the threshold of Bandimere he started jogging at a steady pace, trying to pick up tracks he could follow.

He could tell that everyone had stayed together at first, branching off after they had made some headway into the woods. He could match Grunt's footprints easily, for they left a heavier mark on the grass. He could pick out several spots where one of them had gotten on their knees to inspect the trees for moss.

Soon after, he came upon Koda, Evie, and Grunt backtracking towards Bandimere. Worry was plastered on all their faces. "What's happened?" Dane asked.

"Llanowar and Marleyn have disappeared," Evie replied. "We found their lantern lying on the ground along with the red moss Asira needs. There were a bunch of footprints around it."

"Footprints?"

"Two-legged humanoid for sure," said Koda. "Alive, too. Strides were too consistent to be the dead."

"Then we need to go find them!"

"We were going to deliver the moss to Asira and then come back."

"It could be too late by then," Dane said. "Evelyn, return to Bandimere and tell Pelias and Marek what happened. Tell one of them to come join us. We may need their help."

"Be careful, Dad," Evie said before throwing her arms around his neck. "I have a horrible feeling in my stomach."

Dane could not think of anything comforting to say, as he felt the same thing that his daughter did. He forced a small smile and patted her on the back before nudging her towards Bandimere.

Could this be Braxon? Dane gritted his teeth.

Evie clutched the moss to her chest as she ran, leaping over logs and dodging low branches. It felt like mere moments had passed when she arrived back at the perimeter gates of Bandimere. She tried to catch her breath as quickly as possible as she pounded on the gate.

The guard spied her through a tiny window cut into the wooden wall and said, "Where's the rest of your crew? I already told the other fella that we couldn't have this door open too much."

Evie felt all her patience evaporate and the rage boiled up inside of her. She shouted at the man: "I don't give a damn what you told anyone else! My friend's life is in danger and if he dies because you couldn't be bothered to open this damn thing then you'll have hell to pay! Or am I going to have to climb over the wall and gut you myself?"

The man mumbled something under his breath but made no effort to give a rebuttal. He still made no great hurry, but the gate was opened, and so Evie pushed in and rushed through the streets to return to

Asira's home. The buildings and people were just a blur to her, forming no thought in her mind.

She startled Pelias and Marek as she threw open the door. She flew to Asira's side and held out the moss. "Is this it? Is this what you need?"

Asira glanced at it and nodded before reaching out with one hand and taking it, keeping the other pressed on Caulen's wound. The woman set about crushing the moss into fine pieces and mixing it with different liquids and ingredients until it was a deep red elixir. Never once did she remove her other hand.

Evie pointed at Pelias and Marek. "Llanowar and Marleyn have disappeared in the woods. The others are looking for them, but they need one of you to help them."

The two of them looked at each other, and Pelias shrugged. Marek said, "I'll go," and reached for his trident where it leaned against a nearby table. "Which way?"

"Northeast," Evie replied. "But be careful. We think they were kidnapped by a group of people. It could be Braxon."

"I'll hurry, then." He left the four of them alone in the house.

"Help me with this, child," Asira asked. "Grab the bandages out of the cupboard over there."

Evie did so as quickly as possible. Pelias silently watched from a distance as the young girl wrapped Caulen's leg and Asira gently poured the potion down his throat. He had seen many injured people in his time as a kingsguard, but perhaps due to the overwhelming circumstances and his lack of rest, he seemed to be observing the entire scene from a different plane. Almost as if he was watching himself watching them.

Pelias could not help but think back to the things Marleyn had said to him the previous day. He had failed in all his attempts to help the realm so far, but that did not have to define him. She had told him to find something tangible – something alive – to continue fighting for. Right before his very eyes he saw friends who were doing what they could to save one of their own. He could do little now to help speed Caulen's recovery, but perhaps he could give them more time to do so.

Pelias threw the door open and slammed it shut – dashing down the street with renewed energy and purpose. His armor felt light and he was eager to set out.

"Where the hell is he going?" Asira asked, keeping her eyes on Caulen as she forced more of the elixir into his mouth.

"I don't..." Evie trailed off as she stared intently at the door he had left. She tapped into her powers and sent her thoughts in search of his own. There was only one thing she caught before he was out of range for her powers: *Doompoint.* "Shit!" She jumped towards the door and was about to throw it open when Asira shouted at her.

"I will need your help! There is still more we will have to do, and you are my only other pair of hands!"

Evie's nostrils flared as she huffed and punched the door before returning to the table that Caulen laid on.

* * *

"I can't believe it! This bastard has got to be a vampire!" Koda hissed through gritted teeth as he,

273

Grunt, and Dane surveyed Braxon and The Ravagers. They had tracked them about a mile away from Bandimere and found Llanowar and Marleyn bound in the middle of their small camp. The captives were sitting on tree stumps as the group of barbarians stared at them.

"There's got to be about forty of them," Dane whispered back. "Too many for us..."

"What are we supposed to do?"

"We'll have to be extremely cautious. Grunt, keep watch." Grunt nodded as Dane and Koda sidled back comfortably behind the thickest wall of bushes possible. "Even if both Marek and Pelias joined us, we wouldn't be enough to overpower forty of them. They're undisciplined, but that's part of their strength – they're unpredictable. And Braxon himself is a skilled swordsman."

"Yes, I know all that, but we can't just leave the two of them there."

Dane placed a hand on his shoulder. "I'm not saying we do that; we just need to be as sure in our plan as possible if we're gonna save them."

Just then there was a sharp whistle like a bird off behind them. Grunt glanced over his shoulder, but Dane pointed back towards Braxon's camp to redirect his attention. He remembered that call from his time in the Iron Fox Legion. He had to rack his brain for the response tune. Finally, his memory was refreshed, and he responded in kind. Marek quietly pushed through the foliage – crouched low as if on the prowl.

"I hope I'm not too late," Marek whispered.

"It doesn't matter. There's too many of them." Dane rolled aside to allow Marek to drop to his belly and observe the situation for himself.

"Not good," Marek scowled. "It would be different if this was just the common rabble. The Ravagers are a different animal…"

* * *

"Tell me where you're going," Braxon commanded, leering down at both women with a piercing gaze that made Marleyn look away.

Llanowar snarled at him and said: "Wherever you won't follow. I've done as I've been told so far and kept running, but my legs and feet are beginning to ache. I think I'll put an arrow in each of your eyes and be done with it!"

Braxon — whose arms had been crossed over his chest — gestured to Leyon. The Ravager handed him Llanowar's bow, which he split in half over his knee without so much as blinking as he looked her in the eye. "Not today, you elven whore." He threw the two pieces of the weapon aside. He reached out and grabbed Marleyn by the chin and made her look him in the eyes. "What about you? Do you have the information I want to know?"

Marleyn's breath hitched as she was forced to match his gaze. "I can't help you," she said.

"Sad," Braxon threw her face aside as he let go of her chin. "So then… tell me why I should keep either of you alive? If you were important, you would know what your destination was… You must just be everyone's pack-mules. If you ask me, they should have picked actual mules — they're smarter."

Marleyn stared at her feet as they dangled off the tree stump where she sat. Llanowar glared silently at the general and he glared back.

He leaned over to get directly in her face. "Tell me how many are in your little group now. Surely some of them have drifted off or died..." He grunted when she did not respond.

Rorn approached from behind. "General..." Braxon, Rorn, Leyon, and Aiya shifted away from their captives. "She ain't talkin'." The Ravager leader whispered.

"I realize that, Rorn," Braxon said.

"So, we should slit their throats and be done with it."

"I agree with him," Aiya said, glancing at their hostages. "They're useless. We can just raze Bandimere and be done with it. They won't be able to slip out of that tiny village like they did Etzekel."

"Information is never worthless," Braxon said. He also peered at Llanowar and Marleyn. "The human girl will break. It will just take more convincing..."

"What are you thinkin'?" Rorn asked.

Braxon crossed his arms again as he studied the two women. "Leyon, get your club." He motioned at two of The Ravagers to grab Llanowar as he strode forward.

"What are you doing?" Marleyn asked, sensing the danger that approached.

"Put her hands on the tree stump!" Braxon commanded.

"What? No!" Llanowar was lifted into the air, struggling against the strong arms of the barbarians. She swung her legs, but it made no difference. They shoved her to her knees and forced her arms onto the stump. "Stop! You don't have to do this!"

"That bow is about to be much less useful to you," Braxon said. "Leyon!"

Leyon approached and raised his club, grasping it with both hands above his head. He brought it down with as much ferocity as he could muster. The weapon smashed into Llanowar's right hand with a spine-tingling *crunch*! The elf's eyes squeezed shut and she let out a shrill cry as she felt her hand become mangled and immobilized. Leyon raised his club again and dismantled her left hand with his second swing.

Tears trickled freely down Marleyn's face as she held her eyes shut and her head turned away. Llanowar sobbed to herself as she opened her eyes to see her contorted hands in a pile of shattered bones blanketed in her own blood. The pain pulsed up her arms to her elbows. She wanted to scream, but the entire moment felt like a dream that she was trying to wrestle free from.

Braxon knelt to one knee on the opposite side of the stump from Llanowar. In a voice too calm for the madness that just occurred, he said: "Perhaps now you realize just how serious I am… Would you like to reconsider the answers you've given to the questions I've asked?"

Before anyone could respond, a war cry welled up from the edge of their camp. Koda appeared before them in a flash of black smoke, holding his spear at the ready, a look of pure malice on his face. Dane, Grunt, and Marek were not far from joining him – all of them with their weapons drawn.

Braxon leaped to his feet and drew his longsword. Aiya held the blade of her axe to Marleyn's throat and Leyon planted his foot into Llanowar's back, forcing her to fall over the stump and expose her skull for a strike from his club.

"Dane!' Braxon called. "You will not slip away from me this time. I'm bringing you to justice."

"You shut your mouth!" Koda said. "There will be no forgiveness for what you've done!" He aimed the spearpoint level with Braxon's chest. "Give us our friends before you really piss me off!"

"Your time will come soon. Take us to Bandimere and you can all go to prison together, by order of the king!"

"King Endrew is dead," Marek said. "Your mission is over."

"Lies! I won't fall for such a cheap trick." Braxon almost laughed at the weak ploy.

"It's true. Murdered by a member of his own kingsguard – Sir Eins."

"Bah! You think dropping a name will cause me to lose focus? How pathetic. Sir Eins is dead, anyhow, and far away from Eden."

"He was," Marek nodded. "Doompoint, correct? Killed by bandits?"

"You won't give up, will you? I know you must have been talking to Pelias. Nothing you say is going to convince me otherwise."

"Oh, I didn't learn any of this from Pelias."

The Ravagers glanced from Marek to Braxon and back again. The tension was heavy, but no one moved a muscle.

Marek continued: "It was Wyll – Endrew's steward."

Braxon made no reply this time. He cocked his head slightly to one side.

"Wyll was an informant for the magi the entire time. That's how they could stay a step ahead of you for so long. I got word from him by raven while I was in Etzekel. King Endrew was killed by an undead Sir Eins."

Braxon glared at him for a few moments. Finally, he cleared his throat and said, "Well, I suppose I'll have to clean house once I return to Eden. I had better wrap up my business here." He looked at Aiya and Leyon and nodded.

Aiya drug her axe-blade across Marleyn's throat and Leyon's club rose and fell on Llanowar's skull. Shouts of rage coursed through the forest.

Chapter 13

No one could distinguish how much time passed. Dane, Marek, Koda, and Grunt were scrutinized by the glossy eyes of their dead friends. Marleyn and Llanowar were cast aside by their executioners, appearing to the four compatriots to slump to the ground in slow motion.

"No!" Koda shouted.

"You delusional bastard!" Marek cried at Braxon.

Dane bared his teeth and gripped his longsword in both hands. Grunt took a few steps forward, his large axe warding off the most immediate foes.

"Do not shy away!" Braxon shouted. "Kill them!" The general took charge and rolled under the swipe of Grunt's axe. He lashed out with his longsword and caught Grunt on the back of the thigh. The giant stumbled slightly, the sight of which spurred The Ravagers to rush him.

Grunt decapitated two of his foes in one swing before sending another flying with a ferocious kick to the chest. Another warrior attempted to stab him with a knife, but the giant grabbed him by the wrist and yanked him off his feet. The man screamed as he collided with a tree trunk.

Other Ravagers found their courage and swarmed the others as Braxon fended off the other three with remarkable swordsmanship. His footing was solid as he parried sword, spear, and trident. He dodged to one side and grabbed the shaft of Koda's spear with one hand. He pushed the magi backwards until he was up against a tree.

Braxon was ready to deliver the killing blow, but was disrupted by Dane, who rushed from behind. Braxon threw Koda to the ground and turned just in time to lock swords with Dane. The two glared at each other as they struggled to gain the upper hand.

"I've been waiting to kill you for a while, Dane. I only wish Pelias was here, as well. It would make my job much quicker."

"You've spilled enough blood today," Dane growled. "I won't allow you to continue."

"Finally going to face me like a man, huh? You ran away in Etzekel and left that elf to fight me. You ran away from the arena in Eden. You didn't even so much as bristle when I mouthed off to you years ago at Winter's Edge." Braxon laughed as the surprise crept onto Dane's face. "That's right – I remembered you and Amir both. I don't forget. I never forget!"

Dane was gifted a new surge of strength as Braxon said Amir's name. He used it to push his sword away, deflecting it to the side. He smashed one of the guards of the sword into his face, leaving a gash in the old general's cheek beside his nose.

Though he was consumed by hate for the man, Dane still respected his skill as a warrior. The blow to his face barely fazed Braxon, and he successfully parried each of Dane's attacks in succession. He knew he could not beat him if he was blinded by rage – it would only cause him to falter. He tried to focus on calming himself, but nothing could push out the thought of his dead friend and how much suffering Braxon was responsible for. Not only for Dane himself, but for all the magi affected by his fanatical obsession with wiping them out. So much distress had piled up for so long, and he felt that he could mend some of the pain if he could strike Braxon down.

"You grow weary, Dane," Braxon taunted. "You should have bested me by now."

Dane took a step back - his eyes locked with Braxon's – and inhaled a deep breath. His longsword was still gripped in both hands, the tip pointed at Braxon's chest. He gritted his teeth and prepared to attack again.

"Dane!" Koda shouted. "We need to go! We can't win!"

"Come this way!" Marek said.

Without question, Dane took off toward the voices. He found Marek, Grunt and Koda together, beckoning him on. There were a few bodies on the ground, but they had not thinned The Ravagers' ranks by much.

"After them!" Braxon yelled, leading the chase.

Dane regrouped with his friends and the four of them began sprinting through the forest as fast as possible. "We won't gain enough ground to make it safely inside the walls!" Dane shouted.

"I've got that covered," Marek replied. He slowed his pace until he was last in the pack and Dane saw that his fingertips radiated with the purple energy. Marek threw his arm in a wide arc and the shining lights crossed and formed a large net that flew towards The Ravagers.

Braxon dove to the dirt at the last second, feeling the heat from the energy net on the back of his neck. He looked over his shoulder and saw the nearest Ravagers get diced by the magic rays. They remained nothing but tiny bits of flesh and a cloud of red mist. The grizzled old general could not help but stare for a few moments. Aiya came along and helped him stand. Leyon and Rorn rushed past the two of them, not giving them a second thought. Braxon and Aiya joined them, though the four of them hung back far enough where they could easily dodge Marek's energy net.

Dane and his companions broke through the tree line and sprinted as fast as possible towards Bandimere's gates. "Koda, get the gate!" Dane shouted. Black smoke flashed and Koda was gone, reappearing behind the gate.

"Would you quit that?" The guard shouted, startled. Without a word, Koda threw the bar off the gate and opened just in time for his friends to slide through. It was closed and barred in the blink of an eye.

The guard started in again: "Now, I done told you folks that we try and keep the gate locked. We done opened it too many times for your friends, so I'm gonna have to-"

"Holy hell!" A watchman on top of the wall said. "Who are all *those* people?" He looked down at Dane for answers.

"Get your best archers on them!" Dane said. The watchman blew a short burst on a horn and a dozen men armed with bows and crossbows rushed to join him at his position on the wall.

The gate guard peered through the slot on the wall and gave an audible whimper of fright. He turned and jabbed a finger at Dane. "I knew you folks was bad news! You brought them barbarians here!"

Tanken approached holding a bow and a quiver of arrows. "I heard the horn. What's the matter?"

"These thugs have brought more thugs that wanna attack us!" The guard proclaimed.

Tanken looked at Dane, who said, "It's the same people who chased us from Etzekel. We didn't know they would be able to track us so quickly. I'm sorry."

"You failed to mention you were being hunted," Tanken replied with a hint of disdain in his voice. "Even so, I've offered you asylum and I intend to uphold my promise. That boy with you is not healed, yet. Let's see if

283

we can't deal with these intruders." Tanken looked back at the gate guard. "Rally every fighting man we have. If we can intimidate them with our numbers instead of fight, we should do so."

Dane did not have the heart to tell Tanken that Braxon was not the type of person to bend to intimidation. "Marek," he said. "You and the others stay with Tanken and let me know if anything happens. I'm going to go check on Caulen." Marek and Tanken climbed the ramparts as Dane walked away.

Back at Asira's home, he was relieved to see that Caulen's color was slowly returning. There was an air of calm in the room as his caretakers watched him closely. Evie did not wait long to give her father the bad news.

"Pelias has left," she said.

"Left?" Dane ladled water from the basin and drank deeply. "Has he gone to fetch supplies?"

"No. He stormed out – out of the house and out of the village!"

Dane furrowed his brow. "Where was he going?" He had an inclination of what the answer might be.

"Doompoint..." She looked up at her father with worry in her eyes and she wrenched a rag that she held in her hands.

"You read his thoughts, I suppose?" He stroked the scruff on his face as he pondered.

"The mind doesn't tell lies, Dad..."

Dane sighed. "There's nothing we can do about it right now. Braxon has caught up to us. They're outside the walls as we speak..." He could not bring himself to look his daughter in the eyes.

Evie was quick to pick up on his hesitation. "What are you hiding?" she asked. "I'll find out one way or another."

Dane's sorrowful eyes met hers. "Marleyn and Llanowar are dead."

"No!" Evie screamed. "Are you sure?"

"I saw it with my own eyes."

Evie's nostrils flared and her eyes burned with hate. She shouted again and threw the rag onto the floor as hard as she could.

"Who are these people you speak of?" Asira asked.

"They've been pursuing us for many, many miles," Dane replied. "They've killed some of my friends..."

"They are attacking?" She said with some alarm.

"No, not yet. Tanken is posting archers on the walls to try and keep them at bay."

"I must focus on stabilizing the boy. If a battle is to take place, I will need to be available to care for the wounded."

"We'll leave you to it," Dane said. "Come, Evelyn."

"I'd like to stay and help her watch over Caulen," Evie said.

Dane looked at Asira, who responded: "She may stay. I may need her help. She is gifted with healing hands."

Dane nodded and then smiled at Evie.

* * *

Bren and Harryck slowed their pace to catch their breath. Harryck was incredibly fast, and Bren was a good deal bigger than him. It had been difficult at times for Bren to keep up — especially if there were any hills they had to cross.

"Are you thinking about your friends?" Harryck asked.

Bren shook himself from his own thoughts. "What kind of question is that?"

Harryck laughed. "Oh, I'm sorry. Were you expecting more compassion to come from the guy who was locked inside a cage for months?"

"No, I expected more compassion from the man whom I rescued from said cage."

"I'm ever grateful, but I believe I settled that score when I got us out of that enclosed alleyway."

"By cursing me with beast blood!"

"I've already explained myself," Harryck said, shrugging. "Once you can control your powers, feel free to go search for a cure. Rumor is that there is some ritual you could perform to rid your body of the beast blood."

"Once I have control, I'm joining my friends. That's all that matters."

"For now... You may come to love the lycan village. You'll be a legend there, I promise."

Bren furrowed his brow. "How so?"

"You're already a big guy. When you transformed in Etzekel, you were the biggest lycan I had ever seen. Quite frightening — and I don't cower easily. You'll have your choice of women and I bet you could lead if you choose to do so."

Bren scoffed. "None of that interests me. It's all trivial now."

"We'll see if that holds true."

They both went quiet as they saw a herd of deer scamper off over the hills. Neither of them had even noticed the animals until they darted from the tall grass, swimming through it like the waves of a silver sea

"Wait here," Harryck said as he dropped to all fours. In the blink of an eye, he had converted into his werewolf form: the fur spreading across his body at a rapid pace and his joints and appendages stretching instantly. He bounded over the hill on all fours.

Bren did as he was told and stayed put. He knelt, crossed his arms, and scanned the area around him. He was in a small depression in the field, with hills surrounding him on all sides. If anyone appeared over the rises, he would have little time to react. He wished he had his weapon.

Luckily, Harryck returned quickly – and back in his human form. He dragged a slain deer by its back legs, staining the silver grass with smears of red. He set the beast down in front of Bren, grinning. "Meat! It's been too long since I've sunk my teeth into the juicy flesh of a fresh kill. The wights taste awful!"

"Rotting flesh holds nothing to fresh," Bren remarked.

"Do you think you can stomach the meat raw?"

Bren gave him a disgusted look.

"It is an acquired taste for a lycan. It's quite useful if you want to save time while travelling."

"Eat yours however you please, but it will be a while before I long for raw meat," Bren said.

"Yet another thing you must learn." Harryck chuckled. "Fine. We'll make camp here. In this low spot our campfire will be hidden. I saw a lone tree some ways back. Fetch us some wood."

Bren studied the rises again, unsure of the safety of the place. He decided to trust Harryck's judgement and he left to find the tree. Once there, he pulled some of the smaller branches off to gain enough for a decent fire. When he returned, Harryck had already made great progress skinning his kill. "Where did you get a knife?"

"Stole it from that elf's laboratory." Bren set about building the fire as Harryck continued trimming the meat. He stopped and leaned back on his haunches. He waved his knife over the hills, smiling. "I can't describe to you how great that felt – chasing that game through the grass. After being in a cage so long, that was the best feeling in the world."

"I'm glad you enjoyed yourself. However, if you could continue to fillet that deer..."

"Of course, Master Bren," Harryck said, still smiling.

"It's only that I would prefer we keep travelling as soon as we've filled our bellies. I don't want to meet any of the tribespeople."

"I thought you were of the Bison Tribe?"

"I am. I was... I was born into the tribe, but I was taken from them before I earned my place as a warrior. I will have no bargaining power with them."

"This sounds like a good story. Speak, so we may pass the time more quickly."

"It's a simple story, really. When Endrew came to power, he was not the most popular king the realm has known."

"I'd say he maintained that status fairly well," Harryck quipped.

Bren ignored him. "A rebellion formed early into his rule. The rebels sought to draw Endrew into the open, and there's nowhere more open than the plains. With the Bison Tribe being closest to Eden, they attacked us. I was a young boy – fourteen, I believe, because boys take the warrior's test at fifteen, so I was close.

"I fought. I even killed four of the rebels during the battle, but it reached a point where I saw the overwhelming odds. I watched my people get butchered and raped, and I knew I couldn't win so I ran away south, away from the plains.

"King Endrew found me on his way to assist my tribe. He had formed a counter-offensive as soon as he had heard the news. He took me into his camp without hesitation. He fed me, gave me fresh clothes, and asked me questions about his foes, but I was little help.

"He ordered some of his men to escort me back to the castle at Eden, but I refused. I asked him if he would allow me to join him in his attack for the honor of my people. Against the counsel of his peers, he agreed and had them present me with a sword and shield. I returned to the Bison Tribe with an army at my back and slew thirteen more of the rebels..."

"I'd say that sufficed as a warrior's test," Harryck said.

"It didn't matter to my people." Bren sighed. "The tribespeople are an ancient people bound by tradition. They believed that I had betrayed them by taking up arms with the king. They believed I should have stayed and died fighting. Perhaps they were right, but I had not concerned myself with thoughts such as those in the heat of battle."

"So, they disowned you?"

"That's the short of it."

"Well, what did Endrew say? I bet he was pissed that he spent forces on an ungrateful bunch of savages."

"Wrong," Bren said. "I remember exactly what he said: 'These people may be ungrateful, but we can rest easy with ourselves knowing that we have helped those who could not help themselves. We do not observe their traditions, but we can respect their way.'"

289

Harryck was silent for a few moments, pondering the words. Finally, he said: "That sounds far different from the Endrew I've heard tales of. That doesn't sound like a man who would persecute magi the way he did."

"No, it doesn't." Bren stuck a blade of grass between his teeth. "Being king takes a toll on a person, I suppose…"

"There seems to be a large part of your story missing. How did you go from a boy of the tribes to the Sword of Justice? Surely you did something of note to impress Endrew."

"Not a thing. He watched as I was shunned by my own people and he offered me asylum in his castle. I had nowhere else to go, so I accepted. The decision weighed heavy on me for many days. Even when I made it to Eden, I spent all my time in the room they allowed me to stay in. I would stare out of the window and look on the city as it went through its daily business – a place completely unaware of my emotional turmoil.

"After giving me several days to grieve, Endrew came into my room with his guards. I feared for my life – certain that he had grown tired of my remorse. But he presented me with a breastplate bearing his sigil in front of his own men. He smiled as he watched me run my hand over it.

"He told me, 'I need a new Sword of Justice, and I think an unbiased outsider may be the best choice. Not everyone agrees with a man when he calls an execution, but the last resistance he needs is his own Sword.' His words were poetic in my head, but I think deep down he simply felt sorry for me."

Harryck was distraught. "That's it? You lived happily ever after from then on?"

"Until recently."

Harryck scoffed and then spat. "Some buggers have all the luck."

* * *

"What do you mean he's gone?" Koda stamped his spear into the ground. "Little rat got us good."

"Pelias wouldn't run away from a fight. He left for Doompoint," Dane said. "My words of caution in the forest did little to ease his mind, it seems."

"He should have waited for us. He'll be leagues ahead of us by the time we get out of here."

"If he doesn't wind up dead, first," Marek said.

Grunt growled at the suggestion.

Koda said, "We should just let The Ravagers in so we can be done with them."

No one responded to him. Dane scanned the tree line for a few moments, locking eyes with Braxon, who was bold enough to stand free of cover. A few of The Ravagers had joined him, but most took shelter behind a tree trunk or boulder. Two of The Ravagers were the ones who had executed Llanowar and Marleyn. They stood one on either side of Braxon.

With his arms crossed, Koda nodded his head at the man with the club. "I don't like the look of that one..." The man returned Koda's glare with a jaded stare.

"How do we get out of this one, Dane?" Marek asked.

"We won't — not without bloodshed, I'm afraid," Dane replied. "Something needs to happen soon, though. We can't let Pelias get too far ahead of us."

"Caulen won't be able to travel for at least a few days."

Koda cursed. "If we can deal with these maggots quickly, then perhaps the four of us can continue on to Doompoint while Caulen rests."

"No!" Dane growled through gritted teeth. "I will not be separated from my daughter again."

"This place has proven safe enough, until now."

"No one is staying or going without the others. We have debated this enough!"

Koda flexed his fingers and gathered his composure before his temper erupted. The last thing he wanted was to find himself in an altercation with Dane. "I'm worried about our friend, is all..."

"We *all* are. If we keep level heads and focus on the matters at hand, we can rejoin him soon."

"I could teleport out there and pierce Braxon's heart with my spear."

Dane glanced at him and then surveyed the open space between the two forces. "Is the distance not too far?"

Koda shrugged. "I feel like trying, rather than standing here with our thumbs in our asses."

Dane sighed and scratched at the whiskers on his face. "I don't want you risking your life on a guess, Koda."

Koda scoffed. "Call me when I'm needed, then." With that, he teleported away to some unknown destination.

Marek grinned slightly, stepping forward into Koda's place on the wall. "Tensions grow thicker among our little band."

"Will they ever ease?" Dane replied. "Peace and a simple life seem like a hazy dream, out of reach."

"Don't lose hope, yet." Marek jabbed his chin at Braxon. "If we can rid ourselves of that thorn, I see our lives taking a considerable turn towards the good."

"No." Dane crossed his arms. "We still have Doompoint."

"I don't think we can afford to worry about that now. One thing at a time, brother." Marek waited, expecting a reply. None came. "We will see Pelias safe again. Mark my words."

Dane, Grunt, and Marek stood silent for a while, watching. With a moment to breathe and ponder, Dane realized just how heavy his eyelids were. He rubbed them with his thumb and forefinger and yawned.

Suddenly, a thought struck Dane. He looked at Marek and said, "I can't believe you kept your powers secret all this time."

Marek smirked. "I would've taken that to my grave if Caulen hadn't needed rescuing."

"Why?"

Marek shrugged. "If you, Amir, and the others had known I was a magi, I never would've been treated the same. I just wanted to be one of you, fighting with the others."

"Nothing would've changed."

"I doubt that. I would've been the guy you called on for all the big jobs. I would've been treated like some kind of legend."

"I figure you would've liked that," Dane grinned.

"Oh, I would've milked it, for sure, but I'm happy with the way things went down."

"Me too."

Tanken approached the three of them, eyes fixed upon the intruders across the way. "I've had beds prepared for you in my home. None of your company has slept since you've been here — save for the injured boy. Rest up while you can. I'll wake you up if anything of note happens."

"Thank you," Dane said, clasping forearms with the man. "but I must see to my daughter."

"Not necessary," Tanken replied. "I've already sent a couple of the women to aide Asira should the boy take a turn for the worst. You'll find your girl sound asleep in my home. Don't worry about a thing."

"I'll be hard-pressed to repay your kindness."

"I just ask that you help me defend my home while you utilize it."

"I promise we will. Send word if you need us." Dane gestured to Marek and Grunt and the three of them climbed down from the ramparts.

"Awfully nice of him," Marek commented as they strolled lazily through the streets.

"I miss the days when a stranger's kindness didn't make me uneasy," Dane replied.

Just as Tanken said, Evie was dead asleep on a small cot constructed in the middle of Tanken's home. Dane brushed some of her hair from her face and kissed her on the forehead. Koda was nowhere to be found here – nor had they seen him anywhere in the streets on their way.

Neither Dane, Marek, nor Grunt wasted any time lying down. They wrestled for a time with thoughts of their most recent losses in Llanowar and Marleyn. Though the ache of loss was great, they were too exhausted to remain awake.

Dane once again found himself in the forest outside of Bandimere. He stood with Marek, Grunt, and Koda – Llanowar and Marleyn captive before them. Braxon and The Ravagers stood over them, but no one moved or spoke. Dane felt like a hawk in the sky with an overhead view of the moment. He could even see himself.

There was a flash of light that appeared like lightning, though no whip-crack followed, and no thunder bellowed. He was blinded for a moment, and when his sight returned, he was on the ground with the others, directly between his other self and Braxon. Dane tried to take hold of himself and attack the general, but he could not move.

Braxon nodded to Aiya and Leyon, and then another flash of light. Llanowar and Marleyn lay lifeless, sprawled in their own blood. It seemed like an eternity that Dane was forced to stare at them again. In his dream, he did not blink and could not look away.

Another flash of light and everyone was gone except the two women.

"People keep dying, Dane."

The voice was familiar, but Dane had gone so long without hearing it, he did not believe it was real. His suspicions were appeased when a friendly figure casually strolled in front of him, arms resting behind his back. Amir wore a simple brown tunic. His auburn hair was slicked back, and his beard was trimmed neatly. He grinned the familiar grin that forced Dane to smile in return.

"You come to me in a dream?" Dane asked.

"It's all I can do to help you, I'm afraid." Amir stepped closer, blocking Dane's view of his butchered friends.

"Why have you never done this before?"

"Not many people get to commune with the dead. Are you sure you want to spend the time asking questions?"

"Questions are all I have..."

"Lay them to rest, brother." Amir turned his back and took a few steps away. Llanowar and Marleyn were no longer on the tree stumps – no blood or anything to mark that they were ever there.

"I can't stop people from dying…. I have tried, but it keeps happening. I thought having experience on the battlefield would help me, but I left that life for a reason. I didn't want to die and leave Evelyn with nothing. But nothing has changed. People I call friends are still dying just as they were when we were Iron Foxes, and I'm frightened beyond belief that Evelyn could be one of them."

"You should have learned a long time ago that death waits for no one. Sometimes you can't do anything to save people. When it's their time, it's their time." Amir grinned at him over his shoulder and said, "City life in Eden must have made you soft."

"What do I do? Can you tell me anything about what I can expect in the future?"

Amir laughed. "My friend, I am merely an observer to the world as things happen – a patron at a play. I have no more insight into what may happen than you do."

"So… nothing?" Dane asked in exasperation.

Amir considered for a moment, looking ahead. "Expect death. This won't end without a great deal more death."

Dane felt a lump in his throat that prevented him from speaking. He wanted to ask more questions but was unable.

Amir turned to him, the grin still plastered on his face. "Just make sure you fight your hardest. This is the most important battle we ever took part in."

"*Dane*!" A voice called.

Dane fought the intruder. He did not want to go, to leave his friend again. A bright white light slowly crept between the trees surrounding the two of them.

"Dane!" the voice called again.

The trees started moving towards him and the light was getting brighter. It started closing in around Amir before him.

"Dane!"

Amir strolled towards him and placed a hand on his shoulder. The touch was heavy, and Dane could not believe it was not real. "Thank you for saying the prayer for me," Amir said. The light continued to close in around him until the last thing Dane saw was Amir's smiling face.

"Amir!" Dane's eyes shot open to see Marek, Grunt, and Evie standing over him. He panted heavily as he looked all over the room for Amir before being struck by realization. Had that been a dream or something more?

"Thought you were out for good!" Marek said. "Tanken sent a messenger. Braxon and The Ravagers have disappeared into the forest. There are archers guarding every gate, but night has fallen and Tanken has a feeling that they are going to attack at any moment."

Dane kicked his legs over the side of the bed and picked up his sword, placing thoughts of Amir in the back of his mind. He fastened the belt around his waist and then donned his armor. "Marek, you and I will join Tanken. Grunt, take Evie back to Asira's home. Stay there to guard the girls and Caulen." Dane and Evie embraced before Grunt took her by the hand and led her out of the house. "Where's Koda?"

"Still no sign of him," Marek replied.

Dane cursed under his breath. "Let's just hope he hasn't done anything rash."

The two of them left Tanken's house not long after. Torches were lit throughout Bandimere and they made Dane contemplate how long he had been asleep.

His dream had felt like mere minutes, but clearly, that was not true. He wished he felt as rested as he should.

"Do you think we'll finally be rid of Braxon tonight?" Marek asked.

Dane pondered quietly for a few moments. "After months of dodging the zealot, it's hard to imagine his absence."

"I welcome it, and I haven't been pestered by him nearly as long as you have."

The two of them walked a bit further, occasionally passing someone carrying a pitchfork or a woodcutting axe. Only a few of the villagers appeared to own real weapons, but they were prepared to fight. Once Dane and Marek reached the wall, they noticed that the people there were better equipped.

Tanken and Dane nodded to one another as they approached the man. Tanken pointed into the shadowy forest before them and said: "Those thugs skulked away amongst the trees just as it was growing dark. We haven't seen anything of them since then, but I doubt they've just given up now."

"I assure you they haven't," Dane said.

Tanken turned away to discuss with another man. Marek said, "Dane, have you thought about what comes after this?"

Dane turned and gave him a confused look.

"I mean, after this battle. If Braxon dies, our lives become much easier. We're not so pressed to run anywhere."

"That's true. It'll be a weight off our shoulders, for sure," Dane agreed.

"But what about Pelias?"

The question hit Dane in a peculiar way. He considered for a moment, thumbing his chin, before saying, "I suppose we follow him to Doompoint."

"He made his own choice. Do you think everyone else will follow?"

"I suppose at that point, they don't have to if they don't want to. Pelias made a mistake when he left without us. He needs his friends with him."

"Sounds like it's an easy choice for you."

"No, not at all. But it's the right choice."

Marek made no further comments and Dane leaned on the railing – searching intently for any sign of Braxon.

A few hours of silence passed by. Dane looked at the moon in the sky and guessed it to be around one o'clock in the morning. He glanced at the sentries posted along the wall. A few of them were still alert and actively keeping watch, but most of them were yawning, dozing, or had outright fallen asleep. Dane knew that Braxon would attack soon. The old general knew that the civilians inside the walls were mostly undisciplined and would be at their most vulnerable late in the night.

Just as these thoughts passed through Dane's mind, screams were heard coming from towards the northern gate. The clash of steel was mixed with the savage battle cries of The Ravagers. Tanken ran off to assist them. At the same time, someone shouted, "Hooks! They're using hooks to scale the walls!"

"With hooks, they can climb in from anywhere," Marek said.

Dane drew his longsword and looked out to the forest, but still did not see any movement. He noticed everyone was swarming towards the north. "They're falling right into a trap!" Dane said. "More will come from the south! Let's go, Marek!"

The two of them ran towards the southern gate by themselves, passing several guards who ran the opposite direction. Both Dane and Marek tried to stop them from joining the others, but no one heard their pleas. The southern gate was completely abandoned.

Just as they arrived, multiple grappling hooks landed on the wall before them, being pulled tight until they clutched the railing. Dane made quick work of the ropes by slicing them with his sword. Arrows and stones soared around their heads, forcing them to duck back out of sight. The enemies below had dispersed by the time the two of them had a chance to look.

"They're going to plan B," Marek said.

"We can't hold this entire thing by ourselves! We need to tell Tanken to spread his men out again. Let's go!"

Dane and Marek sprinted towards the northern gate where most of the villagers had posted themselves. They had not gotten there before they realized it was too late. They saw Braxon and The Ravagers marching through the streets, having slipped in unawares...

Chapter 14

Torches were lit.

"Burn everything down!" Braxon commanded. "We're not here to take hostages! We're here to complete a mission!"

The Ravagers dispersed like a pack of wild dogs, howling and reveling in the chaos that was to come. One by one, they started to set fire to the homes of the people of Bandimere. They slaughtered all the livestock they found and put down the people in the same manner without an afterthought.

Dane and Marek wasted no time leaping from atop the wall and rushing to meet their foes in the open streets. "Braxon! Stop this now!" Dane shouted, pointing his sword at the man.

The few Ravagers that had stayed by Braxon's side turned and faced the two men before he did. The general stood with clenched fists resting on his hips, his eyes drinking in the fire. "This is where my crusade ends," he said. "I will finish my business with you pests and return to Eden."

"You still think Endrew awaits you at Eden, don't you?"

"Do you think I would believe your words?" Braxon finally turned. "Enough talk. I should have had your head long ago."

A flash of smoke next to Dane saw Koda standing there with his spear in hand. "I thought I heard your loud mouth over here, Braxon. Tell me where that club-wielding bastard is and I'll leave you alone."

Braxon smirked. "Leyon's gone to crush more skulls around the village. I'll order him to wait if you want to watch the rest of your friends die."

"Wrong answer." Koda teleported again, multiple times in quick succession. Each time he disappeared in a puff of smoke, another Ravager was dead. Koda paused after reappearing between Dane and Braxon. Koda glared at Braxon as he took a deep breath and teleported again.

As soon as Koda disappeared, Braxon sidestepped a short distance. Koda's spear narrowly missed his exposed back. The general reached out and grabbed the spear while he struck Koda with the back of his other fist. The gladiator fell to the ground, his ears ringing from the blow to his chin.

Braxon spun and threw the spear at Dane, who was barely able to knock it out of harm's way with his sword. More Ravagers – including Aiya - joined Braxon and wasted no time attacking Dane and Marek, keeping them preoccupied long enough for the general to turn back to Koda, who was rising from the ground. Braxon put a boot to his face and sent him sprawling out onto the ground, then laid a few punches into his face.

"You're predictable," Braxon said. "Each of those Ravagers you killed you stabbed in the back like a snake. I'm just insulted you thought you could do the same to me. That's a costly mistake."

Braxon stood above Koda and placed his hand on the hilt of his sword. Koda tried to squirm away, but the general dug the heel of his boot into one of his legs. He began to draw his sword, and at the same time an arrow punctured through the soft tissue just above his elbow. The arrow lodged firmly in his lifted arm and stopped short as it pricked the skin on his neck.

Braxon stared dumbstruck. He let his sword slide back into its sheath and stumbled backwards a few steps as he clutched his arm, fingers grasping at the arrow shaft. Koda began to crawl away as Aiya ushered Braxon away from the battle.

The general grimaced and stumbled, fighting to regain control. His head was spinning, whipping in every direction, but the shock was too great. He could not make out any of the faces around him. Aiya muttered consoling words to him, in-between the curses she also spewed.

Braxon's vision was enclosing like a tunnel, and he found it difficult to keep his eyes open. He felt the warm blood dripping from his arm. The last thing he remembered was smelling the harsh, acrid smell of the smoke in the village.

Once Koda was safely away, he looked to see where the arrow had come from. He saw Caulen clutching a bow he had retrieved off a dead body. The young boy leaned on Evie as Grunt kept them protected with his giant battle-axe. Dane and Marek killed all The Ravagers that had attacked them, helped Koda to his feet, and regrouped with the others.

"You're looking much healthier," Marek said to Caulen.

"That woman's magic is exceptional," Caulen said.

"Where is she?" Dane asked.

Evie replied: "She said she couldn't leave without gathering some of her herbs and potions. We *have* to go back for her!"

Dane nodded. "Grunt, Koda, can you get Caulen and Evie to the northern gate?"

Grunt nodded.

"What for?" Koda asked, wiping blood from his mouth.

"Tanken is there. We need to rally and try to save Bandimere. Marek and I will go get Asira."

"I'll go, too!" Evie said.

Dane shook his head. "No."

"I can help her carry her things. It'll be faster for all of us!"

"No!" Dane motioned for them to leave. Koda grabbed Evie by the wrist as Grunt picked Caulen up and began running.

"Asira better still be alive, or this is a waste of time!" Marek called.

Dane ripped his sword out of the bowels of a Ravager who fell to the ground with a heavy sigh. The two of them had encountered a patrol on their way to Asira's home. At this point, The Ravagers were more of a nuisance for the two experienced mercenaries, and they did not believe that there could be too many of them left.

When they finally reached her house, they were relieved to see that it had not been put to fire. However, several of The Ravagers were approaching the building from a different direction. They had not seen Dane or Marek yet, so the two of them took the opportunity to rush them from behind.

Marek threw his trident into the back of one of The Ravagers and then immediately dove over the axe swing of another. Dane lingered and allowed the axe swing to pass him before lopping off the head of the attacker with his sword. The third enemy thrust his spear in rapid succession, forcing Dane to swivel and duck quickly.

Dane used the flat of his sword to redirect the spear tip into the ground. He sliced one of The Ravagers arms off at the elbow and pushed him away, stumbling, before raising his sword high in the air and bringing it down to leave a large gash in his chest.

As Dane did this, Marek had pinned another barbarian to the ground by stabbing his trident through his foot. With his enemy trapped, Marek let loose a volley of rapid punches to the man's face and body before grabbing his head and slamming it against the trident handle, then removing it and letting the man drop to the ground.

Dane threw the door of Asira's home open and called her name. She came from around the corner holding a hatchet and several sacks slung over her shoulder. "I was ready to fight," she said.

"Stay close to us and perhaps you won't have to," Dane said as he held his hand out. She took it without hesitation and the three of them made for the door.

Dane's heart dropped and his blood boiled at the same time as soon as he stepped outside. No more than ten feet away, Rorn had Evie on her knees, a knife held to her throat. The bearded man laughed while Evie glared ahead as she scowled.

Rorn laughed and looked at Dane. "This your daughter? Ya' favor one another." He sucked his ugly black teeth before chuckling again. "You're the one Braxon wants bad, 'sides the kingsguard boy. I should get a good reward for you."

"You won't be getting a reward. Just my sword through your throat." Dane's fingers flexed around the hilt of his blade as he held it in one hand off to his side.

"Tough talk like that don't scare me."

Dane ignored Rorn and looked at his daughter. "Evelyn," he said and nodded to her.

Evie closed her eyes and took a deep breath. Rorn glanced down at her peculiarly before his eyes flickered rapidly and the knife he held moved shakily away from her throat. Dane leapt forward and stabbed Rorn in the throat while Evie dodged to the side. Dane sliced his neck open on one side and brought the sword around to cleave what remained from his shoulders. The headless body slumped to the ground.

Dane helped her to her feet and glared at her. "I told you to stay with Grunt and Koda!"

"I didn't listen," Evie retorted.

"Obviously!"

"We should really keep moving," Marek interjected.

Evie took some of the bags from Asira and the four of them proceeded to the northern gate.

As soon as Koda saw Evie with Dane, he said, "Dane, I'm so sorry. Do you know how quiet she is? Slipped away without my notice."

Dane scowled at him.

"There's also a battle going on, not to mention..." Koda gave a sheepish grin.

Tanken approached them, blood splattering his clothes, and his hair disheveled. "Dane, I'm glad you and your people are still here, but... Bandimere is lost..."

"No! We'll stay and help you win this fight," Dane said.

"You don't understand. What you see here is all that remains. Most people died or fled... We managed to push out the remaining Ravagers, but..."

Dane looked around at the remaining faces that stared at them. There could not be more than ten, and all of them looked dejected and sad – accepting the fact that their homes were gone. Dane looked at the village, brightly ablaze and crumbling. Bandimere was a shell, now a remnant of a sanctuary that had existed mere hours ago.

"Tanken... I'm sorry," Dane said.

Tanken sighed and took in the flames. "We made our choice. Perhaps it wasn't best for us, but we helped you as best we could. That's all we wanted to be – an aid to those who needed us."

"You were." Dane pointed to Caulen. "That boy is alive because of you all. We can't thank you enough."

Tanken gave the smallest of smiles. No one spoke for a while. Several stared silently at the village while a few gathered what little remains they could.

Dane looked at Asira. "Thank you so much for everything you've done."

She bowed her head, smiling. "Where will you go now?"

He looked south, brow furrowed, eyes set. "Into the desert. We have to go find our friend."

"Your friend that ran away?"

"Yes."

"That boy may still need aid," the healer said, nodding towards Caulen, propped against Grunt.

"I'm not leaving my friends," Caulen replied, narrowing his eyes at her.

"Then I will have to go with you," Asira said.

"You don't have to do that," said Dane. "You've done enough."

"I know. I grew up in a desert just like that. I like the sand. I miss it. Plus, I see great potential in your daughter."

"What about the people of Bandimere?"

Tanken cleared his throat and cut in: "She's free to do as she pleases. She's helped us more than we can repay."

"What will you do now?" Dane asked.

"We'll figure something out. There are some farmsteads nearby that are sure to be abandoned. We're not giving up. We'll forge a new home. Join us, if you change your mind."

Dane shook his head. "No. We have business to attend to. In fact, we should be on our way. Thank you again." Dane and Tanken clasped forearms and everyone said their goodbyes.

As Dane, Marek, Evie, Asira, Koda, Grunt, and Caulen left what remained of Bandimere, Marek leaned in toward Dane and muttered: "Do you think Braxon is dead?"

"From an arrow wound? We're not that lucky," Koda responded.

Marek said, "Maybe he got caught up in the other fighting?"

"I pray he did," Dane said under his breath.

The seven companions set their course south towards the Red Crescent Desert, where they hoped to intercept Pelias before he reached Doompoint alone.

Chapter 15

As Bren and Harryck journeyed deeper into the Platinum Plains, they had to be even more cautious than before. The way they travelled took them dangerously close to the people of the Elk Tribe. Patrols had become far more frequent, and some had been difficult for them to dodge – having nearly been caught on two separate occasions.

"We could fight them," Harryck whispered during one of the times they were hidden in the tall grass. "If I transformed, we could rip them to shreds with ease."

"These people have done nothing," Bren countered.

"They would not show *us* mercy if they caught us."

"Then we better not get caught."

It had been several hours since the two of them had seen any of the tribespeople. This realization made both men nervous – expecting to see the elk-riders at any moment. Their heads were kept on a constant swivel and their ears strained to pick up any noises. More than likely – if they paid attention – the two men would smell the elk before any of their other senses warned them of their presence.

"You worry me, you know?" Harryck blurted.

Bren looked at him. "Why?"

"You haven't transformed since the initial infection back in Etzekel. Most people wrestle with it at least every day. It's been almost a week for you."

"What does that mean?" Bren asked.

Harryck shrugged as the two of them slowed their pace to talk. "I don't know. I've never seen it affect anyone quite like this before. We'll have to ask around when we get to my village."

"Should I be worried?"

"Absolutely. I've never known any-" Harryck stopped short his sentence and craned his neck to the side. His nostrils flared as he sniffed the air. "Drop!" He said in a sharp whisper.

Bren followed the order and fell to the ground right where he stood. The grass here was tall and formed around them as they settled into the ground. The place where they hid was a large depression amongst the softly rolling hills of silver grass.

The elk-riders topped a rise near them, marching their beasts in a single-file line. The tribesmen rode their steeds bareback, their legs wrapped tightly around the animals' ribs. Their animal-skin chaps flapped as the elk stamped along at a fair pace.

Most of the tribesmen held spears up in the air, ready to drop and charge at any moment. Their bare chests were dark from the sun and their hair was adorned with feathers that stood erect, forming a crown from the sides of their heads all the way to the back.

They scanned the plains with hard, squinting eyes. Bren and Harryck did not know if that meant they were suspected, but both men instinctively held their breath. The elk flicked their heads and looked down the crater that Bren and Harryck were hiding in.

Bren clutched his stomach as he felt a strange churning deep inside. He clenched his teeth and fought the urge to audibly groan. Harryck looked over and saw his face pinched in pain. Bren looked over at him and the two of them spoke without using words.

Harryck glanced back at the elk-riders. As best he could see through the blades of grass, there were fifteen to twenty of the tribesmen — all mounted and carrying spears or bows. He looked back at Bren, who had begun to slowly curl into a ball as he held his stomach. Beads of sweat dotted his forehead and he bared his teeth in discomfort.

Harryck cursed as he once again looked back towards the elk-riders. Their beasts stamped their hooves and shook their heads in Bren and Harryck's direction. Their large, wide antlers rattled against one another and they snorted in warning.

The tribesmen were now on full alert. They muttered amongst themselves while they adjusted their spears and notched arrows on string. A few of them were motioned forward by the leader and they directed their steeds down the depression where they hid.

By this time, Bren had folded himself up as tightly as possible and the veins in his neck and head protruded so much that they almost looked like growths. A line of blood trickled down his cheek from his nose.

Harryck whispered: "You can't fight it anymore. You'll kill yourself if you do. You're gonna have to turn – and now!"

Through gritted teeth, Bren said, "But... I'll kill them..."

"We'll have to either way. Do it!" Harryck placed his hands on the ground and begun his own transformation.

As the elk-riders set upon them, Harryck's body begun to stretch and contort until he had grown three times in size, and he rose above the grass in his wolf form to tower over the tribesmen on their elk.

The tribesmen halted their beasts and stared at the monster before them in silence. They were not spurred to action until Bren also appeared to float out of the grass. Having already been much taller than Harryck, his wolf form was even more imposing.

The elk-riders near them turned their beasts as quickly as possible and flew away as the remaining members shot at them with arrows from atop the rise. The first few found marks, but Bren found that the skin he donned in his transformed state was much thicker than a human's and he did not feel anything but a sting from the arrows.

A primal rage took over Bren's mind. He was conscious of what he was doing, but he found the animalistic instinct made him more than willing to kill to survive. With his powerful legs, he caught up to the retreating tribesmen in just a few bounds. He reached out with his sharp claws and ripped a rider from his mount, flinging him aside.

He swept two more enemies – mount and all – to the side as if he were swatting flies. The elk blared as they tumbled to the ground, crushing their riders. One brave tribesman attempted to charge at Bren. He made the mistake of holding his spear too low, and Bren leapt into the air with his claws outstretched. He landed on top of the tribesman and brought him to the ground by digging his claws into his torso. Bren threw his arms out and ripped the young man's chest wide open.

Harryck had already bolted ahead of Bren and put himself among the crowd of other riders. He unleashed furious swipes of his claws as he ripped into the legs of the elks with his piercing fangs. His entire body moved like a tornado, ripping off limbs and tearing bodies as he ran amongst the tribesmen.

Bren joined him and together they put down all twenty of the elk-rider patrol. The two of them went about feeding on the feast of elk meat and man-flesh, their wolf-forms unwilling to trouble themselves with differentiating between the two. After they had taken the time to fill their bellies, Bren felt his body begin to morph back into his human form.

He quickly shrank back to his normal size. His hair receded back into his body, and his fangs and claws reshaped into their regular length. His long wolf-snout pressed back into his face and his eyes were once again his own. He blinked several times as he shuddered against the strange skin-crawling sensation he had felt after his first transformation. He looked down at his hands and body and saw that everything had returned to its normal position and size.

Bren looked at Harryck, who had also returned to human form. The man grinned at him and crossed his arms. "Well? Easier coming down this time, right?"

Bren blinked a few times more and said, "A little, I suppose. I can't wait to be over the tingling sensation in my skin. It's strange."

"In time," Harryck said.

"I remember everything this time. Why is that?"

"No lycan remembers their first transformation. It's one of the reasons we have a bad reputation. Many of us go on murder sprees and can't remember a damn thing." Harryck stepped closer and inspected Bren. "I will say, though, that not many lycans can remember their second or third times, either. You may have a real gift for this." He grinned at him again before punching him in the arm.

"A gift I would like to return," Bren said as he looked around with sad eyes at the chaos they had caused. The bodies of both elk and human were ripped apart, blood and guts staining the silver grass of the plain. Bren scowled at the lives he had taken.

"The good news is that we have plenty of meat for the rest of our journey," Harryck said, setting about trimming the elk with his knife. Bren remained silent as he wrested a knife from the body of one of the tribesmen and set about skinning his own elk.

The two of them were silent for a time as they procured the meat. Bren glanced at Harryck occasionally and found a wide grin on his face. Bren tried to ignore it, but there was a slyness behind the expression.

"What?" Bren asked finally, unable to go without knowing the man's thoughts.

"You were ravenous in lycan form! You could be a force unmatched if you decide to embrace your circumstances."

"You don't seem to understand – I have no intention of using this curse. The only reason I'm following you is so I can learn how to control it. I won't have it control *me*."

"You're still bitter about it."

"Did you expect me not to be?"

"After wielding that kind of raw power? Of course! Think of how you could make your foes tremble! No one would ever be able to harm you or your loved ones ever again!"

"That doesn't appear to have worked for you."

Harryck stood up to his full height, clutching his knife in his hand. Bren glanced at the blade before matching Harryck's stare. The shorter man took one step towards him.

"You speak of things you shouldn't. I thought I made the right call for my wife and son back in Etzekel. I was wrong, but now I am set on the correct path. No one can stand in my way. No one." Harryck fondled the hilt of the knife, never breaking eye contact with Bren.

"We should continue collecting provisions," Bren said, turning his back after a moment.

Harryck clutched the knife tightly and drilled holes in the back of Bren's skull with piercing eyes. He sighed and returned to the elk he had been carving. "I will be overjoyed when we arrive at my village and find myself in different company. Perhaps, company that knows how to have fun and enjoy life. Not the soul-sucking brooder you are, Bren."

Bren grinned a little as he went back to trimming the meat for their journey.

* * *

It had been a little over a week since Bren and Harryck had attacked the patrol of elk-riders. The Dragon Fang Mountains ceased to be specks in the distance, as just ahead they began to loom over them like a pride of slowly-rising giants. The snow-capped mountains still lay far off, but the plains transitioned into hilly and then mountainous terrain at a creeping pace.

Bren's hair, which he usually kept shaved closely to his head, was thicker than he liked it. His goatee had formed into an unkempt beard that he could not help but scratch at. He vowed that a haircut and shave would be one of the first things he did when he got to the lycan village.

Harryck looked no worse now than he did when he left Etzekel. His blonde hair and beard were still shaggy and matted. He was still wearing the sack clothing from before, and the dirt and grime of their travels persisted on Harryck's skin more so than Bren's. His own finger and toenails had not grown much longer, and Bren figured it must have something to do with the transformation.

They had seen more patrols as they continued through the Platinum Plains. A few of them they could

315

avoid, but to Bren's chagrin there had been others that they could not. The tribesmen stood no chance. Bren did what he could, but being unable to transform of his own volition, he defended himself however possible while Harryck would ravage their groups before they had time to react.

And so, Bren had no choice but to watch as Harryck murdered with glee. Afterwards, Harryck would transform back and laugh before collecting more meat to carry with them. Bren knew it was getting easier for him to watch the innocent tribesmen be slaughtered...

The two of them slowly climbed to the top of a tall hill. As they cleared the rise, their eyes were cast down on top of an expansive village of modest thatch-roofed homes. The village was nestled comfortably in a sort of natural bowl, hidden by hills and mountains on all sides. Thin trails of smoke rose from campfires that dotted the land, but they evaporated by the time they rose above the hills.

Harryck gestured as he sported his usual grin. "That's it, Bren."

"It's bigger than I expected. Does it have a name?"

"No. We don't bother with naming it. It's just home to us." Harryck descended the mountain in joyous bounds. Bren kept a casual pace, letting him get far ahead. By the time he joined the man, a fair number of people had gathered around him. They all shared hugs and handshakes, smiling.

Bren approached with his pack slung nonchalantly over his shoulder. Harryck put an arm around him and spoke to him as everyone else eyed him suspiciously. "Bren, I'll show you around after I've reunited with my family. Just stay with me until then."

Harryck took the hand of an elderly woman in his hands and looked down at her. "Where is Trithilia?"

The old woman leaned towards him, forcing him to stoop low so she could whisper something in his ear. Harryck gave her a quick hug and bounded off down the street. Bren jogged behind him to create a bit of distance between the two of them.

Harryck led the way through the lycan village, waving to friends as he passed them by. Once they had cut through the entire village, Harryck led him into a cave that lay on the other side. Bren would have never noticed it was there without any investigation, for a thick layer of vines and shrubbery masked the entrance. Harryck pushed through it without hesitation.

There was very little light inside — only what seeped in through the foliage at the cave opening. Even so, Bren noticed he had little difficulty seeing in the darkness, which he attributed as another benefit of the lycan curse. *At least it's not all bad*, he thought.

Bren's eyes roamed the darkness. The cave funneled out until it formed a giant room, with a high ceiling and towering, carved walls. Bren guessed that it was large enough to house the entire village in an emergency.

Bren finally paid attention to Harryck, whose arms were wrapped tightly around a red-haired woman about his height. They held each other silently for some time, and Bren found Harryck's change in demeanor interesting.

In the arms of the woman, Harryck was calm and more reserved. The elation the man felt was evident on his face. The tender interaction made Bren ponder Marleyn. He had not thought of the sweet girl for some time, and he hoped she was safe.

He was snapped from his thoughts as Harryck and Trithilia shifted an arms-length apart to study each other's faces. Seconds later, tears began to trickle down the woman's face. Harryck chuckled and said, "No tears, woman. I'm here now and you're safe in my arms."

Trithilia shook her head and said, "Our son…"

Harryck's grin faded immediately, a pit forming in his stomach. "Erryl? What of him? Where is he?"

Bren's eyes flicked between them both.

Trithilia began to weep openly, putting her face in her hands.

Harryck's nostrils flared and he shook her roughly. "Speak, woman! Erryl! Where is he?"

"He's dead!" Trithilia shouted, wrenching herself out of Harryck's hands and pushing him away. Harryck stood still, dumbfounded, while Bren observed quietly, but with wide eyes. "He died…"

"How?"

"On our journey back from Etzekel… We got trapped by undead. He was bitten while I was shifting into my lycan form."

"Did he turn?"

"Yes… I could not put him down."

Harryck jabbed a finger in her face. "That's *your* fault! I told you months ago that we should have given him the gift!"

"He was eight! It was *his* decision to make! We couldn't force that on him!"

"Now he's out there somewhere – shambling around, dead on his feet."

"I feel horrible enough! Don't point fingers at me!"

Harryck slapped her and she fell to the ground. Bren stepped between them, holding his hands open in peace. Harryck looked up at him before huffing and leaving the cave. Bren turned and looked at Trithilia as she stood and brushed herself off.

"You didn't have to do that. Now he's only going to be angrier."

"I don't like seeing women in trouble."

"Well, don't expect a 'thank you'." She stormed off out of the cave as well.

Bren stood in silence, wondering what he had gotten himself into. He followed Trithilia out of the cave where she and Harryck had continued the argument. They shouted and shoved each other around, and Bren kept his distance.

Others had caught their voices on the wind and came out of the village to inspect. They watched with curious eyes and listened with pricked ears. Some of them eyed Bren suspiciously, suspecting he was the cause of the altercation.

Finally, the shouting match reached its peak, and it ended with Trithilia punching Harryck hard enough in the face that the man fell to the ground. He glared up at her for a moment before she turned and stormed off, parting the crowd with her intense march. Bren's eyes were wide, but no one in the crowd was surprised at the fact that the woman had dropped him with one punch.

Bren crossed his arms and sauntered over to Harryck. Harryck spit into the dirt and looked up at the big man. He motioned in Trithilia's direction. "My wife…"

"She makes quite the impression," Bren quipped.

"Pay no mind to us."

"Is that normal?" Bren offered a hand, which Harryck took.

"It is for us," he said, dusting off the seat of his breeches.

"I'm sorry to hear about your son."

Harryck waved his hand. "I don't want to think about it... Don't mention Erryl again."

Bren nodded solemnly.

Later that day, Harryck showed Bren around the village and introduced him to everyone they saw. Harryck's mind still dwelled on his son, Bren saw, so he tried to make conversation with the strangers as best as he could. Many of them were friendly and accepting of him, but after a while Bren grew weary of telling the story of how he and Harryck had met, though most thought it an exciting tale.

Finally, the sun sank behind the hills and cast a pink and orange wave over them as night approached. Harryck had introduced Bren to nearly everyone and the two men headed for Harryck's home. Bren tried to make light conversation but got nothing but short replies from the other.

Out of ideas, Bren just blurted out a thought he had: "Who is in charge here?"

"We don't have a chieftain or an elder or a ruler. Whatever you wanna call it, we don't have one."

"How does the place function?"

"We're like a family here. Everyone talks and gets along for the most part. If we have problems, we discuss them with one another. It's *that* simple." Bren was intrigued by the notion. "Here's my home. Don't say anything to Trithilia, she's likely on edge."

Bren did not want to be present for whatever was about to take place. He wanted to be anywhere else but here, but he was unfamiliar with the village and its inhabitants, so he decided to stick with Harryck. He followed him inside, where they found Trithilia on her knees in a meditative pose.

"Trithilia... food?" Harryck asked.

Bren took a quiet, deep breath, preparing himself for a violent outburst.

One of the woman's eyes flicked open, glaring at her husband in rage. "We have bread."

Harryck looked around. "Is that all? I brought a guest."

"Wonderful. Perhaps he can fetch us some meat."

"Actually," Bren said, unslinging the pack he had taken from the tribesmen they had slain, "I have elk meat left over from our journey."

Harryck groaned. "I'm tired of elk meat."

"I'm tired of bread," Trithilia retorted, sighing and getting on her feet. "Give me the pack. I will cook the meat." Bren handed it off to her and she threw the bloody flesh onto a table. "What's your name, stranger?"

"Bren."

"Thank you for the food, Bren. I'm glad *someone* is providing."

"I helped, woman," Harryck said, rolling his eyes. He offered Bren a seat and then took one himself.

"So how did you find yourself in the company of my husband?"

Once more, Bren explained the events that had taken place. Leaving Eden, travelling to Etzekel, getting separated from Dane and the others, and getting bitten to be invulnerable to the undead plague.

"Do yourself a favor and forget about your friends," Trithilia said.

Bren shook his head. "I can't do that. They're all I have. And they'll need me."

"Your beast blood could get them killed."

"That's why I'm here — so I can learn to control the beast blood."

Trithilia looked at him over her shoulder, and then at Harryck. "Harryck didn't tell you, did he?"

Bren glanced at Harryck. "Tell me what?"

"It doesn't matter," Harryck said.

Trithilia continued: "You can control the beast blood, but there's also a chance you'll lose your mind in the process. You'll reach a point in your training where your mind and body will be able to tame it, or they will deteriorate and consume you. The beast blood wins at that point."

Harryck glanced at Bren under thick eyebrows to see if he was upset with him, but all Bren said was: "That changes nothing. I'm in trouble either way, so I'll take my chances trying to control the curse."

"Curse?" Trithilia echoed.

"Curse. I didn't ask for it."

Trithilia scoffed. "If you're going to venture back out into the world, you may be grateful for your 'curse' some time very soon."

Bren did not argue, considering Trithilia's loss of her child. He intertwined his fingers and planted his elbows on his knees. He bit his tongue, and there was no more talk among them as she continued to prepare the meal. Even after it was finished, there were only idle attempts at small talk.

Afterwards, Harryck sat with his feet propped on the table and he dug between his teeth with his fingernails while Trithilia cleaned up the table. She smacked the sole of Harryck's foot with a wooden spoon and he drew them off the table in a quick movement.

"Woman!" he shouted as he glared at her.

"Keep your feet off the table. We are civilized people here – in case you've forgotten." She took the dishes away to be cleaned and Harryck growled and muttered quietly to himself.

Bren cleared his throat as he stood. "Thank you for the meal. I'm going to take a walk — explore the village and clear my head. It's been a long couple of weeks."

"Aye." Harryck nodded.

Night had completely enveloped the village. Bren walked down the rickety wooden steps and placed his foot onto the dirt road. He looked both ways and found that most of the village's inhabitants had retreated indoors. The coolness of the dark felt good as it chilled Bren's skin. He picked a direction and began walking.

His thoughts went immediately to his friends. He hoped that all of them had escaped Etzekel and made it to Bandimere safely. He was anxious to begin his training soon, so that he might rejoin them there. Bren's thoughts also turned to Doompoint. If Marek had delivered the message as he was supposed to, everyone knew of Pelias' plan to go to the ruins alone. Perhaps the others had convinced him otherwise, or at the very least accompanied him there. He just hoped he would be able to find them wherever they were. This village was not where he wanted to be.

"Hey, stranger!" someone called, as if to echo his thoughts of loneliness. A slender blonde woman was following behind him. Her hair was wild and unkempt, and her burnished skin was smudged with dirt. Despite her untamed look, her eyes were alight with curiosity and they were accompanied by a playful smile. "Where do you come from, tall stranger?"

"I have travelled across the Platinum Plains with a man named Harryck for a couple weeks to get here. Before that, I wandered the forests of the realm," he replied.

"What might your name be?"

"Bren."

"I like it. Think I might have you for a husband. Would you like that?"

Bren took a step back, holding his hands before him. "I don't know how you do things in this quaint little village you have here, but I am not of this place. You will have to find a husband elsewhere."

"Oy, you don't think I'm pretty?" She extended a taut leg out towards him, grinning.

"I didn't say that. I'm not looking for a bride at the moment, is all." Bren attempted to continue shifting away from her, but she followed him. "Besides, I don't even know your name." He did not know if this woman was crazy or if no one had warned him of some strange custom amongst lycan's.

"Veesha. Now marry me." She jumped at Bren and tried to wrap her arms around his neck in a hug, but his height gave him an advantage. He put his hands on her shoulders and gently pushed her away from him.

"I'm not interested. Thank you."

"I could return to the forest and kill a mountain lion for you. Would that make you love me?"

"That would be impressive, but no," Bren said. The woman scowled.

"Veesha, leave him alone." Harryck strolled up to them, holding a bottle from which he took a long drink.

"Harryck, you're back!" She jumped at him and threw the embrace that Bren had denied onto him. "Have you returned to marry me?"

Harryck chuckled. "Were it that I could, woman. But Trithilia yet lives."

"Remember!" Veesha jabbed a finger into his face. "If she dies, you become mine."

"Run along, woman. Leave me to talk with my friend." Veesha kissed him and then turned and sprinted down the road.

Bren shook his head in awe. "You people have some very strange customs that I will have to get used to."

Harryck laughed and offered Bren the bottle, which he accepted. "That's not a custom. Veesha isn't right in the mind. She stumbled here from somewhere deep in the mountains long ago. She was alone and feral, and on the brink of death. We nursed her back to full health and she ran off back into the mountains. We thought to never see her again, but weeks later she returned with food she had killed. She still disappears for weeks at a time, but she always comes back."

"Is she a lycan?"

"She is. She did not like the idea at first, but once I told her how much more game she could kill and how easily, she changed her mind."

"That's very odd," Bren said.

"She desperately wants a husband for some reason. No one has ever been able to understand why. Perhaps wherever she's from it means something important."

"I wonder where she's from?"

"Deep in the mountains."

"I thought only dwarves lived that far north? They're the only ones who can stand the cold."

Harryck shrugged. "I don't know, and I don't really care. Give me that bottle back." He led the way back in the direction of his house. "You should take a couple days to rest before you start your training. Regain some of your strength and get to know the people here."

"No. We'll start tomorrow."

Harryck sighed. "I knew you would press it. Fine – it makes no difference to me. Don't expect the results you want while you're fatigued, however."

Bren chuckled. "I may surprise you."

* * *

"Pelias went this way, for certain," Marek said. He was the first to muscle through the foliage and into the small clearing where they now stood. The bodies of several undead corpses littered the area densely.

"I wonder how you can tell," Koda quipped, curling his lip at the stench of the dead.

Dane said, "If the bodies weren't cold as they walked about, we might be able to tell how far ahead of us he is."

"Your friend is very skilled to face this many of the demons alone," Asira said.

"He was Chief Commander of the Kingsguard."

"He's still only one person," Caulen said — hoisted in his perch that was Grunt's arms.

"Let's keep pressing on," Dane said.

"We'll be needing water soon," Evie said. "There's just enough for a few sips."

"We're going to need a lot of water. The Red Crescent Desert is a desert for a reason," Koda said. "Luckily for you, I hail from the sand-covered hell. There's a stream not far from here if we divert our path slightly to the west. It won't put us far off course."

"Will we be able to return to Pelias' path?" Dane asked.

"He's leaving quite the trail." Koda swept his arm about. "I also know every location of every oasis in the desert. We won't be long without a reassuring pool."

"Lead the way, then."

"So what exactly is the plan?" Asira asked as they marched on.

"Wouldn't you like to know?" Koda said. "Ha! So would we!"

"We don't know exactly what'll happen once we get to Doompoint, but hopefully we can keep Pelias from doing anything stupid," Dane explained. "The best thing that could happen is we catch him before he even makes it there."

"He believes the source of the undead can be found there?"

"He does. And with good reason, I suppose. Supposedly his friend the prince was banished there for using dark magic, and he believes he's still alive doing it."

Asira furrowed her brow. "Prince Uragon is a magi?"

"I guess so. No one knew it, though."

"Or perhaps he learned how. To think... holding such a vile power. I will stick to my own."

Dane chuckled. "If Pelias' hunch is right, Uragon won't be a problem much longer."

"Will your friend be able to kill *his* friend?"

"If he can't, one of us will," Marek said, scratching at his beard. "Any one of us will be eager to."

"After that, then what?" Asira asked.

"Lady, you've got a lot to learn," Koda said. "We're not really a 'plan ahead' kinda people."

Asira grinned and looked at Dane. He shrugged. "He's right about that."

Koda led them promptly to a cool stream of crisp, clear water. He planted the blunt end of his spear into the ground and leaned on it. He had a self-satisfied look on his face.

Evie walked among everyone, taking the water skins they had. Between the seven of them, they only had four. "We'll have to conserve as much as possible," she said, holding the skins in her arms as she knelt by the stream.

All of them took a moment to relax and spread out from each other. Grunt set Caulen down in the soft grass with his back against a rock. Marek searched the stream for fish he could skewer with his trident while Asira scavenged for any herbs or plants she could harvest for medicinal purposes.

Dane sat in the grass next to Evie as she dipped one of the water skins into the stream, feeling the cool flow of the water. She smiled at him and he smiled back. "I wish there was occasion to smile more often," Dane said. "Your smile makes me happy."

Evie beamed more at that. "I think one day this world will return to its previous state — at least something similar. I hope it will, at least."

Dane nodded and looked away, squinting into the forest. "I do, as well."

Evie removed the first water skin and fitted the cork before submerging the next one. "You never talk about mother."

Dane looked at her, startled. "Where did that come from, Evie?"

"It's difficult to keep her from my thoughts these days. Our lives are filled to the brim with death and decay and mother was the first death I remember." She sighed. "Now, Amir is gone, Etzekel is razed, Bren is missing, Caulen came close to death, Llanowar and Marleyn were beaten to death, and Pelias may very well be on his way to the afterlife."

"Don't speak like that," Dane said, reaching out and placing a caring hand on her back. "We can still get to Pelias, and Bren might be safe somewhere."

Evie shrugged. "I just wish you would talk about mom more. Sometimes I feel like you've forgotten about her."

Dane looked her in the eyes, and they shared a sad gaze. He shook his head. "I could never forget your mother." He propped his hands on his knees and pondered for a moment. "I've seen a lot of death. I've never gotten used to it. Some men can – I cannot. I was a sellsword because I was good at it, but I left that life for you and your mother. Part of me died when that sickness took her. It's not easy for me to talk about."

Evie nodded. "I understand. I'm sorry it's so hard on you. If there's anything I can do for you, Dad..."

Dane chuckled. "I'm *your* father. I take care of you, not the other way around."

Evie grinned. "We're all we have."

"That's not true." He jammed a thumb over his shoulder at the others relaxing away from them. "We have our friends."

"I'm glad to have them." She smiled brighter, and so did Dane.

"Me too."

The two of them sat in silence as Evie filled the third water skin and moved on to the last one. He watched as she flexed her fingers and let the water flow between them. The way she sat on the bank of the stream and the very way she extended her arms was like a vision of the past for Dane.

He said, "You actually remind me of her a lot – your mother."

"I do?"

Dane nodded. "Especially right now. When your mother was pregnant with you, I would accompany her to one of the wells in Eden. The very way you dip the water skins and run your hands through the water reminds me exactly of her. It's uncanny."

"That makes me happy." Evie beamed. "It's silly because it's such a small thing, but..."

"Sometimes the small things mean the most."

"Like this time that we're spending together right now."

Dane and Evie smiled at one another.

Once Evie had finished filling the skins, they both stood, and Dane called everyone back to him. "We're ready for the desert, Koda," he said. "You take point from here on out. We'll follow your lead."

Koda grinned. "Never fear. I've traversed this accursed wasteland more times than I wished to. You all couldn't be safer than you are in my hands." He pointed with his spear off into the forest. "We must pick up Pelias' trail once more so we can make sure he's going in the right direction."

And so, the rest of the company trailed behind Koda as he blazed a fleet-footed path towards the untamed sea of sand.

Chapter 16

Bren heard the door open behind him and Harryck stumble into the sunlight, rubbing his eyes and yawning. He stretched as the sun warmed his stiff body. A grin of smug content spread on his face as he searched for Bren.

Bren took a bite of his peach and scowled as Harryck sauntered to him nonchalantly. "I've already shaved my head and trimmed my goatee this morning. You rise well after the sun," he said.

"For the first time in a long time," Harryck replied. "Surely you won't hold it against me to stay in my wife's arms for as long as possible?"

"I thought you two were currently at odds?"

"Bah!" Harryck waved the thought away. "We'll make up eventually. Then we'll keep you up all night!"

The jest did not amuse Bren. "I hate to think of how much of the day you'll waste the day after."

"It's not a big place. You could have wandered alone."

"I don't know anyone. Am I supposed to ask strangers for help in taming the beast blood? I don't know who can help me and who can't."

"Quit your whining. We can make up for lost time. Let's go."

As the two of them walked down the dusty road into the village, Bren said, "Your demeanor now is very different from when I rescued you in Etzekel."

"I was a caged slave there. Are my lifted spirits a bad thing?" Harryck asked while giving Bren a sideways look.

"Not a bad thing. You just lack the determination you had then."

331

"I will not apologize for losing focus, Bren. I come home to my wife to find that she's gotten my son killed."

"You can't blame her for that."

"Like hell I can't," Harryck muttered.

"Certain things are out of our control, even though we may desperately want to change them. Don't you think Trithilia would go back and prevent that if she could?"

"It doesn't matter now, does it?"

"It does. You're clinging to this grudge."

"Were you in my place, you wouldn't find forgiveness as easy as you think."

"I hope I'm never in your place, Harryck."

"I hope you never are, either, Bren. I don't want to talk about it anymore. There are people you need to speak to."

Several people acknowledged the two men as they walked through the village, but Harryck made no effort to stop and conversate with them. No one was offended by his curt nods and lazy waves, they just continued with their business. Harryck and Bren walked inside a thatch-roofed house that was identical to all the other ones around it.

Inside sat an elderly man and woman, sipping some sort of hot tea and chatting idly. At first, Bren suspected these two to be the elders in charge of the village, but then he remembered what Harryck had said. The two smiled at Harryck and Bren both as they sat down near them.

"You don't look familiar," the woman said, looking at Bren. "New friend, Harryck?"

Looking up, the man interrupted: "A large friend, at that."

Harryck said, "I have brought him here so he can control his lycan form. I had to give him the gift without much choice, and he wants to be able to control his transformations."

Both nodded and looked at Bren. The woman said, "You do realize this is not an easy task, correct?"

"And it may not always work," the man added.

"I do," Bren said.

Both smiled and chuckled at each other. "It requires great will to be able to control the beast inside of you," said the man.

"It will fight you the entire time," the woman added, raising an index finger. "There's a possibility that your lycan form dominates your mind and you will never be able to turn away from it. You will be forced to be a wolf for the rest of your days. Even if that doesn't happen, you may at the very least go insane."

Before Bren could speak, Harryck interjected: "Bregga, he already possesses a strong will. He had no memory loss after just his second transformation. How many people do you know that have done that?"

The woman, Bregga, raised her eyebrows. "Just a few." She glanced at the man.

He shrugged. "We will start your training soon, then. Harryck and I will accompany you into the mountains away from the village. That is for everyone's safety – in case your training doesn't go the way you expect it to."

"I'm not sure *what* to expect," Bren said.

"Good. It's better that way."

Harryck cleared his throat. "Bavin, do I have to go?"

"Of course you do! I'm an old man. I'll need you to help carry my things." He chuckled and grinned mischievously. "Also, if your friend goes mad, I'll need you to protect me."

Bregga laughed. "We both know you could still whip this pup – even as old as you are." Harryck smiled, but Bren remained quiet.

"Stop being so lazy, Harryck. Pack whatever you need. We'll start tomorrow."

"I don't know that we have enough mead for me to take into the mountains," Harryck chuckled.

"Why tomorrow?" Bren asked. "It's early still. We can start this afternoon."

Bavin gave him a quizzical look. "This one's eager," he said to Bregga before returning his gaze to Bren. "Because I'm old! I move slower than you. Tomorrow we start, now shut your mouth and get out of here."

Harryck laughed at Bren's awkward fumbling. He grabbed Bren by the elbow and led him away from the two elders. As they emerged from the house and into the sunlight, Bren said, "That was quite possibly the strangest interaction I've ever had with anyone. They didn't even ask my name."

"Because they don't care, I promise you." Harryck continued to laugh. "The siblings have seen so many people in their lifetime that they no longer choose their words. They speak them as they come to mind."

"A luxury afforded by the elderly," Bren said.

Harryck laughed. "I hope I live to be that old one day. There are quite a few people I would like to tell how I really feel about them."

"You mean you've been holding back?"

Both men laughed together as they returned to Harryck's home.

* * *

"C'mon! He's been laid up for days! He needs to tell us something!"

Leyon sighed as he sat on the ground with one hand propped on the pommel of his club. He was blocking the entrance to one of the few buildings in Bandimere that was still standing.

"We need to know something, Leyon. Most of us are dead now!" The Ravagers had crowded together outside the hut and were growing ever restless.

"I bet Braxon's dead and Leyon doesn't wanna tell us!"

Leyon had never been one to care what people thought of him. He could have corrected them and told them that he had no idea the state of Braxon's health, but he decided to let them think what they wanted. It had no bearing on him.

"Hey, don't ignore us, you maggot!" One human stepped forward – a towering brute with no hair on his head but a bushel of it on his face falling all the way down to his stomach.

Leyon looked up at him and scowled, taking a sip of water. Still he said nothing.

The man's hand came down to swat the water skin out of his hand. The man said, "Tell us about Braxon. He's dead, isn't he?"

Leyon sighed again and looked the man in the eyes. "I don't know anything more than you do. If he was dead, Aiya would tell us. Until that time, assume he's breathing and wait for his command."

"Bugger off, Leyon! You the man's lapdog? Why don't you go in there and lick his wounds for him?"

The man took to laughing before Leyon reached out with his free hand and yanked on the man's beard. His size afforded him an anchor so Leyon could pull himself to his feet while bringing the man down to his size. Leyon brought the club up to smash him in the face. He stumbled backward and Leyon took another swing, and then another, and another.

Soon, nothing remained of the man's face except for a mangled mass of flesh and bone. Leyon leaned on his club like a cane and eyed each of The Ravagers suspiciously. They were not so eager to goad him now.

A couple of The Ravagers creeped forward to remove the fallen human's weapons and valuables, but they kept cautious eyes on Leyon, who glared down at them. He took a quick head count. Nine Ravagers left, not counting himself and Aiya. There were no other warriors of note left, just the bilge of the bunch. Not even Rorn had survived the attack on the little village.

Leyon heard his name called and he turned to see Aiya standing in the doorway of the hut. "Braxon wants to speak with you."

Leyon spit into the grass and hoisted his club onto his shoulder before walking inside. It smelled awful – a mixture of bodily fluids, dirty bandages, and crude elixirs and medicines. Leyon showed no sign of disturbance.

Aiya threw a curtain aside to reveal Braxon sitting up, his arm in a make-shift sling of bandages, stained red. He panted heavily as his gaze rose slowly to meet Leyon. Braxon looked him over and nodded.

"This is the first he's been awake," Aiya said, sitting down on the floor next to him. "He lost a lot of blood. Thought he wasn't gonna pull through."

"You look healthy, Leyon… How did the others fare?" Braxon asked in a raspy voice. He cleared his throat after his sentence ended.

"There are eleven of The Ravagers left," Leyon replied, "including Aiya and myself."

"Good fighters?"

"Compared to the ones we lost? No – shit, all of them."

"Rorn?"

"Dead."

Braxon grunted.

"Good riddance," Aiya said, "he was starting to whine like a woman."

"Are there any other buildings still standing nearby?" Braxon asked.

"Yes. Across the street. It's where the men have been sleeping," Leyon replied.

"I don't want them to see me like this; surrounded by filth. Gather all of them there. I'll be out shortly."

"Braxon's alive, then?" an elf asked.

"He is," Leyon said. "He wants to speak to you all. He lost a lot of blood, so I'm going to go help him across the road." He shut the door and quietly lodged a few wooden wedges around the door frame. When he turned, Aiya was already helping Braxon down the steps – dressed in his old attire and his sword belt on his waist, but his arm in a fresh sling. After a couple steps, Braxon gently shoved her away, staggering, but quickly gathering his footing.

Aiya disappeared inside and Braxon approached Leyon. "Are you sure you want to do this?" Leyon asked.

"Do you hold any of their lives valuable?"

"None," Leyon replied.

Aiya returned holding a burning torch. Braxon took it and immediately tossed it on top of the thatched roof without hesitation. They watched as the fire spread quickly. It took a few moments for the people inside to smell the smoke. Cries of fear and pleading erupted in a short time. Leyon, Aiya, and Braxon watched the fire burn and listened to the screams.

Braxon eventually turned to Leyon. "I trust your evaluation of them was correct. If they were as useless as you say, they would have gotten in the way. With just the three of us, we can move faster, which is what we need now."

"When the fight comes, will we win? Our numbers are smaller than our prey's," Aiya said.

Braxon did not immediately respond. He turned his gaze back to the fire, which had by now engulfed the entire building. The cries for help had turned to cries of pain and anguish, but fewer voices now lent themselves to the wave of screams.

Braxon replied: "Nothing will stand in my way."

Chapter 17

The rays of sunlight sunk down onto the company as if they had weights chained to their arms, legs, and necks as they trudged through the sea of sand. The wind swirled to form small tornados, casting granules around their ankles. They were forced to move at a much slower pace than when they had travelled through shaded forests.

Dane, Marek, Koda, and Grunt were uncomfortable but not unfamiliar with the ways of the desert sun. Caulen and Evie still agonized over the heat and the sweat – even with Caulen being carried by Grunt. The boy swore that he could walk, but Asira warned that it was best to give his leg more time to heal. Asira herself was the least troubled by the heat. She continued calmly, barely sweating at all.

They had picked up Pelias' trail early on once they crossed over into the desert. The expansive wasteland allowed them to see for miles, and they could see the trail of bodies the former Chief Commander had left behind. Only there was something different about these bodies, Koda had pointed out...

"Less and less flesh on the undead," the gladiator said. "They've been dead a long time - all bones."

"If even the skeletons are reanimating, then we know it's not the plague," Caulen said.

"Then that means it *is* magic..." Evie added.

"Your friend Pelias was correct, then," Asira said. "It is no plague at all, but dark magic."

"Look," Dane said, pointing from one skeleton to the next. "Weapons nearby every single one of them. They've never fought with weapons before."

"New tricks," Koda said, scowling.

"We'll just have to be more careful. Uragon has to be stopped."

They continued their march, sweating in silence. A desert lizard scurried away from them and burrowed underneath the sand. Over the rolling dunes, they heard a sand cat crying out.

Marek shifted his trident from one hand to the other as he stepped to match his pace with Grunt. He smiled nervously up at the giant, who glanced down at him. "Back in the desert again, eh, Valyn?"

Grunt glared down at him for a few moments as they continued walking. Caulen glanced from one man to the other, still in the giant man's arms.

"Grunt, then?" Marek asked.

Grunt gave a small grunt and looked ahead.

"Camel Row isn't far from where we're going, I don't think." Marek pointed across the sands. "If we diverted our course a little to the southeast, we would get there."

Grunt made no reply to acknowledge.

"Not that I want to go back," Marek said, looking up at him again. "I know I've already apologized once, but I felt the need to do so again. So, I'm sorry."

Grunt shook his head, keeping his eyes straight ahead.

"Look, I thought the magistrate would honor our agreement. I swear I meant to win you your freedom. He would have killed us all if I had not stayed behind. But I didn't know he would harm you afterwards."

A low rumble welled from Grunt's throat.

"Is it Ivan, then? Did they kill him?"

The giant nodded.

"I can't blame you for being angry about that. I know how much he meant to you. I promise you, if I could take his place, I would. He deserved better."

Grunt glanced at him again, this time with sad eyes.

Caulen said, "I don't know what's happened between the two of you, but I hope you can reconcile."

Grunt now glared at the young boy, who just grinned back at him. Grunt sighed deeply before looking down at Marek. He gave the man a curt nod before locking his gaze straight ahead. That was all Marek needed. He smiled.

"Oh good," Koda scoffed. "Now that we're all friends, we can focus on the task at hand." He rolled his eyes, smirking.

"Don't worry, I'm not taking your only friend away," Marek quipped.

"No, but I was looking forward to watching him crush your skull." Koda grinned at him. Marek laughed. "I still want to know the story with you two someday."

"I don't intend to recount that tale," Marek said.

At the head of the group, Dane looked down at Evie, who held a blanket over herself to create shade. Sweat still glistened on her skin and her breathing was coarse.

"Are you okay?" Dane asked.

"I wasn't prepared for this," Evie replied, quickly adding: "But I can make it."

"It becomes more bearable the longer you're exposed to it."

"How many times have you been in the desert, Dad?"

Dane took a moment to think before he answered: "Eight times. The longest time was five months continuously."

"That sounds horrible!"

"Like I said – you get used to it." Dane grinned, though he too was feeling the weight of the sun more than he remembered.

"I hope I do soon. I hate this." She looked at Asira, who walked quietly on Evie's other side. "Why are you not sweating as much as the rest of us?"

Asira raised her eyebrows as the girl's words startled her out of her thoughts. "My magic allows me to regulate my temperature. I have also spent much time in wastelands such as this. This is much milder than the other deserts I've been in."

Caulen called out from behind them: "Akreya has only one desert."

"Akreya is not the only continent," Asira replied.

Caulen scrunched his face, wondering if she was playing a trick on him. He looked to the others for confirmation, but they all gave him a pitied look.

"You didn't know that?" Evie asked him.

He shook his head. "What do you mean? There are other lands?"

Dane and Evie chuckled, while Koda and Marek burst into laughter.

Caulen scowled. "I wasn't taught these things! Quit laughing at me!"

Asira smiled and nodded. "Yes, there are other lands across the oceans, in all different directions."

Caulen's jaw dropped. "Well how many are there?"

"Tough to say," Asira said. "New continents are being discovered every year."

"Are they different from Akreya?"

"Some of them are. Some are just deserts, some just snow and ice."

"Snow and ice sounds good right about now," Evie muttered, glaring up at the bright sky from underneath her shade.

"Do they all have people just like us?" Caulen asked, eyes wide at the possibilities.

"Some of them were the homes of elves or dwarves. Even humans had their own continents, but as time goes on more races inhabit these places and they become more diverse," Asira said. "Though, there are tales of human-like animals that can speak and carry weapons like people inhabiting other land-masses."

"Wow!" Caulen exclaimed.

Dane raised his eyebrows and cocked his head at Asira. "You've heard stories about these animals?"

"I have heard tales of many strange things, Dane," Asira said, smiling at him. "The world is a much bigger place than any of you know. You Akreyans should make it a point to see more of it."

"I've been to a few places myself during my time with the Iron Fox Legion," Dane said. "Marek as well."

"I like Akreya the best, however," Marek chimed in. "What can I say? My heart is here, my home is here."

"Where have you ventured, Dane?" Asira asked.

"Frenjjya... Ombalisk... Cradin... Kratan..." Dane tried to think. "I believe that's all."

"I have been to all of those. I liked the ice islands of Frenjjya the best."

"Too cold. It was a horrible campaign there," Dane said, his tone full of loathing. Marek grunted in agreement.

"Ice islands?" Evie asked.

"Clumps of ice surrounded by freezing waters off the coast of Frenjjya. All of them close together and connected by bridges. They're quite expansive."

"Who would live there?" Caulen asked.

"It's mostly dwarves because they can handle the cold better than anyone. We were hired to defend it for a time because a fleet of pirates had been harassing the dwarves. We dealt with them in a couple months."

"I didn't know the Iron Fox Legion was so skilled at naval combat," Koda remarked.

"The Iron Fox Legion is the best at all forms of combat," Dane said, grinning slyly back at him.

"I'll attest to that," Marek said.

"So then where is your favorite place?" Asira asked, looking at Dane. He opened his mouth to answer, but she quickly interjected: "Besides Akreya."

Dane closed his mouth and smiled. She had known exactly what his answer would be. "Besides Akreya?"

"Yes."

He thought a moment before answering. "Kratan."

Asira raised an eyebrow. "That is the last place I expected to hear from you. Kratan is nothing but marshes and swamplands. Most of the villages are built on stilts."

"The terrain isn't favorable, but it doesn't bother me. The people are very interesting to me. Their culture promotes respect, discipline, and honor. They are a very humble and quiet people. I like it."

"Humble and quiet?" Marek said, chuckling. "Don't you remember when Oddwen and Spencyr were kidnapped by cultists? Why don't you ask *them* what they think of Kratan?"

Dane laughed. "Besides the cultists, of course."

"Yes, besides a few bad apples, you are not wrong," Asira said. "Perhaps I need to spend more time there."

"I would like to go back some day."

344

"I want to go," said Evie.

Dane smiled at her.

"All of this talk of travel is well and good," Koda said," but you're forgetting one detail. We'll all probably be dead before this is over."

"Don't talk like that," Dane said, glancing at Evie and Caulen.

Koda laughed. "I think both of the children have seen enough death to understand. Better not to get too hopeful and die with regrets as the dead gnaw on our intestines."

"That's enough, Koda," Dane said.

Caulen said, "More bodies..."

"Yes, we're going the right way," Koda said.

"No, I mean the further we go into the desert, the more skeletons there are."

"Perhaps it seems that way because of your vantage point in the air," Marek joked.

"There are typically a lot of bones in the desert, Caulen," Koda said.

"I'm saying that Pelias is having to fight more of them the closer he gets to Doompoint," the boy said, agitated.

"He's right," Dane said as he topped the rise of a dune, looking both ahead and behind him where they had come from. "Uragon knows Pelias is coming for him."

"Do you believe we're going to find that prince still there?" Koda asked.

"I don't know for certain," Dane said. "Pelias' story seems far-fetched, but he isn't a liar. It's also quite a coincidence that the dead reanimated months after Prince Uragon was banished."

"Pelias was telling the truth," Evie said. "I read his thoughts as he told us the story. No deceit. Only sadness and determination."

This time Dane did not scold Evie for using her abilities. He said, "We can't slow down now. We have to catch up to him."

* * *

Pelias panted heavily as he straightened his back and stood with his hands on his hips. The helmet, breastplate, gauntlets, and greaves of the kingsguard were scattered around him, sand wafting and whirling over them. He held his red cloak in his hands for a moment, thumbing the tear where he had ripped off a strip to wipe blood from Cassandra's mouth.

How long ago had that been? He could not remember. The world now did not leave him much time to dwell on the past, and the thoughts of that little girl and her sister had long been vacant from his mind, and he felt a pang of guilt.

He clipped the red cloak around his neck and adjusted his sword belt to hang loosely on his hips. Perhaps it had been a mistake to carry the armor for so long, but he felt bound to it. Only when he realized he would die from the heat did he discard it. He could not fulfill his duty if he were dead.

Pelias' path to Doompoint had been rough — thick with opposition. The undead he faced had gone from freshly killed specimens to the skeletons of those swallowed by the desert. Some of the skeletons wore armor that was so ancient that Pelias did not recognize its origins.

The skeletons still tried to bite into his flesh. When their jaws snapped, there was the clack of bone-on-bone. Through what Pelias could only guess was the power of magic, their skeletal fingers curled around swords, spears, and axes to try and cut him down.

None of this fazed the young knight. The look of the enemy could change but it would never alter the fact that they were obstacles in his path. He would set right everything he had allowed to happen. Too much rested on his success. And so, he would not falter.

Pelias' hand rested on the hilt of his sword as he walked. His entire journey had been plagued by the presence of the dead, and now that he was approaching Doompoint, there were none to be found. His guard was up. He topped a rise and saw the ruins ahead of him.

Nestled in the sea of sand was an elevated stone building that resembled a temple of old. Large stone steps led up to the building. Stone pillars with flat tops lined a stone path that was hidden by sand, but Pelias knew it was there, leading to the steps. He approached from the front of the building.

From the top of the dune that he stood upon, he saw no one. Uragon was nowhere to be seen, and not even a single corpse roamed the wide-open area surrounding the dilapidated temple. Just as it had looked on his last visit, it was a long-abandoned temple with the sand chipping away at the stone for hundreds of years.

Pelias' eyes were squinted in focus as he carefully studied the landscape for a while longer. After making it this far, he could not afford to be caught unawares. It did not look to him like that would happen. He took a quick drink from his water skin and walked on.

There was a large expanse of open desert he had to cover before he even arrived at the stone path between the pillars, and he was careful to keep his head on a swivel so as not to be caught by surprise. He walked at a steady pace, but as he moved, he grew more uneasy. He tried to tell himself it was just fear welling up, but he eventually decided to listen to his gut. He drew his sword and stopped walking. He squinted again and looked all around him. No one.

As he took one more cautious step, a great gust of wind fell upon him, making his red cloak flap wildly, tugging at his neck as he raised his shield to guard his eyes from the swirling sands. The onslaught continued for several moments, and Pelias - eyes clamped shut - grabbed his cloak and brought it around his body to better cover his face.

In an instant, the gale stopped, and Pelias waited a few seconds to allow himself to recover. He tossed his cloak back behind him and slowly opened his eyes. What he saw made him grip his sword even tighter.

Surrounding him was an ocean of skeletons to rival the grains of sand upon which they stood. Some of them wore armor or bore weapons, but they all stared at him with the pitch-black sockets where their eyes were once housed. He shifted a few steps to one side, and then the other. Their heads rotated to follow his movements, but they made no effort to attack him.

All the undead he had faced up until this point had been extremely hostile and had wasted no time trying to accost him, yet these simply stared at him. A few of them repeatedly opened and closed their mouths, and it was not long until more and more joined in. Soon, a wave of chattering noises engulfed Pelias like an onslaught of desert insects. The clacking of bones grew louder and more rapid until it was deafening.

Pelias shoved the blade of his sword into the sand and reached up to unclip the cloak, letting it fall to the wind. He drew his sword from the sands and flexed his fingers around the handle on the inside of his shield. If the dead would not move out of his path, he would part them with sword and shield.

Pelias ran forward, giving a cry of courage as he did so. The skeletons did not react until Pelias brought his sword down into the first one. After that, all of them clutched their weapons and tried to attack. Most of them hit one another in the confusion. He continued to hack with his sword and bash with his shield. All the while, he danced about as if the sand were fire.

Pelias kicked one aside as he slammed another with his shield. He spun in a circle and caught several of them with his sword. He vaulted over one and brought his sword down in a mighty strike to split the weathered skull of one of the bigger undead. Still he remained untouched by them as he got ever closer to Doompoint.

Soon enough he was fighting his way in between the pillars, using them to his advantage as cover and to catch weapon blows intended for his head. As Pelias approached the end of the path and the beginning of the steps, he realized that the fight had been too easy so far. The undead he had met since he had left Bandimere had been more agile and cunning, as if they were better adapting to their reanimated bodies, but these were slow and barely put up any struggle.

While Pelias bounded up the steps, a giant skeleton wearing bright blue armor and wielding two war-axes stepped in his path. Pelias swung his sword at the corpse, but it blocked his blade with one axe before it used the other to hook his shield and rip it from his grasp.

Pelias leapt to the side as one of the war-axes swung at his midriff. He took his sword in both hands and rushed with a stab. The skeleton simply side-stepped and kicked him aside. Pelias ducked under another axe-swing and raised his sword high, yelling as he brought it down.

The undead leaned his head in to catch the blade on his helmet as it hooked its arms between Pelias' and threw them aside. The force with which the ghoul spread his arms caused Pelias to lose his grip on his sword with his left hand. With his arms open and no defense to raise, Pelias stared at the gleaming blade of the war-axe the skeleton raised above him.

The weapon fell, severing Pelias' right arm at the shoulder. He screamed as his entire arm fell to the ground still clutching his sword. As his foe brought his other axe out to his side to sever Pelias' head, all he could think about was the shame that fell upon him for his failures.

Tears welled in the young warrior's eyes and he closed them and lowered his head to receive his death with what little honor remained in him. He did not feel the flat side of the axe strike him in the head and send him rolling down the stone steps, bleeding as he tumbled.

Several of the skeletons skittered forward and clutched at Pelias' limbs and his clothing to pick him up and carry him inside the temple...

Chapter 18

Harryck and Bavin laughed as Bren tumbled in the dirt. The two of them watched him from the boulder they sat upon next to a crystal pool of water. They had ascended deep into the mountains away from the lycan village, and the three of them had made camp in a clearing to begin Bren's training.

This clearing had been used as the training ground of the lycans for several generations. Men and women had come here to tame their beast blood and control their transformations. As Bavin spoke of it, Bren could tell that it was revered as a sacred place to the village.

Harryck poured Bavin another cup of mead as they continued to laugh. Bren lifted himself to his feet and glared up at them. "I believe you're doing this just to make me look like a fool."

"That's not the primary intention – it's only a secondary benefit," Harryck said as he continued to laugh before taking another drink.

"A grown man should *not* be chasing squirrels!"

"You have to make a connection with the beast blood," Bavin said. "You must learn to enjoy the hunt, then you'll tap into the animal nature inside you. Then it will be easier to tame the beast."

"Isn't there another way?"

"I suppose we could have started with bears," Bavin chuckled. "You're a big man, but I would still bet on the bears."

"If we went with bears, he would die – and then we could return home where our mead supplies were more substantial," Harryck said, taking another drink.

Bren glared up at them for a few more moments but decided to hold his tongue. It would only serve to distract him and delay his training. He could not afford that. He turned and looked around for more squirrels to chase.

The moon was high in the sky when Bren found Bavin and Harryck stretched out lazily near the campfire they had made. They both glanced at him, smiling and saying short words of welcome. Bren saw that they had cooked a couple of squirrels over the fire. This made Bren grit his teeth. He had not caught anything all day.

"You were out late," Harryck commented, rolling onto his back and folding his arms behind his head.

"I was trying to catch the damn squirrels. What did you think I was doing?" Bren said as he found where they had laid his pack and began to unroll his blanket.

Bavin chuckled and sipped lightly on some mead. "We weren't sure, considering squirrels aren't nocturnal animals." Both of them chuckled at Bren again.

"I didn't know," Bren replied as calmly as possible.

Harryck said, "What did I tell you, Bavin? Persistence is one of his good qualities."

"I can see that." Bavin smiled at Bren. "Don't fret, young man. Tomorrow, we will make more progress. Today was more of a day for me to learn who you were as a person. If I wanted you to know how to control your gift."

"What do you mean?" Bren asked. "I thought you said I would go insane if I didn't learn how to?"

"That is the truth. But, if you were lazy or had ill intentions, perhaps it would have been the smart thing for me to allow you to turn and then put you down."

"You lycans are all insane, if you ask me, whether you control the beast blood or not," Bren said as he snatched one of the squirrels off the spit over the fire.

"It would serve you well not to separate yourself from us," Bavin said, now looking him in the eye. "The more you deny that you're a lycan, the more difficult it will be to conquer the beast inside you."

"Like it or not, you are a lycan now, brother," Harryck said. This remark was not accompanied by the man's usual chuckle. He rolled onto his side and propped himself onto his elbow. "I'm sorry I had to do this to you. If there had been any other way, I would have taken it. But that's in the past now. Accept what's happened. Accept what you are. Then you can begin to tame the beast blood."

Harryck rolled to his other side and pulled his blanket up to his shoulders. Bavin had laid down already as well, leaving Bren to stare into the fire and contemplate. Did being a lycan make him less of a person? Not if he learned to keep it in check. From what he had seen, the people in the village were not so different from he and his friends.

* * *

Pelias' eyes fluttered open. As they adjusted to the dimly lit stone room he was in, he saw five undead surrounding him, looming over him. He tried to scramble away to safety, but found he was restrained by heavy cords to a stone slab that was elevated about waist high.

He grunted and wrestled against the restraints, but they would not budge. Beads of sweat formed on his forehead, but then he noticed that none of the zombies

353

were moving towards him. They stood as still as statues, just as they had done outside of Doompoint.

Pelias realized that must be where he was – inside the temple of Doompoint.

The first of his watchers to catch his attention was a middle-aged man wearing black armor and a red cape, the same armor Pelias himself had worn for many years. It was clear this man was a member of the kingsguard, by his armor and by the large, two-handed greatsword on his back, but he did not recognize his face, the expression hard, tested. His flesh was sickly-looking, and his eyes were still white, but he was not decayed.

Beside him was a woman dressed in dark blue armor that resembled the scales of a dragon. She wore a plain helm with the visor up, showing a soft face that might have been beautiful if it were not pale with sickness. A blonde ponytail fell from under her helm and draped over her shoulder, while a longsword peeked over the other shoulder.

There were two elves standing side-by-side, wearing long cloaks that covered their entire bodies. By their faces, Pelias guessed they were brothers and that their bodies were packed with lean muscle. Next to them stood a stout dwarf. His body sported a few scars, and two sickles hung from his hips.

None of the five dead beings before him were rotted and stinking like the zombies he had faced before, and they were far from the skeletal beings he had met outside the temple.

Outside!

Pelias suddenly remembered what had happened and looked to the right side of his body. He remembered clearly the lurking ghoul that had lopped off his right arm, but he found it securely reattached to his shoulder. He flexed the fingers and each one responded in kind. He had heard of some people getting their limbs reattached, but there was no stitching in his flesh, just smooth skin.

Pelias' teeth were still gritted tightly, and his eyes were wide as they shifted around the room to each individual undead. He panted slightly, his heart beating a little faster, but none of them made a move to attack him, and even if they had he had no way of defending himself, so it did him no good to panic.

"I see you've made friends with my disciples, Pelias..." The soft-toned voice caught Pelias off guard.

The undead parted like a wave to make way for a cloaked and hooded figure. It was exactly who Pelias had thought the voice belonged to.

Uragon threw the hood back over his shoulders and smiled down at Pelias. Even after months of isolation, with no access to food, Uragon was still just as healthy as Pelias remembered him. No gauntness of cheeks, and though Uragon had always been lean he had somehow maintained his weight. His black hair had not grown any longer and his face was still smooth. The prince's manner had always been imposing, even if physically he was not.

The look in his eyes was all that Pelias noticed. His eyes smiled, shining with glee as he circled the stone slab, peering down at his friend, but there was also a hollowness there, and a madness that was filling that void. He finally stopped at one side and placed a hand on Pelias' bound arm.

"I reassembled you," Uragon said. "Your arm, I mean. I used magic to give it back to you. I hated seeing you bleeding out like that, old friend."

"Uragon..." Pelias did not know what to say. He had believed that Uragon had been alive for quite some time, but it had felt like a distant dream. Now, as he stood eerily over him, no words could do justice to explain how he felt. He was not even certain how he felt anymore.

"Hush, friend, you don't have to thank me." Uragon stood with his hands on his hips as he surveyed all the dead standing before him. "What do you think of my handiwork?"

"My opinion is the same as it was when you first began practicing your dark magic. You should have left it alone. I can tell by your eyes that you are merely a shell of the man I once called brother." Pelias found the words difficult to utter, and almost choked as they caught in his throat.

"You're correct. I am not the same person I was. I am so much more." Uragon made no effort to explain the thought.

Pelias stared warily at the man and slowly said, "Undo my binding, so that we can speak more comfortably."

Without looking at him, a chuckle came from Uragon which soon erupted into full laughter. He continued to inspect the dead as he did. Finally, the laughter stopped, leaving a smile behind. Uragon looked down at Pelias and said, "I have no need for your words, old friend."

Uragon moved around to Pelias' feet and waved his hand to someone behind him. Again, the crowds parted, and into Pelias' view strode the giant skeleton clad in blue armor and wielding the war-axes that had severed Pelias' arm outside the temple. It came to stand next to Uragon, and the man did his best to place his arm around its wide shoulders.

"Do you know who this is?" Uragon asked.

"He cut off my arm," Pelias said through gritted teeth.

A small chuckle from Uragon. "His name is Zenko."

"Zenko," Pelias said, startled. He knew the name. "Zenko the Cradinian Boar?"

"The very same. He founded The Wardens a thousand years ago. He fell here in the Red Crescent Desert while battling the specters that haunted the sands."

Pelias inspected the skeleton. Legend did indeed say that Zenko was a massive human, but Pelias had also met Grunt and Bren, who were large in their own right. He was not sold on the idea that this was Zenko. If it was, how horrible a fate this was for him.

Just as Uragon had mentioned, Zenko had founded The Wardens – an organization of warriors who specialized in fending off threats of the supernatural kind. Though The Wardens had been disbanded for over two hundred years for reasons unknown to most, specters, ghosts, phantoms, demons, ghouls, and even the undead had fallen prey to them over the time of their running. Pelias felt a pang of sadness that this man – who had devoted his life to fighting the supernatural – had himself been turned into one of them.

Uragon faced Zenko and opened his hands, aiming his palms at the skeletal feet. He closed his eyes and took a deep breath before slowly raising his arms up over Zenko's head. A curtain of shadow permeated around the zombie's body, rising as Uragon raised his hands. The thick, black fog swirled around and Uragon took a few steps back and stood beside the stone table Pelias lay on.

After a few moments, the shadows dissipated, whisking away into the air. The skeleton that stood before him was now covered with flesh again. Zenko's legs and arms were slabs of muscle. His face was whole, and Pelias could see he had a broad, flat nose and a mustache that stuck out like the tusks of a boar.

Any doubt that Pelias had about the skeleton's identity was diminished. On the zombie's neck was a scar in the shape of a 'W.' Members of The Wardens were required to have a W scarred, tattooed, or branded somewhere on their bodies. This was no doubt Zenko the Cradinian Boar.

"I've recently mastered full restoration of the body. Soon, I'll be able to recreate every one of my soldiers just as they were when they were alive." Uragon circled Zenko to inspect his work. "Just look at my other work. I call them my Elite."

Uragon swept his arm over the other five undead. He stroked the face of the female wearing the scale armor with the back of his hand. "This is Dovne. She's magnificent. She was a member of The Wardens years after Zenko was. Isn't it fantastic that they're here together? That wouldn't be possible without my magic!

"Ruven and Elandorr do fascinating work together," Uragon said, indicating the two elven brothers. "While you're focused on one, the other will slit your throat. They were the best assassin's money could buy in life, and death hasn't dulled their edges.

"Ulmus here once took down an entire camp of giants by himself. Yes, he's a dwarf, but he's speedy. Finally, there's Honlall, who was the first Chief Commander of the Kingsguard in Akreya. I'm sure you've read about him in the history of your order. His skill and teachings have been the basis of all techniques of the kingsguard, which speaks for itself. No doubt you employ those techniques yourself."

"Uragon, why are you doing this?" Pelias asked, swallowing hard.

"I'm no longer Uragon. Uragon was a weak man, with a soft heart that yearned for his father's approval. I no longer need that. My father is dead."

"You killed him. I know you did, through Sir Eins, right?"

"I had to. It was the ultimate test of my abilities. I had to know that I was strong enough to do what needed to be done. I am Raz-Mikai."

"Raz-Mikai?" Pelias shook his head. "That's a legend."

"The legend has returned." Uragon hunched over to bring his face close to Pelias'. "It took me a long time to realize it. Raz-Mikai was banished because foolish people were too blind to recognize the possibilities – much like my father and yourself.

"I was left here to die, and I had plenty of time to think. With the knowledge I've acquired and the magic I can perform, I realized I was Raz-Mikai reincarnated. I have a chance to do the things I wasn't allowed to in my previous life."

"You're not Raz-Mikai. Your name is Uragon. You were a prince, and you were my friend!"

Uragon straightened and furrowed his brow. He placed a hand over his heart. "Pelias, those are touching words, and I believe you mean what you say; however, they mean nothing to me now. Sentiments like that will only get in the way."

"Damn you!" Tears welled in Pelias' eyes. "What happened to you? You could have done so much good! You could have ruled and made the realm the most prosperous it had ever been, but you chose to forsake all that! Why? Tell me what the hell happened to you!"

"Are you weary of fighting, Pelias?" Uragon's tone was a whisper compared to Pelias' shouting.

Pelias took a few deep breaths. "What do you mean?"

"Are you tired of war? Of battle?"

"Peace is ideal," Pelias responded. "But I'm good at battle. I only fight in the defense of others."

"Such as my father..."

"Yes."

Uragon strolled back to the table and looked down at him. "I hope you don't blame yourself for his death. You could have been there to save him, after all."

"Why have you done all this, Uragon?"

"For peace."

"The realm knows no peace while your pets use Akreya as their hunting grounds."

Uragon smiled. "Try and look at it from my point of view, Pelias, and perhaps you won't be so angry."

"Enlighten me. I want to know your reasons for what you've done."

"As long as society is free and allows people to dream and think, the world will not have true peace. There will always be troublemakers – warmongers, thieves, rapists, murderers, and everything in-between. No one can be allowed to go unchecked.

"Every single one of the dead you've seen walking has been under my control. They do nothing without my command. If I told them to stop attacking and stop feasting, they would."

"Then do it, Uragon! Do the right thing!" Pelias pleaded.

"I'm creating harmony, Pelias, can't you see? I believe in under a year I'll have control of every person's mind in Akreya. With them all under my control, there will be no more war. This land will know true peace!"

"That is insane! Your plan for world peace is to reduce everyone to a walking sack of flesh?"

"Tell me another way for the killing to stop... I've thought it over. I wish we as people could get along without the shackles, but we can't. I don't care what anyone thinks. They can hate me if they want – that's fine. I don't despise any of them for being too weak to take the necessary action. I will do what must be done. My father couldn't, and who knows how many people he would have gotten killed because of Ularon's rebellion?"

"Uragon, you can't do this!"

"I can. There is an empire of bones underneath the sands, and I will raise it from the dead!"

"Let me help you get away from here. I'll help you fix what you've done."

Uragon smiled down at him. "Yes. You will." He swung his arm in an arc to indicate all of the undead. "Every one of the disciples you see before you are one of Akreya's legendary warriors from history. I've drudged them up from all across the realm, and I will use them to quicken my plans."

"Uragon!" Pelias shouted.

Uragon placed a hand over his mouth, still smiling. "Your skill rivals theirs, Pelias." Uragon cocked his head back to indicate the zombies. "You have earned your place among the ranks of my army." His voice was a whisper now. "Unfortunately, for you to fight for me... you have to die."

A knife flashed in Uragon's hands, and Pelias struggled against his restraints with no success. He watched with wide eyes as the point of the blade flew towards him. With a grunt, the knife pierced his heart...

Chapter 19

Bren screamed as his limbs shrunk. The hair receded into his body and the claws on his hands and feet returned to their normal shape. As his snout shifted and was replaced with lips, he vomited.

The puke splashed in the dirt between his hands. He heaved several times before collapsing onto his side. He held his stomach and tucked his legs in. He panted and rolled onto his back, staring up at the sky.

That was the second time he had morphed in the past few days. Both times had only been for a few minutes – much shorter than when he had transformed in the Plains. The frustration mounted within him. The transformations never came when he desired, and he could not hold form for long.

"That's good," Bavin told him, when Bren recovered and pounded his fists into the dirt in frustration. "Your beast blood is resisting."

"Why is that a good thing? If I'm to tame it, I need it to cooperate and listen to me!"

"Does something called 'beast blood' sound like something that wants to be tamed? I think not. It knows you want control. It doesn't want to give it up."

"You talk as if there is some kind of being inside me," Bren said, regaining his calm and sitting with his legs crossed as he looked up at the old man.

"In a way, that's true. There are lots of myths and legends surrounding the lycans, but one of the oldest is that anyone who is given the gift of the beast blood comes under the patronage of the goddess Lycania. She presents us each with a part of her spirit to live within us. The lycan spirits are wild and animalistic. Some allow the beast spirit to take over. But for those more civilized, we must learn to live in harmony with the animal side while maintaining control."

"Do you believe all that?" Bren asked.

Bavin smiled and lowered himself to the ground slowly, as if he were a fragile piece of pottery. "Me? Oh no. But the analogy is good for practical application and to help others learn. If you think of it in terms of trying to tame a spirit inside your body, fighting for control, it may help your mind grasp what needs to be done."

"Hopefully it quickens the pace."

"I think you're getting in your own way, Bren," Harryck said, offering him a jug of mead. Bren took a sip and awaited his explanation. "When you pursue wild animals, you have to be calm. They know when you're in a hurry and they will fight you even more to get you to quit. Same with the spirit of Lycania. All the energy you put toward worrying about how quickly you do this is keeping you from doing it at all."

Bren looked away and pondered the thought. It was true that he wanted to return to his companions as quickly as he mastered his transformation, but it did no good to worry about it. If he focused more of his energy into what he was doing, perhaps the time would not be an issue.

"There may be something that will help you," Bavin said, interrupting his thoughts. Bren looked to the old man. "We will train at night."

"Is he ready for that?" Harryck asked.

"I am," Bren said, scowling at Harryck.

Bavin chuckled. "He is, indeed. Bren, you've already shown superior mastery over your beast blood – at least more than anyone else who may be in your place. For as little time as you've had your gift, you show potential. The goddess Lycania shares a connection with the moon – I'm sure you've heard the myth about how lycans can only shift during a full moon."

Bren nodded.

"While transformations aren't tied to full moons, through Lycania – if one chooses to believe the legends – lycans do have a strong connection with it. It is the lens of a spyglass that Lycania observes the world through. Some claim that's why it magnifies a lycan's powers. Your progress may flourish if we train under the light of the moon."

"Why didn't we do that before, Bavin?" Bren asked.

"Because I needed to know that you were strong enough to even attempt the taming of your beast blood. If I had put you under the moonlight too soon, you could have transformed, and your beast spirit be too strong. You would have been stuck in lycan form permanently..."

"Is there anything I need to do to help me focus?" Bren asked. He stood in a clearing under the bright light of the moon.

Harryck, standing next to Bavin at the edge of the clearing, called out: "Try howling. It always helps me." He raised a jug of mead to his lips.

"Really?" Bren asked.

"Absolutely."

Bren sighed and clenched his fists. He ground his teeth together before looking up at the moon and letting out a loud howl that rivaled that of a real wolf. He only stopped when he heard Harryck and Bavin howling themselves – with laughter.

Bren realized he had been duped. "I'm glad you're entertained, but I'm looking for real advice, you jackasses!"

The two still staggered around, from laughter and drink. "I almost spit out my mead!" Harryck proclaimed.

Bavin raised a hand in peace as he tried to stifle his laughter. "Calm yourself and try to focus on the task at hand."

"I'm not listening to anymore of your advice!" Bren said, pointing at Harryck. He then closed his eyes and tried to think of transforming.

Bren thought about what it felt like when he transformed. Not just to grow and to have his arms and legs elongate and his teeth and nails change to fangs and claws. He thought that maybe it would be more effective to focus on how his mind shifted from his body into someone – something – else.

When he morphed, he could see, smell, taste, hear, and feel everything as normal, but it was almost as if he had no control over what his body did. At the same time, when he wanted to run, the lycan body ran. When he wanted to swing his arms, he did. When he bared his fangs, it was because his human brain had thought of it.

These thoughts led Bren to the idea that when he transformed, it meant the mind of this spirit beast took control. What if his human mind and his beast mind had the same thoughts, but one controlled the body when in his human form, and the other when he was in werewolf form?

Bren shuddered and his neck twitched as a cold sweat broke on his forehead.

Was 'taming the beast blood' simply melding the human and the beast mind into the same thing? That way he would have total control over both his forms? It

365

made sense to him. If he could control the spirit of Lycania inside of him, then there was no risk of transforming when he was not ready. And no chance of harming anyone he did not intend to harm.

Bren grunted and shuddered again. His legs suddenly went numb, as if all the strength in them was zapped away, and he fell to his knees. He clenched his fists as tightly as possible and tensed his neck.

"He's doing it," Harryck said, the jug of mead resting silently in his hand, undisturbed as he watched.

Bavin watched silently, calmly.

Bren had felt the tightness in his stomach before. His muscles quivered and strained as he knelt in the moonlight. The transformation came over him much stronger than any time before. He threw his head back and screamed at the sky above.

Harryck and Bavin watched on as Bren's body grew, his arms and legs stretching, his torso swelling. Hair turned to fur and sprouted along his entire body, and as his mouth expanded to shape into a muzzle, Bren's screaming turned to Howling.

Harryck gave Bavin his mead and took a step forward, squatting low into a ready position. He was prepared to morph at any second and fight Bren if he decided to attack. Harryck's eyes met Bren's, which now glowed red in the darkness.

Steam resonated from Bren's black fur in the crisp night air. He showed the two of them his fangs and slowly turned towards them. A low growl could be heard welling up from inside him. He snarled at Bavin and Harryck.

Harryck dropped to his hands and knees, but before he could transform, Bavin placed a hand on him. Harryck looked up to see Bren bounding through the trees, heading up the mountain, never looking back. The sounds of his paws padding against the dirt died off quickly, the werewolf moving fast.

Harryck straightened, though he did not look away for fear that Bren would return. "Well," Harryck said, "he'll either return successful in human form, or he'll come back in lycan form and I'll have to put him down."

Bavin chuckled and took a drink of Harryck's mead. "He's already won."

"How can you be sure?"

"He didn't even try to eat us."

"He thought about it," Harryck grumbled.

Bavin shrugged and chuckled.

*　*　*

A couple days had passed before Dane and his companions saw Doompoint. Koda had been sure to jump from oasis to oasis as he led them through the sandy wasteland. Grunt fought the wound on his thigh and they had not stopped much, but they could tell Pelias had stopped even less. Where they had hoped to catch up to him, they only were disappointed.

Now Doompoint was straight ahead, and there was still no sign of Pelias – though they had found his armor nestled in the sand. The only beings they saw were a dense crowd of undead around the temple. They were nearly trampling one another as they shuffled mindlessly about. The majority of the crowd were skeletons, but there were a good number of the wights with the rotting flesh the companions were used to seeing.

"We don't have enough people for a battle like this," Caulen said, kneeling in the sand as he inspected the enemy troops. He had finally made it out of Grunt's arms and his leg gave him no issues.

"The Iron Fox Legion has won against worse odds," Marek said with a wry smile.

"That's true, but we're not all fighters here," Dane said, glancing at Evie, Asira, and Caulen. "Plus, the dead have evolved. They've got weapons."

"Then what the hell did we come here for?" Koda hissed quietly through gritted teeth.

"I never dreamed it would be this bad," Dane admitted. However much he hated it, turning back now was not an option.

"Stay here, then," Koda said. "I'll go see if I can find Pelias. Maybe if I'm lucky, Uragon will be here, then I can gut him and finish this mess for all of us." Before anyone could protest, Koda had disappeared in a puff of smoke.

In the blink of an eye, Koda had materialized atop the nearest pillar of stone. He stepped to the edge and looked down at the mob of undead that gazed back up at him with their hollow eyes. Without wasting anymore time, Koda teleported to another pillar closer to the temple. Koda went from pillar to pillar, only pausing for a few seconds atop each one to monitor the movements of the dead.

"This is a bad idea," Evie said. "He can't go in there alone."

"He's just doing a bit of reconnaissance," Marek said.

Dane shook his head. "Koda won't avoid a fight. He'll create one, if he can. We need to get ready to move." He pointed at Evie and Caulen. "Not you two."

He ignored the groans of complaint and looked at Asira. "Watch over them, and make sure they don't follow us."

Asira ushered Caulen and Evie further down the dune as Marek and Grunt sidled up next to Dane. They watched as Koda continued to maneuver the pillars. "That's an awful lot of dead men," Marek commented.

As if in agreement, Grunt removed the giant battle-axe from his back and propped it onto his shoulder. Dane said, "And we're just a few living men. But we're good at killing."

"I should be able to take a lot of them out with my energy net. Save us some trouble."

"Let's go clear out the temple," Dane said, drawing his sword and leading the way.

Koda stopped when he realized that the pillars closest to the temple had toppled over time. He would not be able to teleport far enough to make it on top of the roof. He was focused on studying the temple, and he did not notice that on the ground the undead had begun to crowd together directly behind the pillar he was perched on.

Dane and the others could see it, however. Undead slowly clustered behind Koda's pillar. "What's happening?" Marek asked, squinting at the sight.

"I don't know," Dane replied, "but it can't be good. Koda doesn't see it. Run! Run!"

As soon as the three of them sprinted forward, the undead struck. As if the action had been rehearsed, the crowd of skeletons and zombies lurched forward, colliding into the pillar at the same time, like a giant fist. Koda fell off his heels where he had squatted onto his back. He peered over the edge to see that the dead had struck it, and now it was slowly careening towards the steps of Doompoint.

Koda tried to grasp at the edges of the platform, but with his spear in one hand he was unsuccessful. Dane, Marek, and Grunt watched as Koda slid off the pillar just before it crashed to the ground. In a cloud of sand, they could not see what had happened to him, but they did see several of the undead sprint forward into the cloud.

Dane, Marek, and Grunt sprinted as fast as they could, letting loose war cries as they collided with the mass of skeletons and ghouls. Marek began casting energy nets into the crowd, dicing them up with the powerful magic while fending others off with his trident. Grunt swung his axe in wide arcs, back and forth to meet the exposed skulls of undead. Dane's sword was lively as he fended off multiple opponents, his blade connecting with swords, axes, and other weapons.

The three companions had vanquished many of the dead, but they could tell that the crowd was not lessening. Dane craned his neck to try and find Koda in the madness, but all he saw were more enemies to fight. Dane ducked under an axe swing that almost caught him while he was preoccupied.

"Marek!" Dane shouted. "Put your magic to good use! We need to get to Koda!"

"I'm trying!" Marek replied, quickly shoving his trident down into the sand and summoning his magic powers with both hands to toss the nets into the crowd. Shards of bone mixed with sprays of blood stained the sky and the three companions began to make slow progress towards the temple where they had seen Koda fall.

"Grunt, cover Marek's right side!" Dane shouted. He himself had taken command of the left side of the battlefield. As they drilled deeper into the mob of zombies, their flanks had been put at risk as more of the foul creatures were making their way towards them.

Grunt and Dane fought to keep the flesh-eaters away from Marek as he continued to annihilate them in large numbers. Unfortunately, the further they got, the more the undead began to surround them. One zombie tried to slip by Grunt, but he was able to clip it with his axe and send it careening back into the crowds.

Dane was having a harder time. The undead on his side were less interested in Marek and instead drove toward Dane with full force. His sword whipped through the air with a speed and ferocity that neither Marek nor Grunt had seen matched before.

Even so, it was not enough. Dane was overtaken and tackled to the ground by three zombies at once. He fought to wrestle them off, but they trampled him as they attempted to jump back to their feet. He tried to maneuver away, but he was trapped. He gritted his teeth and growled.

Dane's nostrils flared, and his eyes burned as he glared into empty white eyes of the dead. He kept trying to push his attackers away, but could not. His strength was failing him, but he gave a fierce war cry as the zombies tried to bat at his arms and sink down to where they could finish him off.

His thoughts went to Evie. Surely, she was watching from the dunes, and he wished she did not have to see his demise. He wanted to scream and tell her to run away to safety, but he also wanted to tell her he loved her with his last breath. But all his energy was put into his scream of defiance.

Then a puff of black smoke flared in the sky above him and Koda was falling towards him. In one hand he held his spear in the other was Marek's trident.

Koda fell on top of one of the zombies and stabbed the other two before he hit the ground.

"Marek!" Koda called before tossing him his trident and offering the empty hand to Dane. Dane took it and was back on his feet. He nodded his thanks to Koda before grasping his longsword in both hands and looking around. The horde stopped their assault, shifting and forming a large ring around the four companions.

"What's going on?" Marek asked, grasping his trident tightly.

"I don't know," Koda said. "I couldn't get into the temple. I got surrounded and couldn't even teleport to the stairs. There's too many of them."

"I noticed," Marek said.

"You were right, Dane. We should have waited." Koda said, exasperated, shrugging at Dane, who was scowling at the crowd.

"At least we'll die having heard Koda admit he was wrong," Marek quipped, chuckling.

Grunt grunted loudly and pointed to the stairs of the temple where a young man wearing a hooded cloak had stepped out of the entrance. They looked at the man and knew that by Pelias' story this must be Uragon.

Uragon addressed them directly: "This is my empire of death! It is a young empire but see how vast it already is! I don't know why you are here, but it is unfortunate that you should travel so far only to be denied access to my ranks! But fear not, you may yet find yourselves among my many disciples! There is but one way! Raz-Mikai demands the ultimate showing of faithfulness: Death!"

All four of the companions furrowed their brows at the speech. They had all heard of Raz-Mikai – a legend from long ago that spoke of an elven magi who was the first to reanimate the dead.

Uragon must believe he's the reincarnation of that elf. Dane scoffed at the idea.

"I will take your silence as refusal to take the easy path," Uragon said, breaking their thoughts. "No matter – all come to serve Raz-Mikai eventually, through one mean or another."

"Stop!" Dane shouted.

Uragon ignored the call and walked down the steps. A familiar figure shuffled out of Doompoint. It was Pelias, no longer among the living. The four of them saw that Pelias' eyes were solid white but were fixed on them.

"Shit," Koda growled. Marek stamped his trident into the sand, angry at the sight. Grunt hung his head slightly. Dane watched with a heavy heart as Pelias looked away from them and followed Uragon into the open desert.

The two of them soon disappeared over the dunes. As soon as they were out of sight, the mass of zombies shuddered as one and resumed the attack.

"Shit!" Koda shouted again, stabbing the undead as quickly as he could as he and Dane went back-to-back. Grunt was quickly overtaken, though with his size it took six zombies to get him to stumble.

Marek rushed forward and used his trident to fend some of them off so Grunt could regain his footing. "Dane, Koda! Work your way over here!" Marek called.

Dane and Koda moved as one, covering each other's back from the onslaught. Once they were in range, the four friends formed a circle and were better able to defend themselves and each other.

"This isn't going to work forever!" Koda shouted and he speared two undead through the skull at the same time.

"I know!" Dane shouted back. "I'm thinking!"

"I've already got a plan!" Marek said. "Just watch yourselves!"

Marek slipped his trident into the strap on Grunt's back reserved for his axe. He ran a few steps ahead of them back in the direction they had come from, toward Evie, Caulen, and Asira, his hands glowing purple. He threw his arms out in front of him, sending two energy nets forward to cut a wide swathe out of the thinnest collection of undead in the barrier.

"Go! Go!" Marek shouted, ushering the other three forward. They wasted no time, and once they were out of the clutches of the undead, they turned to check on Marek.

First, they saw that several of the dead were still pursuing them outside the circle, and as they struggled to climb the wall of a high dune, they would soon be upon them. Dane tried to raise his sword as fast as he could, but before he had the chance to fight, one of Marek's energy nets trapped the foes, pulling them away from the three companions.

Dane, Koda, and Grunt watched as Marek casted his largest energy net yet. It arced out of his fingertips high into the air to envelop almost the entire throng of undead that cluttered Doompoint. The three of them watched as Marek gave a strained cry and pulled on the magic strings, drawing the nets towards himself. The purple beams quickly collapsed in on the crowd, retracting back towards Marek.

There was a flash of purple light, and the energy nets were gone – replaced with a cloud of blood and bone as big as the temple of Doompoint itself. The undead had disappeared into nothing but red mist, and Marek with them.

Chapter 20

The six companions had been walking ever since Marek's demise. Not a word had been spoken. Evie, Caulen, and Asira had watched the battle from far away and had seen everything. Caulen sniffled occasionally. Grunt carried his trident, his battle-axe resting in its holder on his back.

Dane had been looking down as he marched under the blazing sun. His mind was filled with thoughts of every friend they had lost up until this point. Marek was just the latest in an ever-growing list.

The thoughts had at first filled Dane with sorrow, but the longer he contemplated all the events, he started to fill with rage. He looked up and saw Koda some ways ahead of everyone else.

"Koda!" Dane called. The man kept trudging along, making no motion to acknowledge him. Dane picked up his pace and began to close the ground between them. "Koda!" Still no reply. Dane reached out and pulled on his shoulder, and Koda shoved his hand away, glaring at him.

"We don't have time to chat, Dane," Koda said, venom behind his words. "We need to keep moving."

Dane stared at him, surprised and angry at Koda's response. "I get that." Dane responded in a slow manner to try and stem the tide of anger inside himself, "But where are we going? We need a plan."

"I have one," Koda said, turning and walking away, this time at a slower pace.

"Would you like to share?" Dane asked as he followed. Everyone else had picked up the pace but remained a distance behind them.

"No, Dane, I wouldn't. You'll disagree and talk the others out of it. I think it's time we followed someone else's plan for once."

Dane gave a short laugh of incredulity, staring at the back of Koda's head. "If there's something you want to say to me, Koda, turn around and say it to my face like a man."

Koda whirled, glaring at Dane for a few moments without saying anything. Dane held the glare. Both of their jaws were gritted tight, as if trying to hold back scalding words. Koda clenched his fist and opened his mouth to speak but shut it quickly.

Koda took a deep breath and said: "We... are running... out of friends, Dane..."

"What are you talking about?"

Koda scoffed. "Our friends keep dying! They keep dying and dying! Ruddell and his little girls, Marleyn, Llanowar, now Pelias and Marek... And let's face it: Bren is gone, too. Bren is dead."

"We don't know that!" Dane said, jabbing a finger in the air towards Koda, his other fist clenched.

"It doesn't matter! We'll never find him now, even if he did survive Etzekel."

"Are you blaming these deaths on me?" Dane asked, taking another step forward.

"*You've* been telling us where to go since we left Eden. Yes, I *am* blaming you!"

"That's not fair!" Evie shouted at Koda, taking a step forward. Grunt placed a hand on her shoulder and pulled her back gently.

Koda glanced at her but looked back at Dane. They were now within arm's reach of each other. "Maybe it's not fair... but that's how I see it. It was your decision to go to Etzekel."

"But when we had to leave, we all took a vote!" Dane said.

"Yes, to go to Bandimere, but when that went to shit, when Pelias left, you didn't ask us – those of us still alive, that is – what we wanted to do. You followed Pelias like a lapdog!"

"He was our friend!"

"Yes. He was. But, he made a shitty decision and when we followed him you put the rest of us at risk. And Marek got killed." Koda put a finger into Dane's chest. "*You* got Marek killed. You. And you killed everyone else, too."

Dane swallowed hard, glaring at Koda. His hand shot up and grabbed the finger that Koda had in his chest and pulled on it, bringing the man into the fist that he brought up to hit him in the face.

Koda reeled back, holding his nose, glaring at Dane. Dane unbuckled his sword belt and threw it into the sand, walking slowly up to Koda. He raised his fists and said, "You want someone to blame, find someone else." He waited for the man to ready himself. Koda wiped the blood from his face and shoved his spear into the ground.

"Should we stop them?" Asira asked.

"Yes, we should! We shouldn't be fighting each other," Caulen said.

Grunt grunted and shook his head as he planted Marek's trident in the sand and placed his free hand on Caulen's shoulder. He held both children in place as Evie shook with anger and Caulen fought against his grip to rush forward and settle the dispute. Asira stood next to Grunt with her arms folded, watching intently.

"Try and hit me again," Koda taunted, his feet in a solid stance, but his arms dangling by his sides. Dane shook his head. He would not fall for any tricks. "Fine,"

Koda said, lurching forward and throwing his hand out in a quick jab.

Dane dodged the punch and threw his leg out to kick him. His leg was only enveloped in black smoke, and behind him Koda reappeared, his arm already drawn back as he glided in mid-air. Dane turned just in time to catch the punch on his jaw.

He rolled to the ground as Koda teleported again – this time above Dane. He came down from the sky ready to stomp on Dane with both feet, but Dane managed to roll to the side, hitting Koda in the thigh with a short kick. Koda fell to one knee as Dane jumped back to his feet.

Dane punched Koda in the cheek and intended to follow up with a knee strike, but Koda disappeared again, this time reappearing low and sweeping Dane's legs out from under him. The two men rolled in the sand as they grappled with one another, trading blows back and forth.

Their four companions watched as Dane finally won the grapple, straddling Koda and unleashing a short volley of blows to his face as fast as possible before he could teleport. The magi did not try and use his powers again. Finally, one of Dane's punches knocked him out, and he got to his feet, flexing his fingers and panting heavily. He looked down at Koda before staggering backwards a few steps and planting himself in the sand.

Dane looked at the others as they approached. He then looked to Koda's unconscious body where Asira had knelt beside him and was using her magic to heal his wounds.

"You got Marek killed. You. And you killed everyone else, too."

Dane put his face in his hands as a mist formed in his eyes.

Evie strode by Koda's unconscious body with her chin high in the air. Caulen glanced at her and then at Dane but decided he would assist Asira in Koda's treatment to give the two of them time to talk. Grunt flicked his eyes between both groups of people but decided to stay away from both, keeping his eyes peeled for approaching enemies.

Evie plopped down into the sand next to her father and put an arm around his shoulders, sitting silently. After a while, she spoke her piece: "Don't listen to Koda. He's a selfish bastard."

Dane rubbed the scar on his chin and looked at her, awaiting an explanation.

"You didn't ask to lead the people who followed you. No one else took charge or led the way. You did what you thought was right, and people followed. They accepted the fact that you made the tough calls. Surely, somewhere in their minds they knew you meant well, even when things didn't go as planned."

"But they're still gone. Those words don't change the fact they got killed," Dane said softly, fighting against the fact that his voice was trying to catch in his throat.

Evie shrugged. "It doesn't. And it's sad that they died, Dad, but if you give up now, you will disrespect them all. They died trusting in you to make the right decisions – or at least the ones you think are right. Quitting now is not the right choice."

Dane linked his fingers and held them in front of his face, his elbows propped on his knees. He said nothing, contemplating his daughter's words as he stared into the vast desert. He swallowed hard and blinked several times.

Evie sighed and squeezed her father tighter. "Dad, if you give up now, then you should have let us all stay in Etzekel. Our fates would be the same..." She kissed her father on the cheek and then stood up, joining Grunt away from the others.

Dane sighed. Her words almost brought tears to Dane's eyes again, but he choked them back. He bowed his head, muttering the prayers he remembered – the ones he only half believed in but hoped did his deceased friends some good. He said them for Pelias and Marek, but also mentioned Amir one more time for good measure.

Looking off into the horizon, he stood slowly – a new air of determination resonating from him. He saw everyone except Evie looking at him with raised eyebrows. He walked to where his sword belt was lying in the sand and picked it up.

As Dane began to cinch it loosely around his waist, he looked at Grunt. "I have to ask you to carry Koda while he's unconscious." Grunt nodded and strolled over to his friend, handing the trident to Asira.

"Where to?" Caulen asked, a small smile on his face as Asira forced Koda's spear into his hands.

"That direction," Dane said, pointing. "Wherever he was leading us."

* * *

Bren's eyes opened so slowly that he swore he could hear them sliding back. The sky above was a vibrant blue with not a single cloud in sight. The shimmering sun above him would have roasted him if he were not lying in a pool of cold water.

Bren sat up and splashed some of the water on his face to bring himself back to life. He noticed he was only wearing a pair of breeches. Apparently, his shirt had been torn from his body, for he found a jagged strip of it still tucked into his breeches.

Bren rubbed his eyes and then ran his hands through his short hair. Nearby was a waterfall that came from an adjacent cliff. He was at the base of a snow-capped mountain and there were many trees surrounding the edge of the pool he was in.

He remembered what happened. He remembered everything. He had spent a day-and-a-half battling the animal spirit inside him. He had wandered deep into the mountains outside of the Lycan village. He had barely rested at all for that length of time. He had fought the urge to kill, and aside from a few deer that he feasted on, he had gotten what he wanted.

Bren had conquered the spirit of Lycania within. It had been a long, grueling test of his willpower, but he had won. He could converse with his beast-side and give it commands to obey. He could stay in control of his lycan form.

He remembered coming to kneel by the pool, but that was the last of it. He must have collapsed from exhaustion right into the water. Bren smiled wryly at the thought of how he could have drowned just after his victory.

Finally, Bren forced himself to stand. His entire body ached, and he rubbed his muscles to give them some relief. With a contented sigh, Bren looked at his surroundings and smiled. Now he could go and join his friends at Bandimere.

Looking at the sun, he oriented himself and headed towards the lycan village.

Bren marched over rough, untrodden terrain for hours. He remembered coming this far, but in his werewolf form it had not taken him very long to travel in leaps and bounds through the mountains. But the slower pace did not bother him.

Bren's hunger grew as he walked. He noticed the emptiness of his stomach, and he stumbled into a clearing where a deer was drinking from a pond. It looked at him with its ears pricked and then skittered away into the tree line.

"Okay, let's try this," Bren said, planting his feet. In his mind, he spoke, *"Spirit of Lycania, listen to me and obey my commands. Come forth!"*

Instantly, he could feel the mind of his werebeast moving from his subconscious to the fore-front of his mind to meld with his own. This brought on the transformation immediately. With his werewolf abilities he chased after the deer. Compared to his supple beast-form, the deer had no chance.

After feasting, Bren said, *"Leave me. I'll summon you again when I need you."*

Just like that, Bren returned to his human form. He looked at the remains of the deer carcass and this brought a grin to his face.

* * *

The sun was going down. Most of the lycan village had already retreated inside their homes after a long, sunny day. Harryck and Bavin were enjoying the cool breeze that had wafted into the town and they shared a jug of mead outside of Harryck's home.

Harryck took a long drink before setting the jug down heavily onto the barrel that was placed between him and Bavin. "I tell you what, Bavin, I really thought Bren had what it took. I tracked him deep into those mountains, but he was gone... Oh well, at least I'm back to a steady supply of mead. What's a friend compared to that?"

Bavin glared at him as he picked up the jug.

"Not you, of course. I would never trade you for mead."

"What about grog?" Bavin asked before taking a drink.

Harryck shrugged. "Grog is good shit."

Bavin chuckled before looking down the street. He blinked and coughed, trying to focus on someone walking towards them. "This mead is really jumbling up my brain today. That looks like Bren."

Harryck looked and jumped off the barrel that he sat on. "That *is* him."

Bren stopped in front of them, smiling. "Are you gonna offer me a drink?" he asked.

Bavin held out the jug with shaky hands, smiling at him. He laughed. "I'm glad you made it."

"So am I." Bren took a drink.

Harryck circled him slowly, looking him up and down. "How are you here?"

"I walked. When I got tired, I transformed and used my beast-body to cover more ground."

"Damn. You were gone for four days. I followed you deep into the mountains – almost to the snow of The Dragon Fangs. We thought you were dead, for sure."

"Plenty of game up there," Bren said, a small smile still on his face.

Harryck looked at him and laughed, clapping him on the shoulders, holding him at arms-length. "That's fantastic. It really is. I knew you could do it."

"Thank you. Both of you." Bren looked at them both, affirming his thanks with a nod. "I'll be heading out tomorrow."

"What? What do you mean?" Harryck asked, yanking the jug out of Bren's hand.

"Don't act surprised. I told you I would be returning to my friends after I tamed the beast spirit. That's still the plan."

"We're your friends now, Bren. You should stay here with us where our kind belongs."

Bren shook his head. "Don't try and switch everything around now. I'll be leaving tomorrow."

"What the hell? So soon?" Harryck growled.

Bavin put a hand on Harryck's arm. "He doesn't have to stay, Harryck."

"But he should! After everything we've done for him!"

Bren held a hand out to calm Harryck. "Look, I'm not asking you to go with me. I'll be fine on my own, but I made a promise to myself that I would rejoin my friends when I could. You knew about this – it was my plan all along."

Harryck took a deep breath to calm himself and smoothed out his beard with one hand. He put the jug of mead down gently on the barrel behind him. "Bavin, go home."

The old man stood, groaning as his bones creaked. "All right, but I'm taking this with me." With that, he snatched the jug and started drinking as he shuffled down the street.

"Bren, I have to be honest with you," Harryck said. Bren listened for the rest. "I don't know if you've noticed the people here. The people in this village are either old and decrepit, or women and children. I'm one

384

of the few capable lycan's left here. There's only a few able-bodied men around."

"Where are the others?" Bren asked, crossing his arms.

"A lot of them have been killed. With news of what's been happening in the realm, they left to gather more information. Not many of them have returned."

"And the ones that haven't been killed?"

Harryck sighed again. He turned and reached for the mead, but cursed Bavin's name when he remembered it was not there. He turned back to Bren and looked into his eyes. Bren saw something he had not often seen in the man's eyes – sorrow. "The rest of them left with me and Trithilia when we went for Etzekel."

"You abandoned the elderly here?"

"We tried to get them to come with us. We would have guided them safely through the Plains, but you know how stubborn the old can be – just look at Bavin. We gave them a choice. Stay or go. They made theirs."

"So what happened?" Bren asked.

"A lot of my friends let the guilt get to them. They turned around halfway through the journey. I couldn't, though. I was doing right by my wife and kid. But I was wrong, and you can see that I've made amends with the people here. Trithilia won't leave them again, and so I made a promise – just like you – that I would protect the people here."

"So you understand what a promise means. Understand that I have to leave."

"I was hoping you would stay and help me preserve the life here. You're a damn good fighter. I could use your help... Please, Bren... I'm asking for you to stay and help me."

Bren shook his head. "I can't forget that you saved my life, Harryck. I owe you for that. But my friends have done the same thing. I owe them first... Tomorrow I'll leave, and once I've helped them, I'll come back and assist you here. I promise."

Harryck looked up at Bren and nodded slowly. The two men clasped forearms and embraced. Harryck said, smiling, "I suppose that's all I can ask. Don't die while you're out there."

Bren smiled and walked towards the house, leaving Harryck alone in the street.

* * *

Nestled in a sling, Braxon's arm was on fire. He kept his teeth gritted and ignored the pain as best he could. It was nothing he could not handle. He used it as motivation to drive forward and bring the traitors to justice.

Braxon, Leyon, and Aiya had pursued Dane and his companions into The Red Crescent Desert. Leyon had done well tracking their prints through the wasteland, but he had prompted Braxon ahead for fear of the tracks washing away in a sandstorm.

Braxon knew that they had to be close to Doompoint. It had been years since he had been there, but he knew how long it took to get there from the direction they had travelled. Bones of the fallen had done well to serve as markers in their travels, and the closer they got to Doompoint, more numerous were those bones.

Aiya had barely left Braxon's side. She was always there if he got tired and needed to lean on her.

386

Braxon was sure she was attracted to him, but things such as that mattered little to him. If she was willing to help, he would take full advantage of that.

Leyon, further ahead than the two of them, called: "Braxon, look here."

Braxon came quickly and bent down to pick up the black kingsguard helm. Braxon smirked. "He shed his armor."

"Doompoint's just over this dune." Leyon pointed.

"Perhaps we'll find Pelias' body. If so, our mission will be done and we can return to Eden. Or you can go wherever the hell you want to."

Leyon did not reply. The three of them cleared the top of the dune and looked upon the temple of Doompoint and the ocean of limbs, flesh, blood, and bone that decorated the area around it.

"What could have happened here?" Aiya murmured, mouth agape at the carnage.

They descended the dune and searched the temple grounds and even inside the temple itself, which was largely abandoned except for a few furnishings, but there was no sign of Pelias' body. They all gathered in the middle of the wreckage, inspecting and thinking.

"Perhaps he lies here somewhere?" Aiya speculated.

"I have to know for certain," Braxon replied, scowling and looking at the ground all around them.

"There's two sets of tracks leading away from the temple. Their deep, so that means they're fresh because there was less time for them to get filled with sand." Leyon pointed in one direction and then another. "The first set is heading northeast toward Jalfothrin-"

"Or Eden," Braxon cut in, looking that way.

Leyon nodded. "It's possible. The second set is heading directly west. That's the shortest way out of the desert."

"What else is that way?"

"Nothing. Just some caves and the ocean. However, the footprints of the giant man they've had with them are going that direction. I can't tell who's going northeast."

Braxon pondered for a few moments. "If Pelias is alive, and Dane and his band were here, then Pelias is with them heading west. That is if he's not here." Braxon indicated the carnage around them. "We follow them west." Braxon winced as a bolt of pain pulsed through his arm. He gritted his teeth and began marching.

Chapter 21

When Koda opened his eyes again, he was flying. He smiled as his arms and legs dangled underneath him. The sun was beating down on his face from the clear sky above. After his eyes focused, he saw Grunt's masked face looking down at him. He saw Dane, Asira, Evie, and Caulen were marching ahead of them.

Grunt put Koda on his feet and let the man take off on his own. They were still in the desert, kicking up sand with each of their footsteps. As Koda walked by Caulen he snatched his spear out of the young boy's hand. "Thanks for holding onto this for me, kid."

Evie – expecting retaliation – immediately used her magic to read Koda's mind. There were no vile thoughts there, and so she kept her mouth shut. She still eyed him suspiciously.

Dane glanced over his shoulder but did not stop walking. "How did you sleep, Koda?"

Koda chuckled. "Better than I have in a while." He matched his pace to Dane's, who was walking briskly. "I don't actually blame you for getting everyone killed. I just said that because I was angry."

"I know. But it helped me decide what to do."

"Which is?"

"This is the direction you were leading us. You must have had an idea in mind."

Koda nodded, propping his spear on his shoulder. "This is the quickest way out of the desert. If we stay this direction, we'll eventually come to the sea. We can find a ship somewhere along the coastline and get out of here."

Koda looked at Dane, awaiting a response. He saw the idea flickering in his eyes. Saw the lines on his face moving as he squinted to better envision the plan. Dane swallowed hard, still marching.

Finally, Dane nodded. "Akreya is lost. Uragon has too strong a hold here and we don't have enough warriors to fight him. If we want to live, we have to abandon this realm..."

"I don't like it any more than you do."

"I know. I just hoped we could save it."

Koda's eyes dropped to the ground. "I'm not a hero, Dane. I'm a survivor. I've always been for myself. And Grunt, because where would he be without me?" Koda grinned.

Dane looked at Koda as they both stopped walking. "That's not true, Koda." Koda looked in Dane's eyes, his smile fading. "You saved Pelias' life in Eden. You killed the cyclops. You saved my life at Doompoint... Maybe you *did* fight for yourself before, but you don't any longer. Stop trying to convince yourself you're something you're not." Dane continued walking.

Koda took a moment to consider his words. He finally chuckled and shook his head in amusement.

Two days later, Koda had led them out of The Red Crescent Desert and into the grasslands that separated the desert from the sea. Another half day and the six companions stood at a cliff's edge overlooking a mass of wrecked ships and smaller boats. Waves swirled and crashed, beating down on the already broken water vessels.

Koda looked dejected. "I'd hoped we'd find an abandoned ship fit enough to sail."

"We won't find it here," Caulen said, staring wide-eyed at the wreckage.

"What now?" Evie asked.

"Make for Yorkenfirth. There's sure to be a ship we can board at Port Trident," Koda said. "Let's stick to the cliffs as we travel, though, just in case we find a ship that's not torn upon the rocks."

Koda led the way and Grunt, Asira, and Caulen followed. Evie held her father's hand to hold him behind. She looked up at him with her hands on her hips. "Aren't you going to say anything?"

"About what?" Dane asked her, resting his hand on the pommel of his sword where it hung loosely from his belt.

"Koda is in charge now? Because he said some cruel words and hurt your feelings?"

Dane chuckled at his daughter, which only made her angrier. "I let Koda take charge because I agree with what he's doing. Evelyn, Akreya is doomed. I would rather we remain safe somewhere else than to die trying to defend a lost cause."

Evie's nostrils flared and she stomped away. Dane sighed and followed away from the rest of the group.

The companions stopped one afternoon to rest in the shade of some nearby trees. The best part of travelling near the coast was the cool breeze that wafted inland. A deer had fallen prey to them the day before, and now they built a fire to cook what was left of their kill. They also munched on some apples they had picked along the way.

"I like this much better than the desert," Caulen said before he bit into the crisp fruit, grinning from ear to ear, juices running down his cheeks.

"You got that right," Dane said. Grunt was standing watch, and so Dane took the opportunity to kick back against the trunk of one of the trees and close his eyes.

Just before Dane was about to doze off, he heard a commanding voice say, "You are surrounded! Don't try anything you'll regret!"

Dane stood up slowly and looked around for where the voices came from. He, Koda, and Grunt all huddled in front of Asira and the two children. The voice had come from the forest ahead, and behind them were the cliffs.

"Do you see anything?" Dane asked them.

Grunt shook his head.

The voice came again: "Throw your weapons down and we'll reveal ourselves!"

Koda looked at Dane and shrugged. Dane replied, "What is your purpose here? Are you bandits? We don't have anything of value."

"Just do as you're told!"

Dane looked back at Evie and the others. Their numbers were too low, and they were all too exhausted to risk a fight. He nodded at Koda and Grunt before unbuckling his sword belt and laying it gently in the grass at his feet. Koda tossed his spear to the ground, and Grunt did the same with his battle-axe and Marek's trident.

Koda glanced at Dane, titling his head. Evie's voice echoed in his head as she relayed Koda's plan to Dane. He could use his powers to quickly grab his spear and kill some of the foes to give them time to get their own weapons. Dane hoped it would not come to that. He did not want to fight. Several days without sleep had left him in no mood for combat.

A band of about ten men stepped out from behind trees, some of them dropping down from branches, and approached with bows drawn and focused on the companions. The men varied in age and race, and a few of them wore mismatched armor.

A couple of the men came forward and seized their weapons. They kept wary eyes on the companions as their friends held their aim steady. Koda looked at Dane, but Dane shook his head. Koda scowled and glared at the elf picking up his spear.

A human man stepped forward, slinging his bow over his shoulder. "Would the six of you come with us?" the man asked, his tone indifferent.

"What's your name?" Dane asked him.

"That doesn't matter."

"Like hell it doesn't," Koda said. "We have somewhere to be. We should know if you're worth our time or not."

The man was not dismayed in the slightest. "This isn't up for debate. I have orders, and I will see them through."

"And those orders are?" Dane asked.

"You'll find out if you just come with us," the man said. "I can't divulge any information, but I promise this is in your best interest."

"My trust runs pretty thin these days," Dane replied. He looked over his shoulder at Evie. Some of the men had moved to surround them, and were aiming their bows at her, Caulen, and Asira. Dane gritted his teeth but raised his eyebrows at his daughter.

Evie blinked her eyes slowly and looked at the man who was obviously in charge. He looked back at her with a questioning look, but after a few moments, Evie looked back at her father. "They are going to take us to their camp to meet their leader..."

"And?" Dane noticed the drop-off in her voice.

"It's Ularon." She glared at one of the men, who drew the string of his bow a little tighter.

"Ularon the Usurper?" Dane said, surprised.

The man in charge was finally pushed out of nonchalance and pointed at Evie. "How does she know that?" No one said a thing, but the man put it together. "She's a magi, isn't she?"

"What difference would it make if she was?" Caulen asked, straightening so he looked as tall as possible.

"You really must come with us now," the man replied. "Ularon is a friend to the magi." He motioned for Evie and the others to follow him. He also signaled for the others to lower their bows, to which they complied.

Dane reached out and put a hand to the man's chest. "If what you say proves to be untrue, and any harm comes to my daughter, know that I will kill you." The man ignored what Dane said, so he grabbed his shoulder and squeezed tightly. "I will even come back from the grave to do it," he added.

The man looked at Dane with a fresh look of indifference and said, "Lots of folks have come back from the grave recently. But it won't come to that. Ularon will treat you all right."

Unaccepting of any further objections, the man turned fast and began striding away from them. The others with them kept their weapons trained on the companions until they started moving. Caulen and Koda glanced back at their food and sighed as the strangers led them into the forest.

It did not take them long – about an hour – to arrive at their destination. Ularon's camp was the most disciplined and well-defended that Dane had seen since the outbreak of the dead. Sharp stakes of wood as thick as the average man's arm were driven into the ground and pointing outward from the camp. Dane knew that many of the undead would be ensnared on these if the camp befell an attack.

Behind the rows of spikes stood armed and armored sentries, evenly distributed every fifteen feet and keeping watch on the entire perimeter of the camp. They were alert to the approaching group but stood down once they recognized the men leading the companions.

Though there were a mass of tents in the camp, and a great deal of people, Dane noticed that no banners were lifted. Dane knew the sigil that Ularon had taken when starting his rebellion – a gold trident against a dark blue background – but the banner was nowhere to be seen. The sigil led Dane's mind to wander to Marek, but he did not allow his heart to grow heavy again, not now. He glanced at Marek's trident - carried by one of the strangers - before clearing his mind.

The people in the camp were a conglomerate of all races, ages, and genders – unlike any rebellion camp Dane had ever witnessed before. Some of the people were warriors, as evidenced by their armor and weapons. However, many of the people who had taken up residency in the camp were peasants and commoners who were cooking, cleaning, and mending clothes.

As the companions were being led through the maze of tents, Dane heard his name called. He snapped his head to the source of the voice and saw two familiar faces sitting on wooden crates. One of them was a man, several years younger than Dane, with short red hair and a kind face, though it had acquired a few scars since the last time Dane had seen him. The other was a bulky dwarf with a thick blonde beard. He smirked up at Dane as he stroked his facial hair in amusement.

Both the human and the dwarf came forward, pushing into the crowd and clasping hands with one another. "You remember me, don't you?" the redheaded man asked, still smiling.

"I couldn't forget that baby face, Spencyr," Dane chuckled, grinning, "though it's a little more battle-worn than I remember it." The younger man smiled and nodded.

The dwarf crossed his arms and cut in: "Well, if you remember him from when he was a poor sapling of a man, you must remember me!"

Dane nodded. "I do, Foggy. Still blowing all your money?"

"Aye! Whores and mead aren't free, m'friend!" The dwarf belted out a laugh.

The man leading them interjected: "You'll have time to catch up with your friends later. Come with me."

Spencyr waved Dane along. "Go ahead, Dane. We'll find you later. We have a lot of catching up to do." He waved goodbye and pulled Foggy away with him so they could continue walking.

"Old friends, huh?" Evie asked her father.

Dane nodded. "They were both in The Iron Fox Legion with me."

"I know." Evie smirked when her father gave a disapproving look.

"Stay focused, Dane," Koda said, cutting his eyes at him.

Most of the men who had rounded the companions up had dispersed one by one as they had mingled through Ularon's camp. Only the leader and two other men remained. They stopped in front of the biggest tent, which was standing in the middle of the camp. Its size was the only thing that differentiated it from the other tents. There were no frills or decorations on it.

The leader of the men stopped and spoke a few words to the guards standing outside of the tent, who responded with whispers. One of the guards poked their head inside, said a few more words, and then stepped aside so they could all enter.

As Dane's eyes were still adjusting to the dim light inside, he was taken aback. He saw a man – perhaps a few years younger than himself – with auburn hair down to his shoulder and an auburn beard much like Amir's. Dane blinked and took a hopeful step forward, but the man turned as his eyes oriented themselves to the light. It was not Amir, but the man did give a small smile that was not unfriendly, which reminded him of his lost friend even more.

So distracted by the Amir imposter, Dane did not notice a familiar face approaching him from the side of the tent. The man smiled at him and held out his arm for a handshake. Dane blinked again at this man, who had a thick mess of short white hair atop his head to match his white goatee.

He clasped forearms with the man and said, "Captain!"

Zuko grinned sheepishly and shook his head. "You mistake me for a proper officer. I abandoned that title when I joined Ularon." Zuko indicated the auburn-haired man.

Ularon came forward and greeted everyone. "Welcome to the camp."

"*Are* we welcome? We weren't told much," Koda said, glaring at the man who had led them here.

Ularon looked at him and shook his head, sighing. "Retyn, we've talked about this. We're not taking prisoners. Don't bring people here against their

397

will. Make sure their weapons are returned to them, as well."

Retyn clasped his hands behind his body. "Sorry, My Lord. The girl's a magi. They weren't listening to reason."

Ularon dismissed Retyn and looked at Evie. "Hello, child." He took one step forward and looked her directly in the eyes. "You don't have to be afraid here."

"I'm not," Evie replied, keeping her chin raised.

Ularon smiled. "Good, there's no reason to be."

"I know."

Ularon chuckled. "Sorry. I was never good with children."

"I'm fourteen, not a child. And I'm not the only magi here."

"Who else?"

"Perhaps we should keep that information to ourselves for now," Dane interjected, glancing back at Evie to silence her. She nodded agreement.

"Very well." Ularon turned and walked back to the table he had been leaning on. The companions saw it was a map of Akreya. Zuko said to Dane: "We haven't seen each other since the Battle of Winter's Edge, have we?"

Dane shook his head. "Obviously much has changed," he said, indicating Ularon.

"Some called me a traitor," Zuko said.

"That's not what I meant. I was a mercenary — you know that. I fought for a lot of people. Balanced both sides of a lot of coins."

"I wish I had time to explain, but Ularon and I were actually in the middle of something." Zuko joined Ularon at the table.

"Like what?" Caulen asked. "Figuring out where to attack Endrew next?"

Ularon chuckled again and shook his head. He looked at Caulen. "No. The rebellion is put on hold for now. I'll deal with Endrew after this… plague… is dealt with."

"Maybe it should be put permanently on hold," Koda said, crossing his arms. "Endrew's dead."

"Koda!" Dane said, glaring at him. Koda shrugged.

Ularon furrowed his brow. Zuko straightened his back, pushing off the table. The knight blinked rapidly. "Is this true?" he asked.

"It is," Dane replied.

"We hadn't heard," Ularon said. "That's unfortunate news."

"Made your job easier," Koda quipped.

"I didn't wish anyone dead."

Koda scoffed. "You started a rebellion. You didn't think anyone would die?"

Ularon looked at Koda. His facial expression was sad, not angry. He said, "I didn't start my rebellion because I hated Endrew. I started it because I love Akreya."

"Now Akreya is in more trouble than we thought." Zuko said. "Endrew was mad, but a realm without a king will devolve into anarchy. At least a bad king can bring people together through mutual hate."

"Nothing's changed our course of action for the moment, Zuko," Ularon replied. "Our main priority is to figure out the safest location to take this camp. We're starting to gather too many civilians and not enough warriors to stay in the wilderness. Sooner or later, we're going to need to find ourselves behind walls."

"Do we need walls that are already standing, or can we build them ourselves?"

"Either way works. We just need tall, strong walls." Ularon stood and gestured at the companions. "You all look tired. You are welcome to food, drink, rest – whatever you need. Don't hesitate to ask anyone. We all look after one another. Retyn will show you where you can sleep."

Zuko chimed in: "Perhaps Dane and his friends could be of some help. I know Dane is a resourceful leader."

Dane nodded his thanks at the compliment. "We don't have much information."

Ularon said, "Whatever help you can provide would be appreciated, but you all deserve a meal and some rest. We'll talk later."

Zuko said, "There's a lot of The Iron Fox Legion here, Dane. Quite a few of them have joined Ularon's cause. I'm sure you'll see more than a few familiar faces around the camp."

Dane nodded and left the tent with the others. The thought of seeing some old friends brought a smile to his face.

* * *

"This is the mess tent, and if you talk to Lelah over there, she'll find you some space to sleep." Retyn stopped and turned towards them after pointing at both tents. "If you're lucky, there's still a tent or two to spare, or maybe you'll be sharing with some of the others. Your weapons are in those chests right there."

Grunt marched directly to the largest chest and lifted the lid, pulling Koda's spear and Marek's trident out, first. As the giant of a man handed his friend his weapon, he squinted at Retyn before inspecting the trident for any signs of damage that may have been sustained while out of his care. A low growl confirmed that all was well, luckily for Retyn. Grunt retrieved his axe, strapping it to his back.

"Thank you," Dane said, looking around, curious to discover any familiar faces.

"You're free to roam the camp as you wish. My job's done here. Gotta take the lads back out into the forest." He started to walk away but said as he passed by: "Sorry about earlier. Just following orders." Dane nodded and Retyn kept walking.

"Well, what now?" Koda asked. "I suppose our plans are on hold. Again." He spit.

Everyone looked around anxiously. There were a couple of people who watched them, but most were not bothered by the newcomers – even one as large as Grunt. Dane could tell by Evie's facial expression that she was attempting to read the thoughts of the people around them. He snapped his fingers to get her attention and then shook his head. She grinned mischievously.

"Why do we not get something to eat, yes?" Asira suggested, gesturing toward the mess tent.

"I could eat," Caulen said, smiling. He led the way to the tent. They were greeted warmly and served hearty portions of pottage – a thick soup of meat and vegetables – and a hunk of bread.

Having been unable to feast on the deer from earlier, the six of them relished the meal. None of them had realized just how hungry they were. The warmth of the food raised their spirits, though Koda insisted on sulking by himself at the end of the table.

As the six of them sat on the ground under cover of the mess tent, several people passed by them. Some murmured greetings or smiled. One of them — a human man — stopped and looked down at Dane. "I know you," he said.

Dane looked up at him as he swallowed the last of his pottage. He sized the man up, gauging his intent. Even with a full belly, Dane still did not want to fight anyone. "Sorry, I don't think you do," Dane replied in a friendly tone. He smiled at the man, but he remained standing before Dane.

"No, actually, I'm sure I do. I'll never forget you. You're a great warrior."

"He's not bad," Koda interjected. "Not as good as I am, but he's alive, if that tells you anything." He chuckled.

Dane shook his head. "I know my way around a sword, but I'm not outstanding. Where do you think you know me from?"

"Winter's Edge. I went behind enemy lines with you, Captain Zuko, Maggard, and your men."

Dane finally remembered his face. "You were the archer. I'm afraid I don't remember your name."

"Alton," the man replied, smiling. "It's okay. I was pretty young then."

"Still, good with a bow."

Alton nodded. "Better now."

"Did you ever get that promotion from Braxon?" Dane smirked as Alton laughed incredulously.

"He tried to promote me. Wanted to make some statement about how brave men were treated in Endrew's army. He didn't care about the dead we lost getting that castle gate open."

"Braxon didn't care about much at all. So, what? Did he make you a corporal? Sergeant?"

"I was a private. Wanted to bump me up to corporal."

"Corporal Alton," Dane said, nodding and smiling.

"I turned it down." Dane raised his eyebrows. "I wasn't pleased that he refused to acknowledge you and The Iron Foxes. Without you guys, I would have most likely been amongst the dead."

Dane gave a small chuckle. "You shouldn't have done that on our account. You would have gotten a pay bump."

Alton shrugged. "Eh, none of that matters now."

"I suppose it doesn't," Dane said.

Caulen said: "Can you teach me how to use a bow?"

Alton looked at him and smiled. "Are you Dane's son?"

Caulen shook his head. "I was supposed to learn to use a bow. A friend was going to teach me, but…"

Alton glanced at Dane, who shrugged. Alton looked back at Caulen and nodded. "Yeah, I can teach you."

"Right now?" The boy grinned.

Alton shrugged. "I've got time."

Caulen jumped up, full of energy. Evie followed them both out of the tent. Asira smiled and looked at Dane. "I will go watch over them."

"Are you sure you don't need any rest?" Dane asked.

"I will be fine." She stood and walked off, leaving Dane, Koda, and Grunt to themselves.

"Well, boys, shall we catch some shut-eye?" Koda asked. The other two men concurred.

When Dane awoke, he found he was alone in the tent. Asira, Evie, and Caulen had found them after the archery lesson and gone to sleep themselves. Dane had been stirred from his sleep at the time but had not stayed awake for but a few seconds.

He lay on his cot for a few minutes. Thoughts of the last few months rushed through his mind, and he realized this was one of the first times he had had a quiet moment to himself. He decided he did not like it. The past could not be changed, and the memories of his dead friends haunted his private thoughts.

Dane slung his legs over the side of the cot and put his boots back on. He reached for his armor, but stopped himself, and after a moment of consideration he told himself he did not need it. His eyes moved to his sword, which was propped against his cot. He shook his head and stood slowly, feeling his sore muscles resist his every movement. He could tell that it was nighttime through the opening of the tent. He rubbed his eyes and approached the flap.

The night air was warm, with a full moon above. A steady breeze meandered through the camp, throwing tent flaps into the air and causing leaves to swirl about. Dane liked it. He knew a storm had to be on its way, but he had always found thunder and lightning soothing to listen to.

He did not notice Spencyr as the younger man approached him. "Did you sleep well?" he asked.

Dane looked at him. "I did. Too long, though. Now I'll be awake all night long."

"Too much rest isn't a bad thing, Dane. I'm guessing it's been a while since you've had any at all."

Dane could not argue with that.

Spencyr clapped him on the back and said: "C'mon, I know what will cheer you up."

Dane followed as the younger man led him through the camp to somewhere near the middle. A large canvas sheet was stretched between four wooden legs. Dane saw a group of people – humans, elves, dwarves, and halflings – all drinking, eating, and laughing loudly with one another. As he ducked his head under the canopy, his jaw dropped.

He saw Foggy stand up and reach out to Dane, taking his arms and leading him to the center of the space. All around him were familiar faces, smiling and greeting him with nods or hugs. Dane had not seen any of these people in years, and it lifted his spirits to see so many of his old mercenary friends still alive and well. He had made peace for many years that most of them were likely dead.

Dane turned to Spencyr and embraced him. "Did you do this?"

Spencyr smiled sheepishly and looked at the ground. "I got all the Foxes together that I could."

Dane rotated and looked at each one of them. There had to be twenty men that he had fought beside all gathered to greet him. He recognized Shibben, a halfling with more tattoos on his face than anyone Dane had met before or since. He raised a mug to Dane.

Also present was a man named Oddwen (though most called him by his nickname: "Odd") and he was one of the few half-elves most of the Iron Foxes had ever met. He had the pointed ears of an elf, but the long shaggy brown hair and a matching, braided beard common among the Tribesmen. Oddwen held his long arms out wide and swallowed Dane in a tight hug.

Another of the men present was a dark-skinned man from the desert with a smoothly-shaved head and body. Tocca had never been fond of garments, choosing to fight in short breeches that stopped just above the knee, plain sandals, and a matching set of leather greaves, bracers, and a chest harness that altogether

405

housed thirty knives. "Captain, it is a pleasure to lay eyes on you again." Tocca smiled and nodded. Dane responded with a smile. It had been a long time since he had been addressed by his rank.

Dane said, "Gentlemen... It's good to see all of you here after such a long time apart. To know that you all are still alive, it... it does me good in these trying times. I know there's several of us missing, and we should have a drink in memory of them, but let's not forget that our friends would want us to celebrate our reunion here tonight. Drink up!"

Cries of merriment erupted as Tocca offered Dane a mug of ale, which he took. He could not help himself from smiling at each of the men as he sat next to Foggy and Spencyr. The others had taken Dane's suggestion and were wasting no time feasting and drinking with one another. Dane sighed with contentment and drunk deeply from the mug.

"How are ya' feeling, m'boy?" Foggy asked, slapping him on the back.

"Overwhelmed," Dane admitted. "I didn't think I would ever see most of them again. That includes both of you."

Foggy laughed. "Well, I'm tough stock. You know that. And Spencyr there, he's lucky 'cause he had me watchin' over him. Hey, you remember how he used to follow you around like a pup? He idolized you!"

Spencyr's face grew red and his eyes dropped to the ground as he smiled shyly. Dane took up for him: "Those days are long gone, Foggy. I'm certain Spencyr is his own man, now. A great warrior."

Foggy spit ale across the canopy, to the dismay of some of the other men, though they were having too good a time to complain long. "Dane, m'boy, you always did have a dry sense of humor!"

406

As Foggy stood to acquire more drink, Spencyr tapped Dane on the arm. "Hey, where's Amir? I'd really like to see him. He left The Legion shortly after you did. I know he planned on meeting up with you. Where is he now? I know you wouldn't leave him — especially not with the way Akreya is now."

"He's dead," Dane replied matter-of-factly. He was tired of thinking about his friend. He could not forget, but he never had a chance to try.

"What? What happened to him?" Spencyr asked, eyes wide.

"He died." Dane took another long dredge from his mug.

"Right, I get that, but-" Spencyr let his voice trail off. "Sorry..." Spencyr got up and walked away to think about the memories he had of Amir.

Dane studied the faces of each man gathered here. Their faces were gnarled, scarred, pockmarked, or marred with tattoos. They were all smiling, having a good time, but in their eyes, Dane noticed something a normal citizen would not — a certain hollowness. Hidden in the deepest depths of their souls, were the horrors of war that they had witnessed.

Some might argue that they had been mercenaries, that they had made that choice willingly, but several of these men had grown up poor or befallen tragic circumstances that left them with little choice. The Iron Fox Legion had been something that these men and men like them were able to turn to and be a part of a brotherhood. That was what it had been for Dane.

Dane was not special — they had all lost friends, and even he had seen countless men die. Friends, acquaintances, or strangers — it was never a pleasant thing to witness death and carnage. But the memory of Amir still lingered. He had been Dane's best friend since his earliest days in The Iron Fox Legion. From that day up until Amir's death, the two of them had been nigh inseparable.

Their first battle had been together, and they had protected one another from that day forward. Amir had been there when Dane had met Tabitha – the woman who would later become his wife. Though Amir had not been present for the birth of his daughter, Evie had always referred to him as "Uncle Amir" and he had played the role well. When Dane started his boat-mending business, Amir had been his first employee and travelled every week with him from Eden to Clifftown and back.

Dane did not figure he would ever find as great and loyal a companion as Amir.

A hand was placed on his shoulder, and Dane saw Koda's face when he looked up. "Play time's over. Ularon says he'd like to speak to all of us, if you're up for it."

Dane cleared his throat, downed the last of the ale, and wiped the froth from his mouth before standing. He gestured for Koda to lead the way. Anything to get his mind off his fallen friend.

Evie turned and threw her arms around Dane's neck as soon as he entered Ularon's command tent. She looked up at him and smiled. "This is a good, safe place, Dad. All the people are friendly. They come from all over the realm. It's just like Etzekel."

Dane squeezed her tightly before stepping away. He hoped it was not exactly like Etzekel. He hoped Ularon was nothing like Renwy.

There were several people encircling the table that the giant map of Akreya rested upon. A plump, older man with gray hair on the sides and back of his head sat there. A well-muscled, middle-aged man with a thick, dark brown beard studied them with an unimpressed look. There was a young man – possibly in his early twenties – with a smooth shaved face and an observant look to him. He smiled softly and nodded at their arrival. The last unknown person was a tall, gaunt-looking man with bright green eyes. He eyed them curiously, appearing nervous at their presence.

Ularon and Zuko both waited patiently as Dane, Evie, Koda, Grunt, Caulen, and Asira took places around the map. Ularon's officers watched them like hawks, with only the youngest one offering any kind of greeting, but Alton was there as the only other familiar face. The archer stood away from the rest of the group but smiled at Dane and the others.

Dane crossed his arms and briefly looked over the map. There were a few stones scattered at random places across the country and other places had giant wooden X's atop them, but no other figures or markers dotted it. Dane assumed that either the stones or the X's represented where Endrew's forces were gathered, but why were they not using figures in the shape of Endrew's sigil to mark them? He also doubted that Endrew's men were still where they were ordered to be since their king had been murdered and the dead were roaming free. He could not be sure what the other marker meant. There were many more X's than flat stones.

"Let me introduce you to my officers," Ularon said. "Aberthol here was a sergeant of the southern district of Eden's city guard. He coordinated efforts to fortify the city and increase security."

The fat officer that was seated dipped his head in greeting.

"Keaton was a lieutenant in the Edenian army during Endrew's rise to power. He helped overthrow the elven rulers before Endrew."

"I brought the violence right to them elvish bastards, and I was damn good at it," the bearded man said matter-of-factly. Evie muttered something under her breath, but no one heard.

"Mayoko here has a gift for intelligence. He's astute and he doesn't miss anything."

The young officer bowed. "You're overly kind. I'm nothing special, just observant."

That left the lanky officer for last. Ularon said, "Cobon has extensive knowledge of the country, and he's an expert at herbalism and plant identification. He was a ranger in Endrew's army before all this."

Cobon offered the slightest of nods. "Hello."

"I'm glad you could join us," Ularon said, addressing the companions. "I'm sorry it's at this time of night, but if I haven't misheard you all got at least some rest."

"We did," Dane replied. "I'm surprised that you and your officers are up now."

Ularon formed a small smile. "We don't get much sleep these days. I'm sure you're familiar with that." Dane nodded, knowing all too well. "I'll be honest with you all – I'm not much for small talk. I like to get right to the important matters. However, if you have any questions about my camp here, feel free to ask."

"How many are in your camp?" Dane asked.

"A little more than five hundred, but we're picking up new people every day. There's no shortage of folks wandering the wilderness, trying to get away from the plague. Most of them are ill-prepared and unequipped to survive on their own."

"Then it's a good thing that you're around to whisk them away to safety," Koda said.

"We don't kidnap anyone. They're free to go at any time, as are you."

Dane glanced at Koda, who shrugged at him and crossed his arms. "Proceed with business," Dane said. He was eager to know what the urgency was that made Ularon host this meeting late in the night.

Ularon nodded. "Thank you... I love this realm, and I'm trying to salvage what I can of it."

"A rebellion is a good way to do that," Koda quipped.

Ularon blinked slowly. "I had reasons."

"Like what?"

"That doesn't matter now. You said so yourself earlier today. There is no more rebellion. There is only the living and the dead. I don't know how these abominations came to be, but they are a bigger threat to Akreya than Endrew ever was."

"Especially now," Koda chuckled.

"How did you come by that information, by the way, that Endrew had been assassinated?" Mayoko asked.

"We learned it from a friend," Dane replied. "He said there was some informant among Endrew's people. Wyll was his name, I believe."

"It was," Koda confirmed. "He was Endrew's steward."

Ularon, Zuko, and all the other officers in the tent were baffled by the news. Aberthol looked at them with raised eyebrows. "Do you speak the truth?"

Dane nodded. "We believe it is."

Ularon sighed and looked at Zuko. "That would make sense."

411

Zuko nodded. "He probably fled Eden soon after Endrew was murdered."

"Do you know this Wyll?" Asira asked.

"We do," Ularon said. "He was an informant for us as well as the magi in Etzekel. He told us whatever he could about Endrew – supply routes and troop movements and such."

"You know about Etzekel?" Dane asked, astonished.

"Of course," Aberthol explained. "Ularon helped establish the magi shelter-city and he organized The New Dawn, with a little of my help. It was a group that helped smuggle magi safely throughout the realm."

"I know what The New Dawn is," Dane said, "I was a part of it." He chuckled incredulously and looked at Ularon and his men.

"I thank you for your contribution to the cause," Ularon said, smiling.

Koda cut in: "Why was this Wyll kid helping you?"

"Because I've been aiding the magi since the beginning of my rebellion."

"But why would this kid care? Being a king's steward would have to be a pretty cushy job. He was probably living the life."

"Wyll's a magi." Ularon pushed away from the table, cracking his knuckles and pacing around the tent. "He can see perfectly in pitch black darkness. It makes him a good spy. I hope the boy is okay."

"He sounds like a traitor to me," Koda scoffed.

"His entire family was murdered by Endrew. You can't blame him for wanting to bring the man down." Cobon said, disgusted.

"How did he get in King Endrew's good graces if he murdered his family?" Evie asked.

"That's a story for another day. I just hope the boy is safe," Ularon repeated, reclaiming his place at the map. "We haven't heard from him in weeks."

"He's probably dead," Koda said.

Ularon glanced at Koda angrily for a moment and then gestured at the map. "The X's are areas where I have forbidden anyone in my camp to travel. You can see I have made The Red Crescent Desert completely off-limits. I think the dead originated from there and migrated in."

"That makes sense," Caulen said. "We've discovered that the undead *did* come from there."

Ularon looked to Dane, who nodded his confirmation. With everything he had learned, Dane decided that Ularon and his men could be trusted. He briefly told them what they knew about Uragon and his army of zombies.

Zuko shook his head. "If I had not already witnessed so many miraculous things in my lifetime, I would have said none of this was possible, but I believe you, Dane."

Ularon said, "So, it was Uragon who funneled the dead to Eden? I don't claim to understand the reasonings of a madman, but unfortunately the sequence of events lines up with the movements of the undead. Look here-"

Ularon moved around the map and stood next to Dane and the companions. He pointed at the desert and said, "Around the time that Endrew was killed, there were reports of a horde of undead moving northeast out of the desert – right towards Jalfothrin and Eden. Now, Jalfothrin is sheltered by heavy, high walls so an attack there would not have panned out the way Uragon would have wanted it to. However, his abominations bypassed it altogether. They swerved around it and went straight for Eden.

"That left only small smatterings of the dead in the rest of the realm, but just recently we've been receiving reports that a second influx of the dead were coming out of the desert and moving north. Uragon is trying to conquer the rest of Akreya now that he has taken the capital from his father."

"It makes sense," Dane said, stroking his beard and studying the map. "What do the stones represent?" The Platinum Plains were covered in stones with just one or two X's. Clifftown in the northeast and Yorkenfirth in the northwest were each marked with a stone, and The Dragon Fang Mountains were stones without a single X.

Zuko answered: "Stones are safe places. Places recently reported to be clear or mostly clear of the dead. I fear with this new information that much of the north will soon be taken over."

Koda pointed and looked at Ularon. "Yorkenfirth. Are you sure it's clear?"

Ularon nodded. "That's my home. I have family there that still reports to me. It's been the victim of only a few stray dead. It's safe, for now."

Koda turned to Dane. "We can go now. We can get a ship and supplies at Yorkenfirth and get the hell out of here."

"You're not staying with us?" Zuko asked, looking at Dane.

"No way, Old Man," Koda replied.

"We're the safest option you have," Zuko pressed.

"It's not safer than leaving the continent."

Zuko pointed at him from across the table. "Listen here you-"

Ularon was suddenly next to Zuko with a hand on his shoulder. "Calm down, my friend."

"I'm sorry, Ularon, but I'm exhausted from watching people run away! If more people fought for this realm, perhaps it wouldn't be in the shit it's in now!"

Koda pointed back at him. "You ran away from your king, you traitorous bastard! Don't lecture me on right and wrong!"

Keaton squared his shoulders and glared at Koda. "You best watch who the hell you're talkin' to, boy!"

Koda raised his middle finger at Keaton. "I'm not talking to *you*, that's for sure."

Dane expected Keaton to hop the table in rage, but he just stared at Koda a moment, his nostrils flaring. Zuko looked at Dane and said, "Dane, I don't know you too well, but I think you're an honorable man. Do the right thing and stay here with us. Fight with us and help us reclaim Akreya for the living!"

Dane looked at each of his friends, who awaited his response. Caulen was wide-eyed at the altercation. Asira and Grunt were indifferent. Evie and Koda both eagerly awaited his response. Dane wanted more than anything to save his home, but he had already made this decision. He looked at them both before shaking his head. "I'm sorry, Zuko. We made this decision together. And we're going to stay that way."

Zuko sighed. Everyone awaited the old man's heated response, but his face was suddenly weighted with sadness. Finally, he said, "Ularon, may I excuse myself from the council?" Ularon nodded and Zuko stood tall, with his chin up. He glared at Koda as he exited the tent, but Dane received a sorrowful glance.

"I think we should call this meeting to a close," Ularon said. "Thank you all for the information you

415

provided. You've put a lot of pieces of the puzzle together for me and my men."

Dane held out his arm and the two men grasped forearms. "I apologize for the trouble. We'll leave at first light."

Ularon waved his hand to dismiss the thought. "Stay and rest up for a few days if you like. As I said, you're all welcome here. I won't make you stay or try to keep you from going. Let me know if you need anything."

"Thank you."

Outside, Dane stopped Koda and pulled him aside. The moonlight was bright enough to illuminate their faces. He let the others distance themselves from the two of them before giving Koda a questioning look.

"What?" Koda asked.

"What's going on with you?" Dane asked.

"Me? Did you hear that old bastard in there? Who does he think he is?"

Dane held up his hands in surrender. "Yes, Zuko was out of line, but so were you. What got you so disparate in there? And what about us? Do we still have a problem?"

Koda rolled his eyes. "Don't take offense to my words, but you've seen a lot of friends here. I was trying to keep us all on track. These people were going to try to get us to stay, or worse yet, split us up entirely."

"I told you, we made this decision together," Dane said. "You've *got* to trust me, Koda."

"I saw the look on your face. You wanted to concede – to stay here with your friends."

"*You* are one of my friends. I made you a promise. I'm sticking to it... Now try not to piss anyone else off while we're here. Me included."

Koda chuckled. "No promises." He was silent for a few moments before looking up at him. "I'm sorry, Dane. I haven't been treating you very fairly."

Dane sighed and shrugged. "Everyone's under a lot of stress. Tensions run high. Everything will be better once we leave Akreya."

"I hope so..."

Chapter 22

"Dad, can I talk to you?"

Dane turned and found Evie standing in the doorway of the tent, holding the flap open and watching him. He had just finished cinching his sword belt around his waist. He put on his fingerless gloves, sat down on his cot, and patted the spot next to him.

"What's on your mind?" he asked.

Evie plopped down and looked up at him. "When we were in the desert - at Doompoint — I heard what Uragon said when he came out of the temple. He mentioned a name... Raz-Mikai. Who is that?"

"That's just a legend," Dane replied. "Raz-Mikai was supposedly the first magi to discover how to use the powers of reanimation. He wanted to try and teach others how, but the elven council that ruled the realm at that time saw what could happen, so they forbade it. Raz-Mikai resisted and a war broke out, though he was eventually defeated."

"So they killed him and it was done with?"

Dane shook his head. "The story goes that they feared he was such a strong magi that even if they did kill him, he would be able to reanimate himself from the dead. So instead, they banished him to an entirely different plane of existence, with him cursing them and swearing he would return to take revenge."

Evie quietly pondered the tale, looking down at the ground with blank eyes. Dane chuckled and said, "It's just a story, sweetheart."

Evie nodded, but tilted her head to the side as she asked, "How does a magi learn more abilities? All of the magi I've met have been born with their powers."

"Some say that the most gifted magi can take on new abilities through study, others say only through a deeper spiritual understanding of the universe can one do that. I think it's just legends."

"I wonder if I'm powerful enough to learn more..." Evie trailed off, a mischievous smile on her face.

Dane grinned and kissed her on the top of the head. "You cause enough trouble as it is with the powers you have now." He stood and picked up a rucksack of supplies by his cot. "Like I said, they're probably just legends."

Evie's face grew serious again. "But, if it's just a legend and Uragon wasn't a magi, how did he do it? How did he raise the dead?"

Dane stared into her eyes for a moment, wracking his brain for an answer. He smiled grimly and shook his head. "There's a lot of mysteries in the world – lots of things we'll never have answers to... I truly don't know, sweetheart."

Evie sat silently on the bed while Dane gathered his final few things.

Another voice said, "Dane, may I speak with you? If I'm not interrupting?"

Dane saw Ularon poking his head inside the tent. "Come in," Dane replied.

"So the rumors are true," Ularon said, dropping the flap behind him as he entered, "you're getting ready to leave."

"We are."

"Your timing is impeccable. I'm preparing to move the entire camp east next week, deeper into the realm." Ularon sat down on one of the cots near Dane.

"I heard. I didn't want to hold you up or cause any problems, so my companions and I decided to leave before you rolled out." Dane took a seat on a separate cot. Evie excused herself, running off to find Caulen.

"I appreciate that. Is your plan still to go to Yorkenfirth?"

"It is. Hopefully there will be a ship there that is setting sail, or we can make some kind of deal to acquire one."

"The people of Yorkenfirth are good. Treat them with respect and you'll receive the same. Mention my name and it may help you, though I'm not sure about these dark times."

Dane nodded his agreement. "You're not going to try and persuade us to stay and help your cause?"

"Our cause is the same, Dane — survival. I'm trying to protect these people, you're trying to protect yours. Same cause, different plans. I pray it goes the way you hope."

"Yours as well."

"Thank you." Ularon stood, and Dane with him. They clasped forearms and Ularon said, "Ask around the camp and see if anyone would like to join you. You may need more numbers to operate a ship properly, and some may not like the direction I'm going. Plus, you already have friends here."

"You'd let me take some of your people?"

"Everyone's free to stay or go. Who am I to tell them otherwise?" Ularon waved and exited the tent.

Dane sat back down on the cot. He thought about how Ularon himself was much different than the stories told about him in Eden. Dane shrugged. Who knew a rebellious warmonger could be such a cordial person?

Zuko poked his head into the tent. "May I speak with you?" he asked.

"Of course," Dane replied, offering him a seat on one of the cots.

The old captain accepted, grunting slightly as he lowered himself to it. He took a moment to gather his thoughts as Dane took a seat near him. "I heard you were getting ready to leave soon, so I wanted to come by and apologize for the way I conducted myself the other night."

"You don't have to apologize, Captain, you're not the first person Koda's provoked." Dane grinned and dismissed the matter with a wave of his hand.

Zuko was unconvinced. "You would think that after all the time I've spent as a soldier that I would have better discipline than I do, but I've always had issues with my temper and... I was never trained for the world we're in now."

"None of us were. The other night is nothing to trouble yourself about. Tensions are high."

Zuko scoffed. "Hell, tensions are always high these days." He sighed, and the resilient soldier became a withered old veteran right before Dane's eyes. "I'm tired, Dane... Tired all the time. I want to quit fighting. I really do... But I'm a soldier. Have been for as long as I can remember. I keep hoping I'll die soon. Either from old age or from battle. There's more danger in Akreya than I've ever seen before. Surely my time is near."

Dane looked Zuko over silently. He had fought with the captain in a few campaigns when Endrew had utilized The Iron Fox Legion but had ever had the opportunity to get too familiar. Braxon had ensured that Endrew's army did not fraternize excessively with mercenaries while they were under his command.

That did not stop stories from spreading like wildfire through the ranks and amongst the mercenaries and army alike. Dane knew that Zuko was the kind of captain that every foot soldier hoped to serve under. Tales of Zuko's compassion and concern for his men were commonplace. He was respected because he made the tough decisions with his soldiers in mind. He would even disobey orders that he knew would get them killed. He was a soldier's man, not an officer's.

Dane then remembered what Ularon had said. "Zuko, you know that there's a place with us if you'd like it."

Zuko looked up, smiling and regaining some of his youth. "What? With you and your lot?"

"Absolutely."

"Absolutely *not*. My place is here, fighting for the realm like I always have. My time is almost up. What kind of soldier would I be if I turned tail so close to the end?" Zuko chuckled and playfully punched Dane in the shoulder.

Dane smiled. "It's a good thing mercenaries have no honor. I don't feel guilty for running."

Zuko wagged a finger at him. "You have more honor and discipline than most of the men I served under. Your men sure as hell respected you, as did I just from the little bit of time we spent around one another. You didn't leave your men to do the dirty work, unlike most of the officers I served with. They could have learned a thing or two from you."

"Thank you."

Zuko clapped Dane on the shoulder as he stood and made for the tent exit. "You know, Dane... I felt bad when I started serving Ularon after all my time in Endrew's army..."

"Don't. It doesn't matter anymore."

"You misunderstand. I felt bad for having served Endrew *at all*. I had no idea what kind of things he was into before I came here. Too many stories about Endrew sending death squads to wipe out people that slandered him. Now all this with his son... Uragon would've never had the chance to do this kind of damage if Endrew had never ascended to the throne. I helped him do that. I helped him enslave Akreya. Now all I can do is play my part to help save it."

Dane nodded. "I hope you do."

"Goodbye, Dane."

"Goodbye," Dane said as Zuko left the tent.

Dane sat for a few moments longer, knowing that this would be the last time he would feel this secure for some time. Finally, after a few deep breaths, he worked up the nerve to stand and make way for the tent exit. Once he stepped outside, he was startled by the large gathering of people that was there. Off to one side were Koda, Grunt, Evie, Caulen, and Asira. Then, before him stood Spencyr, Oddwen, Tocca, and a few of the other Iron Foxes, carrying weapons.

"What's this?" Dane asked, stepping forward.

"Ularon sent word around the camp," Spencyr answered, "that you were looking for people to go with you."

"It was Ularon's idea."

"Yes, he said anyone who wanted to leave with you were free to. That's us."

"We welcome the company." Dane raised his voice and said, "Everyone here knows that this is a one-way trip, right? We're not coming back to Akreya."

"We're all aware of that," Oddwen said. "Akreya's a sinking ship. Hopefully the ship we get in Yorkenfirth will suit us better."

Dane nodded. "I hope so, Odd."

"Hey, Dane," Caulen said. He turned and the boy waved him over. He sighed and looked up at him. "I want to stay with Ularon."

"What?" Evie exclaimed, glaring at him. She slapped him on the shoulder and said, "Explain!"

Koda, Grunt, and Asira had now crowded around him. Caulen looked dejectedly between the five of them. Sighing a second time, he looked up at Dane, who was waiting patiently. "I have a good feeling about Ularon. He seems like a good man. I want to stay and help him. I want to try and save Akreya, because I love it. I don't have any family to care for or to care for me. I want to be here."

"No! You can't stay," Evie said. "You have to come with us. You're my friend."

"We'll still be friends," Caulen replied.

"But we'll never see each other again."

"You don't know that." Caulen grinned at her to try and cheer her up. "Maybe one day I'll come and find you."

Evie crossed her arms, glaring at him. She turned to Dane and said, "Dad!"

Dane smoothed his beard with his fingers as he contemplated. "Are you sure this is what you want, Caulen?"

Caulen acquired a serious expression on his face. "It is. I've gotten close to all of you, but I want to be a part of something meaningful. Alton says I have a knack for archery. He says he'll give me a bow and help me master it… With that I can help them."

Dane looked the boy in the eyes. Growing up in a harsh world had made him more mature than most children his age, but he saw pleading in Caulen's eyes. Dane knew that if he said no, the boy would obey but may also grow to resent him for it.

"Don't let him stay!" Evie said through gritted teeth. She already knew Dane's thoughts.

Dane shook his head and placed a hand on Caulen's shoulder. "This is your decision, Caulen. Make the most of it. Don't let these people down."

Caulen smiled. "I won't. Thank you."

Dane stepped away and Evie moved in front of Caulen. She punched him in the shoulder and glared at him, nostrils flaring as she crossed her arms.

Caulen smiled sheepishly and scratched his head. "I'm sorry, Evie. I want to go with you all, but I want to be here more."

Suddenly, Evie threw her arms around Caulen's neck and squeezed tightly. He smiled and hugged her back. She pushed him away and said, "You'd better come find me someday."

"I will. I promise."

All the other companions said their goodbyes and embraced the boy. Caulen watched them as they left, accompanied by their new allies and supplied with provisions for their travels. Caulen smiled again and stood alone for several minutes before wandering off to find out where he would be most useful.

* * *

Days later, Dane, Koda, Grunt, Evie, and Asira had made great distance accompanied by Spencyr, Oddwen, Tocca, and the other Iron Foxes. Their days of rest and recuperation in Ularon's camp had done them well and allowed them to journey with rejuvenated muscles and eager energy.

When not occupied with cleaving through the undead in their path, Dane had spent his time catching up with the men from his former mercenary band. The ones that knew him were upset when he told them what happened to Amir. Some of the men he had never known well, or at all, though they seemed to know him.

"Some of these men talk to me like they know me," Dane whispered to Tocca, disturbed.

The man grinned. "They do. Lots of tales were told about you around a campfire, Captain. You're a legend."

"You don't have to flatter me, Tocca. What in the world did I do that was so legendary?"

"You led."

"Lots of people did that. I'm not so special," Dane said, chuckling.

"Lots of people gave orders. Not all of them led. And not all of them cared about their men the way you did. We noticed. All of us." Tocca smiled at him and dipped his head.

"Ha!" Dane shook his head, grinning wryly. "Must've had some poor competition if I was the standard."

The conversation dropped, but inside Dane felt a bit of pride in the opinion of his men. They had made it easy to be a good leader. It was because of them; Dane could take no credit.

"What do you think you'll do when we leave Akreya?" Spencyr asked as he trudged alongside Dane. "I mean, what kind of work will you do?"

Dane thought for a few moments. "I may go back to mending boats, if there's a good enough fishing presence where we go."

"I'll join you, if that's okay."

"You don't want to fight anymore?"

Spencyr shook his head. "I want a simpler life for myself. Perhaps a wife to start a family with. If I can find a woman that will have me."

Oddwen, who had been trailing just behind the two of them, interjected: "You'll do yourself a bigger favor if you stay away from women. All they do is cause you grief."

Dane could tell that he was not joking. He remembered that Oddwen had been married to a pretty little elven woman. "What happened to your wife, Odd?" Dane asked, the words escaping his mouth before he took time to think.

Oddwen scoffed. "She abandoned me and went to Jalfothrin. Elves there haven't done a damn thing since this whole mess started. They only allow other elves inside, and they never venture past their walls. And they don't allow half-breeds." Oddwen spit to emphasize his distaste for the elves at Jalfothrin.

"Sorry," Dane said.

"Stay away from 'em, Spencyr," Oddwen reasserted. "Thank me later." He hoisted his pack higher onto his shoulder and shuffled past the two of them.

"Don't take his words to heart," Dane said, looking at Spencyr. "My wife was a very loving woman all the way up until she died. I could not have found a better one." Spencyr nodded.

Asira sidled up next to Dane and pointed off into the distance, through the trees. "Bandimere lies to the east. Do you suppose we can make a detour to acquire some of my medical supplies?"

Dane followed her finger and furrowed his brow. If only their plan had worked, then perhaps Bren would be with them right now on the way to Yorkenfirth. He cursed Braxon in his head, and hoped that Bren was safe somewhere.

Dane shook his head. "We can't delay any longer, if what Ularon said is true. We need to make it to Yorkenfirth before the undead beat us there. I'm sorry. If it's still whole, we'll get you what you need there while we're finding a ship."

Asira nodded and looked off in the direction of Bandimere, as if she could see it through the ocean of trees between her and the settlement.

* * *

Bren stepped through the gates of Bandimere, the village at his back. His hopes of finding his friends there had been disappointing. The place was now abandoned after what looked like a bandit attack. There were bodies strewn everywhere – some of them up and moving - and several of the buildings were collapsed after having been set on fire. One of them had even had many charred corpses housed inside.

After dispatching the undead, Bren had tried to use his beast form to sniff out his friends, but the smell of rotting corpses, blood, and scorched wood was all he could distinguish. None of the bodies he had found had looked familiar, so he knew his friends must have escaped unharmed. There was a large grouping of tracks spilling from the front gate of Bandimere, and Bren took a moment to study them.

After scanning the ground with tentative eyes, Bren sighed. He had never been a great tracker, and he could not make any sense of the marks on the ground. The footprints fanned out in all directions from the village. He planted himself in the dirt and meditated.

Before he could discover his next move, Bren heard someone approaching from the woods. Even though they were some distance away, he heard the tightening as a bowstring was pulled back. He opened his eyes calmly and saw a middle-aged man with a beard standing at the edge of the woods, aiming the weapon at him.

Bren raised his hands casually in surrender before letting them drop to rest on his knees again. "I mean no harm. I'm just looking for some friends."

"What friends?" the man asked, taking a few steps closer into the clearing around Bandimere.

"They're quite the ensemble," Bren said. "Humans, elves, children, adults. One of the men was very large. Even more so than me."

"Carried a big axe? Another fella was a magi with a spear?"

"That's them," Bren said, hopping to his feet and walking towards him.

The man let his bow drop and stowed the arrow in the quiver around his waist. "As long as you're not with those other people, then we don't have a problem."

"Other people?" Bren asked.

"Yeah. Those bandits led by that older warrior. He looked like he was military."

Bren groaned. "I know who you're talking about. Listen, my friends – were they okay?"

The man shook his head. "There were fewer of them when they left than when they first arrived here at my village."

"Your village?"

"My name's Tanken. I was head of Bandimere until it was destroyed. I've come back to gather a few things."

Bren leaned closer, his stomach tight from the horrible news. "What about my friends? What happened?"

"Your friends showed up and brought trouble with them. There was a boy that had gotten ill from their travels. Your friends went into the woods to collect herbs, and... well... not all of them came back."

"How many were there when they left?"

"I don't remember... Dane was still alive. His daughter, too, and that boy. They took my healer with them. The big guy, and his magi friend, too. I think that's all."

Bren hung his head and sighed. His jaw tightened. "Please, where did the others die?"

Tanken shrugged. "I'm not sure." He jabbed a thumb over his shoulder. "Somewhere back that way. Sorry."

Bren nodded and looked over Tanken into the woods. "Can you tell me which way my friends went when they left?"

"They headed south towards the desert. I don't know where their path was taking them, though."

"I do," Bren muttered. He looked south and then walked past Tanken to the edge of the woods. "Thanks for your help."

"You're welcome. Aren't you going to find your friends?" Tanken looked south as he talked to Bren's back.

"I am," Bren replied, wandering into the woods.

He took his time, picking his way through the bushes and sauntering amongst the trees. He had to force himself to keep his breathing calm. Soon, he felt a cold sweat break out on his forehead. His eyes were wide and evermoving.

A short time later, he found two tree stumps near one another. Both of them were drenched in blood, and the body of a mutilated elf was draped over one. Her hands had been mangled, and though her skull had

430

been crushed and she had been dead for some time, he could tell by the red hair that it was Llanowar.

Bren closed his eyes and took a deep breath. Another friend taken from him. He had not known Llanowar well, but she had been dependable and steadfast, and there was not much more needed in a friend in times like these.

But what about the rest of the blood? Who could it have been? Tanken mentioned Dane, Evie, Caulen, Grunt, and Koda, but what about Marleyn? He had not described Pelias or Marek, either. Had they died here, or did they even make it this far from Etzekel?

Bren sighed and knelt in the grass. He ran his fingers over the bloodstains, feeling the coarse wood. He looked south, eyes set. Had the others headed for Doompoint? If so, Pelias must have told them everything.

He looked again at Llanowar's corpse. "I'm sorry this happened to you. You didn't deserve to die like this." He pushed himself to his feet and turned to face the south, his eyes locked on the bloodstain for a moment longer.

When he finally looked in the direction he was facing, he saw her.

Out of the forest came Marleyn, shuffling along. Her eyes were the all too familiar pale white, and her skin the sickly grey. Her throat had been opened, and a curtain of red stained the front of her dress. His eyes caught the flashing silver of Cassandra's old locket, sullied in splotches of red.

Bren swallowed hard and rubbed the stubble atop his head. He could feel the beads of sweat running down his forehead. A gurgle issued from Marleyn's mouth and she stretched a hand out towards him.

Bren cleared his throat. "I came back... Just like I told you I would..."

His fingernails began to extend into claws.

Chapter 23

It had been eight days since the companions had journeyed from Ularon's camp hidden away in the forest. There had been only a few small groupings of zombies along the way, and this raised their hopes of finding Yorkenfirth alive and thriving. The dead that they did encounter proved to be no issue – everyone was skilled enough now and trained in fighting the wights.

Early in their journey they had decided to shift into a pyramid formation, staying near one another, but fanned out enough to give everyone enough striking room for when they did stumble upon any undead. Dane had taken point at the tip of the wedge. Staggered back and to the right was Koda and Spencyr. To the left was Oddwen and Tocca. Grunt and the other Iron Foxes completed the triangle, leaving enough room for Evie and Asira to travel in the middle of the formation, which had proven efficient in the few bouts they had been in.

"Yorkenfirth should be just ahead," Dane called out. "Everyone stay alert. We don't know what this place will be like."

"We haven't had much trouble so far. I think we'll be fine," one of the Iron Foxes said.

"No chances," Dane said. "We're close to the end of the line. No mistakes."

"The best thing we can do is listen to whatever Dane says," Koda said.

Grunt made a loud growling noise and pointed through the canopy of leaves over their heads. Everyone looked up.

"Smoke," Spencyr said.

"It is not too much," Asira said.

"Still… I don't like it," Oddwen said, looking sternly into the sky.

"We won't know until we get there," Dane said. "Let's move. Stay alert."

Everyone's shoulders tensed. They slinked like cats through the remainder of the foliage. Their throats suddenly became as dry as a desert, and their breath was hitched in their lungs.

Weapons drawn, they pushed through the bushes and they were greeted with a sight they had become all too familiar with. Fire, carnage, and destruction. Buildings were collapsed or set ablaze. Bodies abound, dotting the landscape in all manner of grotesque position – arms and legs twisted in unnatural poses from where they had fallen. A throng of undead wandered mindlessly throughout the village of Yorkenfirth, feasting on body after body trying to appease their voracious appetites for flesh. Soon their ranks would swell with the dead that had not been wholly devoured.

"Well… shit," Oddwen said dryly.

"This is fresh," Dane said. "There may still be people alive deeper in the village."

"If they're smart, they ran."

"Look," Evie said, pointing to the left. "Port Trident; and there are still a few ships docked there."

There the Akreyan ocean was, stalwart and threatening, but also a welcome sight to the company. The three-pronged Port Trident appeared intact from here, but there was also a thick mass of zombies directly between them and the port. It appeared most of the citizens of Yorkenfirth had attempted to escape the village but had been swarmed by the dead.

Spencyr said, "No wonder we didn't see many of them on our way. They're all here!"

"Looks like going through the village is safer than going through that field," Koda said.

"Agreed," Dane said. "Everyone, let's cut through the village! Keep the wedge tight and don't stop moving!"

Asira faced away from Grunt and moved her hair out of his way. Grunt used a leather strap to tie Marek's trident behind her. He tested the knot to make sure it was secure and then patted her on the shoulder.

She turned and looked up at him, smiling. "I will keep it safe. Do not worry."

Grunt nodded once and brandished his battle-axe.

Weapons clutched tight in hand, they moved quickly as one great machine with eyes pointed in every direction. The dead took notice of the fresh blood and left their meals to pursue the new prey. Some of them stumbled along slowly as others sprinted at unnatural speeds toward the company.

The companions breached the high wooden perimeter wall through the front gate and checked around each corner as they proceeded down the main street of Yorkenfirth. This village was comparable to Bandimere in size, but slightly bigger. The buildings were made similarly to Bandimere – wooden homes with thatched roofing that were susceptible to the fires already flaring around them.

They found once they were inside the walls that Yorkenfirth had been abandoned by the dead after it had been razed. Only a few stragglers approached them, though they were easily cut down. The company kept their formation tight and stayed on the move.

Tocca looked over his shoulder at the front gate to find the dead clamoring over one another to get back inside the village walls in pursuit of their meal. "They're following us from the field," Tocca said.

"Good!" Koda said. "As long as they're clearing away from the docks."

"We can bar the back gate once we're through and halt most of them from coming for us," Dane shouted.

In Spencyr's hands were two hook swords – thin blades with a sharp back, a pommel shaped into a dagger-point, a sharp, crescent-shaped guard, and a bent end used to catch enemy weapons and interlock to the two blades for swinging. Spencyr spun on one of his heels and decapitated several zombies with his outstretched blades. He locked the blades together and swung them in an arc over his head. The sharpened crescent guard of the second sword bit deep into an undead's skull.

Oddwen brandished a mace in each hand. The studded clubs made short work of the dead. Tocca dug two of his knives into the neck of an undead and spun around his body, pulling it along and pulling the knives free to send it crashing head-first through the window of a nearby building.

"No flourishing!" Dane shouted. "Kill them as quickly as possible and move on. There's no one to impress here." Then Dane shoved the point of his blade through the head of a nearby zombie before removing it and decapitating another.

Koda and Grunt each made short work of any of the demons that came for them, as did the other Iron Foxes. Evie and Asira called out enemy positions and watched everyone's backs.

After cleaving through the undead, the companions finally reached the gate on the opposite end. Luckily, it was already sitting wide-open.

Koda used his powers to teleport through the gate ahead of everyone. He quickly surveyed and dispatched what few zombies were awaiting them. Dane was the next one through and he ushered everyone on. He turned and together with Spencyr, Grunt, and Tocca, they pushed the heavy wooden doors shut.

"Odd!" Dane yelled. "Find something to bar this gate with!"

"On it!" Oddwen replied.

It was not long before the men holding the gate felt fists beating on the other side. They planted their feet and grunted, pushing back. The number of undead they had to resist was growing every moment, and Dane felt beads of sweat forming on his forehead.

The four men held the gate shut while Koda and the other Iron Foxes defended them. Koda's spear jabbed rapidly through the air, the point finding the skull of an undead with every strike. The other men fought with all manner of swords, maces, and spears.

"Help!" Oddwen screamed.

Koda quickly ran off to find him, glancing once at the others holding the gate. Behind a nearby cart laden down with all manner of possessions, he found Oddwen grappling with two of the lifeless beasts. The half-elf held them both by their throats at arms-length. He gritted his teeth and growled as he struggled to hold them back.

Koda ran his spear through the skulls of both zombies and pulled the corpses away, dropping them to the ground and removing his spear. He held a hand out to Oddwen. "Are you hurt? Did they get to you?"

Oddwen waved Koda's hand away. "No, I'm fine. Help me push this."

They both braced their shoulders against the cart, grunting, and pushed. The vehicle dislodged from where it had been stuck in the soft mud, the wheels creaking as they turned. The four that held the gate moved aside as Koda and Oddwen pushed it in place.

The companions stepped away, watching the gate as it pounded against the cart, rocking it slightly. A few deteriorated arms reach through the gap between the doors and clawed at the cart. The hissing and growling coming from the mass of undead was chilling.

Dane heard a scream and turned to see that one of the Iron Foxes had been tackled by a rogue zombie and taken to the ground. Dane sliced into its head and kicked it aside, but he found that the beast had managed to bite into the man's throat already. Dane stood and beckoned his friends to keep moving.

"Go! To the port!" Dane called.

Everyone started running. Waves of the dead were bearing down towards them from either side of Yorkenfirth, having detoured around the village. There were very few zombies between the company and the port, and they ran through them without a hitch in their gait.

"Which ship?" Koda yelled ahead at Dane.

"On the right!" Dane shouted. The ship he indicated was already facing away from land and out toward the sea. The other was facing inland.

Koda disappeared in a flash of smoke and in the blink of an eye was on the ship. He began to hoist up the anchor while the others ran up the boarding ramp. He could see several of the undead had sprinted after them and were now nipping at Grunt's heels.

Grunt turned and smacked one aside with the flat of his battle-axe, never breaking stride. He was the last to make it to the ramp, and as he ran, he placed a hand on the small of Evie's back. With a muscular arm, he pushed her into the air and up the remainder of the way.

At the peak, he turned and cleaved through the closest three zombies, swinging his axe wide and then bringing it back in for the next kill before throwing it out again. Grunt drove the blade of the axe into the railing of the ship and threw his leg out, catching an undead in the chest and throwing him all the way down the ramp onto the dock. He bent down and wrenched the plank out from under another zombie's feet. He threw it aside as the dead began falling into the water, flailing their arms and legs as they ran off the dock.

The rest of the company went about hoisting sails and climbing the masts. Grunt eyed the zombies as they struggled in the water. Their jaws snapped open and shut, bubbles ripping up to break the surface. Their arms flailed wildly, and they sank deeper into the water. The giant ripped his battle-axe from the wooden railing and sheathed the weapon behind his back.

The ship began to gently glide out into the open sea. Once they had the ship sailing smoothly, they gathered on the deck. They stared at Port Trident, where several of the dead had walked up directly to the edge of the dock and stopped, watching the ship sail away with a fierce intensity. Over the calm waters, the company could still hear the hissing and shrieking wafting from the port.

"That's chilling," Spencyr said, being the first to break the silence. A couple people nodded in agreement.

Oddwen said, "If you guys don't need me, I'm going to sleep below deck for a few hours."

Dane nodded. "I think we're fine at the moment. We'll sleep in shifts." Oddwen turned and shuffled across the deck.

One of the Iron Foxes vomited over the railing. "I don't like the shakiness of the sea... When are we going to touch land again?"

"I'm not sure. We haven't even discussed where we want to go." Dane looked at everyone.

"When we were travelling in the desert, you spoke of Kratan," Asira said.

"Yeah," Evie said eagerly. "You said that place was great."

"I enjoyed my time in Kratan," Dane admitted, "but this has to be a decision we all agree on."

"I'm with you, Dane," Koda said. Grunt nodded silently as he worked to undo the strap holding Marek's trident to Asira's back.

"I don't care where we go, as long as we're away from there," Spencyr said, pointing at the ever-shrinking Port Trident.

"I am with you, brother," Tocca said, smiling. "I will find ways to make money anywhere we go." He had already begun sharpening and polishing all his knives, tending even to the ones he had not unsheathed, as he leaned against the railing of the ship.

No one else objected and Dane smiled, excited to revisit the land of Kratan. "Very well. We'll need to adjust our course slightly to the south."

"How much is slightly?" Evie asked.

Dane shrugged. "I can't say." He laughed. "Surely there's a map somewhere on the ship. Evie, check the captain's quarters. Asira, take Spencyr and go check below deck."

They left to fulfill their duties while Dane and the others set about inspecting the ship and adjusting the sails. None of them knew much about sailing, but with their combined knowledge they were able to piece together the more advanced workings of the vessel.

"The good news is," Spencyr said, sliding a barrel aside, "I think we have enough food for our journey."

"Do you know how far Kratan actually is?" Asira asked him.

"Well... No... But there's a lot of food here. It ought to get us somewhere."

Asira giggled and continued to rifle through the belongings. "The people that owned this ship were definitely prepared for a long voyage."

"I wonder if they had the same idea as us, or if it was coincidence." Spencyr walked further down the room and gasped. Leaned against the wall, propped against a sack of flour was Oddwen.

The half-elf looked up at him with hazy eyes. "You sure do make a lot of noise," he said.

"Odd, you're bleeding!" Spencyr knelt and brushed Oddwen's long beard aside. Deep scratch marks ran along his chest. Asira came up to them, stopping in her tracks, seeing Spencyr, Oddwen, and then the wound.

"They got you," Spencyr said.

Asira joined them on the floor and held out her hands. A dim golden light emitted from her palms, illuminating the dark corner Oddwen had chosen to rest in.

"Don't you tell anyone," Oddwen said to Spencyr. He looked at Asira. "You, either."

"Is that a threat?" Asira asked nonchalantly.

"No, Odd wouldn't threaten us," Spencyr interjected.

"If it has to be," Oddwen answered, glaring at Asira.

"Fine." Asira met his eyes. "I will let you die."

Oddwen chuckled, clutching his chest. "I'll die anyway. If you could actually treat this, you would have been doing it for anyone who got bit or scratched. You're just slowing the process, aren't you?"

Asira dropped her eyes to the wound before nodding.

"Oh no," Spencyr said. "What do we do?" He looked at Asira for answers.

Oddwen answered for her: "There's nothing you can do. You've seen what happens. Just because it's me doesn't mean it will be different. Unless halfies are immune to this shit... That would be the first time being a half-breed ever did me any favors..."

"Do you need anything?" Spencyr asked.

"Wine, mead, ale... Any kind of alcohol would be nice."

"I'll go look for some," Asira said. The glowing around her hands stopped as she pulled away and stood.

Oddwen glared as she walked away. He grabbed Spencyr by the wrist and pulled him in. "Follow her. Don't let her tell anyone about me."

"Odd..." Spencyr looked after her.

"Go! Quickly!" He shoved Spencyr and the younger man instinctively followed the order.

Spencyr darted around the barrels strewn across the hull and caught up to Asira just as she began to ascend the steps. He grabbed her arm and spun her to look at him. She saw deep worry and sadness in his eyes. She felt a pang of compassion.

"Don't tell the others. They'll throw him overboard!" Spencyr tried coaxing her off the stairs by tugging on her arm, but she held strong.

"You must not know Dane very well. He would never do that," Asira said.

"Dane might not, but the others will."

"It will be very dangerous to have him here. This ship is not very big."

"I know... Just let me talk to them, okay?"

"What is your plan?"

"I... I don't know. That's why I need time to think."

Asira turned and walked calmly up the steps. Once she was above deck, she started running and Spencyr gave chase. He leapt after her, taking the steps in twos. His feet pounded across the wooden deck as he tried to catch up to her, but they could not carry him fast enough. She was headed for the door outside the captain's quarters where Dane was talking with Tocca.

Asira reached out and grabbed Dane by the arm. Dane smiled at her and saw Spencyr sprinting in their direction. Dane furrowed his brow and looked from one to the other.

"What's happened?" he asked.

"Nothing!" Spencyr replied.

"He is lying," Asira interjected. "We have a problem, but we do not need to overreact."

Dane crossed his arms. "I can't wait to hear this. Problems on land are one thing, but problems at sea are another. What is it?"

Asira flicked her eyes at Tocca, who was smiling innocently. He caught the look in her eyes and bowed his head. "I will take my leave. Find me if you need me." The dark-skinned man walked away, smiling again.

Spencyr replaced him on Dane's other side opposite Asira. He looked at the woman with pleading eyes. "Asira..."

Dane glanced between them. "What happened? Tell me now."

Asira looked up at him and said in a low voice: "Oddwen is wounded. He is below deck resting."

"Wounded? By the dead?" Dane asked.

"Yes," she whispered.

Dane inhaled deeply before sighing. He scratched at the short beard that had grown on his face, matching his black hair. He looked at Spencyr. "Did he ask you not to tell?"

"He asked us both to keep the secret," Spencyr said.

Dane's jaw tensed, and he pondered for a moment. "I'm going to talk to Odd. Don't mention this to anyone else, yet. I'll do it after I talk to him." He rested his palm on the pommel of his sword and marched across the deck, headed below.

Dane found Oddwen with his back against the hull. With one hand he was fumbling with some papers he had found, while the other one clutched his chest where Dane assumed the wound was. Luckily, no one else had made their way below decks so they were free to speak in private. Dane crossed his arms and leaned one shoulder against the hull a few feet away from him.

"Shit..." Oddwen said when he realized Dane was there. "She ratted, didn't she?"

Dane nodded slowly a few times, watching Oddwen fumble with the papers. "Good thing she did. It would be foolish for you not to tell anyone."

"You gonna make me walk the plank?"

"For getting infected? No." Dane walked closer and crouched next to him, lifting Oddwen's hand and inspecting the wound. "I *should* make you walk for trying to hide it. And trying to convince others to lie for you." He replaced Oddwen's hand and glared at him.

Oddwen gave a dry chuckle. "Sorry, Captain. I just wanted to see where this journey ended. Gonna be sooner than I thought."

"I'm sorry, Odd…" He placed a hand on his shoulder.

"You always hated leaving guys behind," Oddwen said, chuckling again.

"I always worried about the men who weren't phased by the notion," Dane replied.

"You mean me? Yeah, I guess I was heartless compared to some of the others. I never wanted to leave anyone either, you know? I just didn't wanna die trying to save them." There was a silent moment between them before Oddwen laughed. "I'm a real hypocrite, eh Cap? I shouldn't ask you to spare me when I wouldn't do the same for you."

"Maybe mercy wasn't your strong suit, but when the tough orders came down, I never had to worry about you following them," Dane said, giving a sideways grin. "Maybe I didn't tell you enough, but that was a great comfort. You were reliable in times when the responsibility was heavy, Odd."

"Reliably violent," Oddwen said, chuckling once more.

Dane laughed and nodded. He looked down to where his fingers were laced together, and he noticed them quivering. In his stomach was a pang of emptiness and his head felt light. He wanted to sleep for days.

Finally, he raised his eyes to Oddwen's and asked, "How do you want to go?"

"Quietly, in my sleep." Oddwen laughed to himself and waved his hand. "I don't wanna chuck myself into the sea. Do you think you can drop me off on the next island we find? If it's uninhabited, I mean. Doesn't have to be a big one."

"I think we can do that. The scratch doesn't appear to be affecting you as quickly is it does some. I'm going to go inform the others. We may have to quarantine you soon."

"Dane, don't let them convince you to kill me too early. I might have a lot of living left to do." He smiled, and the two men clasped forearms, their grip slippery from the blood. "Oh, and I found this," Oddwen added. He held up an unfurled scroll for Dane. "Sorry I got some blood on it."

Dane took the scroll and unrolled it partially. It was a map of the known world. Akreya, Kratan, Frenjjya, Cradin, and Ombalisk all dotted the parchment. Dane rolled it up and tucked it in his belt. "Thank you, Odd."

"Hope it helps..."

Dane nodded, stood, and turned, striding away from where Oddwen lay.

* * *

Caulen placed the bow gently in the notch on the weapon rack. He dusted his hands off, took a step back, and inspected the it once more with his hands on his hips. Alton stood by the open flap of the weapons tent with his arms crossed. He shook his head in amusement.

"You sure are particular, aren't you?" the archer remarked.

Caulen smiled over his shoulder before looking once more at his bow. "I just like knowing I've tended well to my things. Treat your weapon well and it will serve you just the same."

"I didn't know when I gave you my old bow that it would mean so much to you."

"I've never had much of my own. Definitely not a weapon as nice as this. Thank you."

446

Alton did not respond. He did not have the heart to tell the boy that there was nothing impressive or special about the bow, and Alton had no intention of ruining the enjoyment for him.

Outside the tent, people could be heard running and calling to their comrades. An excited energy wafted into the tent from where the camp was now bustling. Everyone was running in one direction.

Alton and Caulen stepped out of the tent together and looked around. Alton stopped someone running by and asked, "Where's everyone going?"

The woman replied, "They're bringing a prisoner into camp."

"Ularon doesn't take prisoners," Alton said.

"This one attacked him while he was out hunting." The woman ran off, eager to see the captive before she missed her chance.

"Let's go see what all the fuss is about." Alton followed the crowd with Caulen following close behind.

At the edge of the rebel camp, the crowd was packed tightly. Alton and Caulen could see Ularon astride a horse with Zuko and a few of his other men. In Zuko's hand was a rope that trailed his horse. Everyone was straining their necks to see who the rope was connected to.

"Please, everyone step aside!" Ularon ordered, slowly steering his horse towards the center of camp, pushing through any opening the crowd was willing to give him.

Caulen slipped away from Alton and separated himself from the crowd. He knew that Ularon and Zuko would have to take their horses this direction. People were yelling and shaking their fists. Some were spitting or throwing mud.

Caulen at first thought that this was strange behavior for everyone to treat a random captive this harshly, but as the horses broke through the mass of people, he realized why they were acting that way.

With his hands bound, Braxon stumbled along, spitting back at the crowd and shouting curses of his own.

Chapter 24

"I remember Marek going on and on about how much he loved the ocean," Dane said. "He loved when The Iron Fox would set sail for a new contract."

Grunt nodded and hummed a low response. He held the trident in both hands, running his thumbs over the metal. He looked from the weapon to the water. The waves lapped gently at their ship, and a cool breeze wrapped around the two of them as they stood by the railing.

"Would you like me to say some words on your behalf?"

Grunt shook his head before looking once more at the trident.

Dane nodded slowly. "Okay... I'll say some on *his* behalf, then." He looked up at his friend. "I understand you may feel guilty for staying distant from Marek because of what happened in your past, but I know personally that he was the forgiving type, and he wouldn't want you to keep that guilt hanging over your head... That's all."

Grunt looked at Dane for a moment, pondering. Finally, he nodded and patted him on the back. Grunt turned the trident around and brought his arm back. He launched the trident into the air and the two men watched it soar before piercing the ocean water.

Oddwen exhaled for a long time. He felt a soothing cool run throughout his body, as if all his muscles and joints were being massaged at the same time. He looked down at the soft golden light resonating from Asira's hands. The foreign woman sat on her heels and inspected the wound as she used her powers on the deep scratch along his chest.

He raised the flagon of wine to his lips. It was not his preferred alcohol, but Dane had brought it to him and said it was all his. He relished the taste like he had never had it before. He just hoped he would live long enough to polish it off.

"How am I doing?" Oddwen finally asked her.

"How do you feel?" Asira asked in a dry manner.

"Good, so far."

"Then you are doing good." She looked up at him. "When you start slipping, you will know it. It will *not* be subtle."

"Damn, woman, you really have a way of comforting your patients."

"Do you want me to lie to you?"

"I suppose not." Oddwen laughed and took another drink. Asira focused on his wound again. "Is Dane making you do this?"

Asira's eyes flicked to his for a moment and she shook her head. "Dane *asked* me if I would tend to you."

"I should say thank you. I know you can't stop it completely, but you're slowing it. So... thanks."

"I do not like seeing people die."

Oddwen chuckled. "You're in the wrong profession."

"I was born with these gifts. It would be wrong of me not to use them."

"I guess you're right." He raised the flagon in the air above his head. "I hope you save many more lives in your time on this world." He downed more of the wine. He wiped the droplets from his beard and asked, "So there hasn't been anywhere you could drop me at?"

"No."

"What happens when I start getting worse? At what point does everyone decide I get a sword in the eye?" His face was now stern.

Asira reached for the flagon. Oddwen did not stop her. She drank deeply and set it back down. She smiled at him and said, "That is why I am here doing what I am doing. We will stall the process, and no one will have to make that decision."

Oddwen sniffed and turned his face to the wall of the ship. "Thank you," he said.

* * *

"Kill that man!"

"I can't."

Caulen shifted to the same side of the table that Ularon was on. He put his hands together in a pleading gesture. "Braxon has caused so much pain across the realm. He *should be* dead!"

"I know he's an awful man." Ularon sat down and offered a chair to Caulen, who accepted so he would not be tempted to pace the entire command tent. "I can't just kill him. He could be very helpful to our operation."

"What operation? You said it yourself: You aren't leading a rebellion anymore. Your enemy is dead and replaced by a new one. What information can Braxon provide you to help you?"

"Caulen, I understand where you're coming from. We won't know what use Braxon holds until we ask, will we? And we can't ask if we behead him. Please give me some time to decide what the best course of action is."

Caulen stood, hands balled into fists. "Braxon didn't give anyone in Etzekel a chance. He didn't give my friends a chance before he slaughtered them in the woods, and he didn't give the people of Bandimere a chance before he butchered them and burnt down their homes. That's the man you're showing mercy to."

Caulen turned and stormed out of the command tent. Ularon called for him, but the boy ignored him. Ularon sighed and rubbed his eyes before looking at the map of Akreya. He looked to Yorkenfirth and prayed that Dane was having an easier time than he.

It was an hour later before Ularon decided to go confront Braxon. Caulen's words had urged him to move faster. He did not want the zealot in his camp any longer than necessary. Many people tried to speak to him as he marched through the camp. He apologized for not having the time for them.

He stopped outside the newly-erected prison tent. Braxon was the rebel's first prisoner in quite some time. Ularon had put Zuko in charge of guarding the man, and the veteran captain had selected several soldiers to form a line around the tent. There was a crowd of people swamped around it. Several in the rebel camp were sheltered magi who knew Braxon as the savage who hunted their kind across the realm. Others were soldiers recruited against King Endrew, who knew him as an enemy general.

Either way, there were many people who wanted to see Braxon dead.

Once Ularon approached, Zuko gave a lax salute. "Have you come to speak to him?" the captain asked.

"I have." Ularon responded, straightening the thick cloak he wore. The sky was darkened by clouds, and he felt the rain approaching.

"You should know the boy came by. He was adamant about speaking to Braxon. I turned him away, but it took some convincing."

"Thank you, Zuko. I'll be sure to speak to him later."

Zuko stepped aside briefly so Ularon could enter the tent. There was nothing inside except Braxon seated in the mud and tied to the main support. The general looked up at him with venom in his eyes. Ularon noticed one of his arms had been injured and in need of a sling.

"You have no friends here, I can tell you that, General," Ularon said, circling the captive casually.

"I don't have any friends at all. Lord Endrew is dead, you killed Aiya when we attacked you in the woods, and that bastard Leyon turned tail like a coward." Braxon spit on the ground. "Bugger all of them."

"Save us both some time. Are you going to help me at all?"

"Ha! Bugger you, too. I won't help you with shit."

Ularon nodded and stopped in front of Braxon. "You realize that if you don't help me, I'll have to kill you. I have no need for prisoners. Especially uncooperative ones."

"Then what are you waiting for?" Braxon kicked mud at him with the heel of his boot, but it did not come close.

"I was giving you one last chance to earn some slight redemption, you bastard. You've tormented, tortured, and killed so many innocents. Do you want to die with that on your conscience?"

"I have no regrets! I have done everything that's been asked of me. Unlike some of you, I know how to obey damned orders!" Braxon looked at the tent flap when he screamed his last sentence, and Ularon knew that it was directed towards Zuko.

Ularon let the old man sit in silent anger for a few moments before stepping closer. He crouched down, balancing on the balls of his feet, his cloak dipping gingerly into the mud. "You perplex me, General. I wish I knew what went on inside your head. I wonder if it would make any sense to me, or if it's all nonsense that you believe to be just and right."

Braxon gritted his teeth. "Don't patronize me, you cur. I've seen more than you ever will. I've fought worse than you'll ever fight. I've butchered, slaughtered, and razed my way through hells you couldn't even begin to imagine! You have the nerve to call me daft, but you won't face me in open combat!"

Ularon gave an emotionless scoff. He looked at Braxon with sad eyes. "I already did in the woods, and you lost. That's why you're here now. You're old and broken down, Braxon. Look at your arm. You'll never hold a sword again."

"Try me, scum!" Braxon spit in his face.

Ularon calmly wiped the spittle from his cheek. He sighed. "I respected you as a warrior and a tactician, Braxon, but there's no reasoning with you. You're beyond redemption. I hope you've made peace with whatever gods you believe in, because you'll be meeting them before nightfall."

Ularon stood and walked out of the tent. The crowd started shouting at once, so he pulled Zuko in close. He told him, "Make an announcement that we'll be executing Braxon just before dusk. Perhaps that will alleviate some of the people."

Ularon strode away so Zuko could spread the news. He searched the camp everywhere, inquiring about where he could find Caulen, but no one had seen him since he had tried to force his way inside the prison tent. Ularon said a silent prayer that the boy had not done anything too rash.

Chapter 25

"To think that Oddwen would fall like this..."

"He feels the same way, I'm certain," Dane replied.

"I haven't had the heart to spend much time with him," Tocca said.

"You should. You've been friends for a long time. Seen a lot together."

Tocca nodded. "I know. When I was younger, I always thought that it would get easier watching my friends die. I know that is a lie now."

Dane nodded. "I think every kid who starts life as a soldier or mercenary tells themselves that. Has to."

"Sometimes... when I really think about it... I still feel like that scared kid."

"That's how Odd feels. Go see him." Tocca walked below deck after Dane patted him on the arm and walked toward the railing of the ship, pulling a map out of his belt.

"Where are we?" Evie asked, glancing from her father to the map as she approached. He was studying it closely. She repeated the question, but his brow remained furrowed as he charted their course. The girl's nostrils flared, and she glared up at Dane.

It was several moments later when he finally tore himself away from the parchment. Dane sighed as he coarsely rolled it up, clenching it tightly in his fist. He gritted his teeth and cast his eyes across the blue waters they travelled. His eyes searched the ocean for answers, and after finding no results, he tucked the map in his belt and put his hands on the railing of the ship.

"There are no islands between where we are and Kratan – big or small," Dane finally said.

"What does that mean for Oddwen?" Evie asked.

"I'm not sure. He's going to die – I know that. We can't kill him too early, but the longer we wait the higher the risk we run of him turning and hurting someone else."

Evie stood silently by her father, helping him search the waters for answers. The wind picked up her black hair and made it flap like a flag on a post. She looked in the direction they were sailing and saw darkness far away in the distance. Hopefully the black clouds would move on as they approached.

"I've had to kill my own men before," Dane said. The sudden harsh words caught Evie off guard. She looked up at him and awaited an explanation. "When I was still a sergeant in The Iron Fox Legion, I had two men – brothers – try and desert the company. We were on Ombalisk. Did I ever tell you this story?"

"No. Go on – I want to hear it."

Dane cleared his throat. "We were on Ombalisk. Do you know much about it?"

"Isn't it a dark world?"

"That's just what people say because it's terrain is made up of obsidian mountains and valleys. It's extremely hot because the black rocks absorb the heat of the sun, and there are volcanoes everywhere. The sky is hazy from all the ash and smoke, but the sun still beats through. We were supposed to be protecting a troupe of treasure hunters from these fire-breathing lizards that inhabit the island-"

"Dragons!" Evie interjected. "You fought dragons?"

Dane laughed. "No. These may be relatives of dragons, but instead of being the size of this ship, they were about the size of a horse."

"That's amazing!"

Dane smiled and continued: "Obsidian is rare in the rest of the world, so lots of treasure hunters go to Ombalisk to mine it. So, besides the lizards, we were also protecting our patrons from rival treasure hunters. If you thought mercenaries were rough, you have no idea. Treasure hunters are cutthroat worse than any sellsword I've ever met."

Evie smiled big, laughing, and said, "They sound like real crazy bastards."

Dane scowled at her and she hid her smile behind her hand. "Anyway," Dane said, "these two brothers – the heat got to them. Everyone had orders to stay hydrated, but because of how hot Ombalisk is, water becomes a valuable currency. Now, the treasure hunters are also extreme gamblers. They love money and any game of chance, and they're good at them – all of them.

"The brothers thought for sure they had one up on the gamblers, and so they bet their water. Some of the Iron Foxes that were there said the treasure hunters cheated, but I don't know. Either way, the brothers lost all their rationings of water. They were embarrassed and hid that they'd lost. Eventually the heat made them go crazy and they tried to run away. They got caught and tried to fight back.

"One of them pulled a knife and stabbed one of my men in the gut. He eventually died from the wound. If they hadn't done that, I would have given them some water and nursed them back to sanity, but I couldn't allow the deliberate harming of an Iron Fox by one of his brothers. The Iron Foxes are supposed to be fiercely loyal, and so if I had given them a pass, I would have had a mutiny on my hands. I had to kill them."

"Wow...

"This is just as tough a decision as that was. It's never easy to kill someone you called a brother, no matter what they've done to force that hand on you."

Evie let Dane ponder for a few more minutes, then she asked, "So what are you going to do about Oddwen?"

Dane sighed and looked down at her. "I still don't know."

Someone behind them cleared their throat to catch their attention. Dane and Evie turned and were greeted by Spencyr. He moved in close and whispered to the two of them. "Odd has taken a drastic turn, almost instantly. His wound is bleeding badly again, he's sweating buckets, and he keeps talking about how hot he feels. He took his shirt off and the skin around the wound is beginning to turn a grey color."

"Asira's in the captain's quarters mixing elixirs out of whatever supplies we have. Take her downstairs and see if she can slow the process down some more. Tocca's down there, so you two watch out for her. If he turns, we don't want him getting a hold on anyone else."

Spencyr nodded and trotted off.

Dane looked at the dark clouds on the horizon before closing his eyes and taking a few deep breaths. Finally, his eyes jumped open and he began to call out to the others. Evie stayed close to him as he went through their plan for storms on the open water.

* * *

Ularon let the tent flap drop from over his shoulder. He blinked several times to allow his eyes to adjust to the darkness. Braxon was watching him with the ferocious eyes of a hungry lion. The general made no sound. He simply watched with fire in his eyes.

"You're out of chances, Braxon," Ularon said. "This is the end of the line for you."

"Get it over with, then," the old man spouted.

"Even in your final moments, you feel no remorse for the evil you've done?"

Braxon spit into the dirt. "I've only done what was asked of me. That's what good soldiers do."

Ularon said, "Maybe at one time you were a good soldier..."

Zuko and another of Ularon's men came inside the tent. They looked to Ularon, who gave a nod, and then they approached Braxon, undoing the ties that bound him to the support of the tent and hoisting him to his feet.

Ularon walked out of the tent with Braxon being led shortly after. The old general pushed and shoved, resisting, until Zuko punched him in the wound on his arm. Braxon cried out and stumbled a little. He looked at the people gathered on each side of him, screaming curses at him, throwing mud, and spitting. When he realized he could not break free of the grip his captors had on him, he resorted to kicking mud at the crowd and spitting back at them.

Ularon glanced over his shoulder as he kept walking. Just as he expected, Braxon's eyes were absent of fear. Only hatred and rage were present. The man bared his teeth and growled like a wild animal, his nostrils flared.

Ularon knew the man was a monster, knew what he had done to countless families. He had hunted, tortured, and executed thousands of magi. He did not know how a man could become so demented. Braxon was a curiosity to him, and Ularon felt a pang of sadness that that was how he had become. But he could not spare him. Not after all the injustice he had caused.

They finally arrived at the wooden platform that his men had hastily constructed. Ularon ascended the wobbly steps and stood to the side as Zuko and the other soldier forced Braxon to stand above the chopping block placed before him.

Alton approached the platform and presented Ularon with a sword in a scabbard. Ularon took off his cloak and handed it to Alton as he drew the sword. Alton stepped away from the platform holding the cloak and sheath, watching with the crowd.

Ularon spoke loudly: "General Braxon of the Edenian Army, you are found to be guilty of the murdering of innocents. I, Ularon of Yorkenfirth, sentence you to death. Do you have any parting words to say?"

Braxon scanned the crowd with squinted eyes. "I don't recognize your authority, Usurper."

Someone from the crowd shouted: "He does you an honor! You should rot in the muck of the stables!"

"You deserve less than to be buried under horseshit!" Another person added.

Braxon's eyes widened like that of an eagle on the prowl. "You're all savages!" he shouted. "Abominations to this great realm! My only words of regret are that I was unable to exterminate all of your ilk!"

"Off with his head!" came multiple calls from the crowd.

"You can take my head, but you will all rot beside me just the same! I will be there when you all descend into the underworld, and I will torment you all for the rest of your miserable afterlives! I will see all of you in He-"

Braxon's words were cut short as an arrow whistled out of the trees behind him and pierced the back of his skull. The point of the arrow protruded out of his mouth and Braxon bit down on the shaft of the projectile. He crumpled to his knees as blood gushed from his mouth, coating his teeth and dripping off the arrow.

Ularon scanned the forest quickly as panicked cries came from the crowd, but saw no one. He looked back to Braxon and raised the sword. When he brought it down, it cut cleanly underneath where the arrow was lodged. The general's head bounced to the edge of the platform and rolled off into the grass. The crowd was uproarious at the display. They cheered and sang and danced as they reveled in the death of their persecutor.

Alton walked around the platform and looked at the severed head. Blood soaked the old general's white goatee, and the open, lifeless eyes still showed the hatred the man had carried in his heart. Ularon walked to the edge of the stage, looked at the head with the arrow still stuck in its mouth, and passed the sword to Alton. Alton took it and handed the cloak up to him.

Alton wiped the blood off the sword with the bottom of his tunic, still studying the head. "That was a good shot," he said.

Ularon sighed and tied the clasp around his neck. He turned, and out of the trees he and Alton saw Caulen marching towards them with a bow in his hand.

Chapter 26

A giant hand of water rose above the ship and slammed down, trying to clutch the vessel in its liquid grasp. Dane, hugging the railing of the ship, watched as the water grabbed one of the Iron Foxes and dragged him to the edge. Dane extended his hand, but the water made it difficult to cling safely. The man's fingers brushed his before he was sucked over the edge of the boat and into the depths of the ocean.

Another man vomited onto the main mast where he held on for dear life. The ship rocked back and forth viciously, and lightning cracked like a whip over their heads. The sails were drawn, and the anchor was dropped. There was nothing any of the company could do while they were bombarded by the storm.

Dane looked about and saw Grunt and Koda motioning him to come from the door of the captain's quarters. He saw Evie peeking between the two men and he was relieved that she had for once followed his instructions to find shelter there. Tocca, Spencyr, and Asira had gone down into the hull of the ship to wait out the storm with Oddwen and to try and ease his pain.

A line broke loose and whipped the man by the main mast in the face. He reeled back and stumbled toward the railing, tipping over the side and into the raging sea. Dane was splashed and shook the water from his face. He felt the cold droplets clinging to his short beard, and he tried to blink the spray out of his eyes. Koda and Evie called to him, and Grunt took a few steady steps further onto the deck, reaching out for Dane.

The ship rocked onto one of its ends and was suspended there for a long time. Finally, Dane felt the bottom drop from his stomach as the vessel tipped the other way. He gripped the railing tighter and panted heavily. Grunt was still standing there, beckoning him forward.

Dane tried to see if the ship was level, but the sky was dark, and the lightning distorted any view he could get. Dane pushed off the railing with all his might and ran towards Grunt as fast as he could on unsteady footing. Grunt extended his muscular arms to steady his friend and the two men made way inside the captain's quarters, where Koda slammed and locked the door from the inside.

"Father!" Evie exclaimed, embracing Dane tightly, despite his soaked clothes.

"Are you all right?" Dane asked. Evie nodded, and he looked to Koda and Grunt, who nodded. "We lost two out on deck. Hopefully the rest are below.

"I don't like being split up," Koda said. "Especially with Oddwen down below."

"Hopefully Asira can keep him stable; at least until the storm passes." Grunt offered a flagon of wine to Dane, who drank deeply as Koda sat down next to him.

"I still say it would have been a good idea to tie him up. Who knows when he'll suddenly turn?" Koda insisted.

"Take it easy," Dane said. "Odd's scared and he knows he's going to die. He's a friend from a long time ago. I couldn't let him spend his last few days tied up like a hog."

"I just hope we don't all die for the sake of his comfort," Koda muttered.

Dane prayed that would not happen. He did not want to cause more death by trying to do good.

* * *

Leyon had observed Braxon's death from the cover of the trees. The old general had been crazy. Leyon had stayed with him for reasons even he did not understand. He had never been one to stick his neck out for anyone else unless it benefitted him in the long run.

Braxon had tried to attack the Usurper, and Aiya had followed blindly because she was attracted to the gruff old zealot. She had taken a spear to the heart and died in the grass. That was when Leyon was sure his time was up. He realized then that Braxon had reached the end of his usefulness.

It was one thing to help Braxon chase after a handful of runaways. It was another to try and attack a rebel with an army behind him. The man himself was not unskilled, and Braxon's injury was still only partially healed, even though Leyon doubted his sword arm would ever be what it once was.

Leyon had counseled against ambushing Ularon, but Braxon had seethed with rage, as he always did. "This would be a bad move," Leyon had said.

"I don't allow traitors to go about freely. The rebels will fall today by my hand," Braxon had said.

Leyon watched from the bushes as Braxon and Aiya leapt into the road, startling Ularon and his men as well as their horses. Braxon had gone straight for Ularon, but the rebel had already had a hunting javelin in his hands. He had thrown it and made Braxon jump to one side of his horse, while he quickly dismounted from the other side.

Braxon came around, holding his sword in his left hand, and being unpracticed with it, Ularon parried and sent the general rolling to the ground. Aiya had tried to jump him from behind, but one of Ularon's captains had shoved a spear right through her heart from behind.

Leyon had slunk deeper into the bushes, shaking his head as he retreated. He pursued Ularon and the captive Braxon to the rebel camp out of mere curiosity. He knew there was nothing he could do by himself.

Then Leyon had watched as they prepared to execute Braxon. He had seen the arrow fly from the trees and lodge in his throat. Leyon looked at the treetops above him and was astonished that he had not heard the boy climbing them.

The boy's boots hit the ground and he strutted confidently towards the camp, proud of his kill. And why should he not? So many before him had tried and failed to kill the grizzled veteran.

Again, Leyon disappeared into the bushes and walked away from the camp. Where was he going? He was not sure.

* * *

Two hundred down; I wonder how many left?

Caulen sighed as he placed the sword into the weapon rack. He looked at all the other weapons in the arms tent and sighed again. He reminded himself that this was worth it. To see that evil man drop to his knees, choking on his own blood.

It was good that Braxon was dead. Caulen had no regrets for taking matters into his own hands. *Sure, he was gonna be executed, but that was too good for him.* The only thing he wished was that the others were still around to feel the same satisfaction he did.

"Don't forget to restring the bows when you're done sharpening the swords, spears, and axes."

Caulen looked over his shoulder and saw Alton grinning at the boy's misfortune. "I already did," Caulen replied. "Sharpening the bladed weapons will take much longer than restringing the bows, so I started with that."

"That's smart. How much do you have left?"

Caulen could hear the teasing tone in his voice, but he chose to ignore it. "I'm not sure how many are here. I've sharpened two hundred swords so far."

"Not bad for two days. Why don't you take a break? Ularon wants to speak to you."

Caulen stopped using the whetstone and looked over his shoulder again. "What about?"

Alton laughed. "He's not gonna kill you, kid. But I wouldn't keep him waiting."

Caulen finished with his two hundred first sword and placed it with the other finished weapons in the rack. He wiped his hands on his tunic and followed Alton to Ularon's command tent. As they walked, Caulen received several smiles and nods from people. The attention he had been given since Braxon's execution had not gone unnoticed by the boy. One woman had even presented him with a basket of fresh-baked biscuits one morning.

When Caulen stepped into the dim lamplight of the command tent, he was surprised to find Ularon alone. He had expected a lecture with all his captains and lieutenants present. The man looked up from the map he constantly studied. He beckoned Caulen closer, and the boy stood on the opposite side of the table from him.

"Is the work going well?" Ularon asked.

"Yes, sir. All of the bows restrung and two hundred of the swords sharpened over the past two days."

Ularon raised his eyebrows. "That's good work for one person." He walked around, producing a sword in a scabbard from somewhere underneath the table. He held it out to Caulen. "Sharpen this, will you?"

Caulen thought for a moment that it may be a trick, or a jibe at the boy's expense, but the look in Ularon's eyes was genuine. Caulen accepted the sword, sitting down in a nearby chair and drawing the weapon from its sheath. Ularon handed him a whetstone and the boy began his work.

"Have you had time to think about things?" Ularon asked.

"I have, sir."

"And?"

"I regret nothing. No matter the consequences." Caulen expected frustration from Ularon, but he nodded thoughtfully.

"I don't blame you. I understand the need for vengeance. I suppose I forgot that in the heat of the moment when I punished you by making you tend to the arms tent."

"It's all right. Actions have consequences. I knew that when I released the arrow."

Ularon smiled and nodded. "I like you, Caulen." He stood and walked back to the other side of the map. "My advisors and I have finally decided a course of action. We won't be in the open woods much longer. We're going to travel to Etzekel, clear out whatever undead are still lingering there and then see if we can make it a livable space again."

Caulen's eyes widened. "Really?"

"Yes. We're going to leave in a couple of days. I want you to be part of my hunting party."

Caulen did not think his eyes could get any wider. "You do?"

Ularon smiled again. "Yes. We need to try and collect as much meat as possible to get us to Etzekel. You're a good shot, and I want you close by from now on. I think you're a good kid, and I sense you could be a great man someday."

"You mean I'll be one of your advisors?"

Ularon chuckled. "Not quite. You're still a little inexperienced for that, but I want you to be exposed to my men and I. They like to bicker, but they're some of the best people I know. I think it will do you good to be around them."

"Thank you, sir, it's an honor." Caulen bowed his head as he handed the sword back to Ularon.

Ularon grasped the sword by the hilt and inspected it. "Well done. Go get your bow and a quiver of arrows. We're to set out hunting within the hour."

Caulen's knuckles were white from gripping the pommel of the saddle as tightly as he could. His knees were clamped to the horse's ribs, and his leg muscles were starting to hurt. He looked over his shoulder and found Alton with a mocking grin on his face. He swayed gently in his saddle as he moved with each of his horse's steps.

Caulen grinned sheepishly and turned his head forward. His face grew hot in embarrassment. It was not his fault that they had given him a thirty-minute crash course on how to ride the beasts. They claimed that they had given him the tamest horse they had, but the animal made him nervous nonetheless. The bow in his hand had a sort of calming presence that counterbalanced the feeling of riding, which he was grateful for.

At the head of their party was Ularon, who had ditched his cloak for some lighter clothes that allowed him full range of motion to hunt in. Zuko was behind him, and several of the officers and soldiers separated Caulen from them. These were the men that Ularon had claimed were the greatest he knew. Caulen recognized the officers that had taken part in the meeting when he and his friends had first arrived at the camp, though he had not yet memorized their names.

Caulen trusted Ularon's instincts and tried to be as observant as possible. He wanted to know everything these men knew, and he wanted to be just like them. Perhaps Ularon did not think he had enough experience to counsel now, but Caulen swore to himself to be one of his trusted men someday.

Some of the men had spears or javelins, others had bows. The men with spears were distributed evenly between the ones who had bows. They had been away from camp for a couple of hours. They had already taken down one boar, two deer, and a couple of the more skilled archers – like Alton – had managed to bag a few rabbits and squirrels.

Caulen had refused to try and bag any of the fleet-footed game. He had killed a squirrel his first time shooting – he remembered Llanowar's surprised and impressed expression. Amongst this company, though, he did not want to risk missing and embarrassing himself.

Though he only heard mumbles from where he rode, Caulen picked up a few words about Braxon here and there. The officers were overjoyed that the general was no longer a threat. A couple times, Ularon's men would glance over their shoulders at him, lowering their voices to whispers. He ignored it as best he could, but deep down he wondered what exactly they were saying about him.

"Sir! Blood – over there." Ularon halted the group with a closed fist and looked back at the man who had spoken, who was pointing.

Ularon guided his horse to the red smear that drenched the flattened grass nearby. "Something is wounded pretty badly. Something big," Ularon said, looking through the trees for any sightings.

"Anyone else hear that?" Alton asked as he craned his neck to look.

"I hear it, unless my old ears deceive me," Zuko replied, squinting his eyes.

Caulen closed his eyes to try and focus on what he could hear. There was a slight breeze, so the leaves above were rustling gently. A stream was somewhere nearby. Then, a deep growl echoed from somewhere not too far off. "I heard it!" Caulen said.

"Sounded like a bear," one of the men said.

"Bear meat's pretty good," another added. "Plenty of it on one, too."

"Let's go find it," Ularon said, waving for them to follow his lead. "Stay alert, though. It sounds wounded, but that will make it even more violent."

Ularon ushered his horse forward at a steady trot as he readjusted his grip on the hunting spear he carried. The others followed closely behind him. Alton guided his horse past Caulen, whispering something about keeping him safe. Caulen reached over his shoulder, drew an arrow, and nocked it in preparation.

They soon found that they were headed in the right direction. The amount of blood on the ground was greater, and the growls and cries of the bear were louder. Claw marks and patches of fur were lodged in the trunks of several trees and some nearby bushes were trampled flat. Thunderous thudding sounds now joined the sounds they had already heard.

Up ahead was a small clearing where two hulking masses of fur – one brown and one black – were tossing one another around. The brown beast was a bear, but the black one was the largest wolf any of the men had ever seen. They all stopped and gaped as the wolf picked the bear up and sent it careening into a tree, which snapped and fell over.

"Look at the wolf's… hands?" Alton pointed shakily.

"It's standing on its back legs!" One of the men said, struggling to keep his voice at a whisper.

"A werewolf!" Caulen said.

"They're extinct," one of the men snapped, not taking his eyes away.

"Obviously not," Zuko replied.

The bear, bleeding heavily from its side, forced itself up from the ground. With the last of its energy, it reared onto its hind legs and roared. The werewolf drew itself to its full height, matching the bear's. It stalked slowly, snarling at its enemy.

The bear swiped weakly with one of its paws, but the werewolf raised a hand to block it. With his other hand, the werewolf clawed the bear in the stomach. The animal's bowels dropped to the ground in a bloody, sloppy mess. The werewolf clamped its jaws on the bears throat and bit down hard, snapping its neck and putting it out of its misery.

"We should leave," Ularon said, backing his horse up. Frightened already, one of the horses let out a neigh as Ularon's horse bumped into it. Everyone held their breath and watched as the werewolf, jowls dripping with blood, looked over its shoulder at them.

The werewolf dropped to all fours and faced them, snarling, ready to launch itself at them at any moment. It kept its body low as it took slow steps towards them. Ularon cursed and gripped the spear tighter once more. "No outrunning him. Follow me."

Ularon kicked his heels into the sides of his horse and hung on tightly as it lurched forward. The other men followed one-by-one, tucking their spears under their arms or hoisting their javelins over their shoulders. Caulen was the last to break the tree line and followed the lead of the other archers as they stayed on the perimeter of the clearing and circled the wolf, trying to get a clear shot around their comrades.

Ularon charged right at the lycan. He braced his spear, but the werewolf dodged to the side and swiped him off his horse with a massive hand. He hit the ground rolling, trying to avoid both the beast and his own men encircling on horseback.

Ularon jumped to his feet and reached for a dagger in his belt and saw the beast sprinting for him with a snarl on his muzzle. An arrow caught it in the shoulder and it stopped to find the pest that had injured it. The werewolf pulled the arrow out of its arm and tossed it aside.

The beast's eyes met with Caulen's – who had launched the arrow – and it hesitated a moment. Caulen drew another arrow and nocked it quickly. He pulled the string and aimed. As he was about to loose, the werewolf held up both of its hands and stumbled backwards.

Before their very eyes, the creature began to shrink. The fur began to recede on its body and his elongated limbs reformed into human appendages. The werewolf was now a tall man with short black hair and a

473

thick goatee with stubble on his cheeks. He looked up at Caulen and the boy's jaw dropped.

He waved his arms in surrender and dropped to his knees, panting heavily. Zuko and the other men continued to circle him and were closing in on him. "Everyone stop!" Caulen shouted, urging his horse forward. He broke through the lines and circled the man himself, protecting him. "Stop! I know this man... I know him. He's a friend."

Still panting, Bren looked up at Caulen and smiled.

* * *

Bren wolfed down the pottage served to him in the mess tent. This was his second bowl, which he had consumed while he listened intently to Caulen retelling the events that he had missed out on. It had taken a couple hours for the boy to convince Ularon, Zuko, Alton, and the others that Bren was not a threat to them. They had drilled him with several questions, which Bren answered simply and politely. Finally, Ularon had ushered everyone out and allowed the two to speak privately.

From their evacuation of Etzekel to their arrival at Bandimere, Bren listened. It was not until the boy began speaking of the last time he saw Llanowar and Marleyn that he stopped eating. He set his bowl down deliberately and listened as Caulen told him what the others had said — how Braxon and his men had brutalized the two women. It was from Caulen that Bren learned the dark-haired woman and the tracker in Braxon's band had been the ones responsible.

"Do we know where they are now?" Bren asked, cutting Caulen off as the boy searched for the most comforting words he could.

"Who?" Caulen asked.

"Braxon, the woman, and the man. The woman especially – the one who slit Marleyn's throat."

"Braxon's dead. I killed him myself a couple of days ago. He got captured when he tried to ambush Ularon. The woman was killed in that ambush. Nobody has seen the tracker since Bandimere."

Bren scowled and moved his bowl to the end of the table so he could plant his elbows on its surface and bury his face in his hands. He took slow, deep breaths. Marleyn had been innocent, yet her life was taken by the woman for no other reason than to be cruel. Now he found the woman to be dead and Bren was unsure what to feel. Vengeance had been attained, but not by his hand. His satisfaction was minimal.

Bren sighed and looked up from his hands. "So they're dead and aren't a problem anymore... Where are the others? Pelias? Dane?"

Caulen told them about how Pelias had fled Bandimere in hopes of sparing his friends more suffering. "We followed him into The Red Crescent, but he got to Doompoint ahead of us. We got there, but it was too late. Pelias was already reanimated and was a part of the dead army. Uragon was there, though..."

Bren nodded slowly, sniffed, and cleared his throat. "So it was exactly how Pelias said... Uragon is behind it all?"

Caulen nodded. "He left Doompoint and Pelias – well, his body – followed by command. We lost Marek trying to get away..."

Bren shook his head and chuckled solemnly. "So much has been lost... Where are the rest, then? Are they out hunting as well?"

Caulen shook his head, frowning. "No. They went to Yorkenfirth to find a ship and sail away from Akreya. I'm the only one who chose to stay."

Bren's eyes were pointing at the empty bowl at the end of the table, but Caulen noticed they were searching the distance and that his thoughts were far from here. Finally, Bren said, "So it's really over..."

"What do you mean?" Caulen asked.

"Pelias... Marleyn... Llanowar... Marek... They're dead, and the others are travelling far away from here, if they aren't dead, too."

"Don't talk like that, Bren! I'm sure they're fine. Maybe they made it to Yorkenfirth and got away safely."

"Maybe they did, but *we're* still here. Not a good place to be, if you haven't noticed."

Caulen leaned forward and looked into his eyes. "Bren... they *wanted* to wait for you. They agonized over it. They just... couldn't." The boy put on a triumphant smile. "But now that you're here, you and I can help Ularon tame the realm. He can do it – I feel it!"

Bren stood and looked down at him. "That's good for you, kid. Good luck. But our paths diverge from here. They already have. I made a promise to someone. I have to leave." He dug something out of his pocket and dropped it onto the table, taking a step away.

Caulen furrowed his brow and snatched up the silver locket from the table. Caulen stood and darted around the table, still holding the locket. "Bren, wait! You didn't even tell me what happened to you after Etzekel. At least stay to fill me in."

"There's no point."

"But..."

Bren leaned in close to Caulen and said in a low voice, "You can come with me, but you can't tell anyone where we're going."

"What?"

"There's a lycan village past the Platinum Plains. You can come with me if you want some familiar company."

"No, I don't want to leave. I believe in what we're doing here."

Bren sighed. "Fine. Stay. If you change your mind, head north to the Black Pillar, and then directly north from there. The village is hidden. Don't tell anyone. And be cautious; the Plains aren't a friendly place either."

"Why is it hidden?"

"Because people don't like werewolves."

"You're not just a werewolf, Bren. You're my friend."

Bren smiled and held out his hand. Caulen took it and the two of them shook. "That's why I'm telling you this secret. If you change your mind, you can come find me. I'll keep you safe."

Caulen nodded. "Thank you, but I'm doing all right myself. I'm making new friends." He offered the locket, but the big man waved it away.

Bren stood tall and smiled down at him. "I hope your new friends do right by you, Caulen. Best of luck."

"Yeah... You too, Bren..."

Chapter 27

Dane awoke with his mind in a haze. He groaned as he shifted on the wooden floor of the ship to a position where he could push himself to his feet. He rubbed his tired eyes and looked around the room. Koda, Grunt, and Evie were scattered around the captain's quarters, splayed in all kinds of positions.

Dane stumbled to a window and looked out. The bright sun in the clear skies jogged his memory. The storm had kept them all awake and alert for a day and a half. When the winds had finally died and the crashing waves ceased, everyone passed out. He did not know how long they had been asleep for.

The others were rousted not long after him. The first thing each of them did was look outside and rub their eyes, yawning as they became reacquainted with the living world. Evie stumbled over and wrapped her arms around her father's waist and squeezed.

"It's good to see the sun," Koda remarked.

Dane nodded, "But we have a problem."

Koda groaned. "What? Can't you just be satisfied with the circumstances for once?"

"No. That storm... I have no idea where we are now." Dane laid the map down on the table in the middle of the room. "I can estimate where we were before, but that storm could have thrown us anywhere."

"Well, we're not marooned, so that's good. And we didn't capsize, so *that's* good. What more could you ask for?"

"A sense of direction." Dane furrowed his brow at the map, planting his fists into the wooden table and leaning over it.

"Your sense of humor could use some work, Dane," Koda said, standing beside him and looking at the map. "Look, let's get outside and get some fresh air before we panic. We can figure something out. We're bound to find land eventually. It might not be Kratan, but as long as there's fresh water and game to hunt, we can work with it."

Dane nodded in agreement and turned as Grunt opened the door and walked out, ducking under the doorframe. The other three followed. They looked up at the blue skies and had to shade their eyes from the sun. The wind was strong, and Grunt went about unfurling the mainsail.

"We should go check on the others below deck," Dane said, beckoning Koda to join him.

The two of them started across the deck of the ship when Evie called out: "Guys, look!"

Grunt stopped what he was doing and stood by Evie. Dane and Koda looked to where she was pointing, and they saw a little speck on the horizon. "A ship?" Koda asked.

"I think so," Dane replied. "Evie, bring me the spyglass out of the captain's quarters."

She returned immediately with the brass telescope and handed it to her father. He extended it out and raised it to his eye. The others looked from him to the horizon and back again.

"Well?" Koda asked.

"It's a ship," Dane answered.

"Friendly?"

"I can't tell. Black sails, no markings." Dane condensed the telescope and handed it back to Evie. "Koda, go check on the others." Koda nodded and walked away. "Grunt, raise the main sail. We need to go. I don't have a good feeling about this." Grunt's heavy feet beat the deck as he quickly returned to what he was doing.

Evie placed the telescope in the satchel on her hip and went about helping Grunt and her father get the ship moving. Dane began cranking the lever to pull the anchor out of the water as Grunt finished hoisting the mainsail. Grunt then set about checking to make sure the lines were secure, and all the sails were open. Dane finished lifting the anchor and regrouped with Evie and Grunt.

"Go! Move!"

The others turned when they heard Koda's voice and saw him rushing Asira and Spencyr above deck. He turned and slammed the trapdoor shut, sliding the iron rod to lock it. The door jumped as something hit it from the other side. Asira and Spencyr ran to Dane and the others and Koda was close behind. He planted his hands on his knees, panting.

"What's happened?" Dane asked, though he had a feeling he knew the answer.

Asira responded calmly, "Tocca was supposed to be watching over Oddwen while we slept, but he fell asleep as well. Oddwen became completely consumed by the curse and he attacked Tocca. We were asleep on the opposite end of the deck and had no idea what had happened."

"That must have happened a while ago. Tocca had already turned," Koda added.

"Some people turn faster than others," Asira said. "I could not tell you when it happened."

"How did they not find you?" Dane asked.

Spencyr answered, "I made a pallet for us out of some supplies. It just happened to be hidden behind a stack of crates and some barrels."

"The dead are not very thorough," Asira said.

"They were just stumbling around down there," Koda said. "They surprised me. Asira and Spencyr came out when they started attacking me."

"You didn't kill them?" Dane asked.

"I didn't have my spear with me. Spencyr and I led them around so Asira could make her way to the stairs, then we followed."

"We'll have to deal with that later. Most of our provisions are trapped with them."

"Why not now?" Spencyr asked.

Dane pointed to the black speck that had formed into a fast-approaching ship. "That's why."

"Oh no," Spencyr muttered.

"Nobody panic," Koda said. "We don't even know if they're hostile or not."

Just as the words had left Koda's mouth, an arrow twice the size of a normal one ripped through their main sail and thudded into the deck near them.

"How is that possible?" Spencyr said. "They're too far away to reach us with bows!"

"Look!" Evie pointed into the sky where several dark figures drifted on the wind. They could not be clearly made out against the brightness of the sun, but what they could see were wings and bows in the hands of the attackers – and they were drawing again.

"Everybody move!" Dane shouted, pulling Evie aside. Everyone dove to cover as a rain of arrows pelted the area where they were just standing, while others continued to tear the sail to shreds. "Get inside the captain's quarters!"

The six of them left the zombies beating on the trapdoor and the arrows assaulting the decks and barricaded themselves inside the captain's quarters. "Trapped in here again," Koda muttered. Grunt and Spencyr slid the desk in front of the door.

"What were those things? Phantoms in the sky?" Evie asked.

"I'm not sure," Dane said.

"Shit!" Koda said, slamming a fist down on the desk. "It was supposed to be safer once we got out to the ocean! You know, smooth sailing? That's the saying, anyway."

"We cannot start panicking now," Asira said, huddling in the corner with Evie. "We must think."

Koda gripped his spear from where he had left it leaning against the wall. "I've got nothing, except kill as many of these bastards as possible."

"How are you going to reach them?" Spencyr asked.

"I'll teleport to the crow's nest and then jump from there." Koda shrugged. "Do you have any better ideas?" Spencyr paused but shook his head.

"Yes," Dane answered. "We might be able to get the upper-hand on them if we have a distraction."

"What distraction?" Koda asked.

"We could release Oddwen and Tocca from below deck."

"We might as well try it," Spencyr agreed.

Suddenly, everyone was thrown to the ground as a massive crash sounded. The ship rocked heavily, and wood could be heard snapping. Dane was the first to his feet and he staggered across the room. His hand dropped to the hilt of his sword to reassure himself it was still there. He offered both Evie and Asira a hand and helped them to their feet.

Dane turned and saw Grunt rubbing his head, a bead of blood trailing down the side of his face. Koda coughed and crawled across the floor, chasing his spear as it rolled across the room. Spencyr was up and had already drawn his hook swords.

"Everybody get up!" Dane ordered. "They've rammed us with their ship! They're gonna try boarding soon. Evie, Asira, stay here. The rest of you come with me! Cover me while I go for the trap door!"

Dane drew his sword and ran for the door. He threw it open and ran outside. To his left was the enemy ship, towering over him where it had collided with their ship and crushed part of it in. The vessel was plain with no markings, no hint of who the threat could be.

He looked around, but no one had boarded their ship yet. He ran as fast as he could, the others funneling out of the captain's quarters behind him. Arrows fell randomly from the sky, but Dane did not take the time to look up. He was focused on the trap door.

His boots thudded on the wooden deck as he ran. He was close. He heard shouts behind him.

"What the hell?"

"Impossible!"

"By the gods!"

Dane did not turn around. He knew if he did, he would not reach the door. This was the only plan they had, and he could not waste time. His friends could hold their own long enough for him to return.

As he got closer, he could see that the collision had not deterred Oddwen and Tocca. They continued to try and push the trap door open without success. Dane was there, in arms-length of it. He reached for the rod that kept the door locked in place. His fingers brushed the metal just as he felt something career into him from the side.

Dane tumbled across the deck – far away from the trap door – with whatever had tackled him. He was bundled up in the strong arms of someone wearing fur armor. He could feel it on his neck as he was wrapped up tightly in their incredibly strong grasp.

Dane struggled to make sense of which way was up and which was down. He blinked his eyes several times. He was yanked off the ground by the collar of his armor and was being dragged across the ship deck. He thought he must have taken a serious blow to the head, because when he looked for his friends, he saw something unbelievable...

Grunt, Koda, and Spencyr were being forced to their knees as Evie and Asira were being shoved out of the captain's quarters by raiders that looked like giant lions! Dane blinked again, but his vision remained the same.

The grand lions donned swords of all kinds – two-handed great swords, longswords, arming swords, and short swords clasped behind their backs or on their hips like a man. Most of them wore simple cloth tunics and kilts, though some appeared just as the lions Dane had seen roaming the wild. They were all adorned in some sort of jewelry – gold necklaces, rings, or bracelets.

All the beasts walked on their two back legs, and their front legs were like those of a human – more like arms instead of another set of legs, with hands instead of paws. Their fur was different colors, though most had pelts of amber that radiated in the sunlight. Some were the color of red clay, others were black like that of tar, and some were grey like stones.

Their eyes inspected each of the prisoners curiously. Dane feared they were about to become food for the beasts. He was oddly calm, and he half-expected to soon be jolted awake from this strange dream, but it only got more perplexing.

From the skies landed half a dozen large birds, dressed similarly to the lions and holding bows larger than those carried by humans. They did not hold the weapons in their wings, but instead had a pair of arms like a human. Their great wings folded together neatly behind their backs.

They resembled eagles and hawks in their shape and feather color, though much larger than their non-humanoid counter-parts. The birds were still shorter than the lions, and they did not wear jewelry like the cat-men did. The birds crossed their arms simultaneously and looked at each of the prisoners with the same sharp eyes befitting birds of prey.

Dane looked again to his friends and was comforted by the fact they were just as shocked as he was. They were dumbfounded and disbelieving. Evie looked to him for answers, but he had none. He looked up at the lion carrying him, his feet dragging the deck.

"He was trying to open that door," the lion growled. His voice was deep, guttural, but he spoke the common tongue.

Dane looked at his friends, who were surprised to hear familiar words. Dane held a finger to his lips to silence them.

"Open it, and see what he was desperate to find," another of the lions said, several golden rings hanging from his round cat-ears.

The lion carrying him set Dane at the end of the line by Spencyr. Another had gone about collecting their weapons. He wrenched Koda's spear out of his hands and then reached for Grunt's battle-axe, which he gave up with a glare.

The one that had tackled Dane turned around and removed the metal rod from the trap door. Before he could open it, the door flew open, and Oddwen and Tocca stumbled out, hissing and groaning. The lion roared as the two undead grabbed at him.

The other lions scattered and ran to help their friend. Grunt leaped up and tackled the lion holding their weapons. Grunt reached for his battle-axe, hoisted it in the air, and brought it down with all his might. The great cat caught Grunt by his forearms and the two stood, grunting and growling at each other.

Koda ran to help, jumping on the lion's back and trying to choke him. The lion roared, showing his sharp teeth. Spencyr and Dane went to collect their weapons, but as they turned to attack, they were met with sharp blades and bows already drawn.

The riot calmed swiftly, as one lion pulled Koda from his friends' back while that one forced Grunt to his knees and forcefully took away his weapon. The lion that was attacked by Oddwen and Tocca had just slammed Oddwen to the ground and was pulling Tocca away from where he had chomped down on his neck. The great beast hurled Tocca over the edge of the boat before turning and crushing Oddwen's skull with a stomp.

Blood matted the fur of the lion as it grabbed its neck. He spit and snarled at his friends. "They trick us!" it shouted. "Let's kill them!" The others moved closer, raising their swords. The birds followed suit, drawing their bows tighter.

Evie called for Dane, and he looked over his shoulder. "I'm sorry, Evie! I'm sorry! Don't look!"

"They speak our language!" One of the birds said, cocking its head curiously at the humans.

"Have you never met a human?" One of the lions asked.

"No, actually."

"We do!" Dane interjected. "We speak your language... Please, kill me and spare my friends. I'm the one who tried to trick you."

"Dane, stop." Koda said through gritted teeth.

"I'll kill all of you!" The bleeding lion growled, stepping close to Dane and baring his teeth.

"No, you won't!" A deep, commanding voice sounded from atop the enemy ship. Dane and his friends looked up to find another lion, wearing a wide-brimmed hat with a purple plume sticking out of the side and a dark blue cloak that was flapping madly in the wind. "Look at his chest, brother. He is friend. He bears the mark of The Iron Fox."

Chapter 28

A rope ladder tumbled down from the enemy ship and clattered against the deck of their own. The lion wearing the hat brushed his cloak free of his arms and revealed he was wearing a green tunic. He sprang over the railing of his ship and grabbed the ladder. He used it to climb halfway down before letting go and landing gracefully – though with a heavy thud. He repositioned his cloak to wrap around him as he turned to face Dane and his companions.

The other lions waited patiently for his command, as did the bird-men. They made way for him, stepping aside, bowing their heads, and holding their weapons out of the way from where they had them pointed at their captives. The leader's tail flicked back-and-forth as his amber eyes looked them over slowly. His wheat-colored pelt would have shone beautifully in the sun if he had not been covered by the cloak and shaded by the large hat he wore. The purple plume whipped in the breeze and appeared like it would be snapped away in the wind at any moment.

Dane could make out the shape of a sword underneath the beast's covering. He still did not believe what he saw, and the looks on his friends faces said that they did not either. Perhaps the storm earlier had been of magical origins and pulled their ship into some sort of strange new plane different from their own? But how did this animal know the symbol of The Iron Fox? Had Brennon been telling the truth this whole time? Surely not. Everyone knew he had been crazy.

Dane rid himself of the thoughts and noticed that the lion captain was standing before him, staring at him thoughtfully. He seemed to care little about his companions – only Dane mattered now. The great cat knelt in front of him, dropping to eye level.

"What... is your name?" the lion asked in a deep purr.

Dane felt crazy to be responding to the cat. "Dane," he replied. Had he died? Was his soul wandering this new realm in the afterlife? He had heard from many different religions about what happened to a person when they died. He could not recall hearing the one about speaking to talking lions.

"My name," the lion spoke slowly and deliberately, "is Xyril. Do you know who I am?"

Dane shook his head slowly, keeping his eyes locked on the lion. "I do not."

"You are familiar with Brennon, yes?" Xyril asked.

Dane almost laughed aloud but held it inside. This was too much of a coincidence. He remembered explaining Brennon to Anandil back in Etzekel. There was no way that the old man had been right this whole time. No one had believed him.

Dane realized the beast was still waiting for his answer. "I knew him, yes," he finally managed to say.

Xyril's muzzle twisted into what Dane could only guess was a smile. "How is he?"

"He's... dead. He has been for some time."

Xyril hissed and shook his head. "A sad day this is to learn of the passing of our old friend Brennon!" The other lions growled softly as the birds shook their heads, ruffling their feathers.

"So... you knew him well?" Dane asked, choosing his words carefully. He was still unsure to what end these beasts would have them.

"Indeed! I am disheartened that he never mentioned us to his kind." Xyril stood, towering over everyone.

One of the other cats replied: "Perhaps that is why we never received any other visitors from his land. *Akreya.*" He said the word as if it left a taste in his mouth like that of a bitter fruit.

"Only Kratan," Xyril said.

"Kratan?" Dane interjected. "You know of Kratan?" The other companions looked from Dane to Xyril with wide eyes.

"Of course. We trade with them regularly."

"Wow!" Dane said. "I'm sorry... Brennon mentioned your kind several times, but like myself, most Akreyans tend to be skeptical of such... concepts."

"What does it mean... *skeptical*?" Xyril said, leaning in close.

"It means finding something hard to believe. See, we found it hard to believe Brennon when he spoke of talking animals, such as yourself."

"Why? Brennon was an honorable man, was he not?" Xyril asked, offended.

Dane grinned and nodded, trying to keep his thoughts from whipping all over the place. "He was. Yes, he was. Very honorable."

"So why would you not believe him when he spoke of us?"

"We just... thought he was... not right in the head..." Dane hoped he was choosing the right words.

"What do you mean?" Xyril asked, squinting perplexedly at Dane.

"He was a strange man."

Another of the lion's interjected, pointing a finger at Dane. "*Strange*! Like my brother! He loves water, much like your kind. Vile stuff! *Strange*, right?"

Dane grinned, chuckling to himself. He thought he was definitely going mad now. "Yes. Yes, that's right. Strange."

"But he was not strange," Xyril said. "Brennon was a nice human. He was the first of your kind we ever met. He showed us how to build many things – houses, armor, boats, and new tools."

"He mentioned that."

"We were the ones who gave him the name, you know? The Iron Fox!" Xyril laughed. "Because he was small like a vulpen - what you call a fox - but quick and fierce, too."

"He trained many people to fight," Dane said. He tapped the sigil on his chest. "He called all of *us* The Iron Foxes."

Xyril laughed again and clapped his hands. "You see?" he asked the other animals, pointing at Dane and the companions. "They are friends!" He reached out and jerked Dane to his feet and embraced him. "You are friends, yes?"

Dane nodded quickly. "Yes. Friends."

The lions and birds helped the others to their feet and clapped them on their backs and shoulders. Dane looked back at them and saw they were giving him looks of bewilderment. He shrugged, grinning in relief.

Xyril said to Dane, "We would very much like to show you our home. In memory of Brennon and all he did for us!"

Dane bowed his head. "We accept." What else was there to do? They had been looking for a place to go, and since they did not know exactly where on the water they were, this was the next best thing to Kratan.

"Fantastic. Men!" Xyril called out and all the lions and birds listened. "Climb aboard! We're going home!" The beasts all cheered and clapped.

The birds immediately took to the skies and were the first ones on the ship. The lions bounded with their muscular legs and leapt halfway up the rope ladder to grab it and finish the climb. Xyril pulled Dane to the back of the line, allowing Evie, Asira, Grunt, Koda, and Spencyr to go before them.

The lion captain put his arm around Dane's shoulder and whispered. "Sorry about your men back there. I have never seen a human fight like an animal before – biting and clawing. Were they *strange*, as you call it?"

Dane looked over his shoulder at Oddwen's body, his face crushed by the lion. He thought a moment, deciding whether he should tell Xyril now about the undead and the plague. Then, a voice in the back of his mind reminded him of what Anandil had told him in Etzekel – about his research into beast blood and how it could be the key to stopping the plague.

He looked ahead and saw Evie staring at him from the bottom of the ladder. He nodded at her, and she smiled before turning and climbing up. Dane looked up at Xyril.

"Yes, they were strange," he said.

"What the hell is going on?" Koda whispered to Dane as he and the companions stood by the railing of the beast-peoples' ship.

Dane shook his head. "I don't have the answers to that question."

"The beast-men are real," Asira said to herself, nodding her head slowly as she accepted the fact.

"They said they trade with Kratan," Spencyr added.

Dane said, "I was in Kratan twenty years ago, and there was nothing like this going on. The Kratanians would've called me crazy if I'd mentioned talking animals."

"Let's just be glad that they're friendly," Evie said. She had barely taken her eyes off the animals as they worked the sails and lines just as humans would – though with more ease given their size. Grunt was the only one of them that compared to them in height and bulk, but they made it look easy even for him.

Spencyr looked at Dane, chuckled, and said, "I'm just glad you still wear the armor."

"Life may have tried to bugger us many times before, but for once we got lucky," Koda said.

"What about the plague?" Spencyr asked. "That one lion may turn soon. You really want to fight one of those things after it's been reanimated?"

"No," Dane said, looking at the cat-man in question. His neck was now bandaged, though he kept wincing and placing his hand on the wound. "No, I don't want to fight it. But we're testing a theory."

"What theory?"

Evie leaned in close and whispered: "We've got reason to believe that beast blood is unaffected by the plague."

"I don't know what exactly makes you think that, but I'm gonna keep my eyes on that one." Spencyr pointed at the lion.

Xyril called to them from the helm of the ship. He waved a hand, beckoning all of them forward. The companions made their way through the crowd of beast-people on deck. The lions and birds gave them barely a glance. Either Xyril's word was law among them, or Brennon truly was revered by these anthromen.

Whichever was true, Dane was grateful for their welcoming attitudes.

Xyril's mane flowed with the wind, and his tail flicked happily back and forth. "We should expect to dock in my homeland sometime tomorrow afternoon."

"Is it a land of only lions, or do the birds live with you, too?" Evie asked.

Xyril looked at her with confusion. "You really do know Brennon!" He laughed. "Lions…" He rolled the word around in his mouth. "I haven't heard us called that in some time. Brennon called all of us Leonin that."

"Leonin?" Dane asked.

"Did Brennon not tell you of our races when he mentioned us?"

"No."

"I see. We corrected him many times. We – the ones you call 'lions' – are called leonin. The other ones with the wings are called avians. What did you call them again?"

"Birds," Spencyr said.

"Very… strange," Xyril said, testing out the new word he had learned. "Anyway, there are others that I will introduce you to when the time comes. Some of the Animalia won't like your human names for them. They will look at you as lower beings."

"There are more? How many more?" Evie asked.

Xyril smiled at her. "Several."

"Do you all come from the same land?"

"Yes. We all live there. In peace, mostly, though some would prefer it other ways."

"I can't wait to see it!" Evie grinned widely.

"I like your energy!" Xyril looked at Dane. "She is your cub?"

Dane smiled and nodded. "She is."

"A proud father, like myself."

494

"How many cubs do you have?" Evie asked.

"Thirteen."

"Wow..."

Xyril yawned, and everyone looked at his fangs with curiosity. "I am excited to be home. We have been at sea for a month. My two youngest cubs will have started their sword training."

"You trained Brennon the same way?" Dane asked.

"Yes."

"Did he teach you how to speak our language?" Koda asked.

The great lion shook his head. "No, he already spoke the Animalian language. He taught us many things, but speaking was not one of them. You should have seen him when he discovered we spoke like he did! The look on his face!" Xyril laughed and looked at them. "Much like all of you when we captured you!" He laughed again.

"Thanks for not killing us," Koda murmured.

Xyril stopped laughing and leaned in close. "My crew is old-fashioned. They are loyal, and they respect tradition. I picked them myself for that reason. When we arrive at my home, stay close to us. Others will not be so kind."

"Does that mean we can have our weapons back?"

"I suppose that would be a good idea. Qalif!" One of the leonin on deck had been chatting with a couple other cat-men but turned when Xyril called. "Return the weapons we took to our new friends." The cat named Qalif walked off to fulfill the order, and Xyril turned back to the companions. "Keep your weapons close."

"Do you think we will be in that much danger?" Dane asked.

"No leonin will give you trouble. I will forbid it. The avians are our closest allies, so they should remain peaceful as well. But news will travel that you two-legs have arrived, and the others will come."

"You're doing a good job keeping us calm," Koda quipped.

"I will keep you safe." Xyril paused several moments, inspecting the water. "But it never hurts to be alert."

* * *

Bren walked unhurried.

I hope the others are safe, wherever they end up.

He thought of Marleyn, picturing her hair and her shy smile. He realized how little he knew about her, and how short a time they had been together. It only served to keep the pain and anger smoldering within him.

Bren stopped at the crest of the hill he had been climbing and looked over his shoulder. The tall grass of The Platinum Plains shimmered all around him, and he pictured himself being swallowed by the sea of silver grass.

He sighed and trudged on. *You made a promise to Harryck. You're a lycan now. You should help look after your own. They'll do the same for you.*

Something beckoned to him in the back of his head, but he ignored it. *I shouldn't have promised. I thought I would find my friends and help them, but they've already gone. I wasted so much time trying to get back to them, but I wasn't quick enough.*

He did not like the feeling of things left unresolved. He marched on. *I'll keep my word...*

*   *   *

Caulen could not keep himself from smiling. After two more days and six more hunting exploits, he had managed to bag three deer, two elk, one rabbit, and one boar – and that was just what he killed on his own. There had been more kills taken down with group efforts.

"I see that smirk," Alton teased. "Don't get too arrogant; you haven't learned everything. Speaking of which, I noticed your bow needs to be restrung."

"Yes, sir." Caulen nodded as he packed the saddlebags on his horse. Ularon had gifted him the horse after his hunting achievements, and he was getting more comfortable with the beast. So far, the boy felt that he had made the right decision to stay in the camp. Still, he thought about Evie and the others often and wondered how they were faring.

The entire camp was buzzing with excitement. Everywhere people were gathering their belongings – clothes, trinkets, food – and putting them either in packs or securing them to any animals that were not already being used for hauling. The rumble of the crowd was loud, and though there were guards posted all around, Caulen wished people would try and keep quiet for fear of attracting the dead. Still, he found it invigorating to see everyone so happy.

"I haven't seen this many excited people in a long time," Caulen remarked.

Alton continued to strap weapons to a mule as he responded, "It's great, isn't it? The people were growing restless. They didn't like being out here in the open. The prospect of Etzekel is enticing to them." He patted the animal as it stomped a hoof impatiently.

"You didn't see Etzekel the way I saw it," Caulen said, sliding a dagger into a sheath built into the saddle. "It was overrun."

Alton rushed over to him and clamped a hand over his mouth. "Keep your mouth shut. You don't wanna spook anyone before we even head out." He let go of the boy.

"I didn't mean anything by it," Caulen shrugged. "I just meant that it might take some time clearing it out. If anyone can do it, we can!"

Alton could not help but smile. "Your enthusiasm's refreshing. I'll trust your instincts. You seem to have good intuition."

"He does, doesn't he?" Ularon said, making his way through the crowd with ease. People gave The Usurper a wide berth. Whether it was from fear or respect, Caulen did not know, though he himself respected the man and was never afraid around him.

Caulen dipped his head quickly. "Thank you, Lord, for your compliment."

Ularon chuckled. "You know, I really don't like it when people call me 'Lord...'"

"Sorry, my...sir?" Caulen wrinkled his nose.

Ularon still chuckled. "Sir is fine, or just Ularon, if you like."

"People will call you lord when you're ruling the realm," Zuko said, appearing out of the crowd from the same direction Ularon had.

"Does that even matter now?" Ularon asked.

Zuko smiled. "It may later."

"I think you would make a good king," Caulen said.

Ularon smiled at the boy. "Thank you for your compliment."

"How close are we to leaving?" Alton asked.

"We're trying to get everything wrapped up now," Zuko said.

"All the tents are down?" Ularon asked.

"Yes."

"Did we have enough steeds for the old to ride on?"

"We did."

"Weapons and supplies in carts?"

"What wouldn't fit in carts are packed on the animals themselves."

"Very good." Ularon clasped his hands behind his cloak and watched the crowd silently for several moments. "Caulen, I want you to ride next to me for this journey. I want you to see what my men and I do."

"Yes, Sir," Caulen replied. He looked at Alton, who smiled at him.

"Don't forget to restring that bow of yours," Alton said.

* * *

The city was a shell. Several of the buildings were collapsed or scorched by flames long-since snuffed out. Papers, clothing, and all manner of trinkets littered the streets among the corpses they surrounded. The sun shined no longer on this place.

"I never imagined this..." the young man said. His companion stood silently behind him, offering no reply.

The two men picked their way carefully through the carnage, stepping over bodies and detouring around fallen structures. A wind blew, carrying dust through the empty streets and tugging at their cloaks as they walked. Finally, they arrived at their destination.

The leading man stopped at the open gate of the castle and looked up at its towers. "It seems like it's been an eternity since I've been here," he said. Again, his companion was silent.

They walked slowly across the drawbridge and through the metal gate left hoisted above them. More bodies were found in the inner courtyard, strewn about as if toys left by a child. The two men stopped walking, and the leader cast his eyes all around at the corpses. They had been killed by blades and fire, that much was apparent.

He threw the hood back from his head and brought his hands together in front of his stomach. He closed his eyes, tilted his head back, and let out a deep breath as he raised his hands in front of his face and spread them widely apart. His hands dropped and the corpses surrounding them stirred as one.

Their fingers twitched; their white eyes opened. They slowly rose to their feet. As one entity, they all turned their heads to face the sorcerer who had resurrected them. Soldiers, stablemen, urchins, and nobles – all stood silent and still, awaiting his command.

The man turned to his companion and said, "Welcome back to Eden, Pelias."

The former kingsguard was unmoving and there was no recollection of this place in his glossy, white eyes.

* * *

"Tell me more about yourself, Caulen."

Caulen was snapped from his thoughts and looked at Ularon. He glanced back at the line of people following their lead. Zuko was right behind them alongside Keaton, their keen eyes scanning through the trees. The boy craned his neck to see Alton, but the man had been positioned too far down the column of travelers.

Caulen looked back at Ularon. "What do you wanna know?"

Ularon shrugged. "Something to pass the time. Stay alert, though... Where are you from originally?"

"I grew up in Jalfothrin."

Ularon raised his eyebrows curiously. "With the elves? I've always known them to keep to themselves. Couldn't even get them to come out from behind their walls whenever the sickness took over."

"They made an exception for me because of my aunt and uncle. My uncle was a talented miner. They said he had the best luck of anyone in the realm, that valuable stones and metals appeared wherever he mined."

"Is that true?"

Caulen chuckled. "My uncle never believed it. He said you just had to know where to look... He wasn't a superstitious man."

"What about your parents? What happened to them?" Ularon asked.

"My mother was my aunt's sister. I don't remember her or my father. My aunt always said that they had been attacked by trolls. Wrecked our cottage, ate our livestock, and killed my parents."

"I'm sorry to hear that."

Caulen shrugged. "It's not too sad. Would've been worse if I had known them, but I didn't. My aunt and uncle fled into the wilderness with my cousin and I."

"Where are they all now?"

"Dead or missing."

"You've suffered a great deal," Ularon said matter-of-factly. "More so than I have. I respect your positivity."

"Bad things have been happening all my life. It doesn't help anything to mope about them."

Ularon chuckled. "Some men never learn that, even well into their years. You're an interesting kid, Caulen."

Even though he had been called a kid, Caulen still took pride in the man's praise. He smiled and straightened his back some more. "What about you?" Caulen asked before he had time to think. He winced, thinking he should not have bothered Ularon with a personal question.

"I'm from Yorkenfirth," he replied. "Have you ever been there?"

Caulen shook his head, and though he wanted to look at the man as he talked, he reminded himself to stay alert to his surroundings. They were in real danger always with wild animals and the dead on the prowl.

"You were at Bandimere, right?" Ularon asked.

"I was."

"Yorkenfirth is like that – small wooden houses, thatched roofs, dirt roads – but bigger. We were a large trading village. We were the only village that far north by the western coast and we had the port, so we got a lot of traffic. It was big, but everyone got along. We were a tight-knit community. Every year we elected one person from the village to lead. That had been my father for fourteen years."

"So, you were like a prince?" Caulen asked.

Ularon laughed. "Only in my dreams. It wasn't like that. My father was harder on me than anyone else because of his position of influence. He was a good man and he didn't want any of his children spoiled by power, even the little power that running a simple trading village brings."

Caulen spoke once again before thinking, and immediately regretted it. "So, what made you venture out and declare war against King Endrew… to become 'The Usurper?'" He cringed as the last words passed his lips. He peeked at Ularon out of the corner of his eye.

"That was never my intention," he said. "I never had dreams of war or fighting or claiming a throne. I was a terrible fighter in my younger days and I never wanted to leave Yorkenfirth. I was content."

"What changed?" Caulen asked, almost at a breathless whisper.

"Endrew caused the death of my father," Ularon replied.

"Oh, sorry," Caulen said. "We don't have to talk about it. Forget I asked."

"No, it's fine," Ularon said. "Most people think I started a rebellion because I wanted the Akreyan throne. I never intended to start a rebellion in the first place, never meant to start a war. I just wanted justice for my father."

Caulen was immediately on the edge of his saddle, eyes on Ularon. "What happened to your father?" he asked, coaxing Ularon.

"You know Endrew came to power through a rebellion, as well, don't you?" Caulen nodded. "He had the support of a lot of people behind him. The previous king – Faylon – was a despicable elf. Absolutely treacherous. Endrew rose up, quickly gained the favor of the people and fought a war to seize the throne.

"My father's name was Yrden. He was honorable, just, and noble in practice – not by birth like some are. He was a fair man, like I said, and so he chose not to pick sides when Endrew's war started. He remained neutral throughout the entire conflict – never dragged Yorkenfirth into it. It was easy because of the northwestern position on the edge of the realm, but we did have the largest port on the western side of the continent.

"My father was bribed, threatened, and cursed by both sides of the war, but he never swayed. He did not have lofty dreams, said his one and only concern was keeping Yorkenfirth safe. Even though he stayed neutral, Endrew never forgot…"

Caulen thought that Endrew had been mad at Yrden for staying out of the conflict entirely and not joining forces with him, but when he looked at Ularon, he could see that the man was trying to work through the details in his head before finishing his story. Caulen took the moment of pause to check their flank. Still nothing stirring amongst the trees. Though their journey was still young, he was unsettled by the lack of activity they had witnessed thus far.

Finally, Ularon spoke: "Endrew eventually claimed the throne, but it took him quite a while to squelch all of the elven king's supporters. They went about terrorizing the realm, trying to make Endrew look weak. He chased them into The Platinum Plains, where they made a pact with the Elk Tribesmen.

"Endrew knew that this was the last of the supporters, and if he could end this battle swiftly, that it would be the end of his problems with them. Yorkenfirth was the nearest ally Endrew had, so he sent a messenger to my father, requesting every able-bodied man report to his camp at The Black Pillar.

"Yrden sent the messenger back empty-handed, claiming that he would not assist the new king because it was a remnant of a previous conflict that he had remained neutral in."

"Endrew was king by this point. Your father should have aided him." Caulen gritted his teeth. He knew that this was for sure going to be the time that his mouth got him in trouble. He was so wrapped up in the story that he did not think before he spoke. He awaited the repercussions, but none came.

Ularon still had a stern look on his face, but that had been present since he began speaking of Endrew. "My father was an honorable man, though not always the most practical. I agree, he should have recognized Endrew as king and sent forces to help him, but he didn't."

"So Endrew resented him for his neutral stance in the war, and then his failure to recognize him as king after the fact..."

"It's even more than that, Caulen, even though most men would not have stood for such insults to begin with... Endrew's brother Koen was a captain in his army. He wanted desperately to lead his brother's forces, but constantly fell short of Braxon's military performances.

"Koen deemed that battle to be the day he would finally prove himself better than Braxon. He took the soldiers under his command ahead without Endrew's or Braxon's approval and attempted to put down the Faylon supporters and the tribespeople who helped them, but Koen and all his men were massacred. It was Braxon who led the next attack – himself personally on the front lines — and put an end to the conflict."

Caulen's eyes were wide at the story. He had not even known that Endrew had a brother. He hoped Koen had died with honorable intentions and was not simply trying to wrest the glory of battle from Braxon. Even if the old general had been a vile man, he had also been a genius tactician.

"Endrew never forgave my father for his lack of support," Ularon continued. "He blamed Yrden for the death of his brother. From that point on, Endrew tried to tax Yorkenfirth dry to get them to turn on my father. He made several other moves to sabotage my father's hard work — mostly political shell games and back-stabbing techniques. They eventually worked, and someone killed my father."

"Who?" Caulen asked.

"A beggar on the street. He had just recently lost his business, his wife had died of sickness because he couldn't afford the medicine, and his two children were starving. Seems strange, doesn't it, that a man who kept his village out of a war was killed by a man living on the streets... I executed that man myself."

"Wow... That's awful. I'm sorry you had to go through that," Caulen said, watching him.

Ularon was still stern-faced. Caulen took another second to observe the woods. Still nothing.

"My father did his best to keep everyone satisfied," Ularon said, "but it was no secret that he was being jammed up by the king. I suppose some people snapped. I took up a sword and declared I would have Endrew's head. I suppose I blamed him for my father's death the same way he blamed my father for Koen's death."

"I don't blame you. I don't think anyone could," Caulen said.

"No?" Ularon looked at him with a small smile. "There were many times I thought I should just give up my crusade, but I never forgot that I was doing it for my father. The most honorable man I knew deserved justice, and I've always believed I was the only one who could deliver that justice. Now, Endrew is dead, there's a plague on the realm, and no one remembers my father..."

Caulen did not know what to say. He nodded grimly and took a deep breath while he cast his eyes to the surrounding forest. He wracked his brain to try and find something comforting to say or change the topic, but nothing sprung to him.

"Thank you, Caulen," Ularon said.

"Thank *me*?" Caulen's head whirled around to look at the man. "What did I do?"

"You let me talk. There's not much time for idle chat or reminiscing these days. Somehow through this rebellion I never intended to start, I gained a following I never wanted to lead to a throne I never coveted. With that responsibility, I had to leave much of myself behind. Not many people have the guts to pry into a 'lord's' past."

Caulen stammered to apologize, fumbling for the right words, before noticing that Ularon was giving him a wry grin. He chuckled as Caulen's face flushed and he scratched his head nervously. "Not guts," Caulen said, "just stubbornness."

"Warriors call that 'perseverance.'"

Ularon and Caulen laughed, and behind them, Zuko smiled to himself.

Chapter 29

The ship rocked gently as it glided over rich blue waters. The wind was strong, urging the vessel along on its journey. The sun beat down on them, illuminating the companions' view for leagues in all directions.

"This weather is perfect! I could just lie down on the deck and take a nap!" Spencyr smiled widely, taking in the rays of sunshine.

"I thought you were going to keep an eye on that cat that got bit?" Koda asked.

Spencyr's mood quickly flattened. He glanced for a moment at the cat, who was drinking a mug of water with a few of his mates, laughing and enjoying themselves. "He hasn't shown any signs of illness," the younger man murmured, "Besides, all of them seem friendly. Why are you so suspicious, Koda?"

"Because," Koda whispered, "even Xyril suggested we be on our guard."

"From the other Animalia of his land," Evie interjected.

"Maybe Xyril trusts his men wholly, but I sure don't. I did *not* make it this far to end up as cat shit."

Dane cut in, "You're all correct. We should keep our eyes open, but we must start relaxing around them. They may be able to sense the tension in us."

"Sleeping in shifts last night did not help," Asira said, her arms crossed as she listened to the conversation off to the side of the group. "I am sure that we appeared paranoid because of that."

"We couldn't risk it," Koda said.

"But they *have* left us all alone for the entire journey, except to offer us food and drink," Evie said.

"Maybe they trust too easily."

Evie glared at him. "We're not going to do anything to betray that trust. Even if they aren't... two-legged like us, we could have happened upon some other undesirable travelers."

"She's right about that," Dane agreed. "They've given us no reason to distrust them. Let's give them a chance."

Koda sighed. "Right... So, what about a plan for when we land?"

"We have no idea what we're up against. We can't plan for much, except keeping our weapons close for the ones Xyril warned us about. Other than that, we'll improvise."

"So, what? We're just gonna lodge with the talking animals for the rest of our lives?"

Dane shrugged, grinned, and clapped Koda on the shoulder. "Maybe. We'll have to see how nice it is."

After around two hours, Dane and his companions could see an island off in the distance. No one knew what they had expected, but they were dismayed that the Animalian island looked the same as any other island. From this distance, all they could make out was a great volcano towering over a forest beyond a large, sandy white beach.

"I'd be lying if I said I wasn't at least a little disappointed," Spencyr confessed.

"I know what you mean," Evie said as Grunt grunted in agreement.

"We'll have to see what awaits us," Dane said. "Remember that Xyril said there were several more animals on the island."

"And some of them not very friendly, so that's exciting," Koda smirked at his joke.

Asira said in a serious tone: "The leonin warrior that was bitten does not seem to be reacting to it. He treats it like it is just another wound."

"That's great," Koda said. "What the hell do we do with that information? It's not like we actually know anything beyond that."

"We don't even know *that* for certain," Evie said. "Perhaps it just takes longer for the Animalia to turn because of their beast blood?"

"That could be right," Asira agreed.

"Then we'd best keep quiet about our suspicions for now," Dane said. "Give it a couple days before we tell Xyril what's going on."

"And if these other beasts eat us before then?" Koda asked.

"Then it won't really matter."

Koda shrugged and leaned on his spear, staring at the far-away island. "I suppose you're right." Grunt patted him on the back before leaning on the railing and joining him in his watch.

"We'll be landing before we know it. Everyone go ahead and check your weapons," Dane suggested, drawing his sword. Grunt eyed the edge on both blades of his battle-axe. Koda checked the point of his spear to make sure it was not dull. Spencyr pulled a cloth to polish his hook swords and gave it to Dane once he was done. Asira pulled two daggers from her satchel and handed one to Evie. Dane eyed her with a disapproving look.

Asira shrugged. "Do you want her to be unprotected?"

"She won't be. We'll all be there," Dane replied.

"But what if?"

"I'll be fine, Dad," Evie said, smiling, before Dane could say anything else. She drew the dagger and looked it over, flipping it from one hand to another. Everyone stopped and watched in surprise except for Asira. Evie stopped and sheathed the dagger, grinning from ear-to-ear. "Marek taught me a few things while I was in Etzekel."

Dane scowled but went back to tending his weapon. Xyril approached them, leaving Qalif to steer the ship safely into port. His tail swished back and forth gently. "I hope you aren't planning anything," the great cat said.

"Just being cautious," Dane replied, "like you said."

Xyril laughed and clapped him on the back with his massive hand. "Good, good. Just try and act calm. They will be able to sense your fear."

"We're not afraid of anything," Koda bluffed.

Xyril sneered and took a step toward Koda, towering over him. Koda remained leaning on his spear, looking up casually at the leonin. "I smell it on you now, the musk of fear. It's nothing to be ashamed of, little one. Fear keeps our wits strong." Without waiting for a reply, Xyril turned away and sniffed the breeze and watched his island grow bigger as they drew closer. "Only a few minutes more, my friends, and you will see our home. You are honored guests here."

"Thank you," Dane said, sheathing his sword and looking at the others to insure they were done with their weapons.

"For what are you thanking me?" Xyril asked, peering over his shoulder.

"For welcoming us so warmly."

Xyril laughed. "Wait until you see it. It may not be to your standards. Brennon seemed to enjoy himself, however." He shrugged.

Koda muttered in Dane's ear: "Wasn't this Brennon guy kinda... insane?"

Dane nodded. "Though, after seeing Xyril, I'm beginning to think he wasn't as far out there as everybody thought."

The companions saw that the beaches were barren, except for several plain wooden piers. There were several ships already docked, but they were also empty of any life. With no one and no buildings around, the companions were unsure what to think. Perhaps the Animalia did not have houses? Though Xyril had mentioned that Brennon taught them how to build them.

They had no time to ask questions, for Xyril began barking orders to his crew, and the leonin and avians scrambled about to draw sails and tie lines. Dane and the others watched as the avians soared to the tops of the masts and the leonin darted across the deck on all-fours, armor and weapons clinking with each step. Xyril stared intently at the tree line of the forest.

Koda sidled up casually next to Dane and leaned in to whisper. "Look in the treetops."

Dane let his eyes drift upwards. At first, he did not see anything unusual, but the longer he focused and squinted, he made out several nests larger than he had ever seen, and eyes watching them from those nests. As if reacting to being spotted, several avians took to the sky, careening towards them at alarming speeds. Xyril waved a massive hand and the birds cut upwards. They congregated above the ship and swirled in the air together like a tornado made up of fowl.

"They're friendly, right?" Spencyr asked nervously.

Xyril nodded and tipped his wide-brimmed hat further back on his mane. "The avians and the leonin have a long-standing alliance. I suspect none of them will bother you humans."

"At least we don't have to worry about the sky," Koda said.

Dane motioned for Evie to come to him. The girl walked over briskly and leaned in close as Dane said, "What is Xyril thinking right now?"

Evie looked up at him with an eyebrow arched. "You *want* me to read his thoughts? You always tell me not to." She grinned slyly.

Dane sighed before his expression hardened to let her know he was not in the mood for her jest. She gave a slight chuckle and turned her focus toward the leonin. Her eyes squinted the tiniest amount as she stared at the cat. Xyril shook his body, ruffling his fur, and turned to look for whatever it was that sent a chill down his spine.

Evie quickly turned back to her father before the leonin's eyes fell on her. "There's nothing there except restlessness. He's just ready to be home."

"No thoughts of danger or trickery?" Dane asked.

Evie shook her head. "I guess I should confess that before you gave me permission, I was tapping into the minds of some of his crew." Dane sighed again, but Evie kept explaining. "Nothing bad from any of them. They just want to be on land again."

Dane crossed his arms as Grunt, Spencyr, and Asira joined the others where they were. The crew was a frenzy as they scuttled about drawing sails and towing lines. They brought the ship to a smooth stop near the dock. Several of the avians on board glided to the pier and caught the lines that the leonin tossed to them. They pulled the ship closer to the dock and the leonin dropped a ramp.

Xyril grinned from ear-to-ear and turned to address his crew. "Welcome home, everyone! Good sailing out there, especially for leonin!" He laughed. "Go to your families and enjoy yourselves. You've earned it!"

Dane and his companions huddled closely together, clinging tightly to one another as the entire ship rumbled with the beating footsteps of the entire crew of leonin sailors running across the deck and leaping over the railing to land on the pier. They roared with excitement, trying to shove past one another to be the first to rejoin their families. Several of the more rambunctious leonin were running on all fours.

Xyril laughed a deep, guttural laugh, watching his crew go. He turned to the companions and motioned for them to follow. "I will lead you myself." As they came down the ramp, they saw that a handful of leonin had stayed to accompany Xyril – Qalif and the lion that was bitten among them.

Xyril led the way and the humans fell in behind him. The other leonin formed a loose barrier around them. Dane looked at Evie for confirmation, and he could tell by the look on her face that she was already using her powers to read each of their thoughts. She smiled at her dad and shook her head. Dane let the tension in his body lessen.

The wounded leonin scratched at the bandage around his neck and then laid a massive arm across Spencyr's shoulders. The younger man flinched and had a pained look on his face. He gave the leonin an uncomfortable look and a forced smile.

The leonin was purring softly as he leaned down to Spencyr's height. "Welcome to our home, human. It is a lovely place. I'm sure you'll take to it." He clapped Spencyr on the back roughly, sending the human reeling forward a few paces. The leonin laughed and Spencyr tried to appear unbothered.

"Ah! Land beneath our paws once again!" Xyril stretched his arms out wide as he trekked through the white sandy beach. He kicked a little in the air out of glee and began purring like the other leonin. He looked back at the humans and said, "Our village is a little way into the forest. It won't take us long to get there."

They found no roads past the tree line, but they did see plenty of tracks, most of them from the leonin and avian. *Of course, they wouldn't need roads*, Dane thought. He looked up into the trees and saw the avian nests, which looked even bigger now that they were directly underneath them. The nests were empty, even though the avians were nowhere to be seen. *Where could they be?* Ambush was the first thought in Dane's mind, and so he made himself even more aware.

The companions found their breath hitch in their throats as they came upon the leonin city. Here, intermingled amidst the trees of the forest was a city bigger than Bandimere or Yorkenfirth made up of log structures for as far as they could see. There were still no roads connecting the random placement of buildings, just paths where the leonin trampled the forest floor.

Here the companions also discovered where the avians had gone. With their help, news of human guests must have been spreading like wildfire through the leonin city. Many of the cats had been whispering amongst one another or to the birds, but quickly hushed when Xyril arrived with his new friends.

The leonin in the city paused whatever they were doing — from carrying jars of water, fashioning boots and sandals, crafting armor and other clothing, or maintaining and polishing weapons — and eyed the humans. The city was full of leonin, and as whispers spread, more of them appeared from inside their homes to marvel at them.

The men wore either light armor or simple tunics, and some wore helmets or hats like Xyril. Some of the females wore dresses or long robes, though others were garbed in battle-dress like the males. Many of the male leonin had several braids in their manes, and almost all the women wore earrings of some sort. Their cat eyes watched with curiosity and suspicion, sizing them up with a precision that the humans could almost feel. It was eerie the way they watched, while the thick forest canopy and buildings shrouded them.

Xyril held his hands out wide in greeting and took a few steps ahead of the others. "Family, friends, it is good to lay eyes on you once more!"

A dozen of the leonin rushed forward and embraced Xyril, some licking his mane or his ears as they knocked his hat to the ground in the scuffle. Xyril bellowed loudly, tossing some of the leonin aside playfully. Some of them were the same size as him, while others were smaller.

"My cubs! I have missed you!" Xyril purred louder than the companions had heard from him so far.

His cubs took a step back, smiling and purring as well. The biggest one, the one closest to Xyril's size, said, "Father, who are these soft-skins you have brought with you?"

"They prefer to be called 'humans,' boy, and they are our friends," Xyril replied. He turned to one of the smaller leonin and said, "Ryndall, you are well-versed in the histories of our people..." Xyril placed a hand on the leonin's shoulder and then pointed at Dane. "Tell the others what the symbol on that man's chest means."

"Everyone knows what that means, Father," the cub replied.

"Remind them."

Ryndall took a deep breath and drew himself to his full height. "That symbol is The Iron Fox, named after the First Human Brennon. He was first of his people to make friends with ours, and he taught all the Animalia many useful things, and we him. It was through this sharing of knowledge that the friendship between Brennon and Animalia formed. We swore to always revere the symbol of The Iron Fox, the title which we gave to Brennon, who accepted it as an honor."

Xyril patted his son on the shoulder. "A good story, though some may prefer not to remember." He stood and addressed the other leonin, who were still skeptical. "This is Dane. He bears the symbol of The Iron Fox, which means he was a trusted friend of Brennon. Anyone Brennon trusted is a friend *we* can trust."

Dane tried to keep his face as plain as possible. He was not about to tell the leonin that his armor that bore The Iron Fox sigil was issued to everyone who joined The Iron Fox Legion. He would play along. And it was not a total lie, with Dane having been a captain in Brennon's legion. He supposed he had been trusted more than some.

One of the leonin voiced his doubts: "How do we know he didn't steal that armor off Brennon's body?"

Xyril drew himself to his full height. "Dane told me he knew Brennon."

Another leonin called, "You always were an over-trusting fool, Xyril."

Xyril eyed the heckler intensely. "Those who are always suspicious of others are often hiding things themselves."

Finally, one of the leonin spoke in Xyril's favor, saying: "Xyril has never led us astray before. No reason his judgement would falter now. That's the end of that." The leonin rose from the campfire he had been seated by and nodded to Xyril. He turned and walked off into the forest. Some of the other leonin followed.

The others waited for the leonin to leave and then one of them said in a soft tone, "Xyril, we all know how much you revere Brennon and want to respect his legacy. But don't you think you should have discussed this with the council before bringing them here?"

"I am a part of the council, and I have lived my life thinking that the council would adhere to The Iron Fox. Anyone bearing that is a friend to our people. That has always been the way of things."

"That's always been a dangerous notion," an avian said, "and one day it could get all of us killed."

"We have been trading with Kratan for years, and they have never once made a move on our people. None of our kind have died in Kratan or by Kratanian hands," Xyril replied.

"Perhaps we shouldn't be pushing our luck."

"So, you would have me put the humans back out in the ocean?"

Another leonin shook his head, his mane waving in the breeze. "I think what everyone is concerned about is not that the humans are here, but what the others will think about it. You know as well as I do that the leonin, avians, and vulpens have respected the tradition. But what of the others? They had begrudgingly allowed us to trade with Kratan, but do you think they will respond peacefully to the humans being here in our land?"

An avian cawed: "You know our alliance with the simians, saurians, and ceratoth is a fragile one. This will break it!"

Xyril sighed. "We will handle that when it happens. For now, we must welcome our human friends."

"You had better be ready to handle it soon, Xyril," one of the leonin snarled. "The avians are spreading the news across the island. They'll hear about it fast, and they'll be here. Probably armed and ready for battle."

"Let my crew and I handle them," Xyril said, trying to convince everyone. The great cat picked his hat up from where it had fallen earlier and dusted it off. He looked at a brown-feathered avian who had been a part of his crew. "Rally the others, and then summon all of the avians and vulpens. Send someone for the loxodon and minotaurs. Tell them to hurry."

The avian nodded and immediately walked deeper into the log city to find the rest of Xyril's crew. The other leonin – some satisfied, some muttering amongst themselves – dispersed throughout. Xyril turned to the companions and smiled.

Evie walked up to him and said, "We're sorry that we're causing you problems, Xyril."

"No, it is I who should be apologizing to you! How quickly some choose to forget old friends and promises. Just remember to be wary. They were not lying when they said that others would show up. And they *will* be angry."

* * *

Though there was tension in the air, the humans were introduced to some of the leonin residents and were welcomed without hesitance. Xyril did his best to reassure everyone that the presence of the humans was a good thing and that he would handle anyone who balked at the idea. Some were easily convinced, while other leonin and avians cut a wide swathe to avoid Dane and his companions.

The humans were brought to Xyril's home and introduced to his wife and thirteen cubs. They were directed to a wash basin and given food and water. None of the companions questioned from what animal the meat they were fed was taken from. They ate it with many thanks, grateful to Xyril and his family for taking them in.

"Brennon always said that you humans like your meat over the fire first," Xyril's wife, Gitra, commented as she cooked. "I never understood why, but I assume you like it the same."

"Yes," Evie said, "thank you." She took the wooden platter from Gitra and served the others for her.

Koda investigated the cup he held and sloshed it around before knocking it back. He swallowed and sighed, looking disappointed. "Xyril, one of these days we'll have to show you and your kind how to make wine."

"My cubs make whine all the time!" Xyril laughed and slapped one of his sons on the shoulder.

Koda muttered something and returned to memories of having strong drink in hand. The others ate and drank happily, enjoying the comforts of being indoors. Then, there was a knock at the door. Gitra let one of the avians from earlier enter.

"Xyril, the simians are headed this way and they're bringing the saurians and ceratoth with them. They're all armed." There was only a hint of apprehension in the bird's tone. He stood awaiting Xyril's answer.

A low growl radiated from Xyril's throat as he peered into the fire that burned in the pit in the middle of his home. "What of the minotaurs, loxodon, and vulpens?"

"The vulpens just arrived. No word from the minotaurs or loxodon."

"Very well." Xyril stood and stretched. "Gitra, help the cubs gather their weapons. There may be a fight." Gitra nodded and began corralling the smallest cubs as the eldest ones began doling out the weapons from their armory.

Xyril led the way outside, taking a deep breath as he stepped into a beam of sunlight that broke through the canopy of leaves above him. There were now more Animalia present, speaking in hushed tones. Besides the leonin and the avians, there were now the vulpens – foxes.

The vulpens were roughly half the size of the leonin, comparable in height to Dane and the other humans. They were sleeker and more nimble-looking. They wore lightweight armor like the leonin and had a multitude of daggers and knives on their belts and strapped to their chests and legs. Most of them had orange fur, but some were grey or black.

Their legs and tails were left uninhibited by any armor or other kinds of clothing. They had the same love of jewelry as the leonin, favoring small gold and silver rings in their ears. They all looked at the humans, most nodding their greetings. When Dane stepped out of Xyril's home, the vulpens took a few steps forward. They studied the Iron Fox on his chest before dropping one-by-one to a knee and bringing their right arms across their torso's and covering their hearts with their fists.

The first vulpen to stand approached Dane, hands hanging casually from the belt around his waist.

His fur was a bright orange and his muzzle was white. Both of his ears had chunks missing where the flesh had been ripped away, and three lines ran from the base of one ear down his neck where the scars prevented the fur from growing again.

The vulpen said, "No doubt you're the one called Dane Iron-Fox. Name's Raudo. Good to meet ya'."

"Yes, you too," Dane said. He struggled to find words, for even though he had met the leonin and the avians, he still was not used to talking animals. "Seeing you, I understand Brennon must have been honored to be named after your kind."

Raudo sniffed and crossed his arms. "If anything, your kind favors the simians. They originally called him 'The Iron Vulpen,' because he was as tall as us, and we're actually the shortest of the Animalia. He didn't even like daggers the way we do, and he asked us to call him 'The Iron Fox,' instead. We did, and he accepted the nickname, saying it was 'a fine compliment to be compared to such fierce and noble warriors.' Brennon was all right in my mind. Sad to hear he's gone."

The vulpen did not waste any time demonstrating that sadness, however. He walked away to bark orders to his kind to spread out amongst the village in defensive positions. Dane watched him as Spencyr approached him.

"He remind you of anyone?" the younger man asked, eyeing Raudo with a small smirk.

"Captain Deller," Dane replied. "He always kept his mind on the next fight. Kept his men on edge and in fighting shape."

"Even when there wasn't a fight on the horizon," Spencyr said. "I guess that's why the Foxes under his command were always the toughest."

Xyril addressed the humans, saying, "Let me do all the talking. Our visitors are quick to anger, but I may be able to keep things peaceful. If I'm wrong, fight. The leonin, avians, and vulpens are with you."

"We won't provoke them," Dane replied.

Xyril raised a furry finger to his lips to silence them and took a few steps away from the humans. His feline hearing must have tipped him off that their visitors were approaching. From the forest, the sound of heavy footsteps and clanging armor wafted into the leonin city, along with the sound of rustling leaves and bushes and sounds of snapping twigs.

Low growls, grunts, and rumblings made the humans' skin crawl. The leonin tensed, hushed growls welling up from their throats. The vulpens' mouths opened and closed in quick, quiet chittering. Some of the avians retreated to the treetops above to observe the coming exchange.

"Xyril!" A deep, angry voice shouted from the trees. "Xyril! Where are you?"

The great cat made no response. He stood in the open with his arms crossed. His tail flicked back and forth in irritation, and Dane saw that his whiskers twitched ever so slightly.

The voice bellowed one last time, "Bring me that mewling bastard!" before pushing his way between two trees which Dane swore he saw bend under the force of his push.

A giant ape even taller than Xyril stomped into the city, locking wide, furious eyes with the great cat. He was clad in a heavy metal breastplate with matching gauntlets and greaves. The armor was painted red, which contrasted the dark black hair covering his body. On his shoulder was propped a two-handed stone hammer that was somehow dwarfed by the sheer size of the beast himself.

There were other simians with this one, though they were all closer in height to the leonin. They also wore their own armor, some painted blue, purple, or gold. All of them carried hammers similar to the leading ape, and all of them appeared just as manic as him.

There were two other kinds of Animalia with the simians. Saurians – which Dane knew as crocodiles – and ceratoth, which fit the description of animals called rhinoceros', which even though Dane had never seen in person, their leathery skin and two horns jutting from their snouts matched the stories he had heard about the animals.

The saurians had dark green or black scales with long, powerful tails, and claw-like nails on their fingers. They wore armor-plated trousers on their legs, but their torsos and heads were free of any coverings, leaving only rings of gold and silver to dangle from their snouts. The saurians coveted the spear, each of them grasping one firmly, the tip pointed straight up into the sky. They were roughly the same height as the leonin.

The ceratoth were shorter than the others - in between the vulpens and the leonin. The stocky, well-muscled beasts brandished metal maces, some with spikes – called morningstars – and were armored similarly to the simians from head to foot, being the only Animalia the humans had seen yet to wear boots. The tips of their horns were painted for ornamentation or intimidation, and some even had cones of gold and silver that capped them.

The leading gorilla stamped closer, his nostrils flaring. Xyril held his stare, but the simian's dark brown eyes shifted to the humans standing behind him as he noticed them for the first time. He bared his teeth and roared, making Dane and his companions shrink back. Xyril remained unflinching.

"Xyril! I had hoped the news we received was part of some jest. I thought surely you and your kind were not so foolish as to bring the soft-skins into our home. I see now that I expected too much of you!"

"Calm yourself, Kurjin, and set your eyes upon this one." Xyril pointed at Dane, but Kurjin only glanced for a moment.

"I saw him... and the vulpen on his chest." The simian's own chest heaved as he fumed.

"Brennon preferred it was called the Iron 'Fox,' after what his people named them. And they are humans, not 'soft-skins.'"

"I do not care on both counts, Xyril. Why are they here? I demand an answer!"

Xyril sighed heavily and looked at the other simians, saurians, and ceratoth that Kurjin had been accompanied by, and then he looked at Dane and the others, the leonin, avians, and vulpens. Something in his eyes said that he was searching for the best words, but Kurjin's eyes said that he did not have the patience. Dane had to fight the urge to put his hand on the hilt of his sword in preparation. He looked at the others and was relieved to see they all kept their hands away from their weapons.

Xyril finally said, "Kurjin, we all know our history. We know what the Iron Fox means. We promised that all who bore that sigil would be unharmed by us. Because of Brennon and all he taught us."

"As you said, we know the history. I understand that. You think I hate the humans, but I do not."

"Then convince my friends here of that. I don't know that they are so sure. We trade with Kratan all the time. Why is this different?"

Kurjin growled and blew a quick breath through his nostrils. He glowered down at the humans for a moment before looking back at Xyril. The gorilla said, "I do not hate the soft-skins. We have benefitted from trading with the ones living in Kratan. I hate that they are *here*. The Iron Fox was the only human that had set foot on our island, and now you have brought them here without discussing it with the council! A council you are a part of, I remind you."

Xyril nodded grimly. "I suppose you are right. It should have been brought to the council, but I did not have time to send a messenger. We crashed their ship and they needed help. That's what we pledged to do for The Iron Fox. Help."

"Your answer does *not* satisfy me," the simian grumbled. "I'm making a formal request that you present yourself and this situation to the council of this island." He swapped the hammer from one shoulder to another.

Xyril blinked several times, staring at Kurjin with a gaze that said he was weighing his response. "Fine," he relented. "I will plead my case to the council."

The two stared in a standoff for several moments, eyes narrowed. Kurjin was suspicious that he had persuaded Xyril to comply so easily. Xyril gazed at him unwaveringly. Finally, Kurjin turned and began to stomp away with heavy, slow steps.

The gorilla said over his shoulder, "Good. I will call the meeting. Be at the mountain summit at an hour past sundown."

Xyril grunted and watched the crowd of saurians and ceratoth turn reluctantly to follow Kurjin. No doubt that most of them were disappointed a fight had not occurred. Dane sighed internally. He could not imagine how difficult a battle that would have been.

Xyril turned to the humans. "I am sorry, my friends. I was hoping this matter would be settled and done, but the council will drag this out."

Dane replied, "Xyril, if we're going to cause you too much trouble, we can leave." He looked to his companions to see if any disagreed, but no one did.

Koda, leaning on his spear, said, "All we need is one of your ships."

Xyril shook his head violently, mane blowing in the breeze. "No, my friends. The Iron Fox means something to me. We made a promise to him, and I intend to honor that."

Without thinking, Dane held out his arm for a shake, "Thank you." To his surprise, the leonin was familiar with the custom and grasped his forearm, his large hand engulfing Dane's own. Dane's hands felt the soft fur on Xyril's own.

"Do not thank me yet," the great cat admitted. "It will be a decision for the council whether or not to let you stay now, but I will fight for you the best I can." He smiled a warm smile, purring. "Come, let me show you around the island, before you are banished from here forever." His laugh reverberated throughout the forest.

Chapter 30

Xyril introduced the humans to many of the leonin in his city, most of which were polite and even sympathetic to them after the altercation that they had witnessed. Earlier, many had been uncomfortable having the strangers near their homes, but now some of them were saddened by the prospect of them leaving.

"The Leonin are good people, mostly," Xyril explained as they left the city, walking to the west, "though some of them need to be reminded of what's important every so often. They have realized that they should be welcoming you all."

"They don't think we're causing trouble?" Evie asked, walking right next to the great cat.

"Perhaps, but they know it's ultimately the decision of the council."

"This council," Dane said, "tell us about it."

Xyril glanced back and saw Grunt, Koda, and Spencyr looking around nervously. "You may lower your guard, my friends. We are going to vulpen territory next." He turned his gaze ahead to the path he walked, though the three men remained observant. "The council is made up of sixteen members – two of each Animalian tribe. We discuss issues and try to reach conclusions we believe are the best for all involved. Sometimes the meetings can turn violent. At the very least, they devolve into shouting matches."

"How do they decide the outcomes of these meetings?" Spencyr asked.

"We take votes."

"What if there is a tie? There's sixteen of you..."

"The one who brings the discussion to the table does not get a vote. That way there is never a tie."

"So, you won't get a vote tonight?" Koda asked. "Great..."

"Never fear, my friends. I will plead my case for you as if I were begging for my own family to stay on the island." He smiled wide. "We already have the avians and vulpens on our side. Raudo liked you, and he's on the council. Speaking of him..."

They came upon another city much like the leonin's. Wooden roofs were built against hollowed out trees to make dens for the vulpens. Some of their homes were simple structures built over holes burrowed into the ground. They did not have much in the way of defenses, since the other Animalia were too large to enter their dens. There were a few vulpen walking about leisurely, but most were underground, Dane guessed.

Up ahead stood Raudo, who was speaking to a giant beast with leathery, grey skin and wide ears fanned out on either side of small, black eyes. Its gigantic ears left much room available for adorning with rings, which the animal took full advantage of.

It had a long, snake-like trunk and two white tusks protruding on either side of it, which were both capped in silver like the ceratoth they had seen earlier. It was twice the size of the leonin, causing the vulpen to appear tiny from the distance they were at. Coiled around a massive fist was a heavy iron chain. On one end of the chain was a spiked iron ball the same size as the beast's fist. Its tail was scrawny compared to the rest of his body.

"Wow!" Evie said breathlessly as she stopped a moment to marvel at the beast.

Dane leaned over and whispered in her ear: "Elephant." He had seen some warriors in foreign countries use them as siege animals, though these were much larger than the ones he had seen.

"It reminds me of that cyclops back in Akreya," Koda said. "Just a little smaller." Spencyr gave a surprised look at hearing about the encounter.

"They are large, but they are not the most courageous of the Animalia," Xyril murmured. "Just don't let them hear you say that." He cleared his throat and walked towards the two. "Daridasa!"

The elephant flinched at the appearance of the leonin. He tried to stammer a response as Raudo dipped silently into a nearby den, but finally resigned to dipping his head in a polite greeting. His black eyes scanned slowly over the humans that accompanied him.

"I'm surprised to find you here, Daridasa. I was just showing our guests around the territories of our allied Animalia." Xyril bowed slightly in return. "I was hoping you would be able to meet them at my city – I sent a messenger for you; did you know that? – but this will do well enough."

Again, the elephant stuttered a response and he had to take a moment to find his answer. "I got your message, Xyril. I was on my way, but I wanted to stop and glean what I could from Raudo's impression of the humans." He gave another polite nod to Dane and the others, who returned it.

"Oh, I see," Xyril said, nodding in understanding. "I could have sworn I told Ja-Rel that your presence was requested urgently when I sent him for you..."

Daridasa looked quickly at the humans and began speaking to avoid Xyril's statement. The leonin smirked when the elephant looked away. "Humans, I am Daridasa. Ambassador for the loxodon. Raudo told me what happened at the leonin city. I apologize for how Kurjin and his friends reacted. They're always angry about something, however. You learn to deal with them."

"So, you will vote to keep the humans on the island?" Xyril asked.

"I, uh, did not say that exactly," Daridasa said, looking away from the humans awkwardly. "The loxodon need more convincing than that. I need to get to know them, see what they're like, and then report my findings to the others."

Xyril growled lightly. "There's no time for that. The council meeting is tonight!"

"Don't be upset, Xyril," Evie said, placing a calming hand on his muscular arm. "We appreciate all that you've done for us, but if the council decides we do not belong here, then we will leave. There will be no misunderstandings."

Xyril looked sadly down at Evie, as if disturbed that she would even suggest the possibility, though he relaxed at her touch. Daridasa also looked at her with surprise, as if he did not expect a human to be so accepting. The girl smiled up at the giant beast as well, and the elephant could not help but smile back at the cheerful little thing.

"So, humans, tell me why you are here," Daridasa said.

Dane replied, "We met Xyril and his crew on the open sea. Our ship took damage, and so he brought us here after seeing this." Dane pointed at his chest, and the loxodon blinked and nodded at the Iron Fox sigil.

Xyril laughed. "That's putting it mildly. I crashed their ship and took them hostage. Lucky for them, Dane had that symbol on display!" The leonin laughed.

"Why were you in that part of the sea?" Daridasa asked.

"We were lost in a storm. We were actually sailing for Kratan."

"Oh! So, if the council votes for you to leave, I'm sure Xyril would happily show you there. We trade with them, you know?" The loxodon chuckled nervously.

"That's rude..." Koda muttered under his breath as he leaned on his spear, looking to the others for confirmation. No one other than him paid the statement any mind.

"Why were you going to Kratan?" Daridasa asked.

Dane flicked his eyes to Koda and the others for a brief second. He coughed and said, "My... uh... family and I just wanted to see a different land, so we set sail." He shrugged and chuckled, trying to seem genuine. He had never been a good liar.

"Do humans *often* do that? Travel to lands that aren't their own to inhabit?"

"Also rude..." Koda muttered again, looking at the others in exasperation.

Dane struggled to find a good answer, but luckily, he was interrupted by the flapping of wings in the sky above. The brown-feathered avian from before stalled in the air and brought himself down to land gently next to Xyril. The bird crossed his arms.

"Ja-Rel, what's wrong?" Xyril asked.

"The minotaur envoys have arrived at your city. You may want to hurry back. They're eager to meet the humans."

"Very good. Thank you." Ja-Rel nodded and took to the skies again. Xyril looked at the loxodon. "We must return to the city. I'm sorry your meeting with the humans was so short. You could accompany us, if you like, and get to know them better."

"Unfortunately, I cannot. I have many preparations to make before the council meeting tonight." The loxodon bowed and took a step away from the humans.

Suddenly, Evie rushed forward and placed a hand on the loxodon's own giant hands. She smiled up at him and said, "Thank you for taking the time to meet us. I regret not having more time to spend with you."

Dane furrowed his brow as his eyes flicked between his daughter and the elephant. The loxodon peered down at her. His shocked expression at her touch slowly morphed into one of cheer. He smiled and nodded. "I wish that, too. Perhaps if you're allowed to stay here, we can." Evie patted his hand and stepped away. Daridasa gave her a small wave and retreated into the trees without giving Xyril or the other humans any recognition.

Xyril took the first steps back in the direction of the leonin city. As the humans followed, Dane leaned down to Evie and whispered in her ear, "What was that all about?"

Evie looked at her father with a mischievous grin and said, "Daridasa will vote in our favor."

Dane was not sure what she meant by that, but he suspected it had something to do with her powers. There was no time for him to make her explain without Xyril hearing, and the leonin was setting a pace that was difficult for him and his companions to match. However, Dane knew that the cat was holding back and could have sprinted off to leave them in the forest if he was so inclined.

Back at the leonin city, the companions were introduced to the last of the Animalia. The minotaurs were bulls that stood roughly the same height as the cats. One of the two minotaurs there was covered in brown hair, while the other was black. Their chests were armored, and they wore gauntlets and greaves of dark, earthy colors. There were gold bands around their tails, and their horns were capped in gold and silver just like the loxodon and ceratoth. They had large gold rings dangling from their snouts. One of the minotaurs had two war-axes tucked into his belt on either hip, and the other had a giant battle-axe – bigger than Grunt's – strapped to his back.

The minotaurs dipped their heads kindly to the humans when Xyril introduced them. Their thick arms were folded over their broad chests, and they looked menacing even though their tones were kind and their attention was focused on them with curiosity.

The bull with brown hair and the battle-axe – who Xyril had introduced as Turmarox - even had an eyepatch that added to his frightening façade. Turmarox turned to Xyril and said, "We apologize for answering your summons so long after it was delivered. We met the simians on our way and had to listen to them bitch about what happened here."

"I hope you've come to me to receive an honest retelling of the story," Xyril chuckled.

A dry chuckle came from the black-haired minotaur – Kingama – who answered, "You know we tolerate the simians. *Only* tolerate."

"He also droned on and on about the council meeting tonight. We wanted to hear your plea now, so we have time to think on it. How did you meet these humans?" Turmarox asked.

Xyril retold the story with an energy that hinted that he was tired of telling it, or that he was trying to save his best performance for the council meeting tonight. As he regaled the minotaurs, Dane noticed something moving out of the corner of his eye. He glanced at it, and saw it was the leonin that had been bitten by Oddwen on the ship. He was still unaffected by the bite and was moving around normally. He even had removed the bandages to air out the wound and Dane could see that it showed no signs of inflammation or deterioration.

Dane elbowed Asira, who looked at him and then followed his pointing finger. She squinted at the wound and nodded satisfactorily. She whispered, "There is no difference between that and a normal piercing wound. I think the elf you met was right. The Animalia are unaffected."

Some of the others had leaned in to listen once they noticed Dane and Asira were whispering. They got the attention of the others when they realized what was happening. There was a wave of calm that came down upon all the companions.

"Do we tell Xyril or what?" Spencyr asked.

"Yes. We owe it to him," Evie said with ardor.

"Are you crazy?" Koda asked. "Animals spook easily. We don't want to ruin any chance we might have of staying on this island."

"Perhaps we should wait until we know the outcome of the council meeting?" Asira suggested.

Dane hushed everyone just as Turmarox acknowledged him with a question: "How long did you fight for Brennon?"

"Fifteen years," Dane replied.

"And which of our fighting styles did the man prefer?"

"Swords. Just like the leonin," Dane responded with confidence.

"You also follow that style?"

"I do. I've always favored the sword."

"Have you seen him fight? Tested his skills?" Turmarox asked Xyril.

The leonin nodded. "Briefly."

"Why did you not ask them to demonstrate?" Kingama asked.

"Brennon would never present that armor to someone who had not earned it," the great cat responded.

"What if he stole it?"

"Dane gave me his word that he didn't."

"That's not good enough for me. You're too trusting!" Kingama said, snorting, and resting his hands firmly on the heads of his war-axes.

"I trust you, Xyril," Turmarox said. "You've always been fair to our kind and your intuition is strong. I'll trust your judgement."

The minotaur and the leonin clasped forearms and Evie stepped forward to place a hand on Turmarox. The minotaur looked down at her. She smiled at him and said, "Thank you for believing us. Xyril's been working very hard on our behalf. It makes me happy that he finds so much support."

The minotaur studied her for a moment before nodding. "You're lucky to have Xyril on your side."

Kingama harrumphed and shook his head. "I'm not convinced. Apologies, but you humans don't understand how things are done here."

"Does honoring the Iron Fox sigil mean nothing to you?" Xyril asked.

"That promise was made in simpler times. We have our own problems to deal with." Kingama looked at the companions with genuine sadness. "Sorry again. I wish I could help you." He turned and stomped off quickly.

Dane saw Evie tense as if she thought about running after him, but Kingama's stride carried him away quickly, and Turmarox and Xyril were in her way. She let her hand drop from Turmarox's and stepped back. The minotaur studied her a moment longer and nodded a farewell to Xyril before taking off in the direction Kingama went. Evie sighed angrily and glanced up at Dane, who gave her a questioning look. She shook her head slightly.

Xyril interrupted everyone's thoughts by saying, "Well, you have at least seen all of the Animalia, and more importantly they have all seen you. That is the best we can hope for before the council meeting. Let's take the next few hours to relax in my home. It has been a long day, and will be longer still..."

Xyril's entire family gathered with the humans and offered them food and drink. Afterwards, they kept everyone entertained by regaling them with the stories of their people, or by teaching them games popular among the leonin.

Dane sipped a cup of cool water and let his eyes scan the room. Evie and Spencyr were learning a leonin game from the smallest cub. Asira was helping Gitra clean the plates and cups while Koda and Grunt listened, enthralled, by one of Xyril's older children telling a story of a leonin legend.

Dane smiled to himself and watched his friends. This was what he had hoped to find when they left Akreya. He had never been certain they would find it, and whatever happiness he imagined did not include talking lions and gorillas. But he was not picky. He and his friends had gone far too long without happiness – true happiness. They had found joy in the occasional warm meal or a bed or cot lent to them for a night or two, but this was their first taste of true peace in a long time.

Thoughts of the friends and loved ones he had lost over the past few months began to creep into his mind, but he smiled harder and focused on the ones around him now, listening to their laughter. Somehow the dark thoughts dissipated. One thing he could not force away were the thoughts of being banished from the island. He took a deep breath and resigned to putting his trust in Xyril.

Dane felt a tap on his shoulder, and he found the big cat standing over him. "May I have words with you privately?" he asked.

"Of course." Dane set his cup down and rose from his seat. He followed the leonin to the door and glanced at the others. They were preoccupied with the other leonin and did not notice his leaving. Dane smiled again.

Outside, there were some leonin scattered around that were sleeping on the ground. Xyril motioned for Dane to follow and said, "We will talk on the beach."

Dane had noticed that Xyril's temperament had changed. As they had reclined inside his house, the leonin had been less talkative and more reflective. His jaw was set, and Dane could see in his eyes that thoughts of the council meeting to take place were working in his mind.

Their entire walk to the beach was in silence. They walked side-by-side, thoughtful and pondering. Finally, they reached the white sands, and Dane recognized the ships from earlier. Seeing that they were finally alone, Xyril asked Dane, "Why did you really leave your land? *Akreya...*"

Dane was surprised and stumbled for an answer. "You heard me tell the minotaur's. We just wanted a change of scenery."

Xyril gave Dane an amused smile. "Dane Iron-Fox, you're a bad liar. That is how I know you to be an honorable man, how I can trust you when I barely know you. You have been honest with me until now. I'm not angry. I want the truth. Tell me here, where no one else can listen."

Dane knew by the way that Xyril watched him with smiling, amused eyes that he was caught. He did not know how the truth would affect the leonin's decision to help him and his companions. He did not want to lie to him, but the truth was fighting him not to come out. In a matter of seconds, he remembered everything that had happened back in Akreya leading up to this moment. Through all the struggles, he had remained strong. He would not lie like a coward again.

"You may find what I'm about to tell you unbelievable."

Xyril chuckled and said kindly, "We do not struggle with surprises the same way you humans do. I have seen Brennon and now you and your friends have to deal with meeting my kind... Say what you have to say."

Dane started slowly, choosing his words as if they were a bridge he was unsure could hold his weight. "My homeland is suffering... There's a plague across the entire realm..."

Dane stopped, expecting Xyril to already have questions or be in a panic at the news, but the leonin nodded thoughtfully and waited for Dane to continue. Perhaps he did not understand what a plague was? "The sickness makes people lose their minds and they gain the hunger for living flesh."

"That is not normal for humans..." Xyril said.

"No, it's not. There is a sorcerer there that controls them. He used magic to raise the dead, and they transfer this mind-rot to living beings they scratch or bite. There aren't many of the living left in Akreya."

Xyril sighed softly. "I mourn for your people and your homeland, Dane."

"Thank you," Dane said. "That's not all, though. Before that, the ruler of our land declared war on all magi – people that have special, unnatural abilities. Evie is a magi, and so I've spent several months keeping her safe from men who hunted us."

"Your daughter is one of these? She is a sweet cub. Who would want to kill her?"

"Evil people. The King hated the magi because his son was the one who raised the dead."

"This man is still ruler?"

"No. His son killed him."

"A shame when sons murder fathers... The boy is still alive?"

"Yes. He controls the realm with his army of the dead."

"I understand now why you left. I also understand why you wanted to hide it."

"You're not upset?" Dane asked.

"Why would I be? I was able to help an Iron Fox in his time of need. I am honored."

"There's something else you should know, then, Xyril." Dane cleared his throat. "In our travels, we met an elf who was testing animal blood. In all his research, the animals were immune to the disease. They did not turn ravenous when exposed to the same treatments as people."

"So, this means..."

"Your kind – leonin, vulpen, all Animalia – can't be turned. You're all safe from the plague!"

Xyril took an index finger and stroked the bridge of his muzzle slowly as he thought. "The human that attacked Icix on the ship – the one that bit his neck – was he one of these...?"

"Undead, yes," Dane replied.

"Icix will not be corrupted?"

"No, he's safe, as far as I know. Unharmed except for the bite itself."

"Hmmm..." Xyril walked past Dane towards the edge of the water. He cast his eyes across the vast sea, in deep thought. Dane said nothing. Finally, Xyril said, "I am glad you have told me this."

Dane was unsure if there was anything else he should say. He waited silently, watching the leonin scan the horizon with his amber eyes. Quite some time went by with no reply, so Dane turned himself toward the water and watched the rolling waves far off in the distance, felt the wind rush around him, carrying with it the scent of the sea. Behind them, the sun was setting, warming their backs.

Dane was glad he told Xyril the truth. He deserved nothing less after all the help he had provided. They would still be lost in the ocean without the leonin's assistance. Even if they were not permitted to stay here, no doubt the cat would help them get to Kratan.

Kratan... It seems like such a long time ago that it was our destination...

"The simians don't just hate you for hate's sake, you know?" Xyril said, interrupting Dane's thoughts.

Dane looked over to see that the leonin had made the statement without taking his eyes off the horizon. Dane waited patiently for the rest of what he had to say.

"The simians, saurians, and ceratoth *are* quick to anger, that's true... But there has been a peace between all Animalia for several years. It's a fragile peace, but there has been less war and bloodshed between us because of it." Xyril took a deep breath and immediately sighed, drawing it out for a while. "The peace began with Brennon, you know?"

The lion finally looked at Dane, who shook his head. The cat planted himself in the sand, drawing his tail near his waist as he did so. Dane sat, out of politeness. Xyril continued: "We lived as beasts, fighting constantly for territory and resources, killing and plotting and killing some more.

"Brennon brought us knowledge – knowledge of tools, which brought knowledge of houses, which brought knowledge of civilization. He taught us how other lands divided their territory and had boundaries to live in. Ships we built took us places we never knew existed and helped us see how other peoples lived. It took us a while to get it right – especially after Brennon left our island - but that's when the peace began..."

"Is that peace dying?" Dane asked. "Are we causing that by being here?"

"No, my friend," Xyril said, smiling at him. "The cracks in the foundation of the alliance were already formed and spreading. You see, with less wars all of the Animalia prospered and multiplied."

"That's good," Dane insisted.

Xyril shrugged. "Yes and no. With more people, there is less room for them all. The island and its resources are finite, and the sea levels are rising. Even less food, even less room, Dane."

Dane nodded slowly as he contemplated, beginning to see the problem.

"The others are just worried, like the rest of us – though they mask it with anger. They think you being here will bring more humans, and soon the island will run out of room for all Animalia. They're frightened for their homes and their families, is all. Do you see, Dane?"

Dane nodded assuredly. "I do. If it's true, then why did *you* choose to help us?"

Xyril turned his gaze back to the water, a reminiscent smile on his face. Dane could see in his eyes that in his mind he was being teleported back in time. Suddenly, he said, "Brennon saved my oldest cub from drowning when he was just a mewling kit."

Dane was shocked at first, but then it all made sense. The Iron Fox meant more to this leonin than any of the other Animalia, and he still intended to honor the debt owed.

Xyril continued, "I was the first to find Brennon when he washed up right here on this beach. I had taken my eldest cub for a walk in the cool morning air, and he was running about, exploring the island, when we discovered Brennon unconscious in the sands. I drew my sword, ready to make sure he was dead, when an avian swooped down from the skies, picked up my cub, and dropped him into the sea.

"This was before our alliance with the avians, mind you. He wanted to take Brennon's body for himself and claim the recognition for finding him. I was in shock, staring at my cub in the water. Leonin can't swim very well, so there was no way for me to go out and retrieve him and bring him back safely to land.

"Suddenly, I see this human dash across the sands, fully awake and diving into the water. The avian pursues him, so I leap into the air and tackle him to the ground, so Brennon can continue into the water. I break the avian's neck and Brennon returns with my cub – soaked but unharmed.

"Brennon hands me my child, and I stare at the human, who stares back, panting and dripping with water. I decide then that I can't kill him. I bring him back to my home and present him as a hero to my family."

"That's amazing," Dane said.

"It was, indeed. It was several weeks before any of the other Animalia were comfortable around him, but he eventually was accepted." Xyril looked at Dane with a wide smile. "I believe the same will happen with you and your friends."

"I hope you're right, Xyril."

"We will find out soon." The leonin turned and began trudging across the sand, his head hanging once again in deep thought.

* * *

When Bren finally returned to the lycan village, it was dark. There were very few torches lit and even less noise. *These people are too confident in their* secret city. *First order of business is to speak to Harryck about scheduling guards and perimeter patrols.*

As if the man could read his thoughts, Harryck appeared out of the dark. "Well, holy shit... Look who it is."

"I told you I'd come back," Bren replied, strolling over to him and snatching the bottle from his hand.

As he took a sip of the mead, Harryck said, "To be honest, I didn't believe you."

"You think my word's not good?" He handed the bottle back.

"I know it is, now." Harryck chuckled and tipped the bottle. He snorted hard and spit phlegm into the dirt. "You find the friends you were looking for?"

"Not all of them..."

Harryck nodded slowly. "Sorry..."

"Doesn't matter. This village does, though, and you're doing a piss-poor job of running it."

Harryck laughed. "You're welcome to take a crack at it."

"I intend to. And you're gonna help me."

Harryck took another long drink and then held the bottle out to Bren, who took it. "Glad you're back, Bren... Shut-eye first, village business tomorrow."

"Yeah." Bren took another drink and looked up at the full moon looming overhead.

* * *

Ularon threw his head back and laughed. Caulen looked at him with a painful smile. The man hit him lightly on the shoulder. Caulen looked over his shoulder to see if they had drawn anyone's attention, but everyone that followed were content to stay in their own conversations. That was fine with Caulen. This was not a discussion he wanted overheard.

Ularon finally got his laughs under control and smirked at the boy. "So you were infatuated with Dane's daughter? Did you tell her?"

Caulen looked again at the people nearby to make sure they were not eavesdropping. He gave Ularon a pained look. "She can read minds..."

"So she knows, but you never told her yourself?"

"I assume she knows... But she never returned the sentiment..."

Ularon laughed again. "Women like to be told things like that. Whether she knew it or not, you needed to tell her."

"Oh..." Caulen hung his head.

"Take heart, my young friend." Ularon placed a hand on his shoulder. "Life is a mysterious machine. Cogs are always turning that you may never even see. There's still a chance you could see her again."

Before Caulen could respond, screams funneled up the line to the two of them. Caulen and Ularon both brought their horses to a stop and looked over their shoulders. Nothing was clear, but people were scattering in all directions some ways down the column.

Ularon kicked his horse into motion and galloped away, careful to dodge anyone who was in his way. Zuko followed him, shouting for Caulen to follow. The boy's bow was already in his hand as he sped down the line, taking a wider path to avoid anyone on foot. An arrow was already drawn from his quiver, and he nocked it as he rode.

Caulen knew immediately what had happened when he came into view of it. Zombies – around twenty of them - had enclosed on the middle of their travelling column from both sides, splitting it into two groups. Some of the civilians were fighting, but most were dodging their grabs and bites while staying close to the rest of the group. A few had outright fled the scene.

Caulen let an arrow fly, and his aim was good. One zombie dropped. Ularon and Zuko had brandished their swords and were cleaving away at the nearest undead. Some of Ularon's other soldiers had come to their aid and were doing their part to round up the people and evacuate them safely from the area. Caulen let loose more arrows, each one bringing down another dead beast.

Caulen leapt from his horse to tackle an undead that had come dangerously close to grabbing hold of a small boy. He rolled and immediately drew another arrow. He fired it into the zombie's skull at point-blank range before reaching out and taking the hand of the child and leading him safely away.

Soon the undead were disposed of and the civilians were being rounded up by the soldiers. Many people embraced one another, while others cried and crumpled on the ground. Caulen caught a glimpse of a woman who had been bitten on the leg. He set his jaw and walked away.

Caulen looked around for his horse but could not find it. Ularon rode up next to him and surveyed the area once more. Finally satisfied, the man looked down at him.

"Well done, Caulen. I saw you save that boy."

"Thank you," Caulen said.

"Lost your horse?"

"I think it got spooked and ran away."

"It may return, yet. In the meantime, we'll see if we have another to spare."

Caulen waved his hand and shook his head. "No, don't bother. Someone else may need it. I don't mind walking." Ularon nodded, more than happy to have one less thing to worry about. Caulen glanced over his shoulder at the woman who had been bitten. There was now a man knelt next to her, crying and holding her.

Zuko joined them on horseback. The old captain took a moment to catch his breath. "Four wounded, Lord," Zuko reported. His eye also caught the wounded woman and he lowered his head respectfully. "Five..."

"All of them bites?" Ularon asked him.

"One clawing, but yes... all wounded by the dead."

Ularon groaned and sighed. "Give them time with their families, if they can still travel. I will lay them to rest myself before we stop for the night." Zuko nodded.

It was an hour later until the column was moving again, this time slower than before. Ularon rode at the front, slumped, Caulen could see. The boy walked next to him. He had followed Ularon silently, his bow clutched in his hand. *Next time*, he vowed, *I'll be ready, and quicker. Maybe no one will get hurt.*

This was the quietest Caulen had ever seen Ularon. He looked up at the man and saw a focused face, contemplative. It was several hours when Caulen noticed that they had travelled later than Ularon usually permitted. The darkness was thick in the forest. He thought about what Ularon had said about the wounded.

Finally, Caulen asked, "Why did you say that *you* would put those people down?"

Ularon had appeared to be in deep thought, but he looked at Caulen as if he had been waiting for the boy to say something, intent on catching every word. "What do you mean?"

"You said you would lay the people to rest... *personally*... You have many men under your command. You could have them do it."

Ularon replied without hesitation: "Go murder those poor people for me."

Caulen gave a start and his jaw dropped. Ularon was not serious, but he was not jesting either. Caulen was at the same time relieved and a bit disturbed.

"You see? I imagine for a moment you thought I was crazy." Caulen nodded. "The way that made you feel... I only expect any man who was halfway decent would feel the same way. And I like to believe my soldiers to all be at least halfway decent. I don't want to put this on anyone else...

"If I choose to lead these men, then I must choose to make all of the difficult decisions. If I make them do it, they won't respect me, and they won't follow me when it counts. Zuko has seen countless battles, and he's killed a great many men. Even he should not be able to kill an innocent without struggle."

Caulen furrowed his brow and stared into the darkness of the forest. Hearing these words made him think. Braxon had not shied from killing anyone, and he was the evilest man Caulen had ever met. He looked back at Ularon, who was casting his gaze over his shoulder at the column behind them.

Caulen saw his hand drop to the hilt of his sword, his fingers rubbing and tapping the pommel nervously. Ularon sighed and dismounted.

"We'll make camp here."

Chapter 31

There was a knock on the door, and one of Xyril's cubs answered. The visitor was M'Kalla – the other leonin member of the Animalian council. He wore a cyan-colored tunic and a grey cloak with the hood down. One sword hung on his left hip, and another on his back. His round ears were pierced, as was the custom.

There were no words exchanged. Xyril had been smiling and enjoying himself. When he saw M'Kalla, he nodded, swallowed the last sip of water from his cup, and then set it down hard.

The *clunk* of the metal cup hitting the wooden table caught everyone's attention – humans and leonin alike. Dane and his companions watched as Xyril drew himself slowly to his feet. The cat's gaze flickered over each of the humans before nodding to them.

Xyril walked to the door and placed a hand on it. He looked over his shoulder and said, "I will do what I can for you, but it's not up to me alone."

"We understand," Evie said, a sad smile on her face. "We thank you for all you have done so far."

Xyril gave a small smile in return. "Cubs, keep these people entertained until I return." He shut the door and strolled through the city with M'Kalla. Other leonin watched them pass, but neither of them said anything to the other until they were well beyond the limits of the city. Xyril finally broke the silence: "Are you upset with me, brother?"

"I respect you and your choice to help the humans," M'Kalla replied, keeping his gaze ahead.

"You have my gratitude, but you don't have to hide your feelings from me. Tell me your thoughts so that we may come to an agreement before the council meeting."

M'Kalla immediately replied, "I don't disagree with your decision to bring them here. Our people have only prospered since we've dealt with the humans – Brennon and the people of Kratan. I just know that it will be difficult to convince the others – especially the simians – to allow them to stay." M'Kalla sighed and placed a hand on Xyril's shoulder. "I just don't want to see you upset if this doesn't go the way you want. What will you do if the humans are forced to leave?"

Xyril did not answer. He kept his eyes low to the ground.

M'Kalla continued: "Xyril, all of the leonin love you and respect you. They would follow you to the Everlasting Hunt with a single command because you have never betrayed their trust. I would be among those to obey. You made peace with the vulpens and the avians, and they have been great allies. *You* did that. Do not be afraid because of me. I will vote in your favor, because I know your intentions are good."

Xyril looked at his friend. "But do you really believe that it is a good thing to allow the humans here?"

M'Kalla shrugged. "Part of me says yes, another part says no. The people of Kratan were gracious to welcome us. Perhaps we should be the same. But I'm also nervous. We know the humans hunt our mute brothers in their lands... It is what they know, but... I'm unsure. We will have to see."

"I understand the hesitancy of the others. I do. But Brennon saved my cub. I made a promise to always honor the ones bearing his sigil. I cannot break that so easily."

M'Kalla nodded. "As I said, I am with you. I'm sure the vulpens and avians will be, also. The simians and their friends are the ones you have to worry about."

"This I know," Xyril said, ending the statement with a long sigh.

An hour later, Xyril stood before all the members of the council atop the highest peak on the island. All the allied Animalia stuck together, separated by the ones that tended to stay neutral between the two alliances. The voices that had been speaking in hushed, hurried tones ceased, and everyone faced Xyril. The meeting had officially begun.

Xyril collected his thoughts as the Animalia waited patiently for him to speak. He took a moment to study the faces of everyone and judge their feelings. His friends stood to the left side of him. M'Kalla was there, along with Raudo and Yuda representing the vulpens, and Gi-Shi and Rhas-Su for the avians. Each of them nodded or smiled at him.

To Xyril's right were those he knew for certain he would have to persuade to his line of thinking. Glowering at him with crossed arms were Kurjin and Sakar for the simians. The saurians – Ollet and Karool - stood beside the simians and imitated the resentful looks their friends gave Xyril. The ceratoth scoffed at the saurians for their eagerness to impress the simians, but Nezog and Bleserek still gave Xyril dirty looks of their own.

Between the two groups were the minotaurs that had visited the leonin city earlier in the day, Turmarox and Kingama. The loxodon – Daridasa and Olgaro – stood behind the minotaurs. They shifted their stances anxiously and wrung their massive, leathery hands. They were the most impatient to proceed.

Xyril finally spoke after looking each of them in the eye, "I will not waste time explaining why we're all here. We know why. Instead, I'll tell you why I've done what I did…"

The others continued waiting patiently with arched eyebrows and expectant looks. Xyril took a deep breath and prepared himself. "I don't want any of you to think that I'm using tragedy for gain, but… Brennon rescued my cub from drowning – you all know this.

"Until you've gone through something like that, you can't know the feeling. And you can try and comprehend the idea of a debt owed for something like that, but you'll never understand. My oldest is alive because a human risked his life for him. I promised him that his kind would be safe."

"You didn't have to bring the humans here, though," Ollet said, the female Saurian crossing her arms.

"They would not have been safe, otherwise," Xyril said. "Here's the story: My crew and I rammed their ship and damaged it beyond repair. We were going to loot them, but the leader of the humans – Dane – was wearing The Iron Fox. I remembered the promise I made to Brennon, and so I brought them to our island."

"We've heard quite enough of your promise, Xyril," Olgaro the loxodon said, holding his hands up peacefully.

"You made the promise, too!" Xyril said, pointing at the giant beast.

"All Animalian kind did. You think we don't want to honor it?" This statement surprisingly came from Kurjin. The simian's demeanor had grown softer, but not by much.

553

"You aren't showing it, I'll admit," Xyril said more calmly.

"You think us savages, but we are not," Kurjin continued. "I value honor and integrity just as much as you, but you can't see it from the pedestal you've placed you and your kind upon."

Xyril held his hands out, pleading. "Then help me see it your way, brother."

Kurjin sized him up, as if he thought the leonin was mocking him. He blew a puff of air out his nostrils and said, "Brennon was a good man. The humans of Kratan have been good men. But good men take up just as much space as bad ones. Our island is not getting any bigger, Xyril, and you just welcome anyone who comes along!"

"Not anyone! An Iron Fox and his family!"

Nezog the ceratoth scoffed and said, "Brennon would understand that we must think of ourselves first. We can't endanger ourselves over the lives of petty humans."

The minotaur Turmarox pointed a finger at him and said, "Watch your words, Ceratoth, or I will break off your horns and shove them up your ass!" Kingama placed a hand on his friends' forearm and forced him to lower it. Both ceratoth glowered at the minotaur.

Rhas-Su spread her hands out. "Enough. We have not accomplished anything, yet. Save your tempers for later. Not here." Everyone shifted uncomfortably until they were calm once more. However, the ceratoth and minotaurs continued to cast dagger-eyes at one another.

"Please, consider this," Xyril said, "if we cast the humans away, we could be dooming them. We would dishonor ourselves, and if we don't act with honor, what does it matter if our island shrinks or grows? We would not be worthy of whatever lives we lead after that…"

Everyone was silent for several moments. Xyril left them to mull his words over.

The grey vulpen Yuda said, "Nothing bad has come from dealing with humans. We have prospered and benefitted from relations with them. Why should we think it any different now?"

"You're focusing on the wrong thing!" Kurjin said. "It has nothing to do with humans, it has to do with *us*! This is our island, and we're outgrowing it on our own!"

"We need to think about ourselves!" Bleserek said.

"Where would the humans even stay?" The other simian – Sakar – asked.

"They would stay with us, the leonin," Xyril answered.

"It would not be difficult to fashion them a house of their own," M'Kalla added.

"And what about when you have more cubs?" Kurjin asked. "Or what about when the humans produce offspring?"

"We can deal with that later," Xyril said.

"It would be foolish not to plan for that now. You claim it would be dishonorable to turn the humans away, but it will be more dishonorable if we must slaughter their young when they begin to grow too numerous!"

"It will *not* come to that!" Xyril growled.

"Will it not?" Kurjin retorted. "I will not displace my simian brethren so I can give the land to the humans! We cannot put ourselves in danger for their sake!"

Xyril's nostrils flared as he glared at the simian. He could say nothing more without risk of shouting threats at the great ape. He looked at M'Kalla and they locked eyes for a moment. M'Kalla smiled sadly at him. There were no words he could offer Xyril.

There were a few whispers amongst the others, but no one spoke outright. Finally, Daridasa cleared his throat and curled his trunk up tightly to his face, as he did when he was nervous. He said, "Perhaps now we should take a vote?" He looked at the others, who all consented.

"Fine," Xyril said, unsatisfied that he had pleaded his case well enough. "All those in favor of letting the humans stay on our island, raise your hand."

M'Kalla was the first to raise his hand. Turmarox raised his next. Both Raudo and Yuda said yes for the vulpens. Gi-Shi and Rhas-Su raised their hands. Daridasa voted yes. Xyril sighed as he finished counting the seven votes. The remaining eight were opposed. He had failed the humans by one.

Turmarox glared at Kingama, and the two minotaurs flared their nostrils at one another. They squared off to one another, as if to fight, but they only locked their violent stares.

Daridasa wrung his hands as Olgaro gave him a strange look. "You approve of the humans being here?" Olgaro asked him.

"I actually met them," Daridasa said. "They're really quite pleasant."

Olgaro crossed his arms and took a deep breath. A short trumpet-like *toot* blared from his trunk.

Xyril growled low, almost inaudibly. He turned on his heel and began to march away from the others.

Kurjin called out, "Xyril, halt!"

The leonin stopped dead in his tracks, took a short breath and turned slowly. "I must be off. Make it quick."

The simian stomped towards him. The look on his face was softer than anyone expected it to be. "I know you are upset. I offer to break the news to the humans for you, if you would like..."

Xyril squinted at him suspiciously. He wanted to roar a vicious threat to him, but all his instincts told him to remain a hold on his composure. He dipped his head to hide his angry eyes. "No. I will tell them myself." With that, Xyril turned again and marched into the darkness alone. M'Kalla glanced at the others before sprinting off after his fellow leonin.

* * *

It was now well after dark. Dane sat on the wooden steps outside of Xyril's home, illuminated in the light of a nearby torch. He whittled with a small knife he had borrowed from Gitra. The laughter and clapping from inside had begun to slowly die down as the leonin bid the humans goodnight.

Dane chipped away at a small branch, lost in his own thoughts. He did not immediately realize that someone had opened the door behind him. He was snapped from his thoughts and looked up to see Evie smiling over him.

"Hey, sweetheart," Dane said, sliding over to make room for her on the step. Evie plopped down next to him and laid her head on his shoulder, heaving a big sigh. He glanced at her but continued shaving away at the branch. "Something wrong?"

"No," Evie said. After thinking for a moment, she added, "I don't think so." Dane gave her a quizzical look and she straightened. "I figured Xyril would be back by now. I'm nervous."

Dane inspected his handiwork before tossing it aside into the darkness. "So am I," he admitted.

"Really?"

Dane nodded. "I suppose it doesn't matter, though. We've done nothing but run for a while now. Won't make a difference to run some more."

"I don't wanna run from here," Evie said. "I like this place. The Animalia are good people."

"All of them?"

"Well no, but neither are all humans good. Or elves or dwarves for that matter."

"You're right about that." The two sat together in silence for a while, listening to the crackle of the torch and the screeching of the nighttime insects. Finally, Dane remembered something and looked at his daughter thoughtfully. "Did you use your powers on that loxodon earlier?"

Evie grinned mischievously and chuckled. "And Turmarox."

Dane grunted and said, "How many times have I told you not to abuse your abilities?"

"A lot," Evie said. "And most the time I don't. I could be much worse, you know?"

"Do you really think that's an excuse? I've raised you better than to take advantage of people."

"I just wanted to help, Father. I'm trying to help us make a home here!"

"I don't like it," Dane grumbled.

"And how many people have you killed to get us here?"

"That's not exactly fair, Evelyn."

"Maybe not," Evie said, standing up so she could look down at him. She curled her fists and placed them firmly on her hips. "The difference is that I don't judge you for it. We wouldn't be alive if you didn't kill people before they killed us."

Dane stared at her for a moment, his mouth slightly ajar. He swallowed and said, "I don't think I like how easily you talk about killing people."

Evie sighed and shook her head. "You're missing the point, Dad. I want to do my part. To help us find a safe home. A place with a future. This could be that place."

"Wherever that place is, whatever you do with it – for it – is up to you. But it's *my* job as your father to get you there. So you leave that to me."

Evie huffed. One of her eyebrows twitched as she looked at him. Just as Dane thought she was about to retort, Xyril appeared from the shadows. His shoulders slumped and he blinked at the brightness of the torch.

Dane stood and greeted the leonin, inviting him to sit on the steps. Xyril waved away the offer, and Dane and Evie remained standing with him. Both wanted to ask how the meeting went, but they did not want to bother him immediately.

Fortunately for them, Xyril could see the questions plastered across their faces. He sighed. "The vote did not pass," he said. "It failed by one. I'm sorry to have failed you, my friends."

Dane scratched at his beard for a moment before pressing his thumb into the scar on his chin. He was sad to have to leave this new sanctuary, but he was glad that the anticipation was gone. They had their answer, and though it was not ideal, they could now begin to plan how to move forward.

Evie walked forward and threw her arms around Xyril's large chest and buried her face in his soft, amber fur. "It's okay, Xyril," she said. "We know you tried your hardest." The great cat purred softly and smiled as he embraced her in return.

"You've been more than kind to us," Dane said. "We don't want to stay if it will cause trouble for you. When should we leave?"

Xyril avoided the question. He let go of Evie and gently shuffled her aside. He took a step toward Dane, looking curiously at him, thoughtful. "Dane... Tell me about your homeland... Akreya."

A puzzled look took over Dane's face, but the leonin waited patiently for an answer. Dane pondered a moment and replied, "It's a great land. It's mostly lush forests, not unlike this one you live in. There are also sweeping grasslands, vast deserts and towns built by the sea.

"There are several cities made of stone that you wouldn't believe until you saw. Animals of all kinds live there, as well as other mystical creatures. Several peoples have made their homes in Akreya. Humans, elves, dwarves, halflings... Why do you ask?"

Again, the question was avoided. "You say that the dead have come to life and taken over?"

"Most of the realm, yes," Dane said, cocking his head to the side in a questioning look at the leonin.

"And we Animalia are immune to this... this..."

"Plague," Evie said.

"*Plague*," Xyril repeated.

"The evidence points to that theory being true," Dane said.

"I see..." Xyril turned his back to them and walked to the edge of the torchlight, as if a barrier prevented him from going into the shadows. He brought one hand up to stroke the fur on his chin, tugging it gently down into a point.

Dane looked expectantly at Evie, who scowled at him. "You just told me you didn't want me using my powers anymore," she muttered.

Dane ignored her and took a step toward the leonin. "Xyril... What are you thinking?"

Xyril let out a long sigh. "I was right, you know? The others – the ones who opposed me – they voted no out of fear because of the overpopulation here on the island... They don't want you taking up space that we desperately need."

Dane said, "It's fine. We understand. The others won't cause issue, I promise."

"I fear for this, too."

Evie said, "We'll be fine, Xyril. And if you don't have to worry about us, you'll be able to focus on helping your people here."

Xyril turned and laid a hand on Evie's shoulder, though he looked Dane straight in the eye. "I think we can help each other, Dane Iron-Fox. Give me time to speak to the others, and I will gather volunteers to bring to your Akreya and help you take back your home."

Dane's eyes widened, and Evie's mouth hung agape. Her eyes flicked quickly between her father and the leonin. Dane's mouth moved to speak, but no words came out. He looked at Evie, but she was no help.

Luckily, Xyril had more to say: "There is one thing I must ask in return... You must promise me that my family and any Animalia that choose to join us will be allowed to settle there."

"To stay in our homeland?" Evie asked.

"I will not be able to convince anyone to fight on your behalf if they get nothing in return. This will solve the overpopulation here and regain your homeland for you. Simple, yes?"

Dane blinked several times. *I wish it* were *that simple, Xyril*, Dane thought. *He has no idea how our society works. Can I give away land that I don't have a right to?*

Dane was tired of fighting. He would much rather stay on this island and learn to live with the Animalia, but he knew he would be a burden to them and he would be unwelcomed by some. Some may even try to kill him. He had already made peace with the memory of Akreya. He had not even thought of returning.

But the idea sparked something in him. To have his home back as it once was? An entire realm rid of a plague that had decimated it? If there was any chance, he had to take it.

Dane straightened and took a deep breath. He locked eyes with Xyril and nodded. "I promise that if you and your kind help me and mine, you may call our home yours. I swear it."

A victorious grin spread across Xyril's face and he held out an arm. Dane clasped the beast's forearm and they shook on it. Evie beamed, grinning from ear-to-ear at the two of them.

Chapter 32

Dane gazed out the window at the leonin going about their chores. It was still early, and while a few of the older cats still lazed around, the others casually scrubbed their clothes or cooked. A blacksmith was setting fire to his forge, yawning in the morning sun that cut through the canopy of leaves over his head.

Dane was awake before any of the others. He had gone to sleep later than them, as well, but his rest was fitful and sporadic. He had spoken to Xyril this morning and the leonin had allowed Dane to use his storehouse to discuss the events of last night with his companions. He had sent Evie to gather the others as they awoke.

Dane rubbed his hands together and flexed his fingers to rid them of the early morning chill. It was either that or the nerves he felt at the coming debate. He did not know how anyone was going to react to the news. His friends were all just as tired of running and fighting as he was, but he was unsure of how Koda especially might take the fact he had agreed to the deal without consulting them.

The flimsy door creaked open and jolted Dane from his thoughts. Evie led Koda, Grunt, Asira, and Spencyr inside. They all gave him suspicious and curious looks, meaning Evie had not divulged any information – just as he had told her not to. There was nowhere to sit except for on top of barrels and crates, so they all gathered around and helped themselves, except for Grunt, who towered behind the others with crossed arms. Dane remained standing before them.

Evie smiled at him and nodded. At least he knew he had his own daughter's support. He looked each of his friends in the face before speaking. No one questioned him.

Dane crossed his arms and cleared his throat. "The council voted... We can't stay here."

Koda threw his hands into the air, and Spencyr groaned. Grunt was unwavering, and Asira eyed both Dane and Evie. Evie still grinned, even in the face of the news, and it caused the healer to narrow her eyes. "What are you not telling us?" the woman asked.

"Xyril has come up with a plan," Evie beamed, "and it's brilliant!" Everyone was silent again. "Tell them, Dad." All eyes shifted back to Dane.

Dane said, "Xyril has offered to gather volunteers to return with us to Akreya and help us reclaim our home."

"Why would he do that?" Spencyr asked.

"I told him that the Animalia are immune to the plague."

"Really?" Koda asked.

"Hold on," Spencyr said, waving his hands. "First off, we don't know one-hundred percent if they *are* all immune - we suspect. Secondly, why would Xyril agree to this? What does he gain from this?"

Dane swallowed hard. "The Animalia are overpopulating the island. They're running out of room, and they're worried they'll outgrow this land. Xyril has agreed to help us if we allow any who desire to settle in Akreya." He opened his eyes.

Everyone was quiet except Spencyr, who laughed incredulously. "How is this a good plan? That sounds ridiculous. What are we supposed to do? Just give away land that we don't own to these... beasts?"

"People," Evie snapped, casting a glare over her shoulder at him.

564

Spencyr raised his hands defensively. "I don't mean that offensively. I like the leonin and their friends. They've been nothing but kind to us. But do you really think we can give them land that we don't own and everyone else in Akreya be fine with these walking, talking animals moving into their homeland unattested? Ridiculous! Tell Xyril we can't do that..." Spencyr laughed once more and shook his head.

Evie looked to her father. He caught her eyes before looking out the window again. He placed a hand on the corner of a nearby crate and braced himself against it, while he rubbed the scar on his chin with the other. No one else had any input, their lips drawn tight as their thoughts ran rampant.

"I already told Xyril we would. We've made an agreement," Dane said. He was certain that if a leaf drifted to the ground, he would have been able to hear it. He had everyone's attention now. All eyes were locked on him.

Spencyr's jaw dropped as he heard Dane's words. He stared at him for a long while before blinking rapidly. "Did I hear you correctly?"

Dane nodded. "I'm sure you did."

"Are you out of your mind? You must go tell him right now that you've made a mistake! We can leave today and be far away from this place by this time tomorrow morning."

"What if we went through with it?" Dane asked.

"You're talking nonsense, Dane! It's not *our* land to give! This would change Akreya for the rest of history!"

"Whose land is it, Spencyr?" Dane asked, pushing off the crate. "Uragon's? Because it will be soon... Unless we do something about it. The way I see it, Akreya's gonna change either way..."

Spencyr stopped and stared, his eyes flickering passionately. "Dane, this isn't our fight... We left Akreya behind..."

"We don't have to. We didn't have this option before. There are still people there fighting for it because they believe in it. Caulen's fighting! My hope for that land was gone, but I've found it again. Should we just leave them to die when we can help them fight?"

"What will they think when our new friends begin setting up camp after it's all said and done?" Spencyr asked. "Who's gonna be in charge to say yay or nay?"

"Who's gonna stop them?" Dane lifted his hands and shrugged.

"That's your argument?" Spencyr asked. He jabbed a finger at Dane and turned to the others. "Is anybody else gonna try and talk sense into him?"

Koda spit and looked at Spencyr. "I thought you respected Dane more than this?"

"You don't think this is crazy? You of all people?"

Koda shrugged. "Maybe it *is* crazy, but you know what else is crazy? Talking animals that walk on two legs like a human, and flesh-eating dead." Koda stood and stretched, looking at Dane. "I'm about tired of being surprised by things anymore. I'm with you, Dane."

Grunt grunted in agreement.

"You're just going along with this?" Spencyr asked. He looked at Asira. The foreign woman had been quiet the entire time. "What about you? Please talk some sense into them."

Asira looked from Spencyr to Evie, then to Koda, Grunt, and finally Dane. She shrugged and said, "I am not from Akreya as you all are, but I have been there for many years. I love the land, and the way I see it is that if

566

the people who *are* from there think this is a good plan, then I agree."

Spencyr buried his face in one of his hands. "By the gods! *I'm* from there. *I* don't think it's a good idea!"

Asira shrugged once again. "I understand your reservations, but as Dane has said, Akreya will change some way. If we do nothing, everyone there will surely die. If we bring the fight back to them, then they have a chance."

"Think of Caulen," Evie said. "He's over there fighting, and he may be optimistic of the outcome, but I'm not. If we can help him and the others, we should. It's a matter of right and wrong."

"You do realize we could still die, don't you?" Spencyr asked. "Even with the Animalia's help?"

"We could die any time," Koda said. "Quite honestly, I'm not sure how any of us are still alive – luck, I suppose – but we won't live forever, so why not die trying to do something good?"

A small smile tugged at Dane's lips.

"Has everyone here gone insane?" Spencyr looked each of them in the face. Their expressions were unflinching.

"You're not obligated to go, Spencyr," Dane said.

"I can't stay *here*."

"Xyril will have to take us to Kratan so we can navigate back to Akreya. You can stay there or go where you please after that. We're not forcing you to join us."

Spencyr looked at the ground and thought for a moment. "I don't know," he finally answered. "I guess I have a little time to decide."

Dane nodded, and Spencyr turned and left the building.

"Do we really want him with us?" Koda asked, chuckling dryly.

"He's always been an anxious kid," Dane said, "but he's okay. Plus, we could use all the skilled warriors we can get."

"We're about to have an army of giant lions behind us, Dane. If that's not enough, I don't know what is."

Just then, there was a knock on the door. A pause, and then Xyril poked his snout inside. "Forgive me, my friends."

"Xyril, I'm glad you're here," Dane said. "I've told everyone the situation. We're in agreement."

Xyril stepped the rest of the way into the door and grinned. "Fantastic! I have already begun to gather allies for our voyage. Come see."

Dane walked between his companions and joined Xyril at the door. The great cat pushed it wide open and found a group of forty Animalia. The mix was made up of leonin, vulpens, and avians, who were all intermingling, talking or gathering supplies and belongings, or sharpening weapons. A few of them looked up and nodded at Dane as he stared at them.

"Holy shit," Koda breathed. Dane's friends had joined him, peeking around him to see the Animalia.

"They're already on our side?" Evie asked, looking up at Xyril.

The leonin nodded. "I still have many more to speak to amongst these people, not to mention the minotaurs and loxodon."

"Are you going to ask the simians? What about the saurians and the ceratoth?"

Xyril grunted. "I doubt any of them would agree."

"You have to ask," Evie pleaded. "You never know until you ask, and we'll need all the help we can get."

Xyril pondered for a moment. "Fine. There are a few who may listen to what I have to say. But right now, I'm going to put some of our allies to the task of building more ships. I'm optimistic that we're going to need many more to take on our journey."

* * *

Bren heard the door *creak* behind him. He had been stroking his goatee, but the noise jolted him from his thoughts and he turned to see Harryck stumbling out of his house. As usual, there was a jug of mead in his hand, dangling at his hip as he swaggered down the steps in front of his house. He rubbed the sleep from his eyes and ran a hand through his shaggy, matted hair.

"You look like you slept well," Bren said.

A quick glare and a frown was Harryck's response. He raised the jug to his lips and took a long drink. He gave a sigh of refreshment and looked at the jug for a moment. Finally, a bit of life crept into the man's eyes. "Trithilia said you wanted to see me. Woke me up to tell me that," Harryck grumbled.

Bren produced two wood-cutting axes from behind his back, forcing one into Harryck's empty hand. "We have work to do. Lots of it."

"I know we talked about this before, but I think we were a little hasty. This can wait until later. After breakfast, and maybe when I have a couple jugs of mead in my belly."

"You need to take this seriously. We can make this place great, but it's going to take a lot of work. I can't do it alone."

569

Harryck grumbled some more, but hoisted the axe up onto his shoulder, taking another sip of mead. "Give me an hour and I'll round up some of the more able-bodied folks to help us."

Bren smiled and nodded. "I'll get more axes."

* * *

An hour later, Bren and Harryck were in the forest north of the village with four other lycans. One of them was younger, not even in his twenties. Another was around the same age as Bren and Harryck, and the other two were several years older, but still healthy enough for manual labor.

Bren instructed the other lycans what trees to begin chopping down, and then he and Harryck began discussing their plans for the village. "Our top priority should be increasing our defenses," Bren said. "There were more wights on my return journey."

"They're migrating north?" Harryck asked.

"They're everywhere. Just some places more than others."

"But surely they won't find our village. We're nestled perfectly in these mountains. I doubt they'll come out here in search of food."

"It won't do us any good to try and *guess* what they'll do, Harryck. It's best if we prepare for the worst. Especially with how under-manned we are. We can't afford to take any risks."

Harryck shrugged and raised the jug to his lips. "So, then what's your plan?"

"Spike traps first, then guard towers. After those, we need to start constructing a wall around the village, so no one can just walk in as they please – including the dead."

"Sounds good to me."

"No objections?" Bren asked.

Harryck tied the jug to his hip and then grabbed his axe with both hands. "You seem to have this all figured out. I'm happy enough just helping what little I can."

"You're no use to me sitting around, drinking mead, and arguing with Trithilia all day," Bren grinned.

Harryck smiled and looked off in the distance. "Nope... But that's the future I'm trying to help you build, buddy." They both laughed and went to chopping trees.

Later, Harryck straightened, his chest and back drenched with sweat. He downed some mead and then leaned on the handle of his axe. "It's going to take a long time to build the defenses with just the six of us cutting the wood," he said.

A little ways off, Bren replied as he continued swinging the axe, "We'll just have to work twice as hard, is all." His shirt clung to his body where the sweat had soaked it. He wanted to take a break and drink some water, but he did not want to stop chopping until he had felled another tree. Their collection was more meager than he would have liked it.

Harryck finally brought down another tree a few minutes later. He took his shirt that he had previously removed and used it to wipe the sweat from his brow. He moved closer to Bren and hacked lazily at another. He kept glancing over at him, a question on his lips, but he hesitated to ask it.

Finally, he broke down. "So there's more undead, huh?"

Bren stopped, panting. "What do you mean?" he asked.

"When you left the last time... Are there more undead than before?"

"It seemed like it."

"More dead than living?"

"I don't know..." Bren put his hands on his hips. "But it seemed like it..."

Harryck nodded. "I guess these defenses are a good idea, then." He chipped away harder at the tree.

*　*　*

Caulen's eyes were on a constant swivel. His heart thudded inside his chest, pounding to get out. He was panting heavily, though he had done nothing strenuous. He told himself to calm down and breathe. He would be no use to anyone if he were to have a panic attack.

Alton dropped from the tree above him and stumbled once he hit the ground. He unslung his bow from across his back and looked through the undergrowth, ignoring Caulen. Once he was sure it was safe, he looked at the boy.

"There's a lot of undead activity, but it's not as bad as we feared it would be," Alton said.

Caulen sighed quiet relief. "Should we return to the others, then?" The two archers had been sent ahead to scout out Etzekel, while the main party had hung back about a mile away.

"You should get a look for yourself," Alton replied.

Caulen swallowed and glanced at the tree Alton had just come from. He looked back at Alton, who gave him a reassuring smile. Caulen slung his bow over his back and began to climb up.

The boy had felt unusually nervous since the attack on the camp several days ago. He hated seeing the families having to say goodbye to their loved ones. The look on Ularon's face as he would lead the sick away into the woods was the worst. It was not a look of fear or sorrow. The scary part to Caulen was the fact that Ularon was able to face those innocent people with such a look of indifference. Perhaps that was required of a good leader – to make tough decisions and face them with a stony expression. Caulen did not think he could ever do that.

After he had climbed halfway up the tree, he maneuvered around to where he could see the city through the branches. It was strange to him to see the great stone city once more. It was almost like a different place. He had been away for so long, with no intention of returning, that the memories he had of Etzekel were like hazy dreams that he could only partially remember.

Caulen had told Ularon, Zuko, and the others approximately how many people had lived in Etzekel, though he could only guess. He had also described in as much detail as possible how the city was laid out, and Ularon had helped fill in any blanks he had drawn, though The Usurper had only been to the city a couple of times. Caulen had then tried to estimate how many of the dead had come into the city when it was attacked, and how many of The Ravagers could have died there. The numbers had not sounded very favorable, but just as Alton said it looked like many of the undead had roamed away from here.

Outside the city walls, Caulen saw several faces that he recognized. Goras the cooper and Abarat the alchemist nearly bumped into one another, while Pyria the priestess – blood soaked into her robes - feasted on the carcass of a deer that had stumbled into the clutches of the zombies. The pang of sadness he felt was becoming too common an emotion, and he feared he would soon lose touch with it. How many friends could he see die before he was no longer disturbed by it?

Caulen shook the thought from his mind and began climbing down the tree. Soon, their plan would be put to motion, and he would not have time to think about his nerves or his sad thoughts.

"What did you think?" Alton asked him, once he planted his feet.

"I feel much better about it now," Caulen replied. "It looked like there were quite a few outside the walls. Hopefully that means there won't be as many inside."

"Better we fight them in the open and not in the streets and alleyways," Alton agreed. "Let's report back."

The two of them took off into the forest, side-stepping tree trunks and hurdling roots and rocks that jutted up from the ground. Alton was running fast, but Caulen had no trouble keeping up with him. The mile they ran passed quicker than any mile they had travelled before.

Ularon, Zuko, and a few of the other officers were awaiting them when they regrouped with the main party. Ularon did not press for their report. Instead, he offered them both skins of water and waited for them to drink before speaking.

"We think there's less opposition than we expected," Alton said.

"And quite a few of them are outside the city walls," Caulen added.

"That's good news," Zuko said. "If we can make quick work of the undead outside the city, then we'll be better prepared for the fight inside the walls."

"Let's try and eliminate the zombies outside as quickly and quietly as possible," Ularon said. "If we don't make much noise, we can move into the city easier. The advantage will be ours." He drew Zuko in. "Pick thirty men to stay here and guard the caravan while we advance on Etzekel."

"Thirty? Are you sure that's enough men?"

"If everything goes according to plan, we'll be able to clean up the city in less than a couple hours. Then we can bring the people inside the city walls. We need to make a good, thorough sweep before we can do that."

Zuko nodded and brought his right fist up to clasp against his chest, over his heart. "I understand."

"When you're done selecting the thirty, return here to us, and bring any soldiers left over. We'll be moving out immediately."

"I'll get it done, Lord."

Ularon clapped Zuko on the back as he ran off to complete his orders. Alton began speaking with one of the other officers, and Ularon turned to Caulen. "How are you feeling?"

"My nerves are a little shaky," Caulen admitted, but he quickly added: "But I'm ready."

Ularon nodded. "I'm nervous, too. I hope we can claim the city without too much loss, and quickly." Caulen gave him a questioning look, and Ularon smiled at him. "You didn't think I would be nervous?"

"You've been a part of battles before, right?" Caulen asked. "Against Endrew's soldiers? Surely they're tougher to fight than the dead?"

"Tougher, maybe... But the dead give me the chills... Are you not afraid of a demon who'll try and eat your flesh?"

"I know they're dangerous, but it's getting easier to get used to them, and I don't like that," Caulen said.

Ularon nodded again. "I understand what you mean."

"Ularon, how long do you think it will take us to rid the realm of the undead?"

Ularon shrugged. "No one can possibly know the answer to that, but I'm hopeful that it will be sooner rather than later." He smiled down at the boy again.

Alton finished talking with the other officers and approached the two of them. "Where do you want Caulen and I to be on the battlefield? Tree tops?"

Ularon shook his head. "Etzekel only has the one gate, so I was thinking that each of you could take some archers to opposite sides of the battlefield and catch most of the dead in a crossfire."

"And you and your men can clean up any stragglers as you move forward?" Alton asked.

"Exactly."

"What about once we're inside the city?" Caulen asked.

"Some of the archers need to clear the tops of the city walls while the rest take to the rooftops and cover those of us on the ground."

"I can take a couple men and clear the walls," Alton said. "It should be light work; won't take us long."

Ularon looked at Caulen. "You can lead the other archers on the rooftops."

"Me?" Caulen asked. "Surely there are more seasoned archers who can lead..."

"Perhaps, but you're already a better shot than most of them," Ularon said.

"Hey!" Alton grinned.

"I said *most*." Ularon punched him lightly in the shoulder. "You'll do fine, Caulen. There won't be any undead on the roofs. Just get the men there and let them pick their own shots. It will be a good first command for you."

"If you say so..." Caulen swallowed hard, averting his eyes.

"Here, take this," Ularon said, undoing the belt that held his dagger to his hip and handing it to Caulen. "You may need it in close quarters."

Caulen began to strap the belt around his waist. "I thought you said there wouldn't be any zombies on the rooftops?"

"Best you be prepared."

Caulen finished cinching the belt and rested a hand on the handle of the dagger. It was not an ornate weapon. Simple, but well-made. He felt comforted by the weight of it on his hip. "How does it look?" Caulen asked, smiling sheepishly.

Ularon chuckled. "It looks fine. Hopefully it gets to stay in its sheath." He paused a moment and studied Caulen's face. The boy hoped he did not show too much fear in his expression. Ularon said, "Don't take any unnecessary risks. Just stay at range and pick the dead off one-by-one. Don't be a hero. Heroes get themselves killed."

The statement caused Caulen to frown slightly, but he looked down at his feet so Ularon would not see it. He only looked up when Zuko approached them.

"That didn't take long," Alton remarked.

Zuko glanced at him, breathing a little heavier than normal. "We shouldn't waste any time. The men are ready to guard the caravan, and the others are regrouping here. We should be ready to move out in less than fifteen minutes."

"Well done, Zuko," Ularon said.

It took less time than that for the soldiers to move on Etzekel. Everyone was ready to be behind walls – even if they proved to be only a little safer. Any occasion they had to breathe a little easier was welcome to them. Their weapons were ready, and their minds were focused.

Ularon led the way, hand on the hilt of his sword, ready to draw at any moment. He had removed the cloak that he was normally found wearing, and he had donned plain leather armor that left him free to move. Zuko still wore his heavy suit of plate armor that he had acquired from fighting in King Endrew's army years before, though the former kings' sigil had been scratched away to almost nothing.

The officer Keaton wore a suit of plate similar to Zuko, but his great big beard erupted from underneath his helm. Cobon and Mayoko were clothed in tough hides. They had crossbows strapped to their backs and quivers of bolts dangling at their hips.

The other soldiers were a mixed bag. Their diverse group was made up of young and old, veterans and newly recruited, men and women. Some wore dense suits of armor, while others preferred loose, unrestrictive clothing with no protection. Some wielded daggers, clubs, swords, or had long-range weapons. A few of them were not even soldiers, just common people with a higher calling to protect the remaining civilians.

Running through the forest with his comrades alleviated even more of Caulen's nerves. One hand was on his bow, while the other rested on the hilt of Ularon's dagger. The boy almost smiled at the upcoming confrontation.

"Caulen! Alton!" Ularon's voice came sharp, but at a whisper. He had halted his lead at the tree line just before the city of Etzekel. The foot soldiers had stopped with him and knelt on one knee to await their orders. Ularon pointed at Alton and Caulen, and then pointed to his left and right.

Alton nodded and pointed at three of the other archers. They followed him as he broke off to the right. Caulen gestured for the other remaining three archers to follow him as he went left. He lined his men up on the edge of the trees and waited until his saw Alton had done the same. The man held one hand straight up into the air.

Caulen nodded and whispered, "Ready your bows. Pick your targets. Wait for Alton's signal." The archers silently followed the command. They nocked their arrows and drew back on the strings. Caulen did the same. Alton's arm dropped, and arrows flew.

The zombies between the two squads had been shambling about mindlessly. Arrows took several of them in the skulls, and their bodies crumpled to the ground. The remaining zombies looked around with their solid white eyes. Their heads turned, and their chilling groans grew louder as they came to be aware of the danger they were in.

Before they had time to register what was happening, a second wave of arrows had come. More dropped, and the undead grew more frantic. A few of them had now noticed the archers on either side of them and began shuffling toward them with grasping arms stretched before them.

Ularon and his soldiers then burst out from among the trees with weapons raised. The men gave no cries of violence but moved silently through the tall grass. The undead, confused, were unable to decide which people to attack, and they were disposed of quickly. One more round of arrows picked off any stragglers. The archers regrouped with the other soldiers in front of the city gates.

"At least the dead don't know how to shut gates," one of Ularon's officers chuckled.

"Lucky for us," Ularon said. "We've done well keeping it quiet so far. Let's keep it up. The deeper we can go into the city without them knowing, the better." He looked at Caulen and Alton. "You two know your jobs. Be quick on the draw."

Ularon wasted no time. He raised his sword high in the air to rally the others as he turned and sprinted through the open gates. Zuko was close on his heels, and the other officers and soldiers were not far behind. Alton took his archers next, and Caulen and his archers brought up the rear.

"Alton!" Caulen said. He pointed at a nearby door built into the side of the wall. "There's a stairwell that leads to the top of the walls."

Alton nodded and waved his men along into the stairwell. Caulen looked at the rooftops and decided that the best way for them to gain access to them was from the top of the walls, so he followed Alton and his men. Once they crested the stairs and were atop the wall, Caulen led his men the opposite way Alton had gone. He knew Alton would follow the wall all the way around in a circle to clear them, so he would take care of any undead this way until they could find a place to get on top of the roofs.

Two zombies were ahead of him. Caulen nocked, drew, and loosed an arrow in as quick and fluid a motion as he could, and the projectile soared true, lodging itself into the eye of the nearest one. One of the soldiers dodged around Caulen and rushed at the remaining undead. He used his bow to push the monster to the edge of the wall before delivering a solid kick to its chest, sending it hurtling over the edge and splattering the ground below.

Caulen continued to lead the way until he reached a section of the wall that was close enough to the rooftops for them to jump. "Right here," Caulen said. He took a few steps away from the edge before running and leaping through the air. His feet planted firmly onto the tile roof. One of the archers jumped and landed beside him.

The next man hesitated. "I can't make that jump!" he said. His hair was solid white, and his skin was dark, wrinkly, and chapped from years in the sun. Caulen guessed he had been a shepherd and not a soldier before the plague.

The other archer put a hand on his shoulder. "Come. I'll help you find some way to cross over." He looked at Caulen for approval, and the boy nodded.

"Be swift!" Caulen called to them as they ran off. He turned to the other archer. "Let's make our way across the rooftops toward the center of the city. We'll be the most useful there."

The two of them walked with unsure steps at first, but once they knew the tiles were solid, they shuffled at a quick pace. Most of the roofs were close enough to one another that they could step from one to the other, but occasionally they had to jump a gap, and others they had to scale a wall to get to a higher position. Whenever they came to an alleyway that produced a chasm too large for them to jump, they were lucky to find beams connecting the two buildings on either side of the alley.

Near the circular courtyard that was the center of the city, Caulen and the other archer spotted Ularon and Zuko below. The two men were weeding their way through the hordes of undead with several other soldiers nearby. The zombies were thickest here, and many of them did not move with the sluggish steps that most did. A lot of them were sprinting violently at speeds that should have been impossible for their frail bodies to reach.

Caulen wasted no time. He dropped to one knee and drew an arrow from his quiver. He nocked, drew, and loosed. The arrow took down a zombie that was reaching for Zuko. With years of experience to test his skills, the captain did not even flinch at the near miss, nor did he drop his guard to track where the arrow had come from.

Nor did Caulen wait for a nod of recognition or thanks from the captain. As soon as he had confirmed his arrow had rang true, his eyes drifted to his next target, at the same time drawing another arrow. The soldier next to him did the same, firing shot after shot.

There were footsteps behind them, and Caulen, unwilling to take risks, whirled on the sound with his bow drawn. It was the archer that had agreed to help the older man find a way to the roofs, and he was alone. He raised his hands in surrender until Caulen recognized it was him. The man knelt next to Caulen and immediately began firing his bow.

"Where is the other man?" Caulen asked as he picked another target.

"Dead," the soldier replied. "One of the abominations grabbed him as we rounded a corner. I couldn't save him."

Caulen said nothing. He clenched his jaw and gritted his teeth with grim resolve. He wished that he had known the man, so he might say a word to the gods on behalf of his soul. Then it dawned on him that he had never met either of these two soldiers before, either.

Ularon and his men on the ground cleaved through the ranks of the dead quickly and efficiently, while Caulen and his men covered their advance. Once the city center was safe, he waved for Caulen to join him on the ground. As Caulen and the other two archers climbed down from the rooftops, Alton and the three archers under him came from a side street.

"City walls are secure, Sir," Alton reported.

"Good," Ularon replied. "Everyone, rally on me." He barely gave his men a chance to draw near. "We're going to split our forces up and clear each street." He pointed a finger. "The main road will probably be the most dangerous, so I'll take that one. I want Caulen, Farrimond, Flynt, and Judd with me."

"Very good, Sir," one of the men replied, though Caulen did not know if it was Farrimond, Flynt, or Judd.

As Ularon continued to dole out commands, Caulen checked his bowstring. His thoughts wandered to the old man that had died under his watch. He looked at all the soldiers around him. He knew the names of the officers, and he knew Alton and Zuko, but most of the lower rank soldiers, he did not. The way Ularon was addressing everyone, assigning each soldier an officer to attend, made Caulen resolve to take time to try and learn the names of every man in Ularon's camp.

Caulen decided his first order of business after the fight would be to learn the names of the three men that had been under his command and thank them for their help. He wanted to admit to Ularon about the old man that had died, but he knew this was not the proper time. He did not need to dwell on that until after the battle was over.

Next thing he knew was that Ularon was charging ahead. Farrimond, Flynt, and Judd had been focused, for they were not far behind. Caulen shook all previous thoughts from his head and ran after them at double time to catch up.

The battle up the main road was difficult for Caulen. Ularon had been right in guessing that it would be more heavily populated, and it was uphill, ascending to meet the tower where the city's most prominent magi had once inhabited. The challenge arose from having to shoot over the other men's heads.

There were more familiar dead on the road. He saw Hilgi and Helby – brother and sister – who used to make money by catching rats in people's houses and taking them away. Caulen had bought them apples and loaves of bread when he found out the siblings were eating the rats they caught. They had thanked him, and then informed him that they liked the taste of the vermin. Caulen put arrows in both of them.

A singer named Henrietta tried to grab Ularon, but Caulen was quick on the draw. When he had first heard her performing in the street, he had been so entranced by the sound of her voice that he told everyone he saw that day about her. Word had spread, and she had collected so much money that she sought Caulen out to thank him. She had explained to him that her mother was sick and she was performing to buy the medicine she needed.

Henrietta's body hit the ground, and became another thought that he had to force from his mind as he drew the string of his bow. He had once believed that battles were fought while the mind was filled with thoughts, but he was discovering that he was often having to purposely clear his mind.

Ularon ducked under the clutches of the closest undead and elbowed it in the back, sending it reeling toward the soldier behind him. The man severed the monster's head with one swipe from his sword. The men stalled in their uphill battle, and Caulen flanked them to an open space to their left. As quickly as he could, he launched arrows into multiple targets, thinning the herd as best he could.

"Caulen, look out!" one of the soldiers shouted, pointing behind him.

Instinctively, Caulen jumped away from where he had pointed. From the building to his left, three of the undead had shuffled out. The closest one had its arms outstretched, and Caulen shivered to think about how close he had come to being grabbed.

Caulen drew the dagger from his belt and drove the blade deep into the first zombie's eye socket. He removed it forcefully, tossing the body to the side, and then he jammed the dagger into the next one's temple. He tugged on the weapon, but it would not dislodge from the zombie's skull.

Caulen pushed the body into the last undead, causing it to flail its arms and stumble around in confusion. With his opponent distracted, Caulen drew an arrow from his quiver. Once the zombie pushed the body aside, Caulen loosed the arrow at point-blank range into its forehead. As it fell to the ground, Caulen was already retrieving his dagger from the other nearby body.

Ularon and the soldiers were finished taking down the nearest undead and were waiting for Caulen to join them. The five of them ascended the street, the tower looming over them, getting closer by the minute. They fought their way up, dodging, slashing, kicking, shoving every undead that got in their way.

Finally, the tower was before them. Caulen stopped and looked up at it, like he had many times before. The memories he had of this city now felt like dreams to him. Dreams that he could not piece together completely, just discombobulated segments of his past that he was not sure if he had experienced or not.

"Come, Caulen!" Ularon ordered, waving him forward. "We can't falter now. We need to secure the tower."

Caulen threw aside the memories and ran to join the others. Farrimond, Flynt, and Judd had already breached the door, and were awaiting Ularon's orders. Ularon shut the door behind them. One of the soldiers had already lit two torches and handed one to one of the other men.

"Caulen and I will go downstairs. You three go up," Ularon said as he took one of the torches from the soldier. "Be cautious, men." With that, Ularon turned, holding the torch in one hand and his sword in the other. Caulen had already slung his bow across his back and drawn his dagger. The cramped, winding staircase would not be ideal for shooting.

Caulen had to keep his wits about him, or else the fright of stumbling on the undead as they descended the stairs would get to him. He had already had a close call with the undead today. He did not intend on having another one. He let Ularon lead the way since he was holding the torch, not wanting to cast a shadow that would be to their disadvantage.

There were only a few zombies in the stairwell. They passed several closed doors on the way down, but they ignored them. They would clear them after they reached the very bottom of the tower. Caulen knew what was down here. It had been Anandil's laboratory, and he remembered Dane saying that they had kept a werewolf in a cage there. He did not expect the werewolf to still be alive after all this time, but a shiver still ran up his spine as he thought about it.

Finally, they reached the bottom and found one last zombie standing in front of the door. Ularon lashed out with one foot, kicking the zombie into the closed laboratory door with a *thud*. Caulen dodged around Ularon and launched himself from the stairs with his dagger out. He buried it into the monster's brain and then pushed him aside from the doorway.

Caulen looked to Ularon, who nodded for him to open the door. Caulen held his dagger up, ready to slash down on anyone or anything that might be lurking behind the door. He pushed the door and it swung open in a haste. It creaked and pounded into the wall, and the two expected the noise to lure any undead present towards them.

Not a sound came from the room. It was pitch black, for every lamp, lantern, and torch had been extinguished in the absence of life. Ularon walked in, raising the torch high in the air. Several books and scrolls lay scattered around, along with many vials and jars of strange-colored liquids and ingredients for alchemy.

Caulen had never been here, but it was exactly what he had imagined it looked like. Finally, his eyes came to the iron cage in the corner. He walked over to it, craning his neck curiously. The lock was lying on the floor, broken by something with much force, and the door was wide open.

The werewolf escaped... Caulen's thoughts of werewolves led him to thinking of Bren. *Bren was here, and so was this werewolf... I wonder if he had anything to do with this one getting away? He didn't say, but it makes sense.*

"Caulen, let's go," Ularon beckoned.

Caulen nodded and left those thoughts at the cage. Yet another clearing of the mind.

The two of them checked every one of the rooms leading up to where the group had split up. They had only found a handful of zombies from where people had tried to hide after being bitten or scratched. It appeared most of the residents had tried to flee the tower when the attack started.

Farrimond, Flynt, and Judd appeared shortly after Caulen and Ularon had finished their search. "Top floor and all rooms above are secure, Lord," said one of the soldiers. Caulen still did not know which one it was.

"Very good. Let's go outside and help the others finish clearing the city," Ularon said. "If all went well, Etzekel will soon be ours."

Outside, a small group of the undead had stumbled to the tower. They turned in sequence when they stepped into the light. Two of them Caulen recognized – the halfling Renwy and the elf Anandil. He had never spoken to either of them much, but he had seen them, and heard people speak of them.

With little remorse, Caulen lodged arrows in both their skulls, one after the other. "Rest in peace," Caulen muttered, not forgetting how Renwy had attempted to use Evie as blackmail against him and his friends.

Zuko joined them after they had disposed of the nearby zombies, coming from a road off to their side. He sheathed his sword and used a gloved hand to wipe blood off his face. Caulen noticed there were two soldiers missing from his squad.

Zuko said, "Western side of the city is secure. Lieutenant Ranald is working on clearing the eastern side."

Ularon nodded. "Well done. I will take Farrimond and Judd with me to help his company. Take Caulen and Flynt with you to gather the citizens. By the time you get them here, the city will be secure. We will have safe places for them to sleep tonight, men."

Chapter 33

The rays of sunlight falling onto the shoulders of the companions was warm and inviting. There were no clouds in sight, and a strong breeze whipped around them, tugging at their cloaks and tousling the fur and feathers of the Animalia. The ships bobbed gently in the waves of the sea. It was a good day to sail.

Xyril stood with the humans and his family. Gitra was rounding their children up near the ramps of the ships. A few of them had been hastily but thoroughly crafted once Xyril's plan was made public, but most of the ships were already in possession of the Animalia.

"Everyone's here," Xyril said, his muscular arms crossed over his broad chest. "Leonin, avians, vulpens, and even some minotaurs and loxodon."

"Not everyone," Dane murmured. Spencyr had not been seen during final preparations this morning. "This is good, Xyril," Dane continued. "Better than good – fantastic." He smiled at the great lion, who emitted a low purr as he inspected his troops, and those whose families had elected to stay on the island and were here to see them off.

"I have a lot of hope for our return journey," Evie said, "and once we land in Akreya, Uragon better begin praying to whatever sick gods he worships."

"I just hope I'm the one to deliver the killing blow," Koda said.

Grunt punched him in the arm and shook his head, tapping his own chest.

"Get lost! You're too slow!" Koda laughed. "Plus, only one of us can teleport, and it ain't you."

Grunt huffed.

"Look, everyone," Asira said, pointing down the shoreline.

Kicking up waves of sand marched a group of simians, saurians, and ceratoth, led by Kurjin. The great ape lumbered along on his knuckles at a steady pace, his eyes locked with Xyril. The crocodiles and rhinos that followed him kept nearby. Their hands were empty, and no weapons could be seen.

"This looks bad," Koda said, wrenching his spear out of the sand where he had left it. Even without weapons, he knew the Animalia could kill with ease.

"Evie, Asira, get on the boat," Dane said. Evie stalled, but Asira forced her up one of the ramps.

Xyril, Raudo, and several of the Animalia stepped between the approaching party and humans. Dane and the others placed hands on their weapons but refrained from drawing them. Spencyr appeared from behind and sidled up next to his friends, and Dane nodded at him.

"Kurjin," Xyril said, "what brings you out on this fine morning?" Dane could tell that the great cat was suspicious, and he respected his restraint.

The simian stood to his full height and looked at the humans before dusting sand off his knuckles. "We have come to bid the humans farewell. We hope that their travels are safe, and that they find somewhere better suited for them."

Dane looked at his friends with a surprised expression. Koda shrugged, Spencyr's eyes were wide, and Grunt stood tall to meet the gaze of the great ape. "That's very kind of you," Dane said, stepping through the crowd of Animalia.

Xyril stepped aside, allowing Kurjin to come closer. The gorilla said, "We also came to apologize for our treatment of you. We have our reasons, and if there was any way that you might make a home here, we would allow it."

"We understand. We never wanted to take your homes away from you. We accept your apology."

Kurjin lowered his head in a bow. Dane placed his right fist over his heart and did the same. "Safe travels, Iron-Fox," Kurjin said again. He looked to Xyril. "That goes for you as well."

"Thank you," Xyril said. The two of them exchanged a bow.

"Most of the cargo is loaded and we're ready to go, sir," M'Kalla said.

"Good!" Xyril turned to the crowd of followers and boomed: "Everyone say goodbye to your loved ones and load the last of your things! We set sail in ten minutes!"

While the Animalia swarmed each other to embrace and say their farewells, the humans took their places aboard the ship with Evie and Asira. They lined up at the railing and watched the mass of creatures mingling, some whimpering, others laughing and sharing a final drink.

Off to the side, away from the others, Kurjin and his band waited with stolid expressions. After watching for a few moments, Kurjin signaled, and the crowd turned and began to leave.

Xyril was the last to board, pausing on the ramp to turn and take in one last surveyance of the island. His eyes scanned the beach and the tree line, the wind tugging at his mane, beckoning him to board. Xyril turned away from his homeland and the ramp was lifted.

* * *

The old fisherman cast his one eye suspiciously at Dane as he handed him the last of his coin. "I ain't never seen you 'round here before," he said through gapped teeth. Dane felt uncomfortable being watched as if he were a thief, when there were giant animals walking on two legs and talking. He pulled his cloak tighter around his body.

"I've actually been to Kratan before," Dane replied.

"But I ain't never seen ya.' Kinda strange that you're with the animals... How'd y'all meet?" The fisherman spit on the ground between his feet. He glared at his sons, who were helping the Animalia carry the barrels of fish aboard their nearby ships. "Why's there so many of 'em?" he asked, forgetting his first question. "Never seen 'em all here at once... Yep... Pretty strange..."

Dane knew there were more questions based on his tone, but all he said was, "I had better return to the others." He nodded a parting goodbye and turned. He could feel the old man's eyes on his back and he heard him sucking on the teeth he had left. Soon, though, he was back to yelling at his sons, just as he had been when Dane had arrived.

He strolled down the village docks at a brisk pace. It was early morning, and a thick fog still hung low to the ground. The sky was dull, with grey clouds blocking the sun. There were some myths that stated that Kratan was always bleak, but Dane knew that was a lie. He had been here several times before, and he had seen the sun shining overhead, even if that was a sparse occurrence. The entire continent was little more than one giant marsh, but the people made do, and they did not let the gloomy weather get the best of them.

The last of the shopkeepers and vendors were just now getting ready for business, though most of them were already open, and they beckoned for Dane's attention, seeing how many of his Animalian companions had hauled off the fisherman's product after he had paid. The Kratanians were known as an industrious people with a variety of skills, and their warriors were revered for their honor and valor. There were very few of those warriors here, however. The village Dane and Xyril had chosen to stop at had several ports to accommodate their ships, even though the village itself was dwarfed by the amount of docks.

A strange feeling fatigued Dane's mind. For several days, he had not known where on a map he could have been located. When the storm on the seas sent them careening off their course, it had left him feeling cut off from the rest of the civilized world. Kratan had been the only place that he and Xyril had both known about. It was not until he had pulled into port that Dane breathed easier, the feeling of involuntary solitude drifting away. Even though he was feeling better, it was still taking him a while to wrap his mind around being back in the known world at the snap of a finger.

Dane shook his head and smiled. *Some things are better left alone. Don't overthink*, he told himself. *You'll just drive yourself mad. You're on Kratan, and soon you'll be on your way home.*

Xyril sidled up next to him, materializing out of the fog. "Sorry, my friend."

"There you are," Dane said. "Thanks for leaving me with that old man."

"He makes me uncomfortable," Xyril said.

"I can see why. I thought Kratanians were supposed to be respectful and friendly?"

594

"I don't think he is from here."

"They say that whoever's suspicious of people stealing is a thief themselves."

"Are you saying he charged us too much for the fish?" Xyril asked.

Dane shrugged. "It's possible, but it doesn't matter. Money is of no concern to me right now. I have more stashed in my old home in Akreya, if our plan works. If not, what does it matter?"

Xyril slapped him on the shoulder. "It will work, my friend. I'm sure of it!"

"Is everyone ready to board again?" Dane asked.

"Yes. We'll set sail as soon as you're ready."

"Then let's go. No reason to waste time."

They walked together silently, grinning and taking in the sights of the docks. Finally, their ships came into view. Three of them took up spots on the piers, while the other ten were anchored away from the bay, waiting for the command to continue sailing. When they approached, several of the avians nodded to them and took to the skies to return to the sea vessels.

Dane followed Xyril up the gangplank of the biggest ship. As they ascended, Xyril shot a nod at M'Kalla and Turmarox, who captained the other two docked ships. The leonin and the minotaur boarded hastily, and the planks of all three ships were brought up simultaneously.

Once aboard, Dane smiled at Evie, who stood with Koda, Grunt, and Asira. Evie gave her father a quick wave, her face beaming. Asira tugged on Evie's sleeve to get her attention, instructing her on some common healing elixirs. Koda and Grunt each gave Dane a small nod.

Dane followed Xyril to the helm where the leonin grasped the wheel with his large hands. "Which way are we heading, Dane Iron-Fox?"

"Northeast," Dane replied, pointing.

Xyril stuck his nose to the air. "Very good, my friend. The wind favors us." He gave the wheel one big spin, and the ship slowly turned its nose to the direction Dane had indicated. "Your cub seems just as eager for this adventure as mine are." The two of them glanced across the deck where Gitra mended a tunic, and Xyril's cubs all assisted in towing the lines.

Dane nodded. "There's a lot to be excited for. We're going home, and we're bringing friends."

Xyril grinned. "I hope the rest of your people are as accepting as you and your friends have been."

Me too, Xyril, Dane thought, but he did not reply. He did not want to disappoint the leonin. Luckily, he was given an opportunity for escape when he saw Spencyr appear out of the hatch from below decks. Dane excused himself and made his way to his friends.

Spencyr shuffled nervously as Dane approached. It was as if he expected Dane to strike him once he was within range. Dane offered nothing but a smile as he got closer.

"I'm glad you decided to come with us," Dane said.

"I'm still not sure this was right," Spencyr replied, looking all around at the Animalia scurrying about the ship, "but I figured what the hell... You convinced all of them to come along on this mad journey."

"Xyril's the one who did all the convincing," Dane corrected.

"Yes... And he even managed to persuade a handful of loxodons too. I can't wait to see them in

596

action." Spencyr laughed. "Look, Dane, even if I don't agree with your decision, I know you didn't make it without weighing the options. I'll trust your judgement." Spencyr crossed his arms, shrugged, and grinned. "Besides, if this works, I wanna be able to say I was there... At the Battle of Eden."

Koda scoffed. "How poetic... Already writing the history, eh?"

"Call it healthy optimism," Spencyr said.

"Let's just see how it goes, first."

Dane drifted from the conversation, cocking his head to inspect each of the Animalia. Leonin, vulpens, avians, minotaurs, and loxodons... He smiled as he thought of Akreya. "I think we have a good chance," he said.

* * *

Bren and the other lycans walked through the gate of the village, driving a team of oxen that pulled their wagon of felled trees. The two older men were seated atop the wagon, one of them holding the reins. Bren was pleased with their work and smiled at each of the four men that had accompanied him and Harryck into the forest.

This was their third day spent cutting trees. Each day, their hauls were bigger than the previous. The village was slowly becoming more fortified. Logs could be found at each of the main entrances, sharpened to points and jutting out of the ground where they were lodged at a forty-five-degree incline. Bren hoped that these basic traps would be what they needed for a first line of defense against the undead.

So far, the lycan village had remained safe. No undead had found their way to their hideout. Some of the villagers were apprehensive about setting up the defenses, claiming that building walls would cause them to be trapped. Others had accepted the news with little more than shrugs, and the more able-bodied ones had helped set the spikes.

Bren's smile faded as soon as he passed into the limits of the village. Harryck raised his eyebrows curiously at him as he took a drink. Bren looked to his left and his right and frowned. Everything appeared normal. Smoke whisked gently from out of the stone chimneys in the homes and other buildings, and people meandered about in the open in a peaceful manner. The other lycans watched Bren with curiosity and confusion.

"All right, I'll bite," Harryck said. "What's the problem?"

"I told Weldon to watch the southern perimeter while we were gone," Bren replied.

"And?" Harryck asked.

"*This* is the southern perimeter."

Harryck shrugged. "Lighten up, Bren. He probably slipped away to take a piss. He'll be back."

"He ain't takin' no piss," one of the older lycans said from atop the wagon. He pointed and said, "He's over there flapping his gums to Layla."

"He's awful smitten with her," the other older man chuckled.

Bren glared at the man. "I don't care if he's smitten with one of these oxen. I made it clear he was not to leave his post." He took a couple stomping steps forward, but Harryck jumped next to him and put a hand on his chest.

"Let me go talk to him," he said. He corked his jug of mead and handed it to Bren.

"You?" Bren furrowed his brow.

Harryck grinned. "Yeah. You say you need my help running this place. This will be something I don't mind doing." He cracked his knuckles and chuckled as he backed away.

"Harryck, that's not exactly what I had in mind." Bren held a hand out to try and stop him.

"Trust me. Weldon's got a thick skull. He doesn't take quickly to tender reprimanding. He'll remember this one!" Harryck laughed and took off at a full sprint down the road.

Bren and the younger two lycans followed. They saw the people in the street jump out of the path Harryck forged. Up ahead, Weldon – a slender man in his early twenties – was smiling and gesticulating rapidly as he talked to Layla – a small woman wearing a bonnet to keep the sun off her face. She was leaned against the face of a building, holding a bucket in front of her, and smiling back at him.

The shouts from the people nearly bowled over by Harryck did not appear to reach the youngsters. They were trapped in their own world and did not turn to see Harryck sprinting right at them. Bren's eyes widened once he realized that Harryck had no intention of slowing down before reaching Weldon.

Harryck lowered his shoulder and wrapped his arms around Weldon's waist as he collided into him. Harryck lifted him off his feet and the two men soared momentarily before crashing into the dirt. Layla gasped and clapped a hand over her mouth, watching with shock.

Weldon groaned and cursed as he writhed on the ground. Harryck rolled immediately to a standing position. He laughed and pointed as the younger man coughed and wallowed in the dirt.

"Harryck! Why would you do that?" Layla shouted. She set down the bucket and dropped to her knees to help Weldon.

"He's supposed to be watching the perimeter," Harryck said. He had quit laughing by now, and the finger he had been pointing in jest was now a stern finger of admonition. "The next time Bren or I tell you to do something, Weldon, you'd better well do it." He did not wait for the younger man to respond, nor could he with the air knocked out of his lungs.

Bren held out the jug of mead to Harryck as he approached. "How'd you like my problem-solving skills?" Harryck asked.

Bren was still watching Weldon squirm on the ground, curled into a ball. "We'll have to see how effective it is... It was certainly a spectacle."

Harryck smiled as he uncorked the jug. "Oh, it'll be effective. You think he's gonna forget being embarrassed in front of Layla? No... He'll be following orders before we give him any, mark my words." He downed the remaining mead in the jug and shook it. "Time for a fresh one."

Bren shook his head. "Remind me to go over our responsibilities and roles with you later so that we have a clear definition of what we *can* and *can't* do."

Harryck laughed and grinned as he walked off. "You know, Bren, I don't think I'm going to mind being your right hand. Let me know next time you need someone roughed up. That's my kind of work."

Harryck ran off and left Bren chuckling and shaking his head. "C'mon, guys, let's go unload these logs. We'll call it a day."

* * *

Caulen looked up at the sky for a moment. No more streaks of red, orange, or purple tore through the clouds. It was almost time for Alton to relieve him of his post. The city would be stirring soon. Even now, he could hear some of the people jostling about.

It had amazed Caulen at how quickly people had taken to making Etzekel a semblance of civilization. Bakers had immediately started making bread and sweets. Tanners had already gone about procuring hides to make leather. Farmers had come together to clear the corpses from the gardens and had wasted no time tilling the land. Smiths had ignited the forges in the city, weavers began making baskets and furniture, tailors went about stitching and crafting new garments for people to wear, and stable hands were pleased to have proper housing for the horses, pigs, and cows that had managed to survive the trek.

Just thinking about it made Caulen smile. He stood straight and propped his bow on one end, with the other pressing into his hands, and his hands under his chin. He sighed and looked at the tree line. In the night, he had taken out four undead while he stood guard atop the city wall. That number was less than the night before. The thought made him happy, but he knew better than to believe the undead were all gone from the forest surrounding them. They would stumble around and clumsily find their way to the walls for weeks. But they could not get in, and there were always guards watching.

Thinking about the undead made him jump when a hand was placed on his shoulder. Caulen whirled around, hand gripping the hilt of the dagger Ularon had given him and slid a full step away. His face went from fierce and determined to ashamed in one instant. Alton stood there, laughing at him. The boy's face turned red.

He pointed at Caulen and spoke through intermittent chuckles. "I'm glad to see that we have such a calm and even-keeled individual guarding us while we sleep." He chuckled some more.

Caulen sighed and shook his head. He took his hand away from the weapon and brushed off his cloak where Alton's hand had been, looking at it as if it was producing a raw stench. "You caught me off-guard, is all," Caulen said. "You were supposed to be here fifteen minutes ago."

"Yeah, I wasn't in a hurry," Alton replied, walking to the edge of the wall and leaning on it. "I was confident you had it under control. Although, after what I just saw, I'm not so sure..." He winked at Caulen and grinned.

"How are you liking the city so far?" Caulen asked as he stood next to him.

"I like it. I like having a warm bed to sleep in, and I like that it's big enough that everyone has room and they don't crowd me. Camps in the wilderness are too small. I like to get away sometimes. I can do that here."

Caulen nodded silently. He had a question to ask, but he was not sure how to approach it. There was an awkward silence for a few moments – at least, awkward for Caulen. Alton was nonchalant as usual, his eyes scanning the trees casually. Caulen screwed up his face, deciding whether he should ask.

Without looking away from the trees, Alton said, "If you have a question to ask, ask it. If not, go on and get some sleep."

Caulen swallowed hard and asked, "Have you ever lost someone under your command?"

Alton looked at him. "Is this about Edmund?"

Caulen nodded. That had been the older man's name – the one from his squad that died. The city had been hectic after it was secure, and the camp was moved in. It had taken Caulen two hours to learn the names of the men he had led – Edmund, Karlyle, and Zekiel. He had found Karlyle and Zekiel after the battle helping direct people to houses they could stay at. They had given Caulen strange looks when he asked to know their names, but they told him and went back to their work.

Farrimond, Flynt, and Judd had been pleasantly surprised when he approached them. It had taken him another two hours to find someone who knew where they were, and when he found them, they were holed up in a small shack near the gate of the city, drinking ale, laughing, and sitting on barrels and crates. They stood when he entered and greeted him with formal titles and bows.

At first, Caulen had thought they were drunk and mocking him, but if they had been affected by the booze, they had sobered up very quickly at his presence. He bowed back, and they relaxed a little. When he had explained that he wanted to ask them their names, they were pleasantly surprised. They thanked him for his consideration and praised him on his skills as a fighter. Caulen let them return to their drinks and left the place smiling. Since then, whenever he saw them around the city, they greeted him.

"Here's the thing about leading people, Caulen," Alton said, "you can't blame yourself. You can mourn, and you can resolve to never make the mistake again, but you can't blame yourself. If you do, you'll go insane. Your mind will cave from the inside out. I've seen it happen. Edmund knew it was a risk."

"He wasn't a soldier," Caulen said.

Alton shook his head. "No, he wasn't. He was just a man fighting for something bigger than himself. Something better."

"Thank you, Alton," Caulen said.

Alton punched him playfully in the arm and shrugged before leaning back on the railing. "I'm no expert by any means. That's just what works for me... Have you talked to Ularon about it?"

Caulen shook his head. "He's been so busy... I don't wanna take up his time."

"He won't mind. He seems to have taken quite a shine to you... For reasons that escape me..." He grinned at Caulen. "Get outta here, kid. Go get some shut-eye."

Caulen left, but he did not feel tired. He made his way towards the tower, where Ularon had taken residence. He passed several people as he walked the city streets. They were always smiling, something that he had noticed since they had secured Etzekel. He was starting to become more well-known, too, evidenced by some of them waving at him, or nodding a greeting. One of the bakers even gave him a freshly-baked loaf of bread as he passed, placing it directly into his hands.

While chewing on a hunk of warm, soft bread, Caulen strolled, smiling to himself. He turned down an alley and walked through to the next connected street. He stepped out of the shadows and into the sunlit street. He stopped dead in his tracks.

Caulen clutched the loaf in both hands in front of him. He looked up, his eyes starting at the top of the roof of the house and scanning down. He studied carefully the windows of the second floor and the attached balcony. His eyes came down to the front door made of solid wood. There were flower boxes mounted just underneath the first-floor windows, though the flowers had been long dead. Memories of his friends prodded his mind. They were almost like echoes in a dark cave – present, but uncertain.

Caulen had been so busy helping get the city in order, that he had not had a moment to spare between sleeping and working to spend it thinking about his friends. Now, with stumbling upon the house where Dane and Evie had stayed, and where all of them had spent time together, he was forced to confront the memories.

He missed Evie. Her smile and her strong personality always cheered him up and alleviated any doubts or fears he might have. Caulen missed spending time with her. He had spent a lot of time exploring the city with her, and he wished to do it again. He sighed. *She was pretty, too… I don't suppose I'll see her again…*

When Evie had told him that her father was in the city, he had been nervous. He worried that Dane would be over-protective since he had been away from his daughter for so long, but he had not been like that at all. Dane had been kind to him and treated him like an adult. He had also been a warrior – strong, focused, and fierce. *If I can learn to be half the man he was, I think I'll be all right…*

Koda and Grunt were also present in his memories. Rarely apart, they made quite a pair. Caulen remembered being amazed at how well the two communicated, even with Grunt's condition. They rarely disagreed on anything, and without that division they were a force to be reckoned with. Koda had always been a skeptic, but Caulen knew he always meant well. While Koda was always doubtful, Grunt was always a stable person to cling to. Powerful, loyal, and determined.

Finally, his thoughts went to Bren; he could not think of Bren without thinking of Marleyn. Sadness set itself upon him, and he felt sorrow for Bren, wandering the wilderness alone. He had said he was part of the lycan village now, but Caulen found it difficult to believe that he had resigned himself to that life without feeling some regret and loss. *Oh, Bren, I hope you* can *find some happiness out there, whatever it is...*

Of course, Caulen could not think of Marleyn without thinking of the other friends he had lost. Marek, Llanowar, and Pelias... He shook his head. He did not want to think of the dead. He took another bite of the bread and turned away from the house. He walked away from it, towards the tower, trying to focus his mind on something – anything – else. But, the thoughts of friends long passed were slow to leave him. He sighed. *How long has it been?* He could not recall the answer.

Luckily, several minutes later he was climbing the steps leading to the top of the magi tower. The thought of speaking to Ularon sobered him against his demons, and he began to plan what he would say. He guessed that Ularon was already aware of Edmund's death, of Caulen's failure. Ularon seemed to know everyone in the city by name, and not only the soldiers. It was one of the reasons he had garnered as much support as he had. With Ularon, everyone felt heard. Everyone had a voice. Caulen liked that about him.

There was a guard clutching a spear on either side of the door outside Ularon's chamber. They both dipped their heads on his arrival, and one of them knocked on the door for him.

"Enter," Caulen heard Ularon answer through the door. The guard pushed the door open, and then pulled it to after Caulen had passed through.

"Greetings, Lord," Caulen said, standing a respectable distance away from the giant map that Ularon was studying. Always studying.

Ularon chuckled lightly. "I've told you - no need to be so formal, Caulen."

"I'd better practice now. I'll have to remember the titles and the formalities when you're ruling."

"So everyone tells me." He smiled grimly. "I don't want people to change how they treat me or how they respond to me just because I might happen to hold a position of power."

"People will have to show you respect."

"Hopefully I'll earn it." He leaned on the table and watched the map with such intensity that Caulen expected the markers to move by themselves. He found himself holding his breath.

"You're always looking at the map, even though we're not facing a living enemy. Can you track their movements that easily?"

"The dead don't seem to be following a specific path, but they are growing in number and spreading across the entire continent. You have to remember that they *are* being controlled by a living enemy. Uragon uses his magic to raise them and he uses it to command them.

"I watch the map to try and predict what he's up to. If there's anything I can do to interrupt his dark schemes, I'll do it. It's difficult, though, because he's sporadic, and there's not very much our little army can do to stop him when his forces span the entire realm. But I stare at it in hopes that something will come to mind."

"Do you think he knows we're here?" Caulen asked, stepping closer to the map.

"I would not be surprised if he did, but I'm not sure how he would. Who can say all the ways he can use his evil magic? If he does know, I think we're in a great position to defend ourselves."

"You think he'll send his undead legions here to retake Etzekel?"

Ularon nodded. "I think he would. This was a great victory for us. Morale is high."

"How long will we stay here?"

"That I do not know." Ularon ran a hand through his auburn hair and scratched at the scruff on his face. "Being here, anyone unwell will get healthy faster and they'll thrive. We can increase our numbers a little by training every single capable person. We'll need them, because we'll need soldiers that can stay here and guard the people in the city while our main force moves on Eden." Ularon looked Caulen in the eye. "Do you think you and Alton can provide archery instructions to the new recruits?"

Caulen raised his eyebrows. "I suppose..." He did not like the idea of being in charge again.

"You have doubts." It was a statement, not a question. Ularon cleared his throat and looked again at the map, pressing his fists into the table. "I heard about Edmund..."

Caulen hung his head. It was just as he had thought. The words he had been prepared to say were meaningless. "That's why I came to talk to you."

"You've lost people before?" Ularon asked.

"I have seen too many of my friends die, yes, but this is different. Edmund was my responsibility. You trusted me to lead..." He took one more step, which brought him to the table. "Why did you give me the command? I wasn't ready for it."

Ularon rubbed the weariness from his eyes and held his face in his hands for a few moments, breathing deeply. "You *are* ready. You have more maturity and humility in you than ninety percent of the soldiers I've encountered in my life. You just don't have experience."

"I don't want to lose anyone else."

Ularon smiled grimly and moved around the table to stand next to Caulen, so he could put a hand on his shoulder. The boy looked up at him, and Ularon said, "That's impossible and you know it. You can't prevent loss. The best you can do is be the greatest leader you can be."

"How do you ever get comfortable with this feeling?" Caulen asked.

"As sad as it is to say, you get used to it. That doesn't mean it hurts less, it just means you learn how to deal with it."

"How do *you* deal with it?"

Ularon frowned and looked at the table. He waved his hand at the map. "I stare at this, and I tell myself I can plan better. I repeat it to myself over-and-over, and eventually I believe it. It gets me by until the next time..."

Caulen looked at the map with a frown and a furrowed brow. It was no longer a pleasant thing for Ularon to spend all his free time staring at the map, studying its pieces and their placements. He would never look at it the same now.

Ularon spoke, breaking up his unpleasant thoughts. "My coping methods will not work for you. Every man must find his own way of grieving. You have to, or it will interfere with your responsibilities and then you'll be even more of a liability to your companions."

"I know that's why some men drink or smoke."

"Those are unhealthy habits that let them escape the weights in their minds for a short time."

There was a long silence as the two of them stared at the table. Finally, Caulen cleared his throat, straightened his clothes and dipped his head. "I'll leave you to your map, Sir." He turned on his heel and marched toward the door.

"Caulen, don't let the guilt tear you down. There are a lot of people relying on you. Don't let them down."

Caulen stared for a moment, saying nothing. Finally, he nodded and pulled the door open. He was already well away down the stairs before he heard the door shut behind him.

*   *   *

Dane watched Evie as she stood at the crest of the ship. The wind tugged at her dress as the ship rocked gently on the sea. Her hands clasped the railing, so she would not stagger while she was deep in thought. She studied the horizon intently, as if she heard a voice calling to her across the waves.

Dane left the conversation he was having with Xyril, Koda, and Asira, and strolled over to stand near her. He placed his hands on the railing next to her. "You know you're not the only mind-reader in the family," he said.

Evie glanced up at him and saw his grin. "Oh yeah? What am I thinking, Dad?"

"You're thinking about home." He gestured out to sea.

She rolled her eyes. "That's obvious. Aren't we all?"

Dane chuckled. "Yeah." He turned around and leaned against the railing, crossing his arms in front of him. "I would guess you're thinking about Caulen. Am I right?" He thought he saw her cheeks flush slightly, and a small smile tug at the corners of her mouth.

Evie looked up at him, a twinkle in her eyes. "It would seem you can indeed read minds." They both laughed.

"I told you I could..." He cleared his throat and looked at her. She had already set her eyes back on the horizon. "Do you, uh... fancy him?"

Evie laughed again. "You're uncomfortable right now."

Dane chuckled and nodded. "You don't need a telepath to tell you that one."

"Nope." She shook her head and thought to herself for a few moments. "I suppose Caulen's okay. I'm not rushing to fall in love and wed, though. He's the only boy my age that's been around, so I don't know if that means anything significant."

"I see." Dane put an arm around her shoulder and brought her in close. "I love you, Evelyn. I want the world for you. Caulen's a fine kid, if you do happen to admire him."

Evie smiled and leaned her head against her father's chest. "Thank you, Dad... I hope he's okay."

"I'm sure he's fine. He's smart, and he's in league with Ularon and his lot. He couldn't be much safer, I expect."

"Did you like Ularon?"

Dane considered a moment before shrugging. "He seemed honorable. He was fair with us. He seemed fine to me. You didn't like him? What, did he have bad thoughts?"

"No, no... None of that. I guess I just worry about Caulen being with anybody else but us."

"We'll see him soon enough, I hope. Should just be a couple days before we land in Akreya, now that we know where we are."

There was a sudden chill in the wind, and Evie gathered her cloak tighter around her shoulders. "How long have we even been away? I tried to calculate it, and I just couldn't."

Dane nodded. "Yeah, that storm really threw us off. I know we couldn't have been lost for more than a day and a half, but time's been running together in one long string since I left Eden to find you."

"Eden... It's been so long since I've been there."

"Longer than me." Dane planted his elbows on the railing and looked down at the churning waters below. "It won't be the same once we return. You know that, right?"

Evie nodded slowly. "Yes. I just hope we can reestablish ourselves quickly. I want a home again."

Dane nodded and they both cast their gaze to the horizon. "Me too, sweetheart."

"Dad..."

Dane looked down at her, eyebrows raised.

Evie did not look back up at him, worry etched on her face. "I still think about Uragon. How did he raise the dead if he's not a magi? Can I learn more magic? Can I *lose* my powers?"

Dane sniffed and crossed his arms. "It doesn't matter, sweetheart. Don't you worry about Uragon. We're going to put a stop to him. I promise."

Chapter 34

It had become ritual in the frosty morning, before the sun was even up, that Bren and Harryck would share breakfast and mead together. The week had been full of hard work, but the results had been fruitful. Spike traps were placed strategically around the village, and a high wall constructed of wooden logs was nearly complete. Soon, Bren would be able to breathe easier.

"Wall should be wrapped up today," Harryck said with a voice that was not fully rid of sleep. To remedy this, he downed a long swig of mead.

Bren nodded and chewed a chunk of cheese. "I think we can afford a rest day tomorrow," he said. "Then we'll need to pick it back up and get the guard towers built."

"Does the work ever end?" Harryck groaned.

"You knew it wouldn't be easy fixing this place up. Even you're not *that* stupid." Bren chuckled, biting into a sausage.

"Can't I just be the guy you get to punch people in the face? I'd like that job, and it would save your feminine hands from getting too tore up." The two men smiled at each other.

"You *can* be that guy, but you'll have to be several others at the same time. We both will."

"It seems to be working so far."

"I was worried that people would butt heads more. With me. With us taking the lead."

Harryck shrugged. "Most of them know that this is for the better. The people here may be isolated, but they're not stupid. They listen and observe. And the ones that venture into the wilderness see the dead for themselves. They know this is safer."

"But I thought they would fight me more."

"You're still thinking like an outsider, Bren." He passed the jug to his friend. "You're a lycan. Simple as that. You gained respect from most of them after Bavin told them how quickly you mastered the transformation."

Bren took a drink and then passed it back to him. "I'm glad you're with me, Harryck. I do still feel like an outsider, like I hardly know these people."

"You make it out to be a bigger crutch than it is. How many kings throughout all of history have known the names of each of their subjects? Probably none." Harryck paused to take a drink. "Don't go getting a big head because I compared you to a king. It's only a metaphor. My point is, you don't have to know everyone personally. You just have to try and do right by them. They can see you want to help and that you had the courage to take charge. Take pride in that, and stop worrying all the damn time, or else you're gonna drive me to drink."

Bren laughed just as Harryck took another long swig. "I wouldn't wanna do that," Bren mocked.

Harryck belched, stood up, and shook the jug. "Well, this appears to be empty. I'm going to fill it before you drag me out into the forest."

* * *

Mid-afternoon, Bren and Harryck hoisted the last log into the back of the wagon. Bren dusted his hands off and smiled while Harryck wiped his face with a towel.

"This should be enough logs to finish the wall. I say we finish the day early, so we can help build and start our rest day."

"Music to my ears, friend." Harryck hollered to the other lycans, "Load up! We're calling it a day!"

As one of the older lycans climbed up to drive the wagon, he pointed off into the distance. "Bren! Harryck! We've got people approaching from the south!"

Bren instinctively grabbed his wood-cutting axe and walked around to the other side of the wagon with Harryck. A group of six men around Bren and Harryck's age were approaching. Bren was certain they were not hostile, because they came out of the tree line and walked towards them in the open, but he remained watchful.

"Son of a..." Harryck trailed off. Bren glanced at him and saw that a wide grin was slowly spreading across his face. He took a few steps forward and held his arms out as the men approached. "You bastards think you can come back here all calm and nonchalant?"

Bren cocked an eyebrow at his friend. He gripped the axe tightly, prepared to spring into action at Harryck's signal. The men slowed and fanned out once they drew close. They studied Harryck, and then Bren, and then the wagon and the other lycans.

They all wore plain hide clothes. Most of them had shaggy hair and untidy beards like Harryck's. One of them had copper skin and sleek black hair. A single, long feather decorated his hair, and his bright blue eyes contrasted the black color. His eyes settled once again on Harryck. He gave one small chuckle and then came forward to embrace him, smiling wide.

"It is good to see you, my friend," the man said.

"You as well, Vokosyrra," Harryck laughed and hugged him tightly. He turned to Bren and introduced him, and the two men shook hands. Harryck introduced the other men, as well, though none moved to shake hands with Bren. They remained standing in a line behind their companion.

Bren loosened his grip on the axe when Harryck began chatting with his friend. While the others were less cordial, he felt they possessed no ill will. Bren took a step closer to join Harryck and Vokosyrra's conversation.

"What are you doing here? I thought I would never see you again," Harryck said.

"The world is a dark place now. We thought we would be safer out there, but we were wrong," Vokosyrra said, folding his arms in front of his belt.

Harryck said to Bren, "These boys here were some of the ones who left the village with me for Etzekel."

"But we've returned." Vokosyrra looked at Harryck. "My friend, we abandoned you and Trithilia alone. We should have stayed the path with you, and we did not. We have realized our error and want to atone for our shame. We didn't know you were still alive. We returned here to try and salvage what we could of the village in your honor."

"Vokosyrra didn't trust me to get us to Etzekel, and so he took the boys and left," Harryck explained, smirking, eyes flicking between Bren and the new arrivals.

"Where did you go?" Bren asked.

"All across the realm, dodging the dead and the living alike. We found very few friends in our travels. Always on the move, always being chased off or hunted... We grew weary and made the decision to return here."

Harryck grinned slyly. "You should have stuck with me, friend. I found Etzekel in the end."

Vokosyrra smiled. "Did you?"

Before Harryck could answer, Bren cut in: "Yes, and he spent most of his time there in a cage."

Vokosyrra and the others laughed at Harryck, who scowled at Bren. "That's a story for another time... For now, come home to the village with us. We have some work to do, but we will be able to celebrate shortly. It will be great to have some more healthy, able-bodied people there. Now, I can take it easy!"

Harryck threw his arm around Vokosyrra's shoulders and waved for the other men to follow as he led him to the wagon. Everyone laughed and smiled, and Bren watched Harryck. He did not know the last time Harryck had been genuinely cheerful.

* * *

Vokosyrra, Harryck, and Bren hoisted the log up and settled it into the hole in the ground. From scaffolding up above, a couple of lycans took to beating it into place with sledgehammers. The three men took a step back and wiped the sweat from their faces.

"I bet you didn't expect to have to work this hard when you returned, eh?" Harryck said.

Without looking away from the wall, Vokosyrra replied, "I was never the one that had a problem putting in hard work."

Bren laughed. "It didn't take me long to figure that out about him."

Vokosyrra ignored him. "Harryck, you've made a lot of changes to the place since I've been gone. Most of them are clever, but is the wall really necessary?"

"It was Bren's idea. He thought the village needed better security, and I agreed."

"I see..." Vokosyrra crossed his arms and walked a few steps away into the shade. "Bren, what made you decide on these changes?"

"You've seen the status of the realm," Bren said. "I didn't think we should be taking any chances for the dead to walk in here. At least with no opposition."

"I would like to see them try." Vokosyrra laughed, seating himself in the back of a wagon nearby. "I think an entire village of lycans would be more than they bargained for."

"It's best we don't take the risk," Bren said, scowling at him.

"How long have you been one of us?"

"A couple of months or so." Bren crossed his arms.

"That's not a very long time..."

"Long enough," Harryck interrupted. "If you have any issues with how we're doing things, speak your mind. Enough of the vague observations."

"I assure you," Bren said, "I have nothing but the best intentions for this place. We should sit down and get to know one another, and you'll see."

Vokosyrra shoved himself off the wagon. "If it's all the same to you, I think we should stay out of each other's way."

"Bren's in charge of this place, now. You'll answer to him," Harryck said.

Vokosyrra scoffed and began to walk away. As he passed Harryck, he whispered, "You should be leading us, and you know it. You have more right than he does."

Bren still heard the words.

"Do I?" Harryck followed, Bren a few steps behind. "I abandoned this place when I should have stayed. If I had a right to begin with, I threw it away then."

Vokosyrra threw a hand up. "Do whatever you like, brother. Come find me when the mead starts flowing."

Harryck and Bren stopped in the street. Bren raised an eyebrow, and Harryck shrugged. "Don't take it personally, Bren. Vokosyrra's always been difficult to get along with. He's bull-headed, but I'm sure everything will work out between the two of you."

Bren said nothing, returning to his work at the wall. Harryck watched Vokosyrra over his shoulder before sighing and following Bren.

* * *

The night was full of cheer and celebration. The arrival of Vokosyrra and his friends had been coupled with the finishing of the wall. After the last log had been placed, there was a weight lifted from the village. No one had spoken of it, but there had been tension since the construction had started. Even those who had been opposed to "caging themselves in" were relieved that it was finished.

Vokosyrra and the boys had jumped right into the work, and because of that they were done hours before they had previously guessed. The rest of the day had been spent with the village crowding Vokosyrra to hear of his adventures out in the wild. Singing, drinking, and dancing had commenced after the villagers had consumed their evening meals.

The elderly – who usually confined themselves indoors well before dark – sat smiling among the younger and healthier members of the village. The young shared drinks with the old, and everyone laughed and sang. They told stories by firelight and played music to dance to.

It was all fantastic to behold, and Harryck smiled as he took it all in. He brought the mead to his lips and tipped it back. He made a refreshing sigh and watched the crowd some more.

"Is that a smile I see on your face?"

The voice was soft, and Harryck turned to see his wife walking towards him. "Trithilia…" She was wearing a white dress with purple frills and her red hair was done up in curls. He offered her the jug of mead and she took it. "You look beautiful," he said as she drank.

Trithilia smiled and handed the mead back to him. "Thank you… I haven't had a reason to fix myself up in quite a while. The whole place seems a lot happier now that Vokosyrra is back, and now that the wall and the spikes are up. I guess we can breathe enough to let our guards down."

Harryck nodded and leaned against a building in the alley he stood in. He looked at the crowd, crossing his arms. "It feels good… being able to smile again, I mean. Whatever happens to the outside world, I feel like we can brave it."

Trithilia smiled softly and stepped close to him. She placed a hand on his crossed forearms and looked up at him. "Whatever good is happening here, you are a big part of it."

Harryck shook his head. "No… Bren's in charge. All this is him."

"Don't give up credit so easily. This past week has been great... I haven't seen you with purpose in a long time. You're happy."

Harryck looked from the villagers to his wife, and a small smile spread across his face. "I am."

Trithilia smiled up at him, locking eyes. They stood in silence for several moments, before Harryck cleared his throat and looked back at the dancing crowd. He expected her to move along shortly after that. He sniffed and swallowed uncomfortably. In his peripheral vision, he could see her sidling up closer to him until they were almost touching.

"Harryck, why won't you look at me?" Trithilia asked.

He blinked several times before he did what she asked. Her eyes were wide, and they scanned his own, as if searching for the answer to a question. Harryck scratched his beard and shifted his weight awkwardly.

"I've been thinking," he said. "I've mistreated you... Ever since I came back to the village... I blamed you for Erryl's death, and that's not fair."

Trithilia's eyes began to water and she buried her face into his chest. "Oh, Harryck! I miss him so much, our little boy..."

Harryck wrapped his arms around her and squeezed her tightly. "I know... I do too... It's not your fault, and I'm sorry..."

Trithilia was now weeping openly, her shoulders shuddering as he held her. Harryck laid his head on top of hers and closed his eyes. He struggled to remember the last time that they had embraced like this. There had been little affection displayed in the last couple months since they had reunited – minimal words spoken, and no romantic gestures made.

Trithilia's crying stopped, though she looked up at him through watery eyes. She smiled and said, "It feels so good to have you back, Harryck. I thought I had lost you..."

"You haven't lost me," Harryck replied. "I lost myself. I think I may be coming back around." They smiled at each other. Harryck glanced at the crowd dancing around the fire. "Would you like to dance?"

"I would like that," she replied.

Harryck gently took her hand and led the way out of the alley. "Do you remember how?" he teased her.

Trithilia smirked at him. "I'll remind you if you forget."

They marched into the throng of people and took each other's hands. The flute and drumbeats were energetic and cheerful. Harryck and Trithilia jumped, twirled, and spun in each other's arms at a fast pace that matched everyone else's. Occasionally they switched partners for a few moments, but they always ended up back with each other, and neither of them left the gaze of the other. There was a slower, more intimate dance that took place afterwards, and they held each other close. Neither of them spoke, simply enjoying the embrace of the other.

After that dance was over, they drifted out of the crowd and into the flickering shadows cast by the fire. For a few silent moments, they stared longingly into each other's eyes, holding each other at arm's length. They smiled and laughed before embracing again.

Trithilia stood on the tips of her toes and whispered into his ear: "Meet me back at the house in an hour. We've been too long without sharing a bed." She smirked and stepped away.

Harryck smirked as well and winked at her before she spun on a heel and walked away. Once she was swallowed by the shadows, he crossed his arms and leaned a shoulder against the support post of a nearby building. He found himself inspecting the smiling faces of the lovers who danced together in the crowd.

Vokosyrra approached and offered Harryck a mug of mead, which he took. "I was watching you and Trithilia dance. It is good to see you – and everyone – in such high spirits."

Harryck nodded. "It really is. It's been too long since our people knew happiness. Bren has brought that to us." He looked at Vokosyrra expectantly.

"*You* are to thank for that." Vokosyrra took a drink, looking at the dancing crowd.

"Trithilia says that, as well, but I'm no fool and no braggart. It's Bren who took the initiative." Harryck indicated Bren with his mug. The big man was across the way, drinking and eating with the lycans who had spent the week chopping trees with them.

"About Bren…" Vokosyrra trailed off.

"You should apologize to him," Harryck said.

Vokosyrra held his hands up. "I like Bren, I do… but… Who does he think he is, taking on the role of chief here? That's not how we've ever done things before."

"And look what happened. The elders were left here nearly defenseless while the young ones ran off like cowards!"

"That was *your* idea, friend," Vokosyrra said.

"I've already admitted that. I'm not blaming you, but don't forget you went with me."

"We were not cowards. We believed we could find a better life than rotting here in the mountains like hermits!"

"You sound like you resent that you came back," Harryck spat.

"I wanted better, but I know now that this is as good as it will get for us... I don't think Bren should be calling the shots. He's not earned his place."

Harryck jabbed a finger into Vokosyrra's chest. "You're pissed off because you had to come running back with your tail tucked between your legs, and you expected to be able to just come back here and run the place the way you wanted."

"That's not true, Harryck," Vokosyrra said, swiping his finger aside.

"It's not? You said before that you didn't know I was alive – that I was here. You meant to come back here and be the big hero for rebuilding the village, eh? Too late. I felt shame for what I did – leaving these people – and I'm trying to make it right. Bren stepped up and helped without any promise of thanks or reward. He's a good man, and I'll stand behind him."

"I have no doubt that he's a good man, Harryck. You need to calm down... All I am saying is that there are people here better suited to lead than him. People who have grown up here, know these people, and know how this place operates."

"You're not even trying to hide your feelings, are you, brother?" Harryck asked, disgusted. He pointed at Bren again. "He's been learning the people and the village. He's doing a good job, and I believe he makes this place safer. If you even *think* about causing any problems for him, I'll be there to stomp your ass." Harryck spit on the ground next to Vokosyrra's feet and stalked off into the shadows.

Vokosyrra's eyes burned with rage as he watched him go. He downed the rest of his mead and threw his mug into the side of the nearest building.

Luckily for him, the sound of the celebration drowned out the clattering. Vokosyrra stormed off with clenched fists. From across the fire, Bren watched with attentive eyes that reflected the glowing of the flames.

* * *

Dane's boots thudded against Port Trident. He was the first one off his ship, and his sword was already in hand. He pushed a nearby zombie off the dock and into the water with a splash. With lightning slashes, he decapitated the two closest undead. He cleaved and sliced to secure his section of the dock as the Animalia and his companions hoisted themselves over the ship's railing.

Dane looked left and right to the other prongs of Port Trident and was pleased to see the Animalia making short work of the undead they found. He raised his sword into the air and shouted, "With me! We must secure Yorkenfirth!"

He turned in time to find another zombie upon him. He ran it through with his blade and forced it to rock back on its heels. He kicked it in the chest and sent it reeling. He flipped his sword in his hands and stabbed down into the creature's skull. It let out a wheezing groan as it dropped lifeless to the ground.

As Dane wrenched his sword from where it was buried, thumping feet rumbled around him. As he stood, leonin and vulpen were rushing by him at speeds faster than a human could move. Above his head, avians danced circles in the sky, raining arrows perfectly down upon the abominations, all without colliding into one another.

Koda ran past him and then disappeared into a cloud of black smoke. He materialized ahead of the Animalia and continued to run, hoisting his spear into the air and calling, "Kill anything that looks like a walking corpse! No sag-skins are to be left moving!" He stormed towards Yorkenfirth.

Dane was captivated by how fast the Animalia moved, and how destructive they were against the undead. Whether it was a minotaur or a loxodon, the rotting demons were dealt with quickly and brutally. A small smile spread across Dane's face as he watched their eclectic army flatten the forces of the dead as an ox tramples grass. They finally had a proper fighting force.

A large hand placed on his shoulder made Dane snap out of his thoughts. He looked up to see Grunt with his gargantuan battle-axe in one of his hands. The masked man nodded down at him and awaited his order.

Dane looked over his shoulder to see Asira and Evie onboard the ship, watching the battle. "You two stay there until we've secured the area," Dane said. "Let's go, Grunt!"

The boots of the two men thumped against the wooden docks as they charged forward. Something burned inside Dane's chest that had not been there before. He had fought and won many battles, but he had never had the same sense of duty inside him as he did now. This battle was not for gold or glory or because he had simply been commanded to fight. This was for his home.

Sure, he had fought for Akreya's safety in the past, but it had always been against a living enemy. The enemy he sought to drive away now was a plague that intended to purge all life from the land. Now that he had the means to oppose the undead, he intended to fight as valiantly as he could until he saw Akreya safe or he saw it with dying eyes. The grip on his sword would not waver until all the evil was thwarted.

The fire in his chest drove his feet on faster. He began outpacing Grunt as soon as they stepped off the docks. The giant man lumbered behind at the quickest pace he could muster. There was no opposition for either of them outside of the village, any dead having already been dealt with by the Animalia. It was not until Dane breached the gate that he found more of the enemy. Even then, the Animalia were making quick work of the biggest forces.

The stragglers that did not bunch together were Dane's biggest concern now. He went about dispatching zombies at one or two at a time. His feet still moved quicker, and his sword swung true. There was not a single missed stroke of his blade – each one caught its target with a fatal strike.

The blows he made were so quick and concise that after a while he felt as if it had become a dance. Cut, stab, cleave, thrust, slice... Zombie skulls split, their guts spilled into the street, and their limbs were sent flying away from the rest of their bodies.

After he had slain at least twenty undead by himself, he turned and saw that Grunt had gone the opposite direction and was making fine work of the zombies. Whole torsos were cleaved in half by the giant man's battle-axe, and any who did not befall his weapon, he would pick up by the throat and slam into the ground before stomping on their heads, popping them like melons.

Dane returned to his own work. His path of slaughter led him down different alleyways and streets – wherever he saw a walking corpse, he pursued. Finally, his trail reconnected with the main street of Yorkenfirth. The battle was dying down. Animalia everywhere were strolling curiously, looking into the windows of the buildings or sniffing around. Just a few of them were still fighting the dead. The avians made passes above them, their keen eyes sighting any opposition to make short work of with their bows.

Dane looked around and a small smile appeared on his face. He cleaned the blood off his sword and returned it to its sheath on his hip. He wiped his face with the back of a gloved hand and strode to meet Xyril, Koda, and Spencyr. Grunt appeared out of an alley shortly after and joined them.

Xyril held his great arms open and smiled, laughing. "Dane! Our first victory!"

Dane nodded. "Yes. Very good, Xyril. You and all the Animalia performed exceptionally."

Xyril clapped a heavy paw on his shoulder. "Your enemy is frightening, but they put up so little a fight. They move so slow and their strength is small!"

"Don't let that fool you, Xyril. In great numbers, they can be dangerous. And they won't always be slow and weak. Some of them can even use weapons. Just be cautious and tell your men to act the same."

"Don't worry, my friend. We won't let you down." Xyril walked away to begin shouting commands.

Dane looked at the others, who were smiling and watching the exploring Animalia with amusement. Spencyr looked at him and said, "That was breathtaking. They handled the dead like they were dolls."

"Does it make you feel better about them being here?" Dane asked.

Spencyr chuckled. "A little... I still think it will cause more problems than you're prepared for."

Dane nodded. "I hear your words, but some things you can't worry about until the time comes." Koda tapped him on the shoulder. Dane looked at the gates where he pointed and saw Evie and Asira walking in carefully, so as not to step on any gore or viscera. Dane went to them and said, "I told you to wait until I'd come back for you."

Evie shook her head. "No, you didn't. You said to wait until it's secure. The avians aren't firing anymore arrows, and there's no more shouting. We knew it was safe."

"It is true," Asira said, "you *did* say that."

Dane sighed and shook his head, but he was too gleeful to be irritated. He made a sweeping motion at Yorkenfirth and stepped beside them. "Welcome back to Akreya," he said.

Dane turned and pointed at Raudo, the vulpen walking around aimlessly, taking in the sights. He called out, "Raudo! Take Turmarox and a few troops and secure both gates. We'll be staying here a few days while we come up with a plan of action."

The vulpen dipped his head. "Yes, Iron-Fox." The veteran fox immediately began barking orders, and the Animalia eagerly followed them.

Asira smirked at Dane playfully. "I did not know that you commanded their forces."

Dane chuckled. "I don't. They follow Xyril, but Xyril has told them that an order from me is also an order from him."

"Just don't let the power go to your head, Dad," Evie teased.

Dane smiled and took another pleased look at the efficient and thorough work the Animalia had done in Yorkenfirth.

Chapter 35

Weeks later, Caulen found himself once again on guard duty atop the wall. It was early morning, and there was a slight chill in the air. Birds had just recently started singing. From his vantage point on the wall, he saw the dew on the grass shimmering like a million shards of broken glass.

Alton had been on watch before him, and he had told him that he had not seen nor heard any undead the whole night. So far, the first couple hours of Caulen's watch had gone the same way. That was the way it had been for two days. People reported fewer and fewer sightings of the dead. That made the citizens and soldiers happy and you could hear it in their voices. They hinted that it was great news, but no one mentioned it outwardly, as if that would bring bad fortune upon themselves.

For reasons he could not explain, Caulen was not sure that less of the undead was a good thing. Something in his stomach said that there was a reason they were not seeing them on the outskirts of the city, and he did not think it was for the better. He sighed and forced himself to think of other things.

The archery training that Ularon had commissioned him and Alton to organize had been going well. It kept the two of them busy when they were not on guard duty, and so far, there had been several promising recruits. The archery lesson had not only been good for training new soldiers, but it was also good for Caulen. Together with Alton, teaching the untrained about the bow and arrow had boosted Caulen's confidence and lessened his hesitancy to lead, command, and instruct.

As far as he knew, the other weapons training had also been going well. Zuko was instructing the recruits on sword techniques and forms. The soldiers had also been trained in a few other types of weapons, and those were handled by Ularon's other officers.

Occasionally, Ularon would appear during the training exercises. He would stand silently to the side and observe for a while, before offering any tips or help he could. The recruits found it energizing to be assisted by their leader, and it made them try even harder. Ularon would always praise the officers for their diligent teachings before he left.

Caulen looked over his shoulder when he heard footsteps. Karlyle – one of the archer's Caulen had commanded - was moving at a nonchalant stride. He yawned and jabbed a thumb over his shoulder. "I was told to come relieve you."

Caulen cocked his head to the side. "What?"

"Ularon wants to see you in his tower." Karlyle crossed his arms and planted his elbows on the stone wall. He spit over the edge and watched the blob fall to the ground far below.

"What about?" Caulen asked.

"Something important is all I was told... You better hurry."

"Thanks," Caulen said, walking away to the stairwell that led to the street. He stopped and added, "I haven't seen any movement so far. No undead." Karlyle acknowledged him with a lazy wave of his hand and spit again, but Caulen did not see any of that – he was already halfway down the steps.

He pushed through the door and stepped onto the street, his bow slung over his shoulder. He pulled his cloak tight around him and quickened his pace. He did not like being unsure of what he was being summoned for. He wanted to get there as quickly as he could and find out.

People were well awake and shuffling about the streets, but they all gave him a wide berth to walk by. Most smiled or nodded, but some greeted him. He responded quickly and as politely as he could, but he did not slow his pace. He was at the base of the tower before he knew it.

Two sentries stood guard at the top of the stairs. They dipped their heads and opened the door for him. Caulen thanked them and went inside. Ularon, Zuko, and the other officers were spread throughout the room. Some were sitting, some were standing. Some of them were smoking pipes and some of them had goblets of wine in their hands. Alton was there, though he looked none too pleased to be. He rubbed sleep from his eyes and looked at Caulen, and the boy knew he had not gotten much rest in between guard duty and his summons to Ularon's tower.

Everyone looked up at Caulen when he entered the room. Mayoko and Cobon nodded to him, but most just watched. They were not unfriendly, but they did not make it a point to go out of their way to talk to him. A couple obviously did not know what to think of him, like Aberthol and Keaton. He guessed that they were unsure about his presence during their meetings, though Ularon vouched for him.

"Everyone's here now," Ularon said. "Take a seat, if you wish, Caulen." He gestured towards an empty chair, which he accepted. Most of them sat, but Ularon and Zuko stood by the table with the map.

"Shall I continue with what I was saying, My Lord?" Aberthol, the plump, balding, officer asked.

Caulen could tell that Ularon grimaced at being called 'My Lord,' but he nodded and replied, "Inform Caulen what he missed out on, Aberthol."

He nodded and folded his arms across his slightly rotund stomach as he looked at Caulen. "I was simply voicing my concerns about the upcoming winter months. They will be upon us before we know it, and we have done nothing to prepare ourselves for them. We do not have enough game preserved and stored, or enough food of any kind for that matter. We haven't even begun to collect wood for fires, nor have we attempted to determine how much wood even to save. If we're not careful, we will trap ourselves inside this city. People will go hungry. Or get sick and die!"

Caulen's eyes were wide. Aberthol spoke with an urgency he had not expected. "We can start preparation immediately!" Caulen said, placing his hands on his knees as if to lurch to his feet and begin the tasks.

"Don't let Aberthol frighten you, boy," Keaton said, his voice a gruff drawl, as he smoothed his thick beard. "Only one he's worried about goin' hungry is his self."

"I hardly think this is the time for jests, Keaton!" Aberthol stammered.

"It ain't even cold, yet. We got time." The man argued.

"Don't be stubborn, Keaton," Mayoko said in his mild tone. His face showed no emotion. He was the youngest person in the room next to Caulen and his face was smoothly shaven. The bearded officer glared at him but said nothing. "The mornings have been getting chillier," Mayoko offered, "and you know it."

"Thank you for agreeing with me, Mayoko," Aberthol said, nodding gratitude. "We need to evacuate – and soon!"

"Wait," Caulen said, "why do we have to leave? Can't we just start getting ready for winter now? Why would leaving make it any better? Would it not be safer to try and prepare for winter here behind safe walls than to get stuck in the wilderness with no options?"

"This boy's speakin' sense," Keaton said, pointing at Caulen. "Anyone who thinks we should bail out is a fool. No way we'll fare any better anywhere else but here!"

"Eden would have everything we would need," Aberthol said. "I'm sure of it."

"No, you *ain't* sure, Aberthol. Stop pretendin' to be smarter than you are." Underneath Keaton's dark brown beard, his cheeks were turning red from frustration.

"Listen to me a moment, you brute," Aberthol snapped. "Eden is plenty large enough to fit the army and the citizens inside. Any buildings we didn't need we could tear down for fuel to burn. That would solve at least one of our problems..."

A few of the officers scoffed, but Cobon said, "That may be true, but have you forgotten that our intel says that Uragon is in Eden? Who knows what he's doing there? We could get everyone killed if we go there without planning."

"See?" Keaton interrupted. "Either we stay here where it's safe and focus on getting through the winter, or we head out on some crusade to retake the capital and get massacred or at the very least trapped in the woods with no walls and no warmth."

"I'm trying to be positive here!" Aberthol said. "I keep offering solutions, and all you buffoons do is create more problems!"

"We may not even have the numbers to fight Uragon at Eden! We have no strategy!" Keaton yelled.

Aberthol opened his mouth to respond, but Cobon intervened calmly, saying, "We're being realistic, Aberthol. We're weighing all options and possibilities."

"Enough." Ularon said. His expression and his tone were calm and collected, but everyone obeyed when he spoke. "Everyone, calm yourselves... We all want the same thing. We want our people to be safe. That's the bottom line. Don't forget that..." His stern eyes drifted from man to man.

All of them were silent for several moments, ashamed at the rebuke.

"Can we send a couple men out to scout Eden?" Mayoko offered to break the quiet.

Zuko glanced at Ularon for silent confirmation before proceeding, "I suppose that's an option... It would be at least a two-week journey."

"While the scouts are gone, the others can be hunting and chopping firewood," Aberthol said in an attempt to appease both sides of the argument.

"That's not a bad idea," Cobon nodded. "There *have* been less sightings of the undead outside the walls."

"That's a good thing and a bad thing," Caulen said quietly.

The officers all looked at him with curious faces. "What do you mean, Caulen?" Ularon asked.

Caulen hesitated, but everyone remained silent for him to speak. Finally, he said, "I believe that Uragon knows somehow that we're here and that we're fortified. I think he believes we're biding our time until we're strong enough to take Eden back and... I don't know... I think the reason we haven't seen any more zombies is because Uragon has summoned them back to Eden. He's pulled all his forces there. He does *not* intend to give up the capital."

"If that's true, we definitely don't have enough soldiers to take the fight to him," Keaton mused, softer than any of his other words.

"What does the capital even mean to Uragon?" Aberthol questioned.

"He probably sees it as a monument to his power," Caulen said, shrugging. Alton nodded thoughtfully in agreement.

"Who cares?" Cobon replied. "Uragon's a madman... has been for a while. We can't waste time trying to predict his motives... only his movements."

"We should send the scouts to confirm, like we discussed," Mayoko said. "Four men? I can lead them..."

"Yes," Ularon nodded. "I think that's the best plan. While the men here prepare for winter and continue with weapons training, we'll send four scouts to bring us information about Eden. Mayoko will lead, and I think Alton, Zekiel, and-"

One of the sentries burst through the door. "Sir! There are visitors at the gate!"

Ularon spun to face him. "Who?"

The sentry shook his head in disbelief. "They didn't... They're... you just have to come see, Lord Ularon!"

Caulen expected Ularon to be irritated by the man, but he must have sensed the urgency in the soldier's tone. Ularon turned to the officers and waved them forward. "With me, gentlemen. Let's go see who our visitors are."

Everyone, including Caulen, leapt to their feet and followed Ularon down the stairs and out of the tower. News of the people at the gate must have travelled fast, for the streets were nearly barren, except for a few people who looked perplexed at the procession of officers making their way through the city.

Caulen wondered what could possibly have this effect on everyone.

He did not have to wait long for an answer. Before he was aware of it, he was climbing the stairs to the top of the wall where he had stood on guard duty less than an hour ago. Up and down the wall, citizens watched with bated breath and terrified looks. Ularon stopped and the officers fanned out around him, peering over the wall to the tree line.

Caulen gasped, and the sound was echoed by the others. They all blinked several times to confirm that what they saw was real. Staring up at them blankly, animals bigger than a human stood on two hind legs. Lions, foxes, bulls, and even elephants formed an immovable wall, their front limbs were identical to a human, and they wore armor and weapons like soldiers.

Immediately Caulen thought of the elf Anandil and his bizarre research into beings such as these. He did not want to admit that the crazy elf that had performed experiments on a caged lycan – the same elf who had assisted Renwy the halfling in blackmailing him and his friends – was right all along. His next thought was that the appearance of these beasts had to be an illusion – more of Uragon's dark magic.

The humanoid beings on the forest's edge made no movements or noises. They watched with keen, unflinching eyes. The citizens atop the wall shuffled nervously and whispered shocked remarks to one another. Ularon and his officers might have been doing the same had the citizens not been looking to them for answers.

Caulen realized that his jaw was dropped, and he swallowed with difficulty after having to remind himself to shut it. Ularon, Zuko, and Mayoko were the only three who stood with resolve and composure. Keaton scowled at the newcomers, and Alton, Aberthol, and Cobon's eyes were wide open.

Caulen saw two of the lions shuffle aside to allow a human in a long cloak to walk through. He could have very well been a taller man, but next to the animals it was impossible to tell. He had lightly tousled black hair and a short black beard. Caulen squinted.

The man was smiling up at him, and he threw his cloak over his shoulders. A wide grin spread unashamedly across Caulen's face when he saw the symbol of the Iron Fox on the front of the man's armor.

"It's Dane!" Caulen said to Ularon, who had recognized him at the same time.

"So it is," Ularon said, smiling. "And look — your other friends."

Caulen looked back as one-by-one, Grunt, Koda, Asira, and Spencyr pushed through the line of Animalia. Caulen's breath hitched in his throat, and he waited unblinking. *Where is she? Please... let her be okay*, he prayed silently.

Finally, Evie appeared, smiling as bright as ever. Caulen cursed himself for the water he felt welling in his eyes. He blinked rapidly several times to rid himself of the tears. Forgetting all formalities, he threw his hand in the air and waved at her. She saw him, grinned wider, and returned the wave.

Dane leaned over and whispered in Koda's ear. With a grin and a nod, Koda vanished, leaving only black smoke. Caulen laughed, happy to see the magi warrior again. However, the laugh was cut short as he felt a powerful arm wrap around his neck while the other one ruffled his hair.

Koda laughed and jerked Caulen around playfully. "What are you doing back here, kid?" he asked.

In a raspy voice, Koda's arm still on his throat, Caulen chuckled and said, "I could ask you the same thing." Koda let him go and spun him around to face him, placing a hand on his shoulder. They both smiled at each other a moment, unaware that the others were watching them peculiarly. Caulen glanced again at the humanoid creatures outside the walls. "I have a few other questions, too, while we're at it."

Koda laughed. "I'll leave that story to Dane. He sent me up here to tell you to open the gates and let us in. We're tired and our feet are sore."

"Umm, well..." Caulen looked over his shoulder at Ularon, who said nothing.

Zuko cut in: "We can't just let you in."

"Why not?" Koda asked, feigning insult.

"Who are..." Zuko pointed at the Animalia. "*What* are they? How do you know they can be trusted?"

"*They* were more welcoming than you lot are." Koda chuckled and crossed his arms. "We've been to their homeland. There's a bunch more like them. The Kratanians trade with them all the time."

"You've gone mad since you've been gone!" Zuko said. He turned to Ularon. "My Lord, I know these are good people, but I don't think it's a good idea to allow them inside... much less their *creatures*..."

"They could have already raided this place if they had wanted to, you know?" Koda said.

"What do you mean, Koda?" Caulen asked.

Koda put his fingers in his mouth and whistled. Like a crashing wave, the trees began to rustle and shake. A swirl of leaves was lifted into the sky as a swarm of large birds appeared out of the foliage. With arms like men, they hovered casually in the air near the wall.

Koda gave a smug look at the others. "We didn't expect to find you all here when we scouted the place earlier. You've fixed the place up nicely..."

"What are you trying to say?" Zuko asked, glaring at Koda.

"Nothing, Captain. I'm just trying to prove that our furry and feathered friends here are not a threat. They come in peace, just like us. If you want the rest of the story, you'll have to let us in – *all* of us - and get it from Dane."

Caulen looked at Ularon, who had a stern yet uneasy look on his face. Ularon looked down at Dane, who stood patiently among the Animalia. Dane met his eyes and nodded to him. Ularon glanced once more at the leonin, vulpens, minotaurs, and loxodons, and then at the avians in the sky above them.

Ularon cleared his throat and said, "Open the gate. Bring our friends inside. Do what you can to keep the people calm. They will be frightened. Bring Dane to the tower. The rest of the humans stay with the animals."

Koda disappeared again, returning to the ground to speak with Dane.

Caulen could not prevent the grin that was spreading across his face. He clenched his fist and pumped it lightly in the air in victory. Before he could celebrate too much, Ularon stopped him by placing a hand on his shoulder.

"Caulen, I want you to stay with your friends," Ularon said. "Reunite with them and see if they'll introduce you to the animal people. It will be good for the people to see you interacting with everyone. Alton, you stay with Caulen."

Alton nodded, and Caulen eagerly copied the man. These were orders he was happy to follow.

Ularon continued, "Zuko, Keaton, Aberthol, Cobon, Mayoko, come with me to the tower. Immediately." Ularon marched away briskly, the other officers in tow.

The gate was just beginning to open, and Caulen darted down the stairs. He wanted to be the first to greet his friends. Alton rushed after him, sighing at the young boy's energy and groaning as his tired joints thumped down the steps.

Caulen slid on the smooth stone pavement just as the iron gate stopped rising and the drawbridge thudded into place. Dane, Evie, Koda, Grunt, Asira, and Spencyr led the way for the Animalia. Dane and his companions all stopped before Caulen.

In a moment of awkwardness and confusion, Caulen bowed stiffly to his friends. He could not remember how long it had been since he had laid eyes on them, but it felt like a lifetime. He straightened and was immediately enveloped in Evie's arms as she leaped towards him.

Caulen laughed and wrapped his arms around her. He closed his eyes and relished the embrace. "You've gotten taller," Evie said.

Caulen blushed and nodded. "You... look the same. Not that that's a bad thing!" he added hastily. Evie chuckled and hit him playfully in the arm.

Dane stepped forward and clasped forearms with him. "I'm glad to see that you're well, Caulen."

"You as well, Dane." Caulen gestured at his own face, as if scratching his cheeks. "The beard suits you."

"Does it?" Dane grinned. "It's a little itchy. I was thinking of shaving it off."

"How did you all know we would be here?" Caulen asked. His mind raced with a thousand questions, and he picked randomly which ones to ask.

"We didn't, honestly," Dane answered.

"We came here to try and find Anandil's notes about the Animalia before we went on to Eden," Evie said. "It was just a pleasant surprise that you were here."

"The best!" Caulen grinned.

"Caulen, are you forgetting anything?" Alton interrupted from behind.

"Oh!" Caulen exclaimed. "Ularon wants you to meet him at the top of the tower."

"Well then, let's go," Dane said to his companions.

"No, just you, Dane." Caulen said.

Dane nodded. "All right."

"Do you need an escort?" Caulen asked.

Dane shook his head. "I remember the way," he said sullenly, before trudging off.

Caulen nodded to Grunt and Asira. "It's good to see you two," he said. Grunt dipped his head and Asira smiled back at him cheerfully. "I owe you two the most for saving my life. Grunt you carried me out of the bog all the way to Bandimere — all the way to Asira's door. And Asira..."

"I am pleased to find you still healthy," the healer said.

While they were talking, the Animalia were making their way around them to peer at the city. This was the biggest city they had seen so far, and they had never seen buildings made of stone before. Many of them observed all of this with mouths agape. They did not attempt to go too deeply into the city, however. Dane and the others had warned them against that. They hoped they would soon be allowed to explore.

Spencyr and Alton moved around the others and shook hands. "Good to see you again," Spencyr said.

"Same to you, Spencyr. We've upgraded our lodging since the last time you were with us," Alton grinned.

"Yeah, I can see that..." Spencyr was curious - not unlike the Animalia – and though he had seen larger cities before, he had never been to Etzekel. "Only the one gate?" he asked.

Alton shrugged. "Built by magi who never planned to leave. It's secure and defensible, but not great if you have to evacuate."

"What happened to the magi that lived here?"

"They needed to evacuate."

"They all died?"

"Not all of them," Koda chimed in, indicating himself and Evie.

"This place is cursed, then..." Spencyr said, looking around again, this time more warily than curiously.

"I didn't know you were superstitious," Alton chuckled.

"Nothing's off the table when the dead walk in the land of the living," Spencyr said dryly, crossing his arms.

"Makes you wish The Wardens were still around, doesn't it?"

"He is right, you know," Asira said. "Supernatural entities were not uncommon in this world hundreds of years ago. Only a few remnants of that time remain, but I would not be so eager to meet them."

"Zombies, you mean?" Alton asked, raising an eyebrow.

"Yes, the undead, ghosts, ghouls, specters... All manner of other-worldly evils - even demons..."

Alton laughed aloud. "Sure... I mean, we are infested by the living dead, but what happened to the demons and ghouls? Where are they now?"

"It is said that The Wardens brokered a deal with the Demon Lord to persuade him to stop allowing his minions to invade our world... But who knows if there is any truth to it?"

"Certainly not me, lady," Alton said. "I don't have time to worry about ghouls from hundreds of years ago, or curses." He glanced at Spencyr. "We were, however, hoping that you would introduce us to the, uh..." He gestured at the two-legged beasts lumbering around aimlessly, their necks craned to look at the tops of the tall buildings.

"They're called Animalia," Evie said. "They're friendly. They've come to help us fight."

"Can we talk to them?" Caulen asked.

"Sure. They speak our language. Come meet Xyril. He's the leader of the Leonin – that's what the lion-people call themselves." Evie took Caulen by the hand and led him away. Alton and the others followed.

Caulen knew that Ularon was relying on him to become friendly with the humanoids, but he was happy to spend time with Evie. Her hand was warm in his and he loved watching her black hair wave in the breeze as she weaved through the throng of people. She finally stopped next to a giant lion with a curved scimitar dangling at his hip and a wide-brimmed hat with a purple plume sticking out of it.

"Xyril," she said, tugging on the sleeve of his dark blue coat.

The great cat peered down at them and smiled a toothy grin. "Evie! This city is amazing!"

"There will be time to explore later. I want you to meet my friend Caulen." She tugged on his hand and he shuffled forward.

Caulen looked up at him and bowed his head. "Hello…"

"Greetings, Caulen," Xyril said. He placed a massive furry hand atop the boy's head and gave it a playful shake. "You are fortunate to be named friend by a cub such as this!"

Caulen glanced at Evie who winked at him. "Caulen, Xyril is the leader of the Leonin people. He's been extremely kind to us."

"It's nothing!" Xyril laughed. "You would do the same for us."

"We'll be able to welcome you more warmly once we have worked a few things out with our people," Caulen said. "Just be patient." He hoped he was not making promises he could not keep.

Xyril waved a hand. "Our people will not cause you any problems. We know how long these things take."

Alton leaned over Caulen's shoulder and whispered: "At least they're polite."

Caulen nodded and looked once more at the Animalia standing idly by. Then he looked again at Evie, who was smiling at him. *No matter what happens, this will be a good day…*

Chapter 36

"Did you expect us to be happy with this?" Aberthol asked. The older man's puffy cheeks were bright red, and beads of sweat were forming on his forehead. "You brought these... these *monsters* here into our homeland, and... and y-you promise them asylum here? What gives you the right?"

Dane stood before Ularon, Zuko, and the other officers in the room atop the tower. Ularon and Zuko stood by the map, Aberthol, Mayoko, and Cobon sat in chairs off to the side, and Keaton leaned against a support beam off to the opposite side of the map. Dane's back was straight, and his shoulders were square. His cloak was thrown over his shoulders and he rested one hand lazily on the pommel of his sword.

He had thought a lot about what he would say to the people that questioned him. He knew he could not please everyone with his decision, nor could he ask them to just accept it. He remained silent for a few moments, pondering how best to respond.

Finally, Dane looked at Zuko. The old captain straightened. "You were angry that I was abandoning the realm. When I left your camp last time, you pleaded me to stay and help you fight. I didn't because I did not believe that there was any hope.

"We didn't have enough men to fight. More people were dying every day. I had to look after my own daughter... When I left, I had no intentions of returning, because I didn't think there would be anything to return to...

"But I found a way to fight. I found soldiers who are unaffected by the curse of the dead... I found new hope in them, and I still believe the only way we'll win is with them. It may not be ideal, and I know I had no right to promise them they could stay here in Akreya, but I stand by my choice. I love this land, and if this is what it will take to save it, then so be it. I'll pay the price for that later. *After* we've reclaimed the realm."

"You see the problem we have, don't you, Dane?" Ularon asked in a steady tone.

"Of course I do. I knew it would cause trouble before I even agreed to it."

"You've made a fool's choice!" Keaton barked from the side.

Dane glared at him. "Perhaps... I won't deny that. But there was no time to mull over the other options. You know why? Because there *were* no other options."

"Now, even if they *can* help us be rid of the dead, we have a *different* kind of infestation." Keaton scowled at Dane.

"These people saved my life when they had no reason to," Dane said. "They sheltered us in their homes, fed us, welcomed us. The ones out there –" Dane pointed in the direction of the gate, "- they left with us because there were others on their island that did not like us being there. Instead of killing us, or sending us off to die, they left *with* us!"

"But not without benefit to them," Mayoko said mildly.

"Of course not," Dane said. "No one does anything without getting something out of it... I believe that this is a small price to pay to save our homes."

"And what if your belief proves to be misplaced?" Cobon asked.

"Hang me." Dane shrugged. "Behead me, fill me with crossbow bolts, parade me across the country shackled behind a team of horses, I don't care. I mean that. I just ask that we don't waste the time that we have dragging our feet.

"Uragon is in Eden. You said so yourself. He's clutched at the throat of Akreya for too long. Now, for the first time, we have the means to fight, where before all we could do was run.

"If you want to stay in your tower and debate the merits and the flaws of my plan, so be it. I'll lead the Animalia myself." Dane looked directly at Ularon. "And even if we win, and Akreya is safe, if you still don't like it, I won't fight you. I just don't want this land to die."

The room was silent as everyone stared at Dane. Ularon gave him a curt nod and said, "Leave us for now. I need to discuss this with my council. Go rejoin your friends. We'll talk to you later."

Dane set his jaw, feeling his words had failed to convince them. He moved to speak a couple of times, but no words came to mind that would do justice to convey his thoughts. He finally nodded and walked away. *No matter what they think*, Dane thought, *I have done this for the right reasons. Perhaps history will see me as a fool and a traitor, but at least I will make sure Akreya will last long enough to see me as such.*

* * *

"Wait! Bren's still alive?" Evie asked, grabbing Caulen by the shoulders. "You're sure?"

"Last time I saw him, he was," Caulen said, fishing the familiar silver locket out of his pocket.

She snatched it from his hand. "That's great!" Evie beamed at Koda and Grunt, who shared the excitement. "Why did you let him leave?"

"There wasn't much I could do. He's... different now, Evie..."

Evie put her hands on her hips, the locket dangling by its chain. "What do you mean 'different'?"

Caulen hesitated. Should he have kept that information to himself? He looked around, biding time so he could think. Koda, Grunt, and Evie had joined him in one of the empty houses where they could stay while they were in Etzekel. Alton had stayed behind with Asira and Spencyr, who were keeping the conversations flowing between the humans and the Animalia.

Caulen took a rag and enthusiastically wiped the dust off of the nearby table. This house had been unattended in the weeks Ularon and his forces had taken up residence. When they had moved in, they had cleaned up the buildings and homes that they needed and left the others alone.

"Caulen," Evie said again. "What do you mean 'different'? What's wrong with Bren?" Her eyes squinted as she studied his face for answers. After thinking for a few moments, her eyes grew wide. "Did he get bitten? Is Bren...?"

Caulen chuckled and shook his head. "It's not like that... I don't think he's in any danger of that anymore..."

"I'll read your thoughts if I have to."

"Just spit it out, kid," Koda said, planting his elbows on the freshly-cleaned table.

A rueful smile spread across Caulen's face. "Bren is... well, he's a werewolf now..."

Grunt made a quick, short growling noise. Evie gasped, and Koda stared at Caulen in disbelief. Koda finally said, while shaking his head, "Good to see that some things still surprise me..."

"He's fine, though," Caulen reassured them. "He told me he's living in some lycan village in the mountains." He shut his mouth, cursing himself on the inside for revealing that.

Dane pushing the door open was just the distraction Caulen hoped for. "Alton told me where I could find you," Dane said. He shut the door and sighed, removing his cloak and dropping into a seat at the table.

"What happened in the tower?" Koda asked him.

Dane ran a hand through his thick black hair and rubbed his eyes. "Is there anything to drink here?" he asked.

Caulen found an empty cup lying on the kitchen counter. He peered inside of it curiously and then took the rag and wiped the dust out of the inside. He placed it on the table with a bottle of wine in front of Dane.

Dane poured himself a cup and then sat back. He knocked the drink back and heaved a sigh of relief. He set the empty cup down on the table. He did not bother pouring himself another drink just yet.

"Ularon and his men are none too pleased about me bringing the Animalia here," Dane finally said.

"No surprise there," Koda said. "We knew that was likely."

"I don't blame them," Dane said. "I tried to explain my reasoning, but I don't feel like I did well enough. They said they were going to discuss it amongst themselves."

"What happens if they don't come to the same agreement we did?" Evie asked. She had taken a seat next to her father.

"Then I leave with Xyril and his troops. I told Ularon as much." His eyes flicked to each of his companions.

Evie squinted at her father and said, "'I,' you said? You don't intend to leave without us, do you?"

"I've prepared myself to pay the consequences alone."

"What does that mean?" Evie asked.

"It's likely that Ularon will be named king once the realm is saved. If he doesn't want to allow the Animalia to stay here, I'll be blamed for the war that will inevitably ensue. I'll be a wanted man, and I don't want that for you all."

"You're joking!" Evie said.

"I'm not. I made the decision alone and you shouldn't have to suffer for that. You all should stay here and obey Ularon's orders. I think I could take Eden with just the Animalia."

Evie opened her mouth to retort, but Koda spoke first: "You're daft if you think we're gonna let you go without us." He pounded his fist into the table to assert his point. "We've discussed this before. We're with you until it's done, and not a moment sooner."

Grunt growled his agreement. Caulen smiled. Dane looked at Grunt, who nodded at him, then to Koda, who did the same. He looked at Evie. She was staring him in the eyes and she drew the dagger from the sheath at her hip.

"I'm ready," she said, slapping it onto the table. "You're fooling yourself if you think you're going to leave without us."

Dane swallowed and looked at his rough, calloused hands. His fingers were intertwined on the table before him. "None of you *have* to do this. None of you owe me anything... We've already been through a lot together..."

"No, we don't owe you," Koda said, grinning at his friend. "I believe we can save this land – just like you – and I don't like the idea of you stealin' all our credit." A small smile spread slowly onto Dane's face. "You're gonna have to learn to share the glory, you bastard!"

Dane and Koda laughed as Evie smiled and sheathed her dagger. Caulen brought more clean cups to the table. Dane poured everyone drinks and looked at each one of them. He raised his cup and said, "Whatever happens, we'll be there together. Thank you…"

The five of them touched their cups together and downed their drinks, smiling and laughing with one another. It felt strange to Dane to be in Etzekel, sitting and enjoying a drink with his friends again. Though strange, it was good. Even if the city itself held bad memories, the people in this room had been present for a lot of the good ones, as well.

There was a knock at the door and Caulen answered. Asira, Spencyr, and Alton walked inside and pulled chairs up to join the others at the table. They accepted cups of wine from Caulen once they had settled.

"Who's staying with Xyril and the Animalia?" Evie asked.

Alton held a hand up, taking a sip of his wine. "No worries. Your Animalia are melding very well with the people here. Makes it easy that our people are so curious about them. Still, we left several men with them to make sure things continue going smoothly."

"Xyril's troops are very patient," Spencyr said.

"Yes. They are very understanding with the humans," added Asira.

"We knew they would be," Evie said smugly, casting a glance at Alton.

"I never doubted it. I just do as I'm told." Alton smiled and raised his cup to Evie before taking a sip.

Evie's eyes suddenly widened, and she looked at Caulen. At first, the boy did not know what she was thinking, but he remembered their previous conversation. He groaned inwardly, wishing that she would just forget. He sighed, knowing that she would be able to read his mind anyway.

Evie looked at her father and said, "You'll never guess who Caulen saw a while back."

Dane looked to Caulen and back to Evie. "Who?" he asked.

"Bren! It was Bren!" She smiled wide and lay the locket down before him.

Dane reached slowly for the silver, his fingers brushing over it. He clutched it and looked at Caulen once more. "Really? He's alive?"

The boy nodded. "He's alive and he's... healthy..."

"Don't be so shy about it, Caulen," Evie interjected, "Tell him what you told us. Why are you being so secretive?"

Caulen heaved a heavy sigh. "Because I wasn't supposed to talk about it! Bren *asked* me to keep it a secret!"

"Keep *what* a secret?" Dane asked, raising an eyebrow.

Caulen's shoulders slumped. He had already let his tongue slip, and he did not want to try and keep secrets from Dane. "Bren is a lycan, now, and he lives in a secret village with others like him."

"Well," Dane said, "that was... unexpected... I'm happy to hear he's still alive, though..." He raised his cup to drink and his eyes danced around the room as he thought. "Was he well? Besides the lycanthropy, I mean."

Caulen shook his head. "I don't know... He was pretty upset that you all left before he could find you. He said he understood. I'm not even sure he would have gone with you, but he wanted to say his goodbyes."

"I would have liked that," Dane said, taking another sip while the others nodded slowly.

Caulen continued, "He was also sad about Marleyn. He found her and Llanowar's bodies in the forest after tracking us to Bandimere."

"Damn," Koda said, shaking his head.

"He was really fond of her," Evie said softly.

"She was of him, too..." Dane said.

There was long silence from everyone. Even Asira and Spencyr, who had never met Bren, remained quiet. The laughter and smiles they had shared not a few minutes ago were far too fleeting.

Caulen had gone too long without his friends, and seeing their cheer die so swiftly was like a blow to his chest from a warhammer. He wracked his brain to think of anything to say to change the topic. In his mind, he began going through everything that had happened since they had all been apart. Finally, he remembered — one thing he was certain would bring everyone back into good spirits.

"Braxon is dead," Caulen said. His words sprang out and felt almost as if they were suspended in the air for a few moments before slowly drifting down to settle on each of his friends.

"Good riddance," Asira hissed while Evie nodded her agreement.

"At least there's one less vile person in this world," Koda said.

"I killed him myself," said Caulen, smiling pridefully.

"Is that so?" Dane asked. "How?"

"He was captured by Ularon. He wanted to execute him before the entire camp. I put an arrow through his throat while he was being led to the chopping block."

"Well done, kid," Koda said, raising his cup to him.

"It would seem that a lot has changed while we were away," Dane said, looking at his friends.

There was a knock at the door, and Caulen went to open it. Ularon nodded at the boy, a grim look on his face. He ducked inside the door and nodded again at everybody inside.

"Wine?" Alton asked, holding the bottle out to the man.

Ularon waved it away. "No, thank you."

"No posse with you?" Dane asked, sliding the silver locket into his pocket.

Ularon shook his head. "There's no reason to drag this out, everyone." He cleared his throat and put his hands behind his back. "I discussed the situation with my officers, and most of them do not agree with what you've done, Dane."

Grunt scoffed. Dane took a moment to answer. He stared into his cup, the wine at the bottom unappealing now. He sighed and nodded slowly. "I understand."

"You've got some real bastards for officers, Ularon," Koda said. "Which ones don't see it the way we do?"

Before Ularon could answer, Dane held a hand out to cut him off. He glanced at Koda. "It doesn't matter. We can't force them to agree."

"You can't, and neither can I," Ularon said. He took one hand and slicked his auburn hair back before returning it behind his back. "I tried to make them see it, Dane... I tried. Your plan is a certainty. The Animalia are big and fast and strong, not to mention their immunity

655

to the plague. The others can't be convinced, though... All they see are monsters. Zuko and I both trust you, but no one else."

"This is ridiculous!" Evie said.

"Ularon, I've spent a few hours with the Animalia," Alton said, "and they seem pure of heart and good intentions."

"I'm afraid that the officers I've chosen have turned out to be cowards," Ularon sighed.

"I'm sick of councils making stupid decisions," Koda muttered.

"Can't you do something about it?" Caulen pleaded. "They're just your advisors! You should be able to make the call!" Caulen clamped his jaw shut, staring at Ularon with worried eyes.

Ularon sighed. There were dark circles under his eyes and his beard was starting to look scraggly, Caulen noticed for the first time. "Caulen," the man said, "I've told you before that I never wanted to be king. It has been thrust upon me – as everyone is fond of reminding me. Well, a king should listen to his advisors."

"You listened," Evie said, "now tell them they're stupid and do the right thing!"

Ularon chuckled dryly. "Perhaps you should rule in my place."

"Gladly," Evie muttered.

"Evelyn," Dane said mildly through gritted teeth. Ularon was unaffected by her words. Dane looked back at him. "Your decision is made. I'm sorry your council couldn't see it the way we do. May we stay here the night? We'll leave before dawn."

Ularon sighed again and shook his head. Everyone else in the room either groaned or scoffed, except for Dane and Alton.

Dane's jaw was set, and he took a deep breath to calm himself. *If we could just get* one thing *to go our way...* "Fine," he said. "We'll be setting up camp outside your walls, and there's nothing you can do about that. We'll be leaving whenever Xyril and his troops feel like it."

"I'll give no argument," Ularon said. He walked to the door. "Alton, Caulen, be at my tower at dawn. We still have things to discuss with the others." He looked at each person in the room and said, "I'm sorry it didn't work out better..."

Koda and Evie glared at him. Asira and Spencyr looked at each other with troubled looks. Caulen and Grunt were both looking out one of the windows, ignoring Ularon. Dane looked back at him and nodded. "Me too," he said.

Alton stood up to leave with Ularon. Caulen stayed with the others, staring at the night sky outside the window with sorrowful eyes. No one else spoke another word. After a while, the Companions gathered what little things they had with them and left the house to go set up camp outside the walls of Etzekel.

Chapter 37

Caulen sat on the floor with his back against the wall. Alton and the officers were seated together around the map in a semicircle, with Ularon and Captain Zuko standing on the opposite side, and one empty seat meant for Caulen. The others had given the boy strange looks after he bypassed the table in favor of the floor. Ularon waved them off when they turned their questioning gaze to him.

"For what it's worth," Cobon stated, "I'm quite impressed with how peacefully the... Animalia... left. I was worried we would have a fight on our hands."

"Which we should be thankful for," Keaton said. "Those were some big bastards. Probably wouldn't've gone in our favor." Keaton's arms were crossed over his broad chest, and he had his usual sour look on his face.

"Don't think we're out of the woods, yet, boys!" Aberthol said, wagging a finger at everyone around the table. "Those beasts are still right outside our gate! Who knows what they're planning? Something devious, no doubt!"

"They're not going to do anything," Caulen said.

Aberthol scoffed. "What would you know, boy? We shouldn't trust those... things!"

"Dane and the others would never do anything that would cause us problems," Caulen argued.

"Oh, it's not the *humans* I'm worried about," Aberthol said before looking back at Ularon. "How long can we expect them to stay here?"

"I don't know," Ularon replied. "But they're not inside - just as you wished."

Aberthol, Cobon, Keaton, and Mayoko glanced at each other. Zuko stood like a stone sentinel next to

Ularon. Alton had his feet kicked up on the table and his chair was leaned back to balance on two legs. His fingers were laced behind his head, and he whistled softly to himself.

"They may not be inside, but they could get in the way," Aberthol said.

"Get in the way of what?" Cobon asked.

"Of… the plan we discussed yesterday! We need to send scouts to Eden while the rest of us winterize the city."

"I was actually thinking some more about that," Mayoko spoke up. "We should send some scouts to Jalfothrin, as well."

"Jalfothrin?" Cobon asked.

"Damn elves," Keaton muttered.

"Why there?" Ularon asked.

"Well," Mayoko said, "Jalfothrin is a very secure city – it always has been. The elves pride themselves on that fact. The moment the plague hit, they locked their gates and no one's heard a word since. We should check it out and see if they'll give us aid."

"Not likely," Keaton said.

"We all know your hate for elves, Keaton," Aberthol said, "but you'll just have to look past that. Whether Mayoko and Alton report that Eden is ripe for the taking or not, there *will* be a battle between us and Uragon at some point. We'll need allies, and the elves in Jalfothrin could be the answer to our prayers."

Caulen scoffed from his place by the wall, but only Ularon acknowledged him with a glance.

"Perhaps they won't help us, but it will only be a minor diversion to check," Mayoko said.

Ularon sighed. "I'll hate sending the scouts out for that long, but it's a good idea. As far as the rest of the plan, we'll need to organize the city into groups so we can divide the workload. I don't want winter preparations to interfere with weapons training, either."

Zuko nodded. "We'll need hunting parties and groups to collect firewood first and foremost," he said.

"And we need to inspect every inch of the wall to make sure there are no weak spots," Ularon said. "If this winter gets bad, I don't want the men to have to be on the wall freezing to death if we can help it."

"Yes, Sir," Zuko replied.

"I want you and Keaton inspecting the wall together. Aberthol, Cobon, I want you both to take stock of our provisions and any firewood we have. Mayoko, get the scouts ready. Take Zekiel and Judd, like we discussed yesterday, but I want Alton to stay here."

Alton looked at Ularon, who met his gaze. The archer shrugged nonchalantly. "Whatever you say, boss."

"Do I have my pick of who I want to replace Alton?" Mayoko asked.

"Yes," Ularon replied.

Mayoko nodded. "Very well."

"You all have your orders," Ularon said. He looked at each man at the table. "We need full effort from everyone so that we can keep these people safe and take back our homes. Dismissed."

The screech of chairs rousted Caulen. He had fallen into a state of only half-listening. He put his hands on the wall he had his back to and pushed himself to his feet, picking up his bow and striding toward the door.

"Caulen, hold a moment," Ularon said.

Caulen stopped dead in his tracks and turned. He kept his back straight and his chin up, but he looked at Ularon with sad eyes. He did not respond, and waited for Ularon to continue.

Ularon sat on the edge of the table and crossed his arms. "I know why you're upset. I understand. But you can't wall yourself off from the rest of us. I need your input in these meetings."

"My input doesn't matter if the others are just going to shoot me down. They think I'm just a kid, anyway. Why should I waste my breath?"

"You bring a necessary balance to the table. The others think that they know everything. Sure, they're experienced but they're not always open-minded, and they're not always right."

"Then why are you listening to them?"

"Like I told you last night, Caulen, a wise king listens to the opinions of his advisors. I promise you, I trust the Animalia, but I can't go against what everyone else tells me is the smart thing to do. Do you understand?"

Caulen looked out of the nearby window. It was a beautiful, bright, sunny day, but inside his heart was gloomy. He bit his lip as he pondered the words he was about to speak.

Ularon sat patiently, awaiting Caulen's response.

Caulen nodded slowly and looked at his feet. "I... I understand... A wise king listens to his advisors... But, perhaps a *good* king does what's right, even if it goes against everything his peers suggest." Caulen mustered the courage to look Ularon in the eyes. "Your advisors are cowards, and you are a coward for listening to them. A just king should do what's right. You know in your heart what the right decision is. You could be damning the entire realm by refusing to act. I don't want any part of it."

Caulen did not wait for Ularon to respond. He dipped his head and then turned on his heel and marched toward the door, flinging it open. The sentinels outside glanced at him curiously as he trudged down the steps before one of them looked inside at Ularon sitting alone, staring at his map.

* * *

"Can you believe this? What bullshit!"

"Scared, Koda?" Dane asked, grinning as he cinched his pack.

Koda glared at him. "I'm not in the mood, Dane. I can't believe they're turning us away! How much do you wanna bet that they're gonna let us do all the fighting and then swoop in and reap the benefits of our victory?"

"I thought you liked fighting?" Spencyr asked.

"I do, and I don't want my glory taken by people that are too busy playing at war to help."

"There's more at stake than glory, my friend," Dane said.

"I realize that. It's just... people are gonna remember these days, and I don't want them remembering it wrong."

Grunt put a hand on Koda's shoulder and made a loud grunting sound.

"Oh yeah?" Koda said. "Well, no one's going to remember you, either, you big oaf!"

All around them, the Animalia were gathering what little things they had. They sharpened their blades, tightened their armor, and finished what was left of their breakfasts. Xyril was speaking to the commanders of each race of Animalia, and they were nodding to him. The leonin leader left the group and made his way to Dane and his companions.

"It is a beautiful day for travel, my friends," he said, smiling.

"You're in good spirits, Xyril," Evie said.

"Why would I not be?"

"I just thought you and your people would be upset when we got turned out of the city."

"Bah!" Xyril waved the thought away. "It's no matter. In truth, I'm more excited that we'll get to see more of your country. I have enjoyed it very much, so far. Beautiful land!"

"It would seem *we're* more bitter than you are," Dane said.

"A great victory is on the horizon, friends. Be happy!" He laughed and walked away.

"Hey, everyone."

Dane and the others turned and Caulen was standing there with a sullen look on his face. Evie walked over without a word and wrapped her arms around his neck. He brought his arms around her and closed his eyes. Her hair smelled like vanilla, and he drank it in.

Once their embrace was over, Caulen approached the rest of them. He said, "I'm sorry I couldn't do more for you."

"There's no need to apologize, Caulen," Dane said, putting a hand on his shoulder. "Ularon's a good man, I believe."

"I don't know any more... I'm not sure I feel welcome here now."

"You could always come with us," Evie said. "It will be just like old times!"

Caulen ignored her suggestion, and said to Dane, "You should go to Jalfothrin and see if the elves will help you. They've been inside their city this whole time. Maybe they'll do more for you than we did."

Dane nodded. "Not a bad idea. Spencyr, go tell Xyril that we'll be making a detour on our way to Eden."

"He'll like that. More to see," Spencyr remarked before walking away.

"So, are you coming with us or not?" Evie asked.

Caulen glanced at her and then shook his head. "No."

"But you said yourself that you don't feel welcome here..."

"I'm not staying here, either," Caulen said.

"You're being secretive, Caulen, and I don't like it."

"I have another plan. I'll meet you guys at Eden. Don't worry." He gave a short wave and tried to hurry along.

"Stop him!" Evie shouted, pointing at Caulen.

One of the minotaur's turned at her command and placed a hand on Caulen's chest.

"Bring him to me."

The bull spun the boy around without a word and marched him back to her. Caulen glared at her, and she glared back. He knew what she was doing, but there was nothing he could do to prevent it. He hung his head as she read his thoughts.

Evie gasped. "He's going to see Bren!"

Dane, Koda, and Grunt all came closer. "What are you up to, kid?" Koda asked.

"Remember he mentioned that he knew where Bren was? He's going to find him and bring him back to fight."

"Are you crazy?" Koda asked. "Bren's a werewolf now. He's probably half-mad! He'll kill you!"

"No, he won't!" Caulen said. "He's the same old Bren. None of you have seen him, but I have. He told me he was in a lycan village in the mountains and told me how to get there. He said if I ever needed him, I could find him. I'd say we need him. We need all the help we can get!"

"You can't go alone, Caulen, it's too dangerous," Dane said.

"You're right, Dad," Evie said, "I'll go with him."

Dane glared at her. "What? No!"

"It'll be less dangerous than going with you to Eden," she said. "You know the dead have left the north. We didn't see many when we came here from Yorkenfirth."

"You can't go into the mountains just the two of you! You don't know what else is out there."

"I could go with them," Asira said. "I have travelled in the north a bit."

Dane turned his glare to her. "We may need your healing magic in Eden."

"If you go to Jalfothrin as you say you are, Father, then that should be enough of a detour that we can meet you in Eden," Evie said. "We may even get there before you," she added matter-of-factly.

"Look," Caulen said, "I wasn't going to say anything because I knew this would happen. I wasn't going to divide the group any more than it already is. I'll just go alone. I'll be fine..."

Dane sighed. "I don't want you to go alone, either, Caulen, and it would be good to have Bren and his lycans on our side. Can't you ask some of Ularon's men to go with you?"

"I'm not going to do that," Caulen said.

"He can't go alone," Evie said, "and it *would* be less dangerous for me. Asira already said she would go, and I would be surprised if you needed her healing powers with the Animalia there to clear the way through any undead to Eden."

Spencyr, who had returned unnoticed, said, "We'll need to make a decision soon, Dane. The Animalia are ready to go."

Dane growled and looked at his daughter. She held his stern look with one of her own. "I don't like the idea of being away from you again," he said, "but you're right about the danger. Spencyr... will you go with them and protect them?"

Spencyr nodded. "I will."

"Thank you." Dane looked at Caulen. "Don't waste any time. Go to Bren and then meet us in the forests west of Eden when you're done."

Caulen nodded. "Yes, Dane."

Dane looked at Asira, who smiled at him. "Thank you, Asira."

"We will be fine, Dane. Stay focused on your task." She smiled at him.

Dane took Evie in his arms and squeezed her tightly. "You're a stubborn girl, you know that?"

Evie giggled. "Yep."

Dane held her at arm's length. "Don't do anything stupid, understand?" She nodded. He smiled at her. "I love you, Evelyn."

She smiled back at him and hugged him again. "I love you too, Dad. Don't worry about us. We can handle this."

"We'd better get going," Caulen said. "We need to reach the Black Pillar as soon as possible."

The rest of the Companions said their goodbyes, before splitting once more.

Chapter 38

"I hope you see now how foolish you were to doubt me..." Uragon stared with hard eyes at the hordes of undead that clogged Eden's city streets below the castle. The corpses stood motionless, not even moving their eyes. There was no room for them to move. They congested the streets, the homes, and even the castle.

Uragon hated calling them all here after he had been gaining so much ground throughout the realm. However, he knew by the fact that his minions had lost some territories to Ularon meant that the man was going to attack soon, and he could not risk losing the capital to the rebel. If he could draw The Usurper to Eden, he would come down on him with the full might of his undead legions.

Uragon spun suddenly and glared. His brow was furrowed, and his lips were curled into a look of disgust and contempt. He thrust an arm behind him and pointed. "You could have had this! You could have had Akreya in the palm of your hand!"

Uragon spit and strode inside, away from the balcony he had been standing on. He reached out and clutched the corpse of his father by the shoulders. Uragon's rage-filled eyes searched Endrew's own eyes for some sort of recognition. The former king's eyes were now solid white, and Uragon could not find the satisfaction he wanted.

Uragon screamed into his father's face, spittle flying, and still no reply came. Uragon wanted something – some sort of acknowledgement from his father, but the dead could not form words. Even something as simple as a wrinkle forming around his lips as he attempted to speak would have pleased his son, but still there was nothing.

Uragon cupped Endrew's face in his hands and screamed, "Speak!" The grey, muddled skin of the corpse was cold to the touch. Uragon squeezed his father's head as hard as he could, hard enough that he thought for sure that his skull would pop like a melon.

Finally, Uragon roared in frustration and grabbed his father by the scruff of his neck, pulling him toward the balcony. Endrew's feet shuffled forward as if he had weights tied about his ankles, or as if he was standing in a bog that came up to his knees. Uragon gritted his teeth and pulled harder, nearly toppling the zombie.

"Look at this!" Uragon - one hand still on his father's neck - leaned him over the balcony and with the other hand gestured at the sea of undead. "This could have been *your* army, but you cast me out as if I was some disease-ridden dog!"

A haggard wheeze escaped through Endrew's teeth, but his glossy eyes were still unmoving.

"Even now you ignore my words... You'll see, father. I promise, you'll see."

A brisk wind kicked up Uragon's coat and whisked through his hair. It tugged at Endrew's brittle strands of hair. Leaves were swept upward from the courtyard that the balcony overlooked. Uragon released his hold on his father's neck, and Endrew stood straight. His dead eyes looking at nothing in the distance.

"*These* soldiers don't have to be fed. They don't need to sleep. They get cut and they keep fighting... And they *always* follow orders..." Uragon smiled as he inspected his army. "Father, if you had simply listened to me... failure would not even have been a possibility..."

Uragon looked once more to his father for recognition. Endrew's eyes were still cloudy, his skin still cold, and his lips still unmoving. In a fit of rage, Uragon grabbed his father by the throat and pulled him in close. He ignored the rotten smell emanating from the corpse's skin.

"Say it, Father…" He squeezed tighter. "Say I was right… Apologize for what you did to me… You should have killed me, but you were a coward… You thought you were sparing me, but you left me in the desert to die! How did that turn out for you, Father? Which one of us is decaying under the autumn sun? *Answer me!*"

Still no twitch of the eye, no blinking. No quivering of the lips, no words. No acknowledgment of any transgressions, no apology, no recognition.

Uragon screamed again and slammed his father's skull into the railing of the balcony – once, twice, three times. Endrew's face was flat, his nose crushed and his eyeballs to the point of exploding out of his head. Uragon let him drape over the railing as he grabbed his father's ankles and tipped him over the edge.

Without a sound, Endrew fell. His body turned several times during the long descent from the balcony of his old bedchamber to the cobblestone courtyard below. Uragon did not look, but there was no mistaking the loud *splat!* of his body splitting apart on impact.

The undead standing in the courtyard made no moves, undisturbed by the altercation.

Uragon spit again and turned back to the bedchamber. It almost startled him to see Pelias standing next to the door, wearing a fresh purple surcoat, a black undershirt and breeches, and silver gauntlets and greaves Uragon had found for him. His sword was belted low on his hip. Uragon had also restored the dead man's blonde military haircut to what it had been during his years of service to the royal family.

"I forgot you were here, old friend," Uragon said, gathering his wits and making his way to a chair and table where several bottles of wine – some full, some empty, and some in-between – were placed. "Did you enjoy the show?"

Uragon uncorked one of the bottles and poured its contents into a goblet. He swirled it around before taking a short drink. He stared at Pelias a moment. "I suppose I'll never again have the luxury of conversing with another living being, will I?"

Again, no answer.

Uragon slapped the cork into the bottle and looked at Pelias. Another pair of dead eyes stared back at him. Uragon cleared his throat and took a longer drink. He crossed his right leg over his left and brought a hand up to his mouth. His fingers scratched mindlessly at the stubble that was growing on his cheeks.

"Don't be so on-edge, my friend..." He pointed over his shoulder to the balcony, where bits of decaying flesh and rotten blood still stained the railing. "*That* won't happen to you... I need you around to protect me."

Uragon grabbed a different bottle, opened it, and poured. "I didn't kill him, you know..." Still no response from Pelias. "My father died when he failed the realm, and he failed the realm when he pissed on my solution to his problems." He held his cup suspended in front of his face and pointed a finger at Pelias.

"I know that your brain is still your own, your *thoughts* still your own... I could have put this entire continent on lockdown. Every citizen would have obeyed. Who would retaliate against the dead? But my father let fear ruin him. He was afraid that I could not control them.

"Tell me – who turned out to be correct on that one? I raised you all from the clutches of death. I sent all of you across the lands, into the plains and into the desert. Then, I summoned you all here, where you currently wait for my command. So, tell me – who was right? My father or me?"

A slow breath escaped from Pelias' mouth, almost like a small sigh.

Uragon nodded. "That's right, Pelias. Me..." He downed the drink and set the goblet gently on the table before standing up. He walked towards Pelias slowly, making a full stop after each step, until finally he was within arm's reach.

Uragon placed his hands on Pelias' shoulders and smoothed the creases out of his shirt. "Relax, my friend, I'm not going to hurt you... Even though I probably should."

His eyes flicked up from where he had been smoothing the material on his chest to meet Pelias' white eyes. "You betrayed me, just like my father... I suppose if you could speak you would defend yourself by saying you were simply following my father's orders. Honor-bound, as always, right? What about your loyalty to me? You were the only friend I had, and you turned your back on me."

Uragon placed both of his hands gently on the sides of Pelias' neck and pulled him in closer. "How easily you forgot what I did for you... When you were nothing but a child on the street, did you ever dream you would end up as Chief Commander of the Kingsguard? And who was the one that made that happen for you? Do you remember?

"Whose idea was it to lie to my father about the 'rabid dog' that attacked me when I snuck out of the castle? Who pitied you enough to claim you saved me from its snapping jaws? My father was eager to welcome his only son's savior into the halls of the castle – practically raised you as his own.

"Think about it, Pelias... It's obviously difficult for you to remember. You must've forgotten a long time ago... Honor, loyalty, morality – these are the things you would prattle on about as if you were better than I. Your whole life in this castle – your very existence here – was based on a lie. How sweet is that?"

Uragon cupped Pelias' head in his hands and brought him closer. He kissed him on the cheek, ignoring the stench of rotting flesh and the sickening taste it left when he licked his lips afterwards.

"But don't worry, my friend. I won't give up on you now. I forgive you. I'll never abandon you... *Friends don't do that, Pelias... Friends never do that...*"

* * *

As Caulen, Evie, Spencyr, and Asira topped a rise, The Black Pillar came into view – still a good distance away, but with the horses they had taken from the stables in Etzekel, they would be there in no time. The sight made Caulen smile, and he brought his horse to a stop, the others following suit. The midday sun shone bright, and a gentle breeze was whisking over the Platinum Plains, tugging at the tall, silver grass.

Caulen shaded his eyes and looked up. He studied the position of the sun and the Pillar before nodding satisfactorily. "Due north – that's what Bren said."

"How far?" Spencyr asked.

"I don't know, exactly," Caulen answered.

672

Spencyr groaned. "I don't like that. We're just supposed to go north until we find a supposed werewolf village? What if we hit snow? We just keep going until we freeze to death? We should turn back."

Evie shot him a glare over her shoulder. "Feel free to do so. We're going to follow Bren's instructions."

"We're not equipped for harsh weather," Spencyr said calmly. "How do you even know your friend Bren can be trusted? You *did* say he had changed."

"We're *not* having this discussion," Evie said. "Don't speak of Bren as if he were a madman."

"She's right, Spencyr," Caulen interjected. "Bren's trustworthy. I don't have any doubts."

"If we hit snow, we're turning back," Spencyr said in a stern tone.

"Fine," Evie sniffed, poking her chin out defiantly and looking ahead at The Black Pillar. She had not a single doubt about Bren. They had all been through too much together, and she would not give up on him now. Not again.

"Have you thought about what you might say to your friend when you see him again?" Asira asked.

"It'll be a long story," Spencyr said, "explaining the Animalia to him without being able to see them will be far-fetched."

"Bren can turn into a wolf," Evie said. "Convincing him may be easier than most."

Caulen added, "Besides, it's Bren. He knows us, knows we're not liars. Why would we travel all this way just to tell him a lie?"

Asira said, "Lycans are very protective of their identities and their homes. And as well they should be, after being hunted as monsters for so long. Do not be surprised if they do not welcome us."

"It's Bren," Caulen said. "Let's stop talking about him like he's a stranger." The thought of Bren turning them away made Caulen sullen. "Let's just keep moving. We could have a long journey ahead of us, and we don't need to waste daylight."

Caulen flicked his horse's reins and the others followed his lead. Once they reached The Black Pillar, they stopped again. There was nothing for them, but Caulen could not help but study it with curiosity.

"Ever seen it before?" Evie asked him.

Caulen shook his head. "You?"

"No."

They both stretched their necks as they looked it up and down. The mysterious black stone that the pillar was shaped from was scarred and weather-beaten. Caulen imagined what it had looked like when it was freshly carved. Of all the stories he had heard about The Three Pillars, no one ever mentioned where they came from.

"The monument to The Arbiter of Souls appears to be neglected," Asira said.

"It seems strange that for so long people believed that The Arbiter judged where their souls went, and now no one cares," Evie mused. "Look at it... No one's cared for a long time..."

"And now the realm's gone to hell," Spencyr said. "Maybe you're on to something, kid."

"There are hundreds of religions," Asira said. "They can't all be right."

"The Three Pillars are here in Akreya, though. People have ignored them, and now there's death everywhere. Sounds suspicious to me." Spencyr shrugged. "Well, if we *have* angered The Arbiter, then we should keep going. Besides, we're in Elk Tribe territory. They don't like outsiders."

There was no argument from the others. They flicked their reins and kicked their heels, sending their horses trotting further into The Platinum Plains.

* * *

The Animalia took no precautions as they trudged through the forest. Their senses would alert them if anyone was coming, and they were confident that they could handle any disruptions to their journey. They still had not come upon any undead since leaving Yorkenfirth. The Animalia sniffed curiously throughout their travels through the forest, though to the humans, the trees and bushes in Akreya looked the same as the ones on their home island.

The last time Dane had travelled through this forest, he had been on constant alert, but with the Animalia around, he was able to relax. He, Koda, and Grunt all walked at a steady pace, without much of a care for anything going on around them. It made Dane realize just how exhausting it had been on his previous travels, having to keep a constant guard up. Now, the Animalia were his alarms, and they were not concerned in the least about being caught unawares.

"I don't think you should have sent them with Caulen," Koda said suddenly.

Dane looked over at him. The two of them were walking side-by-side, with Grunt lumbering closely behind. "I don't like it, either," Dane said.

"Then you shouldn't have done it. We shouldn't have split up. We've been separated too many times, Dane."

675

"I know. But I felt better sending Spencyr and Asira with Caulen. The boy can't travel north into the unknown by himself. Plus, I think Evie will be safer the farther away from Eden she is."

"What does it matter? We're all gonna end up at Eden anyway, if everything goes as planned."

"I think it's important that we try and get Bren," Dane said.

They walked a few more steps without a word, until Koda spoke again: "I was glad to hear he's alive."

"Me too... A part of me feels guilty that we couldn't wait for him in Bandimere."

Koda nodded. "I feel that, too. It's almost like we abandoned him."

"I want him to know that we had no choice. Whether he wants to help us fight Uragon or not, at least he'll know we never forgot him."

"Maybe we all should have gone, then," Koda pondered. "How much worse could Uragon soil the realm in the amount of time it would have taken to find Bren?"

"I don't even want to joke about that," Dane said. "I don't know what all his dark magic allows him to do, but I don't intend on finding out."

"What are you gonna do after this is all over?" Koda asked.

"That depends on how it ends," Dane replied.

"Well, if we don't win, I don't think it'll matter what you plan on doing. We'll all be dead."

"If all goes according to plan, I guess I would go back to my old life. Repairing boats in Clifftown."

"Can we go back to our old lives after this? Even if we rebuild from the plague, who will rule?"

"Ularon, I suppose."

Koda scoffed. "Sounds right. Like I said before – him and his minions are gonna come in after the fighting's done and take all the credit. And what do you think they'll do to us for bringing the Animalia here? I've got to give them respect – letting us do the fighting, come in for the glory, and then imprison or execute us before we can tell anyone what really happened."

"I'm trying to stay as positive as possible, Koda."

"I'm not trying to be negative, just realistic. I thought you would understand that."

"It's not for me," Dane said, scratching at his beard. "Evie deserves to be happy. She's been through a lot in her life."

"But what do you *really* think is gonna happen? After everything is said and done?"

Dane stopped, and so did Koda and Grunt. They waited for his response. Koda leaned on his spear. Dane looked at both before he took a deep breath and cleared his throat. "I may hope everything will go one way, but I expect that, by the end of it, we'll either be dead or fugitives.

"I'll do what I can to get them to spare everyone else, but I made it clear to Ularon and his men that it was *my* idea to bring the Animalia here. I'm sure they'll have my head, but I won't let that happen to you." He looked them both in the eye and nodded to affirm his words.

Grunt and Koda stared at him. Koda's mouth was moving as if trying to form words. Grunt's eyes were searching Dane's face intently. Finally, Koda said: "You're daft if you think we're going to let them do that. We'll run – all of us – before we let them do anything to you."

Dane smiled softly and patted them each on the arm. "Let's hope it won't come to any of that."

* * *

Harryck set his jug of mead on the table and then planted his knuckles into the wood. He leaned forward, looking with urgent eyes at Bren. The big man stood calmly with his arms crossed, giving Harryck a questioning look.

"I'm telling you, Bren," Harryck said. "Vokosyrra doesn't trust you."

"I don't trust anyone that *I* don't know," Bren replied.

"Then you need to listen to me!"

"You want me to send your friend and his gang away?"

"Make them do *something* to earn your trust. They'll eventually come around to you, I'm sure, but I know Vokosyrra. It takes some time for him to trust others."

"Doesn't the saying go 'keep your friends close, but your enemies closer'?" Bren asked, taking the jug away from Harryck and taking a drink for himself.

"If you keep him here, he's going to go stir-crazy. Send him out for something – something that will keep him away for a few days. When he comes back, he'll see the improvements you've made to the village and he might respect you a little more for it."

"Do I need his respect?" Bren held the jug out for Harryck to take, which he did. Harryck took a quick sip and set it back on the table.

"C'mon, Bren. I'm trying to help you here. Don't play games."

"Your friend sounds dangerous, Harryck. He helped us finish the wall, so why is that not enough to prove that I have good intentions?"

"Because, Vokosyrra... he —"

The door opened and Vokosyrra filed inside with his companions. He folded his hands in front of him and stood rigid. He kept distance between himself and Bren, as he did every time they interacted.

"You wanted to see us?" Vokosyrra said, keeping his chin out, looking at Bren.

"I did?" Bren glanced at Harryck who raised his eyebrows and gave him a coaxing look. Bren cleared his throat. "I did... We're going to begin winter-proofing everyone's homes here. We need to repair any weak foundations and frames."

"You need us to go out and cut trees, Boss? Give your arms a break from the chopping?" Vokosyrra asked.

"No," Bren replied. "I'm still handling that. What we need is grass. We can feed it to the animals, use it to insulate roofs, and even burn it if our wood supply runs low. I want you and your boys to go to the Platinum Plains and bring back as much grass as you can."

Vokosyrra furrowed his brow, but he did not move in any other way. "You want us to risk our hides cutting grass?"

Bren raised a hand in peace. "I know it sounds menial, but the silver waves in the Platinum Plains is plentiful, and it grows long. It's our best bet."

"Best bet for collecting grass? You realize that's dangerous territory, right? Tribesmen, undead, who knows what else has festered up in this forsaken realm?"

"I was born a Tribesman. Bison Tribe," Bren said.

"Congratulations," Vokosyrra said. "Maybe *you* should go, then."

"You and your friends here don't even take a shit without the others tagging along. I figure it must've been like that for a long time, eh? You all know each other better than you know yourselves – know how you think and act. Am I right?"

"What does that have to do with anything?" Vokosyrra asked.

"I'm saying that I want you and your boys handling this because I think you're the only ones who could. You'll watch each other's backs from Tribesmen or whatever else you find. I'm sorry if it's not the most desirable job, but these people are counting on you." Bren had kept his eyes locked on Vokosyrra the entire time, and his tone had changed from friendly to impatient. After staring at each other for a moment, he followed up by saying, "Unless you're too afraid to do it, then just run on and abandon these people again. I won't judge you."

Vokosyrra looked at his friends. Some were fuming, staring at Bren with the savage glare of a wolf. Others shrugged when their leader looked to them for their opinions. Vokosyrra looked at Harryck, who stood beside Bren with his arms crossed and a blank look on his face.

"Fine," Vokosyrra said. "How much damn grass do you need?"

"As much as you can possibly carry," Bren answered, this time calmer.

"When do we leave?" he asked in a soft, retrained voice.

"We don't have time to waste. Head out before noon. Can you all handle that?"

"Aye, we can…" Vokosyrra turned and stomped off. A few of his followers continued to glare before turning to leave.

Harryck heaved a sigh of relief after the door was shut. "Gods, Bren... You could have handled that better."

Bren took a drink. "Vokosyrra's a bully. I've seen his kind before. Bullies only respond to aggression."

Harryck shook his head. "He's not a bully, he's just... afraid... Yeah, he's afraid, and that fear makes him unstable. I would hate for you to see it."

"When they found us in the woods, you seemed overjoyed to see him. Talked like you were the best of friends. What changed?"

"We've known each other a long time, and at one point we were thick as thieves, but not anymore... But at this point, I'm excited to see anyone with a pulse!"

Bren laughed and hit Harryck on the arm. "C'mon. Vokosyrra and his boys aren't the only ones with work to do around here."

Harryck put a hand on Bren's chest. "We don't need to leave the village until Vokosyrra and his men are well on their way."

Bren furrowed his brow. "Harryck, you're not doing much to ease my doubts about him."

"He's not an evil person, he's afraid for what you're doing here. Like I said, it'll take him some time to warm up to you."

Bren said, "It better happen sooner rather than later. I have bigger things to worry about than Vokosyrra going berserk inside the village."

"Okay," Harryck said, "just try and tread carefully. He doesn't like you."

"That's obvious," Bren chuckled. "Hey, what were you going to say about him before he walked in earlier?"

Harryck hesitated before shaking his head and answering, "It's not important... I'll keep him in check, don't worry... Just make sure you sprinkle on that Bren charm that I've come to know and love." Harryck grinned and slapped him on the shoulder. "Let's get to that work, shall we?"

"Now I know *for sure* that something's suspicious. You're never in a hurry to work." The two men chuckled and Harryck snatched his jug of mead off the table before they left.

* * *

Four days after leaving Etzekel, Caulen and the others were nearing the end of The Platinum Plains. Now, whenever they topped a rise, across the rolling fields of grass they could see where the plains began to fade away and the mountainous region began to materialize. Even further in the distance, they could see some of the mountains were topped with snow. Secretly, they hoped that they would not have to venture that deeply into The Dragon Fangs.

They had only witnessed two patrols of tribesmen so far in their journey. Both times it had been members of the Elk Tribe passing by. They were moving fast, and Caulen and the others were lucky to find deep gorges where they could hide as they passed.

"Will we be safe from the tribesmen once we're out of The Plains?" Evie asked.

"Not completely, but it will be less likely we'll meet them," Spencyr answered. "Sometimes they venture into the mountains, but that's rare. I'm sure we'll be fine."

"Their camp is to the southeast now," Asira said. "We should not be bothered by them."

"I wonder where all the others were going," Caulen said. "They seemed like they were in a big hurry."

"Probably to or from a hunt," Spencyr answered. "Winter will be here before we know it. They're probably stocking up on game."

"Do you think they knew we were there when they passed us?" Evie asked.

"I doubt it. Tribesmen never pass up an opportunity to kill trespassers."

"Hey, what's that up ahead?" Caulen pointed and the others squinted their eyes.

Finally, they could make out a dozen elk-riders at the top of a rise directly ahead of them. They could hear them shouting war-cries and caught the echoes of the blaring beasts they rode. The tribesmen were flinging their spears or holding them out like lances and charging. They rode in confused circles around one another, kicking up dust that hid the ground around them.

There were other noises coming from where they were scurrying. There were howls and loud roars that sounded like wolves. Through the dust, one of the elks' legs were ripped out from under it, and both beast and man screamed as they were brutalized.

"We need to go," Spencyr said, turning his horse partly away, waiting for the others.

"What? No!" Caulen exclaimed. "That could be Bren over there!"

"And if it's not?"

"I'll find out!" Caulen prodded his horse and the steed took off into a full gallop. Evie followed without hesitation. Asira looked from the kids to Spencyr.

"They're crazy!" Spencyr cursed under his breath and drew one of his hook swords and spurred his horse after the two of them. Asira followed closely behind him.

Caulen had already nocked an arrow to his bowstring. His eyes studied the commotion intently. Out of the cloud of dust, a giant wolf leapt through the air and tackled an elk and its rider, crashing to the ground. All around, men were being pulled from the backs of their beasts or being tossed into the air as if they weighed nothing. Horrible screams resounded across the plains.

Caulen and Evie got to the scene first. Fresh blood tainted the silver of the grass in droves. Steam rose from the fresh carcasses of elk and men alike. There were no survivors, other than the werewolves that patrolled the chaos and inspected their handiwork, six of them milling about. A couple stopped and began eating, but most of them simply sniffed the air. They turned and poised themselves to attack when they caught wind of the horses.

Caulen pulled the reins on his horse and it stopped as abruptly as it could, rearing slightly against the force. Evie stopped hers beside his, and her dagger was in her hand. She immediately began reading each of the werewolves' minds and was surprised when she found mostly a sense of curiosity among them.

Caulen raised his bow above his head in a peaceful gesture. The wolves did not move, but their eyes studied them carefully. The adults finally caught up to them. Spencyr rode his horse between the kids and the lycans.

Spencyr said, "If we get out of this, Caulen, I swear –"

"They're not attacking," Caulen interjected. "Look!"

The wolves began to shrink in size, and their limbs began to retract. The fur on their bodies began to recede back into their skin, and soon there stood six human men in nothing but tattered and torn breeches.

"Pardon our nakedness, Ladies," one of the men said as he fixed a single feather into his sleek, black hair. "We weren't expecting company out here. At least none as lovely as yours."

"Who are you?" Evie asked, still clutching the dagger.

The man with the feather in his hair bowed. "My name is Vokosyrra. These are my companions. I apologize for the mess. The tribesmen instigated, I'm afraid."

"What are you doing out here?" Spencyr asked, still glaring at them hard.

Vokosyrra gave a dry chuckle. "Believe it or not, we've been tasked with collecting grass." He snapped his fingers and pointed to a pack, which one of the other men tossed to him.

"Hey, careful!" Spencyr warned.

Vokosyrra gave him a mocking smile and opened the pack, holding it out for them to see that it was stuffed full of the silver grass. Vokosyrra cinched the pack closed and dropped it on the ground.

"Now," Vokosyrra said, "we've answered your questions. Tell us what *you're* doing out here."

"Do you know Bren?" Caulen blurted.

There was a subtle flicker of anger in Vokosyrra's bright blue eyes, but he maintained a calm expression. He nodded. "I do. What business do you have with him?"

"We knew him before he was a lycan," Evie said, "and we've come to talk to him."

"Have you now?"

"Yes," Caulen said. "He's our friend, and he told me where to find him."

685

"And where might that be?" Vokosyrra asked, annoyance creeping into his voice. He looked over his shoulder at his friends.

"The lycan village," Caulen said.

"I see…" Vokosyrra looked back at them.

"Caulen," Evie said slowly. "Caulen, they're not friends… Watch out!"

Spencyr and Caulen both looked at Evie, and that gave Vokosyrra and his people enough time to act. They had not noticed the subtle movements the lycans had been making, and now daggers and other projectile weapons appeared in their hands.

Spencyr heard a whinny and felt his horse drop from underneath him. The man was able to roll away before his leg was crushed, and he saw a blade sticking out of his animal's throat. He stood quickly and drew his other hook sword. "Run! Get away from here!" he shouted.

He interlocked the hooked ends of the swords and spun them over his head and in a wide circle around him. Vokosyrra approached him calmly, until the moment Spencyr chose to strike. Vokosyrra rolled underneath the first strike, but as the blades came back around in an arc, he jumped over them.

Vokosyrra was soon in striking distance, and he hit Spencyr with a few jabs to the body. Spencyr had a sword in each hand again and tried to swing them independently, but somehow Vokosyrra was able to dodge each attack. Finally, the dark-haired man hit him with an uppercut to the chin and followed up with a solid kick directly to his chest.

Spencyr fell flat on his back, groaning, and Vokosyrra strolled past him casually. He pointed on the ground and looked at his companions. "Subdue him!" Then he set his eyes on Caulen.

Caulen attempted to turn his horse, but it was too late. Vokosyrra was lightning quick, and he jumped up and wrenched Caulen off his horse. Beside them, Evie and Asira were also removed from their steeds and were being bound with rope.

"Don't worry, boy," Vokosyrra said, "you're getting what you wanted. "I'm taking you to Bren. He's going to have some explaining to do..."

Chapter 39

The rest of the day, after having their weapons stripped from them, Caulen and his companions were led as prisoners into the mountains. Ropes chafed their wrists as they were pulled along by Vokosyrra and his men. They did not address their captives, though there was always one or two of them at a time that kept a watchful eye. Caulen and the others did not speak to each other much because of it.

"We should have stayed," one of the captors said. He was a short, wiry man with a patchy beard and tangled hair.

"To cut more grass? Since when did we become glorified gardeners?" Vokosyrra asked mildly, spitting off to the side.

The man continued: "I know you don't like Bren, and I get that. But he's right about the grass. It has a lot of uses."

"Are you afraid of Bren, now, Yancy? That's not like you."

"No. I'm with you, brother, but –"

"Good," Vokosyrra cut him off. "Besides, if 'Lord Bren' isn't pleased with our haul of grass, surely our offering of three healthy horses will make up for it."

"Who cares what Bren's pleased or displeased about?" another of the men asked. "When we show everyone that he's telling outsiders where to find us, they'll tear him limb-from-limb!"

"What's your problem with Bren?" Evie asked.

Vokosyrra cast a look at her. "Never mind, you."

"Whatever you think he did, I promise you he didn't," Caulen said.

"When we get to our village, you tell everyone what you told us. Until then, keep your mouths shut." The other men sneered and chuckled at the captives.

Not another word was spoken by them as they trudged through the forests that blanketed the mountains. They followed a small path that took them up slopes and down ravines, up and down, up and down. The further they went, the more bite was in the air. It was not unbearable, but it was noticeable.

Caulen looked at Evie with concerned eyes. He hated that he involved her in this, even though she had insisted on going. He should have resisted her. Now they were captives to an enemy they did not know.

However, if he was worried, she was not. The look on her face was not nervous or fearful. It was one of angry resolve. He saw in her face that she was trying to formulate a plan of escape, and he knew she would not shy away from violence. Her squinting, focused gaze was locked on Yancy, but he could not think why.

Caulen looked over his shoulder at Spencyr and Asira, whose paths drifted close to one another as they were led by the ropes. They looked at one another, but neither of them spoke. It was evident by the looks on their faces that they were trying to imagine ways to get free. Two of Vokosyrra's men must have seen it too, and gave their lead ropes a rough jerk, sending Spencyr and Asira lurching forward.

Caulen heaved a sigh and wracked his brain for ideas.

"Just a little further," Vokosyrra said, sending a sour look over his shoulder in their direction. "Let's pick up the pace. I wanna get there before dark."

At his urging, Vokosyrra's men moved faster up the path. Caulen and the others were pulled harder by their lead ropes, and their footing wavered for the first few steps as they moved uphill. The horses kept up at a lazy trot. At the crest of the slope, a village was found nestled in the center of a natural bowl formed out of the mountain range.

Vokosyrra and his men wasted no time and they sped down a path leading directly to the village. Caulen tried to take the village in, but he had to keep watching his feet, so he would not slip and fall on the rocky path. He was also distracted by scenarios that flashed through his mind. What would Bren say when he saw them? What would happen when Vokosyrra tried to denigrate Bren in front of the other villagers, and how would those villagers react?

Before Caulen knew it, he was in front of the lycan hideout, waiting for the gate to open before him. The gate and the wall were built from fresh wood and there were spike traps placed strategically nearby all the entrances. A guard peered down at them from over the wall.

"Open the gate!" Vokosyrra commanded. He indicated Caulen and the others. "We have gifts for the village." The guard nodded and a few seconds later they heard the bar being removed from the inside. The doors swung open easily on new hinges.

Word about the newcomers spread quickly, and they had not made it very deep inside the village when a crowd gathered. Humans and elves gathered around them. They looked just like any other of their kind. Nothing of their outward appearance reflected the effects of their beast blood.

Young and old alike watched curiously at the captives being led through the streets. A few of them whispered to one another, but their reactions were much more akin to indifference than anything else.

Slowly, more people approached, though not in any great hurry.

"Oi!" Someone shouted. "Why'd'ya' 'ave them children in binds, eh?"

Vokosyrra kept marching, ignoring the woman. "Where is Bren?" he asked the crowd.

"I'm right here." Bren came slowly down from a nearby porch, his brow furrowed. Harryck was right beside him. "What's going on?" Bren gave a small nod of acknowledgement to Caulen and Evie, but his eyes went back to Vokosyrra immediately.

Vokosyrra's neck stretched as he inspected the gathering around them. "Yes, I suppose this is enough..." He pointed at Caulen and the others. "Our guests have something to say to all of you. Go on, boy, tell them what you told me."

"I don't have anything to say. Not like this," Caulen answered, standing straight, chin jutting out.

Vokosyrra glared at him. "I'm not afraid to gut one of you, boy. Any one of you can tell your story."

"That's enough," Bren said mildly. "Vokosyrra, why don't you explain what's going on, since you're so eager for us to hear a story?"

Vokosyrra pointed at Harryck. "Listen, brother," he said, "these are the first outsiders we've had in our village since it was constructed. This was supposed to be a safe-haven for all lycans – away from the people who would massacre us!"

"So then, why have you brought them here, Vokosyrra?" Trithilia asked from the crowd.

"They were on their way, whether we brought them or not. We intercepted them in The Platinum Plains, and they were coming here! Do you want to know why? Because *Bren* told them how to find us!" Vokosyrra moved the finger to Bren.

"That's ridiculous! Bren wouldn't do that," Harryck said, scoffing.

Bren crossed his arms and Vokosyrra smirked at him. Bren thought for a moment, looking from Vokosyrra to the crowd and then to Caulen and Evie.

Finally, he cleared his throat and said, "It's true. I told Caulen here how to find the village."

Gasps and murmurs flowed through the villagers. "How could you?" someone said.

"After all the good you've done!" another exclaimed.

"Did you really do that?" Harryck asked him.

Bren nodded. "I did. Perhaps it was wrong, but I've been through a lot with Caulen and Evie. I told him where to find me if he ever needed me."

"That was a terrible mistake." Trithilia said. "Bren, if you admit your error, I'm sure we can find a solution."

"I won't."

"You see!" Vokosyrra said. "He's so arrogant that he won't even try and defend himself!"

"Who are you to point fingers, Vokosyrra?" Bren asked. "You abandoned these people and only came back when you had no other choice!"

"Harryck did the same as me!"

"Harryck has atoned for his actions. And *he's* working *with* me to make this village safer."

"Safer?" Vokosyrra spat the word like it was venom from a snake bite. "You build these walls and call us safe? What's next? You give up the wooden walls for bars of steel? Are you going to cage us, next?"

"*I* am a part of this place, now. I wouldn't do anything to intentionally harm these people!"

"You mean like telling outsiders where we are? You're either a fool or you're plotting to take us down!"

"Why the hell would he do that?" Harryck asked. "You're not using your head, brother!"

"We're not here for anyone other than Bren!" Caulen shouted. "Please, let me speak!"

Vokosyrra growled and flung his pack through the air. "Enough talk! Bren, you think you can trap us in here with your walls while you wait for the outsiders to show up and kill us all?"

"You're mad!" Harryck said, moving between Bren and Vokosyrra.

"And you're blind!" Vokosyrra retorted, punching Harryck in the face and sending him sprawling to the ground.

Immediately, Vokosyrra morphed into his wolf form. He raised a giant hand, and sharp claws glinted in the remaining light of the sun. Vokosyrra brought his claws down at Harryck, but before he could cause damage to him, Bren – in wolf form – tackled him and sent him rolling through the dirt street.

Caulen, Evie, Asira, and Spencyr moved out of the way along with the rest of the crowd, which divided one side of the street and the other. Harryck shook the haziness from his head and jumped to his feet. He remained in the street but watched as Bren and Vokosyrra circled one another.

Bren was taller and more muscular, even in wolf form, but Vokosyrra's body itched with rage and aggression. The two black-furred werewolves snarled at each other as they shuffled through the dusty street. Caulen, Evie, and the others leaned forward in anticipation. Which wolf would strike first?

The village was quiet. The indifferent looks from before were still there, and it made Caulen wonder if this was a common occurrence. Looking back at Harryck, he was shocked to see the man yanking the stopper off a jug and drinking without worry, with the fight so close. Did he intend to intervene?

Vokosyrra struck first, raking his claws across Bren's cheek. Bren growled and leapt away from Vokosyrra's second swipe. With so much force behind the swing, Vokosyrra turned slightly when his second attack missed. Bren used both of his hands to drag his claws straight down Vokosyrra's back, before shoving him into the dirt.

Bren stood still, waiting for Vokosyrra to respond. In the dirt, he pushed himself up slowly with both hands. In a flash, he spun to face Bren, and used his back legs and his hands to spring forward and tackle him to the ground with such force that both wolves tumbled several feet away.

Vokosyrra ended up on top. Bren swatted at him, but he deflected all the blows. Finally pinning Bren's arms, he opened his jaws wide and went for his throat. Before he could latch on, Bren used his claws on his feet to dig into his foe's belly and push him away. Vokosyrra's fangs snapped shut on empty air.

Bren tossed him away and drew to his full height, his ears pressed back, and his fangs bared. Vokosyrra snarled and crouched low, like a coiled snake poised to strike. Bren took slow steps towards him, and even through the exposed teeth, he was collected.

Vokosyrra sprung up. Bren curled his fist and struck him in the snout as he was reaching out to grab him with both hands. Vokosyrra rolled through the dirt, but he could not get back up, for Bren had gone on the offensive. He hunched over Vokosyrra and let loose a flurry of punches to the face. Vokosyrra scrambled to get him away, but Bren dug his back claws into the dirt and continued the barrage.

Vokosyrra brought his arms up to cover his face, and Bren countered by ripping his claws across his chest. A yelp of pain escaped Vokosyrra's mouth, and he clutched at the fresh scratches on his torso. Bren returned to beating him in the face with closed fists until Vokosyrra's body went limp and his tongue lolled out of his open mouth.

Bren grabbed him by the throat and opened his jaws wide as he brought the unconscious wolf closer to his face. Bren growled and snapped his jaws shut just before Vokosyrra's face. Bren's wolf-like growls transformed into the growls of a man as his body began to slip back into his human form. He shrunk, and the fur receded into his body. Soon, he could not hold the weight of the werewolf and he let go of the man's throat.

Vokosyrra's body was already reverting to its own human form by the time it hit the ground. The man lay unconscious, his body reshaping itself. The scratches on his back and his chest were still there, and bleeding.

Vokosyrra's friends rushed to his aid, but Bren staggered in front of them, panting, with blood trailing down his cheek where he had been scratched. His body may have been exhausted, but his eyes were still bright with an internal fury. Bren pointed at them first, and then swung his finger at Caulen, Evie, Spencyr, and Asira. "Release them. Now!"

The men did as they were told and cut the ropes holding the four captives. They then joined Vokosyrra, slinking by Bren as if they themselves had taken a part of the beating. Bren glared at them over his shoulder for a moment before allowing himself to relax.

He shuffled forward, and Caulen and the others met him halfway. Evie embraced him, Caulen took his hand to shake, and Bren gave a wearied smile. Behind them, Harryck stood above Vokosyrra and his men, peering down at them with a curious look before strolling across the street to join the others. The crowd was satisfied, and now scattered to return to their chores without a second thought.

"These people are the most unexcitable I've seen in my entire life," Spencyr said.

Harryck answered, "Years of persecution have conditioned them to reserve their emotions. This little squabble was nothing to them. Just a test of power."

"And you won, Bren," Caulen said, grinning.

"Why'd you come here?" Bren asked. "It must've been a dangerous journey."

"First things first," Trithilia said, grabbing Bren's arm. "We need to get you cleaned up. You'll need stitches."

"No, he will not," Asira said. "Let me tend to him. Is there somewhere we can take him?"

"Our home is just over here," Trithilia said.

She and Harryck led the way. Once inside, they pulled chairs up to the table and found some bread, cheese, and mead. They lit a lantern and hung it from a hook suspended over the table. Everyone took their seats and began eating while Trithilia poured the mead for all of them.

Asira ignored the food and drink and began tending to Bren's face first. After peering at it for a bit, and poking around some, she cupped both of her hands over his cheek. She took a sharp breath, and as she exhaled, a soft golden light shone dimly in the lamp-light. Bren eyed her curiously, but he did not shy away from her touch.

Caulen caught himself scratching at the spot on his leg where he had been wounded by the grindylow. He had felt the warm light being emitted from the gentle woman's hands. It had been a pleasant feeling amidst all the pain he had experienced.

Harryck and Trithilia watched her for a minute, but just like the villagers watching the fight, they were not very surprised. Trithilia said, "I don't think I've ever met a magi in the flesh."

"Now you've met two," Bren said, indicating Evie. Asira hushed him for moving while she was working.

Trithilia smiled at Evie. "You're a pretty girl. Now, tell us why you've come."

"For Bren, I assume?" Harryck said.

Caulen nodded, but Evie said, "Can we trust these people, Bren?"

An amused grin appeared on his face. "Yes, they're trustworthy."

Evie looked back at Harryck and Trithilia and shrugged. "Sorry, I had to ask. After your friend Vokosyrra, and all..."

Harryck took a drink and cleared his throat. "You're not hurting *my* feelings. He's not the easiest to get along with..."

"I have a lot of questions," Bren said.

"I have a lot of things to tell you," Evie replied.

She told them about the Animalia and how hospitable they had been on their island. This was the first time the lycan's had shown any emotion. Shock and wide eyes were on the faces of Bren, Trithilia, and Harryck. Then she told them about the council meeting and how Dane had agreed to allow Xyril and anyone else who came along to stay in Akreya if they helped fight the dead. Evie told them about their return to the realm and taking Yorkenfirth with ease. Finally, she told them about their plans to go to Eden and take it back from Uragon.

By the time she had finished her story, Asira removed her hands from Bren's face and squinted at the wound. "You will have a faint scar, but at least you do not require stitches." Finally, she wiped her hands on her dress and sat down to eat.

"Thank you," Bren said to Asira, before looking back at Evie and Caulen. "Dane's taking a big risk," he said.

"He knows," Caulen said. "Ularon and his men already denied him assistance in the battle. We have the Animalia, but that's it."

"Dane's headed to Jalfothrin to seek alliance with the elves," Spencyr said. "No one's heard a peep out of them since the plague hit. Locked their gates and kept them closed."

"Unless Dane intends to take the throne for himself – which I don't believe – then he's also at risk of execution by whoever does," Bren said. "I don't know these Animalia, but I know that the Akreyans won't welcome them as warmly as Dane hopes."

"He knows," Caulen said again. "He didn't have a lot of choices."

Bren nodded contemplatively and scrubbed his hands together slowly. "Sorry Ularon didn't turn out to be the hero you thought he was, Caulen." He gave the boy a sad smile.

Caulen nodded. "I'm not worried about that anymore. I'm helping Dane and Evie."

"So, you're here to ask me if I'll return to Eden with you? To help you fight?"

Evie nodded. "Yes. Will you?"

Bren thought for a moment, looking from Evie and Caulen, to Harryck and Trithilia, who all stared back at him. Finally, Bren shook his head. "No. I can't. I promised Harryck I would help him here. I've made

698

myself a place here. Besides, what good would it do? I'm just one person."

"Well… we were hoping you could bring other lycans with you…"

Bren shook his head again. "No. I can't ask these people to do that. Most of them aren't healthy to begin with, or only now getting better. I can't do it."

"Please, Bren!" Evie pleaded. "We've been through so much together. Help us end this!"

"I can't. I've made a promise."

The table was silent. Harryck swished the mead around in his cup and looked at his wife. She locked eyes with him and nodded. Harryck took a sip and then stared into the remainder of the drink.

Harryck cleared his throat, and everyone looked at him. "You never really fulfilled your first promise, Bren…"

"What do you mean?" Bren asked.

"You told me you made a promise to help your friends. Said they saved your life, and that you owed them all a debt. They've come to collect, brother."

"I wasn't able to. They left. They were supposed to stay away, where it was safer." Bren glared at Caulen and Evie.

"Debts don't go away that easy."

"What are you saying, Harryck?"

"We've built the wall, the spikes, the towers… You've gotten us to a good place. I'm saying go help your friends. I'll manage things while you're gone." He looked at Bren and nodded.

"I can't leave you all again. Especially not with Vokosyrra here," Bren said.

"I can handle him just fine. You need to finish what you started. It'll be here when you get back."

Bren sighed and knuckled his forehead as he thought. Trithilia said, "You've done so much for us already, Bren. You've made this place safer than it's ever been. It will hold together while you're gone, especially with Harryck watching over it." She placed a hand on Bren's arm. "Go..."

"Please, Bren," Caulen said. "We want you to fight alongside us again. We've all missed you."

Still, Bren said nothing. Harryck downed the rest of his mead and set his cup down. "Bren, take the night and think it over, but in the morning, get the hell out of here." He grinned at him.

Bren looked at Harryck and Trithilia smiling at him. He looked at Asira and Spencyr. He did not know them, but he knew that if Evie and Caulen were with them, then they were good people. Finally, he looked at the kids, who sat rigidly, awaiting his response. Their eyes scanned his face, hoping for a clue to his thoughts.

In Bren's mind, he pictured the faces of all the people he had come to know in the lycan village. The place was safer now, but it would not always be so if the undead threat was allowed to grow unchecked. If his friends failed in their attempt, they would eventually find the village, and they would stand no chance. He had to do his part to ensure their success.

A small smile spread across Bren's face. "All right. I'll return with you to Eden, and we'll see this madness finished."

Smiles appeared all around the table. Harryck and Spencyr banged their cups on the table. Asira, Trithilia, and Caulen laughed and clapped their hands, while Evie threw her arms around Bren's neck.

Chapter 40

Three days after leaving Etzekel, Dane, Koda, Grunt, and the Animalia had stationed themselves in the forest just outside of Jalfothrin. They had arrived at night, and after surveying the city they decided that approaching in daylight was the best option. There were torches and armed sentries atop the walls that stayed on the move, their eyes ever vigilant, searching the land around the city. In the pitch blackness of night, the guards would not be able to discern that the Animalia were friends and would be more apt to shoot them.

Dane fastened his sword belt and adjusted it to sit comfortably on his waist. Through a crowd of leonin, vulpens, minotaurs, loxodon, and avians, Xyril approached with Koda walking beside him. Koda offered him a water skin that he had just filled from a nearby creek. Dane accepted and took a refreshing drink.

"They've put out their torches for the day," Koda commented.

Dane looked up at the sky through the canopy of branches above. "Sky's a little dark, but they'll be able to see us just fine." He slipped his gloves on.

"What's the plan?"

Dane shrugged. "We'll tell them the truth. We'll introduce them to Xyril here, and then we'll tell them we need their help at Eden."

"That sounds too simple," Koda scowled.

"I'm hoping a simple idea will work for once."

"These people – elves… What will they say?" Xyril asked.

Dane said, "We can't be sure. Elves in general aren't bad, but the ones in Jalfothrin keep to themselves when the realm *isn't* in turmoil. They do let outsiders in their city, but they interview and inspect every person coming in. The plague hasn't helped their friendliness, I'd guess."

"You did not tell me the people in your land were so unfriendly," Xyril said. "You never said that we would not have any assistance in our fight."

"We might," Dane said. "We can't give up on the elves, yet."

"Dane," Xyril quieted his voice, placed a hand on Dane's shoulder, and leaned in. "I don't want to fight a war with your people. I don't want that for your people or mine."

"I understand," Dane said.

"I hope that you do. We've come here to help you, but we've also come here to settle. I cannot deny my people what they've been promised."

"Xyril..." Dane looked into the cat's eyes. "Whatever happens, I am with you."

"Even if it means fighting your own people?"

"I spent most my life as a sellsword. I've fought people I didn't want to before. I'm with you."

"And don't worry," Koda chimed in, "I was a slave and a gladiator for most of my life. I'm used to killing friends. I'll be right there with you and Dane."

Xyril nodded and smiled grimly. "I'm glad." He straightened and put his hand on the scimitar at his side.

Just then, Grunt stamped up to them, adjusting the mask on his face. He nodded to them and pointed in the direction of the city.

"Is there much stirring inside the city?" Dane asked.

Grunt nodded.

"Then it's time we showed ourselves. I want as many witnesses to this as possible. C'mon." Dane began in the direction of the city with Koda and Grunt on either side, while Xyril rallied the Animalia and fell in behind him.

They picked their way through the trees, but once they began stepping into open space, they spread out to show their numbers. They marched without order or formation, but that did not mean anything to the message they were trying to send. They could already hear gasps and shocked statements coming from atop the walls, where elves began to scurry about.

The city of Jalfothrin had plain stone walls that formed a square shell around a rather large city made up of double and triple-level buildings. Tall towers dotted the wall at each of the four points, where sentries watched with bows and crossbows. Between the towers, elven soldiers patrolled and stood ready to man giant, mounted crossbows called ballistae.

The city was isolated in the center of a large field, though it had not always been so. All parts of the surrounding forests had been trimmed back to give a clear line of sight on all sides of Jalfothrin. Short stumps were all that remained as evidence of that fact.

Bells began to sound in all four of the towers, and people swarmed from the other sections of the city to see the approaching party. Guards nocked their bows and loaded their crossbows with bolts as they gawked at the massive Animalia that towered over the humans. The ballistae were rotated and aimed down at them.

"Don't hesitate. Keep moving, nice and steady," Dane instructed. The Animalia marched on, fearless.

"Stop right there!" One of the sentries called. The elf stood like a statue, casting a look of repulsion down upon them. Dane continued to lead the way, one hand raised in greeting. He locked eyes with the sentry who had spoken. The elf was getting visibly angrier with each step. "I said stop!" the elf shouted.

Dane led them several more steps before bringing everyone to a halt. He shifted his weight to one leg and put his thumbs in his sword belt. Most of the elves were flabbergasted by the force before them. The sentry's lip was curled in disgust.

"I want to speak to whoever's in charge," Dane said to him.

"Who are *you*?" the elf asked.

"*I* am someone who isn't here to waste time. Get me your leader."

"Whoever you are, you are not able to make demands, human."

Dane sighed and jabbed his thumb over his shoulder. "See my friends with the wings? Those aren't just for show, so I suggest you comply. I'm already tired of this conversation."

The avians unslung their bows and held them at the ready, but without drawing any arrows from their quivers. The elves on the wall tensed, and some of them began to draw their own bows prematurely. They looked around and let the string return slowly, realizing no one had given the order to draw.

The elven sentry who had spoken eyed Dane sternly. In his mind he weighed his options. Having never seen the beasts before, he decided to make the safe decision. As much as it annoyed him, he ordered a nearby soldier to find the magistrate.

"Thank you," Dane said, nodding to the sentry.

"Wait patiently," was all the elf said. His eyes still twitched in irritation.

Koda leaned in to whisper to Dane. "Let me teleport up there and put my spear in his heart, eh?" Grunt grunted his agreement.

"No," Dane replied.

"Just him, no one else."

Dane gave Koda a bemused glance before looking at Xyril. The great cat smiled at him and said, "If the leader is anything like this man, I feel we will be fighting this battle on our own."

Dane returned his eyes to the sentry, who continued to stare holes into him. *I hope not...*

The wall of Jalfothrin was now being lined by more elves. These people did not wear the armor of soldiers, however. The new faces were those of commoners, as evidenced by their plain dresses and tunics. No matter soldier or citizen, the elves were all well-groomed and clean.

"All the tales that spoke of how fair elves are were right. You never notice until there's a bunch right in front of you..." Koda said, his words trailing off as his thoughts went to Llanowar. She had always stayed cleaner than the rest of them. If the Companions were covered in dirt or blood, her skin was still pristine. A flash of her red hair appeared in Koda's mind, and he cleared his throat and looked up and down the line of their forces to try and clear his head.

"Out of the way! Out of the way, people!" A sharp, commanding voice bellowed from an unseen place. The elves on the wall quickly shuffled aside, and the soldiers began to usher them away.

A tall elf with short brown hair stopped abruptly in his tracks when he saw the army of Animalia. A tall crown of twenty spikes that tapered slowly as they reached for the sky adorned his head, resting in his hair, though the length of it must have caused it to weigh uncomfortably. He wore a soft beige robe with elaborate mint-colored stitching, and no weapon.

He was frozen where he stood, with only his eyes darting back and forth from one end of the force to the other. The soldiers around him looked to him for guidance, and the elf swallowed hard before stepping the rest of the way to place his hands on the railing of the wall. Not only was he surprised by the Animalia, but he was even more surprised to find three humans leading them.

The elf finally realized his subjects were watching him, and he said, "I am Nevarath, Magistrate of Jalfothrin. I wish to know what business you have here that you believe you can approach us with an army of such... peculiar build."

"My name is Dane. I'm sure that you've noticed the plague that has taken over the realm. We've come to discuss our plans of dealing with it."

Nevarath seemed surprised as he looked at the soldiers to his right and left. "There is no plague here in Jalfothrin. I'm afraid we cannot help you."

"Your act doesn't fool me," Dane said. "I'm not here to judge you for quarantining yourselves, but don't try to feign ignorance."

Nevarath ignored his words. "Who *are* you? Dane...? Anyone important?"

"I can't say that I am. I don't hold a title or a political position."

"Then I have nothing to say to you, I'm afraid." The elven magistrate bowed his head and turned.

"Hold a moment," Dane said. His tone was staunch, but not quite a command. He knew these types, and he knew that he would get nowhere if the elf felt insulted by someone he considered to be lesser.

Nevarath sucked his teeth and glanced at the elven soldiers before turning back around slowly. "Please, be brief."

"The dead now outnumber the living, Magistrate," Dane said. "They're being controlled by Uragon, the son of the former King Endrew. Uragon has gone to Eden, where we believe he is pulling all his forces to. We intend to take our army there and destroy him."

"Your army does not seem so great that you can take them all on, if it's true what you say about their numbers."

"These people – the Animalia – are ferocious warriors, and they're unaffected by the plague. They're immune to the bites and scratches of the dead. One of them is worth ten of a regular soldier, but we're not looking to take chances if we don't have to. We've come to see if you'll join us in our fight."

"We are not interested," Nevarath said without hesitation.

"Consider the glory and recognition you could have," Dane pleaded. "Jalfothrin would be remembered as a great city!"

"Jalfothrin is *already* a great city, and it will remain that way whether you win your little battle or not. Throw your lives away if you wish, but we will not be so foolish. Now, have a good-"

Nevarath's words halted and his eyes squinted at the forest behind the Animalia. Dane, Koda, and Grunt followed where his eyes went, and the Animalia turned and separated to allow the humans to see to the tree line. When the last of the Animalia parted, they could see that they had visitors.

Out of the flora, Ularon, Zuko, Alton, and around ten other soldiers appeared. They marched across the open field directly towards Dane, Koda, and Grunt. They stopped a few feet away, and Ularon bowed his head before smiling and coming forward to clasp forearms with Dane.

"What are you doing here?" Dane asked, smiling.

"Do your advisors know you're here?" Koda quipped.

"Only kings have advisors," Ularon replied. "I'm no king. Let them do as they please, but I'll do what's right. They think the Animalia can't be trusted, but we think they can be. We're here to fight with you." Ularon looked around and his smile dissipated. "Where's Caulen?"

"He went north to find our other allies. Took my daughter and two others with him," Dane said.

"I hope they're safe."

"They'll meet us near Eden, I'm sure."

"Hopefully with Bren," Koda added.

"What is going on down there?" Nevarath called from above. "Did you bring reinforcements to try and intimidate us?"

Ularon glared up at the elf. "Are you mayor of this city?" he asked.

"Magistrate of Jalfothrin, yes," Nevarath corrected him quickly.

"We've come seeking an alliance," Dane explained.

"I believe I've made my standing on that issue very clear."

"You will not help us?" Ularon asked.

"I won't risk the lives of my soldiers. If you were smart, you would follow my lead."

Xyril spoke for the first time, "I promise you that this will be the safest battle you've seen for your soldiers. My people and I will lead the way. Your soldiers will merely clean up any stragglers along the way."

Nevarath shuddered. "Please, don't let that beast speak again. So strange hearing civilized words out of its mouth."

Xyril growled low, glaring up at Nevarath, his tail flicking back and forth. Dane began to turn and speak to try and defuse the situation, but Ularon took several steps ahead of the army and spoke first.

"I promise you that you want to be a part of this battle."

"Why do you say that?" Nevarath asked, chuckling.

"Because we'll win," Ularon said, "and when we do... we'll remember who was there fighting beside us. And we'll remember who cowered behind city walls."

"And that means something to me?"

"Perhaps I'm not putting it plainly enough for you, Magistrate... When we win at Eden and we've handled the plague, we'll return here, and we'll root you out of your city."

One of Nevarath's eyebrows twitched. His eyes blazed with fury at the boldness of the humans. "Your threats don't scare me. None of you will make it out of Eden alive. Enjoy your glorious death." The elf stomped away, his robe flowing in the wind behind him.

The sentry from before stepped up to the wall once more. "Leave now!" he commanded.

Ularon glared him down for a few moments longer before turning to Dane. "Let's move out. Our glorious death awaits." He grinned and marched off, Zuko and Alton close behind him, and Dane, Koda, and Grunt hustled after them.

Over his shoulder, Ularon said, "I'm sorry about the negotiations, Dane. I've had my fill of uncooperative cowards."

"Don't worry," Dane replied. "I'm of a similar mind."

"Are you really going to go back for them after this is over?" Koda asked.

Ularon shrugged. "Who knows? I may not even have the authority to make that call. Hell, I may not even be alive! But it sure felt good to tell that elf off!" Ularon laughed and everyone smiled as they marched towards Eden.

*   *   *

Bren stood in the dirt street just outside of Harryck and Trithilia's home. His pack was slung over his shoulder, and Caulen, Evie, Asira, and Spencyr stood nearby with their own packs. Most of the villagers had gathered around to see them off. Even the elderly and the infirm had made it a point to shuffle into the crowd to say their goodbyes.

"Take care of yourself, young man," an elderly woman said. Bren had to lean down so she could hug his neck.

"You'll come back, won't you?" a pretty, young girl asked, looking up at him with sad eyes.

"Don't stay away too long, Bren!" a man called from amongst the crowd.

"Try not to miss us too badly!" another shouted.

Bren smiled shyly from the attention. To his relief, Harryck and Trithilia muscled their way through the lycans to embrace and shake hands with Bren and the others. Trithilia hugged Bren as Harryck handed packs of food and other supplies to Caulen and Spencyr.

"Be safe, Bren," Trithilia said. "You come back to us in one piece. Harryck will do just fine while you're gone, don't you worry."

Bren nodded. "I'm not worried at all. He can handle it, even if..."

710

"Don't," Trithilia said, locking eyes with him. "Don't you say it."

Bren shut his mouth and nodded, smiling slightly. Harryck came upon him and the two men clasped forearms. "You have plenty of supplies to last you," Harryck said. "I have something else for you, though..."

Harryck made a gesture, indicating something behind Bren. The bigger man turned and saw a group of four lycans standing nearby, waiting to be addressed. One of them was Weldon, the boy that Harryck had thrashed several days ago, and the other three were boys from Vokosyrra's group. All four of them wore travel coats and had packs over their shoulders.

"What's this?" Bren asked.

"They're going with you to Eden. You may need help," Harryck said.

"We can't spare any men. This should be my burden alone."

Harryck waved his statement away. "We've gotten our defenses up. Anything else we need to do before winter comes can be handled by the rest of us. Besides, you'll be back in a week or two, I'm sure, and then I can relax and let you do all the heavy lifting." Harryck grinned.

Bren leaned in closer and whispered, "What about Vokosyrra's men? I don't think they can be trusted."

"Let them explain it to you."

Bren gave Harryck a doubtful look before turning to the three. One of them stepped forward and held out a feather – the same one that Vokosyrra used to decorate his hair. Bren eyed it for a moment before looking back to the man holding it.

"This is a feather from the griffin Ooranoos," the man said slowly. "Vokosyrra's father slew him, and he

711

gave it to his son before he passed. Vokosyrra asked us to present it to you."

"Why?" Bren asked.

Keeping the feather outstretched, he replied, "You've earned his respect. You defended yourself for the good of the people, and you showed Vokosyrra mercy. He wanted us to tell you that he believes you have the village's best interests at heart. When he gets better, he wants to do whatever he can to help you."

Bren studied his face for a few moments before looking again at the feather. Ooranoos had been a terror to The Platinum Plains for decades. The Tribesmen had tried and failed hundreds of times to slay him, and until now Bren had not known who had finally succeeded.

Bren gently plucked the feather from between the man's fingers. He studied it closer before nodding and tying it to a string hanging from his pack. The griffin feather was lifted by the gentle breeze. "Tell Vokosyrra I said thank you, and I look forward to working with him when I return."

"I'll tell him," Harryck said. "You can't delay any longer."

"I still don't think I should bring anyone else along. They could be put to good use here," Bren said. "I won't force them to follow me into battle."

"We're not being forced," Weldon said. "Harryck asked me if I would go. I want to go. I'll prove myself, yet." The girl Layla – whom he had been flirting with the day of Harryck and Weldon's altercation – looked up at the young man with admiration. She clung tighter to his arm.

"Vokosyrra has asked us to journey with you and fight by your side, as a token of good will," another one of Vokosyrra's boys said.

"We're doing it for him," the third one added.

"We'll prove you can trust us," the first one said.

"What are your names?" Bren asked.

"I am Peytah," he replied. "This is Wesa and Waya – brothers."

Bren glanced at Caulen, Evie, Spencyr, and Asira. They stared at him, awaiting his answer. Bren said, "Weldon, Peytah, Wesa, Waya... Let's go. There's a battle to fight, and no time to waste getting there."

Harryck smiled and embraced Bren as Trithilia hugged Caulen and Evie. The crowd waved and shouted their farewells. Minutes later, Bren, Caulen, and Evie walked out of the lycan village headed south with their six companions. What exactly to expect when they got to Eden, none of them knew...

Chapter 41

Dane prodded the campfire with a stick. He sat on the ground, an elbow propped on his knee and his fingers scratching at his short, thick beard, digging through the hair to get to his scar. His fox-tail longsword - nestled in its scabbard - lay on the ground next to him.

Animalia paced about the forest, towering over Dane where he sat. He knew they were restless to begin their fight, but he did not care about any of that at the moment.

Dane stared into the fire as he poked it. His mind journeyed to Eden and he thought about how long he had been away from there. He had travelled a long way, been to many places, but the last time he had been in Eden, Amir and so many others had still been alive. *Amir...*

"This battle could be our last," Amir had said whenever news of a new attack would spread through the ranks of The Iron Fox Legion. After he said the words, there would be a pause, before a chuckle and a playful grin appeared.

Dane smiled wistfully.

Dusk was falling rapidly, and Dane had put in a hard day's work. As he walked down the street to his house, he wiped the sweat off his face with a grimy hand. He reached out for the door handle. Before he could pull it open, a voice said, "Hey... Dane."

Dane, startled, turned to find a grinning Amir, dusty from the road. Amir held his arms out and came forward for an embrace. Dane wrapped his arms around him and the two men laughed. "That was my last battle..."

From that day on, Dane and Amir had worked together every day. Memories flitted through Dane's mind so quickly yet seemed to dwell for an eternity. From the moment they had met, up until that dreaded day in the arena of Eden.

Dane closed his eyes, refusing to dwell on that day. Dane murmured, "My friend... Brother... Maybe this battle will be my last..."

"Dane," Koda said.

Dane looked to him, and the man made no mention of the water he saw welling in his friend's eyes. Grunt, Xyril, Ularon, and Zuko stood with him, waiting quietly.

"We've been camped here for four days," Koda said. "We shouldn't wait any longer."

Dane cleared his throat and swallowed, still coaxing the fire with the stick in his hand. "What's the word on the dead?"

"Still the same."

"Come look for yourself, my friend," Xyril said.

Dane let the stick fall into the fire, grabbed his sword, and got to his feet. He cinched the sword belt as he walked by the others. They fell in line behind him as he picked his way through the forest, skirting bushes and ducking underneath low-hanging branches. Not a minute later, he came to a clearing.

It was a vast opening between them and Eden. There were wrecked carriages and wagons scattered throughout, along with the occasional boulder. The most jarring sight was the hundreds of standing corpses between them and the city.

Still as scarecrows, the dead were silent, their heads hanging low, their bodies slumped. A breeze rolled through the clearing and tugged at the rags covering their bodies, and the Companions could see that they were rotted worse than any of the undead they had seen in their travels so far. Eerily, none of them stirred – no sound, no movement, just dead statues.

They surrounded the entirety of Eden – in the field and even crammed into the half-empty moat. Dane knew it would be worse inside by the fact that the dead were funneled through the city gates. The streets inside would make for close combat. The threats of the zombies were made worse in close quarters by the risk of wounding any allies who fought too close.

Taking all this to mind, Dane hoped that the Animalia would be able to make short work of the dead. He glanced at Xyril. The leonin, thick arms crossed over broad chest, eyes scanning the surroundings, was unfazed.

"The intel was right, it seems," Ularon said. "Uragon is definitely here."

"And he surely knows that we're here now," Zuko added.

"Then we should *attack* now," Koda said.

"We need to wait for Bren, Caulen, and the others," Dane replied. "We'll need every fighting man available for this."

"I'm sure Evie's fine, Dane," Koda persisted. "You don't have to pretend you're not worried about her."

"I can't go into battle with a clouded mind."

"Then stay back. Let Ularon and Zuko lead."

"No!" Dane said. "I won't hang back like a coward while you all do the fighting. Just... Let's just give Evie and the others more time..."

I haven't felt this scared since I left this place to find Evelyn... Dane thought. *Just a little more time.*

"Dane," Xyril said, placing a heavy hand on his shoulder. "I understand what it is to worry for a cub. I would wait here with you for eternity if I could... But the others are growing restless. We need to attack now, or we may never have another chance."

"Evie wouldn't want you giving up this chance," Koda said. "Let's go... We'll capture the city in her honor. Maybe we'll rename it after her, eh?"

Dane heaved a heavy sigh. Squinted eyes scoured the ranks of the undead army once more. He then looked to Koda, who wore a reassuring grin on his face. He felt the warmth and weight of Xyril's hand on his shoulder. Grunt dipped his head to Dane, and Ularon and Zuko stood side-by-side, awaiting his answer.

Dane nodded slowly. "Let's return to camp. Make sure everyone's ready to attack."

"We're more than ready, my friend!" Xyril laughed as he clapped Dane on the back.

He, Ularon, and Zuko stalked off immediately. Koda and Grunt stayed behind while Dane looked at the city for a few moments longer. In his eyes, Dane did not see the dead, the wreckage, or the mess Eden had become. He saw home, and a fire burned in his belly to rid it of the vile corruption.

Finally, snapping himself out of his own thoughts, Dane looked at Koda and Grunt, nodding to each of them, and then marched back into the woods to make sure everything was in order.

It was not long before Dane was kicking dirt over the fire he had previously stoked. Around him, humans and Animalia alike were donning and cinching armor and weapons to their bodies or bidding their friends good luck in the coming fight. Koda, Grunt, Ularon, Zuko, and Alton stood nearby, preparing their own equipment, but Dane felt as if a ring of shadow surrounded him, keeping him from his friends.

His mind wandered, and he fidgeted by loosening his sword in and out of its sheath. He bowed his head and closed his eyes. The ring of darkness that he pictured muffled even sound, for he did not hear people gearing up, did not hear them speaking or marching near.

Whatever gods may be out there, I hope you hear my words. Please safeguard my friends in this coming conflict… You've already taken so many of them from this world… Watch over them and look upon us with favor as we battle these vile creatures of corruption, which you surely look upon with disdain…

Gods – if you even exist – please look upon us with mercy… Whatever we've done for you to turn your backs on us, know that we mean to set it right. Cast your eyes on us, and shower us with your protective covering… Please, don't take any more of my friends from this life…

"Dane," Koda said, tapping him on the shoulder.

Dane opened his eyes. Koda pointed through a wave of bustling Animalia, which parted only slightly to let the newcomers through. Evie, Caulen, Asira, and Spencyr appeared, smiling. They came forward, and Evie hugged her father.

"Were you worried, Dad?" Evie asked, giggling.

"You know I was," he replied, squeezing her tightly. "Were there any troubles?"

"Just a little, but everything's fine now."

Dane did not question it. He closed his eyes and smiled while he embraced her longer. His fears dissipated like fog on a sunny morning.

Nearby, Caulen grinned from ear-to-ear when he saw Ularon, and he bowed deeply. Ularon came forward and placed a hand on his shoulder. The boy looked up at Ularon's smiling face, and the two of them clasped forearms. Alton strolled up to him and punched him lightly in the arm while Zuko nodded warmly to the boy.

Spencyr and Asira greeted Koda and Grunt. Koda began informing them of what they had missed and what to expect. "Typical elves," Spencyr said when Koda told them what had transpired at Jalfothrin. Asira's mouth was agape when he described what Eden looked like, and Spencyr let out a long sigh.

"Look who we've brought with us," Evie grinned as she pointed back the way they had come.

The surging waves of beast-people parted once more, and through the opening, Bren appeared, along with four strangers following his lead. The five of them looked around in wild astonishment at the Animalia, who had grown used to the sight of humans by now and paid them no mind. Finally, Bren's eyes caught Dane, Koda, and Grunt.

A soft smile appeared on Bren's face as he picked his way through the crowds. Dane, Koda, and Grunt grinned and walked towards him. Evie, Caulen, and the others watched with broad smiles as Koda and Grunt each clasped forearms with Bren. Dane opened his arms and the two men chuckled as they embraced.

"Bren... It's good to see you," Dane said.

"It's been an eternity, hasn't it?" Bren said, stepping away and surveying the campsite once more.

"Did the kids explain everything?" Koda asked as he leaned casually on his spear.

"They did, but I'm not sure I understand everything."

"Not important. What's important is that you're here with us. These friends of yours werewolves, too?"

"They prefer lycans," Bren said.

Koda shrugged. "I'll call them whatever they want if they'll help us shred our way through the undead ranks."

"That they can do," Bren laughed. "We'll have no problem, but it looks like we'll be competing for kills against the Animalia."

"Hopefully it'll be that easy," Dane said.

"What can we expect?"

"I'll take you to go see it." Dane looked at Koda and Grunt. "Will you two stay here and make sure we're ready to move out?"

"Whatever you say, Boss," Koda said, giving a lax two-finger salute. "When can we expect that to be?"

"No longer than a half-hour," Dane replied. Koda and Grunt nodded and turned away. Dane motioned for Bren to follow him, and he made his way back to the edge of the forest.

Bren ducked under a branch, and his eyes fell upon the massive legion of zombies surrounding Eden. "This is insane..." He looked from the dead to Dane and back again. "We haven't seen any undead up north in quite a while and now I know why."

"They're all here," Dane said. "All the dead that Uragon could muster with his powers. I don't know if there's a limit to the things he can do."

"It doesn't matter," Bren said, looking at Dane, "it ends here, today." He turned and began marching back towards the camp. "Let's finish this, Dane."

"Bren, wait a moment..."

Bren stopped and turned. He took a few steps closer, furrowing his brow in a questioning look. "What is it?"

"I want you to know that none of us wanted to leave Akreya without you. We didn't have a choice. I know Caulen's already explained to you what happened, but I'm sorry it had to happen the way it did."

Bren sighed. "There's nothing to apologize for, Dane. You couldn't wait for me forever. I'm sorry I wasn't there to help you with everything... Doompoint, Pelias, Bandimere... And Braxon, too. I wish I had been there to help stop all of that, and then maybe Pelias, Marek, Llanowar, and Marleyn would still be alive..."

Dane nodded slowly as both he and Bren stared at the dead. "If it helps any," Dane said, "we'll avenge Pelias and Marek soon, when Uragon is dead. As for Llanowar and Marleyn, Braxon and all his followers are dead, so there's peace in that."

"No," Bren said, hard eyes squinting at the enemy. "Caulen says that the tracker hasn't been seen since Bandimere."

Dane looked at him. "Really? Hopefully he's not breathing anymore."

"I would like to have his head, if he is. Until then, we may never have peace."

Dane dug in his pocket and held out the silver locket that Marleyn had worn after Cassandra's passing. "We can start to claim it with this battle. Fight with me, brother."

Bren looked at Dane and took the locket before shaking Dane's hand. "I'm with you."

Dane and Bren arrived back at camp to find everyone fully armed and armored - Animalia and humans alike. The bustle that had previously overtaken the camp had died, and everyone stood still, waiting for the orders to attack. The silence caught Dane off guard when he returned. All eyes watched him.

The Animalia stood in ranks before him, with the avians off to one side and the leonin, vulpens, minotaurs, and loxodons all together in one group ahead of him. The humans stood with Xyril on his other side. Bren moved around Dane and joined them.

Dane nodded to the Animalia as he strode over to his friends. "Do your people know their jobs?" He asked Xyril.

Xyril grinned. "Aye, they do, my friend. They're ready for this. We won't let you down."

Dane clasped forearms with the great cat. "I know you won't." He motioned Evie and Asira to move closer. "I want you two at the very back of the battle." He looked at Evie and added, "Now, before you argue-"

"I know, Dad," Evie giggled. "Asira's been teaching me some knowledge on medicine. We can help anyone who falls."

Dane smiled at her and then looked at Asira. The woman said, "I knew you would not want her fighting on the front, so I asked her to assist me. This way we still have our uses."

Dane put a hand on Asira's shoulder. "Thank you." He hugged Evie, who squeezed her father tightly. Once she let go, he took another moment to survey their army.

I hope this is enough... Too late now, if it isn't...

"Everyone!" The Animalia straightened, and the humans clutched their weapons tighter, some shifting from one foot to the other repeatedly. "Move out!"

Chapter 42

Once the final word was given, there was no time wasted. Dane and his companions – joined by Xyril - led the Animalia through the trees to the forest's edge. Once there, they stopped once more to analyze the dead. Still no movement, no recognition of their presence. A breeze was blowing through the open ground between the forest and Eden.

"Everyone needs to be aggressive," Dane called. "We have the advantage of speed. Fan out, keep moving. Take out the enemies in front of you, cover the flanks of the soldiers next to you."

Dane looked over his shoulder. On his right stood Koda, Grunt, Ularon, Zuko, and Alton. On his left were Bren, Caulen, Spencyr, and Xyril. Dane met Xyril's eyes last and nodded.

The leonin returned the gesture and hoisted his scimitar into the air. The great cat roared, "Avians!"

The avians burst into the air out of the trees, their shrill cries cutting through the skies. A thick shadow fell over the ground troops as the birds soared in formation. The avians nocked arrows to their bows as they neared the horde of zombies. They drew back and loosed, arrows raining straight down into the skulls of the dead, every shot a hit.

It was not until the assault began that the undead reacted to the invaders. Once the arrows began falling, a surge of energy was mustered amongst the enemy, and they twitched to life. Groans, howls, and frightening screeches erupted across the field just before the undead started moving forward. Some were fast, and some stumbled along, but they were now locking their white, empty eyes on the living, and their jaws snapped hungrily.

Dane drew his sword and held it straight up, letting a war cry ring out. As he brought his sword down and led the charge, the other humans joined in the shout. The leonin roared, the vulpens yipped, the minotaurs bellowed, and the loxodons trumpeted as they shook the ground with their footfalls. Bren and the lycans morphed seamlessly into their wolf forms as they ran, and their animal bodies gifted them with greater speed to catch up to the Animalia. It was not long until the Animalia and the lycans had overtaken the humans and met the undead head-on.

Thunderous crashes erupted all along the battlefield as the beasts and undead collided. The corpses of the dead were thrown far and wide into the air, as if they were ragdolls. The splattering of skulls and brains was all around, along with the snapping of bones and tearing of rotted skin. Howls, growls, roars, hisses, and groans all pooled together in a horrifying song.

Xyril led the Animalia deeper and deeper into enemy-held ground. His scimitar worked in conjunction with his giant, clawed hands and his snapping jaws. The leonin worked their swords with blinding speed and precision. The vulpens' daggers — some thrown, and some in hand - flashed through the air to stab and pierce. The minotaurs used their axes to split and cleave skulls, sever heads, and split the undead in two. The loxodons used flails to smash large numbers of zombies at once, either into the ground or to send them flying into the air above everyone's heads to be grabbed and thrown by the circling avian soldiers.

The humans took up positions behind the Animalia as the beasts mauled their way forward. Dane's sword was focused, never-missing. He separated heads from shoulders and sliced through skulls as he kept moving forward. On one of his sides, Koda beat back zombies with the body of his spear while using the point to impale them. He vanished in black smoke and reappeared some distance away, shoving the point of his spear into the mouth of a zombie as it bit at him, and then he would disappear again, over-and-over.

On Dane's other side, Grunt defended his flank with his battle-axe. The giant man split entire bodies in two while also kicking with such force that it would send the dead crashing into others. Occasionally, he would grip a chomping zombie by the throat and slam it into the ground head-first, splattering his boots and breeches with blood and brain-matter.

Spencyr covered Grunt's flank. His hook swords were conjoined, whipping through the air and leaving gashes in the faces of the enemy, or taking them out at the legs to keep them from reaching the humans. Spencyr pulled his swords apart and spun and twirled from side to side, cutting down the dead left and right.

Ularon and Zuko stayed close together, almost back-to-back. Their swords moved in quick, precise thrusts and slashes. They dispatched of any nearby enemies with clean, controlled strikes.

Bren, Weldon, and the other lycans were scattered amongst the Animalian forces. Their claws slashed ferociously, and their fangs crushed with such force that only one bite was necessary to take down a dead minion. One hit from the werewolves' clawed hands and the zombies were slammed into the ground to be trampled under dozens of feet.

Caulen and Alton covered the others, loosing arrows through any openings their comrades would leave. Arrows whistled by them and pierced the eyes or foreheads of any undead who threatened to grapple with the humans. Everyone pushed forward, following the trails of carnage the Animalia left.

"Xyril!" Dane called, looking around. He slashed through the face of a sprinting zombie headed directly for him and then stabbed another one under the chin, his blade crashing through the top of its soft skull.

Xyril slipped through the line the Animalia held, swiping at a few undead as he did. He was panting greatly, but a sly grin was on his face. "We're cutting through them like a ship through water!" He laughed.

"We need to secure the outer area before we move into the city," Dane shouted over the chaos. He continued to keep his head on a swivel so as not to be taken unawares. "If we try and breach the walls before securing out here, we could get trapped! Tell your forces to split and work their way around the moat! We'll keep them pinched in at the gate while you do!"

"Got it, my friend!" Xyril said, leaping back into the crowd.

"As quickly as possible, Xyril!" Dane called. He looked at his friends around him. Only a smattering of the dead still threatened them in this part of the battlefield. "Everyone on me! We're going to hold the dead at the gates!"

Xyril must have gotten the command through, for the Animalian forces parted and began driving through the undead outside the city walls. Leonin, minotaurs, and others splashed through the water as they cleaved through the undead there. Above, the Avians rained arrows down to thin the opposition.

Dane saw the gates ahead and he took off sprinting through the path before him. The other humans followed close behind. Dane's boots slid in the hard-packed dirt just outside of the gate. The undead were tumbling over one another as they spilled out of the city. Their groans and grumbles welled up as they stumbled towards them. He gripped his sword in both hands and looked quickly over his shoulder. All his friends stood with him.

"Hold the line!" Dane shouted as he hacked at the closest zombie. Blades and arrows pierced flesh and bone, and the undead dropped one at a time.

Dane beheaded the next zombie and immediately followed up with a skull-splitting slash at the next one. As he removed his lodged sword, Caulen fired an arrow that soared over Dane's shoulder and lodged itself in the eye socket of an undead who had been getting dangerously close.

Grunt cut one of the undead in half at the waist and punched another in the jaw. Koda used the body of his spear to redirect the path of a zombie and stabbed the one behind it in the face. The undead he had diverted recovered quicker than he expected, and it grabbed his shoulder.

"Grunt!" Koda shouted. The giant man turned and raised his axe. Koda teleported away and Grunt brought his axe down on the zombie who had been grappling with his friend. Koda reappeared behind Grunt and stabbed an oncoming enemy. "Back-to-back, just like old times!" Koda laughed.

"The Animalia are coming back!" Spencyr shouted as he buried the spear-like point on the bottom of one of his swords into the forehead of a zombie and grabbed another with the hook of his other one. He jerked it to the ground and smashed its face against a rock.

"We should make our way to the castle as soon as we can!" Ularon shouted, still close to Zuko, the two men protecting one another.

Xyril came running up to them, cutting down a zombie on his way, and Bren was not far behind him, having taken his human form again. The other werewolves and a few of the Animalia swooped in to take over guarding the gate, throwing the corpses around as if they were weightless. Seeing this, the avians regrouped and made uniform passes over Eden. The arrows dropped, hammering away at the thick gatherings of the dead.

"The forces outside are nearly gone," Xyril said. "We can push inside, now."

"Be careful," Dane said. "There could be undead around every corner!"

"Yes, my friend."

"Can you have some of your forces cut a path for us to the castle?"

"Whatever you need."

"The rest of your army should focus on spreading out and clearing the streets from the main road."

"I'll have Gi-Shi lead the avians in a path straight towards the castle."

"Good." Dane said, flicking his eyes at the gate to make sure the line was being held. "We'll need a small detachment of Animalia to take inside the castle with us."

"Okay," Xyril said, looking around. "M'Kalla! Raudo! Turmarox!" The leonin, vulpen, and minotaur commanders snapped their heads in the direction of the booming voice. "You three accompany the Iron Fox inside the castle!" The three of them nodded.

"What will you do?" Dane asked him.

"Daridasa, Yuda, and I will lead the rest of the troops."

"I'll leave some of my men with you, Xyril." Dane looked at his men quickly. "Koda, Grunt, Bren, Caulen, and Ularon come with me."

"I should stay with the men," Ularon protested.

"We'll be fine," Zuko said. "Go and see your soon-to-be castle, My Lord." The old captain grinned.

Ularon relented. Dane continued: "It's settled, then. Zuko, Spencyr, and Alton, help Xyril lead the army. Bren, tell your lycans to assist Xyril however he requires."

Bren nodded and ran off towards the gate where the werewolves were still guarding. Dane peered around Xyril and saw Evie and Asira across the field, tending to an injured minotaur. Evie stood up and darted away to offer one of Ularon's wounded soldiers a drink of water.

Dane nodded and refocused his thoughts. "Is everyone ready? Let's go!" The humans and Animalia let loose fierce battle-cries and ran towards the gates of Eden.

"Dammit!" Uragon slammed his fist as hard as he could onto the stone railing of his balcony. The pain reverberating through his wrist all the way up to his shoulder was nothing but an annoyance to him. He gritted his teeth and stared from his tower, unblinking.

The humans and their beastly friends were making their way into the city now. The giant birds were crisscrossing each other above them, providing support from the sky. This made Uragon scream, for while his powers had gotten strong enough for some of the undead to remember how to swing a sword, they did not have the capacity to operate bows and arrows.

"Where did they find these filthy creatures?" Uragon asked. No one answered. His fingernails scraped against the stone. He laughed dryly. "No matter. They won't make it much further. The city streets are packed with my soldiers. They'll be surrounded in no time."

Uragon walked to a nearby table inside the bedchambers. He pulled the stopper out of a bottle of wine and studied it for a moment. He raised the bottle to his lips before reconsidering and picking up a wine cup. He poured until the liquid was near to the brim and set the bottle down next to a loaded crossbow. He brought the cup to his lips and chugged until all its contents were gone.

Uragon's heart was beating wildly, and he brought a hand up to rub his chest. He took several heaving, deep breaths. His eyes darted around the room but did not focus on anything.

The door to his bedchamber opened, startling him so much that he flinched and fell into a chair. Pelias was the first to step through, followed by Zenko, Dovne, and the other members of his personal guard. Uragon's Elites stood rigidly in a line, their weapons ready and in perfect condition.

They bore no rotting flesh, and he had spent a considerable amount of time mustering the energy and focus to resurrect them at full ability. None of their bones were exposed, not even beneath the armor they donned. The only thing that marked them as undead were their greyish, pale skin and lifeless white eyes.

Uragon remained in the chair, panting shallow breaths. A sly smile tugged at the corners of his mouth. He held his arms out wide. "Look at you... My most perfect toys! My Champions!"

The seven elite were silent.

Uragon's attempt at a smile vanished and he poured more wine. He shrugged and downed the contents. "It is a shame that your services won't be needed. These intruders will never make it to the castle.

"But, it's good to see how fantastic my handiwork is. If I keep at it, all the reborn will be like you. Perhaps I can even give you back the ability to speak. That would be lovely. A new world where everyone can speak but won't say anything I don't want to hear."

Uragon laughed and poured another cup. He peered at Pelias over the rim of the cup as he raised it to his lips. "I would like to hear your voice again, my friend... Would you like that?"

Shouts and other sounds of battle wafted in through the balcony. Uragon dropped his cup out of fright and leapt to his feet. He ran to the balcony and nearly shrieked in anger when he saw Dane and the others fighting in the courtyard below the tower.

Uragon turned and cupped his head in his hands, rocking back and forth. "How is this possible?" he shouted in a shrill voice. "You!" he pointed at The Champions. "Get down there and stop them! Now!"

The seven undead ran out of the room single-file. Uragon looked down at the courtyard once more. He saw a werewolf and a few of the giant beasts leading the fight. The guards he had placed in the courtyard, though faster and better armed than the ones outside the castle, were being run through just as easily.

Jolting him from his thoughts were the beating of wings overhead. Uragon ducked back inside as one of the flying monstrosities perched itself on the balcony railing, great talons locking around the stone. Its sharp black eyes zeroed in on him. The feathers on its neck bristled as it prepared to step down, slinging its bow behind its back.

Uragon scooted backwards as fast as he could and snatched the crossbow from the table. The avian warrior took the bolt to the eye and stumbled backwards, tumbling over the edge of the balcony. Uragon tossed the weapon back onto the table and scrambled to his feet. He saw the avian's body crumpled where it had landed.

"Dammit!" Uragon shouted, spittle flying from his lips and dribbling down his chin. His fingernails dug into the stone until they bled and tore.

Dane and his companions burst into the castle from the courtyards and barred the doors. M'Kalla, Raudo, and Turmarox continued to plow through the undead alongside Bren in werewolf form. The interior of Castle Eden was less populated than the city itself.

"Smug bastard obviously didn't expect us to make it this far," Koda said, looking left and right as the Animalia put down the closest remaining zombies.

The doors were being pounded from the other side as the undead clamored to breach inside. The wooden doors creaked and strained with each push. The groans of the dead could be heard coming from outside, and it made Caulen tense. He kept one hand on a nocked arrow, ready to draw at any moment.

"M'Kalla! Raudo! Turmarox! We can handle any opposition ahead of us, but we can't get trapped," Dane said. "I need you three to guard this door. It won't hold forever. Can you do that for me?"

"Yes, Iron-Fox!" Raudo said. "We'll hold this hallway with our lives. C'mon, boys!"

The three Animalia ran past them and took up positions in the wide hallway. The humans joined Bren up ahead, who had reverted to his human form. He pointed down a corridor to their right.

"Throne room's that way," he said. "I bet Uragon's there."

"We'll try it," Dane said, leading the way.

Their footfalls echoed in the empty corridor, and they ran for several minutes before reaching the throne room. Once there, it could not be mistaken. The giant iron doors swung open on old hinges, wailing loudly and announcing their arrival. Once inside, Grunt pushed the doors shut behind them and barred them.

The room was large and mostly empty. A few wooden benches set off to either side of the room, and a thin strip of soft, crimson carpet led the way to the throne ahead. It was simple, made of stone, but with a pillow on the seat and padded leather on the back. The chandeliers hanging above were unlit, and the sunlight streaming in through the windows was the only source of light. Particles of dust floated through the beams of light, and there was a musty smell in the air.

"Not here," Ularon said. The Companions relaxed slightly and took a moment to catch their breaths and collect their thoughts.

"If not here, probably in the bedchambers," Bren said. "That door over there is an access tunnel that goes to the chambers. The King's is at the top of the tower. Everyone else's are at ground level." The door Bren indicated was thrown open violently, and seven armed undead filed in.

"Bastards!" Koda muttered when he saw Pelias leading the way. The others grimaced or took deep breaths when they noticed, as well.

Bren's shoulders sagged a bit as he looked his friend over. His blonde hair and his toned physique was undoubtedly Pelias, and even with the pale skin and cloudy eyes of the dead, his young age was still noticeable, especially in the clean purple surcoat. Bren gritted his teeth and a low growl rumbled from his throat.

A moment later, the door opened again, this time more gently. The head of a young man with black hair peeked out, his eyes – glowing with anger – flicked to each of the Companions individually. He stepped out from behind the door, a sword drawn in his hand, sheathe in the other.

"Uragon!" Bren shouted.

"Bren... Very nice to see you again." Uragon responded in a soft tone, one that did not match the fire in his eyes. "I look forward to adding you to my collection..." He held his arms wide and feigned a smile, though it twitched in irritation. "I welcome all of you, in fact. You worthy fighters will make fine additions to my projects!"

"It's over!" Ularon shouted, raising his sword at the ready.

"Put down your weapon and call off your dogs," Koda said.

"I think not," Uragon replied.

"Fine. I don't mind hurting you."

"Oh, you can try." Uragon scoffed and rolled his eyes. "If you have any last words to each other, or perhaps to Pelias, best to get them out of the way now, though I'm afraid he can't respond."

"This won't end well for you, Uragon," Dane said. "We've made it this far. We'll take you down."

Uragon looked at Dane. "Good luck. I'll laugh in each of your faces once you've become my puppets. Let's not delay. Champions – attack!"

Pelias' sword and shield leapt into his hands. Zenko brandished two war-axes. Ruven and Elandorr threw off their cloaks and drew two knives apiece, though there were more strapped to their bodies. Ulmus drew two sickles, Dovne unsheathed a longsword and slammed the visor down on her helm, and Honlall lifted his large two-handed greatsword. The Elite rushed forward as one, snaking around the throne room, diverging and crossing paths over and over to try and confuse the Companions.

Caulen drew his bow and fired a shot, but in a panic, the arrow deflected off Dovne's helm. "Shit!" the boy shouted, drawing another arrow from his quiver. He rolled out of harm's way, Dane swooping in to distract the Warden, clashing blades with her.

Bren was back in wolf form, and he sprinted on all-fours at Pelias. He swiped the boy aside, sending him crashing into a nearby wall by the force of his hand. Next to him, Grunt's battle-axe came down, but was stopped by Zenko's two war-axes. The two giant men locked down on each other, pushing back and forth, struggling to gain the upper hand.

Zenko tried to swat at him with one of his war-axes while holding Grunt's own weapon at bay with the other but Grunt narrowly avoided the blade. Grunt held up one of his arms to stop the axe and held Zenko's arms apart. The masked giant drove his forehead into the Warden's face and punched him in the gut. He pushed Zenko back and regained his grip on his battle-axe.

Across the room, Ularon ducked under Honlall's giant sword. He rolled aside and landed a small cut on his opponent's leg, which staggered him. The man continued to come at him with his greatsword, swinging in wide arcs. Ularon kept ducking, dodging, and evading, but the undead never tired to allow an opening.

Caulen sent two arrows rapidly, one after another, into Honlall's ribs to distract him, but it did little. As Caulen nocked another arrow, he saw the dwarf Ulmus charging at him with his sickles held out to the sides. Caulen loosed the arrow into his stomach, but he continued his sprint. The boy jumped over the dwarf and tucked his shoulder into a roll as he landed. He nocked two arrows immediately as he came to one knee and shot them into the back of the dwarf.

"Caulen, look out!"

Caulen ducked and rolled when he heard Ularon's voice. Honlall's sword cut through the air above his head, and Caulen scrambled away. Ularon tackled the undead to the ground and the two of them grappled there.

Next to them, the elven brothers were working together to take down Koda. Their knives slashed and stabbed wildly at the air, creating rifts in the black smoke that Koda left in his wake as he teleported. Each time he reappeared, he attempted to strike a fatal blow to either one of them, but they were quick to dodge and counter, forcing him to use his powers to disappear from harm's way.

When Koda reappeared, he kicked Elandorr in the face and stabbed with his spear at Ruven. The elf side-stepped it and slashed Koda in one of his arms. Koda gritted his teeth and teleported again. The two undead brothers turned and put their backs together, waiting for Koda's next attack as they turned in a circle. Koda continued with his relentless assault. Attack, disappear, strike, dissolve, jab, smoke...

Dane stood in the middle of the room, still locked in combat with Dovne. The Warden brought her sword down upon him savagely multiple times, and each time his guarding strength lessened. On her fourth hammer-strike down, he slid to the side and sliced a large gash in her waist. She was unfazed and grabbed the blade of his sword with a gauntleted hand and jerked it away. Luckily, his grip stayed, and he tumbled to the floor, but with the longsword still in his possession.

Dovne stabbed into the carpet where Dane had just been. Hopping to his feet he slashed up, his sword rising with his body. The tip of his blade caught her helm under the chin and threw it off her head. A blonde braid tumbled out from underneath the armor, and for a moment, she was dumbstruck by the attack. A thin line of blood materialized, running up her face, and it began to pool on her chin before dripping to the ground. Dane took the opportunity to send a kick to her chest and throw her off her feet.

Bren stalked up to Pelias, saliva dripping from his fangs, a low growl erupting from his open jaws. The kingsguard got to his feet and sprinted again at the werewolf. Bren swiped again, but this time Pelias skidded to a stop just out of his reach. He slashed Bren in the stomach with his sword and dodged another swing.

Bren raised both his hands and brought them down. Pelias raised his shield and dug his feet into the ground. Bren's claws punctured his shield and lodged themselves there. Pelias cut Bren again in the stomach, and the lycan howled and leapt back, wrenching Pelias' shield away before removing his claws from the metal and slamming it into Pelias' face in retaliation.

Grunt and Zenko had traded blows evenly through their entire fight, but Grunt — slightly bigger than Zenko — finally got the upper hand and kicked one of the Warden's knees out from under him. Grunt smashed one of his own knees into his opponent's chin, snapping his neck back and his arms out, leaving him wide open. With a wild roar, Grunt lifted his battle-axe up and brought it down with all his might into Zenko's forehead. Blood sprayed like a fountain onto Grunt's face and torso. He placed a boot on Zenko's chest and pushed him away as he dislodged his axe.

Grunt looked to either side. Bren was towering over Pelias, who was sprawled on the ground to his left, but to his right, Dane was stabbing down at Dovne. The Warden rolled to the side and jumped back to her feet. Her sword was gone, but she sprinted at Dane, who jumped to the side and let her pass. She ran straight at Grunt, whose fist connected to her face and sent her to the ground.

"Go help Koda!" Dane called. "I've got her!" He ran after the girl, who was already recovering from her blow to the face. Dane slashed and stabbed, but without being encumbered by her sword, Dovne was even more agile. Dane felt his swings becoming less aggressive.

Grunt stomped over to the elven brothers, who still stood back-to-back. He raised his axe, and the two of them separated as his blade bit down between them, splitting them apart like firewood. Koda appeared in a puff of smoke next to Grunt, grinning.

"You two are really pissing me off," Koda said, stamping the butt of his spear into the ground, "but you're done for, now." Koda and Grunt nodded to one another and charged at the brothers. Ruven and Elandorr threw knives at them, and a chase began, with the brothers skirting away from their opponents, keeping a safe distance between them as best they could.

Caulen had forgone his bow now and had drawn the dagger that Ularon had given him. The dwarf was too skilled with his sickles, and so he had resigned to dodging and praying an opening would come. The undead did not tire, and their assaults were relentless.

Caulen did not know how much longer he could keep up his evasion.

Ularon had managed to land only small injuries on Honlall, but none that counted against the undead. His greatsword kept Ularon well at bay, and his inexhaustible energy never left an opening for him to push closer. He hoped the undead would soon make a mistake, if he could just hold out a little longer.

From across the room, Uragon was giddy. He had made himself comfortable on the throne, though he was fidgeting from the excitement. A smile was on his face, and he could not help but cheer for his fighters. "This is what my father could have had! An entire army just like my Champions!" He laughed.

"I wish someone would shut him up!" Koda growled. He tried using his powers to pursue Elandorr, but with each time he teleported, his strikes became slower or weaker, and he could not hit his target.

Grunt's stride had slowed as Ruven led him on a chase, dodging his axe falls or his attempts at grabbing him. The giant man panted heavily underneath his mask. Ruven backed away to where Dovne had recovered her sword and was locked in combat with Dane.

Each of Dane's attacks was blocked or parried, and he knew he was quickly running out of stamina. He could not go on much longer. He saw Grunt coming closer, and an idea popped into his head. His eyes flicked rapidly between Dovne and Grunt, who was being lured over by Ruven.

Dane knew that all his friends were getting fatigued, while their opponents maintained perfect condition. Only drastic measures would win them this fight. They would have to outthink the dead.

Grunt was within range. Dane began leaving openings in his attack - at first small ones, and then more obvious ones. He thought for sure that Dovne would seize one of the opportunities for a killing blow and leave her open for Grunt's axe.

Ruven slipped under the giant's arms, and as Grunt stumbled and turned to follow, Dovne ignored Dane and sliced Grunt in the back of the knee, forcing him to kneel. Ruven then went on the offensive and stabbed Grunt in the stomach with both of his knives.

"No!" Dane shouted. He moved to take out Dovne, but out of nowhere, Pelias – having slipped out of Bren's clutches – appeared to block Dane's strike with his own sword. Bren thundered up to Pelias and swatted him away from the others. Dovne stabbed her sword through Grunt's back, the blade travelling through his body to burst through his stomach. Dane yelled and mustered all his remaining strength into a killing blow, decapitating Dovne and causing her body to double over.

"Grunt!" Koda called. Smoke was left in his wake as he disappeared. Before he could dispatch of Ruven, Elandorr sent his knives soaring through the room and into Grunt's chest.

The giant man roared in pain and held Ruven at bay as Koda materialized in the air above him and drove the point of his spear into the top of his skull as he came down. Koda pulled him away and reached out to Grunt.

"Stay strong, Grunt! Stay with us!" Koda shouted. He did not see Ulmus toss one of his sickles to Elandorr as the elf sprinted at him. The dwarf was not far behind him, forgetting about Caulen entirely to focus on the weaker prey.

Grunt's eyes widened, and he pushed Koda to the side as Elandorr brought the sickle down in an arc. The blow slashed through Grunt's mask, revealing his mutilated, scarred face, blood trickling down. He reached out and grabbed Elandorr by the throat and the wrist of the hand that the sickle was held in.

Grunt squeezed both, shattering the elf's wrist and causing him to drop the weapon, and crushing his neck. Ulmus had caught up to him by now, and Grunt held Elandorr's body like a shield, catching the dwarf's sickle long enough for Caulen to launch an arrow into the back of Ulmus' head. Grunt tossed both bodies of the elf and the dwarf away from him.

Koda ran up to him and put an arm around him. "Hang on! We'll get you to Asira!" Koda looked at Ularon and Honlall, still battling on one side, to Bren and Dane, who had teamed up to take on Pelias, and then to Uragon who's eyes had widened at the turning of the tide of battle.

Koda leaned down and picked up his spear. His nostrils flared as he glared at Uragon. The young man shifted and stood slowly from the throne. Koda prepared to teleport, but Grunt began coughing and spitting blood through the shreds of his mask. Koda supported Grunt so he would not fall, and when he glanced back up, Uragon was slipping out of the room into the tunnel Bren had spoken of before.

Koda cursed and looked around. "Uragon's getting away!" he shouted, but he refused to leave Grunt's side.

The news acted as a rallying cry. Caulen once again drew his dagger and rushed at Honlall, whose back was turned to him in favor of Ularon, who panted as he staggered away. Caulen jumped and stabbed down with the dagger, catching Honlall in the back of the head. The kingsguard fell and Caulen tumbled away onto his back, exhausted. Ularon collapsed to the ground as well, his sword clattering against the stone floor.

Pelias parried Dane's stab, but Dane was prepared. He spun and cleaved his sword into Pelias' waist. With his depleted strength, his sword lodged halfway through the motion. Pelias drew his sword back to stab Dane in the throat, but Bren's large, clawed wolf hand grabbed Pelias by the back of the neck and pulled him away from Dane as he stabbed.

With his other hand, Bren drove his claws into Pelias' back. He opened his jaws wide and sunk his fangs into Pelias' collarbone and shoulder blade. As he bit down, he pulled hard with his hands. Pelias was ripped in two from the base of his neck down his back and to his waist, where Dane had already cut.

Bren threw the two pieces of Pelias across to opposite sides of the room and sunk to the floor. He shifted back to his human form, heaving deep breaths as he clutched at his wounds. Sweat poured down his face as he looked at the carnage riddled throughout the room.

Koda had removed all the blades from Grunt's body and lowered him onto his back. He was no longer breathing. Koda sat beside his body and stared blankly at the ground before him. Bren and Dane looked at one another, exhausted and in shock.

"Uragon's still... still getting away!" Ularon called as he attempted to stand and failed, falling to hands and knees.

Dane forced himself to his aching feet and walked to Bren, offering a hand. Bren took it and rose to his feet, groaning. "Stay here with them, Bren. We're the only ones still able to put up a decent fight."

"You sure you'll be all right?" Bren asked.

Dane looked at Caulen, who was still sprawled on the ground, staring at the ceiling, and Ularon who could not even manage to stand. Koda's eyes were distant as he sat in a pool of his friend's blood.

Dane shrugged and shook his head. "I'll have to be."

"Finish it, Dane." Bren walked past Koda, giving him a moment alone, and tried to coax Caulen and Ularon to their feet.

Dane looked at his friends one more time and then ran to the tunnel leading to the bedchambers. It was empty, but there were a few torches lit to guide his path. In his stomach, he knew Uragon had gone to the top of the tower. Where else could he go?

He found the spiral stairs that led to the king's bedchambers and he took them slowly, one at a time. He did not want to come upon any zombies by surprise, but he also did not want to wear himself out before he found Uragon. He did not know how skilled the prince was with a sword, and Dane had never been one to underestimate an opponent.

Finally, he reached the top of the stairs. The door of the king's bedchamber was left cracked. Dane cocked his head to the side and peered in. He saw nothing, but he knew that someone who was running and hiding would not be so careless as to leave the door open and unlocked.

Dane readjusted his grip on his longsword and struck the door with a mighty kick before leaping to the side and throwing his back against the stone wall of the stairwell. The door flew open violently, and a crossbow bolt whizzed through the opening and clattered down the stairs.

Dane peaked around the corner at Uragon, who held the empty crossbow meekly in his hands. His jaw quivered with anger as Dane strolled leisurely inside, holding his sword to one side.

"Crossbow only holds one bolt at a time," Dane said.

"I could have another!" Uragon hissed, though he made no move.

"You lack the foresight for that kind of planning. That's why we're here now." Dane took a few more steps closer. He noticed that Uragon's sword was on the table next to him, just within arm's reach. "It's over, Uragon. Surrender."

Uragon shook his head slightly. It was plain on his face that he was wracking his brain for a solution. He shook his head faster and let out a horrible cry as he drew his arm back, threw the crossbow and reached across for his sword.

Dane twisted and let the crossbow pass him by as he rushed forward. He raised his sword and brought it down as Uragon gripped his own weapon. Dane's longsword separated Uragon's arm at the elbow and the man screamed in pain, blood splattering the floor, his sword dropping to the ground.

Dane stabbed Uragon in the stomach and drove him back until they were out on the balcony. Uragon's back pressed against the stone and he leaned over the railing, holding on with the only hand he had left. His eyes locked onto Dane's, but his anger had been replaced with confusion.

"I... I..." Uragon choked on the words. "I am Raz-Mikai..."

Dane wrenched his sword out of Uragon's gut and brought it back to slash cleanly through his neck. The man's head disappeared over the edge of the balcony, and his body slumped to the ground, propped against the railing.

Dane lowered his sword as his eyes cast out across Eden. The avians were landing, and the tumult and roaring of battle were beginning to deafen...

Chapter 43

Dane drove the final nail into the doorframe and stepped back, his hands on his hips and a smile on his face. Behind him, people and Animalia alike carried lumber and tools of their own, or passed out food and water to others. The noises of a city being rebuilt and the bustle of its denizens soothed him.

"The house is as good as new."

Dane looked over his shoulder and smiled as Evie strolled up beside him, admiring his handiwork on their old house. "Not quite," Dane replied, looking at the house again. "It still leaks in the far-right corner, and I have to rebuild the chimney. It collapsed somehow while we were gone."

"Then you'll settle in?" Evie asked, holding out a water skin. Her new azure dress swirled in the breeze.

"No. I've got that other thing to tend to." He tossed his hammer into the tool cart nearby and picked up the skin.

"You're sure about that?"

Dane sighed after swallowing the cool, refreshing water. "About the house or the job?"

"Both. Ularon said he wanted you to be one of his advisors on his council. Said he'd give you a room of your own and everything."

Dane shook his head. "I don't want any of that. Promise you'll visit your poor old dad?" He chuckled as she punched him in the arm, both grinning. He wrapped her in his arms and squeezed tightly. "My daughter - an apprentice healer in a fancy castle. Make sure you listen to everything Asira tells you, okay?"

"Of course, Dad." She laid her head on his chest and closed her eyes, hugging him back. "And *you're sure* you need to go?" Evie asked.

Dane nodded. "I'm sure. Besides, it will do Koda some good to get out. He hasn't been doing well these past few weeks, since Grunt..."

Evie nodded. "I understand. Just make sure he comes back. Ularon said he wants him as part of his personal guard."

"We'll be back. I promise." He sauntered over to a pile of bricks that was stacked nearby. Sacks of his personal belongings were leaned against them, and he fished around in one for a moment. "Look at this."

Dane handed her a leatherbound book. Evie opened it and began reading, smiling. "I didn't know you were one for poetry, Dad."

"Your mother loved that book... Take it to the castle with you. Keep it safe for me there, okay?"

"I will."

"There's a bookmark in there, as well. Do me a favor and keep them together, yeah?"

Evie raised an eyebrow and flipped to the middle of the book, where she found a withered buttercup stuck between the pages. She held it gently by the stem between two fingers and held it up. "What's the story behind this?"

Dane smiled. "I'll tell you when I get back. We'll have dinner in the castle and I'll tell you."

"Do you need a healer to tag along?" Asira asked as she approached from behind them, holding a basket of plants, vials of minerals, and jars of other potion ingredients in the crook of her arm.

"Wouldn't wanna take away the castle's official healer," Dane said. "Besides, this'll be the last of it. How pitiful would that be if I died now, after everything that's happened."

"Don't joke about that, Dad!" Evie said, her eyes wide.

"Just be careful," Asira said, smiling. "Even I have my limits, castle quarters or no castle quarters."

"You can't raise me from the dead?" Dane asked, grinning.

"That's over now," the healer said.

"Not quite."

"How long will you be gone?" Evie asked.

"However long it takes."

* * *

Koda's footsteps fell lightly, though the noise echoed in the wide-open area. He turned slowly in a full circle, his eyes taking in the empty stands and the bright blue sky through the open roof above his head. He stopped in the very center of the arena and closed his eyes.

He saw the pumping arms of the crowd as they cheered his name. He heard their roaring, coaxing him on to fight harder, faster, show no mercy. He could smell the fresh blood in the dirt.

A picture of a pool of blood flashed in his mind, but it was on the stony floor of the castle. In his arms, he felt the weight of his friend as he breathed his last. Koda dropped to his knees and curled his fingers around fistfuls of dirt and grass. Tears rolled down his cheeks.

* * *

Spencyr shifted uncomfortably in the black armor. The red cloak seemed to weigh more than he believed it would, tugging at his shoulders with every step. Zuko, Caulen, Xyril, Alton, and Ularon all watched him. He smiled sheepishly, trying not to seem ungrateful.

"This is a new era for Akreya," Zuko said. "We should do away with the old colors."

Ularon nodded. "It may be a while, however. We've got a lot of things to focus on for now."

"I'll make do," Spencyr said, bowing his head. "But, if we do change the design of the armor, I would like to request mine be adapted to accommodate my hook swords." He tapped his fingers on the arming sword scabbard dangling at his waist.

"Of course! You don't have to be so stiff, Spencyr. You're my bodyguard, and I trust you."

"Thank you, Ularon."

Ularon cleared his throat and dropped into a chair, scooting it up to the table. "When Koda gets back from his foray with Dane, I hope he'll accept the position as well. Kingsguard needs good men, and no doubt his magi skills will benefit us, as well. Xyril, how are our people getting along? Any issues?"

The leonin smiled wide. "It's going great! The Edenians have been very welcoming. I've had the avians transporting supplies around the city, while the minotaurs and loxodon help rebuild. The vulpens have been helping dig through and clear the rubble."

"Fantastic," Ularon said, smiling. "Everyone here has fought for this victory – humans, elves, dwarves, Animalia. All of us. I'm concerned about when the people who didn't fight together return to their homes. What will their reactions be?"

"Who cares?" Alton said. "They shouldn't have anything to complain about."

"That's not how people work, I'm afraid."

"Dane needs to be on this council," Xyril said. "He would be invaluable to you."

"I've offered it to him, and I've got Evie trying to talk him into it," Ularon said, grinning.

"You don't think he will accept?" The leonin asked, smoothing out his mane with his hands.

"I doubt it," Caulen said. "This just isn't for him."

Zuko sighed. "One can hope. It's a waste of his talents not being here."

Ularon waved a hand. "He's done his part. In fact, you all have. I couldn't blame any of you if you decided you didn't want any part of this, but I'm grateful for each and every one of you. I don't know how my rule of Akreya will go. I pray to the gods for peace, and I pray that each and every one of you will keep me honest and humble. I couldn't ask for a better council, and I mean that."

King Ularon looked at each one of them and bowed his head in thanks.

"You intend to go back to Jalfothrin for those elves?" Alton asked smirking, kicking his feet up onto the table.

Ularon chuckled. "Maybe... Just to frighten them a little."

Epilogue

Two months later...

"Good hunt, men," Bren said. "Get these deer to Wesa so he can start dressing them."

Bren handed the deer on his shoulder off to Vokosyrra, who disappeared through the gate. Bren looked up at the sky and watched the snowflakes float gently down around him. He smiled at the simple beauty.

Behind him, he heard the clopping of hooves picking their way down from the hill and into the valley their village rested in. The guards at the gate joined him outside and glared at the noise. Bren squinted and saw two familiar faces leading horses, and a third figure with a sack over his head.

"Friends. Visitors for me. Go back inside. I'll be fine." One of the guards turned immediately, but the other stalled before muttering agreement and leaving.

Bren met Dane and Koda half the distance and clasped forearms with both men, all three of them smiling. Koda leaned on his spear, wrapped in a heavy cloak built for the cold. Dane was wearing his Iron Fox Legion armor and his fox-tail longsword, but a cloak was draped over his shoulders, and a hood was pulled over his head.

"I didn't expect to see you so soon," Bren said. He gave the mysterious visitor - whose wrists were bound by thick cord – a sideways glance. The captive's covered head moved at the sound of the voice. A muffled yell for help came from under the sack.

"We brought you a gift." Koda said. He used his spear to knock the prisoner to his knees and then removed the sack from his head.

A skinny, blonde-haired man blinked in the grey, snowy sunlight. A rag was stuffed between his teeth, though a few of them were missing. Small droplets of blood stained his shirt.

"His name is Leyon," Dane said. "He swung the club that killed Llanowar, and he's the last person left alive that had any part in Marleyn's murder."

"The last of Braxon's shit-eater's," Koda said with a smirk.

Bren cast a menacing gaze down at the prisoner. His nostrils flared and his brow furrowed. His hand trailed up and he clutched Marleyn's silver locket, where it hung around his neck.

Dane undid the buckle on his sword belt and pulled it from his waist. He took a step forward and held the weapon out by the sheathe. The hilt faced Bren, who eyed it questioningly.

Dane said, "We've all found our peace, Bren. We want you to have yours."

Bren looked at Dane, then Koda, and then Leyon, whose cold eyes stared at him defiantly. Bren looked again at the sword. He wrapped his fingers around the hilt and drew it.

The End

Acknowledgements

A big thank you to Jeff Seymour for his advice and encouragement. It meant a lot coming from someone in the industry.

Thank you to Donna and Casey for being the first couple of people to encourage me when all I had was a very rough draft and a crippling fear of what you might say about it.

Thank you to Al and Hunter, who were always there to listen and give feedback while I was in the middle of writing it, and whose critiques and reading recommendations really helped me find my stride as an artist.

Thank you to my best friend Jesse, who never once doubted I could do this. Your enthusiasm energized me.

And a very special thank you to Seth, Jaron, and Josiah. They let me read the whole thing to them, gave their honest feedback, and even pretended to enjoy it. Great friends to have.

And to Stephanie − thank you for your notes and excitement. Hopefully, you'll forgive me for the way I treated the elves.

About the Author

Sam Bates was born in Bowling Green, Kentucky in 1995 and began writing stories at 8 years old. His first novel *Doompoint* was published in 2021. He lives in Tennessee with his wife and son.

Made in the USA
Coppell, TX
08 November 2021